Eleanor

by S.F. Burgess

First published in Great Britain in 2013 by Jojosala Publishing Ltd.

Copyright © 2013 by S. F. Burgess

Cover illustrations by Scarlett Rugers
www.scarlettrugers.com

Map by S.F. Burgess

S. F. Burgess has asserted her moral right to be identified as the author of
this work.

A CIP catalogue record of this book is available from the British Library.

ISBN: 978-0-9576996-1-8 (Paperback)
ISBN: 978-0-9576996-0-1 (EPub Edition)

First Edition

For my parents,

Who gave more financial support than they could afford, more love than I ever deserved and who never stopped believing, even when they had no clue what they were believing in. The world is shaped by its quiet heroes and you are mine.

Contents

1

THE END

"Most people's lives begin with their births; mine began with my death."

Direct quote from Eleanor, the 'Extended History of the Five'.

I'm dying.

The thought was followed by a frantic panic that squeezed her chest mercilessly. She struggled even harder to breathe. Blood bubbles clogged her throat, the burning agony intensified, threatening to overwhelm. Cold darkness was moving in from the edges of her vision. It was almost welcome. The instinct to live fought briefly with the excruciating pain and her desire for it to stop. The pain won. The effort too much, body relaxing, she began to let go. A paramedic was kneeling at her side, pushing hard against the centre of her agony. He snapped instructions to his colleague. Most of it went over her head, but some of the words she caught: "Bullet's pierced her lung," "bleeding out."

Overhead, the stark florescent bulbs blurred, and she closed her eyes.

The world faded, she floated. Letting go of the fear, she tried to tune out the pain, a soft lucidity carrying her. Through the background noise of death there was a voice.

Eleanor?

She ignored it – what good could her response do now?

Eleanor!

The voice was hard, insistent, with a strange accent. She forced heavy eyes to open. An oxygen mask covered her mouth. *When did they put that on?* She felt anger, the lucidity momentarily sharper. *Why are they expecting me to talk when I've this thing on my face?* She clutched at the plastic, trying to respond. The paramedic took her hand, replacing the mask offering a kind smile, that stood at odds with the sadness and resignation filling his eyes. *He knows I'm dying.*

"Let us work," he said, his voice raspy and nasal, not the deeper voice with the growl to it she had heard calling her name. Confused, she closed her eyes again.

Eleanor... Eleanor, can you hear me?

Yes. She thought fuzzily. *Why can I hear you?*

I'm in your head, Eleanor.

The absurdity of this statement caused her eyes to snap open, but the intense concentration and hurried movements of the paramedics, their strained faces and the blood she could see from the corner of her eye, spreading in an ever-widening pool across the grey linoleum floor, soon convinced her to close them again.

You're dying, Eleanor.

Tell me something I don't know, she thought bitterly.

I can offer you life.

I'm hallucinating – I'm dying and my mind is trying to lessen the blow, she rationalised.

You're not hallucinating, I'm really here. My offer is real.

Are you an angel? she whispered.

No. I'm someone who needs your help. We need you to join the Five, I need you Eleanor – will you join me?

The five what? I really don't think I should be making decisions at the moment, she answered.

I can feel your life slipping away. Please, Eleanor, join me. Live!

What's the catch?

Pardon?

Well, mystery voice, there's always a catch. Do I get to come back as a bug or something? The voice chuckled and despite everything, Eleanor found the sound captivating.

The catch, since you ask, is that you must leave behind everything you know and join me. This is not an easy life, Eleanor. I have work for you to do.

As Eleanor wondered what 'work' she was going to achieve with two bullets in her chest, the voice interrupted her.

If you choose to join me you will be healed. Please hurry, Eleanor, make your decision.

I'm just a shop assistant, what do you need me for?

You are far more than you think.

How do I know I can trust you?

You don't, but your only other option is dying.

It might help if I knew your name, Eleanor thought, more to herself than to him.

My name is Conlan.

You're not imaginary then. I wouldn't have called you Conlan; I'd have called you Robert or Edward or something… Conlan, that's an odd name…

Eleanor?

Yes?

You're rambling, your mind is faltering. I need your decision. Will you join me?

What's it like… dying?

I have no idea, I've never died.

If I die, will you be with me? Even in her head Eleanor knew her voice sounded small, frightened.

No, you must go alone.

In the end, Eleanor did not care about the consequences, she did not think about what kind of life she would gain or the fact that she knew she deserved the death she was suffering. As the pain drew her deeper, her consciousness fading, she did what any sane person would do – she reached for the light and grabbed at her chance of life. One last thought flickered through her mind before the darkness claimed her:

Yes, Conlan, I'll join you.

Strange dreams chased each other through her mind. There was a strong tugging sensation, like being dragged out to sea by a powerful current. She had agreed to join him, so she relaxed into the current, still not entirely convinced that it was not just her imagination working overtime. There was firelight, shadows, growling and snarling in melodic harmony. Then it was silent, dark and just his voice: Conlan.

"Sleep now, Eleanor, I've got you."

2

SAFETY

Consciousness came back by degrees. Eleanor's eyes felt glued shut. For a while she lay motionless, assessing – infinitesimal flexing of her muscles giving feedback. She was stiff and a little cold, but the pain from before was gone. Her right wrist felt numb, like when she accidentally stopped the circulation to it and there was a vicious headache. She was lying on her back, a hard surface beneath her, something soft under her head. A rough blanket covered her. It smelt of stale animal sweat and campfire smoke. The air was chilly and over the smell of the blanket Eleanor noticed the subtle aroma of pine. She could hear the snapping and rustling of trees moving in the wind, but it seemed distant, high overhead.

I'm outside. Why am I outside?

"I know you're awake, Eleanor."

The voice, she remembered that voice. *Conlan.* She cautiously opened her eyes. Massive pine trees towered above, swaying restlessly, and somewhere a bird let out a screeching call. It was day, but the light was muted and green, the sky hidden by the dense canopy above.

"How do you feel?" His voice again.

Eleanor turned her head carefully, looking at him for the first time. He sat on a log across from her, arms wrapped round his knees; a near-dead campfire lay between them. Intelligent, bright green eyes held hers, scrutinising. His face held the deep tan of someone who spends most of their time outside, yet under this tan he was pale and drained. The skin beneath his eyes was a deep purple, bones sharp over hollowed cheeks. He seemed old, as if life weighed him down. The short-cut brown hair showed no signs of grey, but the several days' worth of stubble did him few favours. Beneath it all Eleanor felt he would have been handsome, but for a thick scar that ran from the corner of his left eye in a deep, livid, jagged line down his face, tearing through his top lip and giving him a menacing look. They stared at each other until Eleanor became uncomfortable with the silence.

"If you're in my mind, shouldn't you know how I feel?"

Conlan shook his head slowly, not taking his eyes off her, as if he were looking for something in her face.

"I was only in your head during the ritual. Your mind is your own once more."

"Then how did you know I was awake? Wait, what ritual?"

"The ritual that was necessary to bring you here. I knew you were awake because your breathing changed." His voice was quiet, but the lack of volume did not hide the strange accent, the soft growling as he spoke – it made him sound angry. Eleanor wondered if he was angry with her.

"And where on Earth is here?" she asked.

Conlan broke eye contact to look at the blended green and brown around them.

"This is Millers Forest."

Eleanor sat up, wincing slightly as she pulled stiff muscles, irritated by his response. He was answering her questions, but there was no actual information in what he was telling her.

"We're not on Earth, or at least not the Earth you know," he added. Green eyes searched her face; again, she wondered what he was looking for. Then what he had actually said hit her. *If I'm no longer on Earth, where am I?* Like a strange reality check, her mind then chose to remind her of the bullets. *I should be writhing in agony or stone-cold dead.* Fear slid an icy hand down her spine, the forest lurched slightly, her heartbeat jumped and her breathing accelerated. Conlan moved to kneel beside her.

"Eleanor, just breathe." he touched her shoulder, but Eleanor jerked away from him, moving out of his reach.

"Don't touch me!" she snarled. "What have you done to me? Where am I? Did my body just disappear? My family are never going to know what happened to me... What have you done?!" As she ranted at him, Eleanor thought she registered pain flash across his face, but he was so quick to hide it she could not be sure. He waited patiently until she had finished, there was no surprise at her outburst. Snapping her mouth shut she glared at him. He stared back, frowning; she forced her breathing to slow down.

"Well?" she said eventually.

"I don't have time to go into all the details right now – we're not safe here and must move soon," he said quietly. Eleanor glanced around the forest, which had taken on a dark and foreboding aspect with his words.

"Why aren't we safe?" her words shot through with the fear she knew was showing on her face. Conlan turned his head away, not looking at her, he appeared to be thinking. Every second of delay in his response increased the terror Eleanor could feel building in her body.

"We're not meant to be here. If we're caught the results could be fatal, so we have to get to safety." Conlan's flat explanation did nothing to calm her.

"Fatal?" she echoed, her terror forcing breaths out of her in short, sharp gasps.

"I didn't mean to scare you," he added almost as an afterthought, his eyes returning to her face, still searching it.

Eleanor raised an eyebrow at him, anger overriding some of her terror.

"Brilliant job on that one! If we're not meant to be here, why did you bring me?"

He stared at her again, the silence stretching along with her nerves. "This is where the ritual took place," he said. "That level of released energy is noticeable. We must leave before it's investigated."

"Investigated by whom?" her question had been calm, but he appeared to notice how much she was shaking. He reached to touch her but then thought better of it, letting his hand drop to his side instead.

"People you really don't want to meet. I know this is difficult for you, but this world is very different from yours and you need to trust me."

"You drag me from my world, to who knows where, to do who knows what, and you won't tell me what's going on and I'm supposed to TRUST you?!" she spat this last part out, her voice rising to a yell.

"I gave you a choice, Eleanor." The tone was calm and reasonable, but there was an edge to it.

"Some choice! Have you done this before? How many choose to die?" Eleanor snapped, her fear fuelling her anger. Conlan stood and turned his back to her. When he spoke, his voice was flat again.

"The first three times this worked, but Earth is different. I've been looking for you for a long time. You're the fourth attempt – and no, nobody chose death in the beginning."

"Three others... where are they?"

Conlan wrapped his arms around his body, holding in his secrets. Eleanor stared at his back, waiting until he answered, unwilling or unable to let this question go.

"They didn't make it," he whispered. His voice sounded so hollow that Eleanor felt the hairs on the back of her neck stand on end. Tears hid threateningly at the edges of her eyes, but she had no idea why she was crying.

"What do you mean, 'didn't make it'? They died? Did you...?" her implied accusation sounded harder than she had intended.

He spun round, anger flashing in his eyes. "I didn't kill them, Eleanor, but I'm responsible. They killed themselves, every one of them. They couldn't handle the shift in reality. They lost all hope. Earth isn't like the others. I chose you because I thought you were stronger."

"Earth?" she asked, confused.

"I really can't get into this right now, so please try to hold it together until we're somewhere safe."

"I'm not losing my mind, Conlan; it's just a lot to take in. You saved my life and I'm grateful." her words sounded calm and in control, but it had taken effort because her grip on what was going on was not nearly as tight as she was pretending.

Conlan laughed a bitter, self-mocking bark, not the soft sound of amusement Eleanor remembered. "I'm not a hero. I brought you here so you could help me. You have no reason to trust me, of course, but now you're here you have no choice but to do so."

There were just too many questions for Eleanor to handle, and she felt that if she demanded that he answered them all, they would never get anywhere. She sighed, deciding.

"OK then, let's go."

Conlan nodded, looking slightly relieved. He reached for the blanket Eleanor had left on the floor and shook out the 'pillow' she had been using. It unfolded into a jacket and he shrugged it on over the once white shirt that covered his slim, muscular torso. In the past this jacket would have been a fine garment, its dark green padded velvet would have been luxuriant, but now it was dusty and worn. One of the elbows had been inexpertly patched with a rough material of muddy green, the stand-up collar was frayed and several of the tarnished silver buttons from the front were missing. There was an insignia stitched in silver thread over his left breast, which looked like a stylized shape, but Eleanor was unable to identify it properly. He noticed her inspection of him and tossed the blanket to her.

"Roll that up, I'll get my horse."

Horse? Oh crap! Eleanor stood frozen in horror as Conlan led a huge grey animal towards her. It was beautiful, from a distance, which is where Eleanor wanted to keep it.

Conlan saw her expression. "Eleanor, this is Rand." He affectionately patted the massive beast's broad neck, and in return it lowered its huge head and rubbed its nose against his master's side.

"I'm... I'm not a great fan of horses," she stammered as memories of failed horse riding lessons flashed through her mind. Horses were too big, too unpredictable and they frightened her. Eleanor saw the amusement in Conlan's eyes.

"You're going to have to learn to deal with them, there are no cars here."

"Can't I just walk?" she stuttered slightly, fear making her voice sharp.

Conlan appeared to consider this proposal. "Yes, you could walk. We're three days' ride from where we need to be, so walking will take maybe a week, possibly longer. That's too long for us to be out in the open, plus it would be long past dark by the time we cleared the edge of the forest. There are wolves here, and without a fire…"

"Wolves?" she asked.

Conlan nodded and calmly returned her incredulous stare for a moment.

In a practiced, fluid motion he mounted and settled himself in the saddle, which also struck Eleanor as being a piece of finery that had seen better days, although its shiny red leather had been better cared for than the jacket. Eleanor rolled up the blanket and handed it to Conlan. He secured it tightly behind the saddle over a couple of matching red leather saddlebags, and he then reached an arm down and with surprising strength hauled Eleanor up until she sat behind him on top of the blanket roll. Wriggling, getting comfortable, she noticed her clothes for the first time. They were not hers. She felt her cheeks redden. Her shop uniform was gone and in its place were baggy, non-descript brown trousers, worn brown boots that slouched around her small feet and a brown shirt several sizes too big for her delicate build.

"Conlan, where are my clothes?"

"You're wearing them," he said, without turning round.

"No, I was wearing my shop uniform. There should be blood…" Her voice dropped off to a whisper. There was a pause, as if Conlan was trying to think of something to say.

"You left your old body behind," he eventually replied. Eleanor looked down. The body felt real, felt like her, but if what Conlan said was true – that it was a different body to the one that was shot? *Is it really different?* She wrestled with her right sleeve.

"What are you doing?" Conlan asked, twisting slightly in the saddle to look at her.

"When I was five I fell off the garage roof into my Dad's scrap pile and there was a piece of wood with a nail in it. The nail went through my arm. I still have the scar…" Having pulled her sleeve up over her elbow, Eleanor examined her forearm. *No scar...* For some reason this did not frighten her as much as she had thought it would. *Perhaps it's because this body feels anything but alien.* On the inside of her wrist the skin was burnt and blistered; it was hard to make out but it looked like a shape had been burnt into it, a radiant-cut diamond seen side-on. It looked like it should hurt. Eleanor gingerly ran her finger over it. *Numb.*

"If this isn't my body, whose is it?" she asked. "And what does this diamond mean? How did it get there?"

"It's your body, Eleanor, it was made for you. The symbol represents the element of Earth; it's a side effect of the ritual that brought you here. Does it hurt?" There was curiosity rather than concern in his question.

She shook her head. "No, it doesn't hurt."

Conlan tilted his head, scrutinising her again. "Let me know if it starts to hurt, OK?"

Eleanor rubbed her left hand up and down her arm. "This body was made for me?"

"How about we leave that as another question for later?"

Eleanor sighed. "Were you this unhelpful with the others? It might explain the suicide rate!" She had meant it as a joke but Conlan did not laugh – the muscles in his jaw tightened but he showed no other signs of emotion as he stared at her before twisting back round in the saddle.

"Put your arms around my waist and hold tight," he ordered. Eleanor obeyed, wondering if she should apologise.

Rand moved at considerable speed through the trees. The ground seemed very far away and Eleanor judged her position to be rather precarious. She gripped a little tighter, feeling the tension in Conlan's body. Leaning her head against his back, closing her eyes, she focused on not falling off and settled into the steady rhythm of the horse and Conlan's movement in the saddle, allowing herself to drift in that pleasant place that comes before sleep.

A sudden change of pace brought her back to reality. Eleanor opened her eyes and found they had cleared the forest and were now moving along a dirt track that snaked into the distance over rolling, grassy hills. Conlan's body tensed as he glanced behind him, frowning at something over the top of Eleanor's head. He gently urged Rand to greater speed. Automatically Eleanor turned to look and gasped. The height of a tall man, weaving a rhythmic dance from side to side on the track behind them, was the tightly spinning cyclone of dirt and dust of a small tornado. Eleanor glanced at the sky. There were no storm clouds, no rain, no wind and no humidity. There was no reason at all for there to be a tornado, which, Eleanor noticed, had increased its forward momentum to match the speed Conlan had just demanded of Rand.

"Is that tornado following us?" Eleanor asked as she bounced up and down with Rand's steady gait.

"Yes."

His response was so matter-of-fact that Eleanor was stunned. "Why?"

"Because Air is curious."

"How can Air be curious?"

"Asks someone who never stops questioning…" Conlan muttered.

"Is it dangerous?" Eleanor asked, ignoring Conlan's aspersion but noticing that he had pushed Rand to greater speed.

"Sometimes. Air is usually quite timid, but I'd rather we didn't get too close."

"You make it sound like a person. Air is just a random collection of atoms; it can't really decide to follow us."

Conlan did not reply and Eleanor suspected it was not because he agreed with the logic of her argument. The tornado continued to follow for several hours, keeping pace with them but never catching up. Eleanor's attempts to get more information from Conlan fell on deaf ears, and irritation pushed her into angry silence. Eventually the tornado disappeared and Conlan relaxed slightly, taking Rand's speed back down to a steady trot. Eleanor looked about her. There was nothing as far as she could see in any direction but grass, hills and trees. The familiarity of it tugged at her memory, reminding her of a trip through France she had taken as a child. The scenery seemed to slip by, like a movie on fast forward. Eleanor watched it, dazed, her head throbbing. Everything was happening too fast.

The quality of the light began to change as the sun started to drop below the horizon, giving the landscape a more pronounced, dreamlike quality. *This isn't real.* Eleanor's thoughts spun until it hurt too much to think, so she went back to drifting, eyes closed, shivering as the failing sun took what little warmth the day had left.

"You're cold."

It was a statement; Conlan had felt her shiver through her arms wrapped tightly around his waist.

I'm also confused, hungry, thirsty and uncomfortable, with what feels like the mother of all hangovers, Eleanor thought, but it was too much effort to explain this to Conlan, so she just nodded her head against his back.

"We have a little way to go before we can stop," he said. She nodded again, wondering if they would be safe when they reached their destination, but she was too tired to ask. He patted her arm locked round his waist, reassuring and friendly. Eleanor felt the muscles in his sides flex as he nudged Rand to a faster pace. She marvelled that he could still move his legs, as she had lost feeling in hers hours ago. A question occurred to her, and the more she thought about it the more urgent became her need to ask.

"Where are we going?"

"We're going to join the others."

Eleanor sighed. "Helpful as ever... other what?"

"The other three people who make up the Five."

The Five – he had mentioned the Five as she was dying. She wanted to know what they were, wondering if she had inadvertently joined some sort of post-death religious cult, but she suspected that in-depth conversations about who they were would not be forthcoming, so she stuck with simple questions.

"Where are they?"

"Hiding in the mountains."

"Hiding from what?"

"The dangers of this world." That same flat, unhelpful tone.

Fear shot through her again. "What dangers? That tornado?" she whispered, as if talking about it might make it suddenly appear.

Silence.

"Conlan?" Eleanor prodded.

"I liked you better when you were quiet," Conlan muttered.

"I bet you did," Eleanor whispered into his back. If he was so reluctant to tell her about what they were running away from, perhaps she was better off not knowing for the moment. She closed her eyes and rested her head on his back, trying again to find the comfortable place between his shoulder blades.

As darkness fell, the temperature dropped even further, and just as Eleanor was thinking holding on was not going to be an option much longer, Conlan reined Rand back to a slow plod. The partial moon lit the road as it wound across the silvery grey landscape of fields and trees into a black horizon. The moon seemed so much brighter than she had ever seen it, resplendent in a sky so full of stars that it reminded her of the black velvet of the diamond tray with a whole bag of the small glittering gems scattered across it, shimmering and mesmerising. Thinking of diamonds took her mind back to a dark place filled with pain and regret, so to distract herself she spoke to Conlan.

"Your stars and moon are so much brighter than ours," she said as she stared up in wonder.

"They're the same stars and moon you have, Eleanor; Amelia says they are just brighter because this world doesn't have much ambient light," he said quietly.

"Ambient light?"

"Your world has street lights, car headlights and so on – it masks the light from the stars," he answered.

"How can we see the same moon and stars and not be on Earth anymore?" Eleanor wondered aloud, not really expecting an answer. "Have you ever been to our world?" she continued.

"No."

"How do you know so much about it then?"

"The others have told me about it and I've watched through the portal." He was beginning to sound irritated.

"The others, they're from my world? What's a portal?" Eleanor asked, trying to get in as many questions as she could before he thought to shut her up.

"Yes, the others are from your world, but the portal is a question for later. Now be quiet!" he ordered. Eleanor sighed, but she was too weary to argue. Conlan brought Rand to a complete stop. "Eleanor, you need to let go so I can get down."

She released her death-like grip on Conlan's waist, her arms throbbing miserably. She tried rubbing normal feeling back into them as Conlan swung his right leg over Rand's head and dropped gracefully to the ground, his many hours in the saddle seeming not to have affected him at all. He looked up at Eleanor expectantly.

"Rand will stand still – slide off, I'll catch you."

Eleanor nodded, doing as instructed and Conlan did indeed catch her, which was a good job because her legs felt like jelly and buckled as she hit the ground, her full weight landing in Conlan's arms. Again she was surprised by his strength as he held her easily while she struggled to find her feet. Rand turned his head to watch as Eleanor forced her legs to take her weight.

"Sorry," she mumbled into Conlan's chest. It seemed like an eternity before she was able to stand up. She noticed Rand still looking at her.

"Is your horse laughing at me?" she asked.

Conlan chuckled, the soft, amused sound Eleanor had liked.

Taking Rand's reins, he led them into a copse of what looked like silver birches at the side of the track. Eleanor stood, shivering in the dark. Conlan sat her on a fallen tree trunk, wrapped the smelly blanket around her and then began pulling bark off the birch trees, after which he collected a good supply of twigs and larger branches for a fire. Once it was blazing merrily, he regarded her silently for a minute.

"I'm going to get us something to eat – stay here."

Eleanor looked at the dark trees around her with apprehension.

"What about the wolves?"

Conlan shook his head. "They won't come this far north, as there are too many people."

Before Eleanor could ask him if she should therefore be scared of the people, he had gone, disappearing into the darkness without a sound. Eleanor pulled the blanket tighter around her narrow shoulders. As the heat from the fire began to warm up her sore, cold body she found it harder and harder to stay awake. Fragmented, half dreams came and went. Her head ached and everything still felt so strange, like a nightmare from which she was unable to wake.

She woke with a start when Conlan dropped two small grey birds at her side, their dead, vacant eyes staring at her. *Wood-pigeons*, she thought distractedly.

"I'm a vegetarian," she said out of habit, more than any real desire to get him to change the menu.

"A what?"

"A vegetarian – I don't eat animals, or birds or fish," she said, trying to decipher his expression.

Conlan regarded her pensively, processing this new information. The firelight moving across his damaged face made him appear even more menacing, but when he spoke his voice was soft, gentle even.

"Why not?"

While she had felt passionately since she was a small child that killing animals was wrong, Eleanor felt stripped of any conviction as she trotted out the reason she had always given. "Why should another living creature have to give up its life to feed me when I can survive just as well without it?"

Conlan continued to stare at her in silence. The quiet, insistent voice in the back of her head told her she still had no idea who this man was. He appeared to notice the fear spreading across her face and his voice was still soft and gentle when he spoke again.

"What do you eat?"

"Vegetables, tofu, rice, fruit, nuts, pasta..." She stopped as it occurred to her that this world most likely lacked pasta. She would miss pasta. All the other things she would miss began to flood though her mind. Her parents, her friends – were they crying somewhere over her shattered former body? Several hours of near silence and she was already craving her iPod and her favourite music, her books, the holiday in the sun she had been planning. Every new loss stabbed at her. She had exchanged a life of comfort for running, frightened, with a man she barely knew and was not sure if she trusted. Perhaps death would have been better. She began to cry, the pain of it all becoming unbearable. Large, bitter tears ran down her face as she hugged her knees to her chest. *If I squeeze hard enough, can I make myself disappear?* She felt a hand on her shoulder, but this time she was too exhausted, too beaten down, to pull away. She raised her head. The look in his eyes stopped her tears instantly. He looked haunted, as if her pain were his own and his words came back to her: "They couldn't handle the shift in reality, they lost all hope." *Was this how it had begun for the others? Does he think I'm going to kill myself, too?* Drying her eyes on her sleeve, Eleanor tried to smile. It must have been a poor effort because it did nothing to dispel the torment in his eyes.

"I can find you something else to eat." He spoke slowly and carefully, as if to a terrorised child, his gaze holding hers.

It's not about having food to eat. She nodded as her grumbling stomach argued against her. "I'm sorry, I'm just tired, and sore, and hungry, and..." It was just all too much. Her throbbing head and tired body felt so disconnected from everything that she was no longer sure that anything was real.

Conlan hung his head. "You have nothing to apologise for. I'll find you something to eat. Will you be OK on your own?" Eleanor felt a hysterical giggle coming on. *Where is he going to get me something to eat? Did I miss the supermarket on the way in to the woods?* She forced herself to nod. Conlan stood but seemed reluctant to leave.

"I'll be fine, Conlan," she said, as much to reassure herself as to reassure him. He nodded once and ghosted into the darkness again. Eleanor pulled the blanket around her and fell asleep almost immediately.

The tantalising aroma of food pulled her from her slumber. There was a small iron pot resting in the embers at the edge of the fire and the most wonderful vegetable stock smell was rising from it. Conlan gave it a slow stir, watching her intently.

"You looked peaceful, I didn't want to wake you. Are you hungry?"

Eleanor nodded. He spooned some of the vegetable stew into a small metal dish and handed it to her with the spoon. Her stomach twisted in anticipation. It tasted as good as it smelt. The tastes were familiar – carrots, parsnips or sweet potato maybe, herbs and mushrooms – every mouthful made her feel better.

"Is it OK?" he asked.

"Conlan, it's wonderful!" This, at least, must have sounded convincing because he smiled. It lit up his eyes, giving them a life and softness she had not expected. Eleanor felt the world lurch again, but this time it had nothing to do with fear. His smile made him a handsome man.

"What?" The inscrutable look was back.

"I was just thinking how different you look when you smile, you should do it more often," she said. He seemed to consider this suggestion but made no further comment, and to Eleanor's disappointment his smile did not return. After another helping of stew and several cupfuls of brackish water Conlan swore was safe to drink, she curled up on her side under the blanket and allowed the crackling of the fire to lull her back to sleep.

She woke with a start, riding the torrent of jumbled memories until she remembered where she was. The fire had died down to glowing embers, and she could just make out Conlan's sleeping form across from her. He lay on his side, his left arm supporting his head, his right arm wrapped into his chest. *He looks cold.* Eleanor realised his jacket was back under her head. *No wonder he's cold.* Quietly she stood, shook the jacket out, and moving around the fire laid it across him. She built up the fire with what was left of the wood he had collected, poking at the embers until the fresh timber caught.

"Are you alright?" He had not moved or even opened his eyes. Eleanor jumped at the sound of his voice.

"Yes," she said, not trusting the tears to stay back if she indulged in a longer response. She curled herself back up into a ball and pulled the blanket over her, but she was no longer exhausted and the hard ground and strange environment kept sleep away. Her parents had never been into camping; her mother preferring 'select' hotels with hot- and cold-running room service, so sleeping outside was a new experience. Over the crackle of the fire, Eleanor could hear the rustling movement of nightlife around her and wondered if this world had any poisonous bugs. A thought, one that had occurred a while ago, but which she had been trying to ignore, kept popping into her head. *If this body is new, do I look the same?* Her shoulder-length wavy, dark brown hair seemed the same unruly mess, but was her face the same? *If I look in a mirror, will I recognise myself?* Her fears went beyond mere vanity, because if her face was hers it would be something familiar – and she desperately needed something familiar. She began to cry again and tears spilled down, dripping onto her shirt where her arm supported her head.

"Eleanor?"

His voice made her jump again.

"Don't you ever sleep?" An irrational anger at being caught crying made her voice harder than she intended. She sat up. He sat up across from her, scrutinising her face again.

"Is there anything I can do to help you?" he asked softly.

"Help me? Can you get me an iPod? A good book? A bed? No, I don't think you can provide any of those things, and that's just what would make me feel better right now. How about getting to say goodbye to my parents? Or telling my friends how much I'll miss them? How about giving me back my life?" She stopped as the pain of reciting what she was missing was threatening to cause tears again.

"If you had died you'd have had none of those things either," he pointed out.

"Don't be so calm and rational! If I'd chosen death I would have moved on, it would have been natural. I certainly wouldn't have been stuck in this wood with you!" Eleanor snapped.

"Moved on?"

"Yes, Conlan, moved on to the afterlife. Heaven? Hell? For all I know the Elysium Fields or Valhalla; anything but here! You don't believe in life after death?" Her voice was still hard, the anger making her feel less pathetic.

"I've never really given it much thought. The shamans believe that your soul can come back and live again if you have further lessons to learn." He was ignoring the fight in her tone, concentrating on answering her questions and keeping his voice calm. With nothing to argue against, Eleanor felt her anger draining.

"Shamans?" she enquired, interested despite her mood.

"Those who live with the ancient gods."

Leaving that cryptic response for a later conversation, Eleanor tried a different tack. "You believe in a soul, right?"

"Of course, your soul is energy. It's what the shaman pulled through from your world, it's what makes you – you." He sounded so very matter of fact about it, so confident, that Eleanor could not help but smile, thinking of all the many philosophers and religious theologians that had argued back and forth about the soul's existence over the years. Conlan watched her suspiciously, as if she was going to throw herself onto the fire at any moment. *Is sudden amusement when considering your soul a sign of insanity and impending suicide?* Eleanor felt her humour evaporate as quickly as it had come; the darkness outside the fire's circle seemed to press in on her from all sides. Three others had gone through this before her, and none had survived it. Was she really stronger than they were?

"I'm here for good, aren't I? Or at least until I die again," she clarified.

"Yes."

"I guess I get to live twice, so that's more than most people get." She stared into the fire for a while until she felt calmer, more in control. Eventually, sleep seemed possible.

"I'm going to try and sleep."

"OK. Eleanor?"

"Yes?"

"What's an iPod?" He sounded genuinely curious.

"It's a device for playing music," she mumbled, not opening her eyes.

"There's music in this world."

She could barely hear his whisper and she doubted very much that this world had anything good enough to rival her favourite bands, so she ignored him, allowing herself to fall into a deep, dreamless sleep.

3

BREMEN

Consciousness was instantaneous, if uncomprehending. Totally disorientated by her rapid jerk from deep sleep, unsure what had woken her, Eleanor stared wildly at the trees around her. *Where am I?* Memories came flooding back. She sat still and with her eyes closed, waited until the onslaught subsided. When her mind had settled down a little she opened her eyes again, noticing with shock that she was alone. Trying not to panic, Eleanor carefully scanned the immediate area. Neither Conlan nor Rand were anywhere in sight. It was raining and in the grey morning light the steady, soaking drizzle blended the edges of the world around her into one grey-green, formless smudge. There was also a strong smell of damp, rotting wood that she had not noticed the night before. The fire had long since died and it was now cold and apparently lifeless. Eleanor pulled the damp blanket tighter around herself.

"Just wonderful!"

Her quiet sarcasm felt loud over the near silence of the world around her and it pushed her fear up a notch. *Now what?* She realised with horror that she had no idea where she was, no idea where she was going and no idea how to survive this world on her own. She was totally dependent on Conlan. She felt fresh tears spring to her eyes and the world blurred further, but before they could fall she heard her mother's angry voice echoing down from her earliest memories.

"Eleanor Mary Murray, self-pity will do you no good. You might not be able to change your circumstances, but you can always change yourself!"

Eleanor smiled. She could sit around and wait to die of hypothermia, or be eaten by a wolf, or she could get on with it and find a way to cope. She wiped away the tears. She was stronger than this, more able, so she would take her mother's advice – if she could not change her circumstances, she would change herself and learn how to survive in this new world.

First, she needed a fire. She could already feel the cold and damp seeping into her bones, but how do you start a fire? She had no equipment and, frankly, no idea. Why had she not paid closer attention to how Conlan had done it? She ignored the frightened little voice in the back of her head that told her she had not paid attention because she had not felt any of this was real. The cold was real, unpleasant and not going to go away. She poked at the fire embers, nearly yelling for joy when she realised that deep under the ash they still glowed faintly. She jumped up and began pulling away the papery bark of the trees around her. This she *had* seen Conlan do. She also swept up in her arms a collection of twigs and a few larger branches, in the hope that the wet bark might catch. By the time she got back to the fire she was soaked, cold rain chilling her further as it ran down her neck. Her teeth chattered uncontrollably. Working carefully, her hands shaking, she uncovered some of the glowing embers from the layers of ash. She held the thin bark strips over the ember and blew gently. At first nothing happened – the ember glowed a brighter orange, but that was all. Getting closer, trying to cover the ember and the bark with her hand to protect them from the rain, she blew again. Smoke curled up from the bark and suddenly there was a small flame; Eleanor stared at it in amazement for a moment and quickly covered the little flame with more bark. Too much bark. It smoked for a few seconds and then went out. Swearing softly to herself, Eleanor uncovered a fresh ember and started the whole process again, but this time she added the bark slowly, allowing the flame to build until the rain no longer threatened to put it out, and she then began slowly adding larger twigs, followed by the branches. The resulting blaze was impressive. She spent a short time collecting a stack of firewood before settling down in front of her masterpiece. She pulled the blanket back over her shoulders. It was still damp, but now it was warm and damp, a far better combination.

Now the fire was lit, Eleanor felt a lot more comfortable, but where was Conlan? She could have excused a short absence, even planned to gloat about her wonderful fire when he got back. *What if he isn't coming back? What if he's in trouble?* Again she felt panic but choked it back down. *Panic is not going to help me*, she told herself firmly. What she needed was a plan. Where could he have gone? Wherever it was he had gone willingly, taking Rand with him. Would he have abandoned her? This seemed unlikely, as he needed her to join the Five. Perhaps he had not meant to be long and had been held up.

As the morning grey turned to a darker afternoon and the fire burned down, Eleanor became more and more worried. She had to do something. As the day wore on, the rain began to ease off and Eleanor finally stood up, covered the fires remnants with earth and looked around. She had some vague notion that she could follow Conlan. She had read about hunters who could track their prey, so could she follow him? She stood where Rand had been tied the night before, his large hoof prints showed clearly through patches of trampled wet grass to the mud below. As she looked at them, Eleanor realised that she could see two distinct tracks, one leading into the copse and another leading out, the rounded front of Rand's hoof clearly showing which was which. This was something she could follow. Trying to keep Rand's hoof imprints in sight at all times, she followed them through the trees and out onto the track. Eleanor swung her gaze up and down the rough road as it stretched into the distance. The recent rain had made the surface wet and impressionable and there were myriad hoof prints and cart tracks heading in both directions, which made sense, as it was a track most likely used by other people. Which prints were Rand's? *I need something to identify him.* She kept following her line of logic, as it was keeping the panic at bay. She moved back a little way into the trees and found an imprint she knew was Rand's. It was large and deep, as Rand was a big horse. *Is that enough to work it out?* Careful not to disturb the print, Eleanor held her hand against it, trying to get an idea of the size. She then moved back to the road and began to measure the prints. It narrowed down the choice, but not enough, as there were large hoof prints going in both directions. Returning to the camp, Eleanor looked carefully for an imprint of each hoof, moving slowly and deliberately so as not to miss anything. She had inspected two different prints before she found what she was looking for. Rand's hooves were shod, and on his back right leg one of the nails holding the shoe on was not straight. The nail's head stuck out at a slight angle, leaving a thin line in the hoof's impression. Surely this pattern was unique to Rand? Elated and rather impressed with herself, Eleanor ran back to the track. She found Rand's hoof mark almost immediately, and turning to the left she found another and then after a few more paces she found it again. She had a trail she could follow.

Once she became used to the hoof marks and the approximate distance they were from each other, Eleanor found that following the trail was almost easy, the imprints jumping out at her as she walked. Several times during her journey other people came down the track, but in the still air Eleanor heard them before they came close and concealed herself until they passed, trembling in her hiding place with Conlan's words ringing in her head: "We're not safe here." However, as she rounded yet another bend it became obvious that eventually she was going to have to deal with the locals, as the track was leading her towards a small village.

The village houses were comprised mostly of wooden huts and Rand's trail appeared to be following the main street. Everything looked shabby, and when compared to the amazing snow-capped mountains in the distance, rather depressing. It began to rain harder as Eleanor came to the edge of the village, but she was grateful as it meant there would be fewer people to encounter. As she walked further down the track the houses became more tightly packed, small gardens disappearing until the houses faced directly onto the muddy street. It reminded her a little of the old Wild West towns. She had gone a fair distance from Rand's last hoof mark before she realised they had vanished. Retracing her steps, she found the last hoof mark; he had stopped here. *Why?* Eleanor looked around her. There was a post to her left that could be used to tie up a horse. The building behind seemed to be one of the larger ones with bigger windows. Moving cautiously, she looked through the grimy glass. There were items on display, tools she did not recognise, a metal skillet she did. Material was draped across a child's chair and a selection of painted wooden toys were scattered across it. They had a lot to learn about window dressing, but it appeared to be a shop. *What had he wanted to buy?* Conlan seemed resourceful, she did not think he would have resorted to buying something unless he had to do so.

Moving back into the street, Eleanor studied Rand's hoof marks again. They had not gone forward. Searching, she noticed them disappearing down an alley on the other side of the street. It looked dark, but if Conlan had gone that way, Eleanor was determined to follow. The alleyway was narrow. Windowless building walls rose above her on both sides, blocking out what little daylight there was, but there was a flickering orange glow at the end of the passageway, and Eleanor moved warily towards it. The alley opened up into a small courtyard, in which lanterns hung from various points, casting eerie shadows in the gathering twilight. At one end of the courtyard stood a large trough into which water ran, while on either side of the courtyard were stables. Eleanor moved towards the water – she had not realised how thirsty she was. She drank hurriedly, and after sating her thirst she began to investigate the stables. She found Rand in the third stall. The red saddle was gone, but it was definitely Rand. He made a soft whiny when he saw her, rubbing his head gently into her stomach. Reassured by his obvious recognition of her and his slow, gentle movements, Eleanor patted his neck, moving to scratch behind his ears as he slowly lowered his head so she could reach. He seemed to be just fine, better then fine in fact, as someone had given him a good brush.

"Nice to see you too, Rand. Any idea where Conlan is?"

He was not with Rand and Eleanor did not think he would have voluntarily left his horse unattended. Stepping out of the stall she closed the door. *One found, one to go.* As she pushed the latch on the door shut, a hand grabbed her arm and yanked her round. The man facing her was quite a bit taller than she was, with thick meaty arms. He smelt strongly of horse; he was also very angry. He yelled in Eleanor's face, grabbing both her arms and shaking her until she felt like her brains were going to rattle out of her head. He yelled some more. Eleanor stared at him – she had no idea what language he was speaking, as it was deep, hard and guttural, as alien a sound as she had ever heard, and in some places it actually sounded like he was snarling and growling. He was looking at her, expecting an answer. Thinking fast, Eleanor pointed at her mouth and shook her head. The man glared at her, his eyes narrowing suspiciously. She again pointed at her mouth and shook her head, making a few gasping sounds to emphasise her point. The man stared at her a moment longer then muttered something in disgust and slapped her in the face, knocking her to the ground.

Eleanor had never been hit before. The experience left her stunned and confused. The man glared at her and then yelled something else, moving back towards her. Ears still ringing and face burning, Eleanor forced herself to her feet and staggered back down the narrow alley, relieved to discover the man did not want to chase her but seemed content to yell what sounded like a few final insults.

At the end of the alley, Eleanor slowed her headlong rush, knowing it would look suspicious if anyone was watching. She walked from the alley as normally as she could manage, not really thinking about where she was going but just wanting to get away from the angry horse man. She continued down the main street, until eventually it opened up into a paved square with a raised stone platform in the middle of it. The main street flowed round the square, with two grey, squat stone buildings flanking the space, facing each other in an eternal stand-off. *Their architecture could use as much help as their window dressing.* The single-storied buildings were drab and ugly, but the stone steps leading up to the large, sturdy-looking wooden doors gave them an air of officiousness. If something unpleasant had happened to Conlan, perhaps an encounter of his own with the horse man, then an official building was the best place to try. However, as she clearly did not speak the language, it was not as if she could just walk in and introduce herself. Eleanor had no idea what to do next. It was raining again and the wind had picked up, pulling at her merger clothing and moaning with soft menace through the gaps and alleyways of the village. She looked around fearfully for a tornado, until she realised she was getting cold and wet as a result of her indecision. Huffing, she moved to investigate the building on the left side of the square first, mostly because there was a lot of light coming from the windows and she would be able to see what was going on inside. Wrapping her arms around her cold, shaking body and pushing her hands into her armpits, eyes carefully sweeping the empty street, Eleanor moved towards the nearest window.

As she reached the building's wall she realised she was not going to be tall enough to see inside. As she stood on her tiptoes trying to pull herself up on the ledge, something grabbed her leg. She yelped in surprise. There was a dirty hand thrust through a small barred hole near the bottom of the wall. Panic and fear twisted in her stomach and she kicked at the arm, falling on her back in the mud in the process. The hand released her and retreated back into the hole. Once her heart rate had slowed a little and Eleanor was quite sure no one was going to come out of the building and investigate the noise she had just made, she peered into the hole, making sure she did not get too close. As her eyes adjusted to the gloom she found two bloodshot eyes staring back at her. It was a man, a dirty, badly dressed man. He appeared to be in some sort of room, as there was a closed door behind him with a barred hole that allowed flickering orange light to spill in from the other side. *It's a prison.* Once Eleanor's mind reached this conclusion it seemed obvious. The man was saying something in that strange growling, snarling language. Eleanor did not understand him any better than she had the horse man, although his tone became more desperate as she moved away. She ignored him; there was nothing she could do. There were other holes with bars across them further along the wall – other cells, she thought. *Maybe Conlan is in one of them.* The next cell was empty and the one after that. The first cell on the other side of the steps contained another dirty man, who was lying spread-eagle on the floor snoring loudly.

She found Conlan in the next cell. He sat with his back to the wall on the right side of his prison, his knees pulled up to his chest, his grey trousers were covered in mud. His forehead rested on arms crossed over his knees. In the dim orange light Eleanor could see blood. It spiked up the hair on the left side of his head, and from what she could see it had run copiously down his face, soaking the collar of his jacket.

"Conlan," she whispered as quietly as possible. He raised his head. Eyes dulled with pain stared at her until his brain registered what he was looking at.

"What are you doing here?" he spat.

Eleanor was taken aback by his anger. He stood stiffly and painfully, the damage sustained clearly not just to his head. He shuffled like an old man until he was under the hole and could look her in the eye.

"I tracked you, Conlan, tracked Rand," Eleanor told him, unable to keep the pride out of her voice.

"Great, *now* you decide you're not helpless!" he snapped. "You were safe where I left you, Eleanor. It's most definitely not safe for you here – go, *immediately!*"

"I don't know where to go." It sounded like a child's whine, even to her own ears, so desperate and pathetic.

Conlan sighed, the anger draining from his face and leaving just the pain.

"Follow the main street towards the mountains and you'll come to a large tree at the edge of town. Stay hidden. I'll find you there tomorrow."

"They'll let you go tomorrow?" Eleanor asked confused. Conlan nodded wearily. She did not understand. If someone had gone to the trouble of imprisoning him, why would they let him go tomorrow?

"Why have they locked you up now? What happened? What were you doing here?"

"Not now, Eleanor – just go!" he ordered.

"No."

"Pardon?"

"No. Conlan, I found you, which was no easy feat, by the way! I'm not going anywhere until you give me a straight answer." She gave him a determined look, or one she hoped made her appear determined.

Eleanor watched the anger move back into his expression.

"I made a mistake," he said with a bitter resignation that gave Eleanor the impression that he did not really believe his current situation was his fault. "Now I'm paying for it, but I don't want you to pay for it as well. So *go!*"

Eleanor shook her head. "Not nearly good enough."

Conlan said something in the growling language the horse man had used. The words meant nothing to Eleanor, but the tone and delivery gave her the impression it had been a string of rather strong profanities.

"Fine, whole story," he said, switching back to English. "There are some things we need that we can't find or make ourselves. Medical supplies mostly. I thought I could visit Bremen and be back before you woke up."

"Bremen?" Eleanor interrupted.

"The town, Eleanor, this is Bremen. They used to be free, but things have changed, particularly as there are Protectors here now. A couple of men tried to steal Rand – nothing I couldn't handle, but the Protectors got involved. I have no papers and neither does Rand, so I was accused of being a horse thief. Rand is confiscated, I get a night in jail and first thing tomorrow morning a public flogging, then they let me go."

"A public flogging? That doesn't sound very pleasant."

"It's not," Conlan agreed, his tone emotionless, but Eleanor saw him shudder.

"Don't you get a trial or something?" Eleanor asked. This was all wrong. Conlan annoyed her, but he seemed to be a good person and he certainly did not deserve this.

Conlan shook his head and Eleanor was sure she saw a flash of terror in his green eyes.

"Bremen has also acquired a resident Enforcer," he whispered.

"Enforcer?" Eleanor felt confusion wash over her again.

Conlan noticed her expression, nodding grimly. "Protectors are mostly thugs, violent bullies, but their power is limited to their strength, numbers and skill at torture. Enforcers, however have the power of the elements at their command, power that's been twisted, power it's very difficult to circumvent. The only force capable of taking down an Enforcer is another Enforcer. They're cunning, vicious and utterly without mercy. It was better to capitulate than have one involved."

"And there's one of those here?" Eleanor whispered, fear cramping her stomach. Conlan nodded again, holding her gaze. *This is why he wants me out of town.* It was a logical order, with her best interests behind it, but Eleanor could no more have obeyed it than she could have stopped breathing.

"Did you steal Rand?" Eleanor asked.

"No!"

The indignant tone was enough to convince Eleanor he was telling the truth. "Then you have to escape," she insisted.

"Eleanor, be quiet," he snapped. "This isn't a game. If they catch you, they'll kill you."

"Why? What did I do?" she asked, totally bewildered. Conlan's head dropped and he stared at the floor for a long moment. When he finally spoke, his voice was flat again, empty.

"You exist... For some people that's enough."

Eleanor felt her fear become terror at his words, but she fought it back, panic would help no one. He watched the expressions move across her face; when he spoke again, his voice was gentle.

"Please, Eleanor, just go to the edge of town. I'll find you. We still have a long way to go, and this really isn't your problem."

Eleanor felt her anger surge at the pity she could see in his eyes. "So I just run away and leave you?" she asked incredulously. "What about Rand?"

Conlan turned his face away to hide the worry, but he could not quite keep it out of his voice. "I don't even know where he is."

Eleanor smiled. "I do."

He turned back, giving her his unfathomable look again. She felt like a bug under a microscope. Whatever conclusions he came to, he kept them to himself.

"Leave him, Eleanor," he said quietly. "Rand isn't worth your life." His resignation was beginning to grate. Clearly the town was a dangerous place to be, but she was not stupid and she could lie low, she could help him. *I'm not going to abandon them.* Conlan and Rand were her friends, she was not going to let them suffer if she could help it.

"Conlan, I can help you. In fact, I'm *going* to help you."

"No, you're *going* to follow my order and leave town now," he barked.

"And how exactly do you intend to make me comply with that order?" she enquired. He glared at her, and Eleanor was suddenly very glad he had no way to reach her.

"What is it with Earth?!" he exploded. "They never take orders. One day on your own tracking hoof prints and you think you're Venusia!"

"I think I'm who?" Eleanor asked, frightened by his anger and totally confused again.

"Venusia. She was a great leader and warrior of the royal bloodline." Some of his anger dissipated as he explained.

"Oh, like Xena?" Eleanor said brightly, as understanding dawned.

"Xena?"

"Yeah! Xena, we have warrior princesses in my world too, you know!"

Conlan gave her another penetrating look, before trying again. "Eleanor, I need you to leave."

"No, you need my help!" she insisted, trying her determined glare on him again.

"No, I need to know you're safe!" he shot back. They regarded each other sternly, but eventually Eleanor looked away, knowing his flashing green eyes were still drilling into her.

"Conlan, I am going to rescue you and Rand, but it might be easier if you helped me plan it," she said, glancing back at him.

"We don't need rescuing!" He was so angry now that he was clenching and unclenching his fists, but he could not reach her and this made Eleanor feel braver.

"Stop being such an arse. Are you always like this when you don't get your own way?" she asked, watching his entire body tense.

"My own way? You have no idea what you're risking! You're an idiot!"

"Thanks so much for the assessment of my intellect!" Eleanor muttered.

Conlan continued to glare at her, but finally he took a deep breath, closing his eyes for a moment. When he spoke, his tone was once again calm and steady; Eleanor wondered how much effort it had taken.

"Eleanor, I brought you here, gave you life. I'm responsible for you. You're going to get plenty of chance to risk yourself in the future without pulling an idiotic rescue mission like this."

"If you're going to be a defeatist about it, I'll just have to rescue you on my own."

As Eleanor stood to leave, Conlan grabbed at her ankle through the bars but she jumped out of the way and ran off into the dark.

She had half a plan forming in her head, but she needed Rand. Using the shadows, she made her way back to the stables. The rain had become a violent storm and the wind seemed to be chasing her, trying to pull her off her feet as it battered with palpable rage against the closed shutters and doors of the deserted village. Rand was where she had left him. She opened the stall door and slipped inside. Again, he seemed pleased to see her, gently nudging his nose against her shoulder. She was going to have to get him out of the stable, across the courtyard and onto the street, but with his metal shoes someone would hear. She needed something to muffle the noise. There was also the matter of when to leave, because if she stole Rand back too soon, someone might raise the alarm before she could rescue Conlan. She would have to wait. Pulling herself into a corner of the stall she drew straw around her, thankful that at least she was dry. Rand stooped to rub his face against hers; she patted him in return, closed her eyes and waited.

Guilt at having slept brought her fully awake in seconds. Someone had opened Rand's stall, flooding it with weak morning light. She froze, not even daring to breathe as a small boy entered and put a nosebag over Rand's head, talking to him softly in the same strange language she had heard before. Fortunately the boy kept Rand between himself and Eleanor, so he failed to notice her partially hidden in the corner. He left as quickly as he had entered, leaving the top half of the stall door open. Working as quickly and quietly as she could, terrified that she had already let Conlan down, Eleanor pulled off the sleeves of her shirt, the seams giving easily. She then tore two uneven strips off the bottom of the shirt, the sound hidden by the noise Rand was making eating the contents of his nosebag. *At least someone's getting breakfast.* Taking the sleeves and two strips of material, she tied one round each of Rand's hooves, stuffing them with straw. The horse stopped eating to watch her, puzzled but remaining perfectly still as she worked. Being careful, Eleanor looked out through the open top of the stall door and found that the courtyard was empty. She had no idea how long this would be the case, but she could not afford to wait. With her heart pounding painfully in her chest she opened the door carefully, removed Rand's nosebag and threw it back into the stall. The animal followed it wistfully with his eyes, but he allowed Eleanor to lead him into the courtyard when she gave his mane a tentative tug. Closing the stall door slowly behind her, she led him towards the alley, relieved to find that his padded hooves made no noise. Near the end of the alley, she stopped and removed the makeshift mufflers. The next bit of her plan was not very well thought through. Could she just walk down the main street with a horse and have nobody comment? *Only one way to find out.* Taking a deep breath she led Rand out onto the muddy track. Head held high, she tried to walk as if she owned the place and had every right to be there, but her act was unnecessary. The street was empty. As she approached the square, Eleanor understood why. It was full of people – practically the whole town must have gathered. There was a party atmosphere as the crowd jostled each other for a better view of the raised stone platform in the centre of the square, which now had a thick length of pole embedded in it pointing upwards to the overcast sky. When they said public flogging, they meant *very* public flogging. Eleanor's stomach twisted until she felt sick. *How can they find pleasure in another's suffering? Why do they want to see this?* More importantly, how was she going to reach Conlan through all those people?

Eleanor was still thinking this problem through when a cheer went up from the crowd. Following the direction of the turning heads, she saw Conlan at the top of the jail steps, squinting in the pale morning light. His hands appeared to be tied behind his back and two stern-looking guards flanked him. They wore matching long, dark-grey jackets, with stand-up collars and two lines of silver buttons running down the chest. *Uniforms? What had Conlan called the guards? Protectors...* Eleanor winced as she saw one of them give Conlan a vicious shove. He tumbled heavily down the steps, landing on his side in the mud at the bottom. The crowd surged forward, kicking and punching at his prone body. Eleanor watched in horror. Would the crowd kill him? She had to act. Pulling Rand towards a small cart, she used its wheel as a step to mount him. Trying not to think about just how far from the ground she was, she wove her fingers through handfuls of Rand's silvery, grey mane. Heart hammering in her chest she tried to work out what to do. The guards broke up the crowd and dragged Conlan back to his feet. They released the binds on his wrists so they could pull his jacket from him. One of the guards looked it over admiringly and tucked it into his belt; the crowd cheered again. The other Protector shoved Conlan back down to his knees and ripped his shirt from him. Even from a distance Eleanor could see the deep purple bruises that covered him. The Protector kicked him in the middle of the back and Conlan pitched forward, putting his hands out instinctively to protect his face. There was more cheering, which had a scary, hysterical edge to it. Again, the Protectors dragged their captive back to his feet. Eleanor realised the crowd around him was thinning, as people began moving to get a better view of the platform and flogging post in the middle of the square. Conlan's hands were still untied and the two Protectors were overconfident, playing to the crowd, distracted. She was not going to get a better chance. Pulling Rand's head round in the direction of his master, Eleanor kicked her heels into the horse's sides with all her strength and grabbing handfuls of mane in a white knuckled grip, clung on.

Rand shot forward. Eleanor had read somewhere that horses did not like to run people down. Obviously Rand had never been told this and charged at full speed into the crowd, most of whom were oblivious until the animal's speeding bulk was upon them. With surprise on her side, Eleanor found that most of those around her panicked and simply wanted to get out of the way. She held on tight as Rand trampled and kicked a path towards Conlan. One slightly more enterprising man tried to pull Eleanor down, but she pistoned her foot ferociously into his face until he let go and was pulled under the thundering hooves, his screams melting into the general chaos. They broke into the small space around Conlan and the Protectors. Rand reared up on his back legs, almost depositing Eleanor on the floor, his hoof kicking out at the nearest Protector's head. It made contact with a sickening, wet, splitting sound, blood splattering in all directions. The man fell to his knees and then toppled over sideways, the whites of his staring blank eyes swimming red. The crowd froze, stunned. Conlan took the opportunity the distraction provided to pull the remaining Protector's own sword on him. Eleanor watched him hammer the hilt into the surprised man's face, yanking his jacket and a small knife out of the man's belt as he crumpled to the floor. He slipped the jacket on, slid the knife down the side of his boot and hauled himself onto Rand's back behind her.

"Eleanor, where's the saddle?"

"I have no idea."

"Then you're about to get a crash course in horse riding; hold on to the mane and grip with your legs." Putting an arm around her waist, he leaned forward, gave Rand a swift kick in the flanks and they were off, heading down the main street out of town at a full gallop.

4

FIGHT OR FLIGHT

Conlan pushed Rand hard towards the mountains in the distance. The wind making her eyes water, Eleanor concentrated on not falling off. She wondered how Rand knew which way to go without Conlan pulling on reins, but as she concentrated she noticed he was flexing and relaxing the muscles in his legs, showing Rand the way by squeezing on one side or the other. Even through her fear Eleanor was impressed by just how well trained Rand was. They rode in silence for what felt like forever. Conlan still seemed angry.

Eleanor's legs began to ache; every part of her body was either sore or numb. The rush of adrenaline that had sustained her through the first few hours of their mad dash was wearing off, leaving behind exhaustion and fear in its place. As the afternoon wore on, the temperature dropped further. Eventually Rand began to falter, and Eleanor tensed at every missed step with the expectation that she would go flying.

"Conlan, we need to stop – Rand is tired."

"We can't, they'll be following us. If you're able to track Rand, you can bet they can." His voice was grim, angry, and his grip tightened on the sword he still held.

"Are they going to catch us?" Eleanor heard the childlike terror in the words.

"I really hope not, Eleanor, because after the mess we left back there, they're going to kill us if they do. What possessed you to ride Rand into those people?"

"I thought it would be OK, that they'd get out of the way. I thought horses didn't run down people," she said, her mind reeling at his anger. She had just rescued him – she had thought he might be grudgingly grateful, she certainly had not expected to have to defend her actions.

"Your whole problem is you *didn't* think," he snapped, a strange snarl slipping into his voice. "Rand is a warhorse, he's trained to do what you just had him do but on a battlefield, against armed soldiers, not against innocent, unarmed people."

"Innocent, unarmed people who were baying for your blood," Eleanor noted.

"Irrelevant. Have you any idea how many you could have killed?"

Eleanor wanted to apologise, an image of the Protector Rand had kicked in the head fresh in her mind, but then she remembered the sound of hysterical cheering the crowd had made as Conlan had been shoved to the ground. They did not deserve her pity – they were ruthless, violent people. It suddenly occurred to her that they were the same people who were chasing them, and fear twisted her stomach so hard she was glad she had not eaten anything recently.

"Conlan, I'm scared," she whispered.

"Good, you should be! Remember this feeling the next time you have the desire to do something suicidally brave!"

"I was just trying to help you," she said, trying very hard not to whine, to sound strong and justified. "You can't tell me you wanted those Protectors to flog you."

"It wouldn't have been the first time."

Eleanor had no response to that and lapsed into silence. Conlan slowed Rand's headlong gallop to a bouncing, bone-jarring trot.

They had been travelling for several miles before Eleanor realised that Conlan's breath was whistling through his teeth at every jolt. As he did it again she turned and caught the grimace of pain on his face.

"You're hurt; you can't keep this pace up," she said.

"I'll manage," came the hard, empty response. Eleanor gently nudged her elbow into his side. Conlan gasped and moaned, his head dropping briefly onto her shoulder as he struggled to catch his breath.

"Oh yeah, Conlan. You're just peachy," she muttered.

As the sun set, the encroaching darkness forced them to slow Rand down to a heavy-footed walk. The animal panted. Sweat had formed a lather that coated his chest and legs, flecks of saliva covered his face and more saliva dripped from his mouth with each panting breath as it steamed in the chilly air.

"Conlan, it's really cold. I'm tired and Rand is all sweaty; shouldn't we stop?" she asked, working hard to keep the complaint out of her voice.

Conlan shook his head slowly. "Our only chance of escape is to run through the night; Protectors don't like to ride at night. It will give us the extra time we need to make it to safety. We can't stop."

The closer they got to the mountains, the colder it became. Snow began to appear in areas that had not been reached by the sun, until they were walking through a blurry, white landscape that glowed eerily pale blue in the moonlight. Eleanor fixed her gaze on the mountains. Her bare arms and hands were numb with cold, her nose and ears were not far behind and her breath came out in small grey clouds. Yet, despite her discomfort, she felt a strange excitement. The mountains were so close now that she could see the snow-covered crags and the path that led up into them. It was so very beautiful that it made her breath catch and brought tears to her eyes. She tried to explain the feeling to herself, but the closest she could get was that it felt like home – which was odd for a place she had never been. The burn on her wrist began to itch. If she could have prised her frozen fingers from Rand's mane to scratch it she would have, but as it was, she simply added it to the list of aches and pains and forgot about it. It began to snow – large, soft, dreamy flakes settling on her head, and then melting and running down her neck. Eventually Rand came to a stop; his head bowed, flanks heaving.

"We walk from here."

Eleanor jumped at Conlan's voice after the miles of silence. She turned to object, to beg for rest, but she met green eyes filled with agony and stern resolve. She promptly shut her mouth. He was pushing himself far harder than he was pushing her, the danger must be very real. He let go of her waist and slid to the ground. The jolt as he landed made him groan, and he crumpled in on himself as he collapsed into the deepening snow, eyes squeezed closed, lips pulled back over clenched teeth. Moving as quickly as her cold, tired body would allow, Eleanor swung her leg over Rand's back and, holding on to his mane, lowered herself to the ground. She knelt in the snow at Conlan's side, with no idea how to help him. Eventually he fought down the pain and glared at her.

"Get me up, we need to move."

Eleanor put her shoulder under his arm and struggled to get him to his feet, as she did she looked back the way they had come. There seemed to be dancing lights in the distance, moving towards them.

"Conlan, what's that?" she asked, pointing back down the trail. Conlan turned to look and his whole body tensed.

"It's them, the Protectors, riding at night. We have to go!"

Eleanor could hear the fear in his voice and it sent a shot of terror through her soul. Turning up the track, away from the lights, Conlan trudged onwards. Eleanor followed, with Rand faithfully bringing up the rear.

The track became steeper, twisting and turning through the crags and revealing some dizzying drops. Eleanor noticed, distractedly, that her wrist had begun to hurt. She rubbed it absently as she looked behind her; the lights seemed closer.

Conlan fell.

Eleanor pulled him up, practically dragging him forwards. *I should be dead on my feet.* Yet, she felt energised, powerful. A strong heat began to radiate through her body, spreading through her frozen limbs and bringing a strange vitality. The exhaustion faded slightly– it was still there, but it did not seem as urgent as it had been.

"I need a moment to catch my breath," Conlan gasped. Eleanor nodded and supported his shaking body as best she could as he panted. The heat in her wrist turned to an intense burning, heating up her muscles and melting the snow that settled on her bare skin. She rubbed at the mark, wincing. Conlan noticed.

"Does it hurt?"

"Yes, it has done for a while and it's getting worse," she said, her voice shaking, although whether that was fear, the bitter cold or the heat she could feel surging through her, she was not sure.

"Good. Eleanor, there's a narrow gap a little further up this trail that leads to a small canyon; we need to get there," his words were barely audible over the pounding in her ears of her frightened heart and his rough voice dissolved into coughs, spasms wracking his body, blood flecking the snow at his feet. Eleanor struggled to keep him upright. As the coughing subsided she pulled more of his weight over her shoulders and dragged him forward. Conlan weakly pointed the way.

Once in the canyon, Eleanor looked around. It was shaped like a stone goldfish bowl. The snow was not as deep here, and in places, where the walls curved inwards, the overhang had stopped any falling at all. Eleanor looked up and saw the stars and moon in the frigid sky through the gap above, filling the canyon with an ethereal, silvery light. She could have made it out of the hole, but Conlan never would and Rand, who stood shivering in the dark shadow under one of the overhangs, would have no hope either. Looking back, she realised that the entrance they had used was also the only exit.

"Conlan, where do we need to go from here?"

"This is where we need to be," came the rasping reply.

"It's a dead-end, we've no escape; we're going to have to fight," she pointed out.

Conlan staggered again and Eleanor lowered him down against the canyon wall under an overhang. He lay with his arms wrapped round his chest, panting. Despite the cold, sweat stood out on his forehead, and his face was drawn, pained. Eleanor gently prised the sword from his cold fingers; he gave her another deep, penetrating look.

"What are you doing?"

"I don't think you're capable of putting up much of a fight right now," she muttered, not voicing her fear that she did not think she was very capable either.

The frown deepened. "Do you even know how to use a sword?"

"I'm sure they'll get my 'point'," she said with a lopsided grin, trying to convey a confidence she did not feel. Conlan nodded, amusement camouflaging the pain in his eyes for a moment.

"You just have to hold them off. Buy us time, Eleanor, help is coming."

Eleanor doubted it, but she got up, again feeling another surge of warmth run through her body, heating her cold muscles and filling her with vitality she was well aware she should not possess. *A concern for later.* Right now, this strange energy was too valuable for her to question its provenance. She gave the sword some experimental swings. She had taken some Kendo classes at summer school years ago, but the heavy metal felt very different to the bamboo 'shinai' swords they had used.

Standing in front of Conlan she faced the narrow entrance to the canyon, raising her weapon as the Protectors entered. There were six of them – they carried lanterns and all drew their swords when they saw her. The slick swish of the metal as they were released from the scabbards made her flesh crawl, a feeling compounded as her gaze tracked the row of sharpened steel glinting in the lantern light. One of the men was talking to her. She had no idea what he was saying, but the gestures he made and the laughing from the other men left little to the imagination. Hers would not be an easy death. Fear made her hand shake, but she fought to control herself as they fanned out around her. She swung her sword at those who moved too close. The two to the right jumped back as she came within a hair's breadth of slicing flesh. The man who had done the talking laughed. He moved forward, casually, then twisted suddenly and aimed a hammer blow straight at her head. Eleanor reacted purely on instinct. Feeling the power surge through her, she raised her own sword to block the blow. The jarring force as it landed made her teeth rattle in her head, the sound of ringing metal momentarily deafening as it echoed around her. A look of surprise flashed briefly across the man's face, before he pulled back and thrust at her side. Eleanor twisted and swung the sword at the back of his neck. He ducked and blocked. He was playing with her, she knew it. He brought another hammer blow down at her head again, but this time she shifted her weight slightly, allowing his blow to slide harmlessly down her blade. As his weapon cleared the tip of hers, Eleanor allowed the tension to release and the sword flicked up. Seeing an opening, she thrust her stolen sword, with all the force she could muster, into her opponent's throat. He looked shocked, but then again, so was she. She watched in amazement as his life blood pumped out of the ruptured main artery. He grabbed the wound with rubbery, useless fingers and collapsed, gurgling his last breaths.

For a moment there was silence and the metallic smell of blood. *I killed a man*, was her first thought. *It was far too easy*, was the second. Horrified, Eleanor looked at the sword. Her hands still trembling, she tightened her grip. Then, raising the wet, glistening weapon again, she turned to stare grimly at the nearest Protector, who stared back in astonishment. The silence was shattered by one of the other men yelling at her, his obvious fury making him sound like an animal as he made his point in his snarling, growling language. She turned slowly. The fight had taken her away from Conlan's side. Her place had been taken by the man doing the yelling – he was thin and wiry, with a nasty grin. Crouched over Conlan, he had pulled his head back by the hair and was holding a wicked-looking knife against his captive's throat, dark malice staring at her from black, hostile eyes. The man said something, looked at Eleanor's sword and then dragged his blade across skin to emphasise the words. A thin line of blood dribbled down Conlan's neck. Despite the barrier of the strange language, she understood exactly what the Knife Man meant and flung her sword away from her. *So much for playing fair.* One of the other men circled behind her. She knew he was there, but there was nothing she could do about it. Forcing herself to breathe slowly, Eleanor concentrated on not showing fear. The man holding the knife to Conlan's throat growled orders. He seemed to be in charge now. Two of the men went to stand by the only exit from the canyon. *Just in case I felt like running for it*, Eleanor thought, fighting back her hysterical panic.

Knife Man called to a younger-looking man, his features soft and frightened; the kid nodded and knelt, holding his own knife to Conlan's exposed neck. Standing slowly, Knife Man moved towards her. He smiled and licked his thin lips, running his gaze up and down her trembling body. Death was coming. Eleanor could see it in his eyes, but first he was going to make her suffer. She had a strong flashback to another life, another man threatening her, gunshots, agony, regret. Knife Man raised his blade and gently, almost as a caress, ran it down her left arm. Thanks to the cold, Eleanor was able to control her reaction; she saw the trickle of blood before the pain hit. It was not a deep cut, but it required her to clamp her teeth together over a cry of pain. She would not give him that satisfaction. Behind them she heard Conlan struggling, yelling something in their growling language. Knife Man barked an order without turning round. There was the dull slap of fists hitting flesh, accompanied by a pitiful, animal-like whimpering and then silence. *Is he dead?* Eleanor could not bring herself to look. If he was, at least it had been quick.

Looking annoyed by the interruption, Knife Man grabbed at her chin with his free hand. Eleanor flinched away, taking an involuntary step back. The other man was there, right behind her. He reached an arm round her chest, pinning her against him. The rank smell of sweaty, unwashed man filled Eleanor's nose, driving her to panic. She struggled, attempting to get free, but the man's arms were like steel. Knife Man sneered at her, growling what appeared to be his amusement at her futile efforts. Anger flared, and with the heel of her foot Eleanor stomped down, hard. The vice-like grip was released and the man howled, landing on his backside as he tried to massage the pain from his crushed toes. Unfortunately, before Eleanor could take advantage of the chance for freedom, the point of Knife Man's blade thrust at her face. Again, instinct kicked in. Raising her arms, Eleanor's right forearm took the force of the jab instead of the eye Knife Man had been aiming for. The pain was immediate, running up her arm and filling her head, lightning flashing through her vision. Crying out, she staggered back, clutching at the injury. An alarming quantity of blood – warm and sticky – oozed between her fingers. She watched it drip, the crimson terrifyingly vivid against the snow. Her body suddenly weak, the situation beyond her comprehension, Eleanor dropped to the ground stunned, shaking uncontrollably. Knife Man stood menacingly over her. In an abstract way she knew death was imminent, but time seemed to have stopped. She raised her head. Knife Man was staring at her, horror and disgust on his face and enough fear in his eyes to reach through Eleanor's shock.

What's he afraid of?

Utterly confused, Eleanor looked about, wondering if the mythical help Conlan had alluded to had suddenly made an appearance.

"Harish!" Knife Man yelled, backing away – the knife held in defence now, not attack. His retreat was halted by a hollow 'thwack'. Knife Man's eyes opened wide, his features frozen in terror. The fletched feathers of the end of an arrow were protruding from the top of his head, like some sort of bizarre headdress. His eyes rolled back in his skull and he collapsed. Behind her, Eleanor heard another 'thwack' and turned as the other man, just having got back on his feet, toppled over, an arrow sticking out of the top of his head. The two by the exit fell with hardly a sound, arrows sticking out of their chests, before they fully realised what was going on. That just left the kid next to Conlan. Eleanor turned to face him. His soft brown eyes flicked around with panicked fear; he gazed at his fallen comrades, promptly flung his sword and knife to the ground and fell to his knees with his hands behind his head.

Eleanor forced herself to stand. Her body continued to shake. Conlan was lying still. She was too far away to tell if he was breathing and too afraid to get closer in case he might not be. Shadows moved across the gap above her – those who had released the arrows, she guessed – but were they friends or more foe? The pain in her wrist became an agony that overwhelmed even the pain of the injury Knife Man had inflicted. She cradled it with her left hand and waited, paralysed, for whatever was coming next. Eleanor jumped when a voice called out from the canyon's entrance.

"You must be Earth. Who taught you to fight?"

Eleanor spun round; a woman and two men were entering the canyon. It was the woman who had spoken. She was tall and willowy, with long black curls tied down her back. Cold grey eyes regarded the world from a beautiful, solemn, ivory-skinned face. The two men could not have been more different. The older one was tall and pale, blond hair and deep-blue eyes in a handsome, rugged face. He moved his lithe, muscular body with a sinuous grace that rivalled Conlan's. The shorter, younger one had skin like polished walnut, a sturdier, stronger looking physique and closely cropped black hair over dark, almost black eyes that shimmered in the lantern light. He had an amused smile and an open, friendly face. They moved towards her with calm confidence, swords at their waists swinging against their legs as they walked. The blond man carried a bow, which he handed to the woman as he passed them, moving quickly towards Conlan. Eleanor felt a surge of relief. She was home and here were her family. She had never met these people before in her life, and yet she felt closer to them than anyone she had ever known. The pain, fear and confusion of the last few days fell away and she smiled through tears she had not realised were falling down her face.

"I'm Eleanor," she managed between sobs, stepping over the dead man at her feet and staggering forwards. The woman almost ran towards her, welcoming her. As they touched, the pain in Eleanor's wrist dropped immediately to a dull throb. Burying her face into the woman's shoulder, she smelt lavender and the vague, comforting impression of incense; the woman stroked her head gently.

"I'm Amelia. We knew you were close when our brands started burning, so we came looking for you. Conlan always said this was a good place for an ambush. He's my man, Will," she said, nodding towards the blond man crouching over Conlan. "The other one's Freddie." Freddie had dragged the cowering young Protector a short distance from them, so that he would not get in Will's way. Eleanor watched anxiously as the blond-haired man gently assessed Conlan's injuries.

"We need to get him out of here," he said.

"Is he going to be OK?" Eleanor asked.

Will nodded without looking up. "He's taken quite a beating and he's exhausted. I think there might be broken ribs, but hopefully he'll heal." He gently pulled his patient into a sitting position; as he did, Conlan's eyes flickered open.

"Hi, Boss, how do you feel?" Will asked.

"Is Eleanor OK?" Conlan's voice was a whisper, and pain danced deep in his eyes as he fought for consciousness, struggling to sit up.

"Yes, she's fine. She put up a great fight," Will said. Conlan stared at Eleanor, the strange look back on his face as he examined her.

"Erm, Boss, what do you want to do with this one?" Freddie called from behind them.

Conlan looked past them to where Freddie stood over the young Protector.

"Will, get me up."

Will shook his head. "You should stay where you are, let Freddie handle it."

Conlan glared, until the blond man sighed.

"Yes, Boss," he muttered, hauling Conlan to his feet, watching him walk painfully towards the Protector.

"Freddie, your sword," Conlan said softly, holding out his hand.

"Yes, Boss." Freddie answered. He unsheathed his weapon, handed it to Conlan and stepped out of the way. The terrified Protector began to babble in his growling language. As the tip of the sword was placed against the man's chest, his babbling intensified, tears ran down his face and he started wringing his hands. Horrified, Eleanor moved to Conlan's side.

"What are you doing?" she demanded.

Conlan looked at her, eyes dark, unreadable. "Killing him."

Eleanor gasped and shook her head. "Let him go, he's just a kid."

"He knows who you are Eleanor, knows you exist – knows we exist. He can't be allowed to live," Conlan said, his voice empty.

"So what if he knows we exist?" she asked, angry at Conlan's sudden casual disregard for life. *Was he not the one who was just berating me for accidentally killing people in Bremen?*

"So when he goes running back he will tell the Enforcers, and we'll be hunted. The minute the snow melts they will be swarming all over this mountain. It will make things very difficult."

"Then it makes things difficult," Eleanor snapped. "Let him go!"

Conlan grabbed her right wrist, giving no care to the still slowly oozing knife wound, and pushed it in front of the kneeling man's face. He growled something at the terrified Protector in his own language. The kid looked horrified, nodded and said something back; it sounded to Eleanor like the word Knife Man had yelled, *harish*. She yanked her hand back, hissing in pain.

"What did you say to him?" she asked.

"I asked him if he knew what you were, if he recognised the symbol on your wrist."

"I take it he did. What's the word he used, 'harish?' "

"The closest Will got it in your language is 'abomination'," Conlan replied.

"He thinks I'm an abomination?"

Conlan nodded. "Yes, he does and that's why he and his kind will hunt us and kill us if they can." As if that was enough of an explanation, Conlan raised the sword. Eleanor stepped quickly in front of the trembling Protector. Alarmingly, the tip of the blade punctured the rough material of Eleanor's shirt, coming to a rest against her skin. It would take very little pressure to force the sword into her belly. She gasped and froze. Conlan glared at her with barely controlled fury; he did not withdraw the sword.

"Eleanor, he has to die," he said quietly.

"So this is what you are? A cold-blooded killer? Don't you think there's been enough blood and pain for today?" Eleanor yelled, her anger giving her courage.

"If you had done as I ordered, the only blood spilled today would have been mine."

His tone was lethal and ice-cold. Eleanor recognised that this was a dangerous situation, that she did not know Conlan well enough to predict if he would actually push the weapon into her, but she was too angry to care.

"You're saying this is my fault for disobeying you? You want to punish me? Punish me! But don't take it out on someone else!"

Conlan tightened his grip on his blade. Eleanor felt the tiny movement against her side, a whisper of menace from the razor-sharp edge, it raised goosebumps across her trembling flesh.

There was no empathy in Conlan's unflinching glare. "You need to understand that your actions have far-reaching consequences – and his death will be one of them. I give orders for a reason, and I expect them to be followed. I need to know I can trust you to do as I say. I'm ordering you to get out of the way so I can clean up your mistake." He spat the words out, clearly not used to having to explain himself.

Eleanor glared back. "I won't mindlessly obey," she yelled. "But this isn't about trust, is it? You need to know you can control me. If that's what you want, someone to follow you around obeying your every command, then please, push that sword into me because I'd rather be dead than someone's lapdog. This human being doesn't deserve to die just because you think I made a mistake." For the longest moment Conlan just stared at her. Amelia walked up to his side.

"You wanted a stronger Earth, Boss. Be careful what you wish for," she said, a small smile on her face. Conlan nodded irritably and said something to the terrified Protector, who began to babble again. The kid took Eleanor's hand, depositing several wet kisses on her brand, getting her blood on his lips in the process and not seeming to care. He muttered something at her, smiled and then ran out of the canyon and into the night. Eleanor watched him go, before returning her gaze back to Conlan's hard face.

"What did you tell him?" she asked.

"I told him an abomination had just risked her life to save his, and that he should reassess his opinion of you," Conlan said in the same lethally cold tone.

"Is that what all the kissing was about?" She wanted to rub her wet wrist against her clothes, wanted to cradle her throbbing arm that was still slowly dripping, a crimson puddle growing in the snow, but she was too afraid to move.

"Indeed – he called you Talukki." Conlan sounded grimly amused.

"What's that?"

"*She* was one of the ancient goddesses."

"So I'm a goddess now?"

"That young Protector certainly seems to think so," Conlan said, not taking his eyes from Eleanor's.

"Great. Well, this goddess would really appreciate it if you'd remove your sword."

Conlan did not respond but just continued to glare at her. With just the tiniest movement, he slowly dragged the blade down, tearing the rough fabric of her shirt. Eleanor felt the tip of the blade run, feather-light, down her flesh. Terrified, she trembled slightly, aware of the skill it must take to rip her clothes yet not mark her now coldly sweating skin; but she was not going to back down. They stared at each other for what seemed to Eleanor like an eternity, before Conlan pulled the blade back and handed it back to Freddie. Giving her one last disgusted look he turned and walked slowly to where Will was holding Rand. Eleanor felt her legs start to collapse under her. An arm caught her before she hit the ground. It was Amelia, and she was grinning from ear to ear.

"What are you smiling about?" Eleanor asked.

"He likes you."

Eleanor shuddered. "I'd hate to see what he does to people he doesn't like."

5

THE FIVE

The snow continued to fall as they moved higher into the mountains. Conlan sat astride Rand, hunched under a thick blanket, while Will and Freddie walked on either side of him, to steady him over uneven ground. It was cold and getting colder, but as Eleanor walked side-by-side with Amelia, following Rand up the path, she barely felt it. This had little to do with the blanket she had wrapped around her shoulders, internally she felt energised, excited and safe all at the same time. The exhaustion was still under the surface and the knife wound ached miserably under the bandage Will had carefully applied while Amelia and Freddie had removed the evidence of the fight, yet nothing could destroy the out-of-place joy she felt.

"Amelia, the others... The ones who killed themselves... Did they go mad first?"

Amelia glanced at her, then turned back to concentrate on the path. "I imagine you've got to be a little disturbed to kill yourself. Why do you ask?"

Eleanor shrugged. "I just have this strange feeling, this bizarre energy; I should be dead on my feet, but I feel like I could run a marathon."

"Well, you're the element of Earth, so your body was made from the soil you're walking on – soil and Conlan's blood. The Earth gives you energy."

Eleanor stopped. Amelia had just given her more information in five seconds than Conlan had managed since she had met him. She blinked rapidly, her mind spinning again. Amelia stood by her side, not hurrying her, letting Eleanor come to terms with this new information in her own time, grey eyes watching her thoughtfully.

Eventually Eleanor found her voice. "So I'm not human anymore?"

Amelia smiled. "Yes and no. You're flesh and bone, with a heart, mind and soul, but you were created, not born."

"From dirt and *his* blood?" Eleanor nodded in Conlan's direction, unable to keep the revulsion from her face.

"He's a good man, Eleanor. He tries so hard to do the right thing," Amelia said.

Eleanor glared at her. Amelia noticed her expression and smiled, as she set off again up the path she called over her shoulder. "I told you, he likes you. Freddie's first week in this world, Conlan broke his arm!"

This news did nothing to quell Eleanor's anger. Sighing, she trotted after Amelia until they were side by side again.

"So how did this creation thing happen?"

Amelia shook her head. "I've no idea. Conlan goes alone to the shamans in Millar's Forest." *Giving up his blood doesn't sound very pleasant.*

"Does it hurt him?"

"Creating us?" Amelia shrugged. "Again, I don't know. He usually comes back exhausted. That's why we came to meet you, in case he needed help, but this is the first time he's come back half-dead and being chased by Protectors. It's a good job Freddie insisted we come armed." Amelia glanced at her curiously. "What have you two been doing?"

Eleanor sighed. "It's a long story and it's mostly my fault, hence why Conlan nearly kill me."

Amelia stopped again, turning towards Eleanor, her face hard. "Is that what you think? If Conlan had wanted to kill you, you'd be a corpse. That was just his idea of discipline. There are some really dangerous things in this world, Eleanor, and he's one of them, but he would never have done you any serious damage."

Remembering the look of fury and menace in Conlan's eyes, Eleanor was not convinced, but Amelia seemed sincere. As they set off walking again, Eleanor's mind, rapidly processing information, came up with another question.

"Are you an element too?"

Amelia nodded. "Air's my thing. You should see how hyper I get when it blows a gale up here."

"How do you make a body out of air and blood?" Eleanor wondered aloud.

"Don't know, I never bothered to ask."

"Freddie and Will?"

"Freddie is fire, Will is water and they tend to clash quite a bit," Amelia said with an unhappy look on her face.

"But Conlan wasn't created?" Eleanor asked, relieved to have finally found someone to answer some of her questions.

"Yes and no," Amelia answered after thinking a moment. "He wasn't created, he had parents, was born, but he's the centre, the spirit that holds the four of us together and directs our focus. He's as much one of us as you are."

"How does he 'direct our focus'?"

Amelia shook her head, and snow flew off in a fine powder. "I've no idea; we've never got it to work."

"Got what to work?" Eleanor asked, confused.

"The connection between us."

"And if we do get this connection turned on, what happens? What does Conlan plan to do with us?" Eleanor asked.

Amelia stopped again, the serious look on her face turning into a frown.

"He plans to save the world."

Eleanor stared at her for a moment in disbelief. "Oh good, I'm glad his aims are realistic!"

Amelia laughed, a light, airy sound. A little further up the path, Will turned back to look at them.

"Come on, you two. You can bond when we're somewhere warmer!"

"We're coming!" Amelia said, grabbing Eleanor's hand and marching off up the path with purpose.

Their last stop had been hours ago. Eleanor had eaten and drunk the meagre provisions she was given in silence. Since then, the only sounds for miles had been her harsh breathing and Rand's occasional snorts. It had stopped snowing and the sky was beginning to lighten as they struggled onto a large ledge. At the back of the ledge was a small gap in the rock, into which Freddie abruptly disappeared. Will carefully eased Conlan off Rand's back, he groaned as his feet touched the ground, but remained standing. Freddie came back out, and then leading Rand, squeezed him through the gap. Will slid his shoulder under Conlan's arm, taking most of his weight, and they too disappeared through the narrow gap. Eleanor bent over to catch her breath. When she was able to stand again she looked out from the ledge at the mountains that spread into the far distance. *It's beautiful.* Moving forward, she felt the familiar squeeze to her insides that any height gave her. It was an irrational fear and she knew it, so whenever possible she forced herself to face it, getting as close to the edge as she could. Amelia was immediately at her side, a warning arm whipped out across her body, and Eleanor was shocked by the haunted look of fear that had darkened her grey eyes. Her tired mind slowly made the connections and she gasped, looking at the dizzying drop into black nothing in front of her.

"One of the others… they jumped from here?" she whispered.

Tears and horror in her eyes, Amelia nodded. Eleanor moved back slowly from the edge and allowed Amelia to guide her through the gap in the rock where the others had gone. The gap opened out into a large cave. Freddie was rekindling a substantial fire in the middle, and as it caught, the light began to chase off the shadows. Eleanor saw entrances to other caves off the main one. She could see Rand moving around in the one closest to her, but the other spaces were still in darkness. The fire quickly blazed into life, and Eleanor shuffled towards its inviting heat.

Will had eased Conlan to the ground. He slumped against the cave wall, eyelids heavy as he fought to stay conscious. Will and Amelia were busy lighting lanterns and depositing them in the caves off the main one. Freddie stoked up the fire and then went to see to Rand. Eleanor continued to watch Conlan. He looked so very tired, hurt and vulnerable. She remembered the blade running down her side. *Not that vulnerable!* Noticing her scrutiny, he raised his head to meet her gaze, a blank expression hiding his thoughts.

"You're really not like the others, are you?" His voice a whisper. Eleanor walked over, kneeling at his side before she responded.

"I don't intend to kill myself, if that's what you mean, but that doesn't mean you won't do it for me," she muttered.

Conlan sighed. "I'm not going to kill you, Eleanor, although beating some sense into you has occurred to me."

"Threatening me with violence isn't a great way to build trust," Eleanor observed.

"I suppose not," he conceded. "Would it help if I said thank you?"

"That depends, do you mean it?" she asked, raising an eyebrow at him. Conlan smiled and her anger melted away.

"Yes, Eleanor, I mean it," he said quietly. "Thank you for rescuing me and for returning Rand. I'm grateful."

She nodded, smiling back. Conlan sighed again and finally allowed his eyes to close, his body slumping further to the side. Eleanor caught him before he hit the ground, gently lowering him down. He whimpered softly but did not wake.

"He *really* likes you. That's the closest I've ever heard him get to apologising."

Eleanor jumped at Amelia's voice. The woman was stood behind her, watching. Eleanor rose to her feet, but she found her eyes straying to Conlan's still body.

"How long have you known him?" she asked.

"Nearly four years now," Amelia said, gazing down at him, concern in her eyes.

"Were you the first he created?"

Amelia shook her head. "No, Will was the first, about ten years ago."

"Excuse me," Will said, not looking at them as he knelt at Conlan's side, checking his pulse. "Freddie, I need help getting Conlan into his bed," he called. Freddie appeared from Rand's cave and between them they carefully carried the unconscious man into one of the smaller hollows. Eleanor followed, but she hung back at the entrance, unsure. This cave was much smaller, and without the fire it was colder than the main cave. It contained five beds made from rough-cut logs and rope. The mattresses looked like straw, but they had thick blankets covering them and inviting pillows. Will and Freddie laid Conlan on one of the beds at the far end of the cave, but he did not stir. Amelia removed his boots and covered him with the blanket. She indicated the bed next to Conlan's.

"This is your bed, Eleanor, do you want to sleep or eat something first?"

She was hungry. The rough bread rolls Amelia had given her on the way up the mountain, though welcome, had done little to satisfy her, but with every muscle and bone in her body screaming for rest, Eleanor looked longingly at the bed.

"I think I need to sleep," she whispered.

Will and Freddie moved back to the main cave, smiling at Eleanor as they left. Amelia patted the mattress, as if beckoning a child. Eleanor walked over wearily, pulled off her boots and climbed under the bed's surprisingly soft blanket; she eased herself down, sinking into the pillow with relief. Amelia picked up the boots, looking at them with distaste.

"Tomorrow we'll get you something more comfortable to wear."

Eleanor nodded, but her eyes were already closing, sleep pulling her away.

"Eleanor..."

The voice was familiar, raising her from the depths of exhausted sleep, but it was the wrong voice; there was no soft growl to it. Eleanor opened her eyes. Will sat on the side of her bed; he smiled at her, deep-blue eyes filled with a gentle concern.

"You've been asleep for over twenty-four hours; we thought you might starve to death if we didn't wake you."

Eleanor nodded in agreement, as she could feel her stomach protesting. She turned her head. Amelia sat on the edge of Conlan's bed. His jacket was gone and the blanket was pulled down to his waist. A bowl of water resting on her knees, Amelia was doing her best to remove some of the blood and dirt that covered him. His body was a sea of purple and green bruises, cuts and abrasions making bloody tracks across his skin. Many were serious enough that they would eventually be adding to the considerable collection of old scars that covered him – mute evidence of abuse he had endured in the past. His sleeping expression was peaceful. He did not stir as Amelia tenderly turned his head to the side so she could wipe the encrusted blood off, once more revealing the long scar that ran down his face.

"He'll be OK," said Will. "He just needs some rest. I've sedated him, so he'll sleep for a while longer yet."

"You're a doctor?" Eleanor asked, her eyes moving to Will from Conlan's slumbering body.

"No, but I *was* a navy diver. I have the basics of first aid and battlefield triage. Come on, there's food ready," he said, helping Eleanor to sit.

He led her out to the main cave. The floor was cold on her bare feet, and through the cave's main entrance Eleanor could see snow falling in the pale daylight. There were several large green cushions on a thick multi-coloured rug, which lay in front of the blazing fire. Will steered her towards the nearest. She settled herself cross-legged and looked around the cave. It seemed bigger than before, but Eleanor realised that she was seeing it fully lit for the first time. She gazed around. A neatly stacked log pile and the crude but sturdy cabinets and table that served as a kitchen gave an air of homely domesticity. Off the larger cave were several smaller spaces that she had glimpsed before in the shadows. In the one nearest to the main entrance Eleanor could see Rand, his head drooped as he dozed. Through the next entrance there appeared to be a large open space. Freddie was moving backwards and forwards inside, swinging his sword in slow, steady, fluid movements. The third cave was too dark for Eleanor to see inside. She turned back to watch Freddie instead.

"He's upped his practice; I think he's a little miffed you got a kill in before he did," Will said, nodding towards Freddie as he handed Eleanor a rough clay bowl with a thick brown stew in it and a wooden spoon. The shocked face of the man she had killed jumped into Eleanor's mind. She placed the bowl down on the rug, her hunger abruptly vanishing, replaced with a cold, clammy, sickly feeling.

"It's not got meat in it," Will said, misinterpreting the look on her face. "Conlan told me on the way up here you were a vegetarian." Still thinking about the dead men, Eleanor looked at the concern in Will's eyes. The thought of Conlan caring enough about her well-being to tell someone about her dietary requirements made her smile.

"What else did Conlan tell you about me?"

"Not much. He's not really one for idle gossip." Will stooped to pick up the bowl of food, holding it out to her. "Please, Eleanor, eat something," he insisted.

She took the bowl out of his hands and began to eat. It was good – almost as good as the stew Conlan had made her in the wood – and she was working her way through a second bowl when Amelia came out of the bedroom, placed the wash bowl and rags on the floor by the kitchen and then made herself comfortable on a cushion by the fire. Will came up behind her and, crouching, wrapped his arms around her, pulling her close to kiss the side of her neck.

"How's our patient?" he enquired, pulling his arms tighter around Amelia, as if they could ward off all the bad things in the world.

Amelia sighed. "He's in a bad way; I've not seen him this beat up since our visit to Nethrus. How much longer can you keep him sedated for?"

"Not much longer. I have no idea what long-term use of these herbs will do to him; besides, he's going to have to eat and drink something eventually," Will said.

"You know what he's like, Will, the minute he wakes up he's going to want to try the connection – and that's draining for him at the best of times. The state he's in right now, it could kill him," Amelia said, fatigue taking the power from her statement.

"We'll leave him asleep until tomorrow," Will agreed. "But he's going to be angry when he finds out."

Amelia gave a resigned nod. "I'd rather have him fuming than dead."

Eleanor watched the casual way they kissed, touched and reassured each other, and she wondered how long they had been a couple. Feeling a little like she was intruding on a private moment, she turned to gaze into the fire. Caught up in her thoughts she jumped when Amelia placed a hand on her shoulder.

"Sorry, you were miles away," she said. "I was just saying, I have a surprise for you."

Amelia took her hand and led her past the cave in which Freddie was still swinging his sword, sweat making his dark skin glisten. Eleanor was led into the cave she had not been able to see into earlier. It was much smaller than any she had so far seen and it was warmer; lanterns lit the small space with their soft orange glow. On the left as they entered were several heavy wooden boxes and over-stuffed bags with items of clothing scattered across them. Towards the rear of the cave there was an ornate wooden screen that looked very out of place in its rough surroundings. Still holding her hand, Amelia pulled Eleanor behind the screen. In front of her was a large metal tub, filled with water so hot she could see the steam coming off it. The soft smell of lavender filled the air.

"A bath! You have a bath," Eleanor squealed, unable to hide her delight.

Amelia nodded. "It's an occasional treat, takes too much fuel, but it keeps me sane." She pointed to a small, private recess in the wall indicating a wooden stool with a hole in it and a metal bucket underneath. She smiled. "There's a toilet too."

Eleanor felt tears welling up.

"Are those tears of joy?" Amelia asked, looking worried. Eleanor nodded but admitted to herself she was not entirely sure. With Amelia's help Eleanor discarded her dirty, torn, ill-fitting clothing and climbed into the steaming water. It was so amazingly good that she felt the urge to cry again. Amelia left her to wash away the dirt, blood and grime of her flight from Bremen. She carefully removed the bandage from her arm, thinking Will would provide a clean one for her when she was washed. The wound, however, looked almost healed. It was going to leave a scar, but the thick scab spoke of days of healing, not hours. Surprised, Eleanor ran her fingers over the injury. *No pain.* There should have been pain, it should have taken some time to heal, perhaps have needed stitches. Puzzled, she began inspecting her body for other differences, but she stopped short as Amelia came back with what looked like a towel.

Shocked and a little frightened, Eleanor looked at her. "Amelia, where's my tummy button?"

"You weren't born – you don't have one."

Eleanor heard the amusement in Amelia's voice, but she found the changes a shock; it was all rather scary.

"I really am different," she murmured. "How did you deal with this?" she asked, her voice trembling.

Amelia thought about the question for a moment before she answered.

"I was an air force pilot before I died; I was used to following orders. Conlan gave orders, I followed them. He said don't ask questions, don't think too much about it, so I didn't, and Will was always there, by my side when it got too much. He just listened and held me while I came to terms with this bizarre new reality. He never complained, although I'm fairly certain I was hell to live with for quite a while, and I fell in love with that strength. He became my world and his world became my reality, then nothing before him mattered anymore. I embraced the new me, because it had brought me Will."

Eleanor smiled. The love in Amelia's voice was so passionate she almost felt a part of it too. "Plus there are advantages," Amelia continued. "We are stronger and faster than the average human being. We have much better immunities and hardly ever get sick. We have a very high pain threshold and heal quickly. We can stand extremes of hot and cold easier and for longer. I don't know if the same will apply to you, but I also don't get periods – can't tell you what a relief that is, living with three guys."

Eleanor picked up the change in her tone; she was trying too hard to make her last comment sound positive.

"We can't have children?" Eleanor deduced.

Amelia shook her head. "Will and I have been together for years, so if it was possible, believe me, it would have happened by now," she said sadly, hiding unshed tears. Clearly Amelia was upset that she could not have children. *Should I be upset about this?* Eleanor had never really considered herself 'mother' material, but she had not discounted that she might have children at some point in the distant future. Having the decision taken from her left her with a cold feeling, but she understood why Conlan might have done it. It would be hard to save the world with a baby in tow; plus, Eleanor suspected even the most ardent 'Earth-Mother' would draw the line at raising a baby in a cave. *Are Will and Freddie incapable of fathering children too?* It seemed a little unfair if it was just her and Amelia, but it was also a question she did not think she wanted to ask.

Amelia held up the large, soft piece of material she had brought as a towel for Eleanor to step into. Wrapped in its cosy warmth, Eleanor sat on the floor while Amelia brushed out her damp hair. Amelia left briefly so Eleanor could use the toilet and when she came back she was carrying a short stick, which she handed to Eleanor.

"Use it to brush your teeth," she explained. "It's not as good as going to the dentist, but it sure beats furry mouth syndrome. I have a good supply of this stuff, but I'll show you which plant it comes from when the snow melts. Now, let's get you something to wear." Eleanor sniffed at the stick. It smelt vaguely minty; she put it into her mouth, chewing the end a little until the bark split, and then rubbed the pulpy innards over her teeth, which tasted minty too. Amelia was right – it was definitely better than furry teeth.

Amelia led her over to the wooden chests and bags, which, it turned out, was her rather extensive wardrobe. Eleanor allowed Amelia to dress her in several outfits, feeling a little like a child's doll, before settling on a pair of overly long, but comfortable trousers with a shirt and jacket. After some rummaging a pair of soft, brown leather boots were found, which Amelia explained were far too small for her. They fit Eleanor perfectly and did a wonderful job of making the trousers look like they fit too. Amelia took a step back, nodded and smiled. Eleanor returned the smile, relived her new friend had stopped playing dress up.

They came and sat back in front of the fire, and Will handed them both mugs of what tasted a lot like sweet, black tea. Warm, clean and comfortable for the first time in what felt like forever, Eleanor became sleepy again. Amelia and Will sat wrapped in each other, whispering softly. As she stared into the fire a little dazed, her mind floating and blessedly not thinking of anything, Freddie sat down beside her. He stared into the fire with her.

"What you did, back in the canyon, it was really brave," he said.

Eleanor shook her head, remembering her trembling body. "I didn't really have much choice."

"It was still really brave," Freddie persisted. "Where did you learn that flicking sword move?"

Eleanor shrugged. "I didn't really learn it anywhere, it was pure dumb luck."

"Brave *and* modest," Freddie said smiling at her.

Eleanor sighed, irritated for some reason by Freddie's friendly conversation. "Whatever, I guess it doesn't make that man any less dead."

All amiable humour fled from Freddie's face. "He was a Protector, Eleanor; he would've killed you and Conlan in a heartbeat and lost no sleep over it. You did the right thing."

"Why do the Protectors hate us? Why do they think we're abominations?" Eleanor asked.

Freddie looked deep into the fire, like he was drawing strength from it. When he spoke, his voice had an angry edge to it.

"Because we *are* Eleanor. We're unnatural. Dead souls reanimated. There are people who run this land, the Lords of Mydren, who have banned us from existing. Conlan defied that law. The Lords have been quietly hunting him – and us – ever since. The Protectors are the Lords' police, their private army, with Enforcers as their generals."

"Mydren?"

"This world, this land, is one huge continent, and they call it Mydren. It means 'blessed' in their language, a misnomer if ever there was one." Bitter misery suffused his voice.

"If we shouldn't exist, why did Conlan create us?" Eleanor asked, confused.

Freddie's face twisted into a sneer. "He has a lot of half-baked delusions of grandeur. I think he's trying to make himself feel better about being disowned by his father. I don't think he has a clue what he's going to do with this 'power' we are meant to provide him with. In the meantime, we're condemned to this." A flick of his hand encompassed the cave.

"Why do you stay here if you feel this way?" Eleanor asked.

"Weren't you listening?" Freddie snapped. "We're abominations, Eleanor, objects of hate and distrust, hunted like animals. Where would I go?"

Eleanor turned to face Amelia and Will; they were both still, listening, they did not seem surprised. Will was glaring at Freddie, but Amelia just looked sad.

"Is it true?" Eleanor asked.

"He's entitled to his opinion, but I think he's being a little unfair," Amelia said, ignoring the sour look Freddie gave her.

"Conlan gave up almost everything he had to create us," Will agreed, watching Freddie intently. "And he truly believes what he is doing is right. I, for one, believe in him."

"What a surprise, always the loyal water boy!" Freddie retorted.

Will sprang to his feet, moving away from Amelia, his eyes wary. Freddie leapt up, the fire blazed higher, spitting sparks. Frightened, Eleanor scrambled out of the way, unconsciously seeking safety with Amelia.

"He's a spoilt little rich boy with daddy issues, why do you insist on defending him?" Freddie yelled.

"He gave you a new life, at the very least that should have earned him your respect. We're in this together, Freddie, please let's not fight about it," Will said gently. Freddie glared for a moment, his eyes blazing, and then he sprung at Will, punching and kicking as he wrestled the taller man to the floor. Will fought back, but Freddie had the upper hand, and straddling the blond man's chest he punched at him repeatedly. Will gave Freddie a vicious punch to the side, Freddie arched back and Will threw him off. The two men struggled to their feet again, circling, looking for an opening. Amelia sobbed with each blow Freddie landed, but she made no move to intervene.

"Amelia, we have to stop them," Eleanor said.

Not taking her eyes off the two men as they fought, Amelia shook her head.

"We can't get involved, Eleanor."

"But they are going to hurt each other."

Amelia nodded, tears running down her face, but she still did not move. Eleanor ran towards the two men, placing herself between them.

"Stop this!" she yelled. "I thought we were on the same side, but you're behaving like children. You're upsetting Amelia and you're frightening me."

A guilty look crossed Will's bruised face, but Freddie just shoved Eleanor out of the way, throwing her off her feet, and launched himself at Will again. Eleanor landed heavily on her back, the breath knocked out of her lungs. Amelia ran to her, cradling her head as she struggled to catch her breath. Will glanced worriedly in their direction, but Freddie's fresh assault forced him back into the fight.

"Enough!"

The order was emphasised by a low, menacing growl. Conlan was glaring at them. He stood with one arm wrapped protectively around him, but even beaten, bare-footed and in just his trousers, Conlan's presence was enough that all four of them froze.

"I need to strengthen the sedative," Will muttered.

If Conlan heard him, he gave no indication. His cold, hard gaze remained riveted on Freddie. Under its scrutiny the fire seemed to go out of his eyes, the flames behind him damping down. Deflated, Freddie moved from Will's bruised, angry look, to Amelia's distraught, tear-stained face, to Eleanor's pained expression; a look of horror crossed his face.

"What have I done?" He sounded small and broken, and so bewildered that Eleanor's heart ached for him.

"You lost control again." Conlan's voice was hard and flat.

Will moved to crouch at Eleanor's side. "Are you OK?"

Eleanor nodded, not trusting her voice to hide her fear. Will's deep-blue eyes looked lovingly at Amelia as he squeezed her hand.

"It's over, Amelia, it's OK."

Unhappy grey eyes looked back. "Over for now, but what about the next time?"

Conlan walked stiffly to Freddie's side and took his arm. Freddie cringed away from him.

Conlan led Freddie into the side cave he had used for sword practice earlier, speaking in a soothing voice. "It's OK, Freddie, you've nothing to fear."

"What's he going to do to Freddie?" Eleanor asked, watching them go.

"Conlan will talk to him," Will said, glancing at her, his attention mostly on Amelia's frightened face. Eleanor did not think 'talking through stuff' was one of Conlan's strong points. Will must have seen her doubt.

"This wasn't Freddie's fault, Eleanor. Conlan knows that, he's not going to hurt him," he assured her.

Eleanor shook her head. "He attacked you, Will, with very little provocation; how is that not his fault?"

"He's the element of fire. Fire is a very destructive and unpredictable force. Since there is nearly always a fire blazing somewhere around him, Freddie feels its pull far more than we feel the pull of our elements. It's a very difficult element to control and can flare up with very little effort."

"I'm surrounded by earth all the time; I haven't lashed out," Eleanor said, confused.

"No, your temper takes far more to bring it to the surface, like the slowly grinding pressure that creates an earthquake – and like an earthquake I imagine it would be just as devastating. Don't be too hard on Freddie; he really does try hard not to let his nature get the better of him."

Will and Amelia were busy in the kitchen preparing food when Conlan came out of the other cave. Intent on what they were doing, neither of them noticed him. Eleanor, having returned to her seat by the fire, took one look at Conlan's face and felt buried under his exhaustion, pain and misery. She felt hot tears spilling down her cheeks. He noticed and with effort smoothed his face into its normal hard, expressionless guise. Staring at him through her tears, Eleanor wondered how he managed to hide so much.

"I'm going to dress," he said, softly announcing his presence. "Then we should eat." Will glanced back at him and nodded absently before returning to his chopping. Conlan walked stiffly back towards the bedroom. Eleanor noticed, with another twist of her stomach, the long, thick, raised red scar tissue. They ran in haphazard, horizontal lines across his shoulders and down the length of his muscular back. *He said the Protectors had flogged him before,* Eleanor thought in horror, wondering at the courage it took to face something like that when you had been through it before. Conlan paused at the entrance to the bedroom, and without turning round he added in a sinister tone, "And Will, if you ever drug me again without my permission, I'll make sure you regret it."

"Ungrateful sod," Will muttered, but there was no real venom in his retort.

Will and Amelia, still organising food, left Eleanor sat by the fire. Before long she began to feel sorry for Freddie. *How awful must he be feeling?* He had not emerged from the other cave and Eleanor's curiosity got the better of her. Getting to her feet she walked over, but at the entrance she stopped, unsure if she should enter. Freddie sat against the far wall, his head in his hands, and he was sobbing softly. She walked over and sat down at his side. Freddie did not raise his head. Not knowing what to say, Eleanor placed a hand on his shoulder. Freddie struggled to get his sobbing under control. When he finally spoke, his voice still sounded broken.

"I'm sorry I hurt you."

"That's OK, you didn't really do any damage," Eleanor said quietly.

He raised his head, eyes full of hope. "You forgive me?"

"Of course I forgive you, Freddie. You didn't mean it," Eleanor said, meeting the grateful, relieved smile that spread across his face with a friendly grin of her own. "I think we're going to have a meal, are you going to join us?"

Freddie's smile fell, replaced with uncertainty. "Do the others want that?"

Eleanor shrugged. "I want it, would that be enough?"

Freddie considered this for a moment and then nodded. Helping Eleanor to her feet, he took her hand and she led him back to the fire. Conlan and Amelia looked up from their food as they sat down, but they said nothing, Will carefully spooned food onto a plate and handed it to Freddie.

"Thank you," Freddie whispered, not able to look Will in the face. Will then gave Eleanor a plate of food from her personnel 'non-meat' pot and for a while they sat in silence, each absorbed in their own thoughts. Eventually Eleanor's constantly churning mind began throwing questions at her again.

"Conlan, you promised that when we were safe you'd tell me what was going on. I'm feeling fairly safe right now, so spill."

Green eyes glared at her. "Do you *ever* stop asking questions?"

Amelia sniggered, and beside her she saw Freddie struggle to keep his face straight. Keeping her expression neutral, Eleanor waited, watching him, until he nodded, sighing heavily.

"OK, where would you have me start?"

Eleanor thought about it – there was really only one place he could start.

"Start at the beginning."

He stared at her for a moment. "The beginning?"

6

FAIRY TALES AND HOKUM

Eleanor snuggled down into the cushions as Will took the empty bowls away. Conlan was staring thoughtfully into the fire. His voice was so quiet when he began that she had to strain to hear.

"In the beginning, when the world was new, the four elements – earth, air, fire and water – held sway. They moved with great force, but no purpose. Great earthquakes shook the mountains, tsunamis crashed against the land, violent winds sent storm clouds racing across permanently grey skies and lightning caused raging fires that incinerated all in their path. And into this terrifying cataclysmic world a portal was opened, a hole from other worlds."

"What other worlds?" Eleanor asked.

"Think of it as parallel universes; all these worlds sit in the same physical place, where earth is, but they exist on top of each other – they are there, but not there," Amelia said.

Eleanor did not quite get it, but asking more questions was probably not going to encourage Conlan to keep talking.

"May I continue?" Conlan asked patiently. Eleanor nodded.

"Thank you. The portal was opened and through it came all manner of creatures, including Dwarves, Elves and eventually men, only realising, once they had come through the portal, that it worked one way and they could never return. Fearing the world around them, the different races put aside their differences and worked together, building a city in which they could feel safe. The Dwarves brought law and a common language, the Elves brought weaponry and magic, and man – man brought purpose."

"Your snarly, growling language… that's the Dwarf's language?" Eleanor asked, surprised.

"Yes." Conlan paused, waiting to see if she was going to interrupt him further, but Eleanor snapped her mouth shut and he continued.

"Man brought purpose. One man in particular, Alaric, saw the terror in which everyone lived and felt it his duty to ease their suffering. He went out into the wilderness to find a way to help his people. Wind buffeted him, floods tried to drown him, fire chased him and the earth shook beneath his feet, but after many years in the wilderness he began to understand the elements around him and he tried to communicate with them. He stood on the beach letting waves crash upon him, sat on mountain tops as the wind raged around him, buried himself in dirt and even let fire burn him. He found he could hear the elements' voices but they were too far removed to hear him. All his attempts to reach the elements failed. Exhausted and broken, all his defences gone, Alaric crawled into a cave thinking only of sleep and eventual release of death. But as he slept, Earth heard his dreams and saw this fragile being resting within her, afraid and alone. Compassion filled her, and seeking to help him she entered his dreams. She told him how he could communicate with the elements; she told him how to create Avatars – beings, in human form, created from the elements themselves, held together by his blood, his passion, but controlled by a human soul."

So I'm an Avatar, at least that's better than an abomination.

"Awakening from his dream, Alaric set to work. Using soft earth and his own blood he fashioned a human shape, but where to find a human soul? Taking his half-finished Avatar with him, Alaric returned to his people, but in their eyes he was a dirty, unkempt mad man, raving about needing to take souls. They destroyed his Avatar and chased him from the city. Alone and bereft he wandered, finding himself in front of the portal. As he watched the other world through it, the thought came to him. Here were souls he could use. He made another Avatar from blood and earth and tried pulling a soul into it. He chose a soul at the moment of its death, believing it to be the more humane option, but the soul was very hard to pull through and the Avatar remained nothing more than blood and dirt. With effort Alaric discovered that it was possible to drag the souls from their bodies, but this caused them untold suffering."

"Untold suffering? That's a rather mild term for what you put me through, don't you think?" Will commented drily.

"You did that to Will, tore his soul from his body?" Eleanor asked, unable to keep the horror out of her voice.

"Yes." Conlan's' voice had the hollow quality to it that made Eleanor shiver. She wanted to ask more questions but she was frightened of the painful memories she might drag up, so she just stared at him.

"It's OK, Eleanor, I got over it a long time ago. Finish the story, Boss," Will said.

Conlan nodded. "After several failed attempts at pulling souls through this way, Alaric decided to try to learn the other world's language so he could talk to the souls, convince them to let go of their bodies voluntarily. Watching the portal he studied hard and learnt what he could, and then finally he was ready."

As the pieces of the puzzle clicked into place, understanding dawned on Eleanor. "You didn't speak his language, that's why you had to drag Will here. You couldn't ask him."

"I didn't have access to the portal, so I had no way of learning and I rushed into something I didn't understand," Conlan said, regret plain in his tone.

"Why? Where was the portal?" Eleanor asked.

"If you let me continue, I'll get to that."

"Sorry," Eleanor said, falling silent again.

"Alaric could now talk to the soul he needed. So he searched for a soul that was appropriate and explained to her what he wanted. To his surprise she said yes; she told him she was dying and was happy to enter a different world where she would be well again. When she awoke, she was the living, breathing Avatar of elemental Earth. Overjoyed with his success Alaric set about creating the other three Avatars. At first they seemed disorientated, confused, but as they got used to their surroundings they began to feel the elements around them, taking on more of their attributes, and as they did so, they became more adept at controlling them. They calmed the world and showed Alaric the five noble virtues, which all men should hold dear: compassion, courage, wisdom, truth and duty. As the Avatars learnt to control their elemental connection, the land became more inhabitable and the people began moving out from the city they had cowered within. They crowned Alaric king, and the Five ruled the land and it flourished. As they grew old the Avatars died and new ones were created, watched over by descendants of Alaric's line who were raised from birth for the important task of ruling the land and communing with the elements. As the old Avatars died, their souls merged with the elemental energy and the people took to worshipping this human energy, giving it the new names Talukki, Paivina, Ethrel and Rana."

Talukki… that's what that Protector called me, Eleanor thought, another question occurring to her.

"So who's who?" she asked.

"Pardon?" Conlan said, not even trying to hide his irritation at being interrupted again.

Eleanor ignored his tone. "Well, I'm the Avatar of Earth and apparently the Goddess Talukki, so the other gods and goddesses, which ones are which?"

Conlan snorted. "You're not a goddess, Eleanor. There are stories about the gods and goddesses that embodied the noble virtues, and if the person requesting contact was pure of spirit then Paivina of Fire, Ethrel of Air and

Rana of Water may well take corporeal form to communicate with them."

"Can you tell us those stories too?" Eleanor asked.

"I'm having enough problems telling this one. May I continue?"

Eleanor nodded.

"Everything was fine in the land for many thousands of years, but over time others became greedy for the power Alaric's bloodline held, and eventually the king was betrayed and the bloodline was lost. Furious battles raged for the crown. The winner was an evil man who knew nothing of virtues, only wanting the power for himself. Once he got it, he destroyed the existing Avatars and made new ones – Avatars like him; mean, power-hungry and vicious. This man ruled the land with terror and menace, demanding the people worship him as a god. His demands became too much and a resistance was formed. The resistance went to the Elves and begged them for help. For a very steep price the Elves provided help by showing the resistance the secret to creating more Avatars. The resistance used this knowledge to create an army of elemental Avatars, but they did not have time to plan and were forced to rip the souls from the bodies on the other side of the portal, in some cases before they were actually dead."

Eleanor saw Will shudder.

"The Avatars they created were driven mad, and they became mindless killers with devastating power. Battles were fought for hundreds of years, following which human beings were almost wiped out. When the dust settled, a new order was in charge. The Lords of Mydren were seen as defenders of the people; they built a tower around the portal and eventually denied its existence."

"So if the portal is hidden, how did you bring our souls through it?" Eleanor asked.

"The Lords may claim the portal no longer exists, but it's still there, and those sensitive enough, like the shamans, can feel it. Despite the tower around the portal, things can still be pulled through it," Conlan said.

"OK, so the soul is pulled through, but isn't it trapped in the tower?" Eleanor wondered.

"Your soul is energy, so it's rather hard to trap and it can't be destroyed – it just has to be guided out. Can I finish?"

Again Eleanor felt confused, but she nodded.

"The portal was hidden, it's existence denied, and people were told that Avatars were evil and to be feared, so that no one would be tempted to create one. Effort was made to control naturally occurring elemental magic, and anyone who displayed the talent was murdered or enslaved." The raw grief in Conlan's voice made Eleanor look up, but he coughed and continued. "The

Lords slowly and insidiously expanded their rule, and where once were free-states or towns, there were now Lord-protected, tax-paying, ground-down people. Now almost the whole land is theirs. It's been seven hundred years since an Avatar walked in this world, and all that really remains in the minds of the people are the names given to the ancient Avatars they worshipped as elemental gods."

Conlan stopped, looking into the fire. The others also seemed caught up in their own thoughts, even Freddie was quiet. Eleanor slowly processed the story, trying to figure out how she now fit into this new life.

"So that's why you brought us here, you want to be king?" she asked after some thought.

"Yep, delusions of grandeur," Freddie muttered.

Conlan glared at him. "No, that's not the reason you're here, Eleanor."

Will flashed him a wicked grin. "Come on, Boss, admit it – some part of you is totally into being king."

Conlan shot Will a warning look and then sighed. "It would make a change from people trying to kill me," he murmured.

A thought occurred to Eleanor and it was out of her mouth before she considered if it was a good idea.

"King Conlan... sounds like a giant ape!"

Next to her Freddie dissolved into such a paroxysm of laughter that the dying fire danced and jumped with his guffaws. Will, a small, tight smile trying to move across his face, made no sound, but his whole body shook with the effort. Amelia had her hand clamped over her mouth, her eyes full of mirth as she fought to contain her own giggles. Conlan looked bewildered from one to the other and then back to Eleanor, who gave him her best wide-eyed innocent look.

His eyes narrowed. "A giant ape?"

Eleanor nodded, still doing her best to look innocent.

"She's talking about a movie character called King Kong. He was a giant ape, a very large version of those little tree climbers we saw in Pendover," Amelia said, slightly quicker than the others to get a hold of herself.

Understanding showed in Conlan's eyes. "Movies, television, moving pictures on a screen... entertainment in your world." Amelia nodded in confirmation; clearly they had had this conversation before. He looked back at Eleanor and for a brief moment she caught a glimpse of the tiger whose tail she had just pulled. He said nothing, made no move towards her, but Eleanor felt the threat as fear turned her skin to ice.

"And what happened to this giant ape?" he asked her softly.

"He was killed, trying to save the woman he loved," Eleanor said, annoyed by the slight tremor in her voice.

Conlan nodded, an amused grin finally showing. "An honourable giant ape..."

Eleanor smiled, relieved he had seen the joke. "If you don't want to be king, what do you want?"

"I want to restore the connection with the elements, before they destroy us all," Conlan said.

"The elements are going to destroy us?" Eleanor asked in horror as images of earthquakes, tsunamis and forest fires ran through her head.

Conlan nodded slowly. "They have been left on their own too long, they're distant and becoming restless. They remember what it felt like to stretch their powers, and the further the link with man fails, the more they move back to that wild state. The Lords pass the storms, flash floods and forest fires off as freak weather conditions, one-off incidents, using their enslaved Enforcers to hold back the worst, but this can't work forever. The shamans have been recording these 'events' for generations and they are getting stronger and more frequent."

"So who, exactly, are the shamans?" Eleanor asked.

"Some of the last free practitioners of elemental magic in Mydren. They use magic in direct violation of the law; they have risked everything to help me," Conlan said.

"How many of them are there?"

"Two."

"Oh." Eleanor considered this, another question occurring to her. "How can the Enforcers be as powerful as you say they are, but be enslaved to the Lords of Maydrin?"

"Mydren," Conlan corrected. "When those with magical talent are found, usually as children, they are forced into an addiction to a drug, the details of which are known only to the Lords. Once addicted, the Lords' will is their only concern."

"How many Enforcers are there?"

Conlan shrugged. "Several hundred, I would assume."

Eleanor paled slightly. "How many Lords are there?"

"Eighty."

"OK then, five of us, two shamans and a warhorse. I think we're a little outnumbered."

Conlan nodded. "Hence my desire to *avoid* drawing attention to ourselves."

Eleanor ignored the rebuke in his tone. "So I'm here to help you communicate with and control the elements by getting this 'connection' thing Amelia was talking about working?"

"That's the plan," Conlan confirmed.

"But I've no idea how to do that," Eleanor said, her voice sounding small again.

"Join the club," Freddie murmured.

"I'm sure it will come to you," Conlan said reassuringly, but Eleanor saw the looks of doubt Will and Amelia gave each other behind his back. Leaving that huge problem for a moment, Eleanor's overactive mind spat another question at him.

"How do you know all this?"

"Pardon?"

Eleanor gave him a scrutinising look. "Well, you said that people didn't remember the past because the Lords hid it from them, so how did you find out about us?"

"My grandfather used to tell me stories about the Five when I was a child," he said, returning her look with calm, emotionless green eyes.

"And how did he know?" Eleanor persisted.

"That, Eleanor, is a whole other story."

Freddie raised his head and glared at Conlan, a bitter edge in his voice as he spoke. "My grandfather used to tell me stories too when I was a kid, but they turned out to be a bunch of fairy tales and hokum, just an old man making up stories to entertain a hyper child. How do we know your grandfather's stories are real?"

"You wouldn't exist if they weren't," Conlan snapped.

"And how do we know that? There could be any number of reasons why we exist that you haven't seen fit to tell us about, like fools dabbling in black magic for instance!"

"I've seen the portal, Freddie, and the shamans have confirmed certain aspects of my grandfather's stories." Conlan's tone was suddenly very calm, rational, like he was trying to talk a jumper off a roof, but Eleanor knew it was too late. Freddie's eyes were blazing again; his fist gripped, knuckles white, to the edge of the cushion as the fire leaped and spat. Conlan watched Freddie carefully as he attempted to get himself back under control.

"Fight it back down, Freddie, control it," he said softly. Cautiously Eleanor reached for Freddie's hand. Conlan shook his head fractionally to warn her off, but she ignored him. Freddie's skin was so hot to the touch that Eleanor almost pulled her hand back, but then he grabbed her. Conlan, Will and Amelia tensed and Eleanor was no longer in the cave, no longer anywhere. She was swept into a swirling orange red inferno, and burning agony poured through every nerve ending of a body that was no longer there. *My body isn't here*, she thought over and over. *I can't be burnt.*

This slowly calmed her down and the agony eased off. *Why isn't my body here? Am I dead?* Stood before her, enveloped in the inferno, was a figure made entirely of flame, just like a stunt in the movies. The figure twisted and writhed in the conflagration. *Freddie?* There was no sound beyond the crackling and roar of the flame, but the figure turned towards her.

Eleanor? I can hear you. What are you doing in my head? Freddie's agonised voice echoed in a skull she did not have, like Conlan's voice had when she had died. She looked the figure up and down.

I have no idea. That must hurt.

Yes it does, Freddie agreed. *But I have to pull the fire back into me to calm it.*

Wouldn't it be better to just to get rid of it?

Get rid of it where? If I just let it go I could hurt someone... again.

Eleanor considered this problem. Her mind spat out all sorts of solutions, but Freddie did not comment on any of them. *Maybe he can't see my thoughts – I can't read his mind, so I guess he can't read mine.* That seemed like a theory to consider later, when Freddie was no longer in pain.

Can it be grounded, like electricity? she said, more to herself than to Freddie.

Send it into the earth? Freddie asked.

Eleanor nodded and then realised how futile the gesture was as she currently did not have a head.

Yes, she said. *After all, you throw earth over a campfire to put it out, so let the earth absorb the fire when you can't.*

There was a pause.

I can't push my energy into the earth, it just bounces back.

Wanting to help, Eleanor reached out for him, as if she had arms with which to smoother Freddie's flames. She felt a strong glowing heat burst through her and the inferno dropped back to the comforting warmth of the campfire.

Her eyes were open and she was lying on her side staring into the fire's glowing depths, her head resting in Amelia's lap. Conlan was kneeling stiffly next to her, concern creating a deep frown between his eyes. Will had dragged Freddie a little distance from her, crouching behind him and holding a restraining arm across his chest. The silence was deafening. Raising her head so she could look Freddie in his now calm black eyes, Eleanor smiled.

Freddie just stared at her.

"Wow!" Was all the acknowledgment he could manage.

"What happened, are you alright?" Amelia asked.

Conlan looked from Freddie to Eleanor and back again, his look of concern changing to surprise and then to an almost religious zeal.

"You connected, didn't you? I didn't even have to get close, you did it all by yourselves."

"Eleanor did it, Boss, and it was *so* much more powerful than anything we've managed before. I didn't just feel her, we spoke, in my head – she took the fire away," Freddie said in awe. Conlan stared at Eleanor, again that strange penetrating look that made her wonder what he was thinking.

"Could you do it again?" he asked.

"Again?" Eleanor asked incredulously. "I have no idea how I did it in the first place."

"Try." There was something alarming about this fevered insistence in a man she associated with cold, calm restraint. She cringed back, but her voice was strong.

"No."

"Let her be, you're scaring her," Amelia said, her tone a little too high-pitched.

I'm not the only one who's frightened, Eleanor thought.

Conlan took a deep, frustrated breath. "OK, but will you try again for me tomorrow?"

Eleanor felt the bone-deep exhaustion that was crawling through her body pushing her towards total collapse. Whatever she had done had practically drained the life out of her. She was not sure she could have done it again straight away, even if she had wanted to, but she needed time to understand what had happened, but perhaps she could use this to get Conlan to take some rest.

"No," she said, trying her best to look determined.

"Why not?" Conlan asked, seeming genuinely surprised.

Eleanor smiled. "Will says you need to rest and heal; if you don't spend at least the next week…"

"Two," Will said, trying to hide his treachery in a cough. Conlan glared at him.

Without missing a beat Eleanor continued, "… two weeks in bed, I'm not going to try to 'connect' to anything ever again."

The chagrin in Conlan's face was almost comical. "You're blackmailing me?"

"Yep!" Eleanor nodded. "Go to bed, stay in bed, get better. The world has waited seven hundred years to be saved, I'm sure two more weeks won't be the end of it."

"She's got you, Boss, just admit defeat gracefully and go back to bed," Will said, unable to keep the grin off his face. Still looking extremely annoyed, Conlan nodded and allowed Will to help him to his feet. They watched him walk stiffly back to bed.

"You are either unbelievably brave or really, really stupid," Freddie commented, shaking his head.

All evidence to the latter.

Eleanor looked up into Amelia's gentle, smiling face. "Amelia, I don't feel so good."

"What's the matter, sweetie?" concern replacing Amelia's smile.

"I'm so exhausted. I've never felt this tired before," she whispered.

"You used your Avatar abilities to connect with Freddie," Will said, sitting at her side. "We aren't human anymore, but our bodies are very similar and they carry more power than they were meant to. Our Avatar energy and our physical energies are linked. When we use our Avatar energy it drains our physical bodies; conversely, if we overtax our physical bodies we drain our Avatar energy to compensate. The balance takes a bit of getting used to, but it will get easier."

"I really am different," Eleanor murmured. Against her wishes, her eyes closed and she slipped into empty black sleep.

7

TRIAL AND ERROR

Conlan's two weeks' enforced rest passed quickly for Eleanor. Freddie became her constant companion, and in-between chores he showed her the mountains' secret wonders. They walked across a lake, frozen to several inches by the winter's icy breath, in the bowl of a mountain top. Stunningly beautiful, Eleanor loved the way the sunlight made the reeds on the bank sparkle like gems in their frosty jackets. They sat on the high bluffs watching eagles swoop and scream. Freddie showed her how to track the hare- and weasel-like creatures that lived around the lake, and he pointed out the tracks left by a frighteningly large cat that he said looked like a puma.

The more time she spent with Freddie, the more Eleanor was able to gauge his moods. When she felt the fire rising within him, she would reach out and smother the flames. This was not like the involuntary connection she had made before, as this required effort, thought and control. It felt like she had a ball of energy in her stomach, and if she closed her eyes she could picture it as a ball of glowing green light. If she pushed hard enough she could force strings of green light out of the ball, sending them sparking off in specific directions. To begin with she had to do this with her eyes shut to keep control, imagining the glowing, pulsing green arcs. With practice she found she could stretch a string towards Freddie and absorb the fire that raged within him, but it was difficult and required a delicate touch. The first time she tried it she knocked Freddie off his feet and exhausted herself so much that she collapsed. Nevertheless, the more she practiced, the more control she acquired, and eventually she was able to push an energy string out to Freddie without having to close her eyes. Through trial and error she discovered a small drip-feed of effort worked the best, just enough to keep the edge off the flames, but not so much that Eleanor could not function afterwards. After a few days, her touch had become so light that Freddie barely noticed her constant small adjustments, although he was enthusiastic about the results, offering Eleanor a gift in return – anything she wanted that was within his power to give. Terrified at the thought of having to face the Protectors, or even worse an Enforcer, Eleanor had asked him to teach her how to fight.

It was early when Freddie woke her. In the soft, wavering light of the guttering candle Amelia liked to have lit at night, Eleanor could see the other three still sleeping soundly. Grinning at Freddie she silently pulled on her boots and jacket, following him out into the crisp, sharp, dark world outside. She was still not fully awake when they reached the frozen lake, and she nearly lost Freddie completely as he deviated off their normal path and had to run to catch up with him.

"Freddie, where are we going?" Her voice sounded muted, muffled by the snow. Freddie did not turn round, but pointed to a black cave mouth at the bottom of the valley they were entering.

Dawn's sunshine was beginning to pour into the valley as they reached the cave's entrance, but its thinner winter light did little to reveal the interior. Eleanor shivered as a strange and very strong primeval fear gripped her. Freddie laughed.

"You're the Avatar of Earth Eleanor, it's just a cave; you've nothing to fear."

It's not the earth I'm worried about, Eleanor thought, images of animals, all teeth and claws, ripping through her mind. Freddie smiled reassuringly and grabbed her hand, leading her into the dark. Once they had gone a few feet, the dark began to fall in around them.

"Eleanor, you know that thing you're doing? Stopping the fire getting too high?" Freddie said.

"Yes."

"Well, could you stop for a moment?"

"Yes, why?" Eleanor asked, as she visualised pulling the string back into the green energy ball.

Freddie pulled something from his pocket. Eleanor saw the sparks as he hit two pieces of flint together, making glowing spots in her eyes that she could still see after the darkness had reclaimed them. Eventually he lit a candle and sat for a moment staring at it.

"Freddie, what are you doing?"

"We have to walk some distance and the candle won't stay lit. The air keeps blowing it out, but if I concentrate on the flame and let the energy build a little, I can see in the dark."

"Really?"

"You think I'm a freak."

Eleanor smiled. "No, I think that's awesome. Seriously, worthy of Spider-Man or Batman or something. I wish I had a power."

Freddie relaxed suddenly and laughed. "You got Conlan to stay in bed for two weeks, that's power right there!"

"Some power – he's going to wait two weeks, jump out of bed and beat me to death!"

"Don't worry, Eleanor; I wouldn't let him do that." Freddie had tried to make the comment light, but Eleanor heard the dark edge to his voice. "OK, I can see now, let me guide you."

Freddie took her hand again, leading her forward. They walked for a while in silence, the darkness so thick it was almost a living thing. Eleanor was finding it difficult to keep her breathing and heart rate under control.

Eventually Freddie stopped, letting go of her hand.

"We're here. I'll light a fire. Stand still, OK?"

Eleanor jumped a mile at the sound of his voice and was profoundly grateful when she saw the sparks fly again as he struck the flints together. They quickly caught, and as the kindling began to burn, the light illuminated the cave around her. *It's a big space*, she thought, looking round, *almost as big as the main cave back home… Home?* She had not been consciously aware of it before, but she realised that she did indeed think of their cave as home. Guilt stabbed at her as she realised she did not really miss her old life; her memories of it had taken on the strange, half-remembered quality of a dream.

"Freddie, do you miss home? The one from before you died?"

"Sometimes I still miss my family and friends, but I'm not homesick anymore."

"How long did it take you to stop being homesick?"

"I'm not sure, about six months, why? Are you missing home or someone special?"

"No, that's just it. I've been here less than a month and I hardly think about before," Eleanor said, unable to keep the guilt out of her voice.

"Maybe your mind is just making it easier for you to adjust. Don't be too hard on yourself, everybody reacts differently to change and frankly you appear to be handling this whole insane mess far better than I am," Freddie said.

The fire was now a roaring blaze. Freddie had lit several candles, and looking around Eleanor realised that the cave had been set up to be lived in – there were blankets, cushions, supplies and wood for the fire already stacked up against the wall.

"You've been here before."

"I was thinking about hiding away for a while, see if I could get a handle on this fire business." Freddie shook his head. "I used to be a fireman, but now I'm fire itself."

"I was working in a jewellery shop." Eleanor shuddered as a dark shadow passed across her mind and strong feelings of shame, guilt and regret rose through her, but she shoved them back down. "But I was saving up to study Geology at university; I've always been fascinated by the Earth."

"I guess that passion is what drew Conlan to our souls in the first place," Freddie said thoughtfully.

"Or maybe this was always our destiny," Eleanor mused.

"You really think so?" Freddie asked.

"Maybe coming here is my reason for being; maybe helping Conlan will allow me the chance to actually make a difference." *Or to atone*, she added silently.

Freddie looked at her, his dark eyes glittering, and Eleanor realised his energy was getting dangerously high; she reached out to smother it, staggering slightly at the effort required to do it. It did not take long for her to recover though, as control was getting easier and easier.

Freddie started her first lesson in unarmed combat; he said it reminded him of the karate he had once taken. They went slowly and carefully to begin with, but as the days went by Freddie pushed her harder and harder. Eleanor discovered that she enjoyed fighting, and she particularly liked the feeling of her body getting stronger and fitter. Freddie was an excellent teacher – steady, patient and knowledgeable – he set up a punishing regime of stretches and core strengthening exercises before each practice, always pushing her that little bit further. As the lessons progressed, Eleanor realised that the more effort she put into it, the more she got out of it.

"You've been doing really well, but your concentration is all over the place today," Freddie said, handing her a cup of water.

It was mid-afternoon and they were taking a five-minute breather. Eleanor could feel the sweat running down her back, but even the energising feeling of pushing her body to the limits could not totally distract her.

"It's his last day in bed, Freddie," she said, unable to keep the fear out of her voice.

"Oh come on, Eleanor, he's not a monster, he's not going to do anything to you. He's irritated, but deep down he knows you did it for his own good."

Eleanor gave him a small smile; ever since she had started curbing Freddie's energy levels, his ambivalent feelings towards Conlan had reduced.

"I know he's not a monster, Freddie, but I'm worried about the 'connection'..." She trailed off into silence, unsure how to articulate her fear.

Freddie shrugged. "It's what we were made for."

Eleanor nodded at his logic, but she found it hard to shake her feelings. She liked to learn about something before she did it, to study and read what others had thought, so working out something so important by trial and error made her uncomfortable.

Amelia smiled at them as they entered the main cave, stamping the snow off their boots.

"Did you have a good afternoon?" she asked.

"It's been fun," Eleanor enthused. Removing her over-jacket she moved to Amelia's side and began helping her to chop the vegetables for dinner. They worked in amiable silence while Freddie warmed himself by the fire. Eleanor was so intent on her task that she did not notice Will was missing until he emerged from the bedroom and spoke.

"Eleanor, Conlan wants to talk to you."

Eleanor nodded, a sick feeling spreading through her stomach. She dried her hands, taking longer than the task required so she had more chance to steel herself. When she could no longer put it off she shoved her fear deep inside and, head held high, walked into the bedroom.

Conlan was sat on his bed, back resting on the pillow and his long legs crossed in front of him. He was reading a small, blue book. Eleanor sighed; she missed reading. Hearing her enter his chamber, Conlan raised his head and she was momentarily stunned by his appearance. He looked younger somehow, a lot younger than Will and younger even than Freddie; he was clean shaven, the exhaustion and pain were gone and his face had filled out a little.

"Hello, Eleanor."

There was no glaring, no angry tone and he actually sounded pleased to see her. Eleanor relaxed a little and smiled.

"You look much better."

"So I'm told. You seem to have been avoiding me. Will tells me you spend your time with Freddie. He's teaching you to fight." There was no accusation or annoyance.

"He's a great teacher," Eleanor confirmed.

Conlan nodded. "Will also tells me that since you and Freddie started spending time together that Freddie hasn't lost control once. He's calmer, happier and more co-operative than any of us ever thought possible."

Eleanor knew he wanted to know how she had managed to help Freddie, but she found she had no idea where to start.

"Maybe he's just happier and maybe you should ask *him* about it," Eleanor said quietly.

"I did, and he told me to ask you."

"Oh," she breathed, staring at her feet and trying to get her thoughts in order. Conlan waited patiently for her to continue. She had no idea what to say, but she knew that sooner or later she would have to say something. "Freddie has a ball of energy inside him that's constantly growing. I drain the excess energy off and sort of absorb it... I think," she said finally.

"How?" He sounded excited.

"Well, it's like I have a ball of energy inside me too, and I can make bits of it stretch out and pull some of Freddie's energy from him. And now I've said it I realise just how totally bizarre that sounds."

Conlan laughed. "Bizarre...welcome to my world."

Eleanor smiled; she had forgotten how much she liked the sound of his laugh. "I don't think I can describe it any better than that."

"You don't have to," Conlan said. "It's the same for me. I've tried to control the Five in the past, and it also feels like I have a ball of energy that I reach out with and pull the energy into me."

"What, from all of us at the same time?" Eleanor asked astonished.

"Well, that's the plan, but it's never worked very well."

"You should be grateful it hasn't. I've only been pulling energy from Freddie and it's exhausting. I couldn't pull energy from anyone else, not that I even know how to – it would knock me senseless or worse."

"Maybe that's because you're not meant to be pulling energy, maybe it's just meant to be me. Maybe with practice I'll be able to handle it," Conlan said, smiling at her.

Distracted by his smile it took Eleanor a moment to realise there were far too many 'maybe's' in his sentence.

"It's not that you haven't been able to get the connection to work. You don't know *how* to make it work, do you?" she deduced.

"It's not like there's anybody around I can ask," Conlan said a little defensively.

"Didn't your grandfather's stories give any details?"

Conlan shrugged. "Not that I remember."

"How about the shamans?"

"The connection is as much a mystery to them as it is to the rest of us. In truth, Eleanor, your connection to Freddie is the closest any of us have ever gotten to making this work."

"Well I'm sorry to disappoint you, but I don't have any great solution," she said, dropping her head, the hope she saw flash through his eyes making her feel uncomfortable.

"Please, Eleanor, I need you to show me how you're doing it," Conlan said, desperation creeping into his voice.

"I can barely explain it to myself. I'm not sure how I'm doing it and I'm not sure it's safe," she said, raising her eyes back to his. "And none of that matters to you, does it?"

"This connection has worked in the past, without doing damage to those concerned. I have to believe that with enough trial and error we can get it to work. Will you help me?" He was smiling at her again and Eleanor felt her resistance fading.

She sighed. "I'd have been happier if you'd just called me in here to yell at me for making you stay in bed. Of course I'll help you, but for the record I think this is a really dangerous idea."

"Duly noted," Conlan said, smiling again.

Deep down, Eleanor knew that what she had agreed to do was a bad idea, but he was smiling at her, making her feel like the centre of the universe again, and she would have agreed to pretty much anything to keep him smiling at her. She was a little shocked by her need to please him. Her brain began trying to formulate a reason for it but Eleanor shut it down quickly, pushing it aside; she did not want to know – it was not something she could deal with right now.

She spent a restless night tossing and turning, unable to get rid of the feeling that she was about to make a huge mistake. As a result, she was only dozing lightly when Conlan woke before dawn the next morning and snuck from his bed. She waited a little while to see if he was coming back, but when he failed to return she got out of bed and followed him. She found him with Rand, talking quietly in his growling language as he gently stroked the horse's nose and neck, scratching him behind the ears. He did not turn as she approached.

"I think he missed you," Eleanor commented.

"The feeling is mutual," Conlan said softly.

"Are we going to try this connection thing today?" Eleanor asked, trying not to sound as worried as she felt.

"This afternoon. Will and Amelia need some time this morning, so I am going to give you a sword-fighting lesson. Freddie says you are ready."

"Erm… ok?"

"Get a good breakfast, you are going to need it," he said, a soft rumble running through the comment, which sounded to Eleanor like amusement.

Conlan was already in the side cave Freddie used for practice when Eleanor arrived. He was loosely swinging a sword around. Even his relaxed warm-up had the deadly, graceful precision and practiced look of a professional. Once they got going, Eleanor started to enjoy herself. The heavy sword felt comfortable in her hand and the steady, flowing movements she was learning were stretching her muscles in new ways. Eventually Conlan moved into attacks and defences, playing the part of the enemy. From one such attack Eleanor tried the flicking sword move she had used to kill the Protector, but Conlan stopped it easily and before she could blink he had swung his sword back, bringing the sharp edge to a stop a hair's breadth from the side of her neck, his implication clear that if he had been a real enemy, he would have taken her head off.

"I got lucky with that Protector, didn't I?" Eleanor said, looking at the sword edge warily.

"You stood your ground against an armed man – that took a lot of courage, but yes, Eleanor, you were very lucky," Conlan said solemnly.

"What should I have done?"

Conlan smiled and began to explain to her how to read the enemy, what to look for in an initial attack and how that might lead on to further moves. His animated conversation and thoughtful guidance gave Eleanor a totally different view of his personality; this was someone she very much liked, someone she could relate to.

After several hours of swinging a sword at her, Conlan moved on to testing the fighting skills she had been learning from Freddie. He pointed out her weaknesses – the lack of strength in her punches and her lack of height and weight – and then he showed her how to make up for those weaknesses. Using her elbow to punch instead of her fist when she could, pushing through with her hips to give extra power and all the delicate points on a human body that could be exploited with a well-aimed elbow or foot were imparted. Conlan then moved on to getting her to use these lessons for real.

His attacks were slow to begin with, allowing her time to think before she reacted, but there was force in his moves, blocking and deflecting them hurt. Not wanting to admit that she could not keep the punishment up much longer, Eleanor began forcibly punching and kicking back, hoping he would back off. It had the opposite effect. Conlan gave her an amused, predatory grin and attacked her with increased force and speed. *I have to stop this before I end up a large walking bruise.* Conlan slung a right-handed punch at her head. Eleanor saw her opportunity and, already moving, blocked with her right hand, span round and planted her left elbow into his stomach, taking grim satisfaction from his sharp exhalation of breath. Her back to him, she pinned his right arm tight into her body, and then pulling hard she dropped onto her right knee, flicking her hips as Freddie had taught her. Following the momentum of his punch, Conlan's body was already twisting in the direction Eleanor had pulled him, so he had no choice but to follow her movement round, his feet coming out from under him. He landed heavily on his back, but before he could recover any sort of composure Eleanor threw a punch and stopped it millimetres from the bridge of his nose.

Conlan stared at her in surprise, a wide, genuine smile spread across his face. Clapping erupted from the cave's entrance, where Amelia stood watching. Conlan got back to his feet; Eleanor gave him a cheeky smirk as he winced. Amelia came over with mugs of water.

"That was great!" Amelia enthused.

"She thinks she's Xena," Conlan said. Amelia did a double take, wide eyes bemused. Conlan gave Eleanor a suspicious sideways glance.

"Xena... a warrior princess of your world," he offered in explanation.

"Yes, Boss, I know who Xena is; I was just trying to figure out how you do," Amelia said, doing her best to hide her amusement. Eleanor dissolved into giggles.

"Eleanor mentioned her once. Is there something funny about it?" he muttered.

"Not really, I just imagine that Eleanor neglected to mention that Xena isn't a real person, she's a character on a television show," Amelia said.

Conlan sighed, looking sternly at Eleanor. "You've obviously watched entirely too much television." His very serious expression and parental tone, not to mention his attitude of absolute authority over something he knew nothing about, just made Eleanor laugh harder.

After a lunch Eleanor was too nervous to do anything other than pick at, they went back to the training room. Freddie, Amelia and Will joined them. Conlan made them sit in a circle and he told them to close their eyes and concentrate on their internal energy. Eleanor did as she was told, feeling the solid ball of energy she imagined in her stomach pulse and twitch with her heartbeat and the constant light pulling on Freddie's energy. As she sat with her eyes closed she gradually became aware of those around her. Amelia was to her left; soft, feathery energy, very nearly non-existent, hidden almost completely in the familiar heat of Freddie's energy on her right. Concentrating harder, Eleanor felt Will. His energy was deep and flowing, and it threatened to suck her in. Next to him was Conlan. Eleanor slowly extended a 'string' from her energy ball and used it to push gently at Conlan. His energy was there, but it was so very different to the others'. It was like his energy was inside a glass ball – she could feel it but not reach it. She tried repeatedly to push her energy through to his, but she did not have the strength to penetrate the barrier. Without warning, Conlan's energy seemingly extended through his shield, attached itself to hers and began pulling. Eleanor gasped. Pain, like someone was forcibly and very clumsily removing her intestines, tore through her. Shocked, Eleanor snapped her energy back, eyes flying open. Conlan was staring at her. They regarded each other in silence while the others sat around with their eyes still closed.

"I felt you," Conlan said softly.

Amelia, Freddie and Will opened their eyes to look at Conlan, who was still staring at Eleanor.

"I felt you too and I didn't like it!" Eleanor said bluntly.

"I never said you were going to like it - let's try again," Conlan said. Nodding reluctantly Eleanor closed her eyes and concentrated. This time she kept her distance from Conlan and concentrated on Will, his energy the strongest next to Freddie's. Eleanor very cautiously extended an energy string towards him. He did not grab but seemed to intertwine around it; there was a tugging sensation, but it was far from uncomfortable. It felt sort of tickly, like getting a bare foot sucked into mud.

Hello, Eleanor.

Will's friendly greeting made her smile. When she had visited Freddie's mind she had seen Freddie burning in front of her, but this was different. It was like Will had an empty, white-washed room in his head and their awareness filled it. She felt his friendly curiosity all around her.

Hello, Will. Are all men's minds this empty?

Will's laughter echoed around the empty space. *No, Eleanor, contrary to popular belief, guys do have occasional thoughts. You're not in my mind. Think of this as an antechamber, a space where we can talk. I can choose what to say to you, what to show you – my thoughts are my own.*

Show me?

I can show you my memories if I wish to, let you feel my emotions, just as you can show me yours if you want to.

Wow, we can mind-meld?

Will laughed again. *Yes, you could call it that. Conlan's right – you have watched too much TV!*

Eleanor giggled. *Can you feel Conlan?*

Sort of... I know he's there, and I've tried reaching him in the past, but there's something blocking me, shielding him from my attempts. If I get too close he tries to pull energy from me. It's not a very pleasant experience. The last time he tried I responded instinctively with such force I almost killed him. Generally, I try to keep my distance.

Eleanor received several flashes of Will's memories, occasions they had tried to connect in the past, with Conlan lying in an unconscious, crumpled heap.

Have you explained this to him? Eleanor felt a strong surge of guilt from Will and even stronger feelings of concern and devotion.

Until you arrived we were never going to get it to work anyway, so I didn't see much point in crushing his hopes, Will said. *We're doing something wrong, aren't we?*

Yes, Eleanor agreed. *I can't imagine we're meant to feel like our insides are being ripped out, so there must be another way. Do you mind if I try pulling your energy from you?* Will's presence faded slightly and Eleanor got the impression he had just taken a mental step away from her.

I'm not sure that's a good idea, Eleanor. I did Conlan quite a bit of damage the last time, I could kill you.

Eleanor shrugged. *I'm willing to take the risk; I need to know what's possible, if I'm going to figure this out.*

Will snorted. *Arrogant, aren't you?*

Eleanor smiled. *No, just determined.*

OK, but be careful, Will warned.

Getting as firm a hold on Will's energy as possible, she carefully began absorbing it. When Will did not react, she focused all her concentration into pulling as much energy from him as she could. It was like drinking water. It felt like her stomach was filling to bursting point with cold liquid, but the more she drank, the more she wanted. The effort it was taking was pushing her towards exhaustion, but she was taking so much energy she found she could keep the fatigue at bay. It was a rather unpleasant feeling having Will's energy slosh around inside her, like her own energy was drowning. She heard voices in the distance, someone yelling her name. A sudden stinging pain snapped her eyes back open. Conlan was kneeling in front of her. He seemed on the edge of panic. *This is very unlike him,* a detached part of Eleanor's mind observed. He slapped her face a second time as he yelled.

"Eleanor! Stop!"

The detached part of her mind knew there must be something wrong, but another, much stronger part felt only the pain. Angry, she fought back, releasing all the energy she had pulled from Will directly at Conlan. His eyes widened in agony as it hit him and coursed through every cell in his body like thousands of volts of electricity. He collapsed writhing onto the floor, his gasping, tormented cries filling Eleanor's head and reverberating through her stupefied brain.

"Eleanor, stop it, you're going to kill him!" Amelia shrieked.

"I'm trying!" Eleanor said through gritted teeth, as she tried desperately to pull the energy back, but once released it flowed from her – she had no control. While there was no let-up in the onslaught Eleanor had unleashed on him, Conlan's movements were getting weaker, his cries reduced to whimpering sobs. Freddie moved to her side.

"Sorry, Eleanor," he whispered, and then he struck her across the head, a teeth-rattling blow administered with something hard and solid. Consciousness did not leave completely, but it was enough to break her focus, making everything distant and hazy. Without focus, the energy she was releasing dissipated around her, making the air crackle with ozone. She slumped forward, feeling blood running with warm lethargy through her hair. Freddie caught her and gently lowered her to the ground, then went to check on Conlan. Eleanor watched, through eyes she could barely keep open, as Conlan stopped writhing. He rolled painfully onto his back, panting. His limbs twitched sporadically, but he waved away Freddie's attempt to assist him.

"Help Will," he insisted, his voice hoarse.

Looking beyond Conlan, Eleanor could see Will. He lay on the ground, eyes closed, unnaturally still; Amelia knelt beside him, frantically moving her hands over his neck and then placing her head on his chest.

"Freddie, he's not breathing," she said, fear making her voice squeak.

Fighting to stay conscious, Eleanor watched Freddie start chest compressions and mouth-to-mouth in an attempt to kick-start Will's automotive responses. *What have I done?* Despite the effort Freddie was putting into his CPR, Will showed no signs of improvement. Eleanor closed her eyes in despair, tears intensifying the throbbing pain in her head. With her eyes closed, she felt something; it was faint, but it was there. Will's string of energy, still entwined with hers, pulsed weakly. *I drained the life from him, literally. I guess our energy isn't limitless.* Although it seemed even a limited amount could do damage. A thought occurred to her that if she could pull his life from him when she pulled his energy, she could help him by giving him energy back. She had none of Will's energy left, as most of it had ripped through Conlan and the rest dissipated around her, but she had her own energy and there was always Freddie's energy. Eleanor tried to focus on Will, but he felt too far away. It was like pushing a huge boulder up a steep hill. *I need to be closer.* She rolled herself onto all fours, and fighting the black wave of nausea and dizziness she forced herself upright. With slow, unsteady steps she walked over to Will, dropping to her knees near his head; she reached out a hand to touch his face. Amelia grabbed it.

"What are you doing? Haven't you done enough damage? Leave him alone!" she yelled, her eyes wet grey stone.

"Let me help," Eleanor whispered, distressed by how tiring uttering just those three words had been.

"How?" Amelia asked suspiciously.

"I don't have time to explain."

For what felt to Eleanor like an eternity, Amelia kept a firm grip on her wrist until Freddie pulled her free, taking Amelia's hand in his.

"He's dying, Amelia, CPR isn't working, let Eleanor try. Will has nothing to lose at this point." Staring down at Will's lifeless body, Amelia nodded, her tears dripping off the end of her nose.

Eleanor placed her hand against Will's face and concentrated on finding the faint pulse of life. She found it, but it was fading fast. She grabbed hold, and with all the force she could muster pushed the glowing green energy from the ball in her stomach into Will. At first nothing happened. Then gradually the pulse strengthened, there was the sensation that her heart was straining, beating for two, as Will's heart jump-started, finding its own rhythm. She took slow, deep breaths until Will's breathing mirrored her own. She pushed more energy into him, surprised at how little effort it took when they were touching – far less than pulling energy out. She felt her own energy level dropping, pushing her rapidly towards the looming darkness, and she realised in dismay that she could not take energy from Freddie because she no longer had the strength to pull it from him. The energy she had would have to be enough. With one last burst of effort, Eleanor sent out as much energy as she could. Not having the strength to hold herself up, she slid slowly down, laying her head gently on Will's shoulder. Her consciousness started spiralling into the silent black, but as it did Eleanor heard the most wonderful sound. It was Will's voice, confused and tired, but very much alive.

"What happened?"

8

POWER

It was the voices that pulled Eleanor up from the bottomless black – loud voices, angry. She was lying in her bed, a thick, hot, itchy bandage wrapped round her head. The fog in her mind lifted slightly and the voices started making sense.

"She nearly killed you!"

A yelling female voice. *Amelia.* Then more conversation, too low for Eleanor to make out the words. *I need to get up; I have to tell them I'm sorry.* That meant opening her eyes and moving. Her whole body ached miserably and there was a steady, mind-numbing pounding in her head. She took a couple of deep breaths and opened her eyes a fraction. A candle burned on the floor beside her bed, casting dancing shadows across the cave. Opening her eyes the rest of the way she squinted in an attempt to bring into focus what she could see, and then she carefully tried to sit up. Her muscles protested and the pain in her head reached a screaming crescendo, but taking short, quick breaths she pushed through the pain, swung her legs off the bed and managed to get herself standing. Walking slowly, feeling sick, Eleanor moved in the direction of the voices. The bandage, made loose by her movement, slipped slightly down her face. She pulled it off, wincing as it rubbed the damage on the back of her head. She probed the area cautiously with her fingers; there was a large raised bruise and a long, scabbed over gash. *What did Freddie hit me with?* She moved into the main cave. Conlan, Will and Amelia were sat round the fire, their backs to her, while Freddie was swinging a sword backwards and forwards in the training cave.

"… didn't mean to hurt me Amelia," Will was saying.

"I don't care whether she meant it or not, she nearly killed you both. She should have known better!" Amelia snapped.

"Why should she have known better?" Conlan asked.

"Will told her it was dangerous…"

"No, I told her it might be dangerous for her," Will corrected.

"The fact still remains that her 'experiments' with Freddie and Will are the closest we have come to getting the connection working. She doesn't follow orders, she follows her own intuition, and as much as you want her punished, Amelia, I don't think beating that out of her is going the help us," Conlan said.

"She left you writhing on the floor in agony while she sucked the life out of Will and you're just going to let that go? Aren't either of you the slightest bit frightened of the power she possesses?" Amelia asked bitterly.

Feeling dread crawl up her back on tiny needle claws, Eleanor stepped a little further forward.

"It was actually the other way round," she said quietly. They turned to look at her, Amelia glaring pure loathing.

"What was the other way round?" Conlan asked, regarding her with a cold, emotionless expression.

"I sucked the life out of Will when I pulled the energy out of him and it was his energy I used to … to…"

"To attack me," Conlan finished flatly.

Amelia, fury in her eyes, jumped to her feet and charged, bringing Eleanor down in a tangle of arms and legs and slamming her head into the ground. Amelia made no sound – she just punched and kicked at every piece of vulnerable flesh she could reach. Dazed and struggling to stay conscious, Eleanor made no attempt to protect herself. This was Amelia and if Amelia was trying to hurt her, it must surely be justified. The beating stopped as Will pulled the furious woman off. He held Amelia close, stroking her hair as she sobbed brokenly into his chest. Eleanor pulled herself up onto her knees, feeling utterly wretched, and forced herself to look at Conlan's face, searching it for some sign that he understood she had not meant to hurt him, had not meant to hurt anyone. All she found was cold disapproval.

"I'm sorry, I'll accept any punishment you want," she whispered, dropping her head, not able to meet Conlan's eyes anymore, not able to deal with the sick feeling churning through her insides. She wanted to say something else, something that would help them understand, but the throbbing in her head was making coherent thoughts difficult. The silence stretched out, and before it ended Eleanor slid gratefully back into unconsciousness. In her last moment of awareness she felt strong arms stop her headlong flight towards the floor.

Eleanor woke again with the feeling that something was wrong, intuition shooting fear through her heart. Although there was no sound, she could feel screeching vibrations through every nerve ending in her body. There was nobody in sight, so moving carefully she got herself standing again. The fuzzy, vomit-inspiring dizziness was less than before, but the throbbing in her head was still a steady, monotonous pounding. She shuffled slowly out into the main cave. Will and Amelia were side by side in the kitchen, preparing food and talking quietly to each other, and they seemed fine. Judging from the noise coming from the training cave, Conlan and Freddie were sparring. Not wanting to risk Amelia's wrath, Eleanor shuffled quietly over to the entrance of the training cave and sat to watch. Conlan and Freddie's swords were a blur as they traded blows backwards and forwards. Freddie seemed to be putting rather more effort into it than was strictly required. Eleanor focused and the vibrations jumped up a gear. Freddie's eyes were blazing, reaching out she felt how dangerously elevated his energy was, and watching his movements she realised he was fighting to win. Conlan seemed oblivious and was clearly enjoying himself. *One slip up and Freddie's going to skewer you.* The thought had no sooner surfaced when Conlan caught his foot on a loose stone. He only lost his balance for a heartbeat, but it was enough. Freddie was on him, heavy overhead blows pushing him further off balance. Panicked, Eleanor reacted instinctively and began siphoning as much of Freddie's energy from him as she was able – far more and far quicker than she ever had before, realising too late that it was not going to naturally dissipate, she was building up power too fast. It was beginning to make her energy ball glow and become hotter; the effort pushed her battered, damaged body towards another shutdown. She silently berated herself while frantically trying to think of a solution to the problem. She wracked her brains and suddenly the image of fork lightning hitting the ground filled her mind.

Pushing a string of energy deep into the earth below her, she pushed Freddie's energy down the string and out into the surrounding earth. It was working; unfortunately, the relentless throbbing in her head made judging the effort she needed to use very tricky. As she pulled at his energy Freddie staggered, his sword dropping from his hand. Conlan froze, concern and confusion on his face. Freddie turned and looked at her, his panicked look turning to understanding. Conlan followed Freddie's gaze and cold fury filled his face. Clearing the distance between them in four long strides he grabbed Eleanor by the collar and dragged her to her feet.

"Stop it!" he hissed.

Still trying her best to pull energy from Freddie while at the same time push it down into the earth, a task akin to patting her head and rubbing her tummy with two sets of arms at the same time, Eleanor was only able to react to this new development with one emotion: terror. Conlan looked back at Freddie, who was now on his knees taking rapid, gulping breaths, giving an even stronger impression of her guilt. Conlan turned back to her, jamming the point of his sword into the soft flesh under her chin, pushing hard enough to break the skin.

"Whatever you're doing, stop it, now… or I will end you," he snarled. Eleanor believed him. Having heard the commotion, Amelia and Will came running through from the main cave. They took one look at Freddie on his knees gasping for breath and Conlan millimetres away from killing her and reached their own conclusions. Will rushed over to help Freddie and Amelia started yelling.

"What's wrong with you? Don't you know the pain you're causing or do you just not care? Freddie has done nothing but help you. Conlan should push that sword right through your sick little brain!"

"No!" Freddie ordered. Not releasing the pressure on the sword, Conlan turned back towards him again. He was still on his knees but he looked far better, his breathing returning to normal. "She was trying to help," he continued, looking ashamed. "With Eleanor not being conscious much the last few days, my energy levels have been raising. I've tried to control it, but... There's a good chance Eleanor just saved your life."

"And you didn't think to mention this sooner?" Conlan asked.

Freddie hung his head. "My thinking becomes different as the energy levels rise. I get paranoid, fearful... angry. It's like all my common sense leaves me."

Conlan removed his hand from Eleanor's collar at the same time as he took the sword away from her chin. She dropped into a heap at his feet, trembling violently and hating herself for it. She watched the steady drip of blood from the cut under her chin as it began to form a puddle on the floor. There was pain, but it just sort of merged with all the other pain, which she was becoming worryingly used to. Having returned Freddie's energy level to a more even keel, she pulled her energy strings back as Will came and crouched down in front of her, firmly pushing a pad of material under her chin to staunch the blood. Eleanor looked into his deep-blue eyes.

"When did I become the enemy?" she whimpered. She felt lost, like the world had just turned upside down for no reason at all. Will gave no answer, but Eleanor felt an energy string gently push up against her. Reaching out with a string of her own she wrapped round it, and Will's cool, calm presence entered her mind.

I know you're not the enemy, Will said, his voice echoing. *The others do, too. You just gave us all a nasty wake up call. I don't think we realised just how dangerous this was going to get. How dangerous we were going to get...*

Eleanor felt him leave her mind and detach his energy from hers. He was still looking at her with emotionless blue eyes and she realised that this was for Amelia's benefit. Eleanor felt profoundly grateful to him for offering her what little comfort he could.

Eleanor was so miserable, she was desperate to escape. Amelia's open loathing exploded if Eleanor so much as caught her eye. Will was careful not to get involved, while Freddie's uncomfortable misery mirrored Eleanor's own. Conlan just did not seem to care; distant and distracted, he seemed to want to spend most of his time on his own, brooding. Freddie came to the rescue, taking her up to the high lake, where she would lie on her back in the snow and just concentrate on her energy. She was going to learn as much as she could, knowledge was power and with it she could ensure she never accidentally hurt anyone again. At first Freddie had tried to talk to her, but when Eleanor made no attempt to respond, he eventually gave up, following her around in silence.

It was up by the lake that she first felt it. Finding her favourite spot Eleanor settled herself back into the snow, watching the clouds roam the sky above her. She lay still, not really thinking of anything, when a thought popped into her head.

Spring is coming!

Eleanor sat up. She looked slowly at the frigid, white world around her. There were no outward indications, no evidence that could have brought her mind to the conclusion that spring was coming. Logically it must come at some point, but this thought had brought with it a certainty, an excitement that spring was imminent. The excitement was not her own – she knew that for a fact – because spring meant the snow would melt and the Protectors and Enforcers would be coming into the mountains looking for them. Spring held no excitement for her.

Fearing for her sanity, she closed her eyes, concentrating on her feelings and turning them over in her mind, looking at them from every angle. As she did, she felt it. She brought it into her conscious thoughts; it was a faint energy string connecting her to the Earth. As she focused on the string it strengthened, vibrating slightly, and the stronger it became, the more information flooded into her mind. She could feel the different types of rock in the ground beneath her, each with stories to tell, and she could feel the seeds and living things of the Earth sleeping, dormant, waiting, sensing that spring was coming. It was their collective excitement she could feel – it was the Earth's excitement at the thought of rebirth and creation. The effort of pushing her energy string deep into the earth became too much and she relaxed, retracting it. Then on a whim Eleanor tried pulling energy from the Earth and was delighted to find this required almost no effort at all. She felt her energy string pulled deep, spreading out like roots of an ancient tree. She had not had to push, she just had to take slow, deep breaths and hold her concentration. Unlike Freddie's energy, which always made her feel like she was burning, or Will's, which had made her feel a little like she was drowning, this energy felt totally natural to her. The green energy ball she imagined in her stomach began growing, stretching, and Eleanor became aware of the unlimited energy at her fingertips; the sense of power was intoxicating.

Distracted by the feeling of omnipotence, she did not notice just how much energy she had accumulated until it was too late. Eleanor discovered that her body was not meant to hold such a large amount of energy; there were side effects. The symptoms came slowly at first, a tingling in her extremities and then numbness. *I have to release the energy.* She pushed it back into the ground, but there was too much. Numbness turned quickly to agonising pain, like acid running through her veins. She gritted her teeth together to keep from yelling out, terrified what might happen if Freddie heard her scream, and she released the energy at him by accident. *Could I release the energy? But where?* She had done it with Will's energy; all she had needed was something to focus on, and unfortunately that had been Conlan. *So, no focusing on human beings... What about something inanimate?* The pain was making it difficult to think, but she pulled herself upright so she could see the lake in front of her with its thick lid of ice. Focusing on a spot in the middle, she released all the energy. It was not the steady stream she had felt when she had released Will's energy. This felt more like flinging a rock with all her strength.

The result was spectacular. The inches-thick ice exploded upwards fifty feet into the air and a deafening, cracking boom echoed around her. Before it had died away it was joined by the gunshot cracks of huge ice chunks and water falling back into the lake. The acid pain drained away and she sat panting, watching in stunned silence as the ice finished falling into what was now a cavernous hole in the middle of the lake.

Freddie came to crouch at her side. "What the hell was that?"

"That was me. Or rather the power I direct," Eleanor said, turning towards him. Freddie was looking at her, concerned.

"Eleanor, you're bleeding."

"I am? Where?" She had not felt any injuries and she was too far away to be hit by the ice. She instinctively rubbed a hand under her chin, but that injury had healed over days ago.

"Your eyes are bleeding," Freddie whispered. Eleanor raised a shaking hand to her eye and rubbed the back of it into the socket. She drew her hand back and looked at the bloody smear.

"Must remember there are side effects," she muttered.

"What?"

"Nothing. Freddie, I need to experiment and I need you to keep a safe distance."

"You just exploded a lake. What if you exploded a rock face down on top of you?" Freddie asked.

"I'll be careful, but this will be easier if I don't have to worry about accidentally exploding you."

Freddie nodded, but he did not seem particularly happy about it. "How come you get the power to explode stuff and I just turn homicidally psychotic at the drop of a hat?"

"Actually, I think we all have similar power, but I need to practice to be sure. Besides, you might turn homicidal, but you've not actually killed anybody yet, have you? I've taken two lives, quite possibly more since I got here, not to mention what I did to Will and Conlan, and I have no out-of-control energy to blame it on."

With Freddie out of sight down the pass that led up to the lake, Eleanor began. As she practiced, the days became warmer and the sun felt stronger. *Spring is coming.* The confirmation of what the earth had already predicted amused her, until she remembered that this meant the Enforcers were coming. Then fear gave her focus, purpose. Her experiments were not just idle knowledge-building exercises; she planned them around being able to use her abilities to fight, if it came to it. She tested pulling small amounts of energy, pulling large amounts, draining it back and exploding it out. Through careful observation she realised that the weak string that constantly linked her to the earth acted like an overflow pipe, helping to keep her energy balanced. She also realised that in extreme situations the overflow pipe would reverse and pull energy from the earth. *Maybe this mechanism is faulty in Freddie...*

Eleanor worked out how to pull tiny amounts of energy from the earth and then release them in small bursts, but there was very little control, and once released there was no calling it back, like a bullet from a gun, she was painfully aware of what would happen if she unleashed this on a person.While she could 'aim', after a fashion, she usually devastated a far larger area than she intended. And the power was immense.

As she lined up rocks along the edge of a rocky outcrop which held mute evidence of previous explosions. She took a deep breath and began pulling energy from the earth, enjoying the feeling of having it build inside her. She relaxed a little, opening herself up to the world around her; she liked this feeling, like anything and everything was possible.

"Eleanor!"

His voice. Angry, demanding. She spun round. Conlan was stood barely ten feet away. Startled and frightened, Eleanor felt her hold slip, releasing the energy as Freddie came charging though the pass. Leaping, he crashed into Conlan, pulling him down to the ground. The mountain wall behind where his head had just been exploded outwards. The rock and dust rained down on them, gradually stopping. There was silence. Images of Freddie and Conlan's crushed, bloody bodies sprang into Eleanor's mind as she ran forward.

"No, no, no!" she moaned, pulling the rocks from them, ripping her hands on unyielding stone in her desperate attempt to reach them.

Thankfully the explosion had been powerful enough that the rocks were not all that large, but there were a lot of them. She saw Freddie first, his body laying protectively over Conlan. She shook him gently, and then disregarding everything she knew about first aid, gripped him under his arms and hauled him towards her, cradling him. His face and hair were grey with dust, a red snake of blood slithering slowly from his hairline to his chin.

"Freddie? Freddie… please, don't be dead, please, Freddie, I'm sorry. Freddie…" she begged. Movement in her peripheral vision made her lift her head. Conlan was struggling to get up, the dust rising in clouds around him, making him cough. Eleanor felt an irrational anger. What was he doing here surprising her? It should be him lying motionless, not Freddie. Then the guilt hit her. Feeling the bottomless pit of despair open up underneath her, she clung to her friend and sobbed softly, begging him to live.

Freddie coughed suddenly, convulsing slightly in her arms. He blinked open his eyes and smiled weakly. Eleanor felt relief wash through her.

"I'm sorry, Freddie. Thank you, thank you for saving Conlan again."

Freddie chuckled. "We seem to be doing this as a favour for each other a lot."

"Eleanor?" Conlan said tentatively. His anger was gone and he sounding wary, frightened even.

"What?" Her voice was hard, empty; not really caring what he wanted.

"Is there something you want to tell me?"

She raised her head. "Tell you? No, Conlan, I don't want to tell you anything; however, if you have questions you want to ask me, I might decide some of them are worth answering."

"You're angry with me." It was a flat statement, with no indication as to how he felt about this fact.

"How observant of you, and here I was thinking you didn't realise I existed. You certainly don't seem to care if Amelia ripped me to shreds," Eleanor snapped.

Conlan looked confused. "Amelia hasn't laid a hand on you in over a week."

"No, currently she's attacking me verbally. Have you *any* idea what it's like to be hated by someone you love?" Eleanor muttered.

"Yes."

This man never ceases to amaze me. Her anger began to melt under the strength of his emotionless gaze.

"But you're not going to tell me about it, are you?"

"No, I'm not," Conlan agreed.

"You're going to have to let me get closer eventually."

"Why?"

"Because, oh mighty leader, you're the reason this connection thing doesn't work!" Eleanor said, taking a perverse pleasure in the shock on his face.

"You don't know that."

Eleanor glared at him. "Yes, I do. I have the bare essentials of how my energy works. I can teach the others how to access and control their own, but I can't reach you. You're trapped in this shield I can't penetrate. I'm fairly certain that you're not meant to pull energy from us, because it hurts us way too much, but the shield stops us sending energy to you. Hence, the connection doesn't work."

"I have a shield around me?"

Eleanor nodded. "Ask Will, if you don't believe me."

"Why didn't he tell me?"

"Because he doesn't want to hurt you. Because up until now it was irrelevant."

"Do you think you can get the connection working?" Conlan asked. Eleanor sighed – he was missing the point.

"I think I can show everybody how to access and deal with their energy..."

"Even me?" Freddie interrupted.

Eleanor nodded, "… but the rest of it, that's up to you Conlan. How far are you willing to trust me? You have to accept that we're in this together."

Conlan stared at her as the moment stretched.

The journey home was silent. They each seemed lost in their own thoughts. So the hysteria that assaulted her as they entered the cave made Eleanor jump. Amelia had taken one look at Freddie and Conlan, covered in dust, blood and bruises, and began screaming in her face, jabbing a finger into her chest like a pneumatic drill as she did so.

"What have you done now? You're not going to be happy until you've killed us all, are you?"

Eleanor took a step backward, coming to a stop against the rough cave wall. Amelia swiftly closed the gap and recommenced her tirade. "Say something. You want to kill us all? Have a go at me and see how far it gets you!" she spat as she raised her fist. Different defensive moves ran through Eleanor's mind, but in the end she discounted them all in favour of simply raising her arms to protect her head and closing her eyes. She could not bring herself to hurt Amelia, and deep down she knew she had no right to. Amelia had a perfectly valid point.

"Stop!" Will's voice was low but commanding. Eleanor opened one eye a fraction. Will stood next to her, his fist wrapped round Amelia's, holding her back.

"You're on her side now?" Amelia snapped. A pained look passed across Will's face.

"Amelia, think for a minute. Stop letting fear get the better of you, think about what you've just said; since when were there sides?"

"Since she started trying to kill us."

Sighing, Will closed his eyes. Eleanor watched Amelia's eyes grow wide in shock and she realised what he was doing; he was talking in her head. *Has he never done this with Amelia before?* Amelia's face froze, glazed eyes staring at nothing. Eventually she blinked rapidly, seeing Eleanor cowering in front of her again. She slowly dropped her fist. Will kissed her lightly on the cheek and moved away. Amelia seemed dazed.

"Are you OK?" Eleanor asked.

"Will showed me exactly what happened, showed me what it cost you to bring him back."

Eleanor sighed. "I'm sorry, Amelia. I never meant to hurt anyone. You have every right to kick me into the middle of next week, but please let me try to make amends. I need you to forgive me."

Amelia glared at her. "What happened today?"

"Conlan surprised me, and to say my 'power' has a hair trigger I'm only just beginning to understand is an understatement. Freddie pushed him out of the way, otherwise I would have taken his head off."

Amelia nodded, her eyes hard. "And what happened with Freddie, before?"

"His energy was getting too high and he wanted Conlan dead. I pulled it back, but thanks to the world's worst headache I pulled a little harder than I should."

Amelia looked appraisingly at her. "This talking in my head, it's... unnatural. Will did it once, but he had promised me he would never try it again. He just broke a promise to me to help you. I love him, so I have to trust he had good reason. You seem to have embraced your 'power' but I've seen the pain and fear you've produced. I don't want any part of it!"

"Amelia, you are what you are. We're no longer human beings, we're Avatars. Ignorance may be bliss, but in this instance what we don't know is going to kill us. Is that what you want? Because if it is, I could quite easily bring this entire mountain down on our heads and end it all now, save us all the pain and trouble," Eleanor snapped, horrified that Amelia thought she could just walk away.

"Eleanor, you can blow things... people... up. No one should have that sort of power," Amelia insisted.

Eleanor winced at Amelia's implications. "Amelia, I think you've got similar power, and ignoring it isn't going to make it go away – it's just going to make it more likely that you let it loose by accident. We can help the people of Mydren, that's what we're here for, and we've been given some powerful 'tools' because I have no doubt we're going to face some difficult challenges." Eleanor placed a hand on Amelia's shoulder. "Sooner or later, if we don't step in, the elements are going to destroy Mydren. I would rather accept my role and try to help this world than sit around in a dark hole, too scared of my own talents to learn to use them. We need you as a fully functioning member of the Five for this to work. Are you really willing to turn your back on us, on everything Conlan is trying to achieve? Make a choice, Amelia, our fate is in your hands."

Eleanor made her way back to the lake, Amelia's desperate sobbing still echoing in her head. She knew bringing Amelia's trust and love of Conlan into the argument had been a low blow, and making her friend cry made her feel nasty and small. She felt sorry for Amelia; she could relate to her fear, but she also knew she had no choice but to rise above it – and Amelia had to grasp this too. Eleanor understood why the other Earths had killed themselves, that this was the turning point: they had preferred death rather than face the darkness within. Eleanor knew she was in no danger of making the same choice, as she was far too attached to the others. She was so wrapped up in her thoughts that she was surprised when Conlan sat down next to her and looked out at the lake.

"Did you make that hole?" he asked.

"Yes."

"Wow!"

"Is Amelia alright?" Eleanor asked, her voice heavy with guilt.

"She's really upset and currently not talking," Conlan said, concern evident on his face and in his tone.

Eleanor sighed. "She's scared of the power inside her. I can understand that but she doesn't want to die, or see us die. Joining us is the only option she really has. So don't worry, your mission is still on track."

Conlan stared at her. "Do you think you are nothing more than a means to an end to me?"

"You were willing to destroy me to protect the others. If Freddie hadn't said something you'd have stuck your sword through my head without even asking me for an explanation. After all, it's far easier to replace one Avatar than four. Not to mention the three Avatars of Earth you went through in quick succession before I arrived. Yes, Conlan, I feel very much like a means to an end," Eleanor said quietly. Conlan was silent as he stared at her. She could see the hurt in his face, but she refused to look him in the eye. When he eventually spoke, his voice was barely a whisper.

"The truth is, I couldn't function without you, I wouldn't feel whole. The four of you and Rand are all I have. If I could spare you what you're going through, attempting to control what I've burdened you with, I would."

They sat in silence while Eleanor digested his words. However much Conlan may regret bringing them all to this point, they were still here and they had some large obstacles to overcome, not least of which was this weird shield around Conlan.

"Conlan, we need more information."

"On what?"

"On you. We need to understand your role in all this."

"I've told you everything I know."

Eleanor thought for a moment. "You said your grandfather told you stories – is he still alive, can we ask him questions?"

Conlan nodded slowly.

Eleanor jumped to her feet. "Good, let's go."

Conlan looked at her, amused. "I'm the one who's meant to be manically obsessed."

Eleanor shrugged. "Guess it's rubbing off on me. Besides, spring is coming, which means the Enforcers will be coming, so we don't have much time."

Conlan slowly shook his head. "We can't leave straight away. Freddie can't come with us, and I don't feel comfortable leaving him with Amelia and Will any more... you're all getting so much stronger... You have to show him how to control his energy before we can go anywhere."

Eleanor smiled. "We'd better get started then."

9

THE BOOK

Freddie was a quick learner, and it took Eleanor less than a week to get him to the point where he could monitor his own energy levels. Being careful to avoid Amelia, who was still not talking to anyone, she asked Will how he was balancing his energy. He had invited her into his mind and demonstrated his control. His energy level could be erratic if he was near open water for any length of time, he had found he was pulling energy from it almost as a reflex reaction. He discovered he could push his energy strings into the ground, to find aquifers and underground rivers to drag away the excess energy, and although it was a lot harder, he could also use rain and snow clouds. Impressed with his knowledge, Eleanor had asked why he had not told all this to Amelia and Freddie. Will protested that he had tried, but neither had wanted to listen.

Armed with this information, Eleanor had explained to Freddie that whenever he was near open fire, which was most of the time, he was unconsciously drawing energy from it and that he had to remember to attach his 'overflow pipe' back into the fire so the energy remained level. She also showed him how to release his energy safely if there was an accident and it did build up. After several practice attempts, he felt confident he could handle himself. Eleanor had also experimented with heating up the water in their bathtub. The first time Freddie just turned the water to super-heated steam, but eventually he had got the hang of it. Will had watched them on one of the more successful attempts. Eleanor noticed him stood by the cave entrance.

"Tell Amelia she can thank me for this later."

"I'm so glad we finally found a use for Freddie," he said drily. Freddie grinned at him.

The sky was just beginning to lighten as they set out. The frighteningly violent storm two days earlier had left Amelia wide-eyed and trembling and

Will twitchy and restless. If she concentrated, Eleanor could feel his energy pulsing. The heavy rain had also melted a lot of snow, and rivers of slush ran down the mountain, in torrents that obliterated trails and washed away vegetation that had struggled to survive the harsh winter.

Conlan led Rand, negotiating the treacherous trail with care. Eleanor followed him, deep in thought. Amelia remained mute. Will's distress was etched into his face and Eleanor had hugged him especially tight when they had said goodbye, but the words he had whispered in her ear had caught her by surprise. 'Look after Conlan for me. He's not nearly as invincible as he pretends to be.' With everything he had to worry about, Eleanor wondered why it was Conlan he feared for. What did he know about where they were going? She had wanted to ask, but Conlan was already walking down the trail and Eleanor knew she would get lost if she did not keep up with him.

The further down the mountains they went, the more evidence they encountered of the storms power. Trees had been ripped from the ground and a rockslide blocked the way, forcing Conlan to backtrack around it; the devastation was extensive. Yet, amid this chaos, spring was already in full swing. Birds chirped and whistled to each other in cheery greeting, and a profusion of small blue flowers erupted in clumps where the snow had melted back to reveal the earth beneath. Eleanor was amazed that something so small and delicate had weathered the storm. The life around her made her smile, gave her hope. As they moved through the mountains' foothills, Eleanor felt the brand on her wrist begin to itch and then burn. Conlan noticed.

"It hurts?"

"Yeah! I guess it's telling me I'm moving away from the others. I was just wondering why it did it and how it worked out the distances," Eleanor said. "I wonder if they feel it too."

"Something to ask them when you get back," Conlan suggested.

As they travelled further away, the pain reached a peak of agony but then dropped off into numbness – information Eleanor stored for later.

As they reached the dirt track road they began passing the occasional village. Eleanor was horrified at the results of the storm. Houses where window shutters, doors and in some cases the whole roof had been torn off were common. Malnourished animals lay dead in fields, half-buried in silt that had obviously poured down from the mountains. In one village the houses on one side of the main dirt track had been washed away completely, leaving only a few posts as evidence to the homes that once existed. People shambled about, looking for possessions, or bodies, shock and resignation stamped on their faces. Others simply sat where they seemed to have fallen and stared.

Conlan stopped to render aid wherever he could. He made no fuss, speaking softly and gently, and moved among the people as if he was one of them, helping to bury the dead, rescue the trapped, patch up the injured and feed the hungry as best he could. He gave words of encouragement to those who took the initiative and set up shelter and rustled up food for those with nothing. Eleanor watched as Conlan held the rough, gnarled hand of a farmer as he died, bloody and in pain, calling out for a wife already dead. In another village he helped a shell-shocked young man bury his baby girl as his wife rocked and wailed, refusing to rise from the mud. Eleanor wondered how the pain, death and chaos did not overwhelm him.

After several more days they passed out from under the mountains' shadow and the destructive path of the storm. Here, life continued as normal, with people apparently unaware of the horrors suffered by their fellow citizens less than a day's ride away. Eleanor thought of the damage and devastation she had seen – so many families without homes, so many dead, crops and animals gone. If their nearest neighbours did not seem to care, what would become of them?

"Who'll help them?" Eleanor whispered.

"We're going to help them, Eleanor," Conlan replied, his voice tight, pained and utterly resolute.

Conlan had explained that his grandfather lived in a city called Baydon. It fell under the jurisdiction of the Northern Tower, home to the Lords of Mydren who controlled the area. They were going to skirt the edge of the mountains, heading east, because it was safer and with fewer people, and then drop down south to Baydon. The journey was going to take them just over three weeks. Conlan brooded, distant and silent, caught up in his own thoughts, and for once Eleanor was glad of the peace. She slowly went through the last week in her mind, trying to come to terms with what she had seen. She had asked Conlan why there had been no official help, no Protectors or Enforcers. Shaking his head, a face full of sorrow, Conlan had explained that life was cheap to the Lords of Mydren, as the fate of inconsequential people would have little impact on their lives. As long as their Enforcers were able to turn away the storms' strength from the rich cities and divert the floods and destruction into areas populated by those too poor to hold influence that was all that mattered.

They had turned south three days previously, with still a day of travel to go when they moved out of the forest they had been travelling through. Eleanor breathed a sigh of relief, as the forest had been a scary place to be followed by the small tornadoes that seemed to appear with such regularity now that Conlan no longer bothered to outrun them. Stretched out in front of them were flat plains as far as the eye could see, neatly divided into a patchwork of green and brown fields, crossed occasionally by a dirt track or a river or cluttered by a small village. It reminded her of the rolling countryside of home, until she saw the huge walled city in the distance; its massive battlements stretched for miles in both directions from a central entrance, guard towers at regular intervals along its structure. Even from many miles away it seemed huge; the walls so high that Eleanor could see only the rooftops of the buildings within. Conlan tensed as he gazed at the city.

"I take it that's Baydon?" Eleanor asked. Conlan nodded.

The closer they got, the more Conlan retreated into even darker, brooding silence. At first Eleanor tried to pull him out of himself, but he just snapped caustic comments at her, so she gave up. For the last few hours of their journey Eleanor could have counted the words he uttered to her on one hand. While they had been able to see the looming walls of the city for the entire day, it was dark when they finally reached them. The massive wooden gates that marked the city's entrance were pulled closed in a stone wall that dwarfed them. Conlan drew Rand to the side and moved down the city wall, towards a small knot of trees. He dismounted, waiting for Eleanor to do the same, and then led Rand forward into the sanctuary provided by the small wood. Eleanor knew the routine well now and started to collect twigs, branches and bark for a fire. The afternoon rain had soaked through the foliage and Eleanor crouched over it, struggling to get it to light. She was on her third attempt when Conlan snatched the flint out of her hand and lit the fire himself.

"I would have got it eventually," Eleanor said, glaring at him.

Conlan's gaze seemed to go right through her, and then he rose and stalked off into the darkness. She set the water to heat, took Rand's saddle and bridal off and tied him up loosely with a guide rope so he could eat the grass. He rubbed his nose into her side. Conlan had been distant with the poor animal as well. She scratched behind his ears, trying to shake off the misery Conlan's mood had forced on her. On instinct she pushed an energy string out towards Rand. His mind was simple; there were thoughts, sort of, but mostly needs. He was tired and hungry, but he was also unhappy because he could feel that the master he loved was unhappy. Digging a little deeper, Eleanor was surprised to discover just how worried Rand was about Conlan. She was pleased to find that the animal liked her, though. Rand lifted his head, staring at her with soft brown eyes; he rested his chin on her shoulder, his mind filling with a need to be scratched behind the ears. Eleanor smiled, acquiescing to his request.

It was hours before Conlan returned. Eleanor had begun to get worried; she raised an eyebrow in question at his absence. He ignored her, preparing the meal in silence. She watched, sensing the waves of hostility coming off him – so different from the sorrow and pain of the last few weeks, it did not seem to be directed specifically at her, just the world in general. Eventually he noticed her scrutiny and looked at her suspiciously.

"What?"

Eleanor shrugged. "I was just wondering what truly terrible thing existed behind these walls; it must be dreadful to be able to get you this screwed up."

Conlan stared at her, his hard face giving no clue as to his thoughts. "This place brings up some bad memories, that's all."

"They must be some really horrendous memories, because that's more words than you've spoken to me all day!"

Conlan's eyes softened and Eleanor caught a glimpse of the emotions churning beneath the surface.

"I just need to get through this and get out of here."

"OK, but Rand and I would appreciate it if you could remember that we're on your side," Eleanor said gently.

Conlan nodded but said nothing more. Eleanor sighed and curled up in a ball to sleep, leaving him to stare distantly into the fire. If he wanted to fight his demons, fine.

He woke her early the next morning, his lack of sleep showing plainly on his tired face. Eleanor smiled reassuringly at him but he offered nothing in return, barely noticing her presence. Feeling a little hurt and very annoyed, she stood, stretching cold, stiff muscles and rubbed life back into her arms. She packed up their meagre belongings and went to saddle Rand.

Conlan shook his head. "We'll leave him here; it's safer."

"Safer?" she asked.

"For once in your miserable existence would you stop asking questions!"

He turned and stalked back along the wall towards the gate. Eleanor followed, trying to swallow her indignation, but it made for an unpleasant meal that settled like a stone at the bottom of her stomach. *What the hell happened to him here?*

Other people were milling around outside the wall, waiting for the gates to open. Some had carts laden with goods, while others carried sacks and boxes – they looked like traders. Eleanor would have asked, but Conlan's expression did not encourage conversation. There was a flurry of activity as the Protectors opened the gate. Hiding within the others entering the city, they walked unchallenged under the massive portcullis. Conlan moved with a purpose, obviously knowing exactly where he was going. Eleanor followed as best she could through unfamiliar streets that thronged with a multitude of dirty, smelly people, all of whom seemed intent on walking into her or blocking her path. After months of just four people for company it was overwhelming. On several occasions Eleanor felt her heart stop as she lost Conlan in the crowd, thankfully his height made it possible to find him again. She saw him disappear down an alley and moved across the busy, filth-strewn street to follow. As she got to the mouth of the alley, he stepped back into the street, grabbed her by the arms and shoved her, none too gently, into the wall in the alley's shadow.

"Keep up," he growled at her.

Eleanor bit back her irritated protest, Conlan's irrational behaviour was scaring her and she had no wish to arouse his anger any further. Nodding mutely, she followed him deeper into the dark alley. Away from the main streets of the city the buildings changed from stone-built to wooden. They became more dilapidated, rotting boards and leaning doors giving the impression of wilful neglect.

"This is where the majority of the city's nameless poor live. These are more of the people the Lords of Mydren have betrayed. They come here for protection from the elements and find only misery, sickness and poverty."

Surprised to find him speaking, Eleanor looked at him – he was angry. She inspected her surroundings. The buildings were several stories high and so tightly packed that they appeared to lean together as they rose, blocking the natural light. Figures shambled through the shadows and children stared at her from dirty faces with large, hungry eyes. Every so often they would walk past a body leaning against a wall or lying in the gutter. Eleanor could not tell if they were alive or dead, but the smell was definitely not a good sign.

They were moving slowly towards the centre of the city, and as they did the properties became more refined and elegant; dirty cramped streets widened into clean, paved avenues with trees down the middle, interspersed with small fountains. The shops that lined these streets had large, clean glass windows displaying expensive-looking merchandise. The crowds also changed, thinning slightly, the people becoming better dressed and groomed. Eleanor spotted the grey uniforms of Protectors patrolling in pairs. Conlan also noticed them, carefully giving them a wide berth. In her worn, crumpled clothes, Eleanor got some slightly disgusted looks from some of the people they walked past, but no one looked at Conlan that way. He just seemed to fit and she understood his attachment to his green velvet jacket, as it gave him a veneer of respectability in this world. By walking as if he owned the place, he gave off an aura of superiority and power that Eleanor suspected few would mess with. They turned down another long avenue, away from the noisy shopping area. Tall, thin, elegant poplars stood at ridged attention down its length, giving privacy to the voluminous, handsome, white-stoned houses that lined either side, glowing a radiant pink in the late morning sun. The avenue was devoid of people as they walked down it towards the palatial residence that stood blocking the end of the street, turning it into a dead-end. As she walked closer, Eleanor noticed that the house at the end of the street seemed much older than those around it. The other houses were nothing more than poor man's copies of the stunning behemoth she was walking towards.

They stood in front of the property's black iron gates. High walls led off from the entrance, following the paved walkway they were stood on. Eleanor could see the elegant garden on the other side of the gates, through which a gravel driveway ran to the imposing front door, wide steps leading up to it. Conlan seemed reluctant to enter; he was staring at the house, his expression haunted. Remembering Will's request, but not knowing what to say, Eleanor reached forward and wove her fingers through his. Conlan glanced at her hand, before looking back at the house, but he did not let go. Eleanor resumed her study of the property, trying to guess at what the inside might look like and wondering what had happened here to cause Conlan so much pain and distress.

"Are we going in?" Eleanor asked eventually.

Conlan shook his head. "No, not yet, we need to wait until dark; besides, I have something I want to show you first."

Giving her hand a gentle squeeze before letting it drop, he walked towards the right-hand side of the gates, following the walkway to the corner of the property. He led her down a narrow alley that ran towards the back of the house and the garden beyond, following the high parameter wall. At the far bottom corner of the property there was an ancient-looking tree, fat and squat, its massive gnarled branches leaning over the wall. Conlan pulled himself up into the tree; he leaned back and offered a hand to Eleanor. Grinning at him, she ignored his hand and jumped up to catch the branch, hauling herself up. Conlan made his way across the tree branches, dropping lightly to the ground on the other side of the wall. Eleanor followed, dangling from a branch for a moment before landing in a crouch next to him. As she stood, the strong, mixed scents of myriad flowers floating on a warm breeze hit her almost like a physical wall. After months of the sterile austerity of snow-covered mountains, it was overpowering. She closed her eyes, breathing slowly and deeply, enjoying the experience.

"Are you alright?"

She opened her eyes again. Conlan looked concerned.

"I'm great, the smell is just wonderful. Where are we?"

She looked around her; they were in the corner of a small, very private garden which was walled in on all four sides. It was overgrown. Flowers grew in random, colourful perfusion – it looked like someone had thrown cans of paint in every direction. It was just possible to see a path, meandering through the chaos, which led to a hexagonal wooden gazebo in the corner, and then to a sturdy-looking wooden door in the wall on the other side of the garden.

"This was my mother's garden." He sounded distant, his mind firmly in the past.

"Was?" Eleanor asked.

"She died when I was a child." He was looking slowly round the garden, seeing something else, someone else. Not wanting to intrude on difficult memories, Eleanor swallowed her questions and moved forward down the path, leaving him in peace. The sun warmed her as she walked among the flowers, occasionally reaching out to stroke the velvety softness of their petals or leaning closer to find their unique smell. She slowly made her way towards the gazebo. Considering that the garden had clearly been neglected, the gazebo was in a surprisingly good state of repair, and on looking inside she found a large, comfortable-looking brown sofa, a footrest in front of it. She pulled the sofa forward a fraction into the sunlight and sank into it. The cushions smelt a little of age but it was not an unpleasant smell, and when mixed with the smell of the flowers the aroma was strangely comforting. Wriggling to get herself settled, she pulled her legs up under her and leaned back, closing her eyes and trying not to think about anything. After a while, she heard Conlan walk onto the gazebo's creaky wooden floor. She kept her eyes shut; she was not sure what to say to him. He sat down next to her, relaxing back into the sofa. She felt him move to lift his legs onto the footrest and then he was still.

"Eleanor, are you asleep?" he asked quietly.

"No."

"I've been rather difficult, haven't I?"

"Yes," she agreed, her eyes still closed.

"Coming here has brought up memories I've tried very hard to bury, but I shouldn't be taking it out on you. I forget sometimes that you're not a warrior, that you didn't ask for any of this. If I'd had the time to tell you the whole truth at the beginning, I'm sure you would have rejected my offer. I will try harder to remember that in future."

Eleanor considered his words – they sounded like an apology. Amelia had said apologising was not something he did, but Amelia was wrong. He did apologise, he just seemed to have an aversion to the word 'sorry'. Thankfully he sounded more at peace with himself; maybe his demons had not bitten as hard as he had thought they would. If she had known the truth at the beginning, would she have rejected him? At the time… probably, but now? She actually liked the thought that she might be able to make a difference to the lives of the people of this world, to help them. Perhaps here she could find forgiveness, make up for her mistakes.

"Eleanor, say something."

She opened her eyes to find him staring at her. She snorted.

"*Now* you want me to talk?" she huffed, holding his gaze for a moment and steeling herself. "OK, why did you choose me?" It was a question that had been wandering through her mind for a while, but she had never had the courage to ask, fearing what the response might be – fearing how much he knew. He blinked, confused by the complete change in conversation topic.

"I mean, there must have been hundreds, if not thousands of people dying in my world at that point, so why me?" she added.

"You don't remember why you died?"

"Yes, I do," Eleanor whispered softly, the shame, regret and guilt suddenly released from where she had hidden it. "A man robbed the jewellery store I worked in and he shot me, twice," she said, wondering if Conlan would add what she had chosen not to say.

"Did anyone else get shot?" he prompted her gently.

Forcing her brain to drag up the memories, Eleanor thought back. "Yes, he shot Elaine, the manager."

Conlan nodded. "In the first instance I didn't choose you at all. I selected Elaine, but as I watched the events, waiting for Elaine's defences to drop so that I could talk to her, I saw you. The man with the gun was threatening one of your colleagues and he was going to kill her. You stepped in front and took the bullets. Amelia, Will, Freddie, they all died heroes' deaths trying to save lives, but that was their job, what they choose to do. You did something far beyond what was expected of you. I moved into your mind; you were accepting of your choice, your death, because your colleague had children and you decided her life was more important than your own. You were too young, too inexperienced and your mind too confusingly complex, but that didn't matter because you were the one I wanted."

Eleanor stared at him, processing his words. Did he know the real reason she had felt her life was so unimportant? Had he seen in her mind how disgusted she had been with herself, how guilty she had felt at her role in the robbery? If he had, he was choosing not to mention it. Eleanor doubted his honour would allow him to associate with her had he known the truth, so perhaps her dark secret was safe after all. He was looking at her, a frown furrowed between his eyes. She was staring at him, saying nothing, arousing suspicion. Comment was required.

"Why was I too young? I'm nineteen," she said finally.

Conlan chuckled. "Everything I've just said, and that's the part you pick up on?"

Eleanor nodded, it was the only part that had made no sense. He chose her because she was willing to give her life for another, but what her age had to do with anything was beyond her.

"What I'm asking you to do is not easy or safe, and if we don't succeed we will die ugly, painful deaths. You are too young to get thrown into this," he said quietly.

"Your mother died when you were a child – you were too young for that. Life doesn't wait until you're ready, life just does and sometimes you have to find the strength to run and catch up."

He smiled at her. Added to the heady smell of the flowers, the afternoon heat and the intensity of his gaze, it was all a little too much and made her feel positively dizzy. She closed her eyes again.

"You're tired. We have a while to wait, so why don't you sleep?" he offered. Eleanor nodded, laying her head back against the cushions. *He doesn't know.* Feeling safe and comfortable she relaxed into a deep, dreamless sleep.

"Eleanor?"

The voice called her awake – his voice, the soft growl emphasising the 'r' on the end of her name. There was a light hand on her shoulder, shaking her. She opened her eyes. She must have moved in her sleep, because she was now lying on her side on the sofa, her head resting on Conlan's thigh, his arm draped over her shoulder.

"It's time," he whispered.

She nodded sleepily and sat up; her stomach rumbled briefly. She tried to ignore it by focusing on getting her eyes accustomed to the limited light. The gazebo and garden were wrapped in shadow, the sky darkening, air chilly and damp. The heavy floral scent was different now, still intoxicating but threatening, and for some reason it made her think of death. Shrugging off this irrational thought and shivering slightly, she got up and followed Conlan. They made their way carefully along the path towards the garden door. Eleanor could see the house as a square of deeper shadow, spotted occasionally by windows, yellow light shining cheerily from them. In front of them, leading up to the house, was a finely manicured garden, its flowers neatly arranged in rows and patterns, small box trees and square little hedges separating them. In the centre, with paths leading from it in all directions, was a perfectly round pool, its water a rippling oily black. It was ordered, symmetrical and tidy, but it was not nearly as beautiful or inspiring as the walled garden had been.

"I prefer your mother's garden," Eleanor said softly.

"Me too," Conlan agreed.

Moving towards the house, there was a paved patio area which sat between the garden and the house. Eleanor noticed several glass doors that opened out onto it from darkened rooms. Conlan was moving towards the last set of glass doors at the far end of the house, the only ones that had light spilling from them. As they moved closer, Conlan pressed himself against the wall of the house and peaked through the glass. He pulled his small knife from his boot and slipped it gently between the doors, wiggling it slightly until there was a soft click.

"You've done that before," Eleanor whispered accusingly.

Conlan grinned at her, replacing his knife. The door opened into a warm, well-lit room. Book shelves lined the walls, filled with row upon row of regimented texts. There were several ceiling-to-floor windows, metallic thread in their curtains' rich pattern catching the light. On the right-hand wall was an imposing marble fireplace that dominated the room, a fire blazing within it and a dark-brown leather sofa resplendent in front of it. Behind the sofa, a substantial desk faced the fireplace, its dark wood polished to a shine; papers, books and writing implements were arranged neatly across its red leather surface. Above the fireplace was the large, gilt-framed painting of a very beautiful woman, her brown hair falling in ringlets around her delicate oval face, the lack of a smile giving the impression that she was concentrating, her green eyes gazing intently at the world. Even if she had not noticed Conlan purposely avoiding looking at it, Eleanor would have known that this was his mother.

"Where are we?" she whispered.

"This is my grandfather's study, he comes here to work alone for a few hours after dinner every night; we need to wait for him."

"What if someone else comes in?"

"We're going to hide."

"Where?" Eleanor asked, looking round a room that seemed to offer no opportunity for concealment.

Conlan walked to the shelves behind the desk, opposite the fire, and running his finger lightly along the spines of the books he found the one he wanted and pulled. There was a click and the shelves swung outwards into the room, revealing a small cupboard behind. There would be just enough room to hide them both. He stepped inside and Eleanor followed him. He pulled the door closed.

"How do you know we can get out?" Eleanor asked as the dark closed in around her.

"I used to hide in this cupboard as a child, there's a catch on the inside."

"Did you spend a lot of time with your grandfather as a child?" Eleanor asked, wondering what it was like to grow up in such splendour.

"My mother and I came to live here just before my brother was born. I was two."

"But not your father?"

"No, my mother came here to get away from my father."

"Why?"

Eleanor felt his body tense and recognised she was stepping into memories she should avoid. "Forget I asked," she said quickly, trying another line of questioning. "What's your brother like?"

"Cruel, cunning, malicious... he takes after my father," Conlan said, a hard edge in his voice.

Sensing another sore point, Eleanor tried a different question. "What about your grandfather?"

"We used to be very close, especially after my mother died; unfortunately my father came to take us away. The law was on his side as the surviving parent and my grandfather had to let us go. I've not seen him since."

"How old were you?"

"Eight."

"Are you nervous about meeting him now?"

"No, he's a good man. I'd have come back to see him sooner, but the need has never outweighed the risk."

"Risk?"

"My father would expect me to return here at some point, so he will have placed spies among the servants. If I was found here, my grandfather would be executed for treason."

"Your father can do that?" Eleanor asked horrified.

"My father's a Lord of Mydren, so he can pretty much do as he pleases – and he usually does."

Eleanor stared into the dark, open mouthed at this information.

Suddenly the comment 'spoilt rich boy with daddy issues' made sense. "Your father is one of the Lords of Mydren, the ones that want to hunt us down and kill us, and you're only mentioning this *now?*"

"It's not something I'm particularly proud of."

"But the others know, right?"

"Yes."

"And nobody told me?" Eleanor asked, a little hurt.

"Would it really have changed anything?" Conlan asked.

"No, I guess not," Eleanor conceded. "But it does make me wonder just how many other secrets you're hiding."

"Many."

"Not helpful; now I'm going to be thinking about what you're *not* telling me, every time you do bother to give me some clue as to what's going on!"

"Eleanor, I can't help it that you're incurably nosey," he said mildly.

Irritated she struggled to keep her voice quiet. "You don't get it. I don't like not knowing the whole picture, it makes all my conclusions suspect. Things have a way of being interconnected, and if I don't have all the information I make mistakes. As the Avatar of Earth, as you are well aware, my mistakes could kill."

"I don't see how knowing who my father is would have affected you attacking me with Will's energy or nearly blowing my head off with your own," Conlan commented.

"No, neither do I," Eleanor agreed reluctantly. "But some other information you're currently withholding from me could have."

This thought pushed them into silence. At least she now knew why they were hiding in a cupboard. She was still deep in thought about what he had told her, trying to ignore the rumblings of hunger in her stomach, when she heard voices in the study. They were too muffled to make out, but it sounded like two men having a conversation. She strained to listen, but all went quiet. They waited a few more minutes, then Conlan released the catch and opened the cupboard door. There was a man stood facing the fire, staring at the picture above it. Conlan said something softly in his growling language. The man whipped round, the startled look on his face turning to joy. He said something back, Conlan walked round the desk and they hugged each other roughly. Eleanor could see the family resemblance immediately. Conlan's grandfather was a tall, slightly portly, handsome man; the lines on his face spoke of great joy and deep suffering. Steel-grey hair gave him an air of gravitas that was immediately destroyed by his wide, slightly mischievous grin and the sparkling delight in his eyes. Conlan said something else, nodding slightly in Eleanor's direction. The older man stared at her, and his eyes held the same fanatical zeal she had once seen in Conlan's. He walked towards her. Eleanor held out a hand for him to shake, but he grasped it and pulled her into a bear hug, crushing her to his broad chest and showering kisses down on the top of her head. Not wanting to offend him, Eleanor tolerated the manhandling until the desire to breathe became too strong and she tried to push him away politely, her predicament not helped by Conlan's laughter behind them. The old man let her go and started talking at her, his excitement and awe writ large on his face.

"What's he saying?" Eleanor asked.

"He's introducing himself," Conlan said.

"Really? He must have a very long name."

Conlan laughed again. "His name is Gregor Baydon. Right now he's listing his lineage, just in case you wanted to know who his great-great-great-grandfather was. He's spent his entire life wanting to meet an Avatar; I think he's a little overexcited."

"Baydon, like the city?"

Conlan nodded. "My ancestors built this city – my mother's family have lived here for hundreds of years."

"If he's spent his entire life wanting to meet me, do you think he might be persuaded to give me something to eat?" Eleanor asked, feeling starvation squeeze her stomach again.

"I'm sure food is a possibility." The amusement in Conlan's eyes changed to deep affection as he watched his grandfather, waiting for him to finish listing those who had come before him.

The old man finished with a little flourished bow and Eleanor smiled at him again, mostly because she had no idea what else to do, she could not have listed her own family beyond her grandparents, and as an Avatar she effectively had no lineage. Thankfully, Conlan started talking and Gregor nodded enthusiastically. He left the room and Eleanor looked questioningly at Conlan.

"He's gone to get you something to eat."

Eleanor smiled. "That's good; did you tell him why we're here?"

"I said we needed to ask him some questions."

Gregor returned with a silver tray piled high with foods Eleanor had resigned herself to never seeing again. There was cheese – five different types in fact – and soft, white, fluffy bread, with real butter. There were also pickles and jams in dishes with little silver spoons, apples, hard boiled eggs and a jug of ice-cold milk, a fragile-looking glass covering its neck. In the corner of the tray, a small flowered plate balanced a mountain of sugar-coated cookies. Eleanor settled cross-legged in front of the fire. Gregor placed the tray in front of her, patting her on the head like a dog, then joined Conlan on the sofa. The conversation flowed one to the other as Eleanor ate. She was making a total pig of herself but was unable to stop – it was cheese, rich, creamy and unbelievable good. Gradually she became aware that the conversation had ceased. She lifted her head to find that both men were staring at her. She painfully swallowed her half-chewed mouthful, feeling a blush raise to her cheeks.

"My grandfather is worried that I keep you half-starved," Conlan said.

Eleanor smiled slightly. "It's cheese, Conlan!" Explanation enough to her mind.

Conlan raised an eyebrow at her. "You're going to make yourself sick."

"Did you get any answers?" she asked, hoping to save some shred of dignity by changing the subject.

"Nothing we didn't already know. My grandfather has a few questions of his own, he wants to know what this 'shield' is like."

"OK, but no grabbing at my energy… promise?"

"No grabbing," Conlan agreed, a smile tugging at the corners of his mouth. Eleanor closed her eyes and pushed an energy string out towards Conlan's shield. He must have felt her, because she heard his sharp intake of breath, but he kept his promise. She pushed her string out over the full surface of the sphere which radiated around his energy. She searched its surface for flaws or cracks, looking for a weak point but found none. As she did so, she felt another subtle energy: Gregor. Moving her focus across, Eleanor reached out and met another shield. Gregor's energy was surrounded just like Conlan's. She pushed against Gregor's shield; it felt weaker than Conlan's, less substantial, but still easily able to resist her efforts to get through. She opened her eyes again, pulling her string back.

"Your grandfather has a shield too. It's not as strong as yours, but it's strong enough to resist me. There's another difference as well. When I touched your shield you felt me, but your grandfather didn't seem to notice."

Conlan said something to Gregor; the older man shook his head. Conlan looked at her thoughtfully. "I've known of my energy from childhood, I've spent hours trying to use it, plus the effort I've put into trying to get the connection to work, so perhaps that's why I'm more aware?"

Eleanor nodded. "That would make sense, but I have no idea why your shields would be different strengths." Eleanor shrugged. "Not that it helps, I can't get through either."

"Maybe you need more energy?" Conlan suggested, the thoughtful look still on his face.

Eleanor started at Conlan in horror. "Are you asking me to pull energy from the Earth to get through? Do you have a death wish?"

"I'm willing to try it if you are," he said, his expression serious.

"I'm not," she said flatly, the thought, or perhaps the cheese, making her feel sick.

Conlan looked at her, the deep analysing expression back on his face. Eleanor felt irritation grind into her.

"Why do you keep looking at me like that?" she snapped.

"I was just wondering what you were thinking."

"That's what the look is about? You're trying to figure out what's going on in my head?" Eleanor snorted. "Good luck with that; I've no idea myself half the time. However, on this occasion, I was wondering if you had any idea of the damage I could cause. Are you insane?"

"Not a good idea then?"

"Now you're just mocking me."

Conlan smiled. Eleanor forced her hands into fists in an attempt to hold onto her anger.

"Stop smiling at me, this isn't funny."

"You once said I should smile more often," he said softly.

"That was before I realised you used it as a weapon."

Conlan's smile vanished. "A weapon?"

"Yes, a weapon that strips me of my resistance, my rational thought. All you have to do is smile at me and you win; I don't want to fight anymore."

"Is that such a bad thing?"

"Yes! It's a bad thing because one day I'm going to agree to something that gets one of us killed on the strength of that smile."

Conlan stared at her; Eleanor refused to back down, her fists still clenched tightly. She had said far more than she had meant to. She had certainly not wanted Conlan to know the effect he had on her, but it had just slipped out.

Gregor had watched this exchange with a shrewd look on his face. As they continued to stare at each other, he spoke briefly. Whatever he said caused Conlan's eyes to snap back to the old man, and he looked extremely uncomfortable as he responded.

"What did he say?" Eleanor asked.

"Nothing."

"Liar."

Confused, Eleanor waited for him to elaborate, but before he could do so, Gregor started talking again. She still had no idea what he was saying, but Conlan had an expression on his face of a little boy caught with his hand in the cookie jar; it was actually rather sweet. *I need to learn this language.* She disliked not knowing what was going on. They continued talking, neither of them raising their voice, but it seemed to Eleanor that they were arguing.

"Conlan?" she said, trying to interrupt. They both ignored her. She tried again, this time a little louder. Conlan looked at her. He appeared frustrated, but his voice was surprisingly calm.

"Yes?"

"I don't know what you're talking about." Eleanor stared at him, expecting some sort of explanation, but after a long moment of silence when none was forthcoming she felt her annoyance building. "It's rude having a conversation in front of someone who has no idea what's going on, and how much time do we have to be here? I know you need to catch up with your grandfather, but we need answers."

"You're right," he agreed. "Answers first, asinine conversation later. Tell me about the shields."

Eleanor's curiosity flickered. She did not think asinine conversation was something Conlan did, grandfather or not, but he did not want to talk about it so she gave him the information he had asked for. "They feel like energy, but they are solid, impenetrable. I didn't find any cracks or weaknesses. I can't push through it, but you know when I'm near to you, so I'm assuming it's connected to you in some way."

"What do you think it's for?"

Eleanor shrugged. "I've no idea. I need more information to make a guess at that – do other people have it? Or is this a family thing? I'm sure the shield has to go, it's in the way, but I've no idea why I'm sure of this; my subconscious must know more than I do right now."

Conlan relayed all this back to his grandfather, who nodded and responded with a lengthy monologue. Eleanor watched him talk, her mind trying to make sense of the syllables, knowing it to be hopeless but unable to stop the process. He finished abruptly, stood, smoothing down his elegant, immaculate trousers, and left the room again.

"Where's he gone?" Eleanor asked.

"He has a book that might help us. Apparently he was told that this book contained all anyone would need to resurrect the power of the Five, so he's gone to get it. He doesn't know anything about the shields, but he says the book contains details about five ancient Talismans that the original Avatars created. He thinks finding these might be what we need."

"Talisman?"

"An object that's meant to have magical power; in its truest form a Talisman is created for protection, but what the Avatars created theirs for I have no idea. My grandfather claims to have told me about them, but I don't remember."

"It's kind of a vital point, Conlan, how could you not remember?"

"I was eight years old the last time I heard those stories, I'm amazed I remember as much as I do."

Gregor came back into the room holding a large black book; he said something to Conlan – the tone made it sound like an order – and then he walked over to Eleanor. Crouching in front of her, he handed over the book, saying something with an earnest look on his face as he did.

Conlan began translating. "He's telling you that this book is very special and has been handed down from generation to generation of his family for hundreds of years. All the information we need has been hidden within its pages. This is the first time the book has been passed outside the family, but he's giving it to you because he believes you're far more likely to figure out its secrets than his stubborn fool of a grandson."

Eleanor smiled. "He called you a stubborn fool?"

"Yes."

"Why?"

Conlan did not answer.

Eleanor sighed. "Why did you bother telling me what he said if you're not going to tell me why he said it?"

"Because my grandfather insisted I tell you," Conlan admitted.

"He can't speak English, he wouldn't have known."

"Yes, he would."

She looked at Gregor; the shrewd look was back on his face. He had wanted her to know that he thought Conlan was being a stubborn fool, but why? He might not understand what was being said, but he was obviously smart enough to know when Conlan was lying. The old man smiled and Eleanor saw the shadow of Conlan's smile in it. He reached a hand out, cupped her face and spoke again. Confused, Eleanor tried to remember the words, hoping to translate them for herself in the future, but they slipped through her fingers like sand. With no meaning attached to them her mind seemed unable to retain them. The old man finished talking and leaned forward to kiss her forehead, then he stood and returned to the sofa, a smug smile on his face.

"Translate, please," Eleanor demanded.

Conlan shook his head. "No."

Eleanor glared at him, but she recognised his expression. She was not going to get him to change his mind any time soon.

"OK, OK, keep your secrets," she muttered at him, working hard to smooth the irritation she knew was showing on her face. She smiled at Gregor instead. "Tell your grandfather, thank you, I will take very good care of the book."

The old man nodded and smiled as Conlan translated Eleanor's words. The two men began talking again – another conversation Conlan showed no signs of translating. Eleanor curled herself around the book, lying in front of the fire. Feeling comfortable, warm and full, sleep claimed her.

"Eleanor, wake up, it's time to go."

Struggling to open her eyes, Eleanor blinked slowly. She could see the pale pre-dawn light through the study windows. Conlan was knelt next to her, a warm hand on her shoulder. Eleanor rose stiffly to her feet, still clutching the book to her chest. Conlan stood up with her; he looked like he wanted to say something, but instead he turned back to his grandfather and spoke to him. Gregor stood and patted Conlan on the back, muttering something that sounded like affectionate admonishment. Conlan offered an apologetic smile. Eleanor was expecting the same breath-squeezing experience as last time and was surprised when Gregor wrapped his arms carefully around her and held her gently. She did not understand the words he spoke, but she could feel the love they held, and letting go of the book with one hand, she hugged the old man back. When he let go there were tears in his eyes.

They left the house the same way they had entered, sticking to the shadows, using the tree to climb back over the wall and running down the alley like thieves. Once they were out on the avenue they slowed to a walk, but Eleanor was conscious of how suspicious they would look if someone saw them. Thankfully, the rich did not seem to be early risers and it was not until they moved into the dirtier part of the city, back towards the slums, that they encountered people.

The streets were not nearly as full as they had been the day before, so as they walked Eleanor half-closed her eyes, extended an energy string and let it trail to the side of her, like using a hand to skim the surface of a river from a slow-moving rowing boat. She felt for the energy of the people she walked past and was amazed to discover that every single person she encountered had an energy shield just like Conlan and Gregor's. She concentrated harder; the shields were of different strengths, but they all seemed to be impervious. With her eyes half-closed and her concentration elsewhere, Eleanor failed to notice that Conlan had taken a slightly different route along the street, until she walked right into the Protectors walking towards her. She tried to step out of their way as her heart jumped to a thundering beat in her throat. The fatter of the two Protectors grabbed her arm and snarled something at her. He was waiting for an answer. Eleanor shook her head slightly, pointed to her mouth and shook her head again, unfortunately revealing the book as she did so. The fat Protector saw and snatched at it, but she pulled back, both arms wrapped protectively around its bulk. Anger flashed through the man's eyes. *Now what do I do?* She could not speak the language, could not reason with them. She was stood in the middle of hostile territory clutching a book to her chest, which, if they found it, would end her life on the spot even if they missed the elemental brand on her wrist. She took another step back, wondering if she could run for it. The Protector grabbed her arm again. Conlan chose that moment to materialise at her side, but her relief at seeing him was short-lived. He grabbed her upper arms roughly with both hands and shook her, pulling her from the Protector's grip as he did so, yelling at her in Dwarfish, fury in his eyes. He let her go and delivered a solid, backhanded blow to the face, knocking her flying. The bright flash of pain left her dazed and hurting at his feet. Conlan turned, with barely a glance at her, to have a calm and polite conversation with the Protectors. The Protector who had grabbed her laughed at whatever Conlan was saying and then produced a thin cane from a clip on his belt, which he flicked. It made a lethal swishing noise as it cut through the air. He gave it to Conlan, who took it, feeling its weight in his hand, his gaze moving to Eleanor's. *Is he going to hit me with that?* The cruel, merciless look in his eyes and evil sneer made her tremble. It was not a look that belonged on his face. Eleanor felt dread grab her insides and twist. Fearing the inevitable she curled herself into a ball around the book, covering her head as best she could in anticipation of the blows. She was surprised when Conlan used the stick to slowly trace the line of her back, down and around the curve of her thigh. He said something again to the Protectors, who both sniggered, nodding to themselves. Conlan handed the stick back and watched as the two men stepped around them and continued on their way.

"Get up!" Conlan snarled through gritted teeth, watching the retreating grey uniforms.

Eleanor pulled herself to her feet. She was still trembling and could feel the skin under her right eye starting to sting and swell. He grabbed her by the back of her collar, marched her down the street and shoved her into the nearest alley. When they were safely in the dark shadows of the city's slums, Conlan let go of her collar and spun her round to face him.

"What was *that* about?" he demanded angrily.

"I wasn't concentrating," she admitted, feeling embarrassed and foolish.

"I nearly had to give you a thrashing, and you're telling me you lost concentration?!" Anger contorted his face, his scar making the expression menacing.

"Why didn't you?" Eleanor asked, watching the anger drain from him.

"You've suffered enough. I won't add to it if I can help it."

Eleanor felt this was a strange reason coming from a man who had once threatened to stick a sword through her head. He was giving her that look, but Eleanor did not feel like discussing what she was thinking.

"What did you tell them?" she asked instead.

"I told them you were a particularly inept servant, prone to daydreaming."

"Particularly inept servant... well that's not far from the mark. You didn't beat me though; they just accepted it, seemed to think it was funny – what did you say?"

Conlan looked uncomfortable. "I simply suggested that there were better ways to punish you that would be more fun if you were in one piece."

Eleanor remembered the feeling of the stick moving slowly down her body, the meaning clear. She raised her eyebrows at him in surprise. "That was very clever."

"I can be occasionally."

Eleanor ignored his sarcasm. "I take it the Protectors don't consider it part of their job to protect servants from being raped by their masters?"

"No. If I'd tried to beat you to death in the street they might have stopped me or perhaps asked me to take it behind closed doors, but there are far too many rich, powerful, well-connected people here. They wouldn't want to risk offending someone over something as minor as punishing an incompetent servant," Conlan said.

"That sucks," Eleanor muttered.

Conlan nodded. "So why weren't you concentrating?"

"I was testing a theory. I was feeling for other people's energy, but every single person I passed, including those two Protectors, has a shield just like yours and Gregor's."

"So it's normal?"

"Well it's not exactly a large pool of data, but the people were of a fairly good cross-section of your society, so yes, with the current information I have I'd conclude that this is a natural part of who you are, but it doesn't change the fact that it has to go."

"So we're back where we started?"

"Yeah, but now I have a new bruise and a headache," Eleanor said, gently pushing the palm of her hand against the swelling.

"Well don't look at me for sympathy!" Conlan said, turning and walking down the alley and further into the slums.

"Wouldn't dream of it," Eleanor muttered at his back as she trudged after him.

They moved through the alleyways in silence. Eleanor clutched the large book tightly to her chest; its stiff, heavy weight and slightly musty smell were comforting and distracted her from the throbbing in her head. As they walked past the hovels, she caught glimpses of some of the inhabitants through open doors and glassless windows. They huddled around mean fires, their slow movements and blank looks speaking of hopelessness and dark despair. *Conlan's right, these people deserve better.*

They reached the outer wall without further incident and passed quickly out of the gate, the bored-looking Protectors waving them through without a second glance. Rand was where they had left him, happily eating grass. After rooting in his saddle bag, Conlan wordlessly thrust a small jar of Will's homemade sticky, jelly-like antiseptic into her hand, waiting as Eleanor gingerly applied some to her face, the sting receding. She smiled gratefully, handing the pot back. He nodded and mounted, hauling Eleanor up behind him. Clutching the book tightly against her with one arm, she put the other around Conlan's waist and laid her throbbing head against his back as they rode off.

They rode until the sunset, and with each mile they put between themselves and Baydon, Conlan relaxed further. The sun dipped below the horizon and Conlan pulled Rand to a stop. They set up camp a little way off the track. Eleanor lit a fire, put water on to heat and saw to Rand while Conlan went to find them something to eat. Her chores done, she sat cross-legged in front of the fire and placed the large book on her lap. The cover was black leather, worn and cracked in places; there was no title, just a large five-pointed star inside a circle embossed in silver on the front. Eleanor traced the points with her finger, then she carefully opened the book, trying not to bend the spine further. The pages crinkled under her hand, whispering their secrets, the paper was a soft brown colour, with small dark-brown spots of age in places. Eleanor was surprised to discover it was hand-written in a steady, even, flowing script that with disappointment she realised she had no hope of reading. *This must be the written language of the Dwarfs.* While the words were a mystery, as she flicked through the pages Eleanor found all sorts of beautifully rendered ink pictures. Near the beginning she found a picture of a man which filled half the page, and even in black and white there was something about him; he had a neatly trimmed beard and a half smile on his face. His intelligent eyes captured her. Eleanor found it most disconcerting; there was something very familiar about the face, but with annoyance she found she had no idea what it was. Moving on through the book she found other pictures; some she recognised, like the mountains she called home, and some she did not, although they all looked like amazing places to visit. There was a picture of a waterfall so high that the water boiled into mist at the bottom as a result of the force of its drop. Another picture showed vast savannah planes, the horizon shimmering in the heat. She also found pictures of what looked like the Talismans they needed; a wand, dark wood twisted round a silver core, a pointed crystal at one end and an egg-shaped one at the other; a sword, a five-pointed star etched into its blade and large stones decorating its hilt; a large oblong diamond on a thick chain; a chalice, tall and elegant, and a crown. It did not look very impressive – a simple band with symbols etched into it – and it was hard to see from the picture but it appeared to be made of silver. *Well, at least we know what to look for.* The book also contained maps, each one of which she studied carefully, hoping to find some indication as to where they could find the Talismans, but nothing obvious revealed itself. However, the illustration at the end of the book held her attention. It was a map of the whole of Mydren and it indicated one huge continent. Eleanor could see the mountains of home cutting a dark swathe across the top of the map and running like a backbone south through the entire length of Mydren. She traced five large rivers that dissected the land, meeting at a central point in the south where a single massive river headed out to sea. There were several large forests shown on the map, and from the distance they had travelled she tried to work out which one was Millar's Forest.

"Find anything interesting?"

Eleanor jumped at Conlan's question as he stepped silently out of the darkness. Settling next to her, dropping his collection of ingredients carefully in front of him, he pulled his small, sharp knife out of his boot and began chopping and peeling.

"I need you to teach me your language," she said, not taking her eyes off the book.

He stopped chopping and stared at her with his unfathomable look.

"What?" Eleanor demanded.

"I was wondering just how good your memory is," he said softly.

He's worried about me figuring out what his grandfather said. Her curiosity flared again. She smiled. "I have a great memory, but you can stop panicking, I don't remember anything your grandfather said – without meaning, the words just don't seem to stick." *Bingo!* Eleanor thought as Conlan's face revealed both his relief and his discomfort that she had known what he was thinking.

"So, will you teach me?" she asked.

Conlan nodded thoughtfully. "OK, but can we eat first?"

After dinner, Conlan presented her with a couple of cookies wrapped carefully in a napkin; they were from the tray of food his grandfather had provided, but she had missed the opportunity to try them. She offered him one, but he simply smiled and insisted they were for her. Resting her back against the fallen tree trunk they had made their camp in front of, Eleanor nibbled the cookies, trying to commit the sweet, delicious taste to memory. Conlan opened the book at the first page and began reading. Running his finger under the words, as if reading to a child, he read the first sentence in Dwarfish. His voice gave the harsh, snarling language a beauty and resonance it did not really possess. He stopped and read the sentence again, translating into English as he went, then he read it again in Dwarfish. After a while, Eleanor recognised what he was reading – it was the story Conlan had told them about the elements and Alaric, the first King of Mydren. Having to repeat the same line several times, they did not get very far into the story, but they did get as far as the picture of the man with the beard.

"Who's that?" Eleanor asked.

"Alaric," Conlan said.

Eleanor stared at the picture, unable to shake the feeling that she was missing something.

Their journey home passed uneventfully. Conlan was more relaxed and Eleanor enjoyed the comfortable companionship they shared, as well as keeping up her sword practice. He took their time together to teach her about Mydren. Eleanor was impressed by the scope of his knowledge on everything from the local flora and fauna, to setting up camp and caring for Rand, to the political structure of the Lord of Mydren's inner council. He was far more patient with her attempts to learn Dwarfish than he was with her attempts to learn to fight. While her stuttering, stammering ineptitude left huge scope for him to mock her, he would only gently correct her. It was not a particularly difficult language structure to learn – the grammar and sentence building were remarkably close to English – but it was just slightly more formal. However, Eleanor found the pronunciation ridiculously complicated, and the rules about when and where one added growls and snarls were incredibly difficult to learn, as they seemed to revolve around who one was talking to and what emotion you wanted to layer into the words. In an attempt to help her learn, Conlan had stopped talking to her in English almost completely, talking to her throughout the day in Dwarfish. Since she wanted to talk to him, to learn about the world she lived in, this actually became Eleanor's biggest incentive to use the language. By the time the mountains of home were in sight once again, he was reading the book in Dwarfish, with Eleanor only interrupting occasionally when there was a word she failed to recognise.

After the story of Alaric creating the Avatars, there were stories of some of the adventures they had had together and how they had shown him the noble virtues. Eleanor found these stories fascinating, as they gave the Avatars much more depth. They were not just tools Alaric used to tame the environment; they had tried to improve the lives of those around them. The book also talked about the Talismans the Avatars had fashioned, but any real information was sadly lacking. While the explanations of what the Talismans were and how important they were to the Avatars left Eleanor in no doubt as to how much they needed them, there was no mention of how they were used. There was also precious little information on how they were meant to work together beyond what they already knew, and there was no mention at all of shields or how to remove them. The way the book presented it, the Avatars were able to connect with Alaric long before they created the Talismans, which enhanced their power. When she mentioned this, Conlan pointed out that his grandfather had thought they needed the Talismans, and since they still had no way to get rid of his shield, at least it would give them something to do while they figured that problem out. Towards the end of the book, the style of writing changed and the tone of the book became almost like a diary, the author writing about the betrayal of the king and how his last loyal servants had tried to carry the six sacred objects to safety. The author became very cryptic about where the objects had gone, saying only that they were 'taken to their hearts'. According to the author, all the servants had succeeded, except for the one carrying the crown. He was captured and the crown fell into the enemy's hands.

"Conlan, how are we meant to find these things?" Eleanor asked in Dwarfish.

He looked at her, confused, and then gave her an amused smile.

Eleanor sighed. "What did I say?"

"You just asked how we were going to find tree stumps," Conlan said, reverting to English.

Eleanor closed her eyes and tried the sentence again. Conlan nodded, switching back to Dwarfish. "You are not going to pass as a native any time soon, but that was much better, and to answer your question I do not know about the other Talismans, but I have seen that wand before."

"Where?"

"The *Jektar* have it."

"What does *Jektar* mean again?" Eleanor asked.

"Elves," he said in English.

"Real Elves?" Eleanor asked, images of handsome, lithe men running through her head.

"Yes, although their blood line has become as corrupted as their features," Conlan said grimly, the Dwarfish allowing him to add an undercurrent of distaste for the topic of discussion.

"Corrupted?"

"It takes a lot of strength to wield magic, Eleanor. Occasionally there are humans born with the natural ability, but not often, and those that are tend to end up dead or under the control of the Lords of Mydren. The Elves are highly magical beings who use both natural and unnatural magic, but through the ages they have mixed their blood line with humans and the magic has twisted and distorted their bodies and – in some – their minds."

"There are two types of magic?" Eleanor asked confused.

"No, magic is magic; it is simply the manipulation of energy, just like the energy you hold within you. It is how you access that energy which makes the difference. For example the magic you practice is natural magic."

Eleanor stared at him. "The magic I practice?"

"Eleanor, you blow holes in solid rock – what did you think you were doing?"

Eleanor felt this needed a reply, but once she had opened her mouth she realised she had no idea what she wanted to say.

Conlan chucked. "You really did not know, did you?"

Eleanor shook her head. "I knew I was doing something, but it never crossed my mind it was magic. It just seemed normal... well, normal for me anyway. Natural magic, unnatural magic, what is the difference?"

Conlan looked thoughtful. "Let me give you an example. I want a piece of wood to fuel my fire. If I used natural magic I would find a seed in the earth and gently encourage it to grow, giving it energy so that it would grow far faster than normal, and when the tree was grown I would cut a branch from it. If I was to use unnatural magic to achieve the same thing I would take the same seed, the building block of life, and through concentration and sheer willpower I would force it to grow and assume the shape of the branch."

"So natural magic is good and unnatural magic is bad?"

Conlan shook his head. "No, Eleanor, magic is just energy. I told you – it is what you do with it that makes it good or bad. All unnatural magic means is that the magician is working outside of the normal rules of nature. This can be very useful on occasion, but it takes a vast amount of strength, knowledge and control to use unnatural magic."

Eleanor's churning mind again provided her with an insight into what Conlan had just said. "That is how you created me, with unnatural magic."

Conlan nodded, smiling at her. "And you did not turn out so bad, did you?"

Eleanor blushed and quickly changed the subject. "So these Elves use a lot of unnatural magic. Are they friendly?"

"No."

"Will we have to steal the wand from them?"

"Perhaps."

"Let me guess: they live in some high, impenetrable tower somewhere?"

Conlan smiled. "No, they live in the Whispering Sands, a vast empty desert."

"Great! We can find them though?"

"If we head out into the desert, they will find us."

"How do you know the Elves have the wand?" Eleanor asked.

"I have a... a friend, an Elf called Trey, I was with him when I saw the wand."

"Why do I get the feeling there is a lot more to this story?"

Conlan sighed. "I met Trey in a town called Drent on the edge of the desert. He had come looking for supplies, I had come looking for the Elves."

"Why?"

"Eleanor, if you want to hear this story, be quiet!"

She nodded, shrugging away her annoyance. Conlan continued. "People do not like Elves and do not trust them, and to be honest they have good reason. I actually had to stop some of the locals beating Trey to death."

Eleanor shuddered as her mind proffered the image of Conlan being attacked by the crowd in Bremen.

"Trey was very grateful. Afterwards we got talking and he seemed friendly enough. I told him I was looking for someone to help me create Avatars and he agreed to take me to his tribe's elders, as he felt sure they could help. On the journey to the meet the elders he asked me about the Avatars and I told him far more than I should have; I was young and stupid, but it was actually pleasant to have someone to talk to who did not mock."

Eleanor smiled, amused that Conlan would admit to ever being young or stupid.

Conlan sighed. "What I did not know was that Trey was a very minor player within his tribe's politics, but that he had big ambitions. I think he saw the power an Avatar would give him as a way of realising those ambitions. The tribal elders listened to my request, and I noticed that one of them had a wand like the one in the book. They refused to help and then banished me back out into the Whispering Sands, effectively a death sentence. Trey came to find me and took me back to Drent. I was not in a particularly healthy state and he convinced me he could help me create an Avatar. I did not see the harm in trying."

"And Will paid the price," Eleanor finished for him. Conlan nodded, his eyes haunted.

"I had made no preparations, taken no time to study his culture. I just ripped him away from it. It nearly drove him mad. It would have destroyed a weaker person. Trey then tried to kill me so he could take control of the power he assumed this new Avatar would possess, but Will fought him off, wounded him, causing him to flee."

"Will defended you?"

Conlan nodded. "I was too weak to protect myself. If he had not, Trey would have killed me. I owe Will a lot."

She could hear the affection and respect in Conlan's voice and it made her smile. She wondered if he had ever told Will how grateful he was. Eleanor stared into the fire, slowly processing this information. A disconcerting realisation hit her, she pulled the book off Conlan, back onto her lap and began running back through the last few pages until she found the part about the sacred objects. And there it was, the author talking about six sacred objects, not five – there was another object that they knew nothing about.

"Conlan, we are missing one," she proclaimed. "The book describes six sacred objects, but we only know about five."

"I know about the sixth object."

She turned to look at him; he was giving her that inscrutable look again, like he was examining her soul. She waited, knowing that badgering him would not make him answer her any quicker.

"The sixth object was a person – the betrayed king's granddaughter, the last of his line, a fifteen-month-old called Fraya," he explained quietly.

"So Alaric's bloodline is not lost."

Conlan shook his head. "No, not lost, just buried by time and secrets."

Eleanor was going to ask what happened to the granddaughter, when everything suddenly slipped into place and the answer flashed through her mind with such clarity there could be no doubt.

"The picture of Alaric… that is why it looks so familiar: it is you! You with a beard; older, but it is still you! Alaric is your ancestor and you are a descendent of the royal bloodline. That is how your grandfather knew all this, why he had the book in the first place," she said, shocked.

Conlan nodded solemnly.

Eleanor stared at him. "Wow, I have never met a king before."

Conlan laughed. "I am as much a king as you are a goddess!"

"Do the others know?"

"Will knows, I had no choice but to tell him."

Eleanor nodded. "Does your father know that you are Alaric's descendent?"

Conlan shook his head. "The secret has been passed on from father to eldest son for generations. My mother was an only child, and my grandfather despaired that the line would die out, but then I turned up and he made me heir to the secret. At this moment in time the Lords of Mydren – and more importantly my father – regard me as an annoyance, a silly boy with an obsession, and they assume I will fail. But announcing myself as the descendent of Alaric would be like declaring war on them. They would take that rather more seriously. I do not need to be king to balance the elements and save Mydren. While nothing would give me greater pleasure than removing from my father and his cronies the power they covet, I am not stupid enough to start a war I have no hope of winning."

Eleanor considered this for a moment. "Why did you have to tell Will?"

Conlan smiled. "Because he is as bright as you and was rapidly coming to his own, slightly inaccurate, conclusions."

"Did you just say I was bright?" Eleanor asked slowly.

"Yes, Eleanor, I said you were bright; deeply annoying, incapable of taking orders and impossible to shut up, but very bright."

"Guess you have to take the good with the bad. You are not exactly the easiest person in the world to deal with either, you know."

"Then I suppose we suit each other well." There was something in his voice – a hint of affection perhaps? Eleanor was not sure, but it made her feel warm inside.

Conlan leaned back against the large log behind them. Eleanor closed the book, and hugging its familiar bulk to her chest she curled herself into a ball, pulling her blanket over her, and watched the fire crackle.

She was tired, but sleep would not come, there was too much information clamouring for her attention. She heard Conlan moving around, stretching himself out behind her, and soon his breathing was a slow, regular rhythm. Eleanor rolled over again slowly, the fire warming her back. He lay on his side in front of her, head on his arm, face peaceful, and she silently admitted that as much as she was missing home, she had liked having Conlan all to herself. Knowing she had to face it sooner or later she let the suppressed thought out from where she had been hiding it. *You're in LOVE with him!* it screamed at the top of its lungs, causing her to catch her breath. It was true of course, she realised as soon as the thought was out. She loved his quiet presence, his ability to absorb the very worst his world hit him with and still be able to care, the impression he gave of strength and control while inside he was hurt and frightened and his stubborn refusals to give in. Eleanor tried to snap herself out of it. *That's more than enough hero worship, it's not as if he's ever going to love me back. How did he describe me? 'Deeply annoying, incapable of taking orders and impossible to shut up...' doesn't sound much like a declaration of love.* The desire to reach out and touch his face was almost irresistible; however, the thought of having to explain herself when he woke up kept her still. Instead she closed her eyes and tried to sleep, a small hope flashing through her head, and she smiled to herself. Maybe she would dream about him.

10

DRAGONS AND DREAMS

"Eleanor... Eleanor?"

The voice, his voice, sounding irritated. She opened her eyes. The light stung, blinding her for a moment. Half-remembered dreams still filled her head. Confused, she sat up, the book falling open into her lap.

"I'm awake," she mumbled, raising her hand to cover her eyes. She had not slept well and her head throbbed and her tongue felt sticky.

"Are you alright?" Conlan asked, irritation heavy in the question.

"Yes," she replied, the irritation mixed with his oddly courteous question confusing her further. "Are you?"

Conlan's irritation seemed to raise a notch. "I'd be better if I'd had more sleep."

Eleanor looked at him blankly, her throbbing brain having problems working out how his lack of sleep and obvious irritation with her were connected.

"You talk in your sleep," Conlan informed her.

Eleanor felt the blood drain from her face. *What did I say?* Her look of horror brought a wry smile to his lips.

"You were talking about something called a 'dragon'," he said. Eleanor knew he had noticed her relief. Desperately looking to hide her embarrassment she began pulling the fragments of her dream together.

"I dreamt about a dragon that lived in a waterfall. It killed me," she whispered.

A frown creased Conlan's forehead. "What's a dragon?"

"A massive lizard-like creature with sharp teeth and even sharper claws –

breathes fire, has wings; kind of hard to miss I would guess," Eleanor replied.

"Traldon?"

Eleanor stared at him perplexed. "Pardon?"

"Enormous flying lizard. I didn't think they still existed. You have these creatures in your world?"

Eleanor shook her head. "Only in books and movies. They are mythical creatures, and there is no evidence to say they ever existed. Then again, in our world Elves are mythical too."

Conlan nodded. "And that's it, you had a dream?"

"Yes, a dream. A vivid, unpleasant dream." Eleanor shuddered. "I'm sorry I kept you awake."

Conlan gave her another irritated glance before getting up and starting to break camp. Eleanor dropped her head so that her hair would hide the expression on her face. How close had she come? *What if I'd said something about him?* Horror at the possibilities for disaster blanked her mind. Her eyes focused on the picture on the page open in front of her, recognition making her jump.

"Conlan, these waterfalls... these are the same waterfalls from my dream."

Conlan stopped what he was doing and crouched next to her, looking at the picture.

"Is that why you dreamt about it?"

"Perhaps." Eleanor studied the picture. Now she knew what she was looking for she found it quickly. Drawn to appear to be the rocks in the side of the waterfall, Eleanor could see the distinct shape of a dragon, a chalice next to it.

"This is where we'll find the chalice," Eleanor said, showing Conlan the outlines.

"How did you do that? I can barely see the dragon and you're pointing it out to me."

"I've no idea, I just can. Is this a real place? Do you think there's a real dragon?" Eleanor asked, looking back at the picture.

"It's a real place, it's where the five rivers meet, but it's a long way from here. The wand would be closer. I didn't think dragons had existed for hundreds of years."

"So we get the wand first and then the chalice – easy," Eleanor said, grinning at him.

"Easy…" Conlan echoed quietly, but he did not smile back.

Eleanor felt her heart sink. "I'm sorry I kept you awake, really. I didn't have any control over it."

Conlan shook his head. "No, I was wrong to snap at you; clearly your dreams were fuelled by the book. I knew this wasn't going to be easy, but I never really considered how difficult it was going to be. Dragons now? How are we meant to deal with that? I thought if I could shoulder the responsibility I could protect you. I should never have dragged you into this."

Eleanor stared at him. He sounded so deeply unhappy that her heart ached for him. She tried to think of something she could say that would make him feel better.

"A dragon is large and scary," she agreed, shuddering as more flashes of her dream came back to her, "but essentially it's still a living, breathing creature and everything dies. Besides, the people who hid the chalice wanted it found eventually, so maybe the dragon will just let us have it." Conlan raised an eyebrow at this and Eleanor shrugged. "You gave us a choice in coming here, Conlan." He snorted his derision, Eleanor ignored it. "I'm willing to do this because I think you're right; the people of Mydren need help." She stopped just short of adding that she would also quite happily skip into the dragon's lair and offer herself for lunch, if it would please him. He smiled, a real smile, and she felt the world wobble on its axis. He stood, moving towards Rand, grabbing the battered brown saddle as he passed it.

"We have lost some time, but if we leave now we should be home by tomorrow night," Conlan said, using Dwarfish to emphasise the word 'home' with a soft growl at the end. Eleanor knew this was a way of subtly expressing pleasure in something, and it made her smile because she was missing home too. While the weeks travelling with Conlan had been enjoyable, she missed Freddie and Will. She was even missing Amelia, but mostly she was looking forward to a hot bath and her bed.

"Do you think Amelia has chosen to be who she is?" Eleanor said, stumbling over the Dwarfish word for 'chosen'.

"I imagine so, it was not really much of a choice… Amelia is a very practical person… I should never have let her attack you for as long as she did."

"She had every right to attack me, I nearly killed the two people she loves most."

"That was an accident, Eleanor, an accident you did your best to fix," he offered. His voice came from behind Rand as he rubbed the animal's neck – more a comfort for him than for Rand, Eleanor suspected.

"No, I would have killed you both if Freddie had not knocked me senseless. I can still hear your screams." She cringed and then switched back to English, her Dwarfish vocabulary not covering what she wanted to say next. "I had no control at all. I unleashed something far more powerful than I could handle and I did it because I was too arrogant to consider the results."

"You did it because you were trying to help me. What is my excuse?" Conlan said with growling Dwarfish subtext, but Eleanor did not understand what he was trying to imply.

Eleanor stared at him. "You are trying to save your world. Besides, if you had not made the choices you did, I would have died. I am grateful for what you have given me. However dangerous this life might be, it is still life and there is joy, love, beauty and friendship. The fact that there is also pain, fear and misery makes the good so much brighter. Truly, Conlan, there is nowhere else in the Universe I would rather be than right here, so stop beating yourself up about it!"

Conlan smiled at her. "Freddie is right, you are amazing when you are angry." A growl emphasised the 'amazing', which Eleanor understood this time as a subtle compliment, indicating that it was not just in this regard he considered her amazing.

"You have never seen me angry," Eleanor said, smiling sweetly, feeling relieved when Conlan laughed.

Eleanor was so tired by the time they reached the mountains' foothills that it was several hours before she felt the throbbing in her wrist. She had been too afraid of 'dragon' nightmares to sleep the night before and she was now paying the price. She had spent the night re-reading the book and trying her best not to torment herself by studying Conlan's sleeping face. When she did finally notice her wrist they were almost home. It had been a relatively easy journey, the snow had nearly all melted and more flowers and fresh tree growth were visible. The weather had been wet but mild and there was not a grey Protector uniform in sight, on the road or anywhere on the mountain.

"Conlan, my wrist is hurting..." she said slowly in Dwarfish.

"We are almost home, so if it has only just started to ache it means they have moved," Conlan said.

"No, it has been aching for a while. My mind is a little slow today, I did not notice."

Conlan turned in the saddle to look at her, concern furrowing a little knot between his eyes; she forced herself to smile at him.

"Are you alright?" he asked.

She nodded. "I am fine, I am just tired."

"We will be home soon."

She nodded again. Still looking worried he turned back in the saddle and pushed Rand to a slightly faster pace. Eleanor laid her head onto his back. She had lied, she knew it; she was not fine. *Normal exhaustion doesn't make me feel like this, certainly not on one night's missed sleep.* She was most definitely not fine. Out of habit she checked her energy level and realised with a shock that it was incredibly low. She had not used her energy since she had left the others. Fear squeezed her insides, her heart racing. *What's wrong with me? Where did all my energy go?* She closed her eyes and tried to pull more energy from the earth, but the effort sent her hurtling down a tunnel into black nothing.

Warm, comfortable, wrapped in a soft cocoon, she cautiously opened her eyes. The flickering glow of a candle illuminated the rough stone above her. Home – she was home in her own bed. She looked round slowly and found that the other beds were empty. Images from her hideous dream still flashed through her throbbing brain, but as she took slow deep breaths they faded.

"Eleanor?"

His voice. He was leaning against the wall. He looked tired but his smile was genuine. She tried to say his name, but her lips were swollen and her jaw ached. The dry rasping of her tongue along the roof of her mouth made her wince. She felt broken. Conlan walked over, and picking up a cup of water from the floor next to her bed he held it for her to drink. The cool liquid ran down her throat, and it felt so good that she tried to drink too much and nearly choked.

"A little at a time, Eleanor, you've not drunk much recently, you're dehydrated," he admonished.

"How long?" she croaked.

"Two days."

Eleanor noticed the concern in Conlan's eyes. *Two days? I've been out of it for two days?* Afraid of what she might find, Eleanor checked her energy. It was still low, very low. Two days' sleep had made no difference.

"What happened?" she asked, attempting to keep her fear from her face.

"You fell off Rand – you were trembling and whimpering. You bit your lip right through and were muttering about dragons and then nothing, for two days."

Using the tip of her tongue, Eleanor gingerly felt the neat line of stitches on the inside of her swollen lower lip. No doubt there would be matching ones on the outside; more scars to add to her collection.

"What's wrong?" Conlan asked.

"I don't know," Eleanor admitted fearfully. "My energy level is really low, but I've not used it and I keep dreaming about dragons killing me."

The concern in Conlan's eyes became full-blown worry.

"Maybe you're ill," he suggested doubtfully.

Eleanor felt tears spring to her eyes and fought them back. *I'm not crying in front of him.*

"I don't feel ill, just very tired."

He reached to squeeze her hand. "I can't help you, can I?"

Eleanor shook her head slowly. "No, I don't think you can. Maybe I just need some more rest."

Conlan frowned, but nodded. "Eleanor, Will and I need to head out to check the passes for Protectors. I don't want to leave you if …"

"Go. I'm not dying, Conlan, I just feel crappy. I'm sure I'll be fine." She gave him a wide smile to hide her fear.

"Can I speak to her, please?" It was Amelia's voice from the doorway.

Eleanor struggled to sit up, reluctantly allowing Conlan to help and feeling pathetic. He placed a pillow behind her back, running a light, comforting hand over her head as he did so. Amelia stood in the entrance; she looked uncertain. Conlan smiled encouragingly and then moved into the main cave, leaving them to stare at each other.

"Amelia, I'm…" Eleanor had been planning to apologise for forcing her to make a difficult decision, for being a dreadful friend, but Amelia held her hand up. Eleanor stuttered to a halt.

"I was so very angry," Amelia whispered. "The thought of losing Will… The anger helped to drive away some of the fear, but then it felt like the anger, the rage, had control and I lashed out at the one person I knew wouldn't fight back. I'm so sorry."

Eleanor could see the tears running down her face, even though Amelia was looking at the floor, and she felt her own tears rise to join them. She opened her arms wide, offering a hug. Amelia almost ran to her and wrapped herself into Eleanor's body as she pulled her close, her head resting on her shoulder.

"I'll stand with you, Eleanor; please forgive me," Amelia begged.

Eleanor smiled and whispered around thick lips. "I never stopped loving you, so there's nothing to forgive." Amelia hugged her tighter. Eleanor held her, stroking her hair. She gasped as she felt Amelia's energy encompass her own – it felt like a cool breeze across sun-warmed skin.

Amelia pulled back, a frown on her tearstained face. "What have you been doing?"

Eleanor shook her head. "Nothing," she wailed.

Amelia rubbed her thumb gently across Eleanor's face, pulling the tears away. "Will and I have been practicing with our energy. I wanted to be able to help if... if... what happened before, happened again. I wanted to know that if Will ever needed energy again I could give it to him."

Eleanor blushed, not wanting to be reminded of the incident, but Amelia held her gaze with earnest sincerity.

"Eleanor, you gave Will your energy to restore him, so maybe I can give you some of mine to help you now?"

Wondering what it would feel like, Eleanor nodded her head slowly. Amelia closed her eyes and Eleanor shivered as the light energy of air blew through her body. It made her own energy leap and pulse; Eleanor could imagine it glowing brighter, and it made her feel rather light-headed. Within moments Amelia had given her enough energy that she had the strength to pull her own. Delighted, Eleanor pushed a string deep into the earth. Strength returned to her limbs and the strange lethargy left her body and mind as the imagined glowing green ball of her energy was returned to its normal size.

Eleanor smiled. "Thank you."

"Did it work? Do you feel better?" Amelia asked, grey eyes carefully observing her.

Eleanor nodded. "Much... I'm starving! Is there anything to eat?"

Eleanor insisted on getting out of bed to eat, so Amelia agreed reluctantly. Conlan and Will were out, watching for Protectors, she assumed. Freddie was affectionate in his welcome as she went to join him by the fire. Amelia handed her a bowl of what looked like stir-fry. *Makes a change from stew*, Eleanor thought, eating slowly.

"I take it Conlan has told you about our trip?" Eleanor asked, once her food was finished.

Freddie looked up from the sword he was polishing, catching Amelia's eye, but Eleanor had no idea what was meant by the look they gave each other.

Amelia took the empty bowl from Eleanor's hand and shook her head. "Not really, no. Since you got back he's spent most of his time either watching over you or out watching the mountains for Protectors and Enforcers."

"So what did you find out?" Freddie asked, putting down his equipment.

Eleanor spent several hours telling them about Conlan's grandfather and Baydon. She read back parts of the book for them in her stilted Dwarfish, translating as she went and showing them the pictures of the Talismans. Freddie had been more impressed with her description of the wonderful meal Gregor had provided her with than his Talisman, but both of them had been stunned into silence when she had explained where they would have to go to get the wand and the chalice.

"Dragon? As in fire-breathing monster?" Freddie asked incredulously, once he had got over his shock enough to speak.

Eleanor nodded. "I've been dreaming about this dragon. I don't remember it all, it's a bit disjointed. I stand in front of the waterfall and he flies out to meet me and asks me questions. No matter what I say he grabs me and slowly forces his claws into my body, eventually ripping open my heart. It's happened twice now."

Amelia looked thoughtful. "Could the dream have something to do with your energy loss?"

"How?" Freddie asked.

"The dragon is draining my energy?" Eleanor murmured. *Is that possible? It would mean the dragon was able to reach me over a vast distance and pull energy from me without me noticing. Then again, if I was asleep...*

"It would be simple to test," Amelia said, bringing Eleanor back from her thoughts. "Your energy is normal now, so if you go to sleep, dream about dragons and then wake up the next day with no energy, I'd say it was the dragon."

"And what if the next time he kills her for real?" Freddie asked. "Drains Eleanor's energy, stops her heart, like she did to Will?"

Amelia looked frightened. "Maybe Will can give you one of his stronger sedatives, to stop you dreaming?"

Eleanor shook her head. "That's no guarantee that the dragon will stop taking energy from me."

"What's no guarantee? And what are you doing out of bed?"

They turned to find Conlan wringing out his sodden jacket. Will stood next to him bone-dry, if a little windblown.

"Benefits of being the Avatar of Water," Will said to assuage Eleanor's confused look.

"You're not well, Eleanor, you need sleep," Conlan said softly as he moved to warm himself by the fire. Will sitting down with Amelia and watching with amusement as Conlan's clothes steamed.

"Actually, I think Amelia's right. I think sleep is leaving me open to the dragon that's draining my energy," Eleanor said.

Will frowned. "Conlan told me about your dreams. If this dragon is getting into your head somehow, maybe I can help."

"How?" Conlan and Amelia said in unison.

Will shrugged. "I can sit inside Eleanor's sleeping mind, so I can watch for this dragon, find out what it wants and perhaps make it go away."

Amelia paled. "That sounds dangerous, Will, what if the dragon takes your energy, too?"

Will shook his head slowly. "The dragon isn't taking Eleanor's energy while she's awake – Eleanor's mind will be asleep, but mine won't be."

"It's worth a try," Conlan said. Amelia opened her mouth to comment and then thought better of it.

"And what if I don't want you in my mind?" Eleanor snapped, her tone harder than she intended. She did not want Will to see her guilt, her crime, and she certainly she did not want him to look at her with disappointment or, even worse, loathing.

Hurt and distress flashed across Will's face, settling in his eyes. "I would never do anything to hurt you, Eleanor. I would never speak of what I learnt about you this way. Don't you trust me?"

Eleanor felt torn. She did trust Will and she did want the dragon gone, but she was also aware of just what Will would know about her. The others were looking at her strangely; Amelia's eyes crinkled in suspicion.

Swallowing hard, her voice barely a whisper, Eleanor made her choice.

"Yes, Will, I trust you."

Smiling, Will stood. "Come on then, let's get you back to bed." He offered

Eleanor a hand up, and she hesitated only a moment before taking it.

She reluctantly crawled under blankets that offered nothing more than the illusion of security. *This is a really bad idea!* Fear whipped violently round her insides. Will positioned himself on the edge of her bed. Amelia stood behind him, a hand on his shoulder, while Conlan and Freddie stood watching curiously. Will ran his hand down her head until it rested gently against her cheek. He closed his eyes, slowing his breathing, and Eleanor felt his energy string brush against her. She pulled him towards her, her mind filling with calm and peace as he entered the space where they could talk. Despite her best intentions, Eleanor cringed from the mental touch.

What are you afraid of?

Eleanor knew she would have to answer him, but her fear kept her silent.

Perhaps it would make you more comfortable if I shared some of the things I've done in my life that I'm not proud of?

Eleanor gasped. *You'd do that? Share your mind with me?*

Yes, if that's what it takes for you to trust me.

Will pushed a memory out to Eleanor, doing nothing to hide the feelings that went with it. It felt like her own experience as she watched it happen from behind Will's eyes. There was an insult, a bar brawl, a fight, a knife was pulled and time seemed to stop as Will saw it heading for his chest. Eleanor felt his terror pulse through her. Then there was someone in front of him, Stephen, his little brother: 'Look out for little Stevie,' his long dead mother's mantra, as the knife embedded itself into Stephen's chest. A searing hot lead weight of grief burned slowly through Will's insides as Stephen died in his arms. Staccato images of gasping, terrified agony branded into Eleanor's mind. The shock still had a firm hold as the memory changed. A dark alley. A man, the man who had thrust the crude knife into Stephen's heart, the man who had escaped justice. The man on his knees, crying, begging for mercy. The first blow of the cricket bat, Stephen's cricket bat, several more blows. Eleanor cringed at the brutal violence, at the fury that went with the memories. Then it was over, a dead body and remorse; killing him had not brought Stephen back, it had just ripped another chunk out of Will's soul. His guilt, self-loathing and distress overwhelmed her; it took a moment for Eleanor to find herself as the memories receded. She felt Will's uncertainty, his fear that she would not understand.

Eleanor had no idea what to say, no clue how to even start a conversation after what she had seen. Her love for Will had not changed, but it had changed her perception of him, in that his passion and determination, even if the result was wrong, did him credit.

Will's fear was growing at Eleanor's silence.

Please, Eleanor, say something…

There was nothing she could say, there was only love for him and distress at his pain. So she sent those feelings, filling his mind. Will gasped, the fear melting away.

I trust you, Will. Eleanor whispered. *My mind is yours.*

Calm pulsed through her head and spread through her whole body, instantly relaxing her and taking everything a little out of focus. She felt him pass through the walls of her mind's defences and was momentarily frightened; instinctively, she tried to push him out. He responded by flooding her mind with such a strong feeling of almost paternal love and security that she sighed, relaxing, drifting, letting Will push deeper into her head. She felt him move through her memories, her thoughts and her dreams. She could hide nothing. Apprehension sank its icy claws into her as she realised someone else was going to know, but she felt only his understanding and acceptance. He was seeing down into her very soul, his mind so close she would have felt his repulsion or disapproval had there been any, but all that existed was a steady flow of warm, safe love. Without further hesitation she gave herself to the feeling, drifting into restful sleep.

Full consciousness came slowly. She was aware of someone calling her name, the black nothing sucking at her. *Will.* Fear for him snapped her eyes open. Candlelight flickered shapes onto the familiar rough stone over her head.

"Will?"

"I am right here, Eleanor."

He was speaking Dwarfish, and her foggy mind took a moment to interpret. She turned her head to the side and saw Will siting on Conlan's bed, leaning back against the cave wall. Amelia slept next to him, curled into a ball at the bottom of the bed, her head resting on his leg.

"What happened, are you alright?" Eleanor asked in Dwarfish, not really sure she wanted to know.

"Yes, are you? The dragon's soul took more of your energy before I could get his attention. He is not a living beast – his body died centuries ago, but his soul is trapped, was trapped by the then Avatar of Earth, and he has a very unhealthy hatred of you, I am afraid. He was trying to get enough energy to escape his prison. We had a 'talk', and he has agreed to leave you alone."

Eleanor stared at him. "In return for what?"

"The dragon's soul has been trapped so long he has gone a little mad, so all he wants now is escape. I have promised him that, once we get the connection working."

What if Will can't keep his promise? Images of her body being ripped apart by dragon's claws flashed through her mind, rapid machine gun fire images of blood, pain and horror.

"We will find a way, Eleanor. If an Avatar trapped him, surely four of us can release him."

Eleanor nodded. "Am I that easy to read?" she asked. It hurt to speak, her voice scratching her throat.

Will chucked. "Not to hear Conlan tell it."

Eleanor smiled at that. "I do not think he tries very hard," she whispered.

Will gave her a knowing look. "You would be surprised."

Did Will know how she felt? Of course he did, he had been inside her mind. Was he trying to encourage her? She noticed Will looking thoughtfully at her shifting expressions – how much was she giving away? Struggling to hide her feelings she changed the subject.

"Why are we talking Dwarfish?" she asked.

"I wanted to know how fluent you were. Conlan mentioned that teaching you had been a good way to keep you occupied on the way back from Baydon."

Eleanor felt a stab of hurt. She had been grateful for the effort Conlan had put into teaching her, had he thought of it as nothing more than a way to kill time?

"He might not have taken his teaching very seriously, but I did," she said bitterly. Will was giving her his thoughtful look again.

"Why has he not yet taught Freddie and Amelia to speak the language?" Eleanor asked.

"We have both tried. Amelia did not take to it as quickly as you have and lost interest, while Freddie's pronunciation was appallingly bad. Unlike you, they both lack a compelling reason to learn."

Blushing and not wanting to get into a discussion about 'compelling reasons', Eleanor changed the subject again. "How long was I out for this time?"

"It has been a few days, but you had moments when you were nearly conscious, so we managed to get water down you, although you spat a fair amount out," Will said. His amused smile was back again, but it felt like he was trying too hard to be normal.

"You know about the robbery, don't you?" Eleanor said, switching back to English in her distress. Her pained whisper was the closest she could get to naming that darkness.

Will nodded. "I understand, Eleanor; my feelings for you haven't changed."

Eleanor smiled weakly. It was what she wanted to hear, but Will would know that.

"I'll never discuss your secrets," Will assured her. "And I would hope you'd never discuss mine." A raised eyebrow added emphasis. Eleanor nodded, rapidly trying to think of something to change the subject to as some of the more disturbing aspects of Will's memories flashed through her mind.

"So does this mean no more dragons?"

"No more dragons." The statement was so heavy that Will seemed to sag under its weight.

"What did he say to you? What's the matter, Will? You look upset." Eleanor's voice rasped in her throat, rubbing it raw. Carefully moving Amelia's head, Will rose stiffly to his feet and lifted a cup from the floor to Eleanor's lips. He leant in to lift her head as he helped her drink. Up close Eleanor was able to see fear and pain deep in Will's eyes.

"Will, something is wrong. Please tell me, maybe I can help."

"Do you trust me, Eleanor?"

"I told you I did."

"Then please let this drop," he begged. "No more talk about what the dragon and I discussed."

She did trust him; she had felt his love for her and was confident he would not hide anything without good reason, but he was clearly upset and she wanted to help.

"The dragon told me some truths about myself I didn't like," Will said carefully, seeing Eleanor's indecision. "I'd rather just forget it."

She held his gaze, wanting to understand, but the dark blue eyes did not back down. Eleanor huffed. "OK, no more talk about dragons, but I'm here if you ever do want to talk about it, and I want something in return."

"You want something from me in return for not pestering me for information that was none of your business in the first place?" Will's incredulous look softened. "What do you want?"

Eleanor shrugged, wondering what she could ask for. An idea occurred, something that may be useful in the future. "One day I'm going to ask you to trust me; no questions, no arguments, just to do as I'm asking you. Agreed?"

Will gave her a tired smile. "Agreed."

"And I want to know how you got into my mind, past my defences."

Will shrugged and his head dropped forward a little. "We all have our 'talents', Eleanor, and that happens to be one of mine. I'm not sure it's something you can learn. Amelia can't do it, and believe me it's not through lack of effort on her part."

"Amelia has tried? Does this mean she has tried using her other 'talents'? " Eleanor asked. This was a very interesting development.

"Didn't she tell you?" Will asked, looking surprised when Eleanor shook her head. "Maybe she was waiting until you felt a little better. Amelia doesn't tend to do things half-heartedly, once she made her decision to fight with us she began doing her best to learn everything she could. Freddie and I taught her what we know, but she's been looking forward to you coming back."

Eleanor wanted to ask more questions, wanted to know what they had been learning, but Will looked so very tired.

"Will, you don't look well, are you alright?"

Will nodded. "You should worry a little more about yourself, you know. Have you any idea how thin and tired *you* look?"

Eleanor sighed. "I'm fine, really. I want to know about Amelia's 'talents'."

"You need to sleep, give your body a chance to recover."

"I want to know what I missed," Eleanor insisted. Will looked at her, concern in his eyes.

"OK, but eat something first?"

Eleanor nodded. She was not particularly hungry, but she could feel how thin her body was getting, skin was stretched tight over bones. Will left and came back with a bowl of what smelt like thick potato soup. Eleanor ate with little enthusiasm, wishing it was cheese, and there was a strange aftertaste to the meal. There was so much she wanted to ask but she felt exhaustion creeping silently through her body. She slumped back into the pillows, struggling to keep her eyes open. The bowl slipped from her fingers; Will, appearing to anticipate this, caught it before it hit the floor.

"You drugged me," Eleanor accused groggily.

"You need to sleep, Eleanor – real sleep, not a dragon-induced coma; you'll feel better tomorrow," Will said, smiling apologetically as his blue eyes faded and sleep claimed her.

She woke slowly, letting herself drift. Warm blankets and the subtle smell of home were comforting. She could hear the slow, steady breathing of others around her, and this too brought a measure of peace, a feeling of security. Will was right, the sleep had done her good; she felt stronger, rested and her energy levels had normalised. She slowly opened her eyes, tracking the familiar pattern of rocks over her bed as they moved in the flickering candlelight. Eventually they came into focus. She looked around her; both Conlan and Freddie's beds were empty. *Did they get up early? Or are they coming to bed late?* The lack of natural light was annoying, as she had no idea what time it was. She would have to get up to investigate. Slowly and quietly she got out of bed, thankful that her body was not as stiff and as sore as she thought it might be. She stoked the cave's main fire, putting water on to heat. She noticed that Rand was missing as she pulled logs from the stack by the wall. Through the gap above the main entrance she could see the sunrise. Pouring hot water into a mug, she stirred in some of the dry tea-like herbs that Will kept as a drink. Eleanor watched as the water turned a reddish-brown, the herbs swirling and sinking slowly. Clutching the mug's reassuring warmth to her chest she walked out of the cave and onto the ledge. Fighting the twist in her stomach at the height, she sat down, her legs dropping over the precipice below. The air was still and cold, the world silent around her, as if all of nature was holding its breath waiting for the sun. The sky slowly turned a soft pink, then orange and then a glowing red as the sun's first rays almost blinded her. It was beautiful – too beautiful to look away – as the light began illuminating the steep mountainsides before her, making them glow a soft orange, the light rushing to meet her and forcing her to close her eyes as it bathed her upturned face in warmth. *Could Freddie draw energy from this? What would it feel like?* Letting her mind drift, she let the warmth and soft cold breeze ease out tension that she had not realised she was holding.

After a while she heard movement behind her.

"Eleanor? Are you alright?"

She smiled. "Yes, Will, I'm fine; just enjoying the morning. Where are Conlan and Freddie?"

"They are watching the area for Protectors. Want some company?"

Eleanor nodded and turned to look at him as he sat down beside her. His face was not as grey and drawn as it had been. The sadness in his eyes remained, but he too appeared more rested. He held her gaze with an air of quiet anticipation. Eleanor realised he was waiting for her to berate him for drugging her, but a swell of affection made her smile.

"Thank you."

"For what?" Will asked, confused.

"For giving me a peaceful night's sleep, for caring enough about me to do what was good for me, even if I didn't want it."

"You're not angry?" He sounded surprised.

"Not really, not once I'd considered why you did it, but I'd appreciate it if you didn't make a habit of it."

Will chuckled. "Conlan could learn a lot from you."

Eleanor gave him a wry smile. They stared out towards the distant mountains in companionable silence. She wondered about the conversation with the dragon that Will was refusing to talk about. Thinking about the possibilities forced a sort of strange melancholy upon her. This home they had created, this safe haven, was not going to last forever, and her memories would be all she had of this beautiful place. Concentrating, she tried to etch every detail of it into her mind.

"Have you two got room for one more?"

Amelia stood behind them, a large grin on her face. Will lifted his arm so she could snuggle up against him.

"It's a beautiful view; I'm going to miss it," Amelia said wistfully. Eleanor was surprised at how much Amelia's thoughts echoed her own.

"We aren't going yet," Will said softly.

"No," Amelia agreed. "But it won't be long now."

Wanting to dispel her dark thoughts, Eleanor looked across at Amelia. "Will said you'd been practicing with your energy. Tell me about it."

"I'd much rather show you; let's have some breakfast and then go up to the lake," she said getting to her feet.

The walk to the lake was bracing, the fresh air still carrying the sharp chill of winter. The sun was making a spring-like effort to push winter's cold back, but Eleanor could feel the strength in the wind and the dark storm clouds gathering in the distance. They would not get long to enjoy the lake. Beside her Amelia shivered.

"Since I started 'practicing' with this energy thing, I feel the air move and it's the most amazing feeling, like the soft caress of a lover, and it makes me feel excited and powerful. There's a gale coming, I can feel it, and I want to be part of it."

Eleanor smiled at the joy she could hear in her friend's voice. "I'm glad you found something to enjoy in all this."

Amelia looked at her, frowning. "Will it make up for the harm I can cause?"

"We can do a lot of good too, you know," Eleanor reminded her softly.

Amelia nodded. "Yes, I'm hoping so."

They walked together up over the grassy hills that surrounded the lake, Eleanor heading for her favourite spot. She lay back on the grass, watching the clouds race across the sky for a while, trying to think about nothing and letting her mind drift. Will's energy string brushing against her brought her back to reality and she reached for it.

Amelia thinks she upset you, he reprimanded. *She desperately wants to show you what she's learnt. She made a difficult decision, Eleanor, and you need to support her.*

Eleanor broke the contact and sat up. The storm clouds were getting closer and a thought occurred to her. Will and Amelia were sat a little further down the hill. Will was looking at her, but Amelia was staring with fascination at the sky above. Reaching an energy string towards her, Eleanor smiled as Amelia gently pulled it in.

Amelia? Can you make those storm clouds dissipate?

Amelia was puzzled. *I don't know... Why would I want to? I like storms.*

Eleanor smiled. *Remember the story of Alaric? The storms were causing deaths, so if we're going to balance the power of the elements, we must learn to control them, which means being able to deflect or stop storms.*

How do I do that? Amelia asked.

You understand how air works; you can feel it, just as I feel the earth. Trust your feelings. Is it possible to push the storm into a higher part of the atmosphere and then direct it somewhere else? Can you manipulate the temperature or moisture content within the clouds so they lose energy and collapse? Can you pull energy directly out of the air and release it down here, somewhere safe? Make sure you have worked through any effects this might have, because dissipating a rain cloud here could cause a hurricane somewhere else — with the weather, everything's connected.

Once Eleanor felt Amelia understood what she was saying, she broke the contact, watching Amelia's face as she closed her eyes.

Amelia must have made some comment to Will, because he was watching the darkening clouds with curiosity. For a very long time nothing seemed to happen. Amelia sat with her eyes closed, her beautiful, solemn face turned up to the dark, broiling clouds as they closed in above them. The wind picked up, lashing Eleanor's hair across her face, but she noticed Amelia's hair was still, as if she was surrounded by her own microcosm of calm weather. The dark clouds were beginning to lighten and disperse, all expect one small cloud high above their heads, which became so dark as to be almost black. It twisted and writhed, a tortured living thing. Then, to Eleanor's amazement, the cloud sank towards them, moving out until it hovered over the lake. Once there it rained heavily and directly into the lake. Eleanor saw her amazement mirrored in Will's expression. Amelia had a small smile on her face as she opened her eyes and watched the rain splatter on the lake's dark surface, causing ripples that moved slowly out towards the lake's rough edges. As the cloud spent its drenching load, it broke apart and dissolved into nothing. Unable to contain herself, Eleanor jumped to her feet, whooping and cheering.

"That was totally awesome!" she enthused, as she came to join Amelia and Will.

Amelia smiled shyly. "It was cool, wasn't it? You're right, everything's connected; I can feel patterns flowing around me. I think, with practice, I could actually predict and manipulate the weather."

"Shame I can't take you back to Britain, we could make a fortune," Will said.

Amelia smiled at him. "And I just thought the shield thing and the pushing thing were the extent of my abilities."

"Wait, what shield thing? What pushing thing?" Eleanor asked.

Amelia gripped her hand. "That's what I wanted to show you."

"Show her the shield," Will prompted.

Looking like a little girl called to answer a question in front of the class, Amelia nodded. She walked a little distance away and closed her eyes.

"Eleanor, go stand over there and pretend I'm a rock you want to explode," Will ordered.

Eleanor's mind froze in horror, but Will just smiled at her. "It's OK," he assured her. Eleanor shook her head – she was not going to aim at Will. Just the thought was making her feel sick with apprehension.

Will sighed. "In that case you stand still and I'll aim at you." Images of Conlan's writhing, tormented body came jumping into her mind, but it was better than accidentally blowing Will up, so she nodded numbly, walking a little distance away. Will said something to Amelia as he walked past. She opened one eye, noticed where Eleanor was standing, and then closed it again.

Will smiled at her. Eleanor was too afraid to move. She just waited for the pain, but it never came. Instead, the air in front of her shimmered, and a rich blue-purple colour spread out like a bruise and faded to nothing. Will repeated the process, but this time his eyes were closed for longer, and as the bruise spread through the air, the colours were so bright that they left dots on her retinas. *He used more energy*, Eleanor thought distractedly. Eleanor could hear a low, almost electric hum. As the colours faded again, Will glanced at Amelia, whose eyes were still closed. Eleanor reached a hand out in front of her and felt the resistance. There was nothing to see, but the air was vibrating slightly, like she was holding her hand against a hard drive as it cycled up. She tried pushing through, but it was solid and caused goosebumps to rise up and down her arm. A slow smile spread over Eleanor's face – now here was something that would be useful in battle. Will smiled, walking back towards her. With no evidence to point to it going, the air was suddenly clear, like nothing had ever been there.

"Want to have a go now?" he asked. Amelia walked over to join them, a smug grin on her face. Eleanor felt her mind starting to ask a million questions at once.

"Amelia, that was awesome, can you make this shield a ball, to protect someone inside? Can it protect someone from normal weapons? Can you make more than one at once? Can energy be fired through it from the other side?"

Amelia frowned. "I could make it a ball, but I need to concentrate really hard to make it at all, and I'd have to worry about the air supply of the person inside. I don't think more than one is possible, plus I have to be able to see where it's needed. It's not easy to move, but I could make one big one to protect us all, if necessary. I've no idea if you can fire energy through it from the inside – I've never tried, but I doubt it because its construction is the same all the way through. It does stop swords and arrows, though."

Eleanor smiled at her. "Congratulations, you have the most useful 'talent' of any of us so far and it seems to be entirely defensive. Maybe if we play with it we can see how far it can go. What's this 'pushing' thing?"

Excited now, Amelia turned towards the lone tree in the apex of the hill. It was the one tree in the immediate vicinity that Eleanor had managed to save from Freddie's practice torching sessions. She had a moment to feel a pang of regret for it before it was ripped from the ground and flung back forty feet, crashing into the mountainside and falling to the ground, its roots reaching plaintively for the sky. It was clearly not an exploding force like her own; it was as Amelia had called it – a 'pushing' force, a very strong pushing force, like the invisible hand of a god. *If we get this connection working, Conlan is going to be the most powerful man alive!*

"That was great! So if we can get this connection thing working, Conlan will be able to explode, electrocute, incinerate and flatten his enemies. Suddenly I'm not so worried about our odds."

They spent the rest of the day by the lake waiting for Conlan and Freddie to return. Eleanor lay on her back concentrated on the book, trying to find answers, playing the pages slowly through her head. Will and Amelia practiced trying to draw and fire energy with their eyes open. Deepening shadows filled the twilight world before they headed back towards home. Eleanor was caught up in the book, her mind elsewhere as Will and Amelia discussed their progress.

"Eleanor!"

Will's sharp tone made her jump. She stopped, trying to bring herself back to the present and out of her rather complicated deliberations on word lengths, position and number theory.

"Yes?" she said, turning to look at them.

Will's concern fought with his irritation. "Are you OK?" he asked. "That's the fourth time I called your name."

"I'm just a little distracted."

Amelia gave her a knowing little smile. "They'll be fine, Conlan knows what he's doing and they can't have gone too far because we've not felt our brands burning."

Eleanor nodded, wondering why Amelia had assumed that was what was distracting her. She was missing them very much. She wanted to talk to Conlan about the book, but she trusted them to take care of each other. She turned back and began walking down the path, humming to herself.

Amelia trotted up to her side.

"What's that tune? You've been humming it to yourself on and off all day."

Eleanor stopped. *What tune?* The minute she focused on it she realised the tune was playing on an almost continuous loop in her head. As she concentrated on it, the music grew louder, like she had heard it before, played on a mournful wind instrument. It swelled through her, pounding through her mind.

"I didn't realise it but it's a tune that seems to have been playing in my head for a while," she said.

"Where have you heard it? I don't recognise it," Amelia said.

Eleanor shook her head. "I *feel* like I've heard it before, but I'm also certain that I haven't."

"Maybe it came out of the book," Will suggested.

Eleanor nodded slowly. "Maybe, but I don't recall seeing music…" That was as far as she got; an energy string came out of nowhere, bursting into her head. She had time to register her body's jarring impact with the ground, before a terrified panic flooded through her.

Eleanor?!

Freddie?

RUN, Eleanor! They're coming, they're really close, don't go back home, they're nearly there; go to our old training cave. Conlan and I will meet you there. Hurry!

Freddie left her head at such speed that it would have knocked her flying had she not already been lying in the dirt. She winced and opened her eyes. Will and Amelia were crouched next to her, faces full of apprehension and concern.

"Help me up, we have to go. Freddie says the Protectors are here," she said, struggling to stand. Will pulled her to her feet. She rocked slightly until the world stopped spinning and then she set off back toward the lake and Freddie's cave.

"Where are we going?" Amelia asked, fear making her voice tremble.

"Somewhere safe," Eleanor replied, saving her breath and pushing her body to move faster.

Panting, sweaty, but chilling rapidly, Eleanor looked at the black void of the cave mouth for a moment. Taking a firm grip of Amelia's hand, as much to reassure herself as her friend, she walked into the darkness, using a hand to feel her way along the tunnel, her breathing loud in her ears.

Eventually she felt the tunnel open out into the main cave.

"Amelia, can you let go of me for a second, so I can light a candle?" Eleanor asked. She was glad that Amelia could not see the look of relief on her face as her fingers were released from the vice-like grip. Moving slowly from memory, testing the way forward with her feet and hands, Eleanor found the stash of flints, kindling and candles. It took a couple of attempts with shaking hands to light the kindling and the first candle, but she managed and lit a couple of others, handing one each to Will and Amelia and then crouched to light a fire.

"You've been here before," Will said, looking around. He found a pile of blankets and wrapped one around Amelia, who was sat staring into the fire. She smiled absently at him.

"It's where Freddie and I used to come to practice my fighting," Eleanor said, finding some water and putting it onto the fire to heat. She put mugs down next to the fire, so she could pour drinks. Her hands were still shaking and she stared at them. *What's wrong with me?* Will took her by the shoulders and led her to the fire, forcing her to sit next to Amelia; he found her a blanket, placing it around her.

"You should rest while you can," he said quietly. She wanted to object, wanted to point out that Conlan and Freddie could arrive at any moment, but something inside her prevented her from doing so. She needed sleep. Curling into a ball, she drifted into oblivion.

"Eleanor?"

A hand shook her shoulder. She emerged from sleep as a drowning man might breach the surface – gasping, frightened and confused - from a dream filled with tunnels, dark underground spaces and the melody in her head crashing through her consciousness in a wall of sound. She had no idea where she was. Panic tore at her. She sat up, scrambling away from the fire in front of her until her back hit the cave wall.

"Eleanor." Will was speaking, saying something. There were words, but she had no idea what they meant; the music held her attention, but it was slowly subsiding.

"I have no idea what you are saying," she said, fighting the fear. Will stuttered to a halt, his eyes wide.

"I was telling you that I can hear movement outside, I think they are here," Will said slowly.

"Then why did you not just say that?" Eleanor snapped, the crashing music receding, a throbbing headache taking the space it had left.

"Eleanor, do you know you are speaking Dwarfish?" Will asked.

He must have been speaking English, but why didn't I understand? Did I forget how to speak English? That's ridiculous, of course I didn't. I'm thinking in English, so Will must have just surprised me; and why won't this stupid music go away?

"I guess I was just a little confused," Eleanor said, switching back to English. "Must have been sleeping too deeply – it's what you wanted, right?" she asked, smiling. Will did not smile back but continued to stare at her, fear for her sanity clear in his eyes. "Will, I'm fine."

"No, you're not."

"OK, I've got a bit of a headache and there's music playing constantly in my head, but it's not as bad as it sounds."

Will sighed. "You're overdoing it; you've been distracted since you got back from Baydon. It's that book, you need to give it a rest."

Eleanor gasped, distress washing through her. "The book, Will, its back home. What if the Protectors find it? I promised Gregor I'd keep it safe."

"Eleanor? Are you OK?" Amelia asked, their conversation having woken her up.

Before she could answer, Conlan walked into the cave, the firelight casting shadows across his grim expression. Freddie followed.

"Where's Rand?" Amelia asked, looking behind them.

"We left him by the mouth of the cave," Conlan said.

"We can't leave him there, someone will see," Eleanor said.

Conlan shook his head. "We're not going to be here long enough; we have to go, now." He thrust a leather satchel at Eleanor, handed Will his medical bag and then walked toward the pile of equipment by the cave wall. Confused, Eleanor opened the bag and realised it had Gergor's book in it. Relieved, she wrapped it back into the bag, making a promise to herself that it would never leave her sight again.

"You went back? How many are there?" Will asked.

"Too many. We got as much of our valuable stuff as we could, but we couldn't stay long, as they were too close," Conlan muttered, not looking round. He was already sorting through the stuff that Freddie had squirrelled away in the cave, looking for things that would be useful.

We have to leave? Although she had known it might be coming, suddenly Eleanor was deathly afraid – this was their home and they were being driven away. *I'm not ready!*

"We could fight," Eleanor said, trying very hard to make it a forceful statement.

"That's what I said, but Conlan has other ideas," Freddie informed her, a look of hurt anger filling his face. Conlan ignored him totally, shoving food and equipment into the bags. Eleanor felt for Freddie; he had a perfectly valid opinion, just as she did. Conlan was simply overriding them. What gave him the right to dictate their every move?

"We don't have to follow Conlan's orders," Eleanor said quietly. Conlan froze. He dropped the bag he was packing and turned slowly to face them.

"You're choosing *now* to question my authority?" he asked incredulously. "Eleanor, there are over a hundred heavily armed Protectors heading this way, and thanks to the Protector you stopped me killing they have a really good idea where to search. Five of us can't take on a hundred men, and even if we did they would just box us in and wait until a thousand Protectors turned up. Life is unimportant to the Lords of Mydren; they will keep coming at us in ever-increasing numbers until they kill us. We have to leave."

A hundred heavily armed men? And it's my fault. On the surface Conlan's argument made sense – five normal people could not take on a hundred and hope to win – but they were not normal people, so why was Conlan ignoring this fact?

"Conlan, I could wipe out a hundred men myself and there are four of us."

He flashed her a dangerous look. "You're talking about annihilating an army, taking lives we don't need to."

"No, that's not what I'm suggesting, I was merely pointing out that I could! What I'm suggesting is frightening them off, getting them to leave. It's going to come to a fight eventually, Conlan. We're too powerful, too much of a threat to the Lords' way of life. Perhaps we could give them a scare they won't forget, make them think twice about coming after us…"

"NO!" Conlan roared, a heavy snarl bouncing off the cave walls. "I did not start this to deliver more senseless deaths. The Protectors are still human beings, with families, loves and lives. I will NOT take that from them!"

Eleanor opened her mouth, but Will shook his head vigorously. Eleanor huffed. "No, Will, I won't just shut up." She turned back to Conlan's furious glare, working hard to hide her fear. "I don't want to kill anyone, I never did, but the Lords of Mydren are hunting us – something you have freely acknowledged. How do you think this is going to end? That we'll get the connection working and it will just be accepted? A big part of their control is the marginal influence they have over the elements, which we would effectively remove. Why can't you see that?"

Conlan's lip curled slightly, a growl starting deep in his throat. "And what, with your vast experience of my world and my people, do you think we should be doing?"

"We should be working towards making you the king you were born to be!" Eleanor yelled.

Thick treacle-like silence filled the cave.

Conlan was coiled so tightly that his body shook with the effort to control himself. Eleanor saw his disgust and fury, and her anger was rapidly fading, regret taking its place. She had overstepped the mark, but she had no idea how to take it back. Freddie and Amelia stood frozen, while Will rolled his eyes in exasperation.

"Is this what you'd prefer?" Conlan demanded of them, pointing at Eleanor. "Would you rather massacre those Protectors than take the peaceful option?"

Amelia paled and Freddie swallowed, eyes wide.

Frustrated, Eleanor tried to explain. "I…"

Conlan whipped round. "Eleanor, you've said enough."

Taking a deep breath, reaching for calm and determined to get her point across, Eleanor tried again. "You can't just shut me up because you say so,

Conlan, just like you can't just give orders without at least consulting us."

"I have more experience, more knowledge and more idea of what is going on than you will *ever* have, Eleanor. I give orders to protect you, because I alone know the ramifications of our actions, and frankly it is highly insulting having you question that," Conlan spat out, switching to Dwarfish, Eleanor assumed, so that he could add his deep growl of contempt for her.

Hurt and embarrassed, Eleanor felt her argument crushed by Conlan's icy glare.

"At the risk of getting my head bitten off too, I would also question the assumption that you are always going to know what is right for us, Conlan." Will's Dwarfish ended in the gentle, quiet bark that requested calm from a superior.

Eleanor watched uncertainty flitter across Conlan's face.

"Have I done such a bad job so far?" Conlan asked. Eleanor noticed the reasonable tone of his dwarfish with which he addressed Will and envied the respect Conlan was according him.

"No, Conlan, that is not what I am saying. Neither was it what Eleanor was saying. I simply believe that as we grow and change, we are moving into new territory and we are going to make a world even you know nothing about. There may even be instances when we are better placed to advise you on the outcome of a course of action than you are to advise us. We need to operate much more as a team."

Conlan narrowed his eyes, a deep suspicious growl through the dwarfish.

"And how would we achieve this?"

"We should vote!" Eleanor blurted out in English, not knowing the Dwarfish word for 'vote'.

"Vote?" Conlan asked confused.

Will smiled slightly. "Not quite what I had in mind, but it will do. We each decide what we want to do in a situation and we agree to go with the majority."

"Will, in a fight that could get us all killed." Conlan looked horrified, the rumbling growl running through dwarfish indicating his level of distress.

"No, in immediate life-and-death situations you will still have the lead, we will always require your expertise in this area," Will reassured him. "But we should get some say as to whether we get into that life-and-death situation in the first place, if possible."

There was more silence as Conlan considered this suggestion.

"If this is a discussion that affects all of us, please can we stick to English?" Freddie asked, looking peeved.

Conlan sighed. "Eleanor and Will were just saying decisions should be made between all of us. We're each going to get a say in a course of action and we'll all then follow the majority. We're going to 'vote'."

"So we get to vote on whether we should drive off the Protectors or run with our tails between our legs?" Freddie asked, ignoring Conlan's sharp look.

Will nodded. "However, we can't vote if we don't understand what we are voting on, so, Conlan, please could you explain why you think we should leave?"

Not looking at all pleased with the request, Conlan thought for a moment.

"There are just five of us. I don't care how powerful you think you are, we don't have the connection working and we therefore can't fight as one – we have weaknesses. Taking on the Protectors now could reveal those weaknesses, which is something I would rather not do. At the moment they have little idea what we are capable of, so hopefully this will make them pause, sap their courage a little, if we find battle with them unavoidable... and I don't want you to kill, any of you, if it can be avoided. Purposefully taking a life is unpleasant, nasty, it does things to you." He looked straight at Eleanor, his voice a whisper. "I never wanted that for you." Conlan looked Freddie, Amelia and Will in the eye in turn as he continued. "As powerful as you believe yourselves to be, you all still have a lot to learn and I can't afford to take the risk that I might lose one or all of you. We don't need to fight a battle we're not ready for, a battle *I'm* not ready for, so we should leave."

Will nodded. "Eleanor, why do you feel we should stay and fight?"

"I... I just wanted to scare them away, a rockslide or a flood, something that would drive them back, maybe not even let them know it was us..." She stopped, realising how childish this idea was. The Protectors would know it was them, and they would know for certain they were out there, that they were dangerous. Conlan was right, there were possible outcomes here she had not considered. When she failed to speak further, Will filled the silence.

"OK, everyone gets one vote. Amelia?"

"I want to leave."

Will nodded, a response he had expected. "Freddie?"

Freddie looked torn, his eyes moving from Eleanor to Conlan. "I didn't want to turn and run, because it felt like the coward's way out, but Conlan's right – we're not ready for this. We should go."

Will nodded again. "I believe we should leave. If we're going to announce ourselves I'd like there to be a solid strategic reason for it. I'm assuming

Conlan that you still want to leave?"

"Definitely."

Will nodded. "Fine, four against one. We're leaving, Eleanor."

"Unfortunately, this little voting thing has taken more time than we had. The sun will have risen by now, we'll have to hide out here until dark and hope they don't find us," Conlan said in a flat, irritable tone.

Feeling like she had been kicked in the stomach, and wanting nothing more than to be far away, Eleanor backed out towards the exit.

"I'll bring Rand further into the cave, so he can't be seen," she said, not looking at any of them.

The tears started falling before she reached Rand. She felt such a fool. They must think her a bloodthirsty, moronic child – not a good combination in someone with the power she carried. She found Rand and gave him an affectionate pat as he snorted his greeting; at least here was a friend who would not judge her. She entered his mind, explaining that she was going to lead him somewhere dark, but that he could trust her. He followed obediently as she felt her way further down the tunnel, stopping as the firelight came into view. She could see the shadows cast by the others, but did not want to join them. Instead she removed the worn, badly fitting saddle and bridle Conlan had cobbled together after Bremen and started giving Rand a good brushing. Enjoying the attention, he relaxed into a doze and time slipped by.

"Have you finished sulking yet?"

Eleanor jumped, turning; Conlan sat on a rock behind her.

She stared at him for a moment. She was not sulking – she was hurt, embarrassed and feeling an utter idiot, but she held no resentment against them for the decision they had made, only anger and disappointment in herself for being so stupid. Unable to explain this, she went back to brushing Rand, ignoring Conlan.

"I wanted to give you something," Conlan said eventually, his voice carefully neutral. Taken totally by surprise by this comment, Eleanor turned to face him again.

"What?" she snapped. "A good beating?"

Conlan's eyes hardened. "I have a lot more reason to be angry about what just happened than you do. I'm trying, so perhaps you could meet me halfway?"

"What do you have to be angry about? You got what you wanted!"

"What I wanted?! That is just one decision, and while I'm glad the majority voted in favour of the sane choice, I just lost what nominal control over our actions I had. Will has asked for a 'sharing' of decision-making responsibility before; I've always managed to talk him round, but this time he had you and you played right into his hands."

"Is it really such a bad idea allowing us some share in the planning and decision-making process?" Eleanor asked, once again feeling there was a whole other level of consequences to her choices that she had not anticipated.

Conlan sighed. "I don't know. I don't know how this will affect things, but all my training tells me that leadership by committee will never work." He looked exhausted, beaten down almost, and Eleanor hated herself for what she had done.

"I'm sorry," she whispered, fighting back the tears.

Conlan shrugged. "It's done. Here, this is what I wanted to give you." He held out a small book to her. Eleanor put down the brush and took it from him; its blue leather binding was soft and smooth. There was no title on the book, just the Dwarfish symbols for 'C.B.' stamped in gold in the bottom corner. Carefully, loving the feel of the thick, little book in her hand, Eleanor opened it, turning the pages. In the dim light she could just make out the title page, which declared the book to be 'A Guide to Successful Campaigns'. Under the title, in tightly flowing, elegant Dwarfish script was an inscription:

For my beloved son,

So you may always win your battles.

Your loving mother.

"Your mother gave you this?"

Conlan nodded.

"I can't take it," Eleanor stammered, shocked by his generosity.

"I want you to have it – I think you'll find it interesting, and if you truly wish to share the responsibility for making decisions, you need a more advanced knowledge of strategy than you currently have," he insisted.

She clutched the book to her chest, touched that he would want to give her such a valuable gift after what she had done and so very grateful that he was still interested in helping her. She wanted to cry again, but fought it back down. Finding her voice, she marshalled a response. "Thank you."

A warm, genuine smile filled his face, a smile that demanded a response that she was only too happy to provide. Standing, Conlan picked up Rand's brush and continued what Eleanor had started. Rand sighed in contentment.

Running her fingers over the book, still a little stunned, Eleanor watched the attention he lavished on his beloved horse and felt a strong surge of adoring affection for the man.

"What was the music you were humming earlier?" Conlan asked, eyeing her over Rand's back.

"What music? When?" Eleanor asked, confused.

"You were humming something while you brushed Rand, I thought I recognised it."

"Oh… that."

The music, as if summoned by Conlan's interest, pounded to the forefront of her mind. Slowly, haltingly, she began to hum along to its beautiful, mournful melody. As she moved into the chorus again, a low voice joined her humming – deep, resonating, perfectly pitched and flawlessly in tone, singing lyrics that went with the melody, that told the story of Dwarves mining for diamonds that would one day change the world. Eleanor did not understand all the words, but Conlan's soft voice as he sang had an intimacy and heart-stopping beauty to it. It gave her goosebumps from the bottom of her feet to the top of her head, making her scalp prickle. He noticed her staring at him and the song came to a stuttering halt. Eleanor continued to stare, until Conlan shrugged uncomfortably.

"It's a song my mother used to sing. Where did you hear it?"

"That was awesome," Eleanor said, amused as Conlan blushed. "I don't know where I've heard it; Will thinks it came from the book, somehow."

"I told you this world had music," he said quietly.

Several things clicked through Eleanor's head. "Conlan, where do the Dwarves live?"

"I'm not sure; deeper into the mountains somewhere, they keep to themselves. I've never met one, why?"

Eleanor smiled. "I think the book is telling us we need to find them."

11

DIAMONDS AND DWARVES

They travelled north, which took them further into the mountains. With every mile they covered, the air became colder. It was as if they were moving back in time, moving back into winter. They were also climbing higher, the altitude making the air thinner. Freddie had asked Conlan how high the mountains were and what they were called, he had shrugged; apparently nobody had ever measured them. He was amused to discover that every mountain in Freddie's world had a known height and that many of them had names.

They had travelled for over a week, the altitude and Rand's difficulty with the terrain making it slow going. With every step Eleanor felt her satchel and sleeping blanket get heavier. She was beginning to regret telling Will she was happy to help him carry some of his medical supplies. They trudged on in near silence, walking and breathing requiring their full attention, and when they made camp each evening they could barely keep their eyes open long enough to eat dinner before they fell into exhausted sleep, only to start all over again as the sun rose the next day. Eleanor knew their food stores were getting low. Will had rationed them almost from the start and hunger pulled constantly at her stomach, but what they had was not going to last much longer. Even Rand was having difficulty finding enough to eat as there was precious little foraging available in the snow-topped peaks and stony valleys they now crossed. Here, winter had permanent control.

The late afternoon sun cast a weak, shadowless light down on them from a grey, rain-laden sky. It was going to pour it down again. Eleanor hated it when it did; her clothes still held the chilling damp from the storm they had walked through two days before. Her nose and cheeks were numb from the biting wind, which had found its way into her clothing with icy fingers so that her teeth chattered uncontrollably. She had been so impressed with the intricate detail of the clues in the book that she really was hoping that somewhere in this barren, cold world there would be more. She and Conlan had worked out that the strange symbols around the picture of the diamond in the book were a way of writing music – it was the song playing in her head. As soon as the concept had registered with her conscious mind, the song had ceased its endless playing. It had been a relief, and now she was concentrating on the mountains before them, looking for something else to help them. She trudged next to Freddie as they followed Rand. Breathing was uncomfortable; it made her feel dizzy and added to the misery of her cold body and grinding stomach. It left her feeling tetchy and irritated. *This was a bad idea.* Next to her she heard Freddie's stomach rumble. She gave him a sympathetic smile.

"Hope we find the Dwarves before we starve to death," Freddie muttered. Eleanor watched him march ahead. *Should we turn back?* Her thoughts were interrupted by Will's energy string brushing against her. She pulled it in as she followed Freddie.

Freddie has a point, Eleanor, we can't stumble around blindly for much longer; we're going to starve to death.

Can I help?

Will pushed an unspoken request into her mind.

Eleanor paled. *You want me to call some poor rabbits to their death.*

I wouldn't ask if it wasn't important, you know that, but this is truly us or them. You can talk to animals – I've seen you talk to Rand. Just find them, call them to me and get them to stay still. I'll do the rest.

Eleanor's heart twisted. *You want me to betray them… to their deaths… to use their innocence against them?*

Please, Eleanor, we're going to starve, we're getting dangerously low on supplies. I don't think we've enough to get back anymore, even if we did decide to turn round. Conlan and I haven't eaten in the last two days in an attempt to make our supplies last longer, but we can't continue like that.

Eleanor felt guilt buzz through her mind – she had not known it was so bad. *Alright, but I don't want the others knowing, I don't want them thinking this is like ordering pizza!*

Fine, we'll do this quietly, on our own.

They made camp early that evening, finding a spot out of the biting wind against the mountain wall, an overhang offering some protection from the steady drizzle that had been falling for hours. Eleanor had asked Amelia if she could get rid of it, but she had smiled apologetically, saying that sometimes it just had to rain. She had offered to create a shield, but Eleanor had declined, knowing how much it drained her. Will casually suggested they split up into groups and forage for food. Conlan and Freddie were to go in one direction, he and Eleanor the other. Amelia would stay to watch Rand

and the fire.

Eleanor moved through the crags following the path of a long-dead stream, Will following her. She could hear his strained panting; the altitude was having more of an effect on him than it was on her. Not wanting him to suffer, she headed for the nearest high spot she could see — a large flat plateau not far from the camp. Once they reached the summit Will stopped, leaning over, hands braced on his knees. He took a couple of heavy gulping breaths and coughed. He eventually managed to get his breathing down to a steady pant and stood up again, looking round. Eleanor walked as close to the edge of the flat rock as she dared, staring out at the mountains and valleys before her as the sun set behind red and gold clouds to her left. The view was stunning and she took a moment to appreciate the beauty around her before dropping to sit on the ground. Closing her eyes, she felt the fading sun on the left side of her face at the same time as she felt the night's biting cold on her right. The power of the moment tingled through her as she opened her mind to the world around her. A large grin spread across her face, she took slow, deep breaths before pushing her strings out into the rock and earth below her. Questing tendrils of energy emanated out from her in an ever-growing radius. She was immediately struck by how little life there was out here. However, because there was so little of it, what she did find pulsed like a lighthouse in the darkness. Moving slowly she located and called three large hares to her. She had spent quite some time searching for a fourth when several of her energy stings found the same thing at once. Life, massive amounts of it, in the distance, deep in the mountain directly in front of her, maybe a day's travel away. She concentrated, focusing on the area, investigating. *The Dwarves?* It had to be. She was too far away to feel individual life forces, but the huge pulsing mass in the distance was like a bonfire to her senses. Excited and relieved, she began pulling her energy back so she could tell Will.

"Will! Guess what!?" Eleanor said, opening her eyes and turning to face him. Will froze, two dead hares at his feet, the third in one hand, his knife, blood dripping from it, in the other.

"Oh," Eleanor murmured, her eyes filling with tears. She quickly turned her head away. They had died because she had asked it of them, because they had trusted her instructions. She had taken them from their families, taken everything from them. She wrapped her arms around herself, sobbing softly.

What have I done?

"I'm sorry, Eleanor, but we need to eat. I was careful, they didn't suffer. I'm going to head back to camp, so you follow when you're ready, OK?" Will said gently.

Eleanor nodded, listening as Will moved away. She sat shivering as it became fully dark, looking to the glittering stars for some sense that she had done the right thing. Her mind became stuck on the warm, gentle thoughts she had found in the animals that had died; they had not deserved death. Which was a stupid thought, as nobody deserved death, but it happened anyway. Finally getting her emotions under control, Eleanor headed back towards the inviting orange flicker of their campfire she could see in the distance. As she got closer she could hear yelling carrying on the chill night air. There was a pause. Eleanor heard nothing, but Will must have said something, judging from Conlan's next outburst.

"I'm not asking *her*, Will, I'm asking you!"

She was close enough now that she could see Conlan pacing in front of the fire; it reminded Eleanor of a wildcat, all graceful, lethal fury. *He just needs a tail to swish!* She could see Will's calm, passive expression in the flickering light.

"You can yell all you like, Conlan; this is something I have no right to discuss with you. The only person who does is Eleanor," he said mildly. "If you paid more attention you would have seen what I did and wouldn't need to ask."

Eleanor stepped into the firelight. She noticed the hares roasting over the fire, the smell filling her nose, so much guilt coursing like acid through her veins that she winced.

"Enjoy," she said flatly, turning and heading back into the darkness. She had wanted to tell the others about finding the Dwarves, but her guilt was an agony, drowning out all other thought and crushing her excitement. She walked a little way from the camp, far enough so that she did not have to listen to the conversation. She found a large rock and climbed on top of it. Pulling her knees up to her chest she stared out at the dark, eerie mountains in front of her. Wanting to reassure herself that she had not imagined it earlier, she sent an energy string into the ground in the direction she had felt the Dwarves and was relieved to discover they were still there.

"Eleanor?"

She jumped, pulling her energy back with an uncomfortable snap.

"Yes, Conlan?"

"Can I talk to you?" He spoke calmly, softly. She nodded and he sat next to her. For a long time he was silent. Eleanor wondered if he was trying to work out what to say, or whether he was just enjoying the silence. She had no wish to push, as she had a feeling she knew what questions were coming.

"Eleanor, what just happened?" he asked eventually. He sounded curious.

"I just provided you with dinner," Eleanor answered without hesitation.

"How?" Conlan asked.

Eleanor stared into the dark. "I don't want to talk about it."

"Eleanor, if this is one of your abilities, I need to know about it," Conlan said, an edge creeping into the words.

"Why do you need to know? Can't you just be thankful you get to eat and leave it at that?"

Conlan sighed. "Eleanor, I'm still in charge. Voting is functional while it's just the five of us, and I tolerate it because you're all happier having your say. But as you pointed out, it's likely that one day I'm going to lead you into battle. No time to vote, just me giving orders that I'll expect you to follow. At that point I'm going to need to know everything I can about you so I'll be able to deploy my forces where they'll have the most impact. So again, what just happened?"

The mention of battle made Eleanor feel like her insides were being rubbed up the wrong way. She saw the logic in his request, but it did not make her feel like any less of a freak when she whispered.

"I instructed the hares to come to me so Will could kill them."

"You talk to animals?" Conlan asked. Eleanor wondered how much effort it had taken to keep the surprise and amusement out of his voice.

"Do I look like Dr Doolittle? No, I don't talk to them. I enter their heads and manipulate their thoughts, although Rand is rather bright, with him it's more like a conversation."

"Rand... you've been in Rand's head?"

"Yes, he worries about you," Eleanor said, remembering the animal's concern over Conlan's state of mind when they visited Baydon. There was more silence.

"Conlan, I think I know where the Dwarves are," Eleanor admitted quietly.

After dinner, Eleanor told them about the Dwarves. She could feel the relief that radiated from her friends. Before she had finished eating her meagre meal, Eleanor was yawning, her body and mind exhausted. She curled herself into a ball by the fire, her head resting on her bag, pulling her blanket tight round her and her eyes dropping heavily. She nearly opened them when Conlan quietly asked Will who Dr Doolittle was, but she was too tired and fell asleep before Will finished his amused explanation.

Now she knew where she was going, Eleanor set a gruelling pace. She forced her body to the limit, her lungs burning, limbs aching, making it necessary to pull energy from the earth to keep herself going. Towards the end of the morning she could hear Will's laboured breathing; not slowing down or looking at him she brushed a string against him. She felt the drop in his energy levels. The rain had cleared up to reveal a chilly and pale-blue sky, but there was no water for him to get his energy from and his straining body was using up what he had. Reaching across, Eleanor realised that Freddie had the same problem. Without thinking about it, she pulled excess energy from the earth and pushed it out to Will, restoring his normal energy level, and then did the same for Freddie. Neither of them said anything, but Will's breathing became easier and they picked up their pace a little. Eleanor kept pushing, giving them more energy when they needed it. Every so often she would send an energy string out to get a distance and directional bearing on what she hoped were the Dwarves. They were so close now that she could feel the individual life forces, many thousands of them. As the sun began to set, Eleanor felt a restraining hand on her arm.

"We need to rest for a while, Eleanor," Will said softly.

"No, Will, we're so close, we can get there in a few hours, if we keep going," Eleanor replied, her eyes shifting from Will's tired face to the mountain they were heading for.

"We need to rest," Will repeated – there was something in his voice, a warning perhaps? Confused Eleanor gave him her full attention. Will shook his head, glancing back. Eleanor followed his gaze. While Will, Freddie and Amelia looked tired, Conlan looked like he was dead on his feet. He was pale and shaking slightly, his breath wheezing in his chest and his eyes staring unfocused at the ground in front of him.

"We *need* to rest," Will said a little more forcefully. Feeling guilty and ashamed for not noticing the state Conlan was in earlier, Eleanor nodded. Too tired to make camp, they just dropped where they were stood. Eleanor moved towards Conlan and led him to a flat piece of dirt against the mountainside, where they slid to the ground.

"Do you want to eat something?" Eleanor asked, concerned over the time it took for his eyes to focus on her face. He shook his head slowly. She should have seen that he was pushing himself too hard, that he was suffering, too. She turned to apologise, but his head dropped onto her shoulder as he struggled to stay awake. She patted her thigh gently, pushing her legs out in front of her and offering him a more comfortable place to lie. He said nothing, but his body slid down, his head resting in her lap. She gently stroked her fingers through his hair as he took a deep relaxed breath, his eyes closing. She watched him sleep as the setting sun took the last of the day's light and warmth. Carefully, so she did not wake him, she slipped off her bag, and pulling the blanket out of its restraints draped it over his still shaking body. Without waking he turned on his side, into his normal sleeping position, pressing his head heavily into her inner thigh. Slowly, Eleanor pulled her legs back in towards her and curled herself protectively around him, resting her head on his shoulder. Closing her eyes, she slept.

Movement woke her in the cold, pale grey before sunrise. Conlan was carefully trying to extract himself. She opened her eyes, rubbing them, pulling herself up as he sat. It was hard to see his expression in the shadowy light, but the tension in his body was hard to miss.

"Conlan, are you OK?" she asked.

"That was wrong of me, it will not happen again," he said in Dwarfish, his underlying growl offering an unspoken apology. His voice was low, but Eleanor could hear the anger. He stood, moving away from her. Eleanor stared after him, totally confused and a little upset. Was this his pride? Was he really angry that he had been weak enough that he had allowed Eleanor to help him? *The whole point of having friends is that you have people to carry you when you are too tired or defeated to carry yourself, just as you carry them when they need it.* Why would he not want her comfort?

In a gesture of supreme optimism, they ate the rest of their supplies in a hearty breakfast and set off again as the sun rose on another beautiful but chilly day. They were climbing so high now that there was heavy snow on the ground, making the path almost impossible to navigate. They had problems getting Rand up the trail – the poor animal did his best – but Eleanor found she had to enter his head on several occasions to give him encouragement. She had even tried sending him some energy, but Rand had not liked it. In the end, Conlan had come up with the idea of a sort of sling, using their blankets so they could haul Rand up after them. Will took one side of the sling and Conlan moved to take the other, but Freddie beat him too it. Conlan glowered at him, but Freddie just smiled until Conlan stalked back to take Rand's bridle and led him forward. Rand quickly settled into the pace. Eleanor pushed into his head; the animal was relieved and quite happy at being half carried up the mountain.

"What's he thinking?" Conlan asked, noticing her distant look.

"He's grateful to have friends to help him in his hour of need, which makes him smarter than you right now."

The mountain stood before her, sheer rock faces rising to dizzying heights. She hoped the Dwarves were inside, but she had no idea how to get in. Moving her eyes slowly she scanned the mountain side.

"What are you looking for?" Conlan asked, an extremely noticeable breathless wheeze in his voice.

"A way in… I don't know, something obvious… A door would be good," Eleanor answered.

"I can't see anything," Conlan said, his eyes scanning the featureless rock as hers were doing.

"I think I might have to climb up there," Eleanor said, a tremor in her voice as she tried not to think about the height.

"No."

Eleanor glanced at him; he had his hard, emotionless expression in place.

"I'll go," Amelia said, coming up behind them.

"No one is climbing up there!" Conlan snapped.

"I used to do a lot of rock climbing and abseiling, I can do it," Amelia said quietly, concentrating on the rock.

"No!" Conlan said again.

"Maybe this is something we need to vote on?" Amelia asked softly, dropping her gaze to Conlan.

"Eleanor, go fetch Freddie and Will," Conlan ordered, not taking his eyes off Amelia. She nodded, jogging back down the path to where Will and Freddie were still struggling with Rand. They both smiled as she approached.

"Amelia wants to climb a mountain, Conlan doesn't want her to. We need to vote," Eleanor told them. Will raised an eyebrow, but they left Rand and followed her.

Conlan and Amelia were staring up at the mountain face when they got back.

"You want to climb up there?" Freddie asked, horrified. Amelia turned to look at him and smiled, nodding her head.

"Can you really do it?" Eleanor asked.

Again Amelia nodded. "Search and Rescue, remember – climbing is as natural as breathing for me."

"But we have no ropes, no equipment, you'd be taking a huge risk," Freddie said.

Amelia shrugged. "It's not as if the Dwarves have a doorbell we can ring. This whole mountain screams 'Go Away!' I can see a ledge up there, so maybe I can get their attention if I reach it. If not, I'll come back down."

"And maybe they'll just push you off," Conlan said. "You don't even speak Dwarfish – what are you going to tell them if you do find them?"

Amelia frowned.

"I'll go with her," Eleanor said.

"Eleanor, you're afraid of heights, I've seen you on the ledge at home. You'd be a liability," Amelia said gently.

"I don't have to go physically, I could just go in your head," Eleanor replied.

"Will, please, talk some sense into her, this is just too dangerous," Conlan said.

Will was studying the mountain thoughtfully. "Amelia, if you're going, you need to go now, or you'll be spending the night once you get up there," he said. Amelia smiled. Conlan stared. Freddie looked shocked.

"Will, she could get herself killed. I thought we were going to vote on this?" Conlan said. Will turned to look at him.

"No, Amelia is very good at this stuff, she'll be fine. Eleanor, Amelia and I are happy for her to climb up there, so majority rule means that Amelia can go. I'll go with her, in her head, to make sure she can talk to the Dwarves if she finds them."

Eleanor opened her mouth to say she was not at all sure she was happy about Amelia climbing so far up the mountainside, but she caught Will's warning glance and closed it again. Amelia moved to Will's side. He kissed her forehead and watched her walk to the base of the cliff to start her climb, before kneeling in the snow and closing his eyes. Eleanor saw Amelia pause as she pulled in Will's energy, and then she began climbing. Freddie and Conlan went back down the path to retrieve Rand while Eleanor knelt at Will's side, watching Amelia's progress.

Amelia moved with slow confidence, stopping every so often for a breather. Occasionally Will would ask Eleanor how far Amelia was from the ledge, but mostly he sat in silence with his eyes closed, his face blank. Behind them, Conlan and Freddie stood in silence, eyes riveted on Amelia, her body made small and vulnerable by the distance.

Several long hours later they let out a collective sigh of relief as Amelia propelled herself over the lip of the ledge. The relief did not last long as they noticed other figures on the ledge with her.

"The Dwarves have found her," Will said.

"Is she alright?" Conlan asked, eyes on the ledge.

"One of them is threatening her with a sword. I need to concentrate," Will said, eyes still closed, frowning. Eleanor jumped when he gasped.

"Will?" Conlan asked. There was no response. Conlan began pacing backwards and forwards, eyes flicking between the ledge high above them and Will's face. Tense minutes crawled by.

"They're taking her to their council. Someone is coming to collect us," Will said eventually.

"What happened?" Conlan asked.

"The Dwarf with the sword stabbed her in the chest because she didn't answer his questions quickly enough," Will said. "It's just a flesh wound, she'll be fine," he added hurriedly, hearing Conlan's sharp intake of breath.

Will opened glazed, distant eyes. He stood up, swaying slightly; Eleanor stepped to his side, steadying him.

"It's tricky being in two places at once," he murmured.

Eleanor gasped as his meaning became clear. "You're not just in Amelia's head, are you? You've gone past her defences, you're in her mind."

"She couldn't grasp the Dwarfish, so it was the only way I could talk for her. I need to concentrate on Amelia, so please make sure I don't walk off any cliffs," Will said, closing his eyes again. Eleanor wrapped a reassuring arm around his waist.

A while later, through the rocks at the base of the mountain, a lone figure walked towards them. Eleanor had expected a short, old, stocky, bearded man, with lots of armour and a battle-axe. *Conlan's right, I watched too much TV.* The Dwarf walking towards them was young, clean-shaven and a little taller than she was. Shaggy, shoulder-length brown hair fell over sharp, brown eyes. His lean, toned body moved under a tight-fitting shirt and breeches, and a sword swung at his side.

"Conlan Baydon?" the Dwarf asked as he reached them. Conlan nodded. The Dwarf continued. "I am Remic, you and your party will come with me."

Conlan gave Will's expression of intense concentration a brief glance.

"Is Amelia well?" he asked Remic, glaring at him, daring him to lie.

Remic held his gaze with a steady one of his own for a moment before answering.

"The Avatar of Air is tired and sustained a slight injury while she was questioned, for which we are sorry, but she is otherwise well. I will take you to join her." Satisfied with Remic's answer, although not looking especially happy about it, Conlan nodded and they followed the Dwarf back the way he had come. Conlan walked in front, at Remic's side, towering over their guide. Eleanor followed with Will and Freddie brought up the rear, leading Rand. Remic led them through a maze of canyons, stopping before what appeared to be a solid rock face, and waited patiently. With a grinding rumble, a large part of the rock face began to move back, revealing a dark entrance way.

"These guys really don't want to be found," Freddie muttered.

Eleanor stepped into the near dark with trepidation. There were lanterns hanging from the walls of the tunnel they had entered, but they only seemed to enhance the shadows. She jumped as the wall closed behind them; the noise stopped and a shiver of fear ran up her spine. Several figures came out of the dark and Eleanor pressed herself against Will.

"You can leave your horse here, he will be well cared for," Remic said.

Freddie handed Rand's reins over to one of the Dwarves that approached him, after Conlan nodded his permission, and they set off again, following Remic. It seemed the whole mountain was dark and strangely warm. They were in a long tunnel, insufficient light coming from the lanterns on the walls.

"It is very dark, how do you see?" Eleanor asked.

"We are a race of the earth, but we have different eyes to those of humans; while we can function in daylight, we prefer subdued lighting and we are also able to see quite well in minimal or no light," Remic replied.

They moved through several twisting, turning tunnels and up several flights of stairs, all carved into the rock. Eleanor caught glimpses of rooms and further tunnels off the ones they walked down, and she noticed the occasional whispered voices and puzzled looks of other Dwarves they met, but nobody stopped them.

"Conlan, can we go faster?" Will said in English, his voice tight and worried. "Amelia's in trouble."

"What sort of trouble?" Conlan asked.

"No time to explain," Will snapped. "We need to go faster."

"Does he require something?" Remic asked.

"Could we get to Amelia faster, please?" Conlan asked. "Freddie, help Eleanor," he added in English. Freddie slipped his shoulder under Will's other arm. Remic nodded and set off at such a ground-eating run down the tunnel that Eleanor had to push herself to keep up with him. Will ran with them, his eyes still closed, trusting her and Freddie completely.

"No, Amelia, no, control it," Will moaned. Freddie cast Eleanor a worried glance and they ran faster.

They heard the sounds of chaos, running and screaming, long before they reached the huge, dome-topped chamber. They stopped in the entranceway, staring at the sight before them. A powerful wind was moving like a tornado around the chamber. It appeared that anything not nailed down, animate or inanimate, had been picked up and was whipping round. Furniture slid along the smooth, polished floor, making harsh scraping noises before the wind lifted it into the air, crashing it into walls, the splinters joining the spinning, churning nightmare. The wind had caught most of the lanterns that had been placed around the chamber, but in the dim light that remained, Eleanor could see frightened faces staring from the chamber's other entrances. At the centre of the vortex, under the apex of the doomed roof high above, stood Amelia. In front of her, included in the oasis of calm she inhabited, was a raised dais on which sat three clearly terrified Dwarves on ornate stone thrones.

"I need to get to her," Will yelled over the noise. His eyes were open, but they held the glazed look that indicated he was still in Amelia's head.

"You can't go in there," Conlan yelled back. "Whatever you have to do to talk her down, you have to do it from here."

Will glared at Conlan. Pushing Eleanor and Freddie away from him he took a step towards the battering, whipping wind. Conlan moved in front of him.

"Dying won't help her, especially when she finds out she's responsible!"

"She's not listening to me."

"Then try harder!" Conlan insisted.

"Yes, boss," Will bit out, before closing his eyes again.

Very slowly the wind began to drop, the noise subsided and the air in the chamber cleared as the debris being flung around dropped to the floor. Eleanor saw Amelia sway, then topple to the ground. Silence. Will shoved Conlan out of the way, and moving as fast as he could through the disaster area he headed for Amelia's inert body.

Eleanor, Freddie, Conlan and Remic followed a little more cautiously. The damage was extensive – wood, metal, stone, paper, candles and bodies were strewn across the floor. As the other Dwarves entered, bringing lanterns with them, moving among the fallen, Eleanor realised that what appeared to be carnage was not as bad as she feared. With assistance, many of the injured were sitting and some were even standing. Will knelt before Amelia, pulling her into his arms. Distracted, Eleanor tripped over something and sprawled on the floor, coming face to face with a pale, unconscious Dwarf. He was pinned under what looked like the marble base of a statue. Eleanor moved to his side, heaving the heavy stone off him. There was a long, deep gash across his shoulder, seeping an alarming amount of blood. Eleanor felt his neck for a pulse and was relieved when she found one. Pulling her jacket off, she made it into a pad, pressing it hard into his wound, the bones beneath her hand moving in an unnatural fashion. *Broken shoulder or collar bone… or both?* The silence was filling as more Dwarves began pulling themselves up, helping each other. Other Dwarves rushed into the chamber, bringing light and first aid to those unable to move. Eleanor looked around; there did not seem to be too many life threatening injuries, and of the ones she could see, the unconscious Dwarf at her side seemed to be in the worst state. Amazingly the three Dwarves on the central dais were unharmed. The Dwarf in the middle appeared to be a woman, with a man on either side of her. They were all old; the men had beards and they were all dressed in rich, colourful robes. They observed in silence as several Dwarves, swords drawn, anger on their faces, circled where Will knelt, cradling Amelia's limp body to his chest. Will watched passively as one of the Dwarfs stepped forward to rest the tip of his blade against his throat.

"**Stop!**"

Conlan's command carried such authority that everybody froze. The silence seemed to rouse the older Dwarves sat on the dais. The female in the middle stood, moving her attention from Will and Amelia to Conlan as he marched towards them.

"Alum, who presumes to give orders in *my* council chamber?" she snapped.

The Dwarf holding his sword to Will's throat turned his head to her. "I believe this is Conlan Baydon, High Lady."

"Apologies for my presumption," Conlan said, although the soft snarl he gave to the word 'apologies' implied unacceptable behaviour on their part, not his. "But knowing how important the law is to your people, I knew you would want to give your prisoners the chance to defend themselves before you did them injury."

"Conlan Baydon… Alaric's heir. Why do you come here?" the High Lady asked. Conlan looked at the female Dwarf in wide-eyed shock. Will caught Eleanor's eye and she knew the surprise on his face was a mirror image of her own. She felt an energy string and pulled it in.

How do the Dwarves know? Will asked.

Eleanor shrugged and Will turned his attention back to the dais. The High Lady was laughing, a dry bark.

"Just because we do not make our presence felt in the world, Conlan Baydon, it does not mean we are unaware of what happens within it."

Conlan's shock rendered him momentarily speechless.

"How do you know, High Lady?" Will asked, speaking for him.

The High Lady glared down at Will.

"Who are you?"

Still holding Amelia, Will got to his feet. Alum allowed him to rise but kept the blade tip at his throat.

"I am Will, Avatar of Water."

Again, Eleanor was struck by the difference in height, as Will looked like he was being threatened by a well-armed child.

"Another Avatar?" The High Lady looked surprised. "How well do you know Mydren's history, Avatar of Water?"

"Do you mean the official version or the real one?" Will asked.

A smile spread across the High Lady's wrinkled face, her dark-brown eyes full of amusement. "We offered *galdener* to the murdered king's granddaughter, and we have watched over the bloodline ever since."

Will, what does galdener mean? Eleanor asked.

Sanctuary.

They hid Fraya with the Dwarves?

So it would seem.

As Will pulled his energy free, the Dwarf next to Eleanor moaned softly, his eyes flickering open. Eleanor could see the agony in them. He struggled weakly, gasping as it intensified his pain, then lay still, panting.

"You have a nasty injury, try not to move," Eleanor cautioned.

"I am Cander," he whispered.

"Eleanor," she offered back. Cander smiled until another spasm of pain forced his face into a grimace. Pushing her hand harder into his shoulder, Eleanor gently stroked his head in an attempt to offer what comfort she could. Remic came to crouch at Cander's side. He felt for a pulse as Eleanor had done, his face blank, horror in his eyes.

"He has a wounded shoulder and I think broken bones underneath," Eleanor said quietly.

Remic nodded, not looking at her. "Why did she do that? We were not hurting her."

Eleanor glanced at Amelia's limp body. "I am sure it was an accident. She is a sweet, gentle, loving person," Eleanor said. Remic did not seem convinced.

The High Lady was looking at Conlan again. "I do not like repeating myself – why do you come here?"

Conlan stared blankly at her for a moment before forcing himself to address the question. "We believe you hold the diamond, the Talisman of Earth, and we have come to claim it."

"The Avatars of Air and Water, the Talismans… Our reports are true, you are attempting to recreate the power of The Five," the High Lady said as gasps and whispers echoed round the chamber.

Conlan nodded. "Yes."

"You must be very sure of yourself, Conlan Baydon, to risk my wrath by allowing your Avatar to destroy my council chamber… with me in it!"

"*Our* council chamber," said the Dwarf sat on the High Lady's right, his tone mild. The High Lady ignored him, glaring at Conlan.

"It was an accident," Will said. "You asked her to prove she was the Avatar of Air. She tried to do that, but her abilities are new to her and she lost control." He winced as Alum shoved his sword forward, breaking the skin, a thin trickle of blood running down his neck. The High Lady watched the blood for a moment before she responded.

"I do not recall asking you to speak, Avatar of Water."

Again, the Dwarf to the High Lady's right spoke. "The Avatar of Water raises a valid point, High Lady; we did ask the Avatar of Air for proof of her claims. Thankfully, nobody seems to have died. The Avatar of Air looks like such a lovely young lady, I am sure she did not mean any harm." His comment carried through the entire chamber, and he regarded Will and Amelia with interest. The High Lady's mouth pinched into a thin line of anger.

"Very well, we will accept the Avatar of Air's attack on us as an accident. It is irrelevant anyway, as even Alaric's heir, Conlan Baydon, has no rights over the Talisman of Earth – only the Avatar of Earth can claim it."

"Then the Avatar of Earth claims the diamond," Conlan said, a small, smug smile tugging at the corner of his mouth. A collective gasp ran round the chamber, the hum of voices dropping to surprised silence.

"The Avatar of Earth is here?"

Eleanor heard a strange catch in the High Lady's voice

"Yes," Conlan replied. The High Lady scanned the silent crowd around them, her eyes moving unseeing over Eleanor as she knelt on the floor at

Cander's side; she saw Freddie and stared at him, appraising him.

Conlan's smile grew a little wider. "This is Freddie, Avatar of Fire. The Avatar of Earth is over there," he said, pointing at Eleanor. Next to her, Cander gasped. Thinking he was in more pain she turned back towards him. The pain in his eyes had been replaced temporarily with awe.

"You are the Avatar of Earth?" he whispered.

"Yes," she answered, embarrassment heating her cheeks.

"Avatar of Earth, approach us," the High Lady commanded, staring down at her.

"Cander is hurt, he needs me to keep pressure on his wound," Eleanor replied. There was another collective gasp from the audience. *Oh, what have I done now?*

"Eleanor, you must not refuse a request from the council," Cander whispered.

"I will help him now, Avatar of Earth," Remic said, applying pressure as she removed her hand.

"Just Eleanor," she muttered as she reluctantly stood and walked to stand in front of the council. She looked at the three old Dwarves sat in front of her; they all looked back with a mixture of awe and surprise.

"You are the Avatar of Earth?" the High Lady asked.

"Yes, my name is Eleanor," she replied, pleased that her fear did not show in her voice; it felt strange to admit her true nature in front of so many strangers. There was silence as the council looked at her.

"I had expected you to be... bigger," the High Lady said seriously.

Eleanor heard Conlan's quiet chuckling behind her.

"Can you prove who you are?" The High Lady sounded a little uncertain, her glance flashing to Amelia. Eleanor looked at the devastation around her.

"I am not sure that would be a good idea, as I have no wish to cause your people further injury," she replied. The High Lady glared at her, and the silence in the chamber seemed to deepen.

"Then it seems we must take you at your word, Avatar of Earth," the High Lady said finally, sounding less than happy about it.

"Eleanor," Eleanor corrected without thinking. The High Lady's eyes narrowed. Eleanor smiled apologetically. "My name is Eleanor, High Lady," she said, putting a soft growl of subservient apology through the sentence and dropping her head.

"Eleanor… You come to claim the Talisman of Earth, but you must prove yourself worthy of this," the High Lady said, smiling at her slyly. Eleanor did not like the look. "You must pass a *maldra scelpa*." There were more gasps from around the chamber, and low-level murmuring broke the silence. Eleanor gave Conlan a questioning look. His concerned frown told her it was not good.

"It's a way of testing people to see if they are worthy to enter your group or tribe. The Elves have these tests for their young to perform before they can consider themselves fully functioning members of the tribe, and it seems Dwarves do too," he said in English.

"What do I have to do?" Eleanor asked, fear tearing through her insides.

"I don't know," he said. Turning to the High Lady, he switched back to Dwarfish. "What must Eleanor do?"

"She must remain for four days and four nights alone within the Earth. While she is there she must ask the Earth for Her song, and when she emerges she must sing the Earth's song for us," the High Lady said solemnly.

"I've got to sing?" Eleanor asked, so horrified she momentarily switched back to English. Conlan looked at her, so many emotions moving rapidly across his face that Eleanor had no hope of working out what he was thinking.

"That's the bit that's worrying you?" he asked, bemused.

"I can't sing, Conlan," Eleanor whispered, feeling the embarrassment turning her cheeks red.

"You don't have to do this," Conlan said quietly.

Eleanor sighed; she did have to do it, if they wanted her Talisman this was the cost, but the fact that Conlan had offered her a way out made her smile. She turned to face the council.

"I will do as required," she said slowly.

The High Lady nodded. "Remic, Alum will care for Cander, so please see that the Avatar… that Eleanor, is prepared for the *maldra scelpa*." Remic nodded to the High Lady as Alum removed his sword from Will's throat and came to take Remic's place, several other Dwarves crowding around Cander. Remic rose and moved to Eleanor's side.

"You have no idea what you have just agreed to," he muttered.

Eleanor felt her fear creeping up a notch as he led her from the chamber, the others following behind.

Remic took them to a large round room, which reminded Eleanor of the main cave at home in size and shape. Benches lined the walls and two tunnels on the far side of the chamber led off from it into ominous darkness.

"Wait here, I will fetch someone to help you," Remic said. Eleanor nodded, taking a seat; it was like sitting and waiting for the dentist. Will sat on one of the benches, still holding Amelia's body to his. Eleanor reached out a hand and gently stroked Amelia's soft black hair.

"Is she OK?"

Will nodded. "She'll be fine, she just needs to sleep for a while."

"Making the air move must be really hard work," Eleanor said. Will did not respond. Eleanor raised her eyes to his, he looked distressed, guilty. Not understanding, Eleanor held his gaze.

"Moving the air didn't cause her to collapse, did it?" Freddie said quietly.

Will dropped his head, shaking it. "I stripped her of her energy," he whispered. Shocked silence filled the room.

"I nearly killed you when I did that," Eleanor said, horrified that Will could do that to Amelia. Will raised his head, anger flashing through his eyes.

"I was careful, Eleanor, but I had no choice. She was lost in the powerful feeling of the air moving around her – she wasn't listening to me and she was going to kill somebody."

"You did the right thing," Conlan said softly. Will nodded, his head dropping again as he hugged Amelia closer to him.

"Yeah, Will, Amelia will be glad you stopped her," Freddie said, placing a reassuring hand on Will's shoulder.

Will lifted his head again, giving Freddie a sad smile. "I hope so."

Freddie turning to Conlan. "So what's going on, Eleanor has to pass some sort of test?"

Conlan nodded. "She has to pass a *maldra scelpa*. She is required to spend four days alone in the Earth, and when she emerges she must sing the 'Earth's Song'."

Freddie raised an eyebrow, turning back to Eleanor. "And you agreed to this?"

She shrugged and nodded.

"Eleanor, have you considered what four days locked up alone is going to do to you?" Freddie asked.

I need your support, Freddie, don't tell me I can't do this.

"She'll be fine," Conlan said, but Eleanor could hear the undercurrent of doubt in his voice, and the others would hear it too.

"Thanks for the vote of confidence," she murmured, unable to look at him. Freddie glared at Conlan and looked as if he was about to say something more when a young Dwarf woman entered the room.

"Avatar of Earth," she said, bowing towards Eleanor. "Please come with me and I will help you prepare." Eleanor stood, walking quickly towards her before anyone could say anything else. Without looking back she followed the woman out of the room.

"My name is Eleanor."

The woman glanced back and smiled. "I am Callie, sister to Cander."

"I am sorry your brother was injured. Is he going to be OK?" Eleanor asked, putting an apologetic growl through her voice.

Callie stopped and turned to look at her. "Our healers are confident that he will recover. Thank you for the care you showed him."

Eleanor smiled. "When you see him, please will you tell him I hope he gets better soon."

Callie nodded, returning the smile.

"That will please him."

They emerged into a small room, a screen blocking the door. Stepping around it, Eleanor was hit by a wall of steam. She soon saw why. In the middle of the floor in front of her was a large circular hole, the sides of which were made from the same polished stone of the council chamber. It was filled with water so hot that the steam was filling the room, condensing on the low ceiling above. Candles lit the room, giving it an inviting glow.

"Before the *maldra scelpa* you must bathe," Callie said. She pointed to where Eleanor could find soap and towels, and then she left her in peace.

Delighted, Eleanor stripped and sank into the hot water. It was almost too hot, her skin quickly turning pink. However, it felt so good that she immersed herself, moving carefully until her body was more acclimatised to the heat. She slowly lathered the soap, washing herself thoroughly and allowing the water to ease away the aches and pains that travelling had created. Once she was satisfied that her body was clean, she bent her head back and washed her hair. She was shocked at how brittle and dry it felt, not to mention how much dirt came out of it, and by the time she had finished the water was dark brown. Hauling herself out, Eleanor grabbed a soft piece of cloth left as a towel and began to dry herself.

"Eleanor, may I enter?" Callie's voice came from behind the screen.

"Yes, Callie," Eleanor responded, wrapping the towel around her. Callie came round the screen; she carried a pair of brown leather sandals and a piece of delicate-looking white material over her arm. Eleanor looked suspiciously at the material; Callie saw the look and smiled.

"These are the clothes you must wear."

She placed the sandals on the floor in front of her and held the material up for Eleanor to see. With a soft swish it dropped to the floor, held up by flimsy shoulder straps in Callie's hand.

"I have to wear this?" Eleanor asked incredulously.

Callie's face dropped. "You do not like it?"

"It is beautiful, Callie, but it's not something I would normally wear; I will feel very... vulnerable in it."

"The test you face is a test of the mind, so what you wear is of little matter to whether you pass or not, but it is considered respectful that you enter the Earth in purity of body and spirit," Callie said. Eleanor sighed, nodding. *In for a penny, in for a pound.* She carefully slipped the dress over her head, and the thin material actually felt pleasant as it fell over her still pink skin. It fitted perfectly, almost like it was made for her, the hem just brushing the tops of her feet. As she moved, the soft, silky material whispered over her. She felt ridiculous. Callie brushed her damp hair using small wooden combs to pull it back off her face, something else Eleanor did not like. When she was done, Callie moved back in front to inspect her work. Smiling, she nodded her approval.

"You are ready," she said, squeezing Eleanor's hand.

No, I'm nowhere near ready, Eleanor thought, but she nodded and followed Callie out of the room.

She was working so hard to fight her growing fear that she did not pay attention to where they were going until she found herself entering the antechamber where she had left the others. As she entered, Freddie and Conlan stood, staring at her. Will raised his head, his eyes getting a little wider as a grin broke over his face. The silence made her feel uncomfortable. Eleanor glared at them.

"I'm going to hit the first person who laughs," she snarled.

"Not laughing, Eleanor, you look... Wow!" Freddie said, a slow, slightly goofy smile spreading across his face. Conlan just stared, his face blank, eyes wide. Feeling utterly embarrassed, Eleanor dropped her head as her cheeks turned crimson.

"It's just a dress, Freddie," she muttered.

"It's not the dress..." Freddie started but then stopped as Eleanor shot him a deeply exasperated look. Remic entered the room; he smiled at Eleanor, his gaze running slowly down and then back up her body, eyes finally coming back to hers full of amused appreciation.

"Follow me," he said, still smiling as he headed towards one of the dark tunnels at the far end of the room. As she walked past him Eleanor glanced at Conlan. The hard, emotionless expression was stamped firmly on his face, but Eleanor could see his tightly clenched fists held rigid at his side; he was not happy about this. She gave him a small smile before the dark tunnel absorbed her.

12

EARTH'S VESSEL

As the darkness flowed around her, Remic reached a hand back for hers, leading her forward. She closed her eyes, trusting him.

"Do not be frightened, Eleanor, I will let you into a secret. It may feel like you are alone, but you will be watched over, you will be safe," he whispered. Eleanor did not respond; instead, she gave his hand a squeeze. They walked a long way. Eleanor could not be sure, but it felt like the tunnel was sloping down. The further they walked, the warmer it got, until Eleanor could feel the sweat running down to the small of her back, collecting around her ribs and under the swell of her breasts. Remic stopped, taking both of Eleanor's hands.

"We are here. We must crawl the rest of the way – if you kneel you will be able to feel the sides of the tunnel we must crawl through," he said. Eleanor stepped away from him, trembling.

"You can do this, Eleanor," Remic said softly. Eleanor nodded, kneeling down, reaching blindly towards the wall in front of her, fingers brushing rough stone. Remic placed his hand on hers and slowly moved it down until she felt the small opening in the rock. The space was just big enough that she could crawl through, her shoulders and head brushing the sides. She began crawling forward gingerly, her progress hampered by the dress; she could hear Remic following at a polite distance. After about thirty feet, she bumped into a solid wall in front of her. The tunnel at this point seemed a little wider, the roof a little higher but not by much; it was still claustrophobic and the heat was stifling.

"Eleanor, turn around," Remic said softly. Shuffling slightly in the tight dress, Eleanor turned around in the small space, her sense of touch and hearing enhanced in the dark.

"This is where you will stay for the next four days and nights. Take a moment to investigate, and then you can ask me any questions you might have. When you are ready I will seal you into this space. You will be alone." His voice was soft, gentle. Eleanor found that she was unable to sit in the small space, so slightly crouched over she used her hands to feel her way around the rough walls that now made up her prison. When she had finished she turned in the direction of Remic's voice.

"If you are going to seal me in, how will I breathe?" she asked, her tight rasping voice filling the black with fear.

"You will be able to breathe; this space allows air to pass through," Remic answered.

"Remic, have you done this?" Eleanor whispered. There was a long pause.

"No," was the flat reply.

"Dwarves do, though, and they survive it?" Eleanor asked, feeling her panic grow in the darkness.

"The last person to do this and come out sane enough to live a normal life was the High Lady. There is a reason she leads the council," Remic said. "You can do this, Eleanor, and when you do you will have the unswerving loyalty of every Dwarf alive, not just Cander and myself."

"And if I cannot...?"

"No, do not allow such thoughts. You are strong enough to do this – I believe in you and your friends believe in you," Remic said, his confidence in her echoing around the small space, making her feel strong.

She smiled. "Thank you, Remic," she said, and then felt him gently stroke her face.

"I will see you soon, Eleanor, do not give in to your fear."

Eleanor nodded, moving back as she heard stone grind against stone. She reached a hand forward and felt the smooth rock that had been moved into place, blocking the tunnel, her only exit from the small space she now inhabited. Unable to sit without hitting her head, Eleanor curled herself into a ball and lay on her side, her body just fitting in the space. *Four days and nights? I'm going to get thirsty.* Having nothing else to do, Eleanor closed her eyes and slept.

She woke with a start and sat up. Too fast – she hit her head against the ceiling, the stinging pain reminding her where she was. How long had she slept? She had no way to measure time. She felt rested. Concentrating, she pushed her energy strings out into the earth. The energy held in the rock around her was immense. Looking for a reason why, she pushed deeper, and then stopped in shock. *This is why it's so hot. It's not a mountain, it's a volcano.* One of her energy strings had run into molten lava, moving sluggishly through an underground river far beneath her. *Was the entire mountain range volcanic?* It was possible; she should have noticed this before. The evidence had been right in front of her in the rocks she had seen, and she had even pointed out the obsidian to Conlan as being a useful rock with which to make tools, as the edge could be knapped to an atom's thickness, making it incredibly sharp. *I'm an utter idiot.* She spent a long time with her energy strings extended, investigating the earth around her, waiting to see if it would sing, but nothing happened. Eventually exhaustion forced her to call her energy strings back and she slept again.

It was thirst and hunger that woke her – mostly thirst; she pushed it to the back of her mind. With nothing to distract her, strange thoughts kept popping into her head. Memories she had not recalled in years were played back. She remembered her grandmother teaching her to ride a bike and her father teaching her to play cards one wet afternoon in a hotel in Wales. Every so often her hunger and thirst would come storming back into her consciousness and she found that the wonderful feast Gregor had provided kept jumping into her mind. Eleanor pushed it back every time, but it was getting harder and harder. She could feel her consciousness slipping; sometimes she was not sure if she was awake or asleep. Her thirst was becoming a raging torment and her throat burned; as it did, her mind began supplying a mix of memory and fantasies to distract her. Conlan featured heavily in these, his strong arms around her, looking at her with love. She knew he was never going to look at her like that, but the dream was pleasant and Eleanor was thankful for the distraction.

Conlan was singing, his beautiful voice filling her head, but it was not the song about the Dwarves; there were no words, just a slow, steady undulating sound that rose and fell in a haunting melody. *Is this the Earth Song?* The thought brought a measure of coherence and with it the shocking realisation that she had unconsciously pushed several energy strings deep into the earth. *When did I do that?* The song flooded through her – *this* was the earth song. She could feel it humming through the rocks around her, the slow blood-like pulse of the molten lava the base beat. As she opened her mind to it, letting it flood every part of her being, desperate to remember it, she felt something else. A presence. Something that felt familiar, drawing her in. It was so powerful that she shied away from it, frightened of losing herself to it. The presence pushed forward, breaking through her mind's barriers as if they were not there. It was so different, so huge, that Eleanor knew resistance would be pointless as the presence filled her mind. It was not threatening as such; Eleanor did not feel it meant her harm, as someone digging a garden does not look to harm the worm. To the presence she was simply inconsequential. Eleanor pulled herself in, retreating to a dark corner of her mind and trying to work out what this presence was and how she could get rid of it.

She felt hands on her body, but she was no longer in command of her movements; the presence that filled her had control. Terrified, Eleanor pulled further into the small corner of her mind that was still hers and watched, powerless, as her body was carried towards the light. The world was blinding at first, and the presence squirmed away from it, raising a hand to block it out. Her body was laid on the floor. The presence sat up, looking around curiously, eyes settling on Conlan. Eleanor felt her mouth pulled into a smile. Conlan came forward and crouched in front of her.

"Eleanor, are you alright?" he asked.

"Alaric..." The presence whispered in Dwarfish, somehow managing to make Eleanor's voice carry a deep rumble. Leaning forward she kissed him. Surprised, Conlan jerked back. Eleanor tried to take back some control, trying to push it out of her head, an action as effective as an ant trying to push over an elephant.

"Eleanor? It is Conlan."

The presence was surprised that Conlan had not called himself Alaric, and its control slipped a little. Eleanor jumped at the opportunity, forcing her own control and using English, her voice a dry whisper.

"Conlan, help, get it out of me."

"Will, I don't think that's just Eleanor," Conlan said quietly. The presence looked at him, not understanding the words. Will moved forward as Eleanor felt her body stand. He pushed an energy string out to her. Not knowing what it was, the presence ignored it. Frowning, Will pushed into her head. The presence reacted instinctively, flinging Will out. Eleanor watched in impotent horror as Will was thrown off his feet, slamming into the wall five feet behind him and collapsed into a heap. Her body marched forward and grasped him round the throat, dragging the weakly struggling man to his feet. *Where did that strength come from?* Eleanor wondered. Dazed, Will stared at her in confusion and fear.

"I did not give you permission to enter my consciousness," Eleanor heard herself say, the same rumble to the Dwarfish words.

"Who are you?" Will asked with difficulty around the fingers digging into his windpipe.

"I am everything."

"You are Earth?" Will chocked out, eyes getting wider. Earth smiled and forcibly skewered Will's mind with an energy string. Memories, dreams, hopes, dreads and fantasies began pouring through Eleanor's head. Will's mind, absorbed into her own. The memories he had already shown her were suddenly given more context, more meaning. Will's life was laid bare before her. It was too much – Eleanor's mind rebelled, pushing the extra information into places she was fairly sure she would never be able to find it again. Was Will's conversation with the dragon part of these memories flashing before her? Would she look at it if it was? Knowing she was walking a fine moral line, Eleanor made the conscious choice to ignore as much of what was pouring through her head as possible. There was a lot of it; would Will be just an empty shell when Earth had finished? Frightened for him, Eleanor once again fought for control. Her struggling made no impact.

"I am everything, little Avatar of Water, and now I am you too," Earth said solemnly, before casually tossing Will across the room. He landed on a bench, his weight shattering the delicate piece of furniture to splinters. Amelia ran to his side. Eleanor had a brief view of Freddie and Remic's terrified faces as Earth turned on Conlan, glaring at him.

"Alaric... left me alone," Earth accused, its voice heavy with grief and loss. Conlan stared blankly. Eleanor could understand his problem, but how does one placate an element? There was a long silence. Conlan's voice was quiet when he spoke.

"Mortals die. Alaric has been dust for a very long time."

Earth shook her head. "Yet I see him before me, I feel his soul."

Conlan smiled. "I am Conlan Baydon, I carry Alaric's blood in my veins; however, I am but a poor echo of the person you once knew."

Earth seemed to consider this information. She reached a hand to stroke his face.

"You are far more than you believe yourself to be; Alaric lives in you... This vessel is important to you?"

Conlan nodded. "Eleanor is very important to me."

Earth sighed. "Then I shall return it to you."

Eleanor felt the presence flow out of her, through her energy strings and back into the earth. Shaking, she pulled back as much of herself as she could and collapsed, Conlan catching her before she hit the floor.

"Eleanor?"

"Yes, Conlan. Is Will OK?" she rasped, her consciousness fading to nothing before he answered.

Noise filled Eleanor's head.

"I do not care what tradition and law demands, she is in no fit state to do anything!" Conlan was saying, his words like hammer blows against an anvil.

"I am warning you, you will show us the proper respect."

Eleanor recognised the angry voice of the High Lady.

"Do you know what your *maldra scelpa* did to her? I know how many Dwarves end up mad after attempting to do this. Respect must be earned, High Lady, and you have done nothing to earn mine," Conlan snapped.

He's been talking to Remic.

"The fact remains that the *maldra scelpa* requires the participant to sing Earth's song within two days of emerging. If Eleanor does not do this, she fails the test and we will send you away without the Talisman. That is the law – and the law is stone." The High Lady's tone had a nasty edge to it. *She wanted me to fail.* Eleanor forced watery eyes to open. She was lying in a bed; soft pillows propped up her head and warm blankets covered her. Conlan and the High Lady stood in the middle of the small room. He towered over the head of the council, but she was holding her own. Amelia sat in a chair next to her; she smiled. Glancing round the room it looked like someone's bedroom; Eleanor could see a chest of drawers, another comfortable looking chair, some shelves with little objects and books on it. There were colourful pieces of material hung against the wall as decoration; they had been carefully matched to the intricate rug she could see on the floor. Candles covered every available surface. This was clearly for their benefit and Eleanor felt a rush of gratitude; whatever the High Lady's problem was, someone was looking after them.

The High Lady turned on her heel and stormed out of the room. The Dwarves did not seem to use doors, but Eleanor was sure if there had been one, the High Lady would have slammed it.

"Will?" she murmured with a thin, fragile voice.

"He's fine," Amelia assured her.

Eleanor blinked, surprised. "No missing memories?"

Relief surged through her as Amelia shook her head.

"How are you feeling?" Conlan asked.

Eleanor shrugged. "Great. What was the harridan yelling about?"

Talking made her cough. Amelia handed her a glass of water, lifted her head and helped her to drink.

Conlan raise an eyebrow at her. "Harridan?"

Eleanor smiled. "If you looked up the word in a dictionary, you'd find a picture of her."

Conlan quirked a smile, before annoyance filled his face. "She was here to tell us you have until sundown to sing the Earth Song, or they won't give up the Talisman."

"Then you'd better give me a lot more water and help me up," Eleanor said, struggling to sit but noticing with relief that she was no longer wearing the stupid white dress. The clothes were not her own, but they fit, were clean and there were trousers. She was irritated when Amelia pushed her back down with hardly any effort at all.

Amelia noticed her look. "Eleanor, you were hijacked by an element, so I really think rest would be a good idea right now," she said quietly. Eleanor took a deep breath, closing her eyes and marshalling her determination.

"Amelia, if you think I just went through all that to fail now, you don't know me very well." She opened her eyes and Amelia looked hurt.

"I do know you, Eleanor, but I had to try."

"Thank you, but I'm not going to let her win," Eleanor insisted. Amelia sighed, helping her up as she forced her tired body to sit. Eleanor saw the concern on Conlan's face, but he wisely chose to keep silent.

Eleanor felt like she had drunk a lake before her voice was in any fit state to even think about singing. She had tried to talk to Amelia about what Will had done to her, but beyond assuring Eleanor that she was fine, she had refused to talk about it. 'He did the right thing,' was Amelia's only comment. At Conlan's unwavering insistence, Eleanor was sat up in bed, attempting to eat some sort of spicy bread and honey, when Remic arrived with Will and Freddie.

"Is that really you?" Freddie teased, grinning at her. Eleanor grinned back. She looked at Will, noticing the deep purple and green bruises that spread across his neck. The smile fell. "I'm sorry, Will, I tried to stop it; it was just too strong," she said.

"It wasn't your fault – sorry about all the junk in your head." His steady gaze seemed to be implying a deeper meaning to his comment, but then he shrugged and smiled. "It was actually kind of cool."

Eleanor caught Amelia rolling her eyes.

"Are you ready?" Remic asked.

Conlan moved to sit on the edge of Eleanor's bed, giving her hand a reassuring squeeze as he did so. "Do you know what you're meant to sing?"

Eleanor nodded slowly. "Yes, I think so, but I'm still not sure I can stand up in front of people and sing it... I really don't think I can sing, Conlan."

Eleanor saw the smile he was trying to keep off his face.

"We're about to find out," he said softly.

The walk back to the council chamber was a terrifying experience for Eleanor; everyone was going to laugh. The terror pounded down on her, crushing what little confidence she had into a pulp. As they walked into the chamber Eleanor came to a frozen stop. The room was full; row upon row of orderly lines of Dwarves, hundreds, perhaps thousands of them, all silently watching her.

"Come on, Eleanor, it's OK," Conlan said softly. Eleanor shook her head, knowing all her terror was showing on her face. She took a step backwards, fighting the urgent compulsion to turn and run.

Will moved up behind her. "Would you like some help, Eleanor?"

She nodded. Will pushed into her mind. The familiar feelings of calm and love spread through her. He moved past her defences effortlessly, pouring more calm through her. Sighing, she felt her body relax. Will moved deeper into her head. She made no move to resist him. Warm, protective love enveloped her, insulating her from her fear. Reality moved out of focus. Eleanor knew what she was doing, but it did not scare her. *Will, living Prozac pill*, she thought, hearing Will chuckling in the back of her head. With a small smile on her face, she ignored the people stood around her and walked down the narrow gap the Dwarves had left so that she could stand in front of the council. When she got there she fixed the High Lady with a glower for a moment and then closed her eyes, allowing the Earth's song to run through her head. She felt Will's appreciation.

Beautiful, isn't it?

Yes, he agreed.

Feeling happy, comfortable and protected, Eleanor began to sing. There were no words; this was just sound, beautiful melodic sound. She gave it her all, doing her best to make her voice match the harmonics running through her head. She knew it was not perfect, but it was not nearly as bad as she had feared. She had no idea how long she was meant to sing for, so as the song came to an end, she started again. This time, another voice swelled to join in, the stunning, resonating sound lifting her attempt. The chamber's acoustics allowed him to layer his voice as the sound echoed off the walls. There were gasps of wonder from the Dwarves. Eleanor put more strength into her singing and kept her eyes closed; she felt his voice flow around her, filling her with such a deep sense of joy that for a moment nothing else mattered. He was singing the harmony for her, bolstering her own voice and helping to make the sound she was making much more like the sound in her head. She felt Will's surprise. *He didn't know Conlan could sing.* The song ended, the remaining sound echoing through her body, making her nerves tingle.

He has an amazing voice, Eleanor thought dreamily.

He's sung for you before? Will asked.

Yes, I think it might be my favourite sound in the whole world, after his laugh.

She felt a rush of amused affection from Will and it cut through some of the fog he had created in her head.

Oh, don't tell him I said that, she blurted out, suddenly embarrassed.

Eleanor opened her eyes and looked back across the chamber. Her eyes locked onto Conlan's, and she smiled gratefully at him. He grinned back and she was still smiling as she turned to face the council. The High Lady was glaring at her, a nasty sneer on her face, but Eleanor did not care – she had passed the test. The diamond was hers.

"Well done, Avatar of Earth," the High Lady said grudgingly. "You have passed the *maldra scelpa*, although we were told that you had some problems when you emerged from the Earth." She smiled in such a condescending and officious manner that Eleanor wanted to slap it off her face.

Eleanor sighed and then said in a loud voice that echoed round the chamber, "Unfortunately, the power of Elemental Earth decided to visit and She used my body to do it; it was a little hard to kick Her out." She heard the gasps that ran round the chamber, and the High Lady stared at her in shocked silence. It was one of the male council members who finally spoke.

"You were a vessel for Earth?" he asked in disbelief. She nodded. "How did you persuade Her to leave you?" He sounded genuinely curious.

Eleanor smiled again. "It was not me," she turned round nodding at Conlan. "He did it." There were further gasps from the crowd. Conlan had his normal emotionless expression on his face, but even from where she stood, Eleanor could see the amusement in his eyes.

"I would like to hear more of this," the old Dwarf said. "Return to your rooms and I will join you shortly."

Eleanor nodded, giving the old Dwarf a friendly smile, and then she turned and marched back to where the others stood, forcing her tired body to give the impression of confidence and strength.

Thank you, Will, I couldn't have done it without you.

"You're welcome," Will said, pulling his energy free.

Remic was full of excitement as he led them back to the rooms in which Eleanor had woken up. He was answering Will and Conlan's endless questions about the council members and Dwarf law, even explaining that they were staying in Callie's home, which she had generously given up for their use. Eleanor was only half listening, as her tired brain was having problems interpreting. As the others chatted in the living room, she slipped into the bedroom and lay back on the bed, staring at the rock above her head; she felt a pang of homesickness and pushed it aside. *One down, four to go.* Victory and relief flooded through her, and she felt the urge to cry but fought it down. Curling on her side she closed her eyes and allowed sleep to take her.

"Eleanor... Eleanor..."

Without opening her eyes Eleanor smiled. "Yes, Conlan?"

"We are eating, are you hungry?"

"No. Did they bring the diamond? Did that council Dwarf come and talk to you yet?" she asked, not liking how weak and whispery her voice sounded.

"The 'council Dwarf' is called Drumar, and yes, we had a talk. I am not sure he believed me about you being Earth's Vessel, but I think that was just a rouse to talk to me. He spent most of the conversation telling me that I should be taking on the Lords of Mydren and bringing back the monarchy, not creeping around in the shadows." Conlan was trying too hard to run an undercurrent of amusement through the Dwarfish.

Drumar's comments are making him think – good.

"There is no sign of the diamond yet," he continued. "You caused quite a stir; the Dwarves are outraged and they are questioning the High Lady's right to rule. They think she should have just given you the diamond, not made you sing for it. You do not sing that badly, by the way."

Eleanor opened her eyes. He was sat on the chair next to her bed, and he looked serious.

"Says the man with the voice of an angel," Eleanor muttered in English.

His eyes held hers. Feeling uncomfortable under his scrutiny, Eleanor sighed and then rolled onto her back, finding it easier to stare at the ceiling rather than at him.

"So have I started a Dwarf civil war?" she asked, switching back to Dwarfish.

"That was a really unsubtle attempt to avoid talking about your singing," Conlan said, and this time Eleanor heard honest amusement in his voice. She turned her head towards him and he laughed at the look of consternation on her face.

"I shall try to be more subtle in the future," she muttered, as he laughed harder.

"Glad you're awake," Freddie said, walking into the room. "Remic and Cander are here to see you."

"Cander? Is he alright?" Eleanor sat up, quickly moving off the bed. Rather too quickly, the room spun around her and she staggered. Freddie stepped forward and caught her before she fell. Eyes closed, she took several slow, deep breaths as Freddie held her up, her forehead resting against his chest.

"Slowly, Eleanor," he admonished.

Pushing herself away gently, she stood unaided and shrugged. "Just need a bit more sleep."

Before either he or Conlan could object, she walked past Freddie into the living room. The comfortable chairs had been pushed back against the walls and large cushions placed around the central low table. Generous platefuls of food had been laid out on it. Eleanor's stomach rumbled. *Maybe I am hungry.* Will and Amelia stood talking to Remic and Cander.

"Cander, how are you?" Eleanor asked. He turned towards her. Physically he looked very similar to Remic, but his dark-brown hair was short and his sharp brown eyes had a cunning that Remic's did not. His left arm was strapped securely across his chest. He looked pale and tired, but his grin was wide and genuine.

"I feel much better, thank you."

Eleanor walked closer to them, and when she got within a few feet both Dwarves dropped gracefully to their knees. Surprised and uncomfortable, Eleanor froze.

Embarrassment flushed her cheeks. "What are you doing?"

Cander glanced up at her from beneath a bowed head, a mischievous grin on his face, putting a finger to his lips. Too stunned to argue, Eleanor nodded.

"Eleanor, Avatar of Earth. We wish to make our loyalty to you official. From today Remic and I swear solemn allegiance to you. Our lives are yours," Cander said slowly, his head bowed like Remic's. Silence followed his words. Moving closer, Eleanor knelt down in front of them. She took their chins and gently raised their heads so she could see their eyes and the looks of trusting devotion on their faces.

"Why?" she asked, confused.

"There are reasons; please accept our loyalties," Cander said, his steady gaze holding hers.

Eleanor nodded. "Erm, thank you?" she said, not sure what the correct response should be. The two Dwarves both looked smugly satisfied. *This is totally insane.*

"We were going to eat, do you wish to join us?" she offered lamely, nodding towards the table laden with food.

Remic smiled apologetically. "We are unable to stay, I was sent to give you the diamond. There are 'problems' in the council. I am needed there and I believe Cander currently has several angry healers trying to find him." He held his hand out, and in his palm was a large, oblong diamond which glittered with blue sparkles in the candlelight. It was housed in a metal setting which looked like silver or perhaps platinum. The thick chain was the same metal. Eleanor took it from him; it was about the size of a double 'A' battery, its heavy weight fitting comfortably into her hand. She closed her fist around it. She was not sure what she had expected, but it just felt like a diamond in her hand. She hid her disappointment and smiled at them.

"Thank you, thank you for everything."

In one fluid movement the Dwarves rose, Remic offering a hand to help her stand. They both bowed to her, Cander still grinning as they headed for the exit. Silence followed their departure. Eleanor looked at the diamond in her hand, aware that the others were staring at her, the diamond giving her the opportunity to avoid looking back.

"Eleanor, do you know what just happened?" Conlan asked eventually, switching back to English, she assumed, for Freddie and Amelia's benefit. Still not looking at him she nodded, her cheeks burning.

"It goes a little deeper," he said, his very serious tone bringing her eyes to his. She looked at him, confused. When he was sure he had her attention, Conlan continued.

"Remic is the closest the Dwarves have to a warlord – he commands the loyalty of the Dwarf army. Where he goes, they will follow, and he just gave that to you, Eleanor. Cander is Drumar's grandson. His is an old and noble family line, and he is being trained to take his grandfather's place on the council. Those two Dwarves just gave you all the resources and power of the Dwarfish nation, something no outsider has ever been given – not even Alaric commanded the Dwarves."

Eleanor stared at him in shock. "Remic said if I passed the *maldra scelpa* I would gain the unswerving loyalty of every Dwarf alive. It never occurred to me that he meant that literally."

It was only Remic, Cander and Callie that came to see them off at dawn the next morning. The extra food and provisions they had been supplied with had turned Rand from a warhorse into a less than happy pack mule. Callie had insisted Eleanor take a whole new wardrobe with her; Conlan had rolled his eyes at the extra bag, but the dirty look Amelia gave him kept him silent. Eleanor hoped that the nightmare white dress was not packed somewhere. Cander and Callie shook her hand and Eleanor thanked them profusely. Remic walked with them for a short distance, out of the shadow of the mountain and into the pale sunlight. He gave Conlan and Will some last-minute instructions on the easiest route to take to find the Elves. He said his farewells and then took Eleanor's arm and gently pulled her to one side, out of the earshot of the others. He took her hands, giving her an encouraging smile before he spoke.

"Our race has spent too long locked away from the problems of this world, and we have become small-minded as a result; the High Lady shows this. Cander and I have been searching for a way to re-enter society, and we see the importance of what Conlan is doing and we wish to help. We are meant to help, which is why we were given the diamond to guard in the first place. Conlan's path *will* bring him into conflict with the Lords of Mydren, and sooner or later he will accept what we both know... Conlan brings a new era, he brings back the glory of kings."

Remic's words made Eleanor shiver, but she nodded firmly. *The Lords have to go, and the only way Conlan can achieve freedom for the people is to become king.* Eleanor wondered how long it would take Conlan to realise that this was where his destiny lay.

"We have watched over Alaric's bloodline for centuries, waiting for this very moment," Remic continued. "However, there are many of the older generation who would not accept a human in charge of the Dwarf army, but you are allied with Earth, have been Earth's vessel, have passed the initiation rite. This way we give Conlan our support, without putting a human in charge."

"Remic, that is very... devious of you. I must say that I am happier knowing that I hold this honour for Conlan."

He pushed something into her hand. Eleanor looked down and found a small, plain dagger lying across her palm. The handle was polished wood, while a worn leather sheath hid the blade and provided a loop so she could hang it from her belt. A brass clasp held the knife in the sheath.

"Look at the blade," Remic said softly. Eleanor released the clasp; it gave easily and she drew out the blade. The wickedly sharp edge tapered to a needlepoint, making it good for slashing or stabbing. While the blade had been cared for, it was obvious that it had been well used. There was decoration on the blade, etched into the metal near the handle; the symbol looked like a mountain with a diamond within it. Eleanor ran a finger over it.

"Look for that symbol in any of the larger towns you visit. If you need to get a message to me or you need immediate assistance, go into one of these shops and mention my name, show them the dagger and they will help you," Remic said. Eleanor stared at him in stunned silence as the implication of his words clicked rapidly through her head.

"Spies... you have spies, a whole network of them, which is how you know about the world, how you have watched Alaric's bloodline," Eleanor whispered in awe.

Remic nodded, smiling. "Cander made a good choice in you."

"This was all Cander's idea?"

Again Remic nodded, his grin widening. "We are more than friends, we are like brothers, but Cander is in charge, his birth and position will always make this the case. He likes to give the impression of quiet deference, always standing to the back, but he is more than capable of leading our people, and all will follow him when the time comes."

Eleanor smiled. "I did not come here expecting to make such good friends. Thank you, Remic, thank you for everything." Remic pulled her into a tight hug, then turned and walked back towards home without looking back. There was no need; they would see each other again.

It took them a week to reach the foothills of the mountain range, but the time seemed to move faster than it had on the journey in. It helped that the further they walked, the easier it got to breathe – their lungs, conditioned to the thinner air, began working overtime, meaning they could push themselves harder and faster. The acquisition of the diamond seemed to have impressed on them all that what before had been nothing more than an idea, was now a very achievable reality. Eleanor looked around her friends' faces and detected a happy glow; even Conlan joined in with the laughter and jokes. She had examined in some detail the diamond that now hung at her neck, discovering that she could send an energy string out into its lattice. She had been surprised when she found there was energy already held in the lattice, trapped and bouncing endlessly within the refractive structure. Who had put the energy in the diamond in the first place? Eleanor decided the only logical assumption was that the energy had been left by the last person to use it, the murdered king's Avatar of Earth, seven hundred odd years ago. Eleanor was aware that energy could not be destroyed, but it was still impressive that the energy trapped in the diamond had not dissipated in seven hundred years. She had attempted to add her own energy to the diamond. It took her a few tries to get it right, as the energy string had to be carefully woven into the lattice structure to make sure the energy was trapped. She had nearly exploded a rock face down on top of herself while figuring that out, but once she was able to safely add energy she decided to see how much the stone would take. Pulling energy from the earth, using her own as a conduit, she transferred it directly into the diamond's lattice. Despite the hours she spent doing this, she never got the impression that the diamond had reached its capacity. She could feel the stone vibrating against her skin, but strangely the massive amount of energy could only be felt with physical contact; to look at it, it was nothing more than a large diamond on a chain.

Her conclusions were that, firstly, this was a way of secretly storing energy, but she could think of absolutely no situation when having this ability would be necessary because she was always connected to the earth, and there was no scenario she could imagine when that energy would not be available to her. The second, more worrying, conclusion was that the diamond had nothing to do with getting the connection to work. While the book made it very clear that they needed the Talismans, whatever they had been created to do, getting rid of Conlan's shield was not it. This thought pushed Eleanor into a bleak pit of despair, made worse by the fact that she knew she could not share her thoughts. The others were happy and hopeful; more importantly, Conlan was happy and hopeful, and she could not take that from them and most certainly would not take it from him. Maybe the hunt for the Talismans would take long enough that they would work out how to get rid of Conlan's shield. With this in mind, she made a massive effort to laugh and smile, pushing her dark thoughts to the back of her consciousness and hoping that Will would not have to go into her head any time soon. At night, though, her dreams turned to nightmares.

13

13

❧ ❧

*J*UDGEMENT

The map and advice Remic gave them brought them out on the east side of Mydren's central mountain range. They then turned south, keeping to the less populated foothills. For several days Conlan's good humour vanished. After he snapped twice at Amelia for no reason at all, Eleanor had asked him what the problem was. When he refused to tell her, she voiced her good-natured but loudly spoken theories that ranged from them being close to some poor woman he had jilted, to haemorrhoids. The others had listened to her badgering him with amused interest. Eleanor was fairly certain that Will and Freddie had a bet going on just how long it would take for Conlan to break. Eleanor had actually been quite impressed with his control, but eventually he had cracked, his gaze practically nailing her to the ground as he grabbed painfully at her upper arm, shaking her, demanding she stop. Despite his livid expression and the bruises she could feel his fingers creating in her arm, she had stood her ground. So he had explained, through gritted teeth, that less than ten days' journey from their position was a tower, in which were the Lords of Mydren that ruled the north, his father being one of them, and that he did not enjoy being as close as he was to the man. Eleanor could plainly see his discomfort and felt sorry for him. It must have shown on her face, because Conlan had taken a very threatening step forward and told her, in a bitter snarl, that he did not want her pity; he just wanted her to shut up. Not wanting to upset him further, and feeling genuinely ashamed of her behaviour, Eleanor had agreed.

They settled into a routine as they travelled, with everyone having their own chores and responsibilities. Conlan was not pushing their pace, estimating it would take them several months to reach Drent. They made camp in the late afternoon, giving them time to practice their fighting, to talk and to generally enjoy each other's company. Eleanor started reading the book Conlan had given her, and when Freddie discovered it was a book about battle he begged her to read it to him. So every evening she read him a chapter and they discussed it, which had the twofold purpose of getting them thinking about battle strategy and helping Eleanor's translation. After several nights of listening in serious silence, Freddie commented that he had read a book much like it, before he died, called the 'Art of War'. Eleanor was amused that two totally different worlds could produce the same book. Freddie laughed, pointing out that human nature and the basic elements of battle did not change, as no matter where they were, humans were motivated by the same emotions. Freddie had a quick and imaginative mind when it came to fighting. Eager to push him to think further, Conlan set up battle scenarios for them, which Eleanor and Freddie spent hours trying to work out. After a few weeks Conlan ran out of set scenarios and began to invent his own. Eleanor found this much more interesting, as his battle plans and ideas were much more intricate and detailed with more complex variables. It was like playing a very involved game of chess.

The further south they travelled, the higher the temperature rose. Eleanor had gone through the clothes that Callie had given her, finding a few tight-fitted, short-sleeved shirts; she had also found a draw-string purse full of thick, heavy coins at the bottom of the clothes bag, with a note from Remic telling her to buy anything Callie had forgotten to pack. Eleanor had smiled at the sweet gesture, especially as she already owed him so much. Conlan had not been happy about her wearing her new shirts and had demanded that she wore something to hide her Avatar brand. Eleanor had ignored him, refusing to back down even when he had tried to back up his argument with violence, by shoving her to the ground. She was becoming less and less inclined to hide what she was, especially out in the wilderness, where their only witnesses were lizards and snakes. Conlan's behaviour, however, was beginning to worry her. She knew she pushed him on occasion, but in the past he had usually been able to resist the urge to actually hurt her. Since their visit to the Dwarfs, more and more of their arguments ended in Eleanor gaining bruises. There was no brooding silence; he was mostly fine with the others, so it was just her he had a short fuse with. The others also seemed to have noticed, as Will and Freddie seemed to materialise near her whenever she and Conlan started arguing.

They were several days away from Drent. The landscape had begun to change, becoming barren and flatter, the sky melting into the horizon. There were no trees, sparse vegetation and cracked dry earth; water became harder to find. The temperature climbed, and Rand began to struggle in the heat, making it necessary for them to walk at night when it was cooler. Skirting several small border towns they saw a few people out on the roads, but nobody gave them so much as a second glance. As they got closer to Drent the traffic on the road became a little heavier. Eleanor had reluctantly agreed to wear a shirt to cover her brand, and it was sticking to her body in the sweltering heat. There was a small breeze, but it came from the desert and it felt to Eleanor like she was being dry baked. Will and Rand looked as miserable as she felt. Amelia and Conlan just appeared to accept the situation with stoicism. Freddie, on the other hand, had a big grin on his face.

"Enjoying the weather?" Eleanor asked, jogging up to his side and feeling the sweat running down her back.

He nodded enthusiastically. "It's wonderful, isn't it? I was getting so sick of the rain and cold – this is brilliant! There is so much heat in the air that I can actually take energy from it."

Eleanor looked at him in surprise. "Really? What does it feel like?"

Freddie looked thoughtful for a moment. "Not like fire – it's subtle, heavy for some reason. I like it."

"Each to their own," Eleanor muttered as Freddie laughed.

Drent was a walled town – as Baydon had been – but unlike Baydon, Eleanor got the impression that the towering battlements were kept in good repair for a reason other than civic pride. As they walked under the shadow of the city gate, in the early afternoon, the three bored guards gave them nothing more than a cursory glance. They were wearing uniforms, but they were not the grey of the Protectors – these guards wore red.

"Are there no Protectors here?" Eleanor whispered to Conlan.

"No, this is a disconnected town; the men in red are the town guard. Drent is a town too threatened to be worth the Lords' trouble taking it."

"Threatened by whom?" Eleanor asked.

"The Elves," came Conlan's terse reply.

Leading Rand, Conlan walked through the busy, sweltering streets. Eleanor looked around her. Unlike her trip to Baydon, she no longer felt out of place, she understood the conversation around her and could hear shopkeepers and street traders yelling their wares. It did not feel as threatening as Baydon had. The people here did not seem to be overly poor or overly rich. The city smelt very different to Baydon: dry and dusty, the air filled with the scents of spice and sweet fried food. Eleanor smiled. She liked Drent, despite the heat, it felt exciting and mysterious; she wanted to explore. Conlan led them to a large inn off one of the main streets. Its long, three storey, white-washed front looked clean and crisp next to its shabby, sand-blown neighbours, balconies drawing sharp lines across its front.

"We'll stay here for tonight and set off for the Elves early tomorrow morning. Will, can you get us rooms? I need to find stabling for Rand; we can't take him into the desert with us," Conlan said, his voice soft and not wanting to draw attention to the fact he was speaking English. He took a small sack of coins from one of his bags and gave it to Will. "There should be more than enough, so get us baths and a meal." Will nodded, disappearing into the inn as Eleanor helped Freddie and Amelia take their bags and equipment off Rand. Eleanor considered the bag of money Remic had given her; it was easily three times the size of the one Conlan had just given Will.

Maybe the coins in my purse are worth less. Will came back out of the inn clutching a room key just as his fellow travellers finally managed to shoulder all the bags Rand had been carrying.

"I got us a suite, it was easier. Room twelve," Will said. Conlan nodded, putting the coin bag in his pocket and leading Rand down the street towards the sign that said 'Stables'. Will showed them to their room. He unlocked the door into a large, airy living room. Its white-washed stone walls and brightly coloured mosaics made Eleanor think of Moroccan interior design. There were several low tables, comfortable chairs and colourful, cushion-strewn sofas, with lamps scattered around. On either side of the room were double doors leading into two further rooms, in each of which Eleanor could see a large double bed covered in brightly coloured throws, along with more comfortable furniture. On the opposite side of the room was a slatted wooden screen that caused stripy light to hit the cool, blue-tiled floor in front of it. Unceremoniously dumping her bags, Eleanor moved to the wooden screen and pulled it; it concertinaed apart to reveal a long, wide balcony that overlooked the street. Eleanor sat, cross-legged and ignoring the heat, watched the life bustle around her. Amelia came to join her. They sat in companionable silence for a while, until eventually Amelia spoke.

"Sometimes I feel so detached from this world... I would love to go shopping. Will and I have been together for three years this summer, and I want to buy him something."

Eleanor reached to squeeze her hand. "I have money. Let's shop!"

"Where did you get money from?"

"Remic gave it to me," Eleanor shrugged.

"I knew that Dwarf had the hots for you!" Amelia said, her voice a little too loud. Eleanor heard Freddie sniggering behind them; she turned to glare at him and he returned to the bag he was rooting through.

"He was just being sweet." She was blushing – she had really liked Remic and Cander, but there was nothing more than friendship involved. She rose to her feet. Walking back to her bags, she dug around until she found the heavy coin purse and brought it back to Amelia, who stared at it with wide, surprised eyes.

"This is a lot of money, Eleanor."

"How much is a lot?" Eleanor asked.

"You could buy a nice house with this," Amelia replied softly, weighing the purse in her hand.

"Would Will like a nice house?" Eleanor inquired, in a conspiratorial whisper.

"I was thinking of something a little easier for him to carry," Amelia said, smiling.

"Then let's go and find him something."

Eleanor had been forced to bribe Freddie with the promise of presents so he would cover for them, but they had finally managed to get away, moving through the streets, looking in shop windows and at the wares of the traders in the stalls they passed, with Amelia asking endless questions in Eleanor's head about what they were saying and selling. Drent was not a large town, and it did not take them long to find the main shopping street. They moved from one shop to the next, Amelia looking dispiritedly at the items for sale but never actually choosing anything. When they had viewed the shops on both sides of the street, Eleanor began to wonder if there would be anything she would think appropriate.

Amelia, do you have something in mind? It might help us find what you are looking for.

I don't know what to get him, I don't know what he would like; there is nothing he really needs and he won't want to carry useless knick-knacks around...

Eleanor could feel her distress. *Would you like some advice on what to get him?* she asked, allowing some of Will's stronger hopes and dreams to drift to the surface of her mind from the dark corner she had shoved them after Earth had rifled through his mind.

Amelia nodded slowly.

He always wanted to draw, Amelia, so get him a sketch pad and some pencils.

Amelia looked at her blankly for a moment. *Really?*

Eleanor nodded. *There's a shop at the far end of the street, it sells that sort of thing.* Taking her hand, Eleanor pulled her towards the shop. Inside it was cool and gloomy. Giving the stock a brief inspection, Amelia picked a medium-sized pad, full of thick, creamy paper, held together by a soft, red-brown leather cover, a long leather thong firmly attached so that it could be wrapped around, holding it closed. The shop sold paints and coloured pencils, but mindful of the weight Amelia selected six beautiful handmade pencils, with lead of various softnesses and a matching red-brown leather case to keep them in. Eleanor asked the shopkeeper, an older man with a friendly smile, to wrap the items, as they were a gift. The man carefully wrapped the items in colourful cloth and ribbon, handing them to Amelia.

Thank you, Amelia said as they exited the shop.

You're welcome. Now we have to get something for Freddie, and I suppose Conlan would be hurt if he's missed out... Is there anything you'd like?

They wandered through the shops again. Eleanor commissioned a new bridal, saddle and saddlebags in red leather for Rand, conscious of the fact that it was her fault the original ones had been lost. She paid the saddler, giving him a description of Rand and telling him which stables he could be found in if he needed to take measurements, hoping it would be finished before they got back from visiting the Elves. She bought Freddie a new sword – she knew she had paid over the odds for it, but it was beautiful, well-balanced, sharp and sleek. Freddie took great care of his old cast-off of Conlan's; he deserved something special of his own. Not wanting to walk the streets holding a sword, she had paid extra to have it delivered to their hotel. She bought Amelia some lavender-smelling soap in a little case and some perfume that had reminded her of Conlan's mother's garden. She bought herself a soft leather wrist cuff so that she could wear short sleeves and still cover her brand. Walking past a jewellery shop, Eleanor noticed the symbol of the mountain with a diamond within it on the corner of the sign over the door, and she thought of Remic and Cander with a smile; she must remember to thank Remic for the fun they were having. She bought Will a pack of what looked like playing cards after noticing that the four suites were diamonds, wands, chalices and swords. Eleanor doubted this was a coincidence.

She now only had Conlan to buy something for; she wanted to get him a book, as he had given her his. The bookshop was down a side street, off the main shopping area. It was quiet and dusty, and the owner, a well-fed matron, slept behind the counter. Amelia and Eleanor moved along the bookshelves looking for something suitable. After some careful consideration, Eleanor had chosen a very old-looking, handwritten book. She had flicked through some of the pages and found that many of the words were new to her, but the general gist of it reminded her of some of the Greek philosophers she had read. It was essays on what constituted good governing and what must be provided for the people to make them happy and prosperous. In short, although the book did not seem to come out and say it, its contents enlightened the reader on what made a good king. Amelia had gasped at the expensive, but the shopkeeper had refused to bargain, explaining that it was one of a kind and a collector's item. She had agreed to warp it, however, and Eleanor put it in her satchel with the other presents.

Happy and relaxed, Eleanor did not notice the men that followed them as they exited the bookshop. It was getting late, and the sun was casting long shadows in the dying heat. As they turned to head back to the hotel, three men stepped in front of them, blocking their way. Eleanor and Amelia froze, then took a couple of steps backwards, only to find two additional men behind them.

"So you are the ones spending money all over town, eh? How about you give us some?" asked the taller of the three men stood in front of the two women.

What does he want? Amelia asked, pushing into Eleanor's head.

Money.

"I am sorry, but we have spent all our money for today," Eleanor answered.

"Then we will take what you have," the man snarled.

Eleanor laughed, a harsh nasty sound intended to convey her contempt. "This is your one and only chance of leaving in one piece – if you lay a hand on either my companion or myself, you will regret it."

The man hesitated for a moment, but then looked at his four accomplices and decided Eleanor and Amelia were too outnumbered to be a threat. He stepped forward, grabbing Eleanor's right arm painfully, just above the elbow. She moved into a fighting stance, twisting her right arm up in a block and punching the man as hard as she could in the stomach with her left hand. She knew it had not been a strong punch, but it was enough that he let go. Staggering back slightly, he swung a right-fisted punch at her head. Using her left hand, Eleanor blocked. Stepping towards him and slipping her arm round his, she jerked back, pulling his shoulder back unnaturally and dragging him to the floor as she kicked one of his legs out from under him. As he landed, she dropped heavily, knee first, onto his chest. Ribs snapped and the man let out a strangled cry. Growling, Eleanor punched him hard in the face. It hurt her hand – a lot – but she heard the satisfying crunch of his nose as blood gushed forth, giving his cries a wet, gurgling quality. Her entire attack had taken seconds. Eleanor jumped back to her feet, noticing the astonished faces of the other four men.

Amelia… RUN!

Grabbing Amelia's hand, she pushed through the two stunned men in front of her and ran down the street in the direction of the inn. It had taken a few moments before Eleanor had heard the slap of feet, as the men recovered their senses enough to chase after them. They were running fast, but the men were gaining on them. Amelia dragged Eleanor down a dark alley, desperate to find them somewhere to hide, but only to discover it was a dead end. Eleanor turned around, her back pushing up against the wall behind her. She could see one man blocking the alley at the end, the other two walking cautiously towards them. *Do I blast them? How much damage would I cause? Or do I try to fight them? They will be ready for it this time!* As various plans and options ran through Eleanor's head, she stepped protectively in front of Amelia. Pulling her small dagger from its sheath, she handed it back to Amelia over her shoulder. When she did not take it, Eleanor turned to look; the taller woman had her grey eyes closed and was chewing on her bottom lip, a look of intense concentration on her face. *She's shielding… OK, not a bad idea, but all that is going to do is create a stand-off, and eventually she is going to drop from exhaustion.* Before Eleanor could make this point, the men came further down the alley; they were talking to each other.

"… so where are they?" a short, bearded man asked.

"It's a dead end, they must be here somewhere," replied the taller, thinner man behind.

The short bearded man nearly walked into Eleanor as he looked around the end of the alley in consternation. *They can't see us… holy crap! Whatever Amelia is doing, they can't see us.*

"Are you sure they came down this alley?" the bearded man asked.

"For the tenth time, yes!" the thin one snapped in reply.

"Well they are obviously not here, they must have used magic to get away!" the bearded man said sarcastically, heading back towards the entrance to the alley. The three men argued for a few moments and then walked away.

"Amelia, I think they've gone," Eleanor whispered as she returned her knife to its sheath. Letting out a slow, tired breath, Amelia opened her eyes and smiled.

Eleanor gave her a hard look. "OK, spill! How long have you known you could do that?" Amelia shrugged. "I didn't, I guess I needed the adrenaline kick to figure it out. I manipulated the energy particles in the shield somehow, split them down and then wrapped them round us. I made the shield at the front project what was being reflected onto the shield at the back – the wall – making it look like we weren't there. The two halves of the particles were still connected somehow, so what affects one, affects the other."

"Wow, I didn't even know that was physically possible. Could you do it again?"

Amelia nodded, a huge grin spreading across her face. A thousand tactical advantages to being invisible went charging through Eleanor's head.

They returned to the inn, stopping at the reception to collect Freddie's sword, which had been delivered for them. Walking slowly back to the room, Eleanor felt strange, as if she were giving up something important, a small piece of freedom maybe. Before she opened the door, she turned to Amelia and whispered.

"I don't think we should mention our little 'adventure', OK? The boys will never let us out of their sight again."

Amelia nodded. "Thank you for a fun afternoon."

Eleanor smiled at her and opened the door to their suite.

Freddie looked up at them miserably from the corner of the room, where he sat on the floor. Will was trying to look stern, but Eleanor could see the relief in his eyes and Conlan was pacing the length of the room. He stopped as they entered and glared at them.

"Hi," Eleanor said, stepping over the threshold and closing the door. Conlan marched towards them, and towering over her he jabbed a finger into her chest.

"Where have you been?" he snarled.

"Shopping," Eleanor said innocently.

"Have you any idea how dangerous this place is?" Conlan snapped. "You were shopping!? Where did you get money?"

Eleanor gave Amelia a sideways glance and they both dissolved into giggles. Conlan grabbed her by the front of her shirt, yanked her forwards and shoved her back, her head bouncing solidly off the door. Her good humour gone, Eleanor glared back at him.

"Being in this room with you right now is the most dangerous thing we've done all afternoon. Take your hands off me," she hissed.

"We were worried about you," Will said, giving Conlan an angry glance.

"I needed to be in the real world for a while, needed to have some fun," Amelia countered, glaring from Will to Conlan and back again. "Eleanor gave me that fun, and now this stupidity has totally ruined my good mood. I don't suppose it has done much for Eleanor either."

"Are we prisoners?" Eleanor asked softly. Conlan shook his head, taking a step away from her. Eleanor glared at him as she continued in the same soft voice. "Then we can come and go as we please. We told Freddie where we were going, if we had not come back in a reasonable length of time, I would expect you to come and find us. Otherwise, I would hope you would trust your training enough to know we can handle most things." There was a long silence. Conlan turned and walked off into the right-hand side bedroom. Once he had left the room the mood seemed to lift. Eleanor stared at the floor, feeling uncomfortable, angry and humiliated.

"So, did you have a good time?" Freddie asked, coming to sit on one of the comfy chairs. Amelia nodded.

"We had fun; Eleanor bought you a present."

Eleanor raised her head in time to see Freddie's eyes light up. She stared at the doors Conlan had just walked through. Seeing her dazed, hurt look,

Amelia took the sword out of her numb fingers and gently eased the bag off her shoulder before sitting with Freddie and Will, giving Eleanor some time to process her thoughts.

Her head hurt, but her heart hurt more. *Why is he so quick to strike at me?* Moving over to Amelia's chair, not taking her eyes off the bedroom door, Eleanor held out her hand, an unspoken request. She felt the book she had bought Conlan placed in it, and not looking at the others, she walked into the bedroom. Conlan sat against the wall. His face held its normal emotionless expression as he stared at nothing. He looked up at her as she walked towards him and held the neatly wrapped book out to him.

"I bought you a present, and to answer your question, Remic gave me the money."

"You want to give me a gift?" He sounded confused.

Eleanor glared. "You're an arse with temper issues, and I'd appreciate it if you kept your hands off me in future." Her gaze softened. "However, I did disappear for several hours with Amelia and then didn't take your concern very seriously. I know I push you too far on occasion."

"I regret my actions," he said in Dwarfish, a soft apologetic snarl rumbling through him, his eyes not leaving the floor.

"Do you really regret your actions?" Eleanor asked in Dwarfish, layering supreme irritation through the question. "Because I had to come and find you for an apology. If you are sorry then fine, I forgive you, so stop sulking, get up and join us."

"Eleanor, I promise I will never lash out at you again."

"Do *not* make promises to me you cannot keep."

Pained green eyes stared at her. "You assume that I am going to hurt you in the future?"

Eleanor shrugged. "Based on past experience, what conclusion would you reach?"

His eyes burned with shame. "I promise, Eleanor, never again."

Eleanor stared at him in silence. *This is a promise he won't be able to keep. I wonder if it's going to hurt him or me more when he breaks it?* He gazed back, waiting anxiously for her reply.

"I suppose never doing it again is the best apology."

She held the book towards him again; he reached for it and noticed her bruised, scraped knuckles as he did.

"You have been fighting."

It was a statement, his voice calm; Eleanor wondered how much effort it had taken to keep it calm.

"Yes, I have. I am not going to talk about it," she said in flat monotone, looking into his eyes and daring him to object. "I am fine, just a bruised hand..." *to match my bruised head.*

"Then we do not need to talk about it any further," he agreed. She could see him forcing down his curiosity and irritation. *He's trying.* Eleanor found herself smiling at him. He stood up and followed her back into the living room. Freddie was moving backwards and forwards swinging his new sword, his face full of childlike glee. There was a knock on the door, and Will went to answer it. Two women entered, struggling under the weight of the trays full of food they were carrying. They lay the food out on the long, low table in the centre of the living room. Eleanor heard her stomach rumble. Conlan heard it too.

"I ordered bread and cheese for you."

He can be thoughtful – when he wants to be.

"I love cheese," she said softly. He smiled at her and she felt all her remaining resentment draining away. They sat and ate, Amelia full of bubbly excitement about what they had seen. Eleanor ate far too much cheese, and it was beginning to make her feel uncomfortably full before she finally forced herself to stop.

After dinner, Amelia took Eleanor to the inn's bathrooms, where tubs of steaming water stood waiting. Eleanor enjoyed washing the travelling off her body, allowing the hot water to relax her. She dressed in a clean short-sleeved top and strapped on her new leather cuff; it covered her wrist and went halfway up her forearm. She inspected it carefully, satisfied that it covered her brand totally. Conlan had noticed the cuff on their return to the room. It was hard to miss, but he said nothing.

At Freddie's request Conlan showed them how to play cards with Will's new deck; the game he taught them was a little like whist. After Freddie won six games in a row, Eleanor and Amelia started cheating, sniggering at Freddie's distress when he lost, doing their best to look innocent as he had accused them of underhand dealing. Several games later Will called a halt by sweeping Amelia up into his arms and, without a word, carrying her into a bedroom, closing the doors firmly behind him as Amelia giggled. Eleanor caught Freddie's look – he gave her a mischievous smirk and she rolled her eyes. Conlan offered Eleanor the other double bed, but she refused to take it, pointing out that she was small enough to sleep comfortably on one of the sofas and his six-foot-odd frame needed more space. Freddie agreed. As Conlan disappeared into the other bedroom, Freddie dropped a few cushions and a blanket onto the floor, next to the sofa where Eleanor was stretched out on, and lay down. She leaned over the sofa's edge.

"Night, Freddie," she whispered.

"Thank you for the sword, Eleanor."

She smiled. "You should thank Remic, he paid for it."

"Yes, but you bought it and you didn't have to. I love it."

"Good, may you win all your battles with it," she intoned solemnly.

Freddie nodded. "I hope so."

Eleanor smiled and lay back, sinking into the plush, comfortable cushions and thinking about the Elves, she dropped into sleep.

Eleanor's dreams were filled with blood, death and mayhem. She woke in the early hours, unable to go back to sleep. She lay still, concentrating on calming her mind and steeling herself to face another day of pretending she was happy and excited about going after the next Talisman. Will had moved silently past her several hours later, unaware that she was awake, and was now having a whispered conversation with Conlan.

"Maybe I should stay here... I think Trey would react rather badly to meeting me again," Will said quietly.

"No, I need you there. Besides, it was a long time ago Will, I am sure he will have forgotten you by now," Conlan said with a reassuring growl.

"I very much doubt it," Will murmured.

"Even if he does remember you, it is not as if you were not justified in giving him a beating. He attacked us," Conlan said, moving to pack up his things and clearly considering the conversation over and done with.

Eleanor sat up and Will quickly hid the guilt and concern on his face. He smiled at her, before moving back towards his bedroom to wake Amelia. Eleanor shuddered as Will's memories of Trey broke free of the place she had shoved them and tore through her mind. It took a supreme effort to force them back. *Will's right, there is no way Trey has forgotten him!* Should she try to help Will, or would that just make him uncomfortable when he realised just how much of him was held in her head? Conlan had been dismissive of Will's concern, but he clearly did not know the full story; it would be hard to change his mind and she doubted Trey would try anything with them all there. Deciding to let the matter drop, as Will seemed to have done, she leant over the sofa she was laying on and gently shook Freddie awake.

They packed little, as Will had arranged for the inn to store the rest of their luggage until they came back. Eleanor took only her satchel, the 'Book of the Five', her sword and her blanket. She tried to leave the blanket, but Conlan insisted she needed it. Too tired to argue, Eleanor nodded, slipping the blanket roll over her shoulder. Conlan seemed surprised it had been that easy.

They headed towards the main gate, and despite the early hour, Eleanor could feel the heat in the sun's first rays; she was not looking forward to the desert. The streets were quiet – a few early traders were setting up stalls, but there was nowhere near the throng it had been the day before. Will walked up to Conlan's side and Amelia put a hand out on Freddie and Eleanor's arms to hold them back a little. Eleanor looked at her in confusion, the expression duplicated on Freddie's face.

"Will wants to talk to Conlan," she said, as if this was explanation enough.

"About what?" Freddie asked, watching the two men walking together further down the street.

"Eleanor," Amelia said, her gaze following Freddie's.

Eleanor stared at Amelia in horror; Will knew too much – what was he saying? Amelia patted her arm gently, her grey eyes giving her a soft sympathetic look.

"Will wants him to stop attacking you; he's warning Conlan that he'll intervene if he tries to hurt you again," Amelia said by way of explanation. Eleanor felt buried under the emotions that dropped on her suddenly: gratitude, affection, anger, frustration and pity. Amelia watched all this in Eleanor's face in confusion. *I really must make more of an effort to stop everything I think and feel showing on my face!*

"It's sweet of Will to try to defend me, but I don't need it, I can fight my own battles where Conlan is concerned. He's already promised not to hurt me again; Will threatening him on my behalf is just going to upset him," she said.

"Eleanor, have you heard yourself? He slammed your head into a door and you're worried about Will upsetting him?" Freddie said incredulously.

Eleanor glared at him. "He apologised, I forgave him, matter closed."

"He apologised?" Amelia asked, giving Eleanor a hard look. *She doesn't believe me.*

"He apologised," she snapped, getting angrier by the second. She pulled away from them and marched down the road toward where Will and Conlan stood. They had noticed her approach before she realised that she had no idea what she was going to say.

"Did you want something, Eleanor?" Will asked.

"What did you say?" she demanded bluntly.

"This is a private conversation between Conlan and I," he replied, glancing down the street to where Amelia and Freddie stood.

Eleanor snorted. "According to Amelia I'm the topic of this conversation."

"Amelia should have kept that information to herself."

"Will, much as I appreciate the gesture, I really don't need protecting. Conlan promised not to hurt me again, end of story." She tried to keep her voice as calm as his, but it was a struggle. Will gave her a long, appraising look.

"Do you trust him to keep that promise?" he asked evenly. Eleanor stared at him in horrified silence. He knew her too well. *I can't lie to him...*

"No," she whispered honestly, giving Conlan an apologetic glance; he looked crushed.

"No, neither do I," Will agreed. "Hence the need for the conversation we just had."

Conlan turned and walked away, his long legs carrying him further down the street, and then he was running, disappearing out of sight down an alleyway that led to the gate.

"That was cruel, Will. I don't want to lie to you, but you're making it very difficult for me!" Eleanor said quietly, turning back to the cold blue eyes that regarded her.

Will sighed. "He needs to learn a little impulse control where you're concerned, and you need to understand that just because you love the man doesn't mean you have to put up with his temper tantrums and frustrations. I know how emotionally messed up he is, but this has got to stop before he takes it too far and accidentally causes you real damage."

Eleanor felt her anger turn to a frigid ball of fury. "Will, mind your own business. I'm not your child. If I want to let Conlan beat me black and blue, that's my right. I know you meant well, but you're making it worse. I want him to open up to me, and this is just going to make him retreat," she said, her voice flat and hard. The depth of the hurt in Will's eyes took her by surprise; she looked at him, bemused by his reaction.

"What did I say?" she asked, slowly running through her words, looking for the problem.

He smiled slightly. "Nothing."

"Oh no, if I can't lie to you, you don't get to lie to me," she said, glaring at him.

He dropped his head. "You just made me realise how much I do think of you as my child. I'm sorry, Eleanor, I just wanted to help."

"Oh... " *Guess it's not just Amelia who wanted children.* "I know you wanted to help, and I'm grateful, truly, but I would appreciate it if, in future, you ran this sort of help by me first to see if I want or need it," she said as gently as she could. Will nodded again and tried to smile at her.

"I take it that didn't go so well?" Amelia asked as she and Freddie came to join them.

"No, not so well... I need to go and talk to him," Eleanor replied, looking back at the alley Conlan had run down.

"He'll have headed for the gate, we can meet him there," Will said, turning to walk down the street. Catching him up, Amelia slipping her hand into his, from the way she kept looking up at him, Eleanor knew they were talking in each other's heads. She followed behind, Freddie walking at her side and giving her concerned glances she did her best to ignore.

Conlan sat on the low wall that led up to the gate. His shoulders were slumped and he stared at the ground as if he were trying to burn a hole through it. Will and Amelia walked by him, out past the guards and down the road a little. Freddie gave Eleanor an odd look, before following them. Feeling sick, hurting for him, Eleanor walked over to stand in front of the angry, miserable man. He knew she was stood there, she had seen his body tense. She ran her fingers lightly down the side of his face, feeling the indentation of his scar. He shivered. *What's he afraid of?* She slipped her hand under his chin, raising his head until she could look into his eyes and felt a stab of pain at the torment she found.

"I am sorry I do not believe you," she said in Dwarfish, conscious of the guards stood nearby. Conlan pulled his head back angrily, away from her hand.

"Stop apologising, Eleanor. Stop being so forgiving; you should be angry, hit me back, hate me!"

"I am what I am, Conlan. I do not like you hurting me, but I do not think bashing my head into a door really qualifies me to hate you," she said calmly. She would use Will's trick – the louder Conlan got, the quieter and milder she was going to get.

"So what would qualify it? Broken bones? Me killing you?" His loud, angry voice was reaching the guards, who were now watching with sniggering interest.

"Death might do it, but I doubt it somehow," Eleanor said softly, unable to keep the amused smile off her face.

"You think this is funny?" he snarled at her.

"Hysterical," she replied flatly.

She reached to touch his face again and he jerked back.

"Do not touch me, Eleanor."

She pulled her hand back, hurt. She had wanted to make him feel better, wanted him to understand that she did not hold his actions against him, but he was too angry with himself to accept the comfort she was offering.

"I do not hate you. You are already doing such a fine job of it, I cannot compete," she whispered. When he remained silent, she continued. "Conlan, your responses to me have been unpleasantly violent since we left the Dwarves – did I do something you did not like? Please, tell me."

Conlan took a slow deep breath, dropping his gaze. "I know you are unhappy, Eleanor," he began. "You might be able to hide it from the others, but I see the look you get sometimes, like you want to be somewhere else – like being with us is painful." Surprised by his perception, Eleanor stared at him as he kept talking. Now he had started, he seemed to have something he wanted to say, something he was pushing himself to say. "You love him, miss him. I know you do. I took you away from him, from the possibility of a safe, comfortable life, and it has made you miserable. It is making me... irrational and I am taking it out on you."

"Conlan, I have no idea what you are talking about. Miss him? Who?" Eleanor asked nonplussed.

"Remic," he muttered miserably.

"Conlan, I did not fall in love with Remic, or any other Dwarf for that matter."

A strange, almost relieved look crossed his face for a moment, before suspicion took its place. "If that is not the reason, why are you unhappy?" he asked.

"I have my reasons. I assume you realise your behaviour is not likely to improve my mood?" Eleanor said softly.

Conlan's body seemed to tighten up even further. "Eleanor, you keep pushing me to tell you how I am feeling, to tell you what I am thinking. I might be more inclined to do this if *you* opened up to *me*."

She sighed. "I am convinced that the Talismans have nothing to do with the connection. I just feel that we could have all five of them and it would still not work. I believe we are wasting time when in fact we should be trying to get rid of your shield."

"Do you know how to get rid of my shield?" Conlan asked.

"No."

"Do you think sitting around thinking about it is going to help you?"

"No, probably not," she conceded.

"Then what is the problem with us looking for the Talismans while we work it out? More importantly, what is the problem with you sharing this with the rest of us? Are you really so arrogant that you believe you are the only one who can fix our problems?" he spat, deep irritation giving his voice a steel edge.

Hurt, Eleanor stared at him. *Why didn't I share this? Is he right?*

She felt tears spring into her eyes, blurring her vision as she walked away through the gate towards where Will, Amelia and Freddie stood watching them, although Will appeared to be paying more attention to the guards.

Freddie gave her a sympathetic smile.

"Are you OK?"

She nodded, not trusting herself to speak, brushing her tears away angrily. Conlan walked up behind them, his face showing its normal, emotionless expression.

"Come on, we're wasting time."

For several hours they walked in silence along the main track from Drent, until Conlan took a side road that Eleanor would have missed, it was so overgrown. From what she had seen, Eleanor would not have called any of the 'roads' in Mydren 'good', but the track they were now walking along was so cracked and pitted it was barely a road. She understood why Conlan had not brought Rand; however, the track was still easier to walk on than the sand that was now in evidence on either side. Some of it had blown in small dunes across their path, and the further they walked, the more sand they encountered. *Follow the Yellow Brick Road*, Eleanor thought, a strong, dark sense of dread flowing through her and making the overly bright day dimmer.

I hate the desert!

Her feet sank deep into the sand with each step, making the simple act of walking an effort. The sand was everywhere, and she could feel it rub and chaff in her boots and other places she was trying not to think about. The dry heat battered at her, desiccating her skin and cracking her lips. She had taken Amelia's advice, as the others had, and brought a shirt to wrap round her head, neck and face, but she was convinced she could feel sunburn tightening her skin, burning her through the thin fabric. She knew she was losing more water in sweat than she was gaining in the small, rationed sips from the water skins Will and Conlan were carrying. The sun's glare off the sand hurt her eyes, and the lack of any sort of smell or sound other than the ones they brought with them made Eleanor nervous and strained her senses. As the sun reached the middle of its daily journey, burning down on them mercilessly, Conlan stopped so they could rest; there was no shade to be had, so they dropped where they stood.

"Water?" Will asked her, nudging her with his foot. She opened her eyes, amused by the 'Lawrence of Arabia' look he had going with one of Amelia's scarves wrapped round his head. His shadow was covering her face as he leaned over and looked down at her. She did want to drink, but the tiny sips she was allowed did nothing other than torment her.

"Not right now, but could you just stand there and block the sun for a few hours?" she asked, her voice grating roughly in her throat. He smiled weakly at her and she noticed just how exhausted he looked. *No water in the desert.* His physical exhaustion would be draining his energy, and there was no way for him to replenish it. Reaching out an energy string she felt his drop in vitality and automatically pulled enough from the earth to restore him to his normal level. He cringed slightly, but nodded his head in thanks and flopped onto the sand next to Amelia. Conlan and Freddie had moved up to the next dune, both of them staring out at the nothing before them. Hauling her tired body back up, Eleanor walked up the sand dune to stand next to them.

"So what's the plan?" Freddie asked Conlan.

"Plan?" Conlan echoed, not looking at him.

"I was kind of hoping we had a plan."

Conlan looked at him. "We walk for a while, and we'll eventually meet an Elf patrol; they'll take us to the Elves' camp."

"That's not a plan, Conlan," Freddie said, anger creeping into his voice. "That's surrender!"

Conlan's entire body stiffened. "It worked with the Dwarves," he said, giving each word a razor sharp edge.

Frustrated, Freddie glared at him. "Chapter two, in the book you gave

Eleanor, 'Know Your Enemy' – what do we know about the Elves?"

Conlan did not reply, just stared at him. Eleanor answered the question.

"From what we know about them, they are sly, devious, untrustworthy and vicious. They have made Drent an unviable option for the Lords of Mydren, so they can fight. They live in the desert, which makes them tough and resourceful, and they don't appear to do anything unless there is something in it for them."

Freddie nodded. "Does *any* of that strike you as a race of people who are going to hand over the wand to a pathetic bunch of losers who got themselves caught? That's assuming we get as far as asking for the wand and they don't just try to kill us the minute they catch us."

"What do you suggest?" Conlan asked with a tone as emotionless as his face.

Freddie looked thoughtful. "We must appear to be strong and in control – we're not asking for the wand, we're demanding it; with violence, if necessary."

"We should avoid the patrols and just march straight into the camp," Eleanor said. Conlan spun round so quickly to glare at her that Freddie's whole body tensed.

"I have no idea where the Elf camp is," Conlan snapped. "It's a camp, it moves. You want to march into it, you find it!"

"Could you do that, Eleanor?" Freddie asked.

"I don't know, this is an immense space to look in. I only found the Dwarves by accident. I guess Conlan's right, we need to find a patrol."

"OK, we need a patrol, but how about we capture them, not the other way around. Force them to take us to the camp?" Freddie suggested.

Conlan shook his head. "They know the desert, we don't. They use magic to shield themselves, so we couldn't sneak up on them, even if we could find them."

"Chapter eight," Eleanor answered, grinning at them as an idea occurred to her.

"'Know how to take and hold the advantage'," Freddie recited from memory.

Eleanor nodded. "I have an idea," she said, heading back down the dune. "Come on, we need to discuss this with Will and Amelia. I think there needs to be a vote."

Eleanor forced her legs to keep moving. The heat was making her feel dizzy and sick. *How much longer before the stupid Elves find us?* Had it not been for the fact that he was in a worse state then she was, she would have complained bitterly to Will as he trudged beside her. She could feel his energy levels were in free-fall and knew he was suffering. Amelia had been topping up his energy, but it was not enough. Eleanor had resorted to sending him a constant, steady flow of energy, just to keep him conscious and moving. *Next time there's a great plan, someone else can be bait!* She and Will had been chosen because Conlan had argued that they were going to look the weakest to the Elves, thus making them overconfident.

"Will, when are the Elves going to get here?" she asked, mostly because the silence was becoming unsettling.

He smiled, glancing at her. "Eleanor, the Elves have been tracking us for over an hour." Eleanor looked about her, squinting against the glare and seeing nothing but sand, sky and heat as it shimmered on the horizon.

"Where?"

"Don't waste time looking, they are using magic to hide themselves, but if you concentrate you'll feel it," Will said quietly. Eleanor kept walking but closed her eyes. *It's not as if I'm going to walk into anything.* Slowly, so she did not miss anything, she pushed her energy strings out into the desert. At first there was nothing, but then she felt a faint pulse to the left of them, moving parallel to their position. Concentrating, without touching the shield they had erected, Eleanor felt for the life it covered.

"There are four of them, out to our left."

"Not quite, there are four adults and a child," Will corrected. Eleanor reached out over the shield. Will was right. She realised she had missed it because the child was using energy; it was a boy, she was sure of it, and his energy was blending with the shield he was creating.

"I can feel the boy; he's the one creating the shield… It must be exhausting for a child."

"I was once told that Elf children often have far more magical talent than their elders. They seem to lose it as they grow older and it corrupts them," Will said.

"If they are following us, why haven't they attacked?"

"A foolish question, Eleanor! Why attack now and risk a confrontation when they can wait until we are too tired to fight back and capture us without risk?" Will said, mimicking the tone she used to lecture Conlan.

"I really am annoying, aren't I?" she muttered.

Will nodded. "Oh yes."

"I'm too tired to fight them now," she said, feeling the ache in her legs and back from walking through sand.

"Not by their standards – you're still standing."

"I can lie down if it speeds this process up," she offered.

Will chuckled but carried on moving. Eleanor walked after him, trying to ignore the sand, the sunburn, the throbbing headache and her dry mouth.

As the sun began to set, Will finally gave up. Trying to walk down a dune, his legs gave out and he rolled down, landing on his back at the bottom. Eleanor loped after him, sinking alarmingly in the deep sand. He was staring at the darkening sky above, watching the stars appear. Eleanor knelt at his side.

"Are you OK?" she asked.

"I hate the desert," he grumbled, closing his eyes.

Eleanor giggled. "Me too. Can you get up?"

"Nope. If the Elves don't show up, I'm here for the night."

Eleanor gasped as she felt warm, sharp metal come to rest against the side of her neck. Will's eyes snapped open. Four cloaked and hooded figures, faces in shadow, had come from nowhere to stand around them.

"Hello there," Will said, as conversationally as Dwarfish would allow. Eleanor felt her skin split, blood seeping thinly as the blade was pushed harder into her neck; she winced.

"Shut up, on your feet," one of the hooded figures ordered, the snarling undertone adding a nasty layer of threat. Eleanor felt no desire to resist their captors; she could feel the air of malevolence that hung around them. She saw the anger in Will's eyes too, but he rose stiffly to his feet. The blade at her neck not moving, Eleanor felt dry fingers grasp a handful of hair, dragging her up.

"Are you OK?" Will asked her quietly in English. One of the hooded figures punched him in the face. Will's head shot back and he collapsed, dazed, onto his back in the sand. Eleanor struggled, wanting to help him. Without warning the Elf with a blade at her neck moved the injury up from a minor scratch to a wound that was going to need stitches. Eleanor clamped her teeth together over the sobbing cry as her eyes filled with tears. She was shocked by the amount of blood she felt running down her neck, soaking her shirt.

"Shut up," ordered the same flat, vicious voice. "Or this one is going to lose her head."

Will nodded, struggling back to his feet. He stood passively, blood from his split, swelling lip dribbling down his chin. A hooded figure disarmed them both and roughly tied Will's hands behind his back. As Will was restrained, a small figure stepped out from behind two of the tall hooded Elves. Eleanor stared at him; she had never seen anything quite so beautiful. His face was angelic, although avenging angel would have better described his current expression. He was her height and had thick, black hair falling across a forehead that held a frown too old for his years. He stared at her with black, knowing eyes, lips pressed into a thin, distrusting line. Eleanor was a little disappointed to note the lack of the pointy Elf ears she had expected.

"They do not look much of a threat, Father," the boy observed quietly.

"Looks can be deceiving," said the hooded figure holding the blade to Eleanor's neck.

"Indeed they can."

Conlan.

Eleanor felt her heart leap in relief as his deep, snarling comment came out of nowhere. Confused, the Elves looked around; Amelia dropped her shield, revealing the three of them, swords drawn. Eleanor saw the pride on Will's face. They wasted not a second of advantage that surprise had given them and leapt at the hooded figures, beating them to the ground before they had the chance to draw their own weapons. Conlan reached the boy, dragging him in front of him and jamming his blade's edge into his throat, turning to face Eleanor and the Elf with the sword at her neck. Eleanor was impressed with the calm expression on the boy's face – he did not even flinch.

"I have no wish to take your lives, but I will if you force me. Let her go and drop your weapon," Conlan growled.

There was silence. Eleanor felt the blade removed, increasing the flow of blood. She resisted the urge to push a hand against it; hands covered with blood were going to get sand coated to them, and it was all too messy to think about. The Elf stepped out from behind her, throwing his sword to the ground at Conlan's feet. His hood had fallen back and Eleanor gasped at the tall Elf's face. It was like he was made of wax and had stood too close to a fire. The right side of his face was pulled down in heavy, sagging folds from his forehead, until it stretched the right corner of his mouth into a look of perpetual misery, the yellow, sickly-looking skin contrasting sharply with his black hair. His right eye was a milky white that clashed with the blazing black of his left. If the Elf noticed Eleanor's appraisal of him, he gave no indication, his gaze fixed on Conlan. Freddie and Amelia had subdued the other three Elves, tying their hands behind their backs with their own ropes and leaving them face down in the sand. Amelia released Will, handing him a water skin.

"Take your sword from my son's throat," the Elf said slowly.

"What is your name?" Conlan asked. The Elf glared at him, and Conlan pushed his blade a little deeper; strangely, he had still not drawn blood. Looking closer, Eleanor realised that Conlan had the blunt edge of his weapon pressed into the boy's neck.

"Adra."

"Adra, you are going to take us to your camp," Conlan ordered. The Elf did not reply, but a nasty, twisted smile spread across the working side of his face as he raised his eyebrow at his son. The boy nodded once and closed his eyes. Softly at first, like the breath of the dying, the breeze brushed against Eleanor's face, then it began to pick up speed. Recognising what the boy was doing, Amelia caught her eye.

"Stop him!" Eleanor ordered sharply over the rapidly worsening sandstorm in which they now stood.

Amelia closed her eyes. Nothing happened. Eleanor felt the wind push against her, the sand coating the wound at her neck, stinging her skin and forcing her to close her eyes. As she did so, she felt the child's energy. Reaching out, she could sense the shield around him. It was different from other shields she had encountered, as it was thinner, almost non-existent. She still could not push through it, but he clearly had no problem pushing his own energy out. Eleanor could feel energy strings pulsating; he appeared to be using one to take energy from the air as he used another to whip the wind around them. Eleanor watched as Amelia grabbed the energy string he was using to stir up the air and pulled it down. The boy resisted, struggling in Amelia's grip. Wanting to help, Eleanor grabbed at his other string and concentrated on drawing energy out. She was careful, as she was much stronger than the boy and instinctively knew that pulling all of his energy would kill him. With Eleanor sapping his energy and Amelia gripping his other energy string, the boy was soon exhausted. The wind stopped so suddenly that Eleanor was able to watch the sand it had whipped up fall back to the ground, like gritty rain, as she opened her eyes. The boy looked pale; he swayed slightly, his eyes rolling back in his head as he slumped forward. Conlan caught him, an arm round his waist, before he hit the sand.

"Dal!" Adra cried in horror, rushing at Conlan, ignoring the danger. Conlan, still holding the unconscious boy, twisted towards him, his sword pointing at the unarmed Elf. Common sense prevailed and Adra came to a halt, the sword tip inches from his distorted face.

"What have you done to my son?" he snarled. "If you have harmed him, I will kill you."

"Your son will be fine," Conlan assured him.

"How?" Suspicion and disbelief plain in the Elf's voice.

"Ask the Avatars," Conlan said, nodding towards Amelia and Eleanor.

Adra turned round, looking at each of them in turn.

"Avatars? All four of them?" He looked shocked as Conlan nodded, then sudden understanding smeared his face into a sneer. "I know of you, Conlan Baydon. You were told not to return."

"I am not very good at doing what I am told," Conlan said mildly.

The sky was a cloudless backdrop of diamonds and the moon shone down coldly, the silvery glow giving the desert an eerie feel. Eleanor felt exposed, vulnerable. They had been walking for so long that Eleanor was beginning to wonder if Adra was leading them deeper into the desert so that they would all die when the sun rose the next morning. It was only the careful, loving way he cradled his son against him as he stumbled along that gave her hope that he would not risk the boy's life in that way. Conlan walked beside him, his sword sheathed at his side. The other three Elves, their hands still tied, walked behind under Freddie and Amelia's vigilant gazes. Their hoods had fallen back, revealing more melted, disfigured faces; Eleanor wondered why they practiced magic and why in particular they made their children practice it, if this is what it did to them. Next to her, Will staggered again. He was exhausted and there was only so long that the energy she and Amelia were giving him would keep him going. If they did not get to the camp soon, they were going to have to carry him. She stopped him for a moment and took the water skin, bag and blanket he was carrying off him, shouldering the load herself. He smiled gratefully. Eleanor gave Conlan a bitter glance, wishing he took her help as easily. Will saw her look, or maybe just sensed her hostility, and she felt his energy brush against her.

What's he done now? he asked with tired exasperation.

It was too complicated to explain, so Eleanor just showed him the pertinent memories and all the thoughts that went with them. She showed him the memory of their earlier argument, even though that was still hurting her.

I'd say there was such a thing as over-sharing, but I'm not sure that applies to us anymore. He sounded amused.

So what am I doing wrong? Eleanor asked.

You're not doing anything wrong, exactly, you're just being you. He has some rather big emotional issues. If you're ever able to get him really drunk, ask him about his childhood, after his mother died, when he went to live with his father.

Why?

Because by our standards his childhood was hell — a constant, unrelenting barrage of physical, mental and emotional abuse as his father tried to replicate himself in his son.

Conlan did his best to resist, using the only weapon he had; defiance. He retreated into himself, learnt not to show emotions that could be used against him. It made him feel stronger, but just because he doesn't show his emotions often, doesn't mean he doesn't have them. It just means he has no idea how to deal with them, so he lashes out. Eleanor, all you are seeing is the hurt you're causing him, but what you don't see is how much you've changed him. He's smiled and laughed more since you turned up than in the whole time I've known him. You've forced him to engage with all of us on an emotional level, and this can only be a good thing. Don't give up trying, Eleanor. You got him singing, everything else should be child's play after that!

Eleanor giggled. The sound was loud, out of place. Amelia and Freddie turned to look at her. She could not see their expressions in the dark, so she just shrugged at them and they turned back. Conlan had ignored her, but even from the back of their little convoy she had seen his body stiffen. *I SO have my work cut out for me!*

Thank you, Will, Avatar of Water, living Prozac pill and Mydren's greatest agony aunt!

Eleanor jumped at the explosion of laughter in her head, impressed that Will had managed to clamp his hand over his mouth quickly enough that all the noises that escaped from him were a few muffled snorts.

They came to the top of the dune they were walking up, and Eleanor would have leapt for joy if she had not been struggling under Will's weight in an attempt to drag him up sand that was trying to suck them both back down. In the distance she could see the inviting, flickering orange of campfires. She nudged Will, nodding towards what she hoped was the Elves' camp. She was actually amazed that Adra knew how to find it in the featureless world they had been walking through; she had assumed he used the stars to navigate. *I wonder if we're going to get to be friends. Maybe then I can ask him.* The boy, Dal, had regained consciousness a short while previously and now walked silently next to his father. He had given her one brief glance, but she had been too far away and it had been too dark to see the look on his face. As they got closer, sentries posted on the camp's perimeter spotted them and moved to intercept. Conlan carefully positioned the boy in front of him, hands on his shoulders, but kept his sword sheathed. Freddie had tied Adra's hands behind his back when he had tried to protect his son. Eleanor felt sorry for Adra, Dal looked so small and vulnerable against Conlan's tall, muscular silhouette. She knew Conlan did not want to hurt the boy, but Adra clearly thought the worst.

The sentries were yelling into the camp. By the time their group walked between the dark shadows of the first tents, they were surrounded. Eleanor's hyperactive brain, much against her wishes, began calculating the very large probability of their whole plan being a bloody failure. Eleanor looked at the faces around her; many of them had features that had slipped, just like Adra's, while some carried deep scars that rivalled Conlan's in their severity. Some of the crowd had weapons drawn and eyed them suspiciously, but

most just seemed openly curious. As they were hoping to convince the Elves
that they were a power to be reckoned with, Will had forced himself to stand
tall as they walked, doing his best to hide his exhaustion, but Eleanor knew
that if it came to a fight he would have no hope, so she stayed by his side at
the back of their group as they moved deeper in the camp. Led by Conlan,
they moved further and further forward. He seemed to be making for a large
fire she could see in the distance. The crowd parted slightly to reveal twelve
cloaked figures sat in a circle near the blazing bonfire. All twelve turned to
look at Conlan. One of the figures stood. The voice sounded female, but
Eleanor would not have known from looking at the distorted face.

"Conlan Baydon, you have disobeyed our order not to return, and you
have compounded this crime further by threatening a child – what do you
hope to gain from this?"

"The wand," Conlan said simply.

"Kill them!" the female Elf ordered. Eleanor pulled her sword from the
scabbard that hung at her waist as she heard hundreds of Elves do the same
thing. Fear shot through her. She faced it for an instant, faced the possibility
of her death, and raised her sword for battle, moving closer to Will.

"No, stop!"

It was a high child's voice, but no less commanding because of it. Conlan
had stepped away from Dal to loosen his sword, and it was the boy who had
spoken. He took a few steps forward towards the twelve Elves that now all
stood staring at him.

"Do not provoke them, they are Avatars. I have felt their power, and we
would not survive a battle with them," the child said with authority.
Everybody froze.

"Is this true, have you succeeded, Conlan Baydon?" the female Elf asked.

"Yes," Conlan confirmed, not taking his eyes off the crowd.

"Then this changes things. We might be willing to trade for the wand."

Conlan flicked his eyes to the Elf in surprise. "The wand belongs to the
Avatar of Air by right; you were given it to protect it, nothing more. As you
have heard, you would not win a battle with us and we will take the wand by
force, if we must. Besides, trade would be difficult, as I am quite certain that
I have nothing you would want."

The Elf stared at Conlan. Seeming to consider this point, she turned back
to the other Elves and then huddled together, muttering.

"YOU!"

The Dwarfish word, full of dark hatred and fury, battered against them.
Eleanor instinctively turned to face the direction it had come from, stepping

in front of Will to do so. She was just in time to see the massive, charging Elf as it flattened her, throwing itself into Will. She made a jarring impact with the ground, a foot stomping on the wrist of her sword arm as the Elf stormed over the top of her. She felt bones chip and crack, a numbness spreading through her arm, but she was too worried about Will to pay it any attention. The enormous Elf knocked him to the ground and crouched over him, pounding him repeatedly in the body and head. Will was in no condition to defend against the juggernaut's savage, frenzied attack. She could see Freddie and Conlan struggling towards them through the surrounding crowd of Elves. Amelia was closer, but she just stared, wide-eyed. Getting to her feet, Eleanor dropped her sword; her right hand was too numb to hold it. Left-handedly she punched at the big Elf's head, but it did little more than distract him as his gigantic fist thrust up into her abdomen, the brute force of it shuddering right through her body, lifting her off her feet and dropping her at Will's side. Will was no longer conscious. Gasping, her vision blurring, Eleanor pulled herself forward, using her body to cover Will's head, neck and chest. She took several punishing blows before the Elf seemed to notice she was there. Eleanor felt a hand grasp round her neck, trying to pull her off, when all three of them were hit by what felt like a fast moving brick wall which sent them sailing through the air.

"Eleanor, are you OK?"

Eyes flickering open, she could just make out Conlan's blurry face. She shook her head. Twisting, leaning over the edge of the bed she was lying on, she retched; water, blood and yellow bile spewing forth onto the sand beneath her. She felt a gentle hand on her head, pulling her hair out of the way and moving down to rub her back. The pain it caused to vomit was intense, and she curled herself into a ball, groaning and grasping her sides. The pain gave no respite. She threw up again, voiding her stomach, and then passed out.

Thirst woke her up. Her throat felt raw, the bitter taste of stomach bile still in her mouth. She opened her eyes, trying to ignore the feeling that someone was attempting to get into her skull with a pneumatic drill. She was in a large, round, off-white tent. The material was thin enough to see daylight through. Her body felt hot and damp. The tent was supported with a central pole, giving a coned roof pulled out by ropes on the outside, creating straight walls of material from where the cone of the roof finished down to the sand. She was lying in a makeshift camp bed, no blanket, not that she would have wanted one, but there was a pillow. She turned her head to the side; the movement made her stomach flip queasily. On the other side of the tent was another makeshift bed. Will was laying in it, motionless, the cuts and bruises on his face vivid against his grey skin. Amelia was knelt at his side, holding his hand. Reaching a string out towards him, Eleanor felt his energy level and was relieved to find it normal. *Amelia or Freddie must be helping him.* Conlan and Freddie were sat at the back of the tent engaged in low conversation. At the end of Will's bed was a table. Eleanor could see a large jug of water sweating in the heat. At the sight of it her thirst wiped out all other thought. Moving slowly she swung her legs over the edge of the bed and tried to sit up, but unfortunately she unthinkingly pushed up with her right hand. What had been a dull throb became a screaming agony. She had not realised how much her leather cuff was supporting the broken bones and controlling the swelling until she had tried to move. She managed to stay sitting, but gasped, cradling her injured arm against her chest as tears slipped down her face. She tilted her head back, closing her eyes, willing the pain back down to a manageable level. Feeling the movement pull open the newly formed scab on her neck, making blood ooze thickly, she ignored it.

"Eleanor?" The soft growl gave her a measure of comfort.

"Yes…" Such a weak, pathetic squeak of a voice.

"Can I help?"

"Water?" she managed. The pain subsided slightly and she opened her eyes, tilting her head slowly forwards again as Conlan handed her a glass of water. She took it and gulped it down. It barely touched the sides, doing nothing to satisfy her burning thirst. She waved the empty glass at Conlan.

"More?"

She nodded, regretting the movement as her stomach tightened and the throbbing in her head took on a shrill whine. He picked the jug off the table and moved back to her. Before he could pour it she dropped the glass to the sand and held her hand out. The sick feeling in her stomach made her lean forward slightly, taking deep breaths as she fixed her gaze on the ground and tried to stop the world from lurching.

"All of it?" he asked.

She waved her hand at him impatiently. The handle of the jug was placed in her outstretched fingers. Taking it, she brought it to her lips and drank greedily, careful not to spill any. She was halfway through the jug before she felt the liquid begin to lubricate her throat. She kept going until the water was gone. Tipping her head back carefully to get the last drops, she noticed Conlan's amused expression as she did so.

"Better?" he asked.

She handed him the empty jug back and nodded, slower this time, looking back at Will. "What happened?" she asked, her voice sounding slightly stronger.

"Amelia stopped the fight," Conlan said.

"Why was there a fight in the first place?"

"Because Trey is holding a grudge," Conlan muttered. Several pieces of information tumbled through Eleanor's pained head.

"Trey? The one who tried to kill you, that Trey? That was the giant that attacked Will and flattened me?"

"Yes, that was Trey. How much damage did he cause you?"

"I think I have a broken wrist, bruises, a concussion and I've bitten the inside of my mouth," she said in flat monotone.

Conlan's jaw muscles clenched as she listed her injuries. "You should lay back and rest," he said.

"So, are they going to feed us to the Almighty Sarlacc?" Eleanor asked.

Freddie chuckled, but Conlan looked confused. "Almighty Sarlacc?"

Eleanor sighed. "Big monster, lots of teeth, slow digestion."

"Eleanor, are you quoting 'Star Wars'?" Will's voice was scratchy and thin, but he sounded amused. She smiled at him. One of his eyes was swollen closed and he looked a mess, but she could see the smile that tugged at his mouth.

"This place makes me think of Tatooine, and you always did remind me of Obe-Wan Kenobi."

Will laughed at this; it made him spasm in pain and cough furiously. Amelia gave her a look.

"I'll go ask for some more water," Conlan muttered, looking totally confused as he took the empty jug to the tent's opening. He lifted the flap and met with the tip of a sword that hovered threateningly in front of his eyes. He asked politely for more water, the jug was taken off him and he was shoved roughly back inside the tent.

Eleanor sighed. "Oh, the Almighty Sarlacc is going to be too good for us," she muttered morosely. Freddie sniggered and Eleanor ignored Amelia's accusing look as Will laughed himself into another coughing fit.

They were left to languish in the tent for hours. Conlan had asked the guards if they would open the tent's flaps to let the air in as the day wore on and the temperature rose further. His request had earned him nothing more than a sharp order to be silent. Will drifted in and out of consciousness and Eleanor lay back on her bed, trying not to think about her discomfort and general misery; in fact, trying not to think about anything. She could hear Freddie and Conlan's occasional whispered conversation, but she could not make out the words. She could hear Amelia's gentle, loving words as she comforted Will. What she could not hear was noise from outside the tent –

hundreds of Elves and not a sound reached her. This scared her.

The light in the tent began to fade. *Sunset.* Thankfully the temperature dropped, too. Eleanor jumped when the tent flaps were thrown open and four Elves strode in. One of them was Trey, his seething, baleful presence seeming to fill the tent. One of the guards brought in some lanterns, giving the tent a soft glow, but Trey's hulking form seemed to take the comfort out of the light.

"Sit, Conlan Baydon, and we will discuss this situation," said one of the newly arrived Elves, a man; his features did not seem to have slipped, but his cheek carried three deep scars, like an animal had scratched his face open.

"There is nothing to discuss, Johan, his life is mine!" Trey growled.

"Your presence here is a courtesy, Trey, not a necessity. If you are unable to be civil you will be removed."

Eleanor recognised the voice as a figure stepped towards Trey, the female who had spoken to them when they had arrived. Trey glared at the woman, but nodded. Watching the huge Elf warily, Conlan sat cross-legged on the sand.

"Let us talk," he said. The four Elves sat themselves in a circle, Trey sitting in front of Eleanor so he could stare at Will as Amelia helped him to sit on his bed. Eleanor was surprised to find that the fourth member of the Elfish party was Adra.

"I am Sarina," the female Elf said by way of introduction. "This is Johan, we speak for the Elf council. Trey has accused a member of your party of a crime. Adra stands as your advocate and advisor in matters of Elf law." Conlan's eyes widened in surprise as he looked at Adra, then narrowed in suspicion. Adra saw the look and sighed.

"You could have killed my son, my whole patrol, but you did not. I will give you honest advice." Conlan nodded, his gaze turning back to Sarina.

"Trey has accused whom of what?" he asked slowly.

"That abomination," Trey snarled, pointing a thick finger to where Will sat. "Took my daughter from me!" The accusation smothered them. Eleanor felt an energy string brush against her.

What did he say? Amelia asked. Eleanor could feel the effort it was taking her to keep calm, and without thinking she gave her an exact translation. Amelia gasped; pulling her energy free with a yank, eyes wide with horror. Will dropped his head in a move that screamed guilty. Conlan looked bewildered. From his point of view Will had been nowhere near Trey's daughter, yet Will's body language indicated he accepted the accusation.

Amelia's voice broke the silence: low, hurt, horrified, disbelieving.

"You killed his child?"

Will brought his eyes to hers; Eleanor could see the agony in them.

"Amelia... I..." he stuttered. He wanted to explain, but he seemed to lack the words. Amelia's disbelief turned to fury. She stood, propelling herself backwards away from him and stumbling. Freddie caught her, helping her up.

"Amelia, Will didn't kill Trey's daughter," Eleanor said.

"Then why is Trey accusing him of it?" Amelia snapped.

"He's not, he's accusing Will of destroying memories of a daughter who had already died, precious memories, memories Trey can't replace." Eleanor said. She did not want to sugar-coat the accusation, as she knew how much Will hated himself for what he had done to Trey, but she also did not want Amelia thinking he went around killing children.

"How do you know this?" Amelia asked. She still sounded hurt.

"Because when Earth attacked him, our minds merged. Occasionally some of Will's stronger memories and feelings break out of where I tried to contain them," Eleanor said. Amelia stared at her, then back at Will, but the look of horror and betrayal did not leave her face. The Elves watched with interest. They might not have understood the words, but the expressions and body language were giving more than enough hints as to what was going on.

"Why?" she demanded.

"Trey was trying to hurt Conlan, trying to kill him, I... reacted. I wasn't thinking straight," Will answered. Eleanor felt her heart squeeze for him. Amelia did not understand. Not 'thinking straight' was a major understatement. Eleanor had lived these memories, carried these memories and knew how much suffering they had caused. Will had been in Mydren for less than an hour. He had been dragged, painfully, from his drowning but still living body. His mind had been a mess; confused, terrified and in agony, he had focused on the only thing that made sense – haunted green eyes. Stephen's eyes. When Trey had attacked he had acted to protect his little brother, fought back, instinctively pushing into the Elf's mind and filling it with his own agony. He had not understood what he was doing or how he was doing it, but the pain he inflicted had been nothing to the pain he found, namely Trey's anguish and grief at the loss of his child. Will had found the memories of the happy, smiling little girl and had ripped them apart, wanting the pain to stop. Will was blaming himself, hating himself, for something that was not his fault.

"Amelia, Will..." Eleanor started, wanting to explain, but Amelia's eyes moved to hers and glared at her with such fury that she stopped speaking.

"Shut up, Eleanor!"

Stunned into silence, Eleanor stared at her.

It was Freddie who broke the silence. "How did Will get into Trey's head? I thought Elves had shields around their energy?"

"Trey doesn't have a shield," Will muttered without raising his head.

"Why not?" Eleanor asked.

"I have no idea, Eleanor, I never got the chance to ask him," Will said, his voice hard, flat and irritated. He raised his damaged face to hers, and she could see his anger. *What did I do?* She looked from Will's ice-cold blue stare to Amelia's furious, brittle, slate-grey eyes.

"OK, shutting up now," she murmured, sitting back heavily on her bed, her churning mind desperately trying to work out how she had managed to make both Will and Amelia mad at her. Amelia sat down with Freddie behind Conlan and continued to glare at Will. Silence followed.

"Are they finished? What were they arguing about?" Sarina asked Conlan.

"Trey's accusation," Conlan said mildly. Sarina raised an eyebrow at him, which made her distorted face look a little less damaged for a moment. She clearly felt there was more to the argument than that. Conlan stared calmly back at her but did not elaborate.

"Very well," Sarina said, sounding a little annoyed. "The accusation that Trey makes is a very serious one. There have been very few of our number with the ability to enter minds, and even then there are only a few minds they are able to enter. We have laws to prevent such intrusions, but no law covers what the Avatar did once he had entered Trey's mind. Destroying memories… this was a horrific abuse of power. This crime makes the Avatar a 'marked' man. He will be considered a criminal until he submits to the Elf council for judgement. We will not be handing the wand over to a criminal, even if you did have something to trade for it," Sarina said solemnly.

"So either we hand Will over for judgement or we leave empty-handed?" Conlan asked.

"*He* is not leaving here alive," Trey snarled. Will raised his head and looked at the Elf. Eleanor could see the resignation – he was not going to fight this, he knew he was guilty and he would give himself up for judgement, accepting whatever they said. He would give his life to atone for what he had done.

"What judgement does the council deliver?" Conlan asked calmly, ignoring Trey's outburst.

"This is a new problem for us, so we wish to know what Trey would consider a suitable punishment," Sarina said, looking at Trey.

"I want his head, you can keep the rest of him!" came the snarling reply.

"No," Conlan said without hesitation. "What Will did was wrong, but there are mitigating circumstances. He was a newly formed Avatar; he had no idea who he was, where he was or what he was capable of. He was frightened and confused. Trey tried to kill me and Will defended me. He made a mistake, but not one he should have to pay for with his life."

"Is this true, Trey? Did you attack this man?" Adra asked. Trey glared at Conlan, but he nodded.

"Then the Avatar's reaction is understandable, although his actions are still not justified. Conlan Baydon is correct, he does not deserve to pay for his crime with his life," Johan said firmly. Eleanor watched every muscle in Trey's body flex as he jumped to his feet; he stood over them, glaring down, his fists clenched. Eleanor felt his fury batter against her, filling the tent.

"And what of my justice? He took my child from me, all I had left." The grief in his voice gave it a hollow, echoing quality.

"What would be acceptable to you, Trey?" Sarina asked. Trey moved to pace backwards and forwards across the tent. He seemed to be thinking but it was hard to tell, as the sagging folds of his face made him look like he was perpetually frowning. He stopped pacing. Turning back to them, there was a twisted attempt at a smile on his face, but Eleanor saw the malicious cunning in his eyes and shuddered.

"This abomination attacked me to protect you," Trey said in a slow, cold, bitter voice, looking down at Conlan. "So he will pay if I make you suffer. He took my child, so you will swear an oath to give me your firstborn child in replacement."

A deep, horrified silence pushed against the tent walls. Eleanor stared at Conlan. His face was blank, eyes empty. Eventually, Johan broke the silence, his voice a hoarse whisper.

"No, Trey, what you ask is not the answer, what you ask is unthinkable."

Trey laughed, a grating sound. "No, not unthinkable. There is precedent." Trey's words knocked into Eleanor's memories, sending a domino effect through her head.

"For a very steep price the Elves provided help by showing the resistance the secret to creating more Avatars," Eleanor whispered, reciting Conlan's words from memory. "The steep price was that you took their children. That was when your bloodline became corrupted, when you brought human children into your tribe. Why did you want them?"

Johan turned to look at Eleanor appraisingly, then sighed. "Not a bright moment in our history, but we were desperate at the time. There were not enough Elves to continue, and we were slowly dying out. We never considered the effect that our use of magic would have on a mixed bloodline. We dealt ourselves as heavy a blow as did the humans who gave up their children. The humans never forgave the deal we forced them to make; we ended up moving into the desert permanently for our own safety, in turn cultivating the belief that we were cruel, merciless monsters in an attempt to protect ourselves. We made a mistake, and it is not one I am in a hurry to repeat."

"This is what I demand. If I cannot have the Avatar's head, I will have Conlan Baydon's firstborn child," Trey said, his voice flat and final.

"He can have my head," Will said quietly, looking at Conlan.

Horrified at the choice, Conlan shuddered and ignored Will completely. "Is the council going to enforce Trey's request as judgement?" he asked, turning to Sarina.

"Johan is right, this is not a decision we would take lightly, but given the rather unique circumstances, it is very likely that the council will uphold Trey's demands for justice," the woman replied.

This news deepened the horrified look on Conlan's face. "Adra, do we have any appeal, any hope of forcing Trey to make another choice?"

Adra looked thoughtful for a moment. "There are some, like Johan, who will disapprove of this judgement, but there will not be enough to sway the council. If you want the wand, you must make a choice – one I do not envy you."

Conlan nodded and looked at Trey. "I do not have children... I may never have them."

Trey sneered at him. "Elves are long-lived, so I can wait. If you do not have children, then that will be my loss, although more yours I suspect. But if you do, you will honour your vow and hand over your firstborn to me within a month of its birth."

Conlan stared at the Elf towering over him. Eleanor felt her heart ache for him; he looked so small, so trapped.

"I need some time," he said, his voice bleached of emotion.

"Of course," Johan said, rising to his feet. "We will leave you, food will be sent. Call for us when you have made a decision."

The four Elves left the tent and a deep, dread-filled silence moved out from Conlan to cover them all.

"So, is someone going to tell us what's going on?" Freddie asked quietly. Eleanor opened her mouth to answer the question.

"Someone *other* than Eleanor," Amelia ordered. Hurt, Eleanor snapped her mouth shut again.

"We have a choice: we can leave without the wand, we can kill every Elf in this camp and take the wand or we can submit to the Elf council's judgement. Trey has made demands, he wants Will's head; if he can't have that, he wants me to hand over my firstborn child," Conlan said in the same emotionless voice, not taking his steady gaze off the sand in front of him. Amelia gasped, starting in horror from Will's miserable expression to Freddie's shock.

"You're not going to let them have Will's head, are you?" Amelia whispered, fear pulsing through her trembling voice.

Conlan turned to glare at her. "I don't know, Amelia; clearly you think me capable of it."

"What are you going to do?" Freddie asked.

"What am *I* going to do? What happened to voting?" Conlan snapped.

"This decision is yours, Conlan; we'll do whatever you want... I'll do whatever you want," Will said quietly.

Conlan slowly shook his head. "So much for sharing the responsibility. I need to think." He pulled himself to his feet, walking towards the tent's exit. As he pulled back the flap a sword tip hovered in front of his face.

"I am going for a walk and she is coming with me," he said, pointing back to Eleanor without looking at her. "If you need permission from Johan or Sarina for this, fine, go get it, otherwise get out of my way." Seeing the look on Conlan's face, the owner of the sword nodded, letting him pass. Surprised at his desire for her company, Eleanor rose painfully off her bed and followed him out of the tent. The night air was cold and pleasant against her skin. She took a couple of slow, deep breaths, feeling the clean air take away her desire to be sick and removing some of the sting from her headache. The tent was a good distance from the main Elf camp and Conlan walked further away, up over the sand dunes, not checking to see if Eleanor was following him. One of their guards tailed them at a discrete distance. On the other side of the dune Conlan stopped and sat down, pulling his knees up to his chest and staring out at the night-shrouded sand that stretched on forever like a silver-black sea.

"I need help, Eleanor," he said in English, his voice a pained whisper as he stared at the horizon.

"How can I help?" she asked, sitting next to him. Her heart jumped, hoping desperately that she would be able to assist him, even as she felt guilty for her pleasure at being asked.

"I need to understand my choices. I want a logical assessment, not emotion. Can you do that?"

"Yes. OK, let's start with the basic options. One – we could forget about the wand for the moment and leave. Two – we could attack the Elves, kill most or all of them and take the wand. Three – we give them Will's head – and four – you agree to hand over your firstborn child. These are your choices, yes?" she asked.

"Yes," Conlan agreed. Eleanor nodded, letting her mind run through these options for a moment and stack up the possible outcomes. Taking a deep breath, she gave Conlan her conclusions.

"Option one. We forget about the wand. This would be the logical choice, as it continues the status quo and nobody has to die or give up their unborn children. However, while I don't believe we need the Talismans to get the connection working, great pains were taken to hide them, so I believe they're important. Simply walking away at this point might be the safest choice, but I'm unsure of how well we would be received by the Elves if we were forced to return for the wand at a later date. It is also worth mentioning that Trey is a wildcard, in that the Elves may let us go, but there is nothing to stop him following us."

Conlan nodded but said nothing, so Eleanor continued.

"Option two. We kill the Elves. This is the option with the most risk. It is also the most morally reprehensible choice. While I believe that Dal is right, that we'd be strong enough to win a fight, heavy losses on our side would be likely, and Conlan I don't think we want to turn our energy on innocent women and children. Plus, if we killed them, we would be losing potential allies. I'm beginning to see a pattern in where the Talismans have been hidden. I think, if we are careful, we will make allies with all the holders of the Talismans. These allies have significant forces positioned out of the Lord of Mydren's reach, and I think this was done on purpose."

"How is the dragon going to be an ally?" Conlan asked, amused.

"Well, I'm not sure about the dragon but maybe we'll find out when we get there. Option three. We let them take Will's head. This would require us having to return to Millar's Forest so you could make a new Avatar of Water, which could take us quite a few months. There would also be the collateral damage to consider. Amelia's response is unlikely to be accepting, and I think that she would either kill herself or kill you – possibly both. Right now, if you made this choice, Will would accept it. He hates himself for what he did, but it really wasn't his fault, he had no clear idea what he was doing or that he was capable of doing it. Losing one Avatar would set us back months, losing two would set us back years and losing you would stop this thing dead. So, emotion aside, this is a poor choice."

Conlan nodded again, and not able to see his expression in the dark, Eleanor kept going.

"Option four. You agree to give up your firstborn child within a month of its birth. This is actually the best choice. The chances of you surviving this 'adventure' you have us on and getting the chance to have children are not great. However, should we somehow succeed and you find some poor woman who is willing to put up with you, giving your child to the Elves would be a brilliant way to strengthen a friendship with them, if you do it right."

"I didn't realise there was a 'right' way to give up a child," Conlan commented, his voice brittle.

Eleanor winced. "Let me rephrase that. If you make this choice, then do it in good faith. You've seen the way Adra protects and cares for his son, and you've witnessed the depths of Trey's grief over his daughter, they clearly love their children. I believe Trey would love yours. Make this a positive thing and make friends with Trey, don't hold a grudge. Make your personal loss a meaningful gain for your people and get the Elves onside. Think like a king, not a man." There was silence. Eleanor sat next to him, letting him think.

"Would you be able to give up your child, Eleanor?" he asked quietly. There was something in his voice, as if her answer was very important.

"It's kind of a stretch, Conlan," she replied softly. "I've never really been the mothering sort, and not being able to have children I've no idea how it would feel to give one up. I don't think it would be very easy, but if I thought it was the right thing to do and I knew the child was going to be loved and live a safe, happy life, then yes, maybe I would."

"What do you mean, you can't have children?" Conlan asked.

"I thought you knew. Amelia and I are biologically incapable of having children," Eleanor said.

"Amelia never told me…"

Eleanor shrugged. "Maybe she assumed, like I did, that it was intentional. After all, it's sort of hard to fight off Protectors with a baby in tow."

"Having children is a part of life – one of the fun, joyful parts for most people, I'm told. I wouldn't intentionally deprive you of that." Eleanor could hear the wistful longing in his voice and realised that if he made a vow to give up his firstborn child, there was going to be a very good chance he would have to follow through on it. He wanted children.

"There is no mention of Avatars having children anywhere in Gregor's book. If it wasn't intentional, then it's just part of our nature. I guess we must be created, not born," Eleanor said. Conlan lapsed back into silence. Eleanor sat with him, listening to his breathing, guilt burning through her. Conlan was going through hell making a difficult decision and she was just happy to get the opportunity to have him to herself again, even for a little while.

"We should go back," Conlan said, but he made no attempt to move.

"There's no rush, we can go back when you're ready," she said, not really wanting to go back to Will and Amelia's glaring.

"Eleanor?"

"Yes?"

"Thank you."

"I want to help you, Conlan, you don't have to thank me," Eleanor said, grateful that the dark was hiding the smile of pleasure his gratitude had brought to her face.

"No, I mean it. Thank you for everything. You put up with me, despite how I've treated you. I don't make it easy. I might not show it all the time, but I'm grateful to have you as a friend," he said softly. Eleanor felt her heart beat harder at his words, the smile getting wider as he continued, oblivious to the joy his words were creating in her as they blossoming out through her whole body, making her feel lighter, even managing to take away some of her pain. "Oh, and thank you for the book," he continued. I've not opened it yet, I was too angry. I didn't think I deserved it, but I'm looking forward to reading it. It's been a very long time since I had a new book."

Not able to get the smile off her face, Eleanor finally managed to find her voice.

"You're welcome."

Conlan stood up, brushing the sand off his clothes. He helped Eleanor back to her feet, mindful of her injuries. They walked past the guard at the top of the dune and back to their tent. At the tent door Conlan turned to the trailing guard.

"I have made my decision, please inform Johan and Sarina." The guard nodded sharply, closing the tent flap in Conlan's face. The others looked up as they entered. Eleanor noticed the food laid out on the table, but only Freddie seemed to be eating. He smiled at her. Both Will and Amelia looked miserable. Eleanor dropped her head as they both glared at her. Conlan saw the looks and irritation marched across his face.

"I'm confused – would someone mind explaining to me why Eleanor is getting glared at?" he asked, looking from Will to Amelia.

"She should learn to keep her mouth shut!" Will snapped.

Conlan smiled. "Not arguing that one with you, but I heard what she said and I don't understand what your problem is."

"She knows more about Will than I do, and she keeps rubbing my face in it. I've had enough," Amelia muttered.

"What has she said?" Conlan asked seriously.

"She told me what present to get him – he loves it – and then she used her knowledge of the inside of his head to try to defend him to me. I should know these things, not her," Amelia said, her voice petering out to a whisper as she seemed to consider how stupid she sounded.

Conlan nodded. "I see the problem. Earth crashed Will's mind into Eleanor's, not something she asked for or wanted, I'm sure. So she has all this extra information in her head that she could happily live without and she is using it maliciously to help you buy Will thoughtful gifts, which she also had the audacity to pay for. To make matters worse, she is now defending Will's actions, trying to help you better understand the man you love – and right after she took a beating to protect him... So, explain to me again why you're glaring at her."

Conlan looked surprised when all four of them stared at him. Eleanor felt such a strong surge of affection that she had to sit, collapsing to the bed.

"What?" Conlan asked. "Am I wrong?"

Will and Amelia shook their heads.

"It's just odd to hear you defend her...," Will said.

Conlan smiled. "She helped me, I thought I'd return the favour. It's not her fault Amelia is jealous, so don't take it out on her. You lectured me about the damage and upset I was causing, please allow me to return that favour, too."

Amelia is jealous. Eleanor found that a lot of confusing looks and comments Amelia had given her in the last few months suddenly made sense.

"You're enjoying being the self-righteous one for a change, aren't you?" Will said. "I take it your good humour means that you're happy with the decision you've made."

Conlan's smile faded. "Happy might be too strong a word. Accepting is a better one."

"Does this mean I get to keep my head?" Will asked. He did not seem all that interested.

Conlan nodded. "You're not much use without it."

Amelia walked across the tent and sat down on Eleanor's bed. "I'm sorry."

Eleanor nodded distractedly, still staring at Conlan, who turned back to look at her and smiled. The world spun at such a dizzying speed that she felt the urge to throw up again, but she smiled back. She heard the tent flaps open, and everybody else turned to look as Johan and Sarina entered. Eleanor saw the movement in her peripheral vision but did not want to take her eyes off Conlan. *He defended me.* The thought gave her such a warm glow that it felt like she was burning from the inside out.

"You have made your choice, Conlan Baydon?" Johan asked.

"Yes, I will swear an oath to give Trey my firstborn child. I would appreciate knowing what you would have me trade for the wand," Conlan said calmly. *He made the right choice.* Eleanor heard Will gasp, a response repeated by Amelia and Freddie when Will translated Conlan's worlds. With effort she dragged her eyes away from Conlan and looked into Amelia's horrified face.

"I thought he'd decided to leave," Amelia whispered. "How can he give up his child?"

Eleanor smiled. "Because he's thinking like a king."

"We want to trade our future for the wand," Johan said. It was such a strange statement that Eleanor's eyes moved to the Elf.

"I do not understand," Conlan said, frowning.

"We do not wish to be stuck on the edge of the world anymore. Most of us do not enjoy the harsh desert life, and we wish to be free to move around Mydren, find new homes, under the protection of a benevolent king," Sarina said.

"I still do not..." Conlan started and stopped as their meaning became clear. He stared at them. "You are asking a man, who is not yet king, to make a decision of state? This is not an easy thing to do. As you have pointed out, humans do not like Elves very much, but time has erased the reasons why from their minds, and all that is left is a vague sense of unease and distrust. Now, it is possible that I can overcome the symptoms of this distrust through the force of law, but this does not actually solve the problem; if anything, it will increase the distrust humans have for you and by extension they will distrust their king for showing unfounded favour."

Johan nodded, frowning. "What do you suggest?"

"Fight with us," Conlan said. "When the time comes, I will call for you and ask for your loyalty, ask you to fight at my side. Do this – fight for me – knowing that if we win you will get what you want, and by fighting at their sides you will be able to show the humans that you are brave and trustworthy allies."

Johan and Sarina looked at each other. "We must talk this through with the council," Johan said. "We will return." And with that they turned and swept out of the tent.

"What happened?" Amelia asked. "What did you say? They looked a bit... shocked."

"I think Conlan just talked another army into following us," Will said, impressed.

"They didn't say yes yet," Conlan said, giving Will a grin.

"I'm confused, how did we get from us having to trade something for the wand, to them agreeing to fight with us?" Freddie asked.

"Because Conlan is thinking like a king," Eleanor repeated, heartened by the smile Conlan gave her.

Eleanor lay in her bed, staring at the apex of the tent's roof. She had wanted to sleep, but her churning mind and pain-wracked body would not let her. Amelia and Will had apologised profusely, but they were now not talking to each other for some reason. Eleanor was too wrung out to care. The sun had risen on a new day. Sarina and Johan had not returned, but they had sent two Elves to tend to their injuries. Eleanor could feel the tight, itchy pull of the stitches in her neck. Will would have done a far neater job. They had bound her wrist, putting the leather cuff over the bandage. They had inspected the large, purple and green bruise that was still spreading across her stomach and halfway up her side, fingers gently pressing in, searching for damage to the organs beneath. They had found nothing to cause them concern and had moved on to Will, leaving her panting in agony. The pain had eventually receded to a dull throb and she began going through Gregor's book in her head again, as she had not thought about it in a while. The sun rose higher and the temperature became too much for logical thought and she had begun to feel sick once more, so now she was staring at the roof, not thinking about anything. She felt an energy string brush against her and reached for it.

Sorry.

I told you, Will; don't worry about it. Now I understand that I'm making Amelia jealous I'll make sure I don't mention stuff I know about you in front of her.

No, just carry on as you are – Amelia needs to deal with her jealousy. She's still really angry with me; she wants me to show her the memories of what happened with Trey.

Then show her.

Will sighed. *I wanted to protect her from that.*

Amelia is stronger than you give her credit for!

Eleanor felt another energy string brush against her and winced as Amelia's angry presence filled her head. She felt Will try to leave and gripped firmly to his energy string.

What are you and Will talking about?

Eleanor could hear the suspicion.

Will was telling me you want to know about what happened with Trey, experience his memories; your request is making him uncomfortable.

Why? Amelia's anger rising.

Because he's frightened that if you know the truth about him that you'll stop loving him.

Eleanor felt Will's shock. *You pretend to yourself that you are protecting Amelia, not damaging her delicate sensibilities, but you don't want to risk losing her. I know, Will, I understand, do you really think that someone who loves you as much as Amelia does is going to be any less understanding?*

There was silence in her head. It felt profoundly odd, especially as there were currently three of them in there. Frustrated, Eleanor grabbed Will and Amelia's energy strings, wove them firmly round each other and then pushed the combined string out of her head.

"Talk to each other!" she practically yelled, sitting up and glaring at them.

Will and Amelia flinched. Slowly Amelia stood and moved to sit next to Will. Freddie and Conlan watched them in surprise. They closed their eyes and Eleanor hoped she had been right, hoped that Amelia was going to understand. She watched them, realising she was holding her breath uncomfortably. Amelia jerked and gasped, tears began running down her face. Will opened his eyes and looked at her in miserable, guilty torment. *Oh… what have I done?* Amelia stared at Will, trembling as the tears fell. Will dropped his head, unable to look at the distress he had caused. With a few hiccupping sobs, Amelia brought herself under control and gently reached a hand out, raising Will's bruised face to hers.

"I never understood," she said. "When you said being dragged here nearly drove you mad, I never thought you meant it that literally… I love you." She threw herself into Will's arms, and Eleanor saw the poor man wince at the pain she caused him. Wrapping his arms around her he pulled her tight against him, tilting her head so he could kiss her. Eleanor sighed in relief and lay back on her bed, staring at the roof again and trying to give them as much privacy as possible. Another energy string brushed against her. Confident that Will and Amelia were far too occupied to be talking to her, she pulled the string in.

Hello, Freddie. Are you and Conlan having marital difficulties, too? Dr Eleanor is currently in session.

Freddie laughed. *Conlan and I were going to see if we could get out of the 'Tent O'Love' before this gets any more serious. Want to escape with us?*

Eleanor listened to sounds of passionate kissing from across the tent.

Get me out of here!

It had actually been far easier to leave the tent than they had imagined, as the guards seemed unsure about their status – were they prisoners or potential allies? They let them go, one of the guards following. In silence they walked over the dunes towards the Elves' main camp. It was quiet, as people had retreated to the shade of their tents to avoid the heat of the day. Walking through the deserted camp they came across a large, open-sided awning. Under it were five Elf children, who seemed to be playing. Wanting to stand out of the blazing sun, Eleanor moved closer. The guard placed a restraining hand on her shoulder. Conlan and Freddie scowled at him.

"It is for her protection," the guard said, hastily removing his hand. Slightly mystified by this statement, Eleanor looked back at the children. As she did so, one of them flung a knife at the other; she tensed in shock and then watched in amazement as the tumbling knife's journey slowed, as if it was moving through water. Energy dissipated, it fell to the ground at the feet of the grinning child it had been thrown at. Eleanor and Freddie exchanged looks. Could they do that? Getting as close as the guard would allow them, they watched as the beautiful, unmarred children practiced their magic. They sent large round balls that looked very heavy flying through the air and, like the knife, stopped them. They created invisibility shields, winking in and out of sight as they did so, giggling. One child stood to the side, eyes closed, a look of concentration on her delicate face while several tiny tornadoes of sand danced around her feet.

"Can all Elf children do this?" Conlan asked the guard.

The guard shook his head sadly. "No, Dal is out with his father on patrol and Johan's son, Grell, refuses to use his abilities. With those two exceptions, you are looking at all the Elf children that show magical talent."

Eleanor stared back at the five children, wondering how long it would take their use of magic to twist and pull their beautiful faces into masks of permanent misery; it seemed a heavy price to pay for the advantages it offered. Being careful not to disturb them, Eleanor pushed an energy string out towards the children. After investigation she discovered that every single one of them was pulling energy from the air, and she wondered whether or not this was a conscious choice. Of the four elements, earth and air were most likely to provide them with a continuous supply of energy, and she wondered if they could use the other elements, if necessary. The guard was beginning to become uncomfortable, not happy about them being this close to the children, especially as he seemed unsure as to whether he should have allowed them out in the first place.

"Think we've given Will and Amelia enough time?" Eleanor asked in English of no one in particular.

"No," Conlan and Freddie said together, both of them sounding so certain that Eleanor burst out laughing; startling the children, five pairs of eyes suddenly regarded them with suspicion.

The guard hustled them away. They wandered on through the camp. Walking past one of the many identical off-white tents that surrounded them, the flaps were thrown back and a large Elf exited in such a hurry that he marched straight into Eleanor, knocking her off her feet. She gasped as pain shot through her, black fireworks exploding through her head at the jolt.

"What are you doing here?" came a familiar snarling voice.

Trey.

"We needed some air. Can you get up, Eleanor?" Conlan asked, kneeling at her side, gentle hands helping her to sit. She could feel the waves of anger and hostility coming off Trey – she felt it literally.

Can I feel it because he doesn't have a shield?

It made her angry.

"Enough, Trey!" she snapped. "The man is willing to give you his child, I believe that should at least have earned him your respect."

She felt Trey's surprise. "I am sorry, have I hurt you?" he asked, leaning over her. The tent flap opened again and a tall, beautiful woman stepped out. Her face was unmarked, and large blue eyes stared down, her mouth pressed into a look of extreme displeasure. She hit Trey on the arm, extremely hard.

"What have you done now, you *drallup*?" she hissed.

Eleanor had no idea what *drallup* meant, but the woman's tone did not make it sound like a term of endearment. The woman moved forward, kneeling on Eleanor's other side, the soft, delicate, colourful fabric of her loose clothes billowing out slightly as she did so.

"I am Brydra, Trey's wife. You are Conlan Baydon," she said, staring at Conlan over Eleanor's head. Conlan nodded in acknowledgement. "Would you like to bring the Avatar inside? She does not look well," Brydra asked, ignoring Trey's huff of annoyance.

"I am sure she will be fine," Conlan said stiffly.

"I am sitting right here, you know," Eleanor muttered. Neither of them looked at her.

"Please, I would like to talk with you," Brydra said, an earnest look on her face. *This is a good thing; this woman will be the mother of his child, he should get to know her.*

Conlan hesitated. "No, I…" he began.

Thinking fast, Eleanor took the very desperate step of making herself look pathetic. With a totally faked, shuddering groan, she closed her eyes and collapsed into a limp heap, knowing that Conlan would catch her.

"Oh, poor little thing, bring her inside," Brydra said, gently stroking the hair back from Eleanor's face. Eleanor felt her body lifted as an energy string brushed against her and Freddie's amused presence filled her head.

Faker! What are you doing?

This is Trey's wife. Eleanor replied. *She will be the mother of Conlan's child, if and when he has to give it up, and she wants to talk to him. I thought that was a really good idea.*

Oh… Conlan isn't fooled, you know.

I know, but this was easier than arguing with him.

Freddie's laughter echoed round her head as he pulled his energy free. Conlan carried her into the cool shadow of Trey's tent and laid her down on a pile of cushions offered by Brydra. Eleanor allowed her eyes to flicker open, letting out a groan that in truth was not entirely faked. Conlan was knelt at her side, his face blank and eyes flashing irritation. Tension suffused the tent. Trey watched, every muscle in his body screaming his annoyance. Their guard stood just inside the door, eyeing Trey.

Bet he's wondering who he is meant to protect from whom.

Brydra came forward and dropped to her knees next to Conlan, offering a glass of water.

Eleanor sat up, taking the water with a smile.

"Thank you," she said, drinking it quickly and handing back the glass.

Brydra dropped her head, looking embarrassed and uncomfortable.

"Bry… I did not mean to hurt the girl, she got in the way," Trey said, his voice pleading.

"If you *ever* want the privilege of touching me again, Trey, you will keep your mouth shut or leave!" Brydra snarled, angry eyes glaring up at the big Elf. Trey stared at her in misery, then turned and stormed out of the tent.

Eleanor watched their guard visibly relax as he left.

Brydra sighed. "He is a good man, but losing Remie changed him. He lost too much. I am sorry for what he is demanding of you. I have tried to change his mind, but he will not be swayed." She looked at Conlan; Eleanor could feel his body tense as he attempted to control what he was feeling, keeping his face blank. Hidden under the cushions and material she was lying on, she reached for his hand, holding it tightly and giving what comfort she could.

"My child, do you want it too?" His voice's hollow whisper made Eleanor's hairs stand on end. The woman's blue eyes filled with pity and distress.

"There were complications when Remie was born. She was never a healthy child, and her birth left me unable to have more children. I would give anything not to have Trey do this to you, but you must know that your child would not want for love and attention. I would love it as my own. I know that it is hard for you to believe, but Trey would also love your child – he was a wonderful, doting father to Remie. I know he longs to be that again. His motivations may appear vengeful, but he is just a grieving father trying to get back what he lost. I am so sorry that he must hurt you to do it."

"Maybe I would have done the same thing in his position," Conlan allowed, giving Brydra a sad smile.

"No, Conlan Baydon. I believe you are too honourable to have done this to someone, but it is generous of you to say so," Brydra said, smiling back.

Once Brydra was convinced that Eleanor was not going to drop dead in her tent, she insisted on feeding them. Bringing out small, dried, date-like fruits and a sticky, brown paste in a bowl, with flat bread to dip into it, she set this on a small table in front of them. Eleanor looked round the tent as Brydra prepared the meal. It was the same size as the tent they had been held in, but it seemed smaller because there was more in it. The mountain of brightly coloured cushions and material on which they sat filled one side of the tent, with a thick dark brown rug underneath covering the sand. There was not much furniture – the table in front of them, several trunks against the tent walls and a couple of small cabinets that seemed to serve as a kitchen. *A simple life, but it does not look deprived*, Eleanor thought, a memory of Baydon's miserable hovels springing to mind.

Moving with slow deference, Brydra poured Conlan a glass of black liquid from a large jug and handed it to him. He gave her a genuine smile of thanks. Much to her delight, Eleanor discovered that the brown paste tasted a lot like peanut butter and she tucked in with gusto, feeling giddy as the sugar rushed through her battered body. The black liquid was a bitter, cold, coffee-like drink that Freddie loved. He begged Eleanor to ask Brydra to give them some to take back with them. Eleanor refused, pointing out it was bad manners and that it would be more weight to carry back through all that sand, a prospect she was not looking forward to. The slightly more relaxed atmosphere gave Conlan the opportunity to ask questions about Trey and Brydra, about life in the desert, about Elf children and magic. Brydra answer all of his questions in a slow, thoughtful manner, asking some of her own about what they were doing and about the Talismans. Eleanor liked the woman, as she was intelligent, caring and knew her own mind, and she clearly loved Trey, even if she was currently furious with him.

The paste was beginning to make her feel sick again, so Eleanor distracted herself by asking Brydra about Trey's missing shield. The Elf woman told her as much as she knew; at some point just after Remie's death, Trey's shield had disappeared, but she had no idea why and he refused to discuss it. Eleanor asked about other Elves that may have lost their shields in the past – was there something that had happened to all of them that could cause it? Had they all lost children? Brydra thought about this, shaking her head, it happened rarely and there was no obvious underlying reason. With a puzzled look on her face she had asked why it was important. Eleanor explained, as best she could. It felt very odd telling a stranger about Conlan's shield, kind of personal, but she gave him several glances as she explained, and he did not look annoyed.

Does this mean he likes Brydra, too? I hope so.

Their conversation stopped when Trey appeared back in the tent, their bored guard leaping to his feet as the Elf entered.

"Johan and Sarina are looking for them, they should return to their tent," he said, not taking his eyes off the dark-brown rug. Conlan rose, Eleanor and Freddie getting up with him, and Brydra got gracefully to her feet. The smile she gave them contrasted sharply with the heartache in her eyes.

"Thank you, Brydra, for your hospitality and your honesty. I am grateful," Conlan said, holding the woman's steady gaze. She nodded. Turning to leave, they walked past Trey. As they exited the tent Conlan stopped, an odd look on his face. He turned round and moved back to face Trey. Panic flashed through the eyes of their guard.

Doesn't want to get between Conlan and Trey in a fight... I don't blame him, Eleanor thought, wondering what Conlan was doing. He made no aggressive moves, he just stood before the Elf, watching him and waited. Eventually Trey raised his eyes from the floor and looked back. Conlan spoke, very quietly, almost a whisper, but the words carried a lethal threat that made Eleanor shiver.

"You will not allow *my* child to grow up hating me for a decision you forced me to make."

Trey shook his head slowly, the folds of skin hanging down his face sagging and wobbling.

"Your child will not hate you, although it may never forgive me."

"Yet you still wish to go through with this?" Conlan asked.

"Love is a funny thing. If you could replace someone you had lost, would you not take that opportunity?" Trey asked. Conlan's face paled slightly and Eleanor knew who he was thinking about.

"Perhaps," he said, his voice strained. "But I would hope that I would have the strength to resist, if it meant hurting others."

Trey sighed. "I am not that strong."

Conlan stared at the Elf for a moment, then walked past him, back towards their tent at such a quick pace that Eleanor had to jog to keep up, her body protesting every step.

The sun was setting as Conlan opened the tent flap. Will and Amelia smiled at them; Eleanor tried not to think about what she knew they had been doing for the last few hours, trying to give them the illusion of privacy. Freddie, of course, had no such scruples.

"Did you have fun making up?" he asked with a wicked grin. Amelia blushed and Will glared, but Freddie laughed. Irritated, Will began giving Freddie a lecture on manners, but his remonstrations lacked heart. Like Eleanor, he had noticed Conlan's dark brooding presence sat at the back of the tent, staring at the sand. He kept glancing at him with a worried frown. Eleanor went to sit down next to the miserable man.

"How do I do this?" he whispered.

"Like a king. Do it with dignity, strength and power. Make a few demands of your own, and make Trey swear to them. Make sure that everybody knows you are doing this because you choose to, not because you think you have to," Eleanor said quietly.

Conlan smiled, but it did not reach his eyes, the normal bright green dulled by the haunted look of despair deep within them. Before they could speak further the tent flaps opened and Johan and Sarina marched in. Conlan pulled himself to his feet, unconsciously offering a hand to help Eleanor but not taking his eyes off the two Elves.

"Conlan Baydon, we will give you the wand and fight at your side when you call on us. In return you will swear that once you are king, you will do everything in your power to improve our lives, giving us your protection and the freedom to roam Mydren as we wish. Are these terms acceptable to you?" Johan asked solemnly.

"Yes," Conlan said.

"Very well, then please join our people so that you can swear this in front of them and swear your oath to Trey," Johan continued.

The two Elves turned and walked from the tent. Pulling himself up to his full height, straightening his shoulders and taking a deep breath, Conlan followed. As Eleanor walked with the others behind him through the evening twilight, she saw the change in him. Just as he had done as they had walked the streets of Baydon, he was projecting a strong sense of power and determination.

They were led back to the main camp fire. The council members stood to the side, the licking orange flames dancing over their disfigured features. Around them stood a sea of faces. Eleanor could see Brydra and Trey, stood with Adra and Dal, and it was good to see some friends. Johan and Sarina went to join the council, and the silence filled the growing dark for a moment. Johan spoke, his voice ringing clearly in the deathly hush.

"Conlan Baydon, you have asked for the wand on behalf of the Avatar of Air and you have asked for the Elves to fight at your side in the coming battles with the Lords of Mydren." A strangled gasp of shock travelled through the crowd. Johan ignored it and continued.

"What do you trade in return?"

Conlan stepped forward. "In return for the wand and your loyalty, I swear my protection to you. Once I am King of Mydren, the Elves will be free to leave the desert, if they wish, without fear of attack, reprisals or discrimination."

There was silence again as Johan allowed Conlan's words to sink in to the minds of the crowd, letting them understand what they would be gaining. When Johan began to hear excited whispering, he spoke again, silencing it.

"Very well. Conlan Baydon, future King of Mydren, we accept this trade." Johan walked forward and handed something to Conlan, which Eleanor assumed was the wand. Johan walked back to the council and Conlan stepped back a few paces, handing the wand to Amelia. The crowd began to grow restless, whispering amongst themselves – obviously they had an idea what was coming next. Again Johan spoke, bringing instant silence.

"Trey, of the family Melat, you have a grievance to bring before this council?"

Trey stepped forward. "I accuse Will, Avatar of Water, of violently entering my mind and destroying the memories of my precious Remie." This time the gasps and whispering that erupted were loud and persistent.

"Silence!" Sarina ordered, and a deathly hush dropped over the crowd again.

"Will, Avatar of Water, step forward," Johan ordered. Will walked towards the council, his injuries making him look like one of them in the flickering firelight.

"You have heard the accusation against you, are you guilty of this crime?" Johan asked.

"Yes," Will said, so much pain and remorse in the word, that beside her, Eleanor heard Amelia start to sob softly. Not taking her eyes off what was unfolding before her, Eleanor reached a hand out. Amelia took it, squeezing tightly. On the other side of her Freddie wrapped an arm round Amelia's shaking shoulders.

"Conlan Baydon, you have agreed to face council judgement on behalf of the Avatar of Water?" Johan asked.

Conlan moved to Will's side. "Yes, I have." His voice was strong, firm and emotionless. Eleanor saw Will's shoulders drop as he hung his head.

"Trey, of the family Melat, what do you demand in compensation for this crime against you?" Johan asked.

"I demand that Conlan Baydon swear a blood oath, that within a month of its birth, he will give his firstborn child to me to raise as my own," Trey said slowly and clearly. Eleanor had expected furious whispering to follow this statement, but the crowd just stared in stunned silence.

"The council upholds this request as judgment. Do you accept it, Conlan Baydon?" Johan asked. There was a pause.

"Yes," Conlan said finally. "However, I ask the council's patience, as before I do this, I have some requests of my own." Johan looked at Conlan, unsure, as this was not something they had discussed, but he nodded.

"What requests do you have?"

"When I hand my child over, I must officially disown it, thus removing any future claim it or its offspring may have to my crown. While humans may be able to accept Elves moving among them, they are very unlikely to accept one as a king, and I wish to protect Mydren from the possibility of further war. While officially the child will no longer be mine, this does not mean that I will have no interest in it. I require Trey to swear an oath to me that my child will be loved and cared for, that any gifts and assistance I may send will be given to it, that lines of communication will be kept open and if, in the future, the child wishes to approach me, it will not be discouraged. Are you willing to swear this, Trey, of the family Melat?"

His voice was strong and commanding, his words reminding everybody that while he planned to be a king first, he was also a man – a man who cared about the child he was reluctantly giving up. Eleanor felt her heart bursting with pride; this was someone fit to rule.

"I will so swear," Trey said, sounding weak and pathetic after Conlan's deep, powerful voice. He stepped forward, dropping to his knees at Conlan's feet. Pulling a knife from his belt he dragged it hard across the palm of his hand, grunting at the pain. Making his hand a fist he held it out over the sand and allowed the blood to drip down, black in the firelight, and bowed his head.

"I, Trey, of the family Melat, do this day swear to Conlan Baydon, on my life blood, that the child he entrusts to my care will be loved, protected and cared for – treasured for its entire life. This child will know of and respect Conlan Baydon for the difficult decision he has made. Any gifts or assistance Conlan Baydon may send will be given to the child without reservation. Lines of communication will be kept open, and should the child ever express an interest in approaching Conlan Baydon, a meeting will be arranged."

A heavy silence fell. Trey rose to his feet, handing the knife to Conlan. The significance of the move was not lost on Eleanor. He was giving Conlan the means to kill him, if he had wished to. In front of everyone present he was showing his trust in Conlan as a man of his word. Conlan looked at the knife for a moment, then dropped gracefully to his knees, pulling the blade deeply across his palm, making no sound. He held his fist out as Trey had done, allowing the blood to fall. Keeping his head raised, he stared Trey in the eye as he spoke his oath in a slow, steady voice that rang with authority.

"I, Conlan Baydon, do this day swear to Trey, of the family Melat, on my life blood, that within a month of the birth of my first child, I will entrust it to his care, giving up all claim upon it and allowing Trey, of the family Melat, to raise the child as his own."

The silence became deafening. In one fluid movement, Conlan sprang back to his feet, handing the knife back to Trey. Eleanor watched the blood from his clenched fist continue to drip to the sand as he turned back to face the council. To anyone watching he looked strong, in control, regal, but Eleanor could see how stiff and uncomfortable his body was, she knew how much this was hurting him. This vow could end up preventing him from getting married – could mean he never had children – but Eleanor knew he had made the right choice, because his quiet acceptance of their judgement was why the Elf council had agreed to fight with him, not what he had promised in return. He had gained their loyalty from the moment he said yes to Trey's demands.

Johan stepped forward again. "Will, Avatar of Water, Conlan Baydon has paid your debt to Trey, of the family Melat. You are no longer a 'marked' man. All oaths and judgements made here tonight will be recorded in the tribe's history for all time. The council would remind all present that breaking these oaths will bring an immediate death sentence. Conlan Baydon, you are free to leave, although we extend our hospitality to you, should you wish to stay."

"Thank you for your offer, Johan, but we must be moving on. We would prefer to leave now, to make the most of the cooler night air," Conlan replied.

"Very well," Johan said. He sounded sad. "Return to your tent and we shall bring your bags to you and a guide to ensure you leave the desert safely."

Conlan nodded, and turning sharply marched back to their tent. Eleanor and the others moved quickly after him. Once inside, hidden from view, Conlan allowed his guard to drop slightly. He sat on Eleanor's bed, staring at nothing with vacant eyes, body shaking, blood dripping from his still clenched fist. Instinctively respecting his silence, Eleanor took the jug of water from the table and gently inspected the damage to his hand. He did not resist, unclenching his fist when she carefully prised the fingers apart. She poured some of the water over the deep gash, flushing out the blood and cleaning it. He did not flinch. Eleanor heard the ripping of material as Will tore a strip off the bottom of his shirt, handing it to her. Carefully, Eleanor wrapped the strip around Conlan's hand. She had just tied off the end as Johan and Sarina walked through the tent flaps, followed by Adra and Dal, who carried their bags. They collected their things quickly. Eleanor smiled as she watched the joyful way Freddie silently greeted his sword, tucking it safely back into the middle of his blanket roll. They said their goodbyes, Conlan saying the absolute minimum required to be considered polite, and they left, marching out in silence across the dark sand with Adra as their guide. Conlan set a hard pace; Eleanor got the impression that he would have preferred it if they had run. They left Adra as they joined the main road back to Drent a few hours after dawn, a sad look on his twisted face as he turned and headed back into the sand. They should have made faster time once they reached the main track, but Eleanor was exhausted, and from listening to Will's panting she knew she was not the only one. They began to slow down, the gap between Conlan and the four of them getting longer and longer as he pounded on ahead, oblivious or maybe not caring. If she could have caught up with him, offered him comfort, she would have done so, but just putting one foot in front of the other was an effort, so she concentrated on that.

As they entered Drent's town gate, Conlan sat waiting for them on the low wall. His shoulders were slumped and his eyes were as empty as his voice when he spoke.

"I'll get Rand. You go to the inn and get the rest of our baggage; I'll meet you there."

"We're leaving straight away?" Amelia asked, disappointed.

"We can't afford to stay here, we have to get back out to where foraging is possible," Conlan said, sounding irritated that he was having to explain himself. Eleanor was grateful to hear any emotion in his voice. She reached into her bag and pulled out the large purse of money Remic had given her and handed it to Conlan.

"We're staying," she said flatly. She waited for the argument, waited for the explosion of irritation, waited for him to object in some way, but he nodded and led them back to the inn. They were able to get their old suite back. Conlan stalked across to the bedroom, slamming the doors shut behind him as soon as they got inside. The inn staff brought their bags back and Will ordered them food and baths, flashing the occasional guilty glance at Conlan's closed bedroom doors.

It was three days before Conlan answered one of their polite knocks on his door, asking him if he wanted to eat. He emerged looking haggard and spent; thick stubble added years to him. His face was gaunt and drawn and exhausted, bloodshot eyes stared at them with disinterest. He had pulled the bandage off his hand, and even from across the room Eleanor could see the deep purple and fiery red of infection. Will saw it too, and grabbing his medical bag manoeuvred Conlan into a chair so that he could inspect the injury. Conlan did not resist and said nothing as Will cleaned the wound as best he could, rubbing liberal amounts of his homemade antiseptic into it. Eleanor knew from experience that the stuff made any cut sting and burn. On Conlan's hand it must have been agony, but he gave no outward indication of the pain.

"Promise me you won't take this off," Will said, patting the clean bandage.

"I've sworn enough oaths for you," Conlan snapped, bitter resentment pouring from him. Eleanor saw Will's body flinch as if struck.

"That's not fair… " Amelia started, coming to an abrupt halt as Conlan stood and turned his eyes on her with a look so malevolent that Amelia began to shake. Eleanor knew she was right – this was not Will's fault, not really anybody's fault – but Conlan was not ready to hear that yet.

"Is there anything else I should be sacrificing to make me a better king?" he asked them. His question met with uncomfortable silence. Turning, he stalked back to his room, slamming the door again.

"Will, I need you to make up some sedative, enough to give him twenty-four hours of oblivion," Eleanor ordered. She picked up a plate and began putting food on it, realising she had no idea what he liked. By the time she finished, Will had prepared a glass of the medication and handed it to her. She took a deep breath, opened the bedroom door and stepped inside. The closed blinds made it gloomy. Eleanor stood for a moment, waiting for her eyes to adjust. The bed had not been slept in, but from Conlan's condition that did not surprise her.

"What do you want?" He sat in the corner of the room, scowling.

"I want you to eat something, then I want you to drink this sedative and then I want you to sleep," Eleanor said quietly.

"And if I don't want to?" The fight was back in his tone.

"There are four of us, if I have to get Will and Freddie to sit on you while I pour this stuff down your throat, I will do," she said, sounding a lot calmer than she felt. When he did not make any more threatening responses, Eleanor walked over to him. Sitting down she handed him the plate of food and watched him eat. When he had done, she gave him the sedative; he looked at it suspiciously but swallowed the entire glass in three large gulps.

"Happy now?" he muttered.

"No. You need to lie down, Will's sedatives are strong and you're too heavy for me to lift, so get up and get yourself into bed," Eleanor ordered.

Sighing with annoyance, Conlan lumbered to his feet and moved towards the bed, stumbling as the sedative began to take effect. Eleanor put a shoulder under his arm, helping him. He made it – just – and collapsed back into the pillows, dragging Eleanor with him. She untangled herself and pulled his boots off, lifting his legs onto the bed. He gazed at her, his eyes glassy, eyelids trying to drop as he fought the drug.

"I hated him for doing that to me," he said thickly. *Hated who? Does he mean Will?*

"Hated who for what?" Eleanor asked.

"My father. I hated him for disowning me, and now I've done it to a child I've not even met."

Eleanor sat next to him on the edge of the bed, her heart aching at the pain and misery in his voice.

"Your child won't hate you, Conlan, your child will understand," she said softly. She saw the doubt in his eyes, but he stopped fighting and allowed the sedative to drag him away. She watched his peaceful sleep for a while, wondering if she was right, if his child would forgive him, would understand. She leaned forward and gave his forehead a soothing kiss, feeling a little guilty, knowing he would have objected if he had been conscious.

14

THE CHALICE

They stayed in Drent for several weeks. Eleanor welcomed the time to recover, as her wrist itched and throbbed and she still felt sick if she overtaxed herself or strained the muscles in her stomach. Conlan retreated into brooding silence, rarely leaving his room, but he ate and drank what they brought him with little more than an irritated glance. Sleep and decent meals had a positive effect and he began to look better, even if his mood did not improve. The evening before they left, Eleanor had insisted that Conlan leave his room, have a bath, shave and change his clothes. Will had redressed his hand. Eleanor had been relieved to see that the infection had died down, leaving just a raw, ugly wound. Instead of retreating back to his room, they had been surprised when he had chosen to sit and eat with them. He said nothing, but it was not an unpleasant, distancing silence; he looked comfortable, relaxed in their presence as they laughed and talked around him, content to just be there without having to engage.

As they packed up the next morning, it occurred to Eleanor that Conlan would not get to enjoy his new saddle, because they were going to turn Rand into a pack mule again. This seemed a little unfair, so she gave him Remic's coin bag again and asked him to buy them all horses, pointing out it was time she learnt to ride and that it would make travel far quicker. He nodded, taking the money from her and asking Will to accompany him to the stables to help.

Eleanor stood outside the inn with Amelia and Freddie, waiting in the mid-morning heat, when they heard hooves approaching down the street. Rand came towards them. The animal was so ecstatic to be back with Conlan that he was almost skipping, his beautiful grey coat and silvery mane shining and his new saddle and bridle standing out against his muscular body, silver studs reflecting dazzling flashes of sunlight. Rand's steps were precise and fluid and sat proudly on his back Conlan moved with him, as if they were one, the animal's movements an extension of his own. Eleanor knew she was staring at him, but she did not feel so bad when she realised that Amelia stood next to her doing the same thing.

"Wow," she breathed. "He really can look the part when he wants to."

Eleanor nodded, awestruck.

As they got closer, they saw Will behind him on a large, black, grumpy-looking horse of his own, holding the reins to three others. Eleanor did not waste much time looking at the other animals, as she had eyes only for Conlan; he gently halted Rand at her side and looked at her, a genuine, happy, stunning smile spreading across his face, lighting up his bright green eyes. *This is why women in those silly romantic novels swoon*, Eleanor thought as her heart pounded nosily in her chest and the dusty street spun around her. She returned the smile, grinning stupidly at him because suddenly there were no thoughts in her head, not a single one. His smile, after so many weeks of misery, was like finding flowers in the desert; an unexpected miracle that she was struggling to appreciate fully.

"Thank you for the new saddle, Rand looks very handsome in it," he said. She nodded dumbly, still smiling like a moron and profoundly grateful when Amelia dragged her away under the pretence of helping her mount her horse.

"You cheered him up, well done, but unless you *want* to take this moment to declare undying love for him, I suggest you pull yourself together," Amelia whispered in her ear as she pulled her towards the small caramel-coloured horse that Will had indicated was Eleanor's. Eleanor froze and stared at the taller woman. Amelia smiled at her.

"Oh sweetie, how could I not know? We all know, it's so obvious; how Conlan's missing it is beyond me. Why don't you just tell him?"

Eleanor's panicked mind flooded her with answers to this question and they all came tumbling out in a whispered, breathless rush. "Because he'll laugh at me, because he needs a queen, because he wants children and I can't have them, because his rejection will destroy me."

Amelia stared at her. "OK, you have reasons, but not especially valid ones. Have you thought that he might actually love you back?"

Eleanor raised an eyebrow at Amelia and the woman shrugged.

"Well maybe not," she agreed. "But he might want to, if you tell him how you feel."

Eleanor shook her head violently and Amelia sighed. Saying nothing more on the matter, she showed Eleanor how to mount her horse, giving her quick instruction on how to hold the reins and guide the animal. What she was saying was familiar to Eleanor, as she had ridden Rand, but this would be the first time she would be fully in control and it gave her a thrill of fear and excitement, helping distract her mind from Conlan. She pushed into the animal's head and was pleased with what she found – it might be a small horse, but the mare was brave and dependable. Eleanor sent her feelings of affection, liking the way the animal's body relaxed as she did so. She gently sent a question, asking the animal for her name. The reply was the Dwarfish word for 'horse'. Eleanor smiled, as a horse called 'Horse' seemed very appropriate. They headed out of town and Eleanor felt a pang of loss. She had liked Drent, but with every mile they travelled Conlan's mood improved, so she found it hard to miss the place. Eleanor had studied the map of Mydren in Gregor's book and had been surprised when Conlan had told them they needed to go north along the central mountain range, before they could turn west across the mountains to where the five rivers met. Eleanor had questioned this, earning herself a look of supreme irritation as Conlan had explained that if they moved directly west from Drent they would have to negotiate volcanoes active enough to spit fire, which had confirmed her suspicions about Mydren's underlying plate tectonics. So they headed north for three weeks and then turned west.

Mydren's central mountains were not as high or as barren as the mountains of the north, which Eleanor still considered home. They were gently sloped and mostly covered in a thick blanket of dark green grass, which looked so inviting that when Eleanor had first seen it she had insisted on getting off her horse and running through it barefoot, its spongy, tickling softness a pure delight. It was high summer. Beautiful blue-sky days, a floral scent heavy in the languid air, the soft, light breeze and the sounds of insects and birds gave way to sultry evenings and warm peaceful nights. Even when it rained, it was light and pleasant, leaving them feeling refreshed and cooled. Foraging was plentiful and hunting was good, and without Eleanor's help they ate well for a change, not pushing themselves too hard and sleeping in on some mornings until the sun had fully risen. Eleanor began to feel truly connected to the earth and felt its power pulse through her; she felt so very much alive that she did not seem to be able to stop smiling.

At Amelia's insistence they had begun using some of their free time to explore their abilities. They spent an hour every morning sat together in quiet meditation, their energy strings woven tightly together as they explored the world around them, pushing their energy strings far out across Mydren. Eleanor was amazed to discover just how far they could reach when they used their energies together. Individually they were powerful, but together they were unstoppable. They learnt to feel the energies of their own and each other's elements, learning how to balance them and how to manipulate the flow. Amelia had been their teacher – the solid, skilful grasp she had of her own abilities when it came to manipulating the weather was their best instruction. It soon became obvious to them that balancing the elements required the delicate attention of all four of them working in harmony; for instance, it was no use Freddie attempting to stop a forest fire if air was fighting against him, and Will was unable to stop a raging flood without Eleanor giving him somewhere to divert the water. When it came to balancing the earth Eleanor needed all the help she could get. Once they got the hang of it they worked together in silence – there was no need for conversation, in their heads or anywhere else, as they were so close they could feel the thoughts of the others. Conlan had asked them to explain what it felt like, a curious look on his face. They had tried, but it was difficult, as they were not reading each other's minds, rather each other's intentions, instinctively knowing what the others needed to provide balance. It felt like riding Rand; Eleanor had tried to explain that it felt like a balance of control and power aligned with the pure joy of letting go sometimes and allowing yourself to get carried along. Conlan had smiled at that, a feeling he could understand.

As they travelled they discussed aspects of their old world that could be replicated in Mydren, insights they could bring to their adopted world. This had been prompted by Eleanor asking Conlan what was beyond the sea that surrounded Mydren's land mass in the maps. He had looked at her blankly; Eleanor had been horrified that nobody had ever thought to look. She had explained the very serious spirit of discovery that most people had on her world. Conlan had asked where the benefit lay in knowing how tall a mountain was or what was on the other side of an ocean. Eleanor had smiled and told him that the spirit of exploration had taken men from her world to the moon, pushing forward the boundaries of medicine and science, hugely expanding human knowledge. Conlan had pointed out, unhappily, that the hard work of surviving broke most people's spirits and that the Lords of Mydren, who had the time and wealth to explore, were far too busy stabbing each other in the back, sometimes literally. Will had told Conlan that education, research and learning were something he could encourage as king, the concept driving Conlan into a deep, thoughtful silence that had lasted several days.

The journey east across the mountains took them several months, and Eleanor knew she had never felt happier. She pushed all her dark and unpleasant thoughts about the future to the back of her mind, and she even tried not to think about the book and Conlan's shield. Instead, she concentrated on enjoying each day, the beauty of the world around her and the company of those she loved. As they came out of the mountains, the fun stopped abruptly. Will and Conlan started having quiet, serious conversations that Eleanor could not hear. After three days of their odd behaviour she wanted an explanation. Pulling Horse to a stop, she dismounted and stared at the whispering men, until they noticed her.

"What is it?" Conlan asked.

"I want to know what you and Will are whispering about, it's making me nervous," she said bluntly.

"We're trying to decide the best way to get to where we're going," Will answered.

"If all you are doing is plotting a course, why can't the rest of us help you decide?" Eleanor asked.

"Because it's not as simple as that, Eleanor," Conlan said, his jaw muscles tensing with the flash of irritation in his eyes.

"No," Eleanor agreed. "It never is."

Conlan swung himself off Rand's back and marched towards her, Freddie seeming to appear out of nowhere as he moved closer.

"Eleanor, get my grandfather's book out," Conlan ordered, giving Freddie an irritated look as he stood at Eleanor's side, arms crossed over his chest. Turning to her horse, Eleanor rummaged in a bag and pulled out the book. Conlan snatched it off her, and moving to the back he quickly flicked through until he found the map of Mydren. Holding it out in front of her, he pointed.

"This is where we are now." He moved his finger. "This is where we need to be; in between these two points is the Central Tower, the main seat of power for the Lords of Mydren, and around it hundreds of towns and villages, along with thousands of Protectors. We are trying to work out a safe way through."

Eleanor frowned and then looked at the map. "Will, lend me one of your pencils, please."

Will walked over, handed her a pencil and looked over at the map enquiringly. Carefully, she drew a thin line, plotting a straight course from their position to the five rivers, straight through the middle of Protector territory and taking them within three or four miles of the Central Tower. Conlan looked at her, slightly perplexed. Eleanor smiled.

"They have no idea who we are, so nobody is looking specifically for us. If the area we are going to walk through is as populated as you say, we'll just be five more in a multitude. As long as we don't do anything to draw attention to ourselves, we should just be able to blend in. I don't think we're that important to the Lords of Mydren yet, and frankly we should take advantage of this situation for as long as it lasts."

"I'm sorry, Conlan, but I don't think I can fault her logic," Will said.

"Me neither – if we can take the quick route, let's do it," Freddie agreed.

Conlan glared at her and then at Will; closing the book with a sharp snap, he thrust it back into Eleanor's hands.

They did not exactly sneak past the Central Tower, but Eleanor felt like that was what they were doing, coming close enough that she could see its soaring height in the distance. Conlan and Will were wound up so tightly that

Eleanor could feel their anxiety creeping through her body, leaving her tense and fearful and jumping at every unfamiliar noise or movement. They travelled mostly in silence; the conversations they did have were terse and whispered. Eleanor found that they were talking in each other's heads more and more; Conlan noticed and did not seem particularly happy about it. The denser population meant that finding out-of-the-way places to camp was becoming harder and harder, and they were forced to use Eleanor's dwindling supply of money to stay in various inns in the towns and villages they moved through.

Had she not been in an almost constantly elevated state of fear, Eleanor would have found their journey fascinating. The landscape was a slowly undulating, neat patchwork of fields stretching out in front of her. She had no idea what the crops were, but fields of dark yellow, purple and gold stood out among the greens and browns. Eleanor had quietly asked Conlan if he knew what was being grown; she decided he probably did, although his response of 'Do I look like a farmer?' had not been very helpful. The towns they moved through ranged from opulent, on the level of the richer parts of Baydon, to miserably impoverished. After Conlan's comments she had expected broken, despairing people like those she had seen in Baydon's slums, and while this was certainly the case in some places, it was not true of everyone they met. The main roads were busy with merchants moving carts and wagons between the thronging towns, well-dressed men and women riding past on beautiful, highly-strung horses and large dogs trotting obediently at their sides. Farmers moving herds of cows and black-horned sheep occasionally blocked the way. They even passed a troop of brightly dressed players who practiced their juggling skills in time to the cheerful sound of a flute. Nearly everyone they passed smiled and nodded polite greetings or, in the case of the merchants, tried to sell them something. They also met patrols of twenty or thirty Protectors, who forced all traffic on the road into the ditches on either side as they marched past, but not a single Protector gave them so much as a sideways glance.

Five weeks of hard riding during the day and they made it through the area Conlan considered 'dangerous' and out the other side. Eleanor had no idea what they were going to do on the way back, as she had money left for maybe one or two nights in an inn for the five of them, but that was a worry for later. The towns and villages they passed through became sporadic and spaced further apart, and they were able to start camping again. Signs of cottage industry and agriculture began to disappear from the landscape, and Mydren reverted to the natural beauty Eleanor loved – vast virgin forests, grassy, rolling hills and a profusion of wild flowers. They travelled west for several weeks, eventually meeting a wide, fast-flowing river. This was one of the five rivers that led to the waterfall she had seen in her dreams and in the book; they followed it southwest along its banks.

The sun had dipped to the warm, golden glow that preceded sunset, when they saw the great lake in the distance. Fed by five separate rivers, the lake sat in a bowl of land, steep sloping hills rising up on all sides. It reminded Eleanor of the high lake at home and she felt a pang of homesickness; how beautiful their lake would look in the warm summer sun. At the far side there was a gap in the hills, and the water ran up to the edge, looking like an enormous infinity pool. *The waterfall.* The land where the lake sat and the rivers met dropped away on the other side of the waterfall, a cliff edge slipping hundreds of feet straight down. *God's front doorstep.* Instinctively reaching out an energy string, Eleanor investigated the underlying rock strata and found, far below them, a fault line where the earth had just slipped at some point. Eleanor tried to work out from the rocks how long ago that had been, but the strata was too messed up, too complicated – the earth was singing in the wrong key. It felt stable now, as the pressure was currently much further east. She had felt it in their morning meditations, but she also felt how easy it would be to destabilise the fault, to apply a small amount of energy in the right place and Mydren would split itself apart. This was something they were going to have to factor in to their balancing efforts.

They moved round the edge of the water towards the waterfall, having to cross two of the wide, deep, lazily-flowing rivers which fed the lake. At the first river Eleanor was pleased to discover that Horse was an excellent swimmer and followed as she was led across with little trouble, although Eleanor felt an idiot with a bag on her head holding her books, sword and dagger so they did not get wet. Conlan, of course, had no problems at all, because Rand was a marvel on four legs. He did not even have to dismount and sat waist-high in water, holding his book, boot knife and sword above his head, a smug grin on his face. Freddie and Amelia had some difficulties, but they eventually managed to negotiate the water. Unfortunately Will's horse was having none of it and refused point blank to get so much as a hoof wet. Stripping Rand of everything but his bridal in an effort to reduce water damage, Conlan headed back across the river. Will handed him his sketchpad, pencils, playing cards and sword so that Conlan could ferry them back across the river to the safety of dry land. Then Will tried dragging the moody, black animal into the water. Freddie laughed until he cried over Will's efforts and Conlan's dry comment on the irony of the Avatar of Water's horse being afraid to swim almost finished him off. Wanting to be slightly more helpful, Amelia suggested from the far bank that Will go into the horse's mind and encourage it to cross the river. As he tried this, the horse reared back and then plunged forward and bit his arm, pulling as far back from him as Will's grip on the reins would allow, eyes wild and nostrils flaring. After giving them a dirty look from across the water, he shrugged a 'what now?' expression. Wondering what was wrong with the animal, Eleanor warned Will that she was going to try talking to it and he should watch out, just in case it tried to bite him again. Gently, carefully, Eleanor entered the frightened creature's mind. It was a spinning tornado of terror and confusion. Sending out a steady stream of calming, encouraging feelings the spinning finally slowed down, revealing a memory of falling into a river and nearly drowning when the horse had been a foal. All water was bad and to be avoided. While the horse liked Will he was not going in the water for him. Using Will's trick, Eleanor wrapped the animal's consciousness in a soft, numbing cocoon of calming love, insulating it from its fear and separating it from reality – lightly anaesthetising it. She then very softly but insistently called it to her. She watched, focused on nothing but the horse, as it walked slowly into the water, its wide eyes holding a relaxed, vacant look. It had a brief moment of panic as the riverbed fell away and it had to swim, but Eleanor sent it calm instructions on what to do, adding layers to the insulation she had placed around its mind. It reached the bank, pulling itself out of the water to stand in front of her, dripping, shivering and confused as to how it got there. Will, who had swum after it, pulled himself out of the water and up the bank, giving Eleanor an odd look.

"What?" she asked.

"How did you do that? How do you even make sense of what's in its head?" he asked, taking the animal's reins and giving it an exasperated glance.

"I just looked at its thoughts, they're mostly pictures," Eleanor answered.

"I couldn't do it, it was like trying to understand modern art; I know I should be able to see something in it, but it's just a confusing mess. I could see the nasty beast had thoughts, but they made no sense," Will said as Amelia tried to inspect the bite on his arm.

Eleanor frowned. "He's not nasty; in fact, he likes you and feels guilty about biting you. He was just frightened. He fell in a river as a baby and nearly drowned, so now he quite sensibly avoids water."

"Oh… How did you know that? I'm meant to be the mind-meld guy, so why couldn't I see that?" Will asked, irritated with himself. Eleanor shrugged.

"Maybe you can just talk to fish," Conlan ventured with a totally straight face, looking mildly surprised when Freddie fell over laughing again.

At the next river Will waited until they had all crossed, and when Eleanor offered to help him he gave her a smug smile and closed his eyes. Eleanor watched in amazement as the river in front of her began to slow. It was as if Will had drawn a line across the water – the river on one side of it stopped flowing, the water on the other side continued to move, draining away into the lake and leaving a wall of water, the river on one side and an almost dry riverbed on the other. Not opening his eyes, his face a mask of total concentration, Will kicked his heels, urging his horse forward. The animal gave the wall of water, gently tumbling and rolling in on itself, a frightened glance, but did as it was told, Will trusting it to pick its way across the riverbed and up the bank. The horse stopped when it reached the other side, and with a shuddering sigh Will let his concentration go. The wall of water collapsed and the river rushed in to fill the void, soon resuming its normal pace, as if it had never been stopped.

"Show off," Conlan said, but he did not look surprised. *He's seen Will do this before*, Eleanor realised, still trying to understand what she had just witnessed. Freddie's look of impressed amazement matched her own; Amelia, however, looked worried and annoyed.

"Wow, that was so cool!" Freddie said, staring at Will in admiration.

"If you can do that, why are we getting wet?" Eleanor asked.

"Because what he just did takes every ounce of his strength and he shouldn't be doing it at all," Amelia muttered, moving her horse towards Will as he slumped forward in his saddle. She managed to reach him before he fell to the ground and helped him to stay upright while he took slow deep breaths.

Freddie was still staring. "Really, Will, very cool – just like Moses."

Will raised his head and smiled faintly, his eyes unfocused.

"I don't understand," Eleanor said, her ever-churning mind spitting out questions and filling her head with confusion. "In our balancing sessions I've felt Will manipulate the water flow of far bigger stretches of water, and that didn't do this to him."

Will gave her a long appraising look. "Eleanor, changing the flow of water is easy; a small nudge, an alternative route, letting it do what it does anyway but just in a different direction. What I just did was stop the flow, I made water do something it doesn't naturally do. Could you stop the earth turning?" Eleanor shook her head, shocked by the concept. Will nodded and continued in a slow, tired voice. "When I stopped the river flowing I held back the weight of the whole river, held the molecules within it, from here all the way to the river's source. That's a lot of water, and it takes a lot of effort."

"Really? Totally awesome," Freddie whispered as Amelia glared at him.

"Don't encourage him!" she snapped.

There was an uncomfortable silence, broken by Conlan's confused question.

"Who is Moses?"

They set up camp under a large tree by the side of the lake, where the bank slid gently into the water via a rocky beach. They built a large fire and made racks so they could dry their clothes and bags. Eleanor, still damp, pulled her boots and leather wrist cuff off and went swimming with Amelia and Freddie. The water was cool, deliciously so, and made her nerves tingle, washing away the dust and aches of travel. Without having to worry about Horse or getting her books wet, Eleanor was able to enjoy the experience. Amelia tried to get Will to rest, but it lasted ten minutes before he came to join them, unable to resist the obvious pleasure that being immersed in water gave him. After much badgering they even convinced Conlan to stop oiling Rand's saddle and get wet again, splashing and playing, Conlan trying and failing to beat Will in a swimming race. Moving away from the boisterous play of the others Eleanor relaxed, floating on her back, her soaking clothes sticking to her body and trapping air bubbles so they tickled as they moved around her body, looking for release. Above her the delicate pinks and oranges of sunset streaked the sky with colour. *So beautiful.* She could feel the tug of the current as it moved towards the waterfall's deadly drop, but she was too far away for it to be a concern, as their little beach was sheltered by a small, natural harbour. The sun dropped and Eleanor began to feel cold; the fire looked inviting and she swam to shore, avoiding Freddie who seemed to be on a mission to dunk everyone. *A strange quest for the Avatar of Fire.* Clothes heavy, dripping and clinging, and hair plastered back against her head, Eleanor pulled herself out of the water. As she stood up she was able to see out over the lip of the waterfall to the land hundreds of feet below. She could hear the water crashing down, recognising the noise from her dreams with a shudder.

The next morning, Conlan and Freddie spent several hours scouting out a way down to the bottom of the waterfall as Eleanor, Will and Amelia packed up the camp. To take the easiest route they travelled several miles down from the waterfall, where the cliffs were not as steep. They moved carefully, leading their horses while moving along narrow, rock-strewn pathways. It took the better part of the day to reach the bottom, but fortunately it was not as hot as it had been; the sky now overcast with threatening dark-grey clouds. Conlan asked Amelia if she could stop the imminent storm, as it was hard enough moving down the cliffside without water making everything slippery. Amelia examined the clouds and was confident that they would make it to the bottom before it started raining. The entire journey was a terrifying, nerve-wracking experience for Eleanor, as the drops were horrendous and the ground rushed to meet her from dizzying heights. She kept a firm hold of Horse's reins, letting the brave animal offer her comfort and support and trying her best to focus on just the ground in front of her.

Eleanor was relieved when they finally reached the flat terrain at the bottom of the cliff and made their way back to the foot of the waterfall. That relief vanished quickly, though, replaced by a gut-churning dread as she watched the water crash onto the rocks in the pool. It was just as it had been in her dream. *No, something is different… I can't smell rotting dragon.* This realisation brought her some comfort, but Eleanor still shuddered as she looked up and saw the grassy ledge high above them that the dragon had always appeared from in her dreams. Will noticed her look, his eyes filling with sympathy and pity, and she shrugged and smiled in return.

"So where is the chalice?" Conlan asked.

"In a cave, behind the waterfall," Will said, watching the pounding and crashing water thoughtfully.

"We're going to get wet again," Conlan said with an air of resignation.

Will shook his head. "Not necessarily."

"Will, no!" Amelia said in horror. "That much water, are you insane?!"

"I'm not going to stop it, Amelia, I don't think I could. I was just thinking I could divert it so we could get past easier," Will said, frowning at the worry on Amelia's face.

They left the horses in a small stand of trees, a short distance down the riverbank. Eleanor told Horse and Rand what they were doing, smiling when both of them gave her the impression that she should be careful. Moving slowly across the slippery, slimy rocks, they made their way towards the waterfall, getting as close as they could. The noise was too loud to allow conversation, so Conlan raised a questioning eyebrow at Will, who nodded and closed his eyes. Nothing happened. Will screwed his eyes tight, biting his bottom lip, his hands clenched in tight fists. A rippling shudder went through the solid wall of falling water in front of them and echoed in Will's body. Slowly, the flow moved, as if a giant hand was pulling it aside like a curtain. The water splattered down onto the rocks and bank on the far side of the pool. With the water flowing out to the side, a large, black cave opened before them, and they stared into unblinking darkness. Eleanor shivered. Conlan led them forward, Eleanor and Amelia each taking one of Will's arms so they could guide him forward so he did not have to break the effort he was giving to diverting the waterfall. Negotiating the rocks and ledge with Will was difficult, but they made it eventually. As he released the water slowly back into place, Will's full weight collapsed into Amelia. She staggered, struggling to hold him up. Freddie moved to her side, supporting them both as Will sank to his knees, eyes glazed, taking slow deep breaths. With the water back in place, it was gloomy, cold and noisy. Eleanor knew Will and Amelia were talking in each other's heads, although given the expression on Amelia's face, maybe they were arguing. Conlan saw the same thing Eleanor did and frowned. Will forced himself back up and glared at Amelia as a look of hurt misery filled her eyes. He spun away from her and marched towards the cave's forbidding void. A single tear ran slowly down Amelia's face as she watched him; she saw Eleanor looking at her and brushed it away irritably. At the entrance to the tunnel, Freddie was fiddling with the flints he had brought with him, sparks flying. There was a blaze of orange light, which after the gloom left spots on Eleanor's retinas when she closed her eyes. A pile of torches lay by the wall, so Freddie lit five and handed them out. *Where did these come from?* Eleanor used her energy to examine the wood; it had been cut within the last few years. Apprehension gripped her – there was something wrong. She reached out for Freddie.

That's the first time I've ever seen Will purposely hurt Amelia. Freddie sounded uncomfortable, like his worldview had been shaken.

Freddie, something's not right.

Yeah! Will and Amelia are arguing.

No! Don't worry about Will and Amelia – they love each other, they'll get over it. This is important. We have a problem.

What?

Look at the torch you're carrying. That's new wood, a few years old.

So?

So who put it here?

Silence.

We need to warn Conlan, Freddie said.

Then we need to get further into this cave, because he's not going to hear anything we try to yell over this noise.

OK, what do you think they were arguing about?

Eleanor shook her head. *I don't know.*

The cave turned out to be a long tunnel which had been naturally carved by water at some point, making the floor uneven and difficult to walk on. While the blazing flames of the torches lit the way, they also left them feeling blind and disorientated if they looked at them. Eleanor held her torch high above her head, trying to get a balance so she could see where she was treading without losing sight. *If someone attacks, I'm going to need all the advantage I can get,* she thought grimly as she ran her hand over Remic's knife hanging at her waist, thankful she never let it out of her sight. She knew Will and Conlan had similar small knives concealed on their person. She assumed Freddie did too, as the man loved his weapons, so it would be Amelia who was unarmed, only wearing her sword when she had to. Amelia would have to shield herself while they dealt with the problem.

At the end of the tunnel, they emerged into a voluminous cave. The roof was invisible in the darkness high above them and the far side was as equally hard to see.

"We need to be careful – someone else comes here," Conlan said, his deep voice echoing through the cave.

Freddie and Eleanor looked at each other in surprise.

"How do you know?" Eleanor asked.

Conlan turned to look at her. "These torches are new, there are foot marks in the slime on the rocks outside and I can feel it."

They fanned out across the cave, looking for... well, they had no idea, something out of place perhaps.

Deep in thought, Eleanor jumped a mile when Amelia screamed a sharp, shrill, terrified sound that echoed around the cave and made it hard to work out where it had come from. Turning around wildly, she moved as fast as she could in the direction she thought was right. She found Amelia sat on the ground in front of the cave wall, where she seemed to have collapsed, her torch lying at her side. Eleanor was the first one to reach her, skidding to a halt on the loose rocks. She dropped to her side.

"Amelia, what happened? Are you all right?"

Amelia said nothing, her grey eyes black with fear and staring in front of her in terror. Slowly, feeling fear run up and down her spine in stilettos, Eleanor turned her head to follow Amelia's gaze. As the flickering light of the torches fell on the cave wall she froze at the monster in front of her. From high above the dragon stared down at her with hate-filled yellow eyes.

Conlan, Will and Freddie arrived shortly afterwards. Amelia and Eleanor were still staring in shock at the beast before them. It was the dragon, just as Eleanor remembered him, face frozen in an eternal snarl and claws extended. The cave wall was clear, see-through almost, like the dragon had been dipped in plastic or was the surprise in a child's bar of soap. Still not able to form a coherent sentence, Eleanor pulled herself shakily to her feet and walked towards the wall, resting her hand against its smooth, cold, polished surface and pushing an energy string into it. It was crystal – the dragon had been encased in a solid tomb of crystal. This was how the Avatar of Earth had trapped his soul; it was stuck in the crystal's lattice. The creature may be dead, but Eleanor could still feel its life force and snapped her energy free, not wanting to be dragged into the dragon's mind again.

"That's the dragon? The one that attacked you?" Amelia whispered. Eleanor turned and nodded. Amelia still looked horrified.

"It's dead, Amelia, it can't hurt you," Eleanor said quietly, wanting to reassure her frightened friend.

"It managed to hurt you," Freddie commented.

Eleanor gave him an irritated glance. "Yes, but I don't think it wants to hurt anyone else."

Amelia pulled herself to her feet. "Why does everybody assume that everything I think and say is motivated by fear?" Her loud, angry voice repeating itself across the cave.

"Because mostly it is," Will said. Eleanor was shocked by the low, hard, angry tone.

Amelia glared at him. "Maybe if I wasn't so dependent on you I wouldn't be quite so terrified of losing you all the time," Amelia spat back.

Eleanor was confused; their conversation was out of place, and how had they gone from the dragon to being dependent on Will? She decided that this must be a continuation of the argument they had started outside the cave.

"You don't have to be dependent on me," Will snapped. "Do what Eleanor did, learn to survive. Learn how to take care of yourself."

Amelia stared at Will, her eyes betraying the hurt coursing through her body. "Is that what you want?"

"I want you to be happy, I want you to be able to relax, but mostly I want you to accept the truth," Will said quietly, holding her angry gaze with one of his own.

"What truth?"

"That everybody dies, Amelia, even Avatars. You can't stop it or hide from it. The only thing you can do is accept it and not let it ruin the joy that life can bring you in the meantime. I would rather have one day loving you, knowing it would end, than an eternity without you."

Silence. Amelia stared at Will as heavy, slow tears slipped over and began to run down her face. Conlan and Freddie looked extremely uncomfortable, as if they were intruding on something far too private, but Will had wanted them to hear what he was saying and Eleanor wondered why.

"Erm... Can I interrupt?" Freddie asked, looking from Amelia to Will.

"What is it, Freddie?" Will asked, his eyes not leaving Amelia's face as she worked to control her hurt.

"I think I've found the chalice," Freddie said quietly. He nodded to the bottom of the wall in which the dragon was entombed. Underneath the massive creature, a small alcove had been carved into the crystal – and within lay the chalice. Will finally took his eyes off Amelia's face and walked to the wall, taking the chalice out and giving the dragon a wary glance as he did so.

"Well that was easier than I expected," Conlan murmured.

Eleanor turned, intending to give him a mouthful for tempting fate, when she realised she was too late. Conlan saw her expression, or perhaps her hand's instinctive move to her knife, and whipped round to see what she did. Figures. Twelve of them. They were some distance away but getting rapidly closer, and it took Eleanor a moment to realise why she could see them in the dark. They were glowing. The sickly green light radiated out of their skin, giving each a slight luminous corona.

"*What* are *they*?" Freddie whispered in surprise.

"I have no clue," Conlan whispered back, sounding just as astonished.

The tall, skeletal figures stopped in front of them, fanning out in a semi-circle around the group. Eleanor stared. They were the oddest things she had ever seen. They had the basic look of humans —arms, legs, torso and head — but thereafter the similarity ended. Their skin looked like it had scales, not dragon scales but small, soft, translucent fish scales. They all had large, black, cold eyes, like those of a shark, and when they blinked the eyelids moved horizontally across their eyes like shutters. They had bumps where their faces should have had noses, but this clearly no longer served any biological function. *A genetic trait left over from a common heritage*, Eleanor thought, noticing the lack of ears, the gill-like slits in their necks and their webbed fingers. They had mouths framed with thin, hard-looking lips and Eleanor could see rows of short, vicious-looking, needle-like teeth. Their bald heads and bright flowing robes made Eleanor think of soaking wet Buddhist monks – an image totally ruined by the heavy, lethal-looking spears they all carried, sharp gold spearheads reflecting their green glow.

"Who are they?" Will asked quietly, coming up behind them, the chalice in one hand and a small dagger in the other. Eleanor noticed sharp blades had appeared in both of Freddie's hands. Conlan had not drawn a weapon, so Eleanor followed his lead.

"I don't know," Conlan said, his voice low, he gave Will an odd look.

"What do we do?" Freddie whispered.

"I'm open to suggestions," Conlan said.

Eleanor snorted. "Well that's a first!" she spluttered, her loud, sarcastic voice echoing across the cave. The reaction in the beings in front of them was startling. They cringed back for a moment, then hissed deep in their throats, raised their spears and ran at them.

It all happened so quickly that they had no time to make a plan. The green beings were too close and moving too quickly to give Amelia time to shield or to give any of them time to use their energy without risking hurting each other, so all five of them reacted on instinct honed by hours and hours of Conlan's combat training. They spread out as the green bodies flowed between them. Freddie moved to Amelia's side, handing her one of his knives as he did so. Eleanor contemplated drawing her knife, but she knew she would fight better without it. If she had been carrying her sword it would have been a different matter. Two glowing green blurs bore down on her. She stepped lightly out of the way of the one on the right's spear, punching it hard where its ribs should be as it moved past. It staggered, gasping. The being on the left stopped and whirled round, stabbing down at her, but she moved to the side at the last second, allowing the force the creature had given to the move to overbalance it, driving its spear into the cave floor. Eleanor gave the spear's shaft a strong side-kick, splintering the wood. The creature pulled itself upright to find the spearhead still buried in the cave floor and just a wooden stick in its hand. The creature she had punched had recovered enough that it was coming at her again. It thrust towards her, but she twisted out of the way, feeling a sharp stinging pain as the spear's razor-sharp head grazed her side. *Too close.* As she span around, she grabbed the spear's shaft with both hands and whipped it out of the creature's hands. Still turning, she brought it up and slammed the handle into the creature's head with a bone-cracking thwack. She felt movement behind her, and glancing over her shoulder she pushed the spear back under her arm and into the stomach of the other creature as it used the spear's shaft she had left it with to bludgeon her, a heavy crack across her back. White-hot pain flashed and black spots swam through her vision. The creature she had hit in the head toppled to the ground and lay still. With a yank, Eleanor tore the spear from the hissing creature behind her and twisted to face it, whipping the spear around in a relaxed, ready grip. The creature staggered, clutched its stomach and fell to its knees, green and light blue gloop oozing through its fingers. Eleanor raised the spear's deadly point to its neck, intent on finishing it off.

"STOP!"

Will's voice was so commanding that Eleanor froze. She turned her head. Conlan stood nearest to her, three creatures lying at his feet. He had frozen in the process of punching the lights out on the fourth. He had not even worked up a sweat. Freddie and Amelia stood back to back, two creatures at their feet, clearly dead. A third watched them warily, also frozen. A creature was curled up in a ball against the cave wall, shaking, as it watched with cold, emotionless eyes. Eleanor could not work out from its expression if it was injured or just afraid. Another body lay face down, dead, near the cave's exit, Conlan's boot knife sticking out of its back. Will was standing over one of the beings – he had its own spear jammed into its neck, but he had an odd expression on his face, as if he was listening intently. Slowly, he lowered the spear, dropped it to the ground and reached a hand out to the green being, offering it assistance to stand. A firm, webbed green hand took Will's and the being stood. Surprised, Conlan released the robe of the creature he held and dropped his raised fist. The creature staggered back, tripping over the body of an unconscious comrade and landing on its back, staring at Conlan in terror, Eleanor assumed, but it was tricky to tell; their faces did not show emotion in a way she understood.

Eleanor watched numbly as the green beings silently checked their dead and wounded. They made no noise, but they were clearly communicating with each other and Will. *Maybe they don't like noise.* Every so often one would approach Will, tilt its head to one side and they would stare at each other for a moment. Will would nod or shake his head. *Why are they just talking to Will?* Considering who they attacked, Eleanor decided the beings had got off lightly. Conlan had not been trying to kill them, or they would have suffered far heavier losses. As it was, they had three dead and Eleanor was doubtful the creature she had stabbed in the stomach would survive. She felt guilt wash over her whenever she looked at it lying on the ground and surrounded by its friends. *Are they friends? Are they family?* The dead creatures did not lose their green glow when they died, and Eleanor tried very hard not to look at their eerily glowing lifeless bodies as the others fussed around them. *Bioluminescence caused by some enzyme in the skin?* It was not something created by their energy, as Eleanor could feel that was gone. She remained where she was, as the others did, watching as the green beings flowed around them.

Eventually Conlan's curiosity got the better of him.

"Will, what's going on?"

His voice was calm and soft, but the creatures froze, all eyes turned towards him, and Eleanor unconsciously tightened her grip on the spear she was still holding. Will looked at Conlan and shook his head slowly. Looking extremely irritated, Conlan nodded once and said nothing more. The green being that had been trembling against the cave wall was carefully and reverently helped to its feet. Something in the way the other creatures touched it made Eleanor think this was someone special, important almost. The being was smaller than the others and moved with more noticeable grace. *Is this a female?* It walked towards Will, stopping in front of him. They stared at each other for a long time. Eventually Will raised his head and looked at Conlan, his gaze intense.

"Whatever happens next," he whispered. "Don't intervene."

Conlan nodded his agreement. Will returned his gaze to the being in front of him, and to Eleanor's surprise dropped to his knees before it. Green hands were raised, webbed fingers spreading out like green baseball gloves, and Will's head was gripped firmly between them. Almost immediately his face screwed up in pain – his eyes rolled and his hands grasped the being's forearms as his body shook violently. Amelia sobbed involuntarily and made a move towards him. Freddie grabbed her arm, shaking his head. Their eyes glazed over as they argued. Whatever Freddie said, Amelia was finally convinced and slumped against him sobbing softly, unable to watch Will's obvious agony. Head still trapped between the glowing green hands, Will's jerks and twitches were becoming weaker. He whimpered as his arms fell to his sides, and Eleanor got the impression that he was only upright because he was being held there. His breath was coming out in short, strained pants, and blood ran from his nose and eyes. Terrified that they were going to kill him, Eleanor dropped her spear and ran forward. Conlan grabbed at her, pulling her off her feet and pinning her to him, his strong arms wrapped securely around her waist and chest. She squirmed in his grip, kicking and flailing with her arms and legs. She heard his grunts of pain as her heels and elbows struck him, but she could see Will dying in front of her – she had to help.

"Let go of me," she hissed.

"Will asked us not to intervene. Trust him," Conlan whispered harshly as he struggled to hold on to her.

"But they're hurting him," Eleanor moaned softly, looking at Will – face pale, eyes closed. He no longer looked conscious.

"And do you think you're the only one finding that hard to take?" Conlan whispered in her ear. Eleanor froze at the pain in his words.

When he felt certain she was not going to struggle any further, Conlan lowered her feet to the ground but kept a firm arm around her. Eleanor found it comforting. With no visible sense of ending, Will's head was released from the being's grip and he toppled to his side, lying still. Eleanor felt Conlan's body tense. For several heartbeats nobody moved, and then Amelia tore herself from Freddie's grip and ran to Will's side, trembling fingers touching his face.

"Is he OK?" Conlan whispered. Amelia turned a tear-stained face to his, her doubt and fear burning in her eyes, then turned back to Will, gently stroking his hair. The green beings began moving around them again as if nothing had happened. Will twitched and slowly opened his eyes, and with Amelia's help he pulled himself up to sit upright. He looked awful. Even after he had wiped the blood from his face, he was pale and shaking, and he gazed at them from unfocused, bloodshot eyes. Eleanor felt a strong energy string brush against her and pulled it in, realising that Freddie, Amelia and Will had combined their energy strings so they could all talk together.

OK, what's going on?

Not now, Eleanor, Will said, sounding remarkably like Conlan. *We need to leave – as slowly and as silently as we can manage.*

A million questions and thoughts whirled round Eleanor's head. Hurt by Will's rebuke she would have kept quiet, but one persistent thought needed to be aired before they left.

Will, I think we are meant to make these people our allies. I think that's why the chalice was placed here.

Making these people our allies is not an option right now. If we're lucky we might get out of here alive, Will countered.

We were doing a pretty good job of kicking their glowing green butts before you told us to stop, Freddie commented.

Will glared at Freddie. *This is the advanced party... any minute now hundreds of these green creatures are going to show up, and I do* NOT *want to be around for that. I made a deal – these guys will let us go, along with the chalice, although they are not happy about it and they're not sure how the others will react when they arrive. We need to get away from the water so they don't follow us.*

What deal? What did they do to you? Eleanor asked suspiciously.

I won't say it again, Eleanor, NOT *now!* Will snapped.

His anger leaving her thoroughly dispirited, Eleanor nodded and headed with the others towards the cave's exit, making sure to take silent, careful steps. Conlan retrieved his small knife, still coated in glowing green goo, and then had the presence of mind to pick up a torch. They crowded together to walk down the tunnel back towards the waterfall, the lack of light increasing Eleanor's fear. Will moved the wall of water aside so they could get out. Amelia said nothing but left it to Freddie and Eleanor to lead him from the ledge and out of the way while he concentrated on keeping the water back. As Will let his hold on the water go, he staggered again, but Freddie was ready for it and supported him. It took him longer to recover this time, and Eleanor could see his exhaustion. Amelia saw it too, worry for him clear in her eyes. *Maybe Will should be grateful someone cares so much about him.*

They stepped from the waterfall into a heavy rain storm, wind whipping up around them and ponderous dark-grey clouds casting a gloomy pall over the land. Will hustled them away from the waterfall and the river and they made their way back to the horses. Eleanor quietly greeted Horse as Conlan's irritation and curiosity finally exploded.

"What was *that* about?" he asked, looking at Will.

"They are natives of Mydren; they evolved here, they didn't come through the portal. They live out under the sea. They worship the dragon and we just violated their sacred space. Every year, hundreds of their people come here in groups on a pilgrimage up the river to the waterfall, to talk to the dragon. In return, he tells them the future," Will said in a slow, tired voice.

"Can't be very good at it – he didn't tell them we were coming!" Freddie commented.

"Why did they only talk to you?" Eleanor asked, ignoring Freddie.

"They said they tried, but you didn't recognise their presence in your minds. I was the only one that did," Will said.

"So you *can* talk to fish," Freddie said, a grin spreading across his face.

Will gave him an irritated scowl. "They're not fish, Freddie, they're people and we killed them for no real reason."

"I think we were supposed to make allies of them," Conlan said softly.

Will raised an eyebrow at him in surprise. "So Eleanor said, but I don't think that's possible right now. Maybe in a few decades when they've calmed down."

"Maybe if they hadn't attacked us, we wouldn't have had to defend ourselves. Can't we explain that?" Eleanor asked.

"They interpreted you yelling as an act of aggression, Eleanor – they thought *they* were defending themselves," Will said.

"Oh." Eleanor felt her guilt crash over her again. "I didn't know."

"Maybe this will teach you to think before you open your mouth," Will said, hard eyes and stern tone making Eleanor cringe. She dropped her head as the wind and rain plastered her hair across her face. She had lost Conlan potential allies because she was unable to keep her sarcastic comments to herself. Shame burnt through her.

"So what was that 'person' doing to you?" Conlan asked.

"Ransacking my head," Will said, holding Conlan's gaze, his expression saying several things that Eleanor did not understand.

"Looked like it hurt," Freddie said.

Not taking his eyes off Conlan, Will nodded. "I don't think our minds were entirely compatible; she certainly didn't intend to hurt me."

"But you knew she was going to?" Amelia asked in a quiet emotionless voice.

"Yes."

"Then why did you do it?" Amelia snapped. Will finally moved his gaze from Conlan to Amelia, his tired blue eyes holding hers.

"They're as curious about us as we are about them; she wanted to know about us. I offered her a deal – my memories for our lives and the chalice."

"She stripped you of your memories?" Freddie asked, horrified.

Will shook his head. "No, she sort of copied them, like Earth did when she stormed through my head. To be honest, I have no idea how much she saw, which is a little worrying because I'm not exactly the best ambassador for Avatars, or human beings in general for that matter."

"What was her mind like?" Conlan asked.

"Discussion for a little later, out of the rain perhaps, when I don't have a headache that feels like it's going to rip my skull in two," Will said, looking pointedly at Conlan again.

"OK, so where to next?" Freddie asked.

"I don't know," Eleanor said in a small guilty voice. "I haven't been able to work out the location of the sword."

"Then we should find somewhere we can rest for a while to give you some time to think," Conlan said, his tone soft, reassuring and very welcome after Will's rebuke. Eleanor smiled at him, and before she knew how it happened her world was turned upside down.

Eleanor registered Conlan's eyes widening in shock, registered the arrow that flew past her head close enough for her to feel the fletching brush her face. She registered Amelia shriek Conlan's name, saw her move in front of him and watched in paralysed horror as the projectile thudded deep into her chest, pushing her back into Conlan with such force that she knocked them both off their feet. Still unable to move, Eleanor saw them land, the air 'whoomphing' out of Conlan's lungs as Amelia landed on top of him. Freddie yelled Eleanor's name and she turned in time to see the arrow that should have pierced her skull fall inert to the ground as it hit solid air in front of her. *Amelia is shielding, she's not dead.* Eleanor turned back to her stricken friend. Conlan had sat her up, cradling her slumped body, a look of horror on his face. Amelia was pale. A thin line of blood dribbled from the corner of her mouth and her eyes burned with agony as she fought for consciousness. She pushed herself to keep shielding them, to keep protecting them. More arrows struck the shield. Overhead lightning flashed and the sky rumbled its sympathy for its wounded Avatar. Will stared; he made no move towards Amelia but dropped to his knees, wrapping his arms around himself, wretched devastation etched into his face.

"Where are the arrows coming from?" Freddie asked, coming up to Eleanor's side.

"Amelia," Eleanor moaned. It was currently as far as her thoughts went. Putting a hand on either side of her face, Freddie wrenched her eyes away from Amelia and forced her to look at him.

"Eleanor, Amelia is not going to keep shielding us forever – we need to find out who's trying to kill us before our protection fails," Freddie said.

"You mean before Amelia dies!" Eleanor snapped, pulling away from his hands.

"Eleanor, please don't make me do this by myself," Freddie said, looking hurt.

Eleanor felt her anger fade away, knowing that Freddie needed her. Moving to Horse, she pulled her sword from her blanket roll and strapped it to her waist, watching Freddie do the same. She glanced briefly at Amelia; Conlan was talking softly to her, comforting her, tenderly stroking her hair and bending his head over her to keep the rain from her face. Will was still knelt to the side, watching them. It was hard to tell in the rain, but Eleanor suspected he was crying. The arrows continued to crash against Amelia's shield, and the frequency made Eleanor think they were dealing with more than one archer. Moving carefully they discovered that Amelia had only erected a shield in a horseshoe shape around them, so using the trees and shrubs for cover they moved towards the river, creeping silently downstream. Freddie reached for Eleanor's hand, gripping it tightly. They had not travelled far before they heard voices. Nodding grimly, Freddie headed towards the sound, pulling Eleanor after him. Moving closer, Eleanor found she could hear what they were saying.

"It is them, I am telling you; six summers of waiting and it is them. Cannot believe I got one... think we will get a bonus when we take their bodies back?" The voice sounded excited.

"We were told not to kill the one with the scar down his face... that had better not be the one you hit," another voice growled.

"Will you two shut up and pay attention. Keep firing at that shield. When it fails you are going to have to make those arrows count. I do not want you to kill any of them yet, so just wound them," a strong, commanding voice ordered.

"I think I lost two of them, did you hit them?" the excited voice asked, uncertainty creeping into the tone.

"No, you idiot, there is a shield up. Where did you lose them?" the growling voice demanded.

Eleanor listened to the conversation in confusion. Why had they been waiting for them for six summers? How did they know who they were? How did they know where they were going to be? She pushed the questions to the back of her churning mind for later and tried to concentrate on what she was doing. Moving slowly, they emerged at the edge of a camp —quite a permanent camp by the looks of it. They had built sturdy shelters, and Eleanor could see bedrolls and personal effects within them. The fire had a permanent-looking metal grill secured over its embers, and Eleanor could see rustic handmade chairs placed in front of it. There was a lot of 'stuff'; they had been here a long time, maybe the six summers they were talking about. She needed to talk to these men, to ask them who had sent them and what they were doing here. The three men stood with their backs to them. Two had bows raised and were taking it in turns to loose arrows out in the direction of where they had left the others. Eleanor was just about to tell Freddie they needed to talk to the men, when the fire started to jump and hiss, the embers bursting into roaring flame. In the split second she realised what Freddie was doing, it was too late. His eyes blazing, he released all his energy at the three men, watching dispassionately as they turned into jerking, screaming fireballs, the slightly sweet and sickly smell of burnt flesh filling the air. They stumbled, flailing around their camp in agony and setting fire to their shelters. Eleanor felt the extreme heat and raised an arm to protect her face, feeling the cut on her side scream in protest as she did so. The men dropped, their bodies continuing to burn. Feeling a little sick, Eleanor snatched her hand away from Freddie's and walked around the blazing camp and back towards where they had left the others. *Freddie didn't need me for that, why did I have to watch?* She felt empty, emotionally blank. She knew she would be angry with Freddie later, but right now all she could see was Amelia's pale face.

Amelia was just as she had left her. Conlan tenderly held her and amazingly she was still conscious. Will was still knelt to the side, his face and eyes now blank. Amelia's shield was gone, and Eleanor wondered distractedly how close they had cut it; maybe Freddie had done the right thing by burning their attackers on the spot. Conlan noticed her and raised his head, eyes filled with agony.

"Eleanor, shake Will out of it – Amelia needs help." Conlan's voice was rough, hurt. Eleanor nodded, moved to Will and then dropped to the wet, muddy ground in front of him.

"Will?"

Blank eyes saw her, but they looked right through her. She slapped him hard, his head snapped to the side. Shuddering as if shaking himself awake, recognition coming back into his expression, he brought his gaze back to hers.

"Will, Amelia needs medical help. You're the only one who can give it, so help her!" Eleanor ordered in as hard a voice as she could manage. Nodding dumbly, he crawled the short distance to Amelia's side. Solemn grey eyes watched him, glassy and pain-filled. Gently he inspected the arrow where it had entered her chest beneath the left shoulder.

"Freddie, the fire? Are they dead? Was it Protectors?" Conlan asked, looking over Eleanor's shoulder. Freddie stood behind her, his face devoid of emotion.

"They're dead. I don't know who they were," Freddie admitted.

"Why not?" Conlan looked confused.

"Because he turned them into human torches before we had the chance to ask them," Eleanor murmured.

"If we don't know who they were, we don't know if there will be more, or how they found us. We need to get out of here, and right now! Will, can Amelia be moved or do you need to treat her first?" Conlan asked, giving Freddie an irritated glance before looking at Will.

"Has the arrow head come out the other side?" Will asked in a flat voice, looking at the arrow and not Conlan.

Moving slowly and carefully, Conlan moved his hand over Amelia's back, supporting her with his arm. Although he tried not to jostle her, Amelia gasped at the pain and coughed weakly, more blood leaking out of the corner of her mouth.

"No," Conlan said, gently easing Amelia back into place.

Will looked at Amelia. "I can't fix this; the arrow is too close to your heart."

Amelia nodded and reached for his hand. He grasped it and kissed it tenderly.

"I can't live without you, Amelia," he moaned. Amelia gave him a small smile.

"This terror you're feeling over losing me. This is what I live with every minute of every day. Do you understand now?" she asked, her voice a rustling whisper, like newspaper dragged along a pavement by the breeze.

"I'm sorry," Will said, agony ripping through his words.

"I don't want your apologies. I need your understanding." Amelia's words hung between them. Will nodded and Amelia's smile lit up her face for a moment, a brief view of the sun between clouds.

"I love you," she breathed.

Running a gentle hand down her face, Will leaned in and kissed her.

"I love you too, please don't give up. We'll find a way to help you."

Amelia nodded and sighed, her eyes closing, Will moved his hand down to her neck, feeling for a pulse.

"She's not dead," Freddie said, and Eleanor jumped at the sound, the empty voice of a stranger.

"How do you know?" Eleanor asked; Amelia certainly looked dead.

"When the other Earths died we felt it. It was agony. You'll know when

Amelia dies," Freddie said.

"No!" Will snapped angrily, not turning round. "Amelia is not going to die!"

"You said you couldn't help her," Conlan said gently.

"I can't, but I know someone who can," Will said, and Eleanor heard the ruthless tone.

"Who?" Conlan asked.

"Jarrick," Will answered, raising his head to look at Conlan, who had tensed in wide-eyed shock.

There was a tense silence and Conlan slowly shook his head.

"Will... Jarrick won't help."

"Yes he will. We're going to take Amelia to him. Nethrus is only a day's ride from here. You're going to do or agree to whatever he asks to get him to help," Will said, his voice hard and cold.

"You have no idea what you're asking," Conlan said quietly.

"Yes I do, and I don't care. Amelia is dying because she saved your life; you're going to help her. I have followed you through one nightmare after another – never questioned, never doubted – and so has Amelia. I don't care what it costs you, you will help her!" Will demanded. Conlan stared at him in disbelief, and then looking down into Amelia's face he nodded.

"I'll do whatever he asks," he echoed softly. Eleanor wondered if anybody else had noticed how hard he was shaking.

15

JARRICK

They cut down a couple of thin trees, and using their blankets they made a stretcher for Amelia, Eleanor making a hood from branches and one of her jackets to protect her face from the rain. Will and Freddie's horses were about the same height, so they carefully suspended Amelia's stretcher between them so she was spared some of the bouncing of the journey. Under dark, evil-looking storm clouds they set off for Nethrus. Freddie and Will rode in front while Eleanor and Conlan followed, Conlan leading Amelia's horse after him.

"Conlan," Eleanor said softly. "Who's Jarrick?"

Conlan turned to look at her, loathing deep in his eyes. "My brother. He hates me."

"Then why are we going to him for help?"

Conlan sighed. "Jarrick has a healer, a very good one. I made a deal with Jarrick once before, when Will got stabbed in a fight. I think Will is hoping I can make a similar deal."

"What sort of a deal?" Eleanor asked suspiciously as her brain provided her with the memory of Amelia talking about Nethrus.

"Jarrick agreed to help Will and I allowed Jarrick to give me a beating," Conlan said flatly.

Eleanor stared at him. "What?! That's totally ridiculous! You can't make that deal again; Will has no right to ask it of you! What…"

"Eleanor, shut up." The order was low and quiet, but there was something in his tone, as if he was down to his last thread of self-control and she was doing little to help him keep a grip on it. She snapped her mouth shut, staring at him. He ignored her and kept his eyes firmly in front.

"Amelia won't want this," Eleanor noted. She had expected him to tell her to shut up again or maybe yell at her, but his shoulders slumped and he turned his head to look at her. The rain and the gloom gave shadow and depth to the despair that filled his face.

"I can't let her die, Eleanor. I owe her too much, owe Will too much..." he whispered, and Eleanor saw the fear he was trying so hard to hide.

"Maybe we can make a different deal," Eleanor said gently. "We're Avatars, we have powers, perhaps your brother would like ..."

"NO!"

Conlan's yell was so loud that both Rand and Horse jumped, but not nearly as high as Eleanor did. Freddie turned in his saddle to watch them. Conlan's eyes blazed as he leaned across the gap between them, his voice a harsh whisper.

"Eleanor, my brother is a dangerous man – a nasty, devious, vicious monster."

Eleanor stared at him incredulously. Conlan glared at her still, but she could see him attempting to get his anger under control.

"If you tell my brother what you are capable of, he will want that power for himself – and he can be very 'persuasive'. You're not going anywhere near him!"

Angry at his stubborn refusal to even think about other possibilities, Eleanor glared back. "I'm not going to let you just hand yourself over to some monster, not when there are other options."

"You have no idea what you're talking about, Eleanor." He pulled himself upright and turned away from her.

She would stop him, find another way. Closing her eyes and trusting Horse to follow the others, she tried to work it out, but how would she know what deal to make if she did not know what Jarrick might want? She doubted Conlan was going to give her the information she needed, so she was going to have to find a way to meet Jarrick herself.

Will pushed them through the afternoon storm and on through the night, heading south, stopping every few hours to check on Amelia. He said nothing. Eleanor had tried to talk in his head, but he had refused, which added more anger and frustration to what she was already feeling. The clouds broke as the sun rose the next morning. The bright light was dazzling, and Eleanor rode in a tired, miserable daze. When she felt an energy string brush against her, she thought her slightly addled mind was imagining it, but when she pulled it in and felt Amelia's light presence fill her head, she was certain she was hallucinating.

Amelia?

Eleanor, you're right, I don't want him doing this. In her head, Amelia's voice sounded strong and determined.

Amelia, you should be saving your energy...

Eleanor, please listen to me, you have to stop Conlan.

I'm not happy about it either, Amelia, but I'd rather he got his arse kicked than you died.

You don't understand. Will was pretty out of it the last time, he doesn't really remember. I was the one who nursed Conlan. Jarrick didn't just give him a beating, he tortured him... for days. What he suffered... He had nightmares for weeks. Jarrick tried to kill him last time, and this time I think he'll make sure. We're all expendable, apart from Conlan; he can make a new Avatar of Air. I would rather die than put him in Jarrick's hands again.

Eleanor shuddered as Amelia sent her memories: Conlan's broken, pain-ravaged body, the pitiful sounds he made in his sleep as he relived the torture, the wide-eyed terror when he woke, gasping, his body shaking with remembered agony.

How do I stop him? Eleanor whispered.

I don't know, but you have to think of something, please Eleanor. I was willing to give my life to save his, and Will is going to take that from him.

As Amelia's presence left her mind, Eleanor realised she was crying, tears running down her face and dripping off her chin. She turned to look at Conlan. His eyes held hers; she saw the understanding in them. He knew, knew what Amelia had just shown her. For one frozen minute Eleanor saw all his terror and despair at what was coming, then, with effort, he pulled his hard, emotionless mask into place and turned his head, leaving Eleanor sobbing for him in wretched misery.

They began seeing signs of habitation in the landscape – the odd farm, walled fields and domestic animals. They saw a track cutting across the hills and heading off north, and they joined it, making faster time on the easier surface. It was late afternoon before Will pulled them off the track, heading towards woodland Eleanor could see in the distance. He was still silent, ignoring all attempts made to talk to him. They dismounted as they walked under the trees. It was cooler here, and the flecked green light and the sounds of trees swaying gently in the breeze eased away some of the tension. With great care Will lifted Amelia, cringing as she gasped and moaned in pain, her eyelids fluttering, but she did not regain consciousness. Leaving Freddie to dismantle the stretcher and lead his horse, Will walked deeper into the trees.

They emerged from the tight crowd of vegetation around them into a wide clearing, trees standing regimental guard in a circle around it. While it was overgrown, there was evidence of a previous camp – a filled-in fire pit, logs now rotted, that had been pulled around it. To her left Eleanor could hear the gurgling flow of a fast-moving stream. Will moved forward with purpose, laying Amelia gently on the ground next to where the fire had been. *He's been here before.* Eleanor watched him run a hand down Amelia's pale cheek, then standing he turned to Conlan, a look of single-minded determination on his face.

"Go and talk to Jarrick, we'll wait here for you," he ordered. His face blank, Conlan nodded and turned to lead Rand back out of the wood. Panicked, Eleanor dropped Horse's reins and darted in front of him. He looked down at her with one of his deep looks she did not understand, frowning slightly.

"Get out of my way, Eleanor" he said, not unkindly.

Eleanor slowly shook her head. "I'm coming with you."

"No, you are going to stay here, out of the way," he answered, his voice still quiet.

"I know what Jarrick did to you, Amelia showed me. I can help you. Let me meet this monster, let me work out what he would rather have than your pain."

"There's nothing he would rather have..." Conlan whispered, his fear showing again for a moment, before he pulled himself together, his voice harder. "You can't help me, Eleanor, and I told you I don't want you anywhere near him. Amelia doesn't have time for this. Now sit down and shut up."

"No! If you won't take me with you I'll just follow you. You can't stop me!" she blustered, her voice just as hard as his had been.

Conlan dropped his head and took a slow, deep breath. "I *can* stop you, Eleanor."

Reflexes sharpened by months of practice saw his fist fly at her head an instant before it hit. He had been aiming for her temple, a solid blow that would have knocked her senseless but done no permanent damage. However, anticipating it, Eleanor had instinctively begun to rock back on her feet and his fist made contact with her face under her left eye instead. He was still holding Rand's reins and Eleanor felt one of the silver studs tear a bloody rent into the skin across her cheekbone as her head rocketed back and her vision exploded into a dazzling multi-coloured kaleidoscope. *Like he's ripped a rainbow apart in my skull.* She dropped back, thudding to the ground, the darkness moving in on her. *He broke his promise,* was her last miserable thought.

Pain dragged her back to consciousness, a groan escaping dry lips. Her head felt full of needles, stabbing into her brain with every breath. Gingerly she raised her hand to her face, feeling the tackiness of drying blood where it had run down her cheek and neck and the bruising that was threatening to swell her left eye shut. Gentle hands pulled hers away.

"Don't touch, Eleanor, you'll make it worse."

She slowly opened her eyes. It was dark. She was lying beside a fire, Freddie sat by her head, leaning over her, his upside down, blurry face holding a deep, concerned frown.

"He broke his promise," Eleanor said in a voice of shattered glass, the words shredding her as the memories came back. She felt self-pitying tears spring to her eyes.

"And he'll never forgive himself for it. Why can't you just take no for an answer?" Will's tone was hard, cold and bitter. Eleanor forced herself to sit, irritably slapping away Freddie's efforts to stop her. Will sat across the fire from her. Amelia was cradled in his lap, the arrow still protruding from her chest and moving slightly with the rise and fall of her lungs; still features, grey and lifeless. Will's face was stone, eyes brittle, sparking sapphire as he glared at her. Conlan and Rand were gone.

"Don't make him do this," Eleanor said slowly.

"I won't let Amelia die!" Will snapped.

"So Conlan dies instead? What if we're too late and lose them both?" Eleanor tried to reason.

"This is the only chance Amelia has of pulling through – and I'm taking it."

"But Will, Amelia doesn't want you to."

He looked surprised. "How do you know what Amelia wants?"

"Because she told me, on the way here."

Will's eyes narrowed in suspicion. "She hasn't spoken to me."

Eleanor shrugged. "Maybe she didn't have strength for the protracted argument she knew she would end up having with you. Maybe she thought it would be easier for you if I was the one arguing for her death."

"Is that what you're arguing for?" Will's voice was low, edged with lethal fury. She ignored it.

"Amelia was willing to die to save Conlan; she still is, and you're making her sacrifice meaningless!"

"She is not going to die, Eleanor," he said from between clenched teeth.

"Maybe she is, maybe she isn't; either way, if you force Conlan to hand himself over to his brother he *is* going to die," Eleanor snapped.

"I don't think Jarrick wants him dead, or he would have killed him last time."

Eleanor stared at him. "You're betting his life on an assumption? Even if Jarrick doesn't want to kill him, just because he survived it once doesn't mean it's OK to put him through it again! Do you even know what Jarrick made him suffer?"

Will finally dropped his gaze from hers. "I don't care."

Fuming, Eleanor pulled herself to her feet, ignoring the hot needles stabbing into her brain, the wave of nausea that washed over her and Freddie's more insistent attempts to stop her. Grabbing Will's hair and pulling back his head roughly, she forced his deep-blue eyes to meet hers and yelled at him.

"He's your friend. Of course you care! I know you do! Jarrick tortured him, Will, and from the injuries Amelia showed me he was lucky to survive. It was probably an oversight on Jarrick's part, I'm sure, but it's not one he is going to make again."

Will grabbed her hand, twisting it into a lock. Her wrist, weakened from having been broken once before, screamed in protest. She whimpered and let go of his hair, but he did not release her. Pulling her arm down in front of him, adding slowly to the pressure, he forced her to drop forward until the damaged side of her face was pressing into the dirt. Eleanor groaned in pain, her arm strained to the limit of bone and sinew, feeling blood run as the wound on her side split open again.

"Let her go."

Freddie.

Eleanor heard the anger in his voice.

"Stay out of this," Will snarled at him.

"You're going to break her wrist," Freddie protested. "Will, please, you're holding Amelia, Eleanor can't fight back. I can't stop you, please... You don't want to do this. You're in pain, I can see that, but Eleanor's right – and you know it. Amelia can be replaced, we are all expendable, but Conlan isn't.

Think about what you are doing."

Will laughed, a sharp, vicious noise. "Do you think I care about Mydren? About any of this? Do you think for one second that any of you mean more to me than Amelia does? If she dies I am done with this whole sorry mess, do you understand me?"

Freddie stared at him in shock.

"I know you care," Eleanor whispered, concentrating on keeping the pain and fear out of her voice and trying to replicate Will's own calm, steady tone. "Stephen died because of you; do you really want to be responsible for another brother's death?"

Through his grip on her hand, Eleanor felt Will shudder. He released the pressure on her wrist and she collapsed. Freddie reached for her, helping her to sit and letting her lean against him. Her wrist throbbed and her head ached, but for an instant she saw Will's agony, saw his hurt and the impossible position in which he felt trapped. Then the remorse and sympathy were gone and he held her gaze with cold, calculating determination.

"You're bleeding," Freddie noticed. Eleanor followed his gaze to the small, dark-red puddle she had left on the ground.

"Yes," she agreed, returning her eyes to Will. She was past caring.

"You should have said. When did you get hurt?" asked Freddie.

Eleanor shook her head. "It doesn't matter."

Freddie took her chin and turned her head to face him, the life and humour gone. "You're bleeding, Eleanor, of course it matters."

"Really? Why?" Eleanor asked in lifeless monotone. "Amelia is most likely going to die, at which point it sounds like Will is planning to kill himself, having first handed Conlan over so Jarrick can torture him to death. I am going to lose most of my family in one go, including the man I love, along with all hope of saving this world. You and I will be left hunted and alone, so tell me, Freddie, why do you think a little blood matters?"

Freddie stared at her for a moment, then wrapping his arms around her and burying his head into her hair he sobbed. Too emotionally battered to comfort him, Eleanor let him cry while watching Will. He stared back at her and Eleanor waited, hoping that eventually her words would reach through his desperation and grief, that he would realise what he was doing was not the answer.

Freddie's crying had dropped to sporadic hiccupping and the odd sob, although he was still clutching tightly to Eleanor, when they heard the sound of hooves. Pulling away from Freddie, Eleanor rolled herself onto all fours and stood. Conlan's silhouette walked through the trees and out into the clearing, an insubstantial shadow. A feeling of dread and death made Eleanor shiver. He did not step into the fire's circle of light, instead staying hidden in the dark.

"Jarrick will help Amelia. Will and I will take her. Freddie, you stay here with Eleanor – look after her. She is not, under any circumstances, to follow us. Is that clear?" Conlan ordered, his tone giving no room for argument. Freddie nodded his agreement as he came to stand behind her. Eleanor glared at him. *I don't need looking after.* Stepping around the fire towards Conlan, her voice trembling along with her body, she made another attempt to get through to him.

"What did he make you agree to? Is he going to take his pound of flesh?"

There was a long pause, and when Conlan finally spoke, his voice was the terrible hollow sound that tore at her heart. "He gets to give me another beating, but he has promised to let us leave alive, if I give him Rand."

Eleanor gasped, a tornado of emotions whipping through her mind. "And you believe him? How do you even know he'll keep his word?" she demanded. "There's nothing stopping him from killing you and using Amelia as leverage to get Will to do whatever he wants – or the other way round."

"Jarrick is a monster, but he is a man of his word," Conlan said with conviction.

"Don't do this, Conlan, you're making a mistake. Let me help you," she pleaded. Will walked past her, past Rand and Conlan, and out of the clearing clutching Amelia to his chest, leading his horse behind him.

"Let's go, Conlan," he ordered over his shoulder.

Conlan hesitated for a moment, his face still in shadow. Eleanor took a few more steps towards him.

"Are you just going to leave?" she asked. "You have no idea if you're going to survive this. Aren't you even going to say goodbye?" Tears washed lines through the blood on her face, dripping pink onto the front of her shirt.

"Goodbye, Eleanor."

Two words. So much meaning was held in them that Eleanor felt she was being buried under their weight. The pain in his words stripped her of her strength, and as Conlan turned to follow Will, she sank to her knees. He was already a ghost, a dark wraith moving through the trees, fading and then gone completely.

For a long time Eleanor remained kneeling on the ground, arms wrapped round herself and tears falling, her mind blank at the horror of what she might be losing. Freddie tried to offer comfort, but she pushed him away. She did not need comfort, and she most certainly was not going to accept this. She needed to think. Forcing her fear and grief down, she stood and began pacing in front of the fire. Her mind made up, she turned and began following in the direction Conlan had taken back to the track. She had almost made it to the edge of the clearing before Freddie ran in front of her, blocking her path.

"No, Eleanor, you have to stay here," he said, placing a restraining hand in the middle of her chest. Eleanor looked down at it, not understanding. Surely he wanted to help her?

"Freddie, we can do this the easy way or the hard way. I'm going. I would prefer to do it with your help, but I'll do it without, if I must," she said, keeping her tone calm and controlled.

"Conlan said you were to stay here."

"When did Conlan's orders become law again? Use your common sense, Freddie; we can help him."

Freddie shook his head. "Eleanor, there are some things you just can't fix."

Eleanor stared at him. "How do we know what we can and can't fix until we try? Conlan is going to suffer unless we do something, so please, I'm begging you, help me."

"No."

"Do you really hate him so much you would let Jarrick torture him?"

Freddie looked hurt. "No, Eleanor, I don't hate him. I don't want him to suffer. I just want what he does, to protect you from Jarrick." Eleanor felt rage crawl through her guts and she shoved Freddie back with both hands, catching him so much off guard that he fell to the ground. Eleanor stepped round him quickly. Turning back, she looked down at him.

"I don't need protecting," she snarled.

"Eleanor…" he began to implore, but something caught his attention and his eyes flickered behind her head, opening wide in shock. Sensing movement, Eleanor turned in time to see a blurry object moving at speed towards the side of her head. She reacted by trying to step back, but Freddie was in the way and the long, thin object crashed across the side of her head, rattling her teeth and dropping her into black oblivion from a great height.

Breathing was difficult, and something was crushing her lungs, forcing her to take short, shallow gasps. Oblivion pulled back a little. Something was very wrong. Her hands and feet were tied and restraints bit deeply into her flesh. Her arms and legs had been tied firmly, securing her over something,

something that was moving. *I'm tied over a horse.* As more awareness came back, the situation became clearer. She was face down, head to the ground, over the back of a moving horse. The raised pommel of the saddle was digging mercilessly into her chest and stomach; so much pain filled her head that Eleanor was surprised it had not exploded. She tried to struggle, to call out, but all she managed was a strangled groan. She froze as she felt a hand run firmly down her back to rest on her buttocks. Someone was sat behind her in the saddle.

"Now, now, Princess," said a soft, nasty growl in Dwarfish. "You should not be awake yet." The hand gave her rear a squeeze, making her whole body tense, and then a booted foot kicked the side of her head. It was not a particularly hard blow, but it made contact with the bruises she already had, the pain clamping down like a vice and the oblivion coming back in a rush to claim her.

"She is a mess, Perry! And so was the other one. Did I not give you clear instructions that they were not to be injured?" The Dwarfish was cold, commanding.

"She was already in this state when we got there, and you saw the power of the other one – it took a lot to take him down." This voice was familiar: it was the man who had touched her and called her 'Princess'. Forcing down the pain and the fear, Eleanor opened her eyes. She could only get her left to half-mast, but she decided under the circumstances that this was good enough. The bright lantern light made her wince and blink tears until she could deal with it. Eventually her vision cleared and she found herself looking at a winged horse. *Too many blows to the head*, she thought groggily, shutting her eyes and counting to five before she opened them again. The winged horse was still there, flying above her. It took her far longer than it should have to work out that she was looking at a beautiful painting on the ceiling of the room she was in. She was lying on a comfortable couch, a pillow under her head. A man sat on a chair next to her, another man stood behind him. The man in the chair smiled, his watery pale-blue eyes full of sympathy. It was a kind smile, an encouraging smile. He had a large round face, its podgy and undefined features making the eyes look small. Even relaxed, his mouth gave the impression of petulance, and his weak chin and bad teeth gave him a slightly pathetic air. Sat comfortably in his chair, expensively cut black trousers and white shirt not able to hide his heavy frame and thick, fat fingers held delicately on his crossed knee, he was assessing her, too.

"Hello, I am Jarrick," he said softly, giving his introduction a quiet growl that indicated a meeting of equals.

Eleanor froze, instinctively wanting to get as far away from him as possible. Adrenaline overriding every ache and pain she scrambled up, drawing her legs into her chest, cringing into the corner of the sofa and watching him with suspicion. If Jarrick was upset or surprised by this he hid it well, instead he cocked an amused eyebrow at her.

"I see you have heard of me."

Eleanor stared. *You got your wish, moron, Jarrick is sat in front of you. Now what are you going to do?* A million questions poured through her brain, but taking slow deep breaths she managed to bring herself under control.

"How did I get here?" she asked, giving the man stood behind Jarrick's chair an angry look. A predatory smile spread across his pinched, thin face, his brown eyes full of lust. Frightened, Eleanor dropped her eyes back to Jarrick's face.

"Conlan is a bad liar. I knew there were more Avatars out there so I sent some men to follow him. They found you and your friend and brought you back here," Jarrick said.

"What is an Avatar?" Eleanor asked, playing dumb while trying to work out what Jarrick already knew.

He smiled at her. "Elemental conduits. Which one are you?"

"I do not know what you mean," Eleanor said.

"You are no better at lying than my brother," Jarrick advised conversationally.

"Where are my friends?" Eleanor asked. Jarrick nodded, as if this was a question he had expected.

"Your lady friend is being tended to by my healer, who was able to remove the arrow. I am told she may yet live – the next few days will be critical. The desperate blond-haired man is with her. The friend you arrived with has been locked up, as he was a little angry when he regained consciousness and tried to set people on fire. The Avatar of Fire, I presume…"

"Where is Conlan?" Eleanor whispered, not sure she wanted to know the answer.

"Conlan is strung up, awaiting me. Your return to consciousness forced a delay in our 'conversation', but I am anxious to resume it," he said, as if they were discussing an interruption to a sporting event he was watching. Eleanor cringed, her stomach twisting at his words and sending electric sparks of pain through the entire length of her body.

The sympathy returned to the pale-blue eyes. "I am sorry if hurting him upsets you, but he has brought it on himself."

Eleanor stared at him, not understanding. "What did he do?"

Jarrick narrowed his eyes slightly.

"How much do you know about Conlan?" he asked.

Eleanor shook her head. "Not very much, he is sort of private."

Jarrick chuckled. "Private? No, he just has too much to hide." He looked at Eleanor for a moment, his face draining of humour, and when he spoke his voice was hard and cold. "When our mother died, our father came to claim us and took us to the North Tower – not a place to raise small children. From almost the moment we arrived, Conlan ignored me. He would spend hours talking with our father in his study, and when he was not there he was out in the training ground being taught the arts of a gentlemen by some of the finest swordsmen and warlords who ever lived. In short, he was given a full and extensive education. I was left totally by myself. There were no other children in the tower and nobody had time for me. I was six years old and everything I loved had been taken from me. I tried to approach Conlan, tried to reach out to him, but he pushed me away, that hard, cold emotionless look on his face... I can see you know the one I mean."

Eleanor winced. She was giving too much away again, she concentrated on making her face blank as Jarrick continued. "Conlan has no compassion, pity or empathy; he is selfish and cruel. I will make him hurt as I did, for the nightmare he put me through." Jarrick gazed intently into Eleanor's eyes, the shadow of a desperate, lonely, miserable child clear. *He really does believe this, believes that Conlan hurt him on purpose.*

"Conlan would not have meant to hurt you," she replied. "Maybe he just did not understand, but regardless, what he did to you does not justify what you are doing to him now. He is a good man, give him the chance to explain himself," Eleanor said.

Jarrick laughed a harsh bitter bark – Conlan made a sound like it occasionally, but it did not suit him; coming from Jarrick, however, it seemed to fit. "You are defending him?" he asked incredulously. "Why? He dragged you into this world so that he could force you into giving him energy, force you to fight for him, kill for him, force you into making him king. My father's ambitions drove him as far as ruling North Tower, but Conlan wants the whole of Mydren – and you do not think that is a problem?"

Angry, Eleanor leant forward on the sofa. "You know nothing about him – that is not what he wants at all!"

Jarrick looked at her balefully, a flash of steel in his watery blue eyes. "Really? Did he tell you about our mother? Did he tell you he was responsible, that he betrayed her to her death? Even my father was angry at him for that. I saw him once, he made Conlan kneel before his desk and forced him to say he was sorry for killing her. My brother took everything from me, and he is going to pay for that."

He never uses the word 'sorry', Eleanor thought, wondering how many times his father had forced him to say it. She ignored Jarrick's comments about Conlan's part in his mother's death. Jarrick was wrong. Conlan loved his mother, grieved for her, even now; he would not have purposely caused her death.

"What would it take for you to stop hurting him?" Eleanor asked, wondering if the direct approach would work. Jarrick looked a little confused by the change in conversation, and Eleanor saw Conlan's echo in the expression.

"I have everything I want in life, tearing my brother apart is just an added pleasure. Consequently, there is nothing you can give me that I cannot take for myself," Jarrick said, the wide and friendly smile back on his face. *He's totally insane. I have nothing to bargain with… Conlan said he was a violent man, so perhaps he would understand violence better than deals. How would he respond to threats? What could I take off him that he would miss?*

She looked around. They were in a large oblong room, a library. Several expensive, comfortable, delicate-looking chairs and sofas were placed over a brightly coloured, tightly woven carpet on the floor. Book shelves lined the wall behind her, and down each side wall, in front of her, were floor-to-ceiling windows that looked out onto a large square courtyard, lanterns placed around it allowing her to see across the space. There were lots of doors and windows facing into the courtyard, and a large, closed wooden gate stood firmly in the wall at the far end, directly across from the library's windows. There seemed to be lots of people standing motionless in the enclosed space, watching the dawn as it began to appear over the red-tiled roof of the continuous block of buildings that enclosed the courtyard. Curious, Eleanor unfolded herself and stood, swaying a little as her head complained bitterly. She took a couple of deep breaths, waiting until her body could handle being upright. When neither man made a move towards her, she walked to the windows, looking out at the people. *Statues.* They filled the courtyard. Turning and looking back into the library from the windows Eleanor realised there were several in the room with her. *I wonder how much he values them?* The nearest was in the left-hand corner. Eleanor moved towards it. The stone was a beautiful polished pink and had obviously been chosen to enhance the subject matter carved into it. The statue showed a naked woman with rounded hips and large breasts, a massive snake wrapped around her. Its jaws were wide open and ready to bite, but the woman seemed unafraid – her face held a look of almost sexual pleasure.

"She is very special," Jarrick said as he appeared at her side. He was gazing adoringly into the woman's face. *He loves this statue.* Eleanor reached a hand out and ran her fingers along the stone's smooth, cold surface, automatically pushing an energy string out to it.

"This statue is hundreds of years old; it once resided in Alaric's palace. Do you know who Alaric was?" Jarrick asked. Only half-listening to him, her concentration on the stone, Eleanor nodded, wondering if Jarrick knew he was related to him – she doubted it. The stone sang to her, of life and its creation, of all the events that had brought it to its current position. Jarrick was wrong. She turned to him, pulling back her energy string, a small smile on her face.

"I think I may have found something to bargain with."

"Really?" he sounded intrigued.

"This statue is not old. In fact, it was created only a few months before you stole it. I am the Avatar of Earth, Jarrick. Stone talks to me, tells me its secrets and retains a memory of everything that has happened to it. I can tell you which of your statues are fake, if you like... or I can just destroy them." Pulling energy from the earth as she turned, Eleanor released it at the statue of a man coiled in battle pose and ready to strike, which stood in the opposite corner of the room. The statue exploded outwards with a cracking boom that blew the windows out into the courtyard. The statue's fragments shredded through the book shelves behind it and the furniture in front of it, filling the room with noise, dust and grit. It took all of Eleanor's self-control not to flinch, not to duck as stone fragments flew at her and not to raise her arms to protect her face. She forced herself to stand still, unconcerned, amongst the devastation she had wrought. She was stunned when nothing actually hit her, so when Perry came at her through the confusion and grabbed her upper arms, holding her in front of Jarrick, she did not resist.

"Be careful, Perry," she said softly as the dust settled. "I am far from defenceless; I can do to you what I just did to that statue. Is that what you want?"

Eleanor's arms were released, but Perry remained behind her. There was the sound of running feet and the library door burst open. Men spilled into the room, all of them coming up short at the mess before them. Jarrick stopped coughing at the dust and turned to them.

"Are you alright, Jarrick?" asked a short man in front, confusion on his face.

Jarrick nodded. "I am fine, leave – all of you – Perry can deal with this."

Bowing, the short man stepped out of the room. The others followed him, closing the doors behind them. Eleanor could tell how angry Jarrick was, even under his layers of fat. As his body tensed, he whipped around, glaring at her, rage coursing like lightning through his eyes.

"Have you any idea how old that statue was?" he demanded loudly.

Eleanor was impressed. He was yelling at her; fully aware of the destruction she could cause, the man was no coward. She extended an energy string out to one of the pieces at her feet and smiled smugly at him.

"Approximately four hundred years old. Oops, I guess that one was not a fake!"

He slapped her face, hard, and the cut beneath her eye started to bleed again. Dazed, she dropped to the floor like a bag of jelly. Her head felt like it was splitting in two, but forcing herself to focus she turned to look through Perry's legs, out of the splintered windows and exploded the first statue she laid eyes on. The boom echoed around the courtyard, followed by the pitter-patter of falling chunks of rock, the shock wave knocking over several other statues. She turned back to Jarrick, his face a mask of indignant fury.

"Hit me again and I will do that to you," Eleanor said flatly. He glared at her but made no attempt to stop her as she staggered back to her feet. Eleanor could feel the exhaustion and pain pushing her towards shutdown, but her fear was shooting massive doses of adrenaline straight into her heart. She felt strong, in control. She held Jarrick's malignant gaze, and when she spoke she was pleased to discover her voice was cold, calm and steady.

"You have no idea what I am capable of unleashing. You have no hope of controlling it and no chance of stopping it. I have a new deal for you, and I strongly suggest you take it. You will let Conlan go, you will heal Amelia and you will let the five of us leave without harming so much as a hair on our heads. In return I will refrain from blowing up any more of your statues. I may even tell you which ones are fakes. Do we have a deal?"

A slow, evil smile spread across Jarrick's face. "Or I could just kill you!"

Eleanor had anticipated this retort, knew that Perry was stood very close behind her. Turning her head a fraction, she saw the movement in her peripheral vision as he pulled a knife. He thrust it at her, aiming round and up, intent on stabbing her through the ribs. Eleanor reacted. Turning into the thrust, she blocked down with her left arm, stopping the knife's trajectory with bruising force, and using the heel of her hand she punched up under his chin, his head flying back. Bouncing back lightly on both feet, she gave the man a solid front kick to the stomach and he staggered back, bending over and gasping as the air ejected from his lungs. *Jarrick understands violence... show him some.* Eleanor drew energy from the earth and released it at Perry. The man never knew what hit him – not that this gave Eleanor any comfort. With a wet snapping and ripping sound, his body went from being whole to being in pieces in a fraction of a second; bone fragments, flesh, gore and blood splattered onto the carpet and out through the broken windows into the courtyard. The shockwave took most of the remaining window frame with it. The violence of it took her breath away.

Eleanor took a second to ensure that none of the remorse and horror she felt was showing on her face and then turned to Jarrick, who stared at her in wide-eyed shock.

"Yes," she answered, as if considering his suggestion. "You could kill me. However, you are going to need to call those men back. Do you think they can get from the door to me before I annihilate them? I should also warn you that I have some powerful friends, if you do somehow manage to bring about my death, you are going to have three really ticked off Avatars on your hands. I guarantee you, you would not survive that. If you do not let Conlan go, I will destroy every one of your statues. Do we have a deal?"

Jarrick pulled himself together. Standing over her, his shock gone, a dark fury filled his face and he took a step towards her. Eleanor overrode her body's desire to step back – it would not be a good idea to show this man weakness. She saw his expression change, as if something had just occurred to him. A look of cunning surfaced in his eyes, and he smiled a friendly, charming smile. "You are very impressive," he purred. "Conlan must be very proud of you. I know I would be unwise to provoke you; however, I have a request of my own to make," he said, the words a silky, smooth veneer of polite respect.

Eleanor raised an eyebrow at him; the man had a lot of courage. "What do you want?"

Jarrick's smile widened. "I will promise that Conlan will leave here with no more than the slight 'damage' he already has, but I would ask that you allow me to keep him locked up on his own. He will have no contact with any of you until you are ready to leave. You are right – I should make some attempt to talk to him, but he is going to have to be a captive audience to listen to me. Would this be possible?"

Eleanor frowned at him. She did not believe for one minute that Jarrick had any intention of making up with Conlan, but if all he wanted to do was talk to him, what possible damage could he do? Conlan was quite capable of withstanding a little taunting and name-calling, and if it kept Jarrick happy…

Eleanor nodded. "Alright, but you are not to hurt so much as a hair on his head and I wish to see him. I will assess his 'damage' for myself, to ensure you do not go back on your word. Should I find that you have, I will give you very little time to regret it. I also give you fair warning that if you *ever* hurt him again I will wipe you from the face of the earth, do you understand?"

Jarrick nodded, still smiling at her genially. "He will have to be restrained, of course, for my safety. Some of the things we have to say to each other will not be kind."

Eleanor blenched. *What is he planning?* So long as Conlan came out of it unscathed, she was not sure it mattered. *How much damage can he do with words?* However, Jarrick had a point. Conlan had a habit of lashing out, and if he did, his brother would have an excuse to hurt him again. She reluctantly nodded her agreement once more.

"Good, would you like to see Conlan now?" Jarrick asked, still smiling.

"No, I want to see Freddie first – the Avatar of Fire – where is he?" Eleanor said.

Jarrick took her to see Freddie himself, leading her across the statue-filled courtyard as the rising sun illuminated the damage she had caused. Trying hard not to look at the bits of Perry scattered around, Eleanor carefully picked her way through the debris. On the right-hand side of the courtyard Jarrick opened a door and led her down a short, scruffy corridor with several doors on each side. Two men stood outside one door and jumped to attention when they noticed Jarrick walking towards them.

"Open the door!" he ordered. One of the guards pulled a key from his pocket and unlocked the door. Eleanor followed Jarrick into the room. From the light emanating from the corridor she could see a small, windowless storage space. With the exception of Freddie, it was empty. He sat against the back wall, hate-filled eyes glaring at Jarrick as he entered. Eleanor was relieved when, despite the cuts and bruises she could see, a delighted grin of recognition spread across his face.

"I take it that was you I heard?" he asked.

Eleanor nodded. "Are you OK?"

"I'm fine, does this mean we have a new plan?" he asked, getting stiffly to his feet.

"Yes, Freddie, we have a new plan."

"I'm sorry I tried to stop you."

"I'm sorry I shoved you... still friends?" Eleanor asked.

"Always."

Eleanor turned back to Jarrick, who was watching them with genuine curiosity, a look so much like Conlan's that Eleanor felt her heart squeeze.

"You really are from another world," he said softly.

"Where are Will and Amelia?" Eleanor snapped, ignoring his comment.

Jarrick led them further down the right-hand side of the courtyard, away from the library windows. Eleanor heard Freddie gasp at the damage, but he said nothing. Jarrick opened another door which led into a wider corridor; there were fewer doors leading off, indicating larger rooms behind them. This corridor had a carpet and painted walls with lights hung at regular intervals – it felt 'lived in'. There were guards here, too, jumping to attention at their approach. Jarrick stopped in front of the first door on the left.

"Hannad, open this door," Jarrick ordered. The door was unlocked and Jarrick walked in, Eleanor and Freddie following. It was a bedroom. A rich-blue carpet covered the floor, the walls were painted the dark blue of a winter twilight sky and a window on the left-hand wall showed the courtyard beyond, a generous armchair before it. In the middle of the back wall was an impressive double bed, in which Eleanor could see Amelia lying, her face blending with the white sheets drawn across her chest. She was so still that Eleanor froze in panic. She pushed a string out and was relieved when she felt the weak fluttering of her friend's energy. The arrow was gone and a bandage covered the wound. A shocking red stain showed beneath the material, the colour exaggerated by the crisp white of the sheets and the translucent white of Amelia's skin. Dragging her eyes away from her injured friend, Eleanor swept the rest of the room. There were small tables with lanterns burning on them at each side of the bed and a large chest of drawers just inside the door. On the right-hand side wall was another door, slightly ajar, with what appeared to be a bathroom beyond.

"Eleanor? No..."

Eleanor looked in the direction of the broken, horrified voice. Will was sat on the floor, behind the door they had entered through. Fear, exhaustion and misery filled his face.

"It's OK, Will," she said, her voice empty. Using the wall for support, Will got to his feet.

"That was you exploding the building?" Will asked.

"Exploding people," Freddie said softly. Eleanor felt shame and guilt burn through her and dropped her head.

"I'm sorry, Eleanor, I should have listened. I heard him... heard him screaming..." he stuttered, his words catching in his throat. He stopped. Eleanor raised her head. Tears ran slowly down Will's haggard face, his body shaking and his torment making his eyes the colour of a stormy sea. Not able to deal with Will's guilt and remorse, and feeling her stomach flash sympathetic pain through her, Eleanor turned back to Jarrick.

"Freddie is going to stay here. I want to see Conlan, now," she ordered. Jarrick nodded, the wide and friendly smile still on his face. Turning back, Eleanor followed Jarrick out of the room.

He took her further down the corridor to the last door on the right. The guard unlocked it and Eleanor entered a large, windowless bathroom with a floor of polished black stone. The bathtub, toilet bucket and washstand had been moved into the corner next to the door, leaving the main part of the room empty. Eleanor could smell blood, sweat and the nauseating reek of burnt flesh.

Conlan knelt before her.

He was being kept upright, his arms wrenched painfully behind his back, tied together at the elbows and attached to a rope suspended from a metal candelabra fitting in the ceiling. His shirt and velvet jacket were in a pile by the door. His head sagged forward, chin resting on the pale skin of his chest. To the side of him was a large comfortable chair, which looked like it had come from the library. On a low table beside the chair, in Conlan's line of sight, were a lot of sharp, scary-looking metal instruments, glittering with evil promise in the flickering lantern light. A large, round brazier stood bolted to the floor a small distance from the other side of the chair. Embers glowed deep, ominous red within. Normally used to heat water for bathing, this one had been used to heat a couple of two-foot-long metal pokers. From what Eleanor could see of the injuries that ran down Conlan's left side from under his arm to the waist of his trousers, this was where the torture had started. Eleanor rushed forward, dropping to her knees. Conlan's face was grey, his eyes were closed and sweat dripped from his lank hair. His chest rose and fell slightly with each shallow breath, but otherwise his body was lifeless. Eleanor rested her hand gently against the clammy skin of his cheek.

"Cut him down, now!" she snarled at Jarrick, without looking at him. She heard him walk across the room and pick up one of the metal instruments off the table. Moving behind Conlan he sliced through the ropes at his elbows. The restraints fell away and Conlan dropped forward, a dead weight into Eleanor's waiting embrace. The movement, or perhaps the pain of feeling returning to his arms, brought Conlan back to consciousness. As gently as she was able, Eleanor lowered him to the floor. He moaned pitifully, the sound ripping at her heart. Body shuddering, he jerked weakly and struggled to wake. His eyes fluttered open, unseeing and full of terror. Eleanor noted the bruises on his face and body, but they were nothing compared to the thick lines of burnt, blistered flesh; cracked, raw skin seeped blood which ran down his side. In some places the lesions were so numerous that they merged together.

"Conlan," she whispered softly in English. "This is going to stop now, there'll be no more pain". At the sound of her voice, Conlan shook himself and fought to focus. Recognition appeared in his dazed eyes.

"Eleanor, you shouldn't be here..." he managed, his low voice rough and strained.

Will's words played through her head: '*I heard him screaming...*'

Wanting to bring some comfort she smiled.

"You're here, why would I want to be anywhere else?" she asked, knowing how close she was coming to saying something she should not.

"Your Avatar made a more 'persuasive' deal," Jarrick said, interrupting. Eleanor saw hate burning in Conlan's eyes as he looked up at his brother. Jarrick smiled at him and continued. "This, sadly, means I am unable to finish teaching you the error of your ways."

"What deal?" Conlan ground out.

Ignoring him, Jarrick addressed Eleanor.

"You have seen his injuries. I promise there will be no more damage than this when you are ready to leave. I will see to it he is fed. Put this on him." He held out his hand, in which was a heavy metal band, hinged in the middle so it opened out into two halves. Sturdy looking rings protruded from the ends of the band where it split apart. Eleanor took it, looking at it in confusion.

Jarrick smiled, as if it was the best joke in the world.

"It goes around his neck, to restrain him."

Jarrick's meaning punched through her numbed brain. *He's going to chain you up like a dog... Oh Conlan, I'm sorry.* Nodding, Eleanor opened the collar and placed it round Conlan's neck. It was tight, but not so tight that he could not breathe. Jarrick handed her a padlock that filled her hand and the end of a metal chain. Eleanor slipped the lock though the collar's rings and the last link in the chain and closed it, turning the small key, the sharp click making Conlan tense. Removing the key, Eleanor placed it in Jarrick's waiting hand; thick, meaty fingers closed over it, as if Conlan's humiliation and imprisonment were precious gifts. Eleanor shuddered, for Jarrick they most likely were. Conlan had offered no resistance to her actions, but she could not bring herself to look him in the eye. As Jarrick took the other end of the chain and spent a few moments securing it to the base of the brazier, Conlan placed a cold hand gently over hers.

"Look at me, Eleanor," he whispered. With effort she did as he asked; the pain and fear she found made her want to cry. "You're shaking," he told her distractedly. "What deal did you make with Jarrick?"

She stared blankly at him. *Am I shaking?* She glanced at her hands. Yes, she was. She tried to get her cotton wool-filled, aching head to formulate a short answer that would explain everything for him. Instead, her mind kept wandering off on strange tangents. Was Jarrick going to keep his word? Was the collar she had put round Conlan's neck going to hurt him? Had she done the right thing? Was Amelia going to live? Along with the discordant thoughts came flashes of Perry's face, his body exploding. Eleanor flinched at the memory, feeling a dull ache in her stomach.

"Eleanor!" he croaked, his weak, grating whisper as insistent as he could make it. "What deal did you make?"

Before she could answer, she felt hands on her upper arms – gentle, reassuring and helping her up. Jarrick stood behind her, one hand now resting lightly on her shoulder and the other gently stroking her hair. *Strange that he can care for me and yet show such violence towards his brother,* Eleanor thought numbly. She did not like the feeling and cringed again, but she was too shell-shocked by recent events to pull away from him.

"Your Avatar has shown herself to be brave, intelligent and resourceful. I shall enjoy getting to know her," Jarrick said, sounding oddly amused – smug almost. With effort, Conlan pulled himself into a crouch, his face twisting into a mask of pain as he whimpered. Getting himself under control he looked at Jarrick with loathing and fury.

"If you hurt her, I will destroy you," he said, his attempt at a threatening tone making him cough.

"It's OK, Conlan," Eleanor whispered, unsure why she felt it was OK.

He dropped his gaze to her face, agony crying out from his eyes. It took her a moment to realise he was frightened for her, that he was terrified Jarrick was going to hurt her. She tried to find something to say, something to reassure him, but before she could, Jarrick was gently leading her out of the room, an arm around her shoulders. He stopped at the door, looking back.

"I will be back to talk to you later, brother. I shall tell you all about the deal we made."

There was an unpleasant gloating in his words, which did not make sense. Eleanor heard the metal chain skitter rapidly across the stone floor; she turned in time to see it reach its limit, the sudden stop pulling Conlan to the ground.

"No, Eleanor, please!" he choked, trying to get up and tugging in desperate futility at the chain. Taking hold of her shoulders in a tighter grip, Jarrick steered her from the room and the door was locked behind her.

"He really likes you," Jarrick commented, amused. He guided her back to the room where they had left the others. Giving her a small shove inside, he closed the door. Eleanor listened for the key turning in the lock, but it never came. She stood, staring at the blue carpet and taking slow deep breaths, trying to get her trembling body under control. The adrenaline was fading and the exhaustion was bearing down on her, along with all the guilt and fear.

"Eleanor?"

She raised her head and saw Freddie stood beside her.

"What happened? Is Conlan alright?" he asked.

Unable to find words for her misery, Eleanor pushed into Freddie's head and sent him her memories, all of it from the moment she had regained consciousness, knowing all her feelings were leaking through with them but not caring. She just wanted someone to understand. Freddie's eyes glazed over as he watched her personal hell playing through his mind. As the memories finished, Eleanor pulled her string free and hung her head.

"Oh," Freddie breathed, wrapping his arms around her and pulling her tight to his chest. She wanted to cry, wanted to purge herself of her bitter, dark, twisted feelings to cleanse herself, but the tears would not come. She was beyond tears now, beyond pain and rational thought. Still holding her, Freddie led her to the wall by the window and sat her down, sitting next to her, an arm round her shoulders.

She stared blankly at the blue carpet. The colour matched Will's eyes. Unbidden, her mind moved into overdrive. There were thirty-two statues in the courtyard, not including the one she had exploded. The chain Conlan had been tied up with had sixty-seven links. Jarrick's short hair was the same colour as his brother's, but while Conlan's was soft and wavy, with a mind of its own, Jarrick's lay flat to his head, like a thin, greasy cap. The guard, Hannad, only had three fingers and a thumb on his right hand. She had seen books in the library on art, mathematics and philosophy. Either Jarrick had attempted to educate himself or he wanted people to think he had. Perry's face flashed into her mind again, and all thought ceased for a moment as she saw his body rip apart. She pushed it away and the barrage of random information restarted. The courtyard was perfectly square. There were forty-three windows facing in to it, and fourteen doors.

With a small, detached part of her brain, Eleanor had an idea what was happening. Her mind had done this a lot when she was a child, before she learnt how to control it. Everything she empirically experienced or thought, her mind stored in perfect crystal clarity, ready for instantaneous recall. When she was younger her mind would spit this data out in nonsensical order, especially when she became upset, frightened or stressed, often causing her to recite meaningless strings of information in babbling incoherence that led many family members to suspect she was insane. Over time she had learnt to control her mind, turning it from an aggressive monster which gave her headaches and stopped her sleeping, to a valuable tool she relied on totally. *My control is slipping.* Panicking, she tried to take command of her faculties again, but the tighter she gripped, the more it felt like things were slipping through her fingers, tidal waves of information crashing over her. *I'm losing myself.* Desperate to stay afloat she reached for the only life preserver she had, the only one she wanted. Conlan. As her mind seethed around her, she retreated and took her memories of him with her – the way his cheek fit perfectly into her hand; the intelligent curiosity in his bright green eyes; *the fresh colour of new leaves;* the way his laugh captivated her; his unique smell – light and masculine, which made her think of warm, sunny days and the smell of saddle leather, horse sweat and campfire smoke – she had to be close to smell it and for her it was more intoxicating than the most expensive perfumes; the feel of his fingers laced through hers as they had stood before his grandfather's house; the almost painful surge of joy, when he had sung with her, his beautiful voice wrapping round hers and supporting it, raising it above ordinary – just as he had done to her soul, bringing her to Mydren, raising her above ordinary.

His stunning, heart-stopping smile filled her head. Slowly she felt her mind calm, and letting go of her fear and panic she imagined him sat next to her, his quiet presence reassuring her. She imagined listening to him breathing as she had done in the desert. The chaos in her mind dropped and the dull throb of her headache returned. She recognised this discomfort – understood it, even. The familiar pain was a strange comfort. Closing her eyes she let her body slip sideways to the floor, Freddie's arm falling away. Resting her head on the soft carpet, holding her feelings for Conlan close to her like warm, protective armour, she gave in to her exhaustion and slept.

The days passed. They did not leave the room. Will would not leave Amelia's side, and Eleanor did not want to be any further away from Conlan than she already was. Freddie went with the majority. Food came at regular intervals throughout the day, as did Jarrick's healer, Kona. He was not the wise, stooped old man Eleanor had expected. He was tall enough to look Will in the eye and appeared to be about the same age; a thin, fragile body supported a head that seemed too big for it. Everything about him was soft – his voice, his expressions, his touch, his light-brown eyes. Will treated the man with deference and awe-filled respect, asking him quiet questions as he hovered at Amelia's side and watched Kona check her pulse, change her bandages and apply salves and pastes that filled the room with a pungent antiseptic smell. At Will's polite request, Kona had treated Eleanor injuries, too. Taking her into the bathroom for privacy, he inspected the cut on her side, which had finally stopped bleeding, and touched the scabbed-over tear beneath her eye and the bruising on her head with practiced, kind, professional fingers.

"Your friend – Conlan – Jarrick permitted me to treat his injuries. I was not allowed to speak to him, but he spoke to me. He worries for you," Kona said, watching her face for signs of pain as he probed the lump on the side of her head.

"Is he going to be alright?" Eleanor asked, Kona's words better medicine than anything else he could do for her.

"He will be fine," he answered. "Jarrick is now treating him well – he visits him every so often and they talk. No further acts of violence have been committed against him."

Eleanor looked at the healer. "Why do you do it? Why do you work for a monster like Jarrick?"

Kona smiled at her. "He is not a monster. He has a good heart and he treats his employees like family. Perry's death wounded him deeply. He may be a criminal, but he is respected. He is known to be a man of his word, and whilst he is harsh, he is fair. He saved my life and saw value in my skills where most did not and has become my friend. Please try not to judge him on his current actions – the pain of his childhood has left him irrational and hate-filled when it comes to his brother, turning him back into the lonely, frightened, grieving little boy he once was."

In the days that followed, as Amelia slipped in and out of fevered, unknowing consciousness, Eleanor thought a lot about what Kona had said, so when Jarrick knocked politely on their door one afternoon and inquired if Eleanor would take a walk with him, she agreed without hesitation.

In the courtyard, all signs of the destruction she had caused were gone. Even the library windows had been replaced; she could smell new wood and paint on the warm, restless breeze.

"We did not get off to the best of starts, did we? I was hoping we might be friends," Jarrick said, an underlying growl of apology in his voice.

"I am sorry for the hurt I caused you," Eleanor said quietly, watching his face, trying to judge his response and looking for the truth in what Kona had told her. She saw him wince, grief and pain flashing through his eyes. He noticed her studying his reactions and his friendly, relaxed smile returned immediately to his face.

"His death was my fault, I gave you no choice. I underestimated a force of nature and sadly Perry paid the price. I shall miss him," he said softly.

"What are you and Conlan talking about?" Eleanor asked, realising her mistake as Jarrick's body tensed, the muscles in his jaw flexing.

"Lots of things... you mostly," he replied. It appeared to have taken him some effort to stay calm.

"Me?"

Jarrick smiled at her, and there was something dark underneath his countenance that Eleanor did not like. "I have told him what you did, how truly impressive you are. He seems to think that you are weak and foolish, that you made a mistake trying to help him. He is angry that you disobeyed him. I have tried to reason with him, but I am certain you know how stubborn he is."

Eleanor stared at the podgy man stood next to her. He seemed sincere, worried for her almost. She did not trust him to tell her the truth, as what he had just said could have been designed to make her think badly of Conlan and better of him, except that all Jarrick had really done was confirm the fears she already had about Conlan's current state of mind. This would not be the first time he had thought her a fool for trying to help him. Jarrick watched the expressions on her face for a moment before speaking.

"I have upset you, I am sorry. How about we avoid conversation about Conlan in the future?" he asked, looking at her with concern. Eleanor nodded. At least if they did not talk about Conlan she would not have to try to work out if Jarrick was lying to her or not.

"Kona tells me you have a nasty injury on your side as well as the cuts and bruises on your face. May I ask what you have been doing?" Jarrick asked, changing the subject.

"Not moving fast enough," Eleanor muttered, but she smiled at his concern and told him about the battle with the glowing green people, leaving out the bit about the chalice, the Talismans and how important they were. She reluctantly admitted that Conlan had given her the cut under her eye and Jarrick quickly changed the subject again, asking her about her life and some of the things she had seen on her travels across Mydren. He asked her several times why they were making the journeys, but Eleanor refused to answer the question. To her surprise Jarrick simply nodded and smiled and did not push for an answer. He seemed relaxed and comfortable in her presence, and he gave the impression of genuine interest in the responses to the questions he asked her and would accept her refusal not to answer certain inquires with nothing more than a shrug. Eleanor actually found herself liking the man. He was bright and educated, with a quick wit and a ready laugh. She asked him questions about his criminal activities and he answered all of them with what felt like open honesty. He did not try to hide or apologise for his activities, but he did not sound as if he was especially proud of himself either – it was business and he would kill to protect what was his, but he took no pleasure in it. His men loved him and he clearly cared a lot for them; he knew everything about them and trusted them implicitly. On returning her to her room, Jarrick asked if she would spend some time with him every day, and much to Will's surprise – and Freddie's when he found out – Eleanor agreed. She spent several hours every afternoon walking through the courtyard with Jarrick. They discussed philosophy and science, Eleanor telling Jarrick about the wonders of her world; he listened in rapt attention, arguing the occasional point without irritation or anger and never telling her to shut up, which for Eleanor made a refreshing change. She even helped him catalogue his statues, giving him the age and provenance of every one, while he told her why each one was special to him. She felt guilty for enjoying Jarrick's company, but when she was with him he was able to distract her from the dark and miserable thoughts which had become normal for her. While her mind was engaged with his light, friendly conversation, she rarely saw Perry's face or grisly demise. Jarrick kept the horror at bay, which Eleanor found ironic.

Eleanor returned from a walk with Jarrick one afternoon to discover Amelia awake, lucid and sitting up, pillows stacked behind her. Overjoyed, she rushed forward, wrapping her arms around her friend's body, which felt as substantial as a dried-out leaf, as if she could crumble to dust and blow away at any minute. Nevertheless, she was alive, awake and returning the hug.

"Careful, Eleanor, she's not up to that!" Will chided, his voice harder than it needed to be. Eleanor had not really spoken to Will, even though they had been living in the same room for weeks. She suspected Freddie had shown him her memories of the state in which Jarrick had left Conlan, but he had made no attempt to discuss it with her, as his focus had been solely on Amelia. Will's silence had been part of the reason Jarrick's attention had been so welcome – he was someone to talk to, someone to listen who did not want to judge her. Will's rebuke hurt, she *was* being careful – she could see how fragile Amelia was, she was not stupid. Gently releasing Amelia, Eleanor pulled back.

"I'm sorry," she whispered, fighting the tears she could feel crowding her eyes. "Did I hurt you?"

Smiling, Amelia took Eleanor's face in her hands. "No, sweetie, but Will has hurt you, hasn't he?"

The tears began spilling over and Eleanor nodded. Amelia patted the bed next to her and Eleanor climbed up, curling into Amelia's side, her head resting on her lap.

"Amelia, I don't think..." Will started.

"No," Amelia interrupted. "You don't think, do you?!"

Eleanor closed her eyes, blocking out Will's irritated expression. Amelia stroked her head, a loving, comforting feeling. When Amelia brushed an energy string against her, Eleanor pulled it in.

Show me, Eleanor, show me what caused the damage I can see on your face and in your eyes.

Searching back through her memories, Eleanor dragged them forward and played them from the moment the arrow had struck. Holding nothing back, she gave Amelia everything – all the pain, fear, guilt and heartache. She heard Amelia gasp as she watched Perry explode, and she whimpered in sympathy, her hand squeezing painfully tight to Eleanor's shoulder, when she saw Conlan's injuries. Showing Amelia made Eleanor feel lighter and happier, as if sharing her pain with her friend somehow made it less dark. Amelia was getting better, they would be able to leave soon and she could see Conlan again. She felt a small something burst to life within her, something that had been missing – hope. She retracted her energy string and opened her eyes. Amelia continued to stroke her head.

"What are you thinking?" Eleanor asked her softly. From where he was sat, back to the wall by the door, Will raised his head to look at Amelia.

"I was thinking Will owes you all an apology, and I was wondering who tried to kill us and why. I saw the men in your memories, but I didn't understand what they were saying. Translate for me," Amelia said.

Eleanor ran through the conversation she had overheard, before Freddie had turned the archers into chargrilled corpses, and recited it back to Amelia in English.

"They'd been waiting for us for years?" Freddie asked. Eleanor lifted her head off Amelia's lap to find him sprawled across the chair by the window, legs hanging over one of the arms.

"So they said," she answered.

"Were they Protectors?" Will asked.

Eleanor sat up, wriggling slightly as she crossed her legs and got comfortable. "I don't know. I don't think so, as they were talking about getting bonuses for bringing our bodies back."

"Back where?" Freddie asked.

Eleanor gave him an irritated look. "I don't know, Freddie; you turned them into ash before I got the chance to ask them."

"Sorry," Freddie mumbled, looking ashamed.

"If they weren't Protectors, that means we have a new enemy, a rather worryingly well-informed enemy…" Amelia mused.

"I vote Jarrick," Freddie said.

Eleanor could see where Freddie's logic was coming from. Jarrick definitely had a motive, and they had been attacked near Jarrick's home by men who, while not Protectors, were clearly being paid. Jarrick would have no problem hiring that sort of help – he had the money to pay for it and he had seen the book as a child, so he might have remembered certain parts of it. This all made sense, but her own logic did not agree; things she knew about Jarrick gave her the feeling that Freddie was wrong.

She shook her head. "I'm not sure it's Jarrick."

"Oh really? Please tell us why your new friend, who is quite happy to torture his brother to death, would not be willing to destroy all he stood for if he got the chance," Will asked, lacing his question with sneering sarcasm.

Eleanor sighed. She should have known better than to expect understanding from Will on this. He was still beating himself up over what he had forced Conlan to do, so the thought of handing some of the responsibility off to someone else was probably quite appealing. "Jarrick hates his father and the Lords of Mydren nearly as much as he hates Conlan," she explained. "He's actually quite happy that Conlan is a thorn in their sides."

"He can't have cared that much if he was going to torture Conlan to death," Freddie muttered.

"I think Will was right, I don't think Jarrick ever intended to take Conlan's life," Eleanor said slowly, letting her words hang in the silent room like bodies on the gallows. Will raised his head and stared at her, but Eleanor failed to read the look on his face. Freddie stared at her open-mouthed, and even Amelia looked shocked.

"Eleanor, I think you've been spending too much time fraternising with the enemy," Freddie said with quiet concern.

"Jarrick wants the Lords of Mydren gone," Eleanor continued doggedly. "He wants his father dead, and killing his brother won't achieve this. Don't get me wrong, I think he fully intended to inflict agonising pain on Conlan, but Jarrick has had a lot of practice at torture. He could quite easily take Conlan to breaking point, without actually killing him."

"Eleanor, you are defending a monster who wants to rip apart the man you love – doesn't that strike you as a little odd?" Amelia asked softly. Eleanor turned to look into Amelia's pained grey eyes. Was she defending Jarrick?

"I'm not justifying his behaviour, Amelia, and if he ever hurts Conlan again I'll kill him and he knows that, but I don't think he was responsible for the men who attacked us. I don't want us to think we have found a solution. I know it's convenient and comforting to blame Jarrick, but if he was planning to kill us all, the waiting men would have reported back to him and he would have ambushed us himself on the road."

"He'd have taken on four Avatars?" Freddie asked.

Eleanor nodded. "He saw the damage I caused and still yelled at me, still hit me. The man has courage."

"Oh yeah, lots of courage. Hitting a small, unarmed, defenceless gi..." Freddie said loudly, stopping when he caught sight of Eleanor's rapidly deepening scowl of indignation. A slow, cheeky grin eased itself onto Freddie's face. Eleanor tried to keep her hard look, but it was too much effort to resist Freddie's smile and she grinned back at him.

"So, we still have no idea who attacked us," Amelia said quietly. The comment wiped away Eleanor's smile. She turned back to look at Amelia, noticing the worry and fear before she answered.

"The men talked about having orders not to 'kill the one with the scar', so whoever it is wants us dead, but Conlan alive. I think we can assume this enemy knows Conlan."

"We're going to have to be more careful when we work out where the sword and crown are, as there could be more traps," Freddie said quietly.

Amelia sighed. "Just what we need, more enemies…"

Eleanor smiled at her apologetically. Amelia's eyelids began to drop, clearly the conversation had exhausted her. Will was at her side immediately, fussing with the pillows so she could lie back. He shooed Eleanor off the bed without looking at her.

"She can stay if she wants," Amelia whispered weakly, eyes closed. One look at Will's face told Eleanor everything she needed to know about his thoughts on the matter, and she carefully climbed off the bed.

"That's OK, Amelia, you need to rest," she reassured her quietly, but Amelia did not respond, her breathing already giving way to the slow, regular sound of sleep. Will tenderly brushed a stray hair from Amelia's face and leaned to kiss her forehead. Then he returned to his position on the floor behind the door, back against the wall, his eyes watching Amelia's face with an almost unnatural intensity. *I need to talk to him.* Eleanor did not relish the thought, as his attitude towards her had stripped her confidence. Would he want to talk to her? She loved him and did not like him being angry with her, so she was going to try.

She sat next to him. He ignored her. She pushed an energy string out to him. He ignored that, too. She knew she could have pushed into his head, but that did not seem the best way to start a reconciliation talk; besides, if he flung her out it would hurt. Will was too strong to fight.

"I just want to talk to you..." Eleanor whispered. She felt Will take her energy string.

OK, talk!

I'm worried about you. I want to make sure you're OK. You look so unhappy all the time. Is there anything I can do to help? There was silence. She gave him some time, wondering what he was thinking.

You want to know if you can help me?

Well... yes. You're my friend, I love you and you've just been through hell thinking Amelia might die, seeing her in pain. I know how much that hurts. I just thought you might want to talk about it. I know you're angry with me, and I know it sounded like I was arguing for you to give Amelia's life for Conlan's, but I would never have done that — we would always have found a way to save them both, but you didn't trust me. More silence followed Eleanor's speech, and she cringed as Will's disbelief crashed over her.

I emotionally blackmailed the man you love into handing himself over to be tortured, I refused to listen to reason, I hurt you... and you're upset because you think I don't trust you? Will asked incredulously.

Pretty much, Eleanor muttered. There was another long silence.

I have no idea where to start with this, Will whispered.

Sorry, I didn't want to upset you again.

Conlan's right, you say sorry far too much.

Well Conlan doesn't say it at all, so I'm just making up for him, Eleanor reasoned, and relief filled her as Will chuckled.

Eleanor, are you interested in knowing why I didn't want to talk to you?

I… yes, she stuttered, wondering if she was going to end up feeling hurt again.

I thought you were going to tear me apart for what I did to Conlan, for making it necessary for you to kill that man – you have every right to, but I don't think I can take it just now.

Eleanor heard the misery and felt Will's guilt and remorse.

You said you were sorry. I believed you. I understand why you did what you did, but I don't understand why you didn't trust me. I trust you.

Will sighed. *I guess I just never thought anybody could love and care for Amelia as I do, and I assumed you would put Conlan first, as I was doing with Amelia. I thought this was the only course of action. I had some ill-conceived plan to rescue Conlan once I knew Amelia was going to be OK, but it never actually occurred to me to threaten Jarrick. It's not that I didn't trust you, I just underestimated you…*

Good answer.

The truth usually is. I'm sorry, I won't underestimate you again.

Eleanor giggled. *Oh good! One down, three more to convince.*

Eleanor…

Eleanor was shocked by the pain that accompanied Will's soft utterance of her name.

Yes?

I nearly lost her, you know? If she hadn't been an Avatar she'd have died. The voice in her head was a whimpering sob.

Yes, I know, Eleanor replied, gently taking Will's trembling hand and squeezing it.

I was so full of pompous advice when Amelia was afraid of losing me. I told her one day of loving her was worth the risk, but I wouldn't have wanted to survive her death.

Eleanor sighed. *As with all things in life, Will, you have a choice. If Amelia's death had driven you to suicide, that would have been your choice. But you're stronger than that, I've felt it. Leaving us like that, just to escape your own pain, is selfish – and that's not who you are. You gave Amelia good advice. Love with all your heart while you have the chance, as it's the only armour you'll have with which to face the darkness.*

Once she was awake and able to eat and drink without a tube down her throat, Amelia's recovery was rapid. In anticipation of their departure, Jarrick had returned their bags to them. Eleanor knew hers had been rifled through, which meant everybody else's most likely had as well, but nothing seemed to be missing. She bathed, changed her clothes and strapped Remic's knife back round her waist – the blade tapped against her thigh as she moved, a comfort she had missed. It was a bright, sunny morning when Kona arrived, followed by Jarrick, to give Amelia a clean bill of health and declare she was fit to leave. Will shook Kona's hand and thanked him, then demanded Jarrick immediately bring their horses out and release Conlan so they could go. Jarrick agreed without hesitation. Eleanor had spent enough time with Jarrick to know there was more going on than his smiling face showed. The man had an air of malicious anticipation that set her nerves on edge, making her suspicious and fearful. Trying to work out what Jarrick might be planning, Eleanor brushed an energy string against Amelia.

Amelia, if we needed you to shield, do you think you could?

Yes, Amelia said cautiously, picking up on Eleanor's fear and anxiety. *Well, for a little while… this is too easy, isn't it… Jarrick's up to something.*

Yes, he is.

It says a lot about our lives that the minute something good happens we immediately assume the worst.

Eleanor had no answer to that, as the thought left her feeling a little depressed and no less frightened. She pulled her energy free and followed the others into the courtyard. There were quite a few men present. Eleanor had never seen a woman the whole time they had been in Jarrick's compound. Some of the men were holding their saddled, loaded horses, but most just seemed to be standing around. *Jarrick wants an audience.* Eleanor's stomach tightened and she caught Will's eye. He had reached the same conclusion and was moving to his horse so he was within grabbing distance of his sword; he looked at the men warily.

"Where is Conlan?" Eleanor asked, annoyed at the tremble she heard in her voice. Jarrick smiled and approached her, holding out his hand. As he moved closer, Eleanor realised that the small key to Conlan's collar was in it. She took it off him, her apprehension moving up a level.

"I will fetch him," he said, smiling cheerfully.

Eleanor watched Jarrick disappear through the door, back towards Conlan's prison. When he emerged several minutes later he had Conlan's shirt and jacket in one hand and his chain in the other. The bright daylight caused Conlan to wince and slow down, momentarily blinded. Jarrick grinned and yanked the chain, forcing him to stumble forward. There were sniggers from the surrounding men. He pulled Conlan to a stop like an unruly horse, in front of Eleanor.

"As you can see, no further damage," Jarrick said. Eleanor ran her eyes over Conlan's body, looking for signs of abuse. He was pale and significantly thinner, but the injuries on his side were mostly healed, no doubt thanks to

Kona's skill, and she saw no evidence of further torture. Yet the way he held himself gave the impression of a beaten man. He looked fragile, and he purposely turned his head so he would not have to look at her. Confused, Eleanor nodded at Jarrick, who then turned back to Conlan.

"Get down on your knees, you fool, she cannot reach if you are stood," Jarrick ordered, yanking the chain sharply down to emphasise his command. Conlan sank to his knees; there was more laughter from Jarrick's men. With shaking hands, Eleanor opened the padlock and pulled the collar off. The skin underneath was rubbed red raw and bleeding thinly in places. Guilt crashed over her and she fought the urge to cry; unthinking, she brushed gentle fingers against the damage.

"I'm sorry, Conlan," she whispered in English. Still not looking at her, he angrily slapped her hand away. Hurt, Eleanor wrapped her arms around herself, staring at him.

"You should show your Avatar a little more respect," Jarrick said softly. "She suffered a lot to protect you."

Not understanding, Eleanor looked from Jarrick's smug expression to Conlan's bowed head and shaking body, his fists clenched at his side. *What am I missing?* Jarrick tossed Conlan his clothes, staring balefully while he dressed and saying nothing when he stood up again. As Conlan rose, his eyes found Amelia and relief filled his face. Two quick steps and he pulled her into his arms, resting his head on her shoulder. Amelia returned the gesture, looking surprised. The image stabbed at Eleanor's heart – he had no problem hugging Amelia, but he would not even let her touch him.

"Are you OK?" Conlan asked Amelia, as he reluctantly released her. She nodded, running a hand down his face.

"Are you?" she asked. He nodded slowly. "Then let's get out of here," she whispered, looking anxiously at the men around them. They made for their horses, Conlan greeting Rand with a gentle rub along his neck. Still feeling hurt and bewildered, Eleanor did not move immediately, so from a distance she was able to see what Conlan did not. Rand was stood strangely. His legs were pushed out, like a cheap plastic chair with too much weight on it. His head hung down and his sides heaved. Slowly stroking Rand's nose, Conlan sensed what Eleanor could see. Rand was ill. Feeling her anger grip her, Eleanor spun round to Jarrick.

"What did you do? What did you do to Rand?!" she demanded of him, voice echoing around the courtyard. No one was sniggering now. Jarrick gave her a smug, self-satisfied smile.

"Poisoned him." He sounded exceptionally pleased with himself.

Eleanor was stunned, her body went numb and her mind reeled in blind rage. "Why?!" she screamed. "He is an innocent animal; he has done nothing to you. Surely you know I will kill you for this?" she spat, bile rising to her throat. The threat was one thing, but could she actually carry it out?

Jarrick still had the smug, satisfied look that made Eleanor want to rip at his face with her bare hands. "The deal you made ensured that the five of you would leave with not a hair on your heads damaged. You made no provision for Rand. Did you really think I would just let Conlan walk away? Besides, Rand was my horse – something else Conlan took from me – I am just reclaiming my property."

Unable to deal with his calm, matter-of-fact tone, his utter lack of remorse over what he had done, Eleanor stepped away from him. Turning back to the stricken animal, she watched as Conlan removed Rand's saddle and saddle bags and gently slipped the red bridle over the horse's head. Rand shuddered. Wanting to comfort the ailing creature, Eleanor pushed into his head. Rand was dying and he knew it. She felt his pain as the poison slowly eroded away his internal organs. Through his agony, Eleanor felt his love and concern for Conlan. Rand had seen the men surrounding them and recognised the danger – how would Conlan escape if he was dead?

"Jarrick, help him, please help him," Eleanor pleaded, tears falling, not able to take her eyes off Rand.

"Oh no, Eleanor, I have no intention of helping Rand. I want the pleasure of watching Conlan witness the death of the wretched beast. The poison is slow and Rand is a strong horse; it will take him many hours of agony to succumb." Jarrick's voice was vicious, all pretence at civility gone. Eleanor glanced at him and he smiled back gleefully. Eleanor took a deep breath and tried to reason with him.

"Jarrick, this is wrong. Move on, make a life free of the hate you are carrying. Conlan may have failed you, but it does not justify this course of action. You could have chosen to forgive him and been the bigger man, not a small, petty, pathetic child."

A shadow passed over Jarrick's face. It could have been remorse or perhaps regret, but whatever it was, it was not there long enough for Eleanor to decide before the gleeful grin returned once more.

"Why would I want to forgive him? This is much more fun!"

Sickened, Eleanor turned away from his smug grin and looked back towards Rand. Conlan stood at his side, forehead resting gently against Rand's neck, his hand tenderly stroking his nose.

"Eleanor, I need Rand to lie down – tell him," Conlan ordered in English.

Walking hesitantly towards them, Eleanor gave Rand the impression that he should get down on the floor. He resisted, again his worry for Conlan surging through him, as he knew he could not protect his master while lying down. Eleanor felt her heart twist.

"Conlan, he doesn't want to, he wants to protect you – he can't do that from the floor," Eleanor managed to get out between sobs. Conlan wrapped an arm around Rand's neck, gently scratching him behind the ears.

"You have done your best to protect me, old friend, and now it is time for me to help you," Conlan said softly. Eleanor tried again to get Rand to lie down as another acid wave of agony flooded through him; he shuddered and complied, dropping clumsily to his knees, then lying on his side, body shaking. Conlan dropped with him, supporting his head and resting it across his lap, tenderly stroking Rand's cheek.

"Eleanor, can you calm him, help him with the pain?" Conlan asked, his voice empty. He still had not looked at her.

"Yes."

Closing her eyes so she could concentrate, Eleanor pushed back into Rand's head, carefully taking his consciousness and wrapping it in warm, comfortable love, insulating him from the pain, fear and worry. She heard him take a slow, relaxed breath.

"Eleanor, I want him to know how much he means to me," Conlan whispered in English. Nodding, Eleanor pushed out her memories of Conlan's love for his horse, the way the two of them had moved as one in the street in Drent, the trust Conlan had in Rand and how happy he was to see him when they had been separated, filling the dying animal's mind. Rand sent back the love, devotion and adoration he had for Conlan, and countless memories flashing through Eleanor's mind of simple kindnesses that meant so much – the affectionate pat, the gentle tone. Rand did not understand why he was in pain or why he was dying, but he trusted, absolutely, that Conlan would help him. His innocent faith tore at Eleanor's soul.

"He trusts you to help him, Conlan" Eleanor managed before the sobs tore at her throat and made speech impossible.

"Will, I need my sword," Conlan said quietly.

Eleanor knew what was coming. There was no hope for Rand, and the only way Conlan could help him was to end his pain. She did not argue, did not try to stop him. She could feel the damage the poison had already done, and she knew that Rand's swift death would be a merciful act. Screwing her eyes tight and concentrating, she wrapped Rand's mind in layer after layer of loving support, doing what small thing she could to help make the animal's death easier for him. She heard the sword drawn from its scabbard, and the metallic swish made the hairs on the back of her neck stand up.

Eleanor felt Conlan thrust the sword into Rand's chest to the hilt, angling it exactly so he forced the blade through the animal's labouring heart. Rand noticed and for a moment was confused by the lack of pain. She felt his body relax and his consciousness fade, his last thought one of love for the master who had helped him. That feeling of love remained, even after

Eleanor knew Rand's body was dead. How could this feeling still exist? Slowly, confusion gave way to understanding. Her energy string was still wrapped around Rand's energy; it had diminished to almost nothing with his death, almost. What remained had no thought, but it was where the love was coming from. *His soul*, Eleanor realised with shock. *I'm holding Rand's soul.* She pulled back her string and released the small spark of energy, feeling it move away as if drifting on the wind. She wondered where it went.

For a long time there was silence. Eleanor opened her eyes slowly. At some point she had fallen to the ground. Conlan sat in front of her, Rand's head still resting in his lap and blood spreading in a pool to the side of him. Conlan was covered in it, but he did not seem to care. He stared ahead, at nothing, as he absently stroked Rand, his right hand still holding the sword hilt. Rand's eyes were closed and his face was peaceful; had it not been for the blood he would have looked like he was sleeping. Eleanor knew the others were stood around her, but her only interest was in Conlan. She pulled herself up and walked towards him on shaking legs, wanting to offer him comfort. She placed a hand on his shoulder and was shocked by the sudden rage that poured through her body. More than rage – rage was a part of it – but there was also grief, pain and uncomprehending desolation; the rage moved up a level into something else, a white-hot feeling, the urge to destroy, the single-minded overwhelming desire to hack, stab and tear and to bring those who would cause these feelings to their knees. Eleanor knew the feelings were not her own, that they were Conlan's, and she had a brief moment of lucidity when she realised she should not be able to feel his emotions. Then all thought was swept aside in another crashing, bruising wave of tormented agony. The feelings were overriding her own, and before she even knew what she was doing Eleanor pushed energy strings deep into the earth, trying to force the emotions deep into the ground as she did unwanted energy. She pushed deeper and deeper, her body shaking with the effort, his pain giving her more strength than she had ever thought possible. She felt her energy punch through to the boiling, seething, pulsating liquid core and she staggered back as a familiar presence surged through her mind.

Hello again, little Avatar, Earth purred.

Fear flashed through her, but this time it was different. This time Eleanor was carrying Conlan's emotions – strong, powerful, rage-fuelled feelings. They gave her strength and control. Acting purely on instinct and Conlan's desire for destruction, she pulled Earth's consciousness to her, trapping it, holding it and bending it to her will. Earth struggled, but Eleanor knew that she was stronger. The feeling of omnipotent power flowed through her body, making her feel like she was glowing. Her eyes snapped open and she turned to face Jarrick, his expression full of malicious joy. Conlan was suffering, so he was happy. The smug grin was still on his face. Eleanor stepped towards him menacingly. Jarrick looked at her and fear showed in his eyes for the first time.

"We made a deal, I have not broken it," he stammered. Eleanor looked at him, all of Conlan's rage tearing through her insides.

"You have broken it as surely as killing any one of us. I warned you what would happen if you hurt him again. There will be no mercy," Eleanor said, hearing her deep, Earth-assisted voice echo forebodingly around the courtyard. She dropped her head, closed her eyes and gave in to Conlan's desire for the total destruction of his enemies. That was when the rumbling started.

It started deep in the ground below them, slowly rising and getting louder. It sounded like a ferocious beast moving through the ground towards them. Around them the buildings began to vibrate, slates flew from the roof and birds scattered startled from the eves. Behind her Eleanor heard their horses move with skittish fear, and without thinking she reached for them all at once, putting them into a gentle sleep and allowing them to drop slowly to the ground. It was not something she had ever done before, or even thought of doing, but it was as simple as breathing. The power was total; she felt it pump through her veins, fuelled by righteous fury. *He will pay, my love*, she thought as she brought her head up to glare at Jarrick. The buildings around them began to shake; the statues around the garden jittered and toppled, crushing several of Jarrick's men as they attempted to escape. Windows cracked and glass fell, and from inside the buildings came the sound of falling furniture, ceilings and light fittings dropping, all accompanied by the occasional scream. As the earth bucked and rolled beneath her, Eleanor found it was easy to keep her feet because she could anticipate the apparent chaos of the movement and move lightly on the balls of her feet – it was like standing upright on the deck of a ship in a storm. Jarrick, however, was knocked off his feet as the main building behind him collapsed, the library windows once again blown out. The fast-moving shards of glass should have ripped them to pieces, but they got half way across the courtyard and stopped, falling to the ground in a tinkling background noise to the rumbling destruction of the earthquake. *Amelia is shielding*, which a detached part of Eleanor's mind registered as a very good thing as the building to the right exploded. An enormous fireball washed over them, briefly engulfing the protected sphere in which they stood in a ball of red and orange, before the flames, finding nothing to sustain them, moved on to devour the books in Jarrick's library. The rumbling and shaking increased its intensity at Eleanor's simple thought that she would not leave a single wall standing. In front of her, protected by Amelia's shield, Jarrick cowered on the ground and stared in horror as his world was destroyed before his disbelieving eyes.

"Eleanor… Stop!"

Someone was stood in front of her, yelling and blocking her view of Jarrick. The growl in the voice reached her and made her heart jump for him. *Conlan*. Complying without hesitation, she released Earth, who pulled away from her by using Eleanor's own energy strings to escape back from where she had been pulled. As she did so, Eleanor felt something else. A possibility. She could follow and merge herself with Earth – merge herself with that power. She understood now, and she was strong enough to retain her identity, her control. The temptation was impossible to resist and so she let go a little, pulling all her energy together so she could push it down into the earth, her last act as an Avatar and her first as Earth.

"Please, Eleanor, stop!"

She hesitated, halfway between two existences. She could not do this to him, he needed her help, now more than ever. She loved him too much. As much as she wanted the joy of that formidable power and total sovereignty of the earth, she wanted him more. With effort she dragged herself back, retracting her energy strings as the shaking around her dissipated and then stopped. Fires still blazed and there were still crashes and bangs of buildings collapsing, but after the deafening noise of the earthquake all she could hear was white noise. It felt like silence.

Reality came back to her slowly, shaking body revealing her exhaustion. She looked up into Conlan's face; green eyes held hers, and horror, pain and grief looked down at her, but the anger, the white-hot fury, was gone.

"Why did you do that?" Jarrick cried, disbelieving shock echoing through his voice. Conlan turned. Jarrick was still on the ground, raised up on one elbow; his face showed fear and a deep, malignant hatred. Jarrick ignored Conlan and stared at Eleanor. "There are other people here," Jarrick continued. "This compound is in the centre of a busy town – do you have any idea how many you have killed? You lecture me on right and wrong; my revenge killed a horse, but yours has killed hundreds, maybe thousands of innocent people."

Eleanor stared at the man, and there was only one more thing to do. Very softly she said, "Then I guess one more will not make a difference." She released her energy and Jarrick's body went from being whole, terror just having a chance to hit his face, to a splattered wet collection of body parts in a fraction of a second. She and Conlan regarded the mess in silence for several long moments.

"Can we *please* get out of here?" Amelia asked. She sounded tired and empty, as if the shock had taken her spirit. Eleanor nodded, and turning from the blood revenge she had carried out, she walked back to the others. Horse was waking up and looked dazed and confused. Eleanor ran a gentle hand down the mare's neck, the warm, soft sensation giving her a moment of peace. They stood in a perfect circle of calm; rubble, broken glass and roof tiles mapped out the limit of Amelia's shield. Conlan caught sight of Rand's body and his shoulders slumped.

"I should bury him," he said quietly, regret and grief filling his voice. Saying nothing, Freddie stepped forward and gazed at the fallen animal, then he stepped back as Rand's body was engulfed in a violent inferno, the heat so intense that from several feet away Eleanor could feel it singe her hair. The pyre blazed, a writhing inferno, for minutes, causing the courtyard's paving slabs underneath Rand to split and crack. Rand's body collapsed in on itself, crumpling to ash before Eleanor's eyes. The fire died to nothing as quickly as it had started, and a small breeze picked up, swirling around the ash and lifting it up, raising it in a gentle dancing cloud. *Amelia.* Turning her head, Eleanor saw the distant look on her friend's tired face, the small smile. Rand's ashes moved lazily before them as the breeze blew them higher, through the smoke and up towards the cloudless blue sky above, leaving them for somewhere new. Eleanor felt Conlan's pain and grief crash through her already weakened defences.

"Goodbye, Rand," Conlan murmured, watching the ashes disappear.

At first Eleanor had been horrified at the chaos and destruction her earthquake had caused, but as each new harrowing sight tore at her, the feelings moved to unendurable and finally, blessedly, complete numbness. They moved carefully through the devastated streets, sometimes having to retrace their steps to find another way when they discovered a collapsed building in front of them. The dead lay around them, open, staring eyes frozen in that last moment of terror. They stopped to offer aid whenever they could, but there were so many in need. The wounded and dying cried out pitifully for help. Screams of suffering filled the air, the lamenting wail of grief the living gave for the dead, and Eleanor let the sound crash over her, let it rip at her, because she needed to hear it, to suffer with them, even if it was only an echo of their agony; they should not have to suffer alone. She deserved the pain.

16

CONSEQUENCES

They eventually managed to work their way through the maze of destruction until they arrived at the half-collapsed city gate, once proud, heavy wooden gates leaning at improbable angles. They walked around the gate, over the rubble of the wall at the side and out into the countryside. Eleanor had no idea where they were going and did not really care; so long as it was away from the death, blood, pain and misery that she had caused – that was fine by her. She could not get used to seeing Conlan on Amelia's horse, Rand's saddle tied to the back, and every time they caught her eye she felt reality lurch, until she had to stop looking at him or risk throwing up. He did not seem to want to look at her either, so ignoring him seemed fair. Will cradled Amelia across his saddle as she slept. Eleanor knew she should feel guilty for the extra strain she had put on her friend, but she felt so much guilt for everything else that there was simply no room for Amelia. Conlan and Will rode side by side, a little further ahead, talking quietly to each other. Eleanor could not hear what they were saying, but at one point Conlan reached across and gently patted Will on the shoulder. She assumed Will had apologised and Conlan had forgiven him. With a shudder Eleanor thought of all the people she had just killed – who was going to forgive her? Could she ever actually be forgiven? The thought sent her into a downward spiral of silent despair.

They had been riding for several hours before Eleanor finally recognised where they were. They were heading back towards the forest. Eleanor would have preferred to have kept going, she had a strong desire to get as far away from Nethrus as possible, but she knew Amelia was tired and needed to rest, so she swallowed her distress and followed the others.

The sun was dipping low on the horizon as they arrived at the edge of the wood. As before, they led their horses through the tangle of bushes and trees, towards the isolated clearing. Once there, Will placed Amelia carefully on the ground and began lighting a fire while Freddie began tethering up his and Will's horses, taking off their saddles and their bags. Conlan stood next to Amelia's horse, staring blankly at the ground in front of him. Eleanor stood a few feet away, leaning against Horse and allowing the solid little mare to support her. She was confused by the familiar activity before her; it seemed so banal, so routine after the horror.

"Is nobody going to say it?" she asked. Will and Freddie turned to look at her.

"Say what, Eleanor?" Will asked carefully.

"That I just committed mass murder," she said flatly.

"You're a monster – you just killed hundreds of innocent people to avenge the death of one horse," Conlan said coldly.

"That's not fair," said Freddie, stepping towards Eleanor. Dropping the reins he still held, Conlan ran at Freddie, intercepting him a few feet in front of Eleanor, tackling him to the ground and sitting on his chest while he punched repeatedly at his face. Freddie tried to fight back but Conlan just kept going, all control gone, snarling with animal ferocity. Too stunned to react, Eleanor stared blankly; what was he doing? *Does he really want to do that to me? Does he think Freddie is a better choice to take his rage out on?* Moving swiftly, Will put an arm across Conlan's chest and dragged him off Freddie, taking a couple of bruising elbows to the ribs in the process but stubbornly refusing to let go.

"Stop it!" Amelia shrieked, wide-eyed, as she was woken by the noise. "What are you doing?" she demanded.

Looking at Freddie with hatred, Conlan struggled against Will. Realising he was not going to get free, he yelled at the stunned man instead.

"What was the last thing I said to you, Freddie? I told you to look after her, told you NOT to let her follow us. You are too stupid to obey a simple order! What has Eleanor suffered, because of you?" There was silence. Coming slowly forward, Eleanor left the quiet comfort of Horse and crouched at Freddie's side. He looked at her in hurt bewilderment. She turned to glare at Conlan.

"Freddie tried to carry out your order. Jarrick didn't believe you when you said there were no more Avatars. He sent men to get us. They knocked us senseless and carried us back to the compound. Freddie didn't do anything wrong." Eleanor concentrated on making her voice as cold and hard as she could. The anger drained from Conlan's face, leaving it an empty void. He struggled in Will's arms again, and this time Will let him go. Getting to his feet, Conlan turned and stalked off into the trees, his whole body rigid. Watching him go, Eleanor sighed. *Nothing is ever easy where that man is concerned.* She looked back at Freddie.

"Are you OK?"

Freddie shrugged, wiping blood from his lip with the back of his hand. "I'll live. What was that about? He went from calling you a monster to hitting me for not protecting you."

"He's a complicated man," Eleanor said, helping Freddie to sit. "I think there is more going on than he's telling us. I need to go and talk to him."

"Leave him be, Eleanor, he needs some time," Will said. He was still sat on the ground, watching the trees through which Conlan had disappeared.

"He's suffering, Will. I don't want him to have to do that on his own," Eleanor said.

"That's his choice," Will replied.

"Maybe he thinks it's his only choice," Eleanor said as she stood and followed Conlan.

Conlan was not in sight. Reaching out a string, Eleanor felt for him and found his energy. As she brushed against it she realised with a shock that his shield was thinner. It had faded, she was quite sure. Was this why she had felt his strong emotions? Was it losing Rand or something Jarrick had said or done to him? Had grief done it? Trey had lost his shield after his daughter died. Maybe the loss of a loved one did it: *That could be a problem; the only loved ones Conlan has left are us and Gregor... I can't really test that.* Not knowing when his shield had lost its strength meant that conjecture was pointless, but at least she now knew that it could be reduced. He had walked a long way from the camp. Eleanor followed his energy to the edge of a stream; he had washed Rand's blood from his hands and arms and stood with his forehead resting against the trunk of a giant tree. With a steady monotony he was pounding the wide trunk with his right fist. The only sounds were the flowing water and the dull thud as he made contact. Eleanor walked a little closer.

"Go away!"

Hard, flat and angry, his voice made her jump. Eleanor stopped, but she could not bring herself to obey. *I can feel his pain.* It was flowing out from him in pulsing waves. He continued pounding on the tree and Eleanor could see the blood splattered across the bark from his damaged knuckles. She had no idea what to say, was not sure there was anything she could say. She knelt down, feeling the damp vegetation soak through her trousers. Fat tears crowded her eyes, blurring her vision and slowly running down her cheeks. She quickly brushed them away.

"Please stop that," she begged.

"I. Told. You. To. Go," he snarled, punctuating each word with a jab to the tree, each one with increasing force.

"Please don't, don't hurt yourself anymore," she whispered, the tears coming too fast to hide now.

"Why do you care?" he muttered, still hitting the tree. The answer burst out of the place she had hidden it like the evils in Pandora's Box. *If I tell him, will it help?* She had no answer to that. It might distract him. He might even care enough for her that he would stop hurting himself once he knew it hurt her too.

With a hiccupping sob, Eleanor whispered, "Because I'm in love with you. I can feel your pain."

She had said it. It had slipped out so easily.

He stopped punching, letting his hand drop to his side, and he stood in silence, his head still resting against the blood-splattered bark. Eleanor was not sure what she had expected from him, but the sudden silence was eerie. He rolled slightly so he was facing away from her, his shoulder resting against the tree, and slowly he let his legs fold under him. Eleanor got the impression it was only the support offered by the victimised tree that was stopping him collapsing completely. She sat in numb confusion for so long that it became fully dark. All she could see was Conlan's outline blending with the tree, the only sounds the endless hurry of the stream and her own pounding heartbeat. She could still feel his pain washing over her, sharp stabs from which she had no protection. Speaking softly she tried once more to offer him comfort.

"Conlan..."

"Go away, Eleanor," he pleaded.

"Are you going to keep hurting yourself?" she asked bluntly. He shook his head, wrapping his arms around himself, as if he might fall apart at any moment.

"You don't have to go through this alone," she said.

"Please, Eleanor, go away." His voice was now barely a whisper and she could hear the grief in it. Eleanor stood, but instead of moving away she found herself walking towards him. Reaching a trembling hand out she gently placed it on his shoulder. He shrugged away from her. Hurt and paralysed by the depth of his pain as it battered her, she froze, staring at him. When he spoke, his voice was hard, cold and remorseless.

"I don't love you, Eleanor, how could I after what you did? I don't want you or your pity. Leave me alone." Each word was like a physical blow. She staggered back, feeling her heart split in a jagged, bloody line down the middle. The pain of it took her breath away. What did he mean, 'after what you did'? Did he mean the earthquake? Was he so horrified by the deaths she had caused that it had erased any feeling he might have had for her? Or was he upset about his brother? Jarrick had loathed him, but perhaps the feeling had not been mutual. Did he hate her for destroying one of his last links to his family? She had expected him to reject her, even humiliate her, but this anger was not something she had considered, and it was definitely not something she understood.

"I'm sorry about Jarrick," she whispered, making a guess at what had caused his reaction.

Pushing himself to his feet he turned on her, his expression shrouded by the dark, but she felt the waves of disgust, hurt and rage as they flowed out of him. He pushed her roughly down to the ground, standing over her, his fists clenched.

"What were you thinking?!" he yelled. "You let him... touch you! Why? To stop him torturing me? Are you insane? No agony he could have inflicted would hurt more than the mental torture he put me through or the way I feel right now. You *should* get to feel my pain, Eleanor, because you caused it! I can't look at you without seeing his twisted, scornful face. Get out of my sight!"

Eleanor stared at him, stunned. "What did Jarrick tell you?" she asked.

"Why does it matter?" Conlan snapped.

"It matters."

Eleanor felt Conlan's suspicion and could imagine the look on his face – his eyes narrowed, an expression so much like Jarrick's.

"He told me he'd made a deal with my pretty little whore. I got to leave unharmed if he got to sample your 'many delights', as he put it. He would visit me and tell me in great detail about all the hideous things he was doing to you, how much you loathed it..." Conlan said, his voice empty.

Eleanor stared, incredulous. "And you believed him?"

"I... you looked so shaken when I saw you and refused to answer my question about the deal you'd made. I already knew about Jarrick's proclivity for rape... and he knew things... about you, about your life... about your body..." Conlan's explanation dropped to a pained whisper.

Eleanor glared at him, a dark bitter anger twisting the broken pieces of her heart. "I was in shock when you saw me, Conlan. Yes, I did make a deal with Jarrick. In exchange for his promise not to cause you any further injury, I promised to stop blowing up his precious statues. He knew things about me because we talked a little, *just* talked. I imagine he knew things about my body because Kona told him. He couldn't hurt you physically without breaking our agreement, so he found different ways to hurt you..."

"That was the only deal you made?" he asked, suspicion still plain in his tone.

Eleanor nodded, anger and a strong sense of betrayal overwhelming the pity she had felt for him. "Yes, but if there had been nothing else I could have bargained with, if I'd been desperate enough to sacrifice my body, my self-respect, in order to protect you, this would have been your response? I just gave you my heart, Conlan. I don't expect you to love me, but have you *no* care for what you've created."

He stood silently in front of her, and Eleanor felt grateful that it was too dark to see his face because it meant he would not be able to see the devastation on hers. She rose on shaking legs. If she had given everything for him, he would have despised her for it. Her love was clearly wasted on the man. The thought was a fresh agony, because she knew she could love no other. Unable to bare the torment of being so close and yet so far away from him she fled, heading for the flickering orange glow of the fire she could see through the trees. She forced herself to keep her eyes focused in front of her, although she could feel his gaze on her back.

Will looked at her questioningly as she stepped into the firelight. Amelia was curled up against him, fast asleep. Eleanor envied her that quiet comfort. Freddie was snoring softly on the other side of the fire. Too angry to explain, Eleanor pushed roughly into Will's head, not waiting for him to accept her and ignoring the shock on his face. She then played back the memory of her conversation with Conlan, along with all the anger, disgust and betrayal. The memory finished and she yanked her string back, watching with an emotionless stare as Will winced at the discomfort.

"I agree, he's an idiot on occasion, but there's no need to take it out on me," Will said with a reproachful look.

Eleanor felt guilt begin to beat down on her. As her anger left, so did her strength. She dropped heavily to the ground. Pulling her knees up to her chest, she knew the hurt was coming and she would just have to endure it.

"Sorry," she mumbled, unable to meet the deep-blue eyes she could feel boring into her. "I just don't understand. Does he think I have no self-respect? He believed Jarrick, believed that I would have handed myself over to that merciless monster to do with me as he pleased, just to protect him."

"Of course he believed Jarrick. He believed you would give yourself up to protect him because he would willingly have done it for you," Will said.

"Then he's an even bigger idiot than I thought," Eleanor muttered.

"Because he wants to protect you?"

Eleanor nodded and felt her anger returning. "I'm quite capable of looking after myself. If I'd really felt threatened by Jarrick, I could have reduced him to a bloody pulp a lot sooner than I did. The only one who really needs protecting here is Conlan, and mostly he needs protecting from himself."

Will was silent but was looking at her intently, a small smile on his face and a knowing look in his eyes.

"For a clever person, you can be unbelievably obtuse," he commented.

Eleanor glared at him. "Care to give this moron a clue as to what she's missing?"

Will chuckled. "Don't you see it? The evidence has been right in front of you since day one. Conlan has pandered to your every wish. That Protector he spared because you insisted. Taking you to see his grandfather – he could have travelled far quicker, safer and easier on his own, but he took you because he wanted you to meet the only family he cares about and, I suspect, so that he had an excuse to spend time with you. The voting thing, he gave up way too easily. Did you think you were the first one of us to try that line of argument? Your decision to travel though the middle of Protector territory? Another risk he accepted on your say so. I've known him for nearly ten years, but he's allowed you to get closer than any of the rest of us ever have a hope of getting. He's put so much effort into training you that Amelia and Freddie are jealous. He taught you to speak Dwarfish, before you turned up he was more into brooding than conversation. He seeks you out, listens to your counsel, trusts your judgements; he's never so much as expressed doubt to me, but he confides his fears and regrets to you."

Eleanor sighed. "He listens to you too, more than you think, he has every respect for you."

Will smiled. "What I'm trying to tell you, Eleanor, is that the man loves you, far more than I think even he is aware of, and the thought of Jarrick getting his hands on you has devastated him. If you'd left him alone, as I suggested, he might have calmed down enough to have a rational conversation about it, but you caught him at his most vulnerable and he said some things he doesn't really mean."

Eleanor felt the fragments of her heart twitch at Will's words. Did Conlan love her? *He has no reason to lie.* Eleanor shook her head.

"He doesn't love me, Will. He thinks I'm a monster for destroying Nethrus. He thinks I'm annoying and stubborn and impossible to shut up. I don't follow orders and I make too many mistakes. He put effort into training me because I needed it; I was a liability until I could fight. He taught me his language because I need to know it to interpret the book, and he's only interested in my 'counsel' because he thinks I can figure out how the 'connection' works. I'm a means to an end."

Will shrugged. "You're wrong."

"I want very much to be wrong, but after his last outburst, I'm not willing to hope anymore," she whispered. Pulling her blanket out from her things and covering herself with it she closed her eyes and curled into a ball. Despite the fire's heat she felt cold, a steady chill spreading through her body and emanating from her damaged heart. She shivered slightly, pulling the blanket tighter round her. She was too wound up to sleep, so she concentrated on slowing down her breathing and calming her mind. Maybe sleep would come.

The fire had died down to the deep penetrating heat of glowing ashes; Eleanor listened to Freddie's gentle snoring, finding it strangely comforting.

"I was wondering when you were going to come back," Will said quietly.

"I take it Eleanor told you what happened?"

"Yes, she did. Want to talk about it?"

"No."

There was silence. Eleanor heard movement as Conlan sat at Will's side. Then more silence.

Will sighed. "Fine, I'll talk, you listen. It's OK, she's been asleep for hours, they all have; it's just you and me. You're making a huge mistake – she loves you. I've been inside her head, and no matter how hard she tries she can't hide her feelings for you; they run through her every thought." Eleanor felt her cheeks heating, Will had no right to tell Conlan about things that were private. She had just about worked up the courage to say something, when Will asked a question that froze her.

"Do you love her?"

There was heavy silence, and Eleanor felt apprehension make her limbs tremble as she forced herself to keep her eyes shut.

"No," Conlan said eventually, his tired voice empty of emotion. Eleanor felt her heart shatter further, causing her to catch her breath, the pain of it momentarily filling her world.

"Liar," Will accused.

"She's just so young, too young."

Will chuckled. "That line of argument might work on the others, but you forget who you're talking to, Conlan Baydon. I don't believe you."

"I don't love her, at least not in the way she wants or deserves. I don't think I'm capable."

"Really? And how does she want to be loved? Have you asked her?" Will snapped.

"All I've done since I dragged Eleanor into this mess is inflict pain on her. She's better off without me," Conlan whispered, and Eleanor heard the acidic self-hatred in his words.

"But she's not without you, Conlan. She deals with you every day. Let her in. *She* wants to protect *you*! She's trying to anyway, but at the moment she has to fight you every step of the way. Despite your faults she loves you, and I don't understand why you would throw that away."

"I don't love her, Will."

Will sighed. "Are you trying to make Eleanor hate you?"

"It would be safer for her if she did."

"You don't know her very well, do you? Eleanor isn't the type to hate. You need to understand, even if you don't love her back, that her love for you has consequences. Causing that earthquake? She did that for you. She saw your pain and reacted, and I don't think she even had any control over it. She needs your support and understanding, not your condemnation. What she did hasn't hit her yet, but when it does I don't think it's going to be pretty."

Silence.

He doesn't love me. The thought ricocheted around her head, leaving a blinding agony every time it struck. Eleanor realised she was holding her breath and so she slowly let it out, trying to make her breathing sound like the slow, regular imitation of sleep.

"This is not a conversation I want to have ever again."

"You're a stubborn fool, Conlan," Will muttered.

Conlan sighed. "So people keep telling me."

Eleanor remembered Gregor's words; he had called Conlan a stubborn fool, too. Eleanor wondered if Gregor had realised she loved Conlan and had said something – it would certainly explain Conlan's reluctance to translate. Eleanor heard the clink of bottles.

"Freddie stole these on one of his escapes. The man can see in the dark, which makes him useful for night-time recognisance," Will said. Eleanor gasped – Freddie had been creeping around Jarrick's compound at night, but why? Why had he and Will not told her?

"Did he find out anything interesting?" Conlan asked, sounding relieved to be changing the subject.

"He was looking for evidence that Jarrick was responsible for attacking us," Will said.

"That wasn't Jarrick," Conlan said softly. "I've had far too much time to think recently. Hiding, attacking from the bushes – that's not Jarrick. No, we have a new, unknown enemy." Eleanor heard the squeak of corks being pulled from bottles.

"So what do we do now?" Will asked.

"I think we're safe here, so we should stay for a while and figure out where the sword is, give Amelia a little more time to recover," Conlan said.

"If we're going to stay we should build a shelter. Amelia says that autumn storms are on their way," Will said. There was more silence. When Will spoke again his voice was full of such gentle concern that Eleanor thought he was talking to Amelia. "What's the matter?"

"I'm tired, Will," Conlan whispered. "I just want it to stop for a while."

"I have a solution for that problem; here, have a bottle." Eleanor could hear the smile in Will's voice. "Let's drink to Rand, the finest horse that ever lived." The bottles were gently clinked together again.

"To Rand," Conlan said solemnly, the fresh, raw grief seeping through his words. They drank in silence for a while. When conversation started again, they talked about Rand, reminding each other of all the times he had raced them away from danger and chuckling at some of their more outrageous exploits.

Eleanor woke to brilliant sunlight. It was long past dawn. Strange, violent dreams made her feel tired and crabby. Sitting up, she stretched and yawned. Conlan was lying on his back, one arm across his face hiding his eyes and the other arm cuddling the empty bottle. Will lay on his side snoring – they looked rather comical. Amelia and Freddie were sat a little distance away, eating breakfast. They both gave her amused grins. Moving quietly, Eleanor walked over to them.

"Guess they drank a little too much last night."

Amelia giggled. "We were beginning to wonder if you'd joined them."

"No, I was just tired."

Amelia nodded and Eleanor was glad to see that the horror and fear from yesterday seemed to have faded a little from her eyes.

"So do we wake them up?" Freddie asked.

"Do we need to? They look so peaceful," Amelia remonstrated slightly, regarding Will's sleeping form lovingly.

Not able to bring herself to look at Conlan, Eleanor nodded. "Let them sleep."

They moved away from the two slumbering men so that their voices would not disturb them, but close enough to protect them from danger, if necessary. At Amelia's instigation she and Freddie began to practise her shielding. Amelia would manipulate the air in front of Eleanor into a thick shield and Freddie would bombard it with his energy. The colours were beautiful. Amelia got her to pace up and down slowly as she practised moving the shield with her and Freddie practised hitting a moving target. Amelia was getting very good at getting her shield to keep pace, while Freddie was mostly just setting fire to the shrubbery. It was not a game and required total concentration from Freddie and Amelia, but as the 'target' Eleanor had nothing to do, and time to think was not something she wanted. Amelia moved on from practising her shielding to practising stopping a knife thrown at a target. Eleanor had told her about the Elf children doing it and Amelia had been trying for months, with some success.

It was almost midday before Will finally stirred, moaning softly as he struggled to sit up and shading his eyes from the sun. Amelia took him a mug of water.

"Was it a good year?" she asked innocently, eyeing the empty bottle. Will smirked at her and rubbed absently at his temple as he drank, wincing slightly. Eleanor watched the care and love they showed each other and it ripped at the pieces of her heart. She had to leave or she was going to cry. *I need an excuse.* Her desperate mind remembered something Conlan had told her about a plant that had the ability to alleviate headaches and other minor aches and pains, although its name escaped her. However, she could see an image of it clearly in her head – small purple flowers and roots filled with something that worked like aspirin. Leaving before Conlan awoke, Eleanor moved off into the woods to look for the plant. They were much further south than she had been before, but most of the other plants and animals had been the same, so maybe the small flower was here somewhere. The wood was quiet, with only the occasional birdcall to disrupt the peace. Eleanor was enjoying the walk as she moved carefully, studying the ground and scanning it for the flower she needed. *Lepdrac*, she thought, *he had called it* lepdrac. The memory of Conlan's animated face as he had taught her about his world jumped into her mind. He had seemed happy, and she wanted to go back to that time. He did care, she was sure of it, and as she concentrated on this belief, letting it fill her mind, she felt her anger start to fade.

She eventually found a small crop of the purple flowers and got down on her hands and knees to dig out the roots. She was so intent on her work that she failed to hear the approaching footsteps until the figure stood in front of her, blocking the sun. She smelt smoke, blood, alcohol and unkempt bodies. Fear raced through her as she stood, the plants she had collected dropping from trembling fingers.

17

$\sim \!\! \sim \!\! \sim$

DUNCAN

The man standing in front of her was tall and thin, almost gaunt. He had a pleasant smile on a face that could have done with a wash and a shave. Hard, black eyes spoke of sly intelligence as his gaze slowly undressed her. Rusty sword drawn, he raised the tip to sit snuggly against her breast bone as she stood. His clothing was an eclectic mix of rough-sewn peasant garb with pieces of ill-fitting richer clothing here and there.

"Well, you are a wonderful sight this fine afternoon. Did you escape Nethrus, too? We are going to have some fun with you," he said, grinning rakishly at her. At the mention of Nethrus, images of bodies began flicking through Eleanor's mind like an out of control slide projector, and with a sickening twist of her stomach she realised where this man had got his mismatched outfit from – he had stolen clothing from the dead. Her fear became terror. There were five, equally strangely dressed, half-starved wretches behind him, who sniggered and grinned, one of them licking his cracked lips as he stared at her. The man threatening her pulled his sword back and used the point to force her chin up. Eleanor took a step back, coming up against a tree trunk.

"Nowhere to run, darling, but do not worry, we will be gentle," the rogue said, closing the gap between them. He forced his mouth against hers and pushed his tongue inside while hands roamed across her body. Eleanor froze. Tasting alcohol and corruption on his breath, she wanted to fight back, wanted to stop him, but her mind refused to assist. All she could see were the faces of those she had killed. In desperation she bit down hard on his tongue, her mouth filling with blood as the man howled and wrenched himself free. He glared at Eleanor for a moment before punching her violently to the ground, pain pulsing flashing lights behind her eyes and leaving her momentarily blinded.

"Leave her alone, Nic, this is not right," a trembling voice spoke up.

As Eleanor's vision cleared, she watched the other four men step away from the one who appeared to have spoken, physically distancing themselves from his comment.

Her attacker looked over his shoulder. "You pathetic excuse for a man," he snarled.

Hoping to take advantage of the distraction, Eleanor attempted to stand, but Nic turned back to her and delivered a hefty kick to her ribs.

"Stay there, girl, I will deal with you in a moment," Nic snapped. Eleanor curled into the sharp pain that spread through her left side, gasping for breath.

He turned back to the dissident member of his group. "You came to me and asked me to take you in, so you do as I say," Nic said, a dangerously threatening growl piercing through the Dwarfish.

"Thieves, that is what you said we were. I had no issue with that, but this is wrong. She is little more than a child, and I will not be part of this."

Without warning, Nic sprang forward, punching the man in the face with his sword hilt. He staggered back and Nic stabbed him forcefully in the gut with his sword. As he pulled the weapon free, the man dropped to his knees, eyes wide, and then toppled over, making a few agonised sobs before he lay silent and still. A cold, vicious smile on his face, Nic turned back to look at Eleanor.

"I think I prefer to play rough," he growled, spitting blood at her.

His weight dropped on top of her and she struggled violently. He struck her across the face again and Eleanor felt his knees digging painfully into her thighs as he forced her legs apart. She twisted her body to the side, pushing the man off balance. Getting a leg free she drove it up between his legs, once, twice, and at the third blow the man let her go, rolling onto his back, gasping and clutching at himself. Eleanor scrambled away, trying to get to her feet. She was knocked back down by one of the other men who had moved behind her. Nic pulled himself up.

"You are going to regret that," he hissed.

"Leave me alone or I will kill you," Eleanor replied as calmly as she could manage. The men laughed. Eleanor felt her pain and fear evaporate as anger pounded through her brain and she welcomed it, its fiery heat removing the faces of those she had killed. The anger also brought a strange calm as she stared at the men, thinking of all the ways she could reduce them to gibbering wrecks. *I want to kill them; I want to cause as much damage as possible.* Shocked by her own bloodlust, Eleanor took a few deep breaths and felt the anger turning to rage, her body shaking as she tried to calm it down. She was allowed back to her feet as Nic moved towards her menacingly, his weapon pointing at her eyes. Feeling her control snap and recognising an opening, Eleanor grabbed his sword hand, snapping his wrist back with such force she heard the bones break. Then stepping forward she slammed her elbow up into his chin and cut off his agonised scream. She wrenched the sword from his hand, stepped round him and gave him a vicious side-kick to the knee, smiling as she heard bones crack there, too. He collapsed in a whimpering, sobbing heap.

"I think I prefer it rough, too," she growled at him as she thrust the blade between his ribs, through his heart and yanked it swiftly free. She weighted the sword in her hand; it was well made and would once have been a fine weapon. She swung it in lazy figures of eight around her body. Its two-handed grip was smooth and bound in supple red leather; it was worn, but fitted her fingers comfortably. It was well-balanced and offered a gentle flex down its length. The blade, however, had been neglected through sheer laziness; its once carefully honed edge was rough, pitted and rusty. *No slashing then, just thrusting stabs.* This suited her perfectly. The other men were looking at her apprehensively. One behind her drew his sword carefully, considering his options, while the others just seemed content to watch. *Idiots, you'd have more of a chance if you came at me together.* He raised his sword in a clumsy overhead attack. *Why is he moving so slowly?* Eleanor twisted lightly, the sword dropping down behind her back, the stranger falling forward. Spinning, she repositioned the blade as she moved, bringing the point down hard into the back of his neck and pushing through the spine. The weight of his dead body falling released the sword's red glistening length and Eleanor turned round to face the remaining men. Finally catching on that they should stick together, the two on the right rushed her. One aimed at her skull, the other her stomach. She deflected the blade inches from her abdomen and dropped low as the other sword whistled over her head. From this angle she was able to sweep one man's legs out from under him, kicking him in the face as he met the ground and breaking his nose. As she rose she jammed her sword's point into the other man's groin, watching his face distort into a soundless scream and not feeling the slightest flicker of remorse. As he doubled over she used her foot on his shoulder to pull the blade free with a slurping, squishy sound. He collapsed, twitching weakly, blood quickly pooling between his legs, and then ceased moving altogether. *Must have hit an artery.* The thought was detached, her observations clinical, and the only emotion she felt was her pulsing rage. She thrust her sword, without looking, through the neck of the man still clutching his broken nose. He let loose a gurgling gasp that dropped to a sort of whimpering, then silence. Stepping over his dead body she faced the last man standing. She casually flicked the sword down its length, creating a fine spray of blood on the forest detritus at her feet. As she was not intending to use the blade to slash, it would make no improvement to the weapon's efficiency, but she was well aware of the impact the cold, precise movement would have on her final enemy. His eyes grew wide in his already frightened face, and shrieking he dropped his weapon and ran. Eleanor briefly contemplated throwing her sword through his back, but Conlan's mantra – 'Never willingly let go of your weapon' – ran though her head. These six might not be the only refugees from Nethrus roaming the woods. So she watched him run.

It was a moment before the roar of battle left her and a movement on the edge of her vision told her she was being watched. She turned and found Conlan staring at her with his usual unreadable expression. *Bet he's thinking of all the mistakes I made.* She felt guilt simmering beneath the surface at the carnage she had caused, but she swallowed it down. It was like drinking acid. *I'm not going to apologise to him any more for being what he has created.* Keeping her face as hard and as calm as possible, she moved towards him, stooping to pick up the flowers she had collected. As she walked past, she looked him in the eye.

"Still think I need protecting?" she hissed. The look of shock, distress and disappointment on his face gave her such a strong feeling of satisfaction it was almost worth all the guilt she was going to feel for killing a bunch of incompetent, disorganised, half-starved morons. She stepped round him and walked back to the camp. Conlan did not follow and Eleanor tried hard to hold on to the feeling that she did not care. Will, Freddie and Amelia were halfway through building a large three-sided shelter when she arrived; they looked surprised that she had come back alone.

"Did Conlan find you?" Freddie asked. "He wasn't impressed you'd wandered off by yourself."

"Yes, Conlan found me," Eleanor said, noticing Amelia eyeing the bloody sword in horror.

Will looked with alarm at the sword and the crimson streaks that covered her hands and arms. "You didn't kill him, did you?" he asked, not entirely in jest. Eleanor felt the ghost of a smile drift across her face at the joke and handed the plants over to Will.

"Chew the roots; it will help with the headache," she said quietly. Will looked down in surprise.

"You found *lepdrac*? How did you know about this?"

Eleanor shrugged. "Conlan told me," she said flatly.

"What happened?" Freddie asked, his gaze travelling from the sword to her bruised face and then to her eyes.

Eleanor shook her head and walked away, heading towards the stream. She felt numb, as if someone had shoved a sword through her, and she was just waiting for the agony. The stream ran past lazily, and she dropped to her knees at its edge. Rubbing the gore off her hands she cupped them and sipping the clear, cold water she washing the taste of blood out of her mouth. The incriminating red stains continued up her sleeves and she wanted it off. Leaning forward she plunged her arms into the water's icy depths, watching as the steady flow dragged the blood away with it, spreading dark clouds through the water for a moment before it cleared. The cold water was numbing her hands and arms to match the rest of her – and it felt right. She had killed them, just like she had killed the people of Nethrus; killed another four men, just because she could. The rage had made her want to kill them. She wanted the world to see how she felt inside, to have someone else experience her pain. Her anger had made her powerful and able to deal with looking at Conlan; her anger was a wall which had kept him out. She remembered the distress and disappointment she had seen in his eyes. *He gave you a gift, the ability to protect yourself and to defend others, and you betrayed him.* She shied away from that thought, pushing it deep inside her along with her guilt and all the other emotions that threatened to drop her into sobbing hysteria. He would not see her weeping and full of remorse. *I am stronger than this.* She smiled as the thought made her feel stronger; anger was a way to deal with her hurt. She heard movement behind her and grabbed her sword. She spun round into a crouch, flexed and ready to pounce, if necessary. Freddie stared at her, fear on his face.

"What happened?" he asked again.

Eleanor allowed herself to relax ever so slightly as she stood and calmly returned his gaze.

"I met a few would-be rapists and killed them."

Freddie's eyes grew wider. "How many?"

"Six attackers, I left four dead." Eleanor felt the guilt crash against her as she recited her crime, but the wall she had created held; she would not have to deal with the guilt just yet. Freddie stared at her but said nothing. She pushed past him, heading back to the camp, but she stopped short as the trees opened into the clearing. Conlan was walking into the camp from the other side, the body of one of her attackers, the one who had spoken out, resting over his shoulders. *What's he brought the body here for?* He knelt down and gently lowered his burden to the ground in front of the shelter. As he did so, the man moaned and clutched at the wound in his stomach. *He's still alive.* Her anger came surging back and removed all her guilt. She welcomed the feeling, he would pay for attacking her. Coming up behind her, Freddie gasped.

"Make that four dead and one soon to be dead," Eleanor murmured, marching forward.

"Who's that?" Will was asking Conlan.

"A survivor. I'm going to need your help burying the other bodies," Conlan muttered.

"Bodies? A survivor of what?" Will asked, confused.

"Me," Eleanor said.

Conlan turned to stare at her and she glared back, feeling the anger fill her with strength.

"You left him for dead," Conlan said.

"My mistake," Eleanor sneered. "But one I can fix."

She matched towards the injured man, raising her sword. He was conscious and saw her coming. Holding out a blood-stained hand in a pitiful attempt to defend himself, he whimpered, tears carving rivers into his dirty face. She brought the sword down, aiming at his head. It was not a subtle blow. She had not wanted it to be, as she did not want the man's death added to her list of crimes, but to keep herself in one piece she must keep the anger going, must fuel it. If she was slow and clumsy in her attack, perhaps one of the others would stop her. As her blade sliced through the air, another weapon came up to meet it, stopping it an inch short of the trembling man's head with the resounding clamour of striking metal. Eleanor recognised the blade and turned slowly to face Conlan, green eyes iridescent with fury. Silently she stepped back into the open, away from the injured man and the fire, giving herself room to manoeuvre. She raised her sword, waiting.

"I don't want to fight you, Eleanor," Conlan said, although his twitching sword hand indicated otherwise.

Eleanor narrowed her eyes.

"Afraid I might beat you?"

He did not rise to the taunt but just stared back at her passively. This pushed Eleanor's anger up another notch. It felt good to be this strong, not a pathetic wailing woman weeping over a broken heart. She moved back threateningly towards the injured man. Conlan stepped between them, raising his sword.

"You'll regret this," he cautioned quietly.

She smiled grimly. "I'm not really in the regretting mood."

She sprang towards him, feigning a thrust to his face. The point of her weapon heading for his eyes, Conlan was forced to react by blocking the blade. As he did, Eleanor pushed her arms out, slapping his sword to the side. If her blade had been sharp she would have pulled back and sliced into his neck. A killing blow if she had the aim right, but with the blade's dull, rusty edge she was forced to swing it back as a blunt instrument. Using her hand on the hilt as a fulcrum she flicked the pommel of the sword away from her, the see-saw motion snapping the blade back towards Conlan. A hammer blow to the side of his head. She felt the impact vibrate along the blade's length. He staggered back, dropping to one knee, his body slumping and stopping himself collapsing completely with his outstretched sword hand. His body trembled as he pushed the palm of his other hand into his scalp. He looked shocked when it came away streaked in blood. Eleanor felt cold, hard victory course through her body as she held her sword comfortably in a relaxed two-handed grip and stared at Conlan. There was no pity, no mercy, no guilt. All those cumbersome, painful emotions were buried deep inside. His sword hand was supporting his body. He was kneeling, vulnerable. She moved cautiously towards him and placed the tip of her blade against his throat. He stared up at her, his eyes unfocused. Slowly he stood, leaving his weapon at her feet; she let him up but kept the blade tip resting against his skin.

"You want me dead? Do it," he said, his voice empty and the hard, unreadable expression back on his face.

"You really shouldn't tempt me," Eleanor said, surprised by the menace she could hear in her voice. *Who am I? What am I doing?* She saw movement in her peripheral vision. *It's a distraction.* She quickly took several steps away from Conlan, swinging her weapon to the right as Will came towards her, his open hands held out to the sides in a universal sign of surrender. However, Conlan had not surrendered, and as Eleanor turned to face Will, her sword raised, he charged her. Eleanor caught his movement, and as he launched himself she dropped her sword, grabbed both his arms and rolled back onto the ground, pulling him down with her. She curled her legs into her chest and planted her feet firmly into his stomach, and as he came up over her head she pushed out hard with her legs, releasing her grip on him. He sailed over her, crashing into and through a group of saplings ten feet across the clearing. She continued her movement, rolling over her shoulder and back onto her feet into a crouch, grabbing her sword again as she did. She brought the point back to face Will, who had frozen, staring at her in utter amazement.

"Eleanor? It's OK, calm down," Will said quietly.

"I'm perfectly calm, thank you!" she snapped, jumping to her feet. There was a groan from the trees into which Eleanor had flung Conlan, and both she and Will turned to look. The trees trembled and rustled as Conlan hauled himself up, using a snapped tree trunk for support.

"Some great warrior you are," Eleanor sniped at him as he stood. He stared. There was silence, a lengthy silence. Eleanor began to think she was missing something again. She looked at Will, who was still looking at her in shocked amazement.

"What?" she demanded.

"You're just so incredibly fast," he whispered.

"And strong," Conlan finished as he walked towards them, his hands now raised in surrender as Will's had been.

"I was well trained," she sneered, daring Conlan to accept responsibility. He continued to walk towards her. "Don't come any closer!" she ordered when he was still comfortably out of her range. He froze. Eleanor wondered if he realised that she had given him the order to protect him, not because she was afraid of him. He was still staring at her, and he spoke quietly.

"No, Eleanor, this is beyond training, this is something else. Your movements are precise and economical, but when you fought those men you used moves I've never seen and adapted your approach immediately for the limitations of your weapon. You made it look easy... graceful. If you were thinking your way through that fight, not acting purely on instinct, then your reaction times are truly astonishing."

So he saw me fight. His words sounded like a compliment, but why could she see fear in his eyes? Will was regarding her in much the same way he had the dragon. Looking behind her, Amelia was knelt beside the still whimpering man, but her terrified eyes were fixed on Eleanor's bloody sword. Like Will, Freddie managed to look both impressed and fearful at the same time. What was Conlan trying to say? *I'm not behaving like myself.* She was actually behaving like Freddie with his energy too high. She cautiously examined her own energy. It was higher than normal, a lot higher. It was not causing pain, but holding onto even a small amount of excess energy was turning her into a total psycho. An image of Earth using her body to fling Will across the room sprang into her head. *More energy, enhanced strength and speed?* Even understanding what was happening did not take away the desire to rip Conlan's head off, and anger flared as she looked back at him. Her energy jumped once more. *That's the trigger; my anger is pulling more energy from the earth, knocking my internal balance out.* She took slow, deep breaths and tried to relax by releasing the excess energy into the ground. It was working, until Conlan spoke again.

"You can put your sword down, Eleanor, I'm not going to let you murder an unarmed, injured man." His usual hard look was back on his face and Eleanor felt her hands jerk with the urge to ram his words back down his throat.

"But when you want to murder an unarmed kid just because he's a Protector, that's OK?" She bit the words out, the buzz of fury filling her ears and her energy leaping up again.

"No, that wasn't right either, but I had you to stop me from doing something I would regret. It's a favour I'm trying to return," he said, his intense gaze not leaving her face.

"I do not think you could stop me," Eleanor said slowly in Dwarfish, relishing the feeling of power over him she took from delivering the words in his own language and knowing them to be true. He stared at her and then glanced at Will. She could not read the look that passed between them.

"No," he agreed, responding in Dwarfish. "I do not think I could, but you will have to kill me to reach him."

He would do it. Eleanor marvelled at the stupidity of the man; he would throw his life away for some useless nobody, just to make a point. She struggled for a moment to fight down her anger and to focus on something good, something she loved about him. A deluge of images filled her mind. *Just one*, she thought distractedly. Obediently her mind brought one image into sharp focus: Conlan's soft smile, eyes full of affection as he watched his grandfather recite his family line. His feeling for this man he had not seen in years, someone he admired, made her feel warm inside. *I want him to look at me like that*, Eleanor realised. She held the image in her head as she allowed the little voice in the back of her mind to become a yelling insistence: *I don't want to kill you, Conlan, I love you.* The warm glow the image brought forth took the place of some of her anger. A little too much, though. She needed to get away from him, her anger was draining and taking her resolve and her strength with it. The guilt and the pain were coming – and she would not show that in front of him.

Eleanor sighed. "Neither of you are worth the effort."

She dropped her sword and turned away from them all, walking out into the woods. She had walked a long way before her defences finally crumbled and she stopped, the trees spinning around her. She felt bile surge through her stomach and retched, throwing up against a tree. She staggered on a little further, not really caring where she was going. She collapsed to the ground and curled into a tight ball. She was vaguely aware of a presence, someone gently shaking her, but she was too caught up in her torment to acknowledge it. Dropping her defences totally, Eleanor let the emotions she had been suppressing take hold. Fear, betrayal, longing, misery and the guilt for all the lives she had taken blanked her mind and tore at her soul. Her body trembled at the onslaught as her tears fell.

"Freddie?"

"We're over here, Will," Freddie said from somewhere close.

"Freddie, you've been out here hours, is she OK?" Amelia asked.

"I don't know." His voice sounded small and unhappy.

It was dark and cold, heavy, determined rain pounded her. Eleanor opened her eyes, blinking out the water that ran into them. At least it would wash away the evidence of her tears. *I'm soaking wet… when did that happen?* Will crouched in front of her, placing a lantern at her side, the rain hissing off its hot cover. She allowed him to sit her up and to pour water down her throat from a reused alcohol bottle. It eased the burning she had not even registered was raging in her throat. Amelia and Freddie stood behind him. Freddie looked soaking wet, cold and miserable. Amelia's eyes were filled with pity. Pity for her, Eleanor realised.

"Why didn't you come back and get us?" Will asked.

"I didn't want to leave her alone, what if the man she let go came back? She's not in any state to defend herself at the moment," Freddie answered.

"You could have brought her back with you," Will said.

"I tried, but she struggled too hard," Freddie whispered.

"Well she's not struggling now," Amelia commented.

"Eleanor? Eleanor…" Will said, staring into her face. She tried to focus and to formulate a response, but it was too difficult. "You're really cold and wet," he continued as she tried to pull her scattered thoughts together. "You might be an Avatar but you can still get sick. We need to take you back to the camp." *Not the camp. Conlan will be at the camp...*

"I am not sure I can face him," Eleanor whispered.

"What did she say?" Amelia asked.

"I've no idea, she's speaking Dwarfish," Freddie said.

Will took her face in his hands; they were so hot that it felt like he was branding her cheeks. *No, he's not hot – I'm so very cold.* She felt him push into her mind and she put up no resistance. *Make me forget, Will, please, take it all away,* she begged, feeling his shock.

What would you want to forget? he asked softly.

Everything, I want to forget murdering those men, I want to forget Rand dying, I want to forget destroying that town, killing all those people… I want to forget that I love him.

Why would you want to do that?

She laughed bitterly. *Because unrequited love sucks? Because I don't want to remember I'm an efficient, cold-blooded killer or that Conlan doesn't care about me.*

Eleanor, removing memories is a serious business. I've only done it once and you know how that turned out. Almost every thought you've had since you got here has been tied up with Conlan. Your love for him runs through all of it, everything you have learnt would be gone. All the control you have of your energy, the skill you have with a sword and your ability to speak Dwarfish would all go – and that's the best-case scenario. Worst case, I turn you into a drooling vegetable… permanently. Chances of that are fifty-fifty.

I don't care; I want the pain to stop, please, Will.

You might not care, but I do. We don't have time to start you back at the beginning. A wise person once told me, 'Leaving us like that, just to escape your own pain, is selfish'. You're stronger than that as well, Eleanor, I've felt it. As you pointed out to Amelia, our fates are linked, what affects one of us, affects all of us. If we lose you we're vulnerable, you hold us together. Don't give up on us, Eleanor, we need you and you're strong enough to handle this. You've given Amelia courage, Freddie peace and Conlan hope, please don't take that away.

Eleanor felt her guilt as a flooding torrent that threatened to drown her. She could not abandon them.

I have no right to risk all our lives just because I'm a coward and can't deal with my guilt and a broken heart, but don't expect me to be little miss cheery for a while.

Not a problem; in fact, if you want to take a few more shots at Conlan I'm not going to stop you. He's being an idiot. We can handle you miserable and angry.

But can you forgive me?

If my forgiveness helps, you have it. I know you didn't mean to kill all those people. Conlan knows it too – for all his many issues he does care about you.

He's got a funny way of showing it.

Will sighed. *I can't really argue with you on that point.*

The man drives me insane and I still love him, but I guess I can learn to deal with it.

We'll help, I promise.

Eleanor felt Will exit her head. He was still holding her face, and as she opened her eyes he smiled at her.

"Thank you," he whispered. She nodded, seeing Amelia and Freddie's concerned faces behind him.

"Hi," she said. "I guess Will told you what happened last night?" They nodded. Eleanor smiled at them, doing her best to make them believe it was real. "Did he also tell you about the conversation he had with Conlan later on?" Again they nodded.

"You heard that?" Will asked, a concerned frown deepening the lines across his forehead.

"My mother always told me you never heard anything good if you eavesdropped, and she was right," Eleanor said, feeling the pain of the memory stabbing at her again. "I'm sorry, has that man died?"

"No, he's hanging on," Will said, not sounding very happy about it.

"He tried to stop the other men raping me; he doesn't deserve to die for it," Eleanor said.

Will nodded. "I'll do my best to keep him alive."

"Will, sitting in the rain like this is not good for any of us, and Eleanor is freezing cold," Amelia said softly as she took Eleanor's hand.

"OK, let's take her back to the camp," Will said. He helped Eleanor to her feet, but dizziness and nausea hit her so hard that her legs collapsed out from under her. Freddie caught her, picked her up and cradled her gently against his chest. She felt safe and comfortable and felt the warmth of his body heat up her own. They walked back to the camp. Exhaustion was adding lead to her eyelids; she needed to sleep. She drifted as Freddie walked, not thinking, just floating, numb. She heard the crackling of the fire before she felt its warmth. Freddie sat her down beside it and she slumped against Amelia's shoulder. Amelia put an arm around her and she slipped down further, resting her head on Amelia's thigh. Across the fire, through the flames, she could see Conlan adding extra branches as insulation to the shelter. The injured man was already inside and looked dead, his face pale and drawn, eyes closed. Eleanor felt a sort of abstract pity, but her heart was too broken and her mind too battered for anything deeper. Will came back and crouched in front of her.

"Come on, Eleanor, let's get you out of the rain."

She nodded, allowing him to help her to her feet and guide her under the shelter's steep sloping roof. The floor had been swept clean, and given the weather it was surprisingly dry and warm. She was too tired to care about how close the injured man was to her, and curled up into a shivering ball, the fire's heat not yet penetrating her cold, wet clothes. Amelia arrived and coxed her into dry clothes, taking her wet garments with her when she left. Freddie came and lay down at her side, offering his arm for her head. She smiled gratefully, wriggling closer to his warm body, her back resting against his chest. He covered her with a blanket and rested his hand lightly round her waist; it was comforting, reassuring.

"Are you OK with her?" Will asked as she closed her eyes.

"I'm fine, I'll call if I need you," Freddie whispered.

"I'm not going to murder you in your sleep, Freddie," she muttered, without opening her eyes. Will chuckled as he stood and turned to move back to the fire.

"Is she going to be OK?" It was Conlan's voice. It sounded strained.

"Eventually," Will snorted. "Only you could take a sweet, innocent, gentle girl and turn her into a raging psychopath." There was silence and Eleanor opened her eyes. Will had gone to sit with Amelia. Conlan stood in front of the shelter, his head bowed and rain dripping off the end of his nose. From her position on the floor Eleanor could see the hurt on his face, and despite everything she felt sorry for him — how could she blame him for not loving her? *This is all my fault.* Self-pity and misery filled her and her tears started falling again. Freddie pulled her closer, his breath on her neck.

"It'll be OK, Eleanor, please don't cry," he whispered.

She could hear his pain. *I'm hurting him, too.* She struggled for control, fighting back the tears and allowing exhaustion to pull her down into sleep.

Her dreams were chaotic and unclear. An African landscape swam into focus; she felt dry air scorch her lungs and the dull drone of insects fill her ears, the horizon shimmering in the heat. But as she looked, she realised something was wrong. Some of the trees were strange and the colour of the sky was off. As Eleanor looked around, she recognised where she was from the picture in Gregor's book — it was the southern savannah, not in Africa but in Mydren. Suddenly Conlan stood in front of her; he smiled and then lunged forward, forcing a sword through her chest and into her heart. She tensed, expecting pain, but none came and she knew why.

"I have no heart, Conlan, I gave it to you."

He smiled again. "A gift beyond measure."

His whispering voice held such love that she started crying for what she could not have.

"I'm here, Eleanor, it's OK," Freddie whispered again.

She looked down at the sword in her chest. The hilt was familiar; this was the sword from the book. Then Freddie spoke again.

> "A silver sword in south freedom's hands,
> A gift beyond measure, to enter their lands,
> A heart for a heart, a price to be paid,
> Think to the future, a deal to be made."

Eleanor looked up. She was alone again. She called for Conlan, her voice rent with sorrow, the place where her heart should be a cold, dark pit.

"Please don't cry, Eleanor, it'll be OK," Freddie whispered.

Comforted by his words, she relaxed and her dreams became less acute and more blurry. Finally she drifted into deeper, dreamless sleep.

She woke with the distinctly uncomfortable feeling that someone was watching her. Her eyes flew open to find Conlan staring back. He was sat with his back resting against one of the tree trunks they had used as a support post for the shelter. It was nearly dawn and a bird was slicing the half-dark with sharp, lonely cries. The trees swayed in weary unison with a biting wind. The rain had stopped, but there was a damp chill in the air. Eleanor felt the warm, solid comfort of Freddie holding her close and felt a rush of grateful affection. Conlan looked cold, tired and miserable, his body drawn in on itself. Her love for him filled her with a radiating glow, before she remembered he had not wanted it, her hopes became dust, an empty, hurt feeling spreading through her all over again.

"Conlan, I'm so sorry, I... "

"Don't..." His voice was a whisper. "Eleanor, look at me."

She felt his anger punch through her fragile defences and cringed. *I've made a mistake.* She had inadvertently made a fundamental change and there was no turning back. The tears started up and she felt the broken pieces of her heart fall and crack into even smaller shards at his continued rejection. *Make it stop.* She closed her eyes, pushing her face into Freddie's arm.

"No," she replied, her voice muffled by Freddie's shirt sleeve. *Please, make it stop*. She was incapable of dealing with this any longer, and she could not put herself through the pain of having him reject her again. "Conlan, I killed people – hundreds of them – and I know I deserve whatever punishment you want to give me, and I also know I made a fool out of myself doing nothing more than adding to your misery, but I can't take much more, so please leave me alone." She felt his hand on her shoulder and she recoiled, pushing herself into Freddie's reassuring bulk and whimpering at the surge of love that that single touch forced through her. His hand flinched away, as if she had stung him.

"Leave her alone, she's not ready to deal with recriminations right now," Freddie said in a low, menacing voice. *How long has he been awake?* There was silence, but Eleanor could feel the tension in Freddie's body.

"I just want to talk to her," replied Conlan, his tone of voice pulled tight, controlled and flat. He was doing his best to sound rational and calm, although Eleanor suspected this was not how he felt.

"Eleanor, do you want to talk to Conlan?" Freddie asked gently. She shook her head, keeping her face pressed into Freddie's arm and her eyes tightly closed. "Leave her alone," Freddie ordered, his voice once more hard and cold. "She just tried talking to you and you shut her out. That's the only chance you're going to get for now."

More silence, and then she heard Conlan move away.

"He's gone, Eleanor, are you OK?" Freddie whispered after a moment.

"No," she moaned. "If he wants nothing to do with me, why was he watching me?"

"He's been watching you all night. You were calling out for him in your sleep, and he didn't look very happy about it," Freddie said.

Eleanor felt embarrassment heat her cheeks. "I bet he didn't. Why does this hurt so much? I knew he wouldn't want me, but I love him, my heart is his. This is killing me, Freddie."

"I'm sorry he's hurting you." There was such pain in Freddie's voice that Eleanor turned to look at him. The pain was also in his black eyes, taking away some of the life that normally burned within them. "I have a really strong urge to beat the crap out of Conlan right now," he muttered.

"Don't, please don't, I feel guilty enough about the pain I've caused him."

Freddie gave her a lopsided grin, the pain still in his eyes. "He doesn't deserve you."

Eleanor smiled and rolled slightly, curling into Freddie's body. "I think you'll find it's the other way round, but I appreciate the thought."

Freddie hugged her close to him.

"Thank you for being here for me," she whispered. He leaned forward slightly, pulled her closer and gently kissed her cheek.

"You're welcome," he whispered back.

Days began to crawl by. The injured man dropped in and out of consciousness, but he stubbornly refused to die. Sitting around doing nothing did not sit well with any of them, least of all Conlan. After a while he started pacing the clearing's radius, like a tiger trapped in a cage. Will had suggested he use his obvious pent-up energy to practise his sword fighting, seeing as Eleanor had kicked his arse. The suggestion had not gone down well and Conlan had disappeared for two days. Worrying them all. When he finally returned he started training, silently swinging his sword for hours on end with an energy-draining repetition that made Eleanor tired just watching; sweat dripping from him, he was totally focused never once faltering,. Eleanor tried to keep busy by practising her sword fighting and unarmed combat with Freddie, but she resisted all requests from the others to practise with her energy or join them when they did. Every time she pulled energy from the earth, all she could see were the people she had killed. It made her shake to the point of collapse, reality fading into the distance as the slide show of horror started up in her head, leaving her senseless and sobbing until it passed. She did, however, join in their morning balancing meditations. She knew this activity was important and could save lives, so she did not have quite the same reaction as she did with the more violent disciplines. Unfortunately the reaction she did have was not without its problems. The others were all now intimately aware of how she had started the earthquake, had been repeatedly dragged through her memories of the fight with the vagabonds and Conlan and had been forced to relive Rand's death several times as Eleanor's shaky defences crumbled, filling their minds with the nightmares she could not escape. They had been gentle and understanding with her and gradually, time and the morning meditation brought Eleanor a semblance of calm – not enough that she was ready to use her energy, but enough so that the night terrors became less frequent. What, at one point, had been the regular occurrence of her waking screaming, was now getting rarer and rarer. When it did happen Freddie was always there by her side, whispering gentle reassurance until she could function again.

To distract herself Eleanor concentrated on the book. Spending hours sitting by the fire with her eyes closed, she went through it a page at a time. The words of her dream came back to her again and again, and as she concentrated on the pages she found the words jumping out at her. Every twenty-fifth word of the fourth and eight chapters, the chapters that talked about the Avatar of Fire and the sword, the words gave her the verse she had heard in her dream.

> A silver sword in south freedom's hands,
> A gift beyond measure, to enter their lands,
> A heart for a heart, a price to be paid,
> Think to the future, a deal to be made.

The sword was in the southern savannah, somewhere, and 'south freedom's hands' made it sound like a person. She really wanted to talk to Conlan about it, but the others were being very protective of her, especially Freddie, who she felt was almost glued to her side. She was never left alone, and if Conlan accidentally got within a few feet of her, someone would glare at him until he backed off. He and Freddie had nearly come to blows over the one further attempt he had made to talk to her. She could not bring herself to look at him, but she was aware of him staring at her occasionally as waves of anger flowed out of him; it made her shudder. He had fallen into a dark, brooding silence that made her feel just as miserable as he seemed to be. If she happened to raise her voice above a whisper or laugh at something Freddie had said, he would stare at her before stalking off by himself, sometimes for hours at a time.

Will and Amelia, while just as protective of her as Freddie, were slightly more occupied with the injured vagabond. Will had taken the risky step of operating on the man, cutting his side open and doing his best to stitch up the hole in his stomach. Eleanor was amazed when the man survived the procedure. The grey, lifeless pallor left his skin and for some of his conscious moments he was lucid. He managed to drink and even gave Will his name. Duncan, he had called himself, or something that sounded very much like it in Dwarfish. If this miraculous recovery pleased Conlan at all, he did not show it, although Eleanor did notice him frequently staring at the injured man with a dark malevolence.

As he got stronger, Duncan began to take more interest in what was going on around him, and Eleanor caught him watching her more than once, a wary respect in his eyes. She knew she would have to talk to him. The opportunity finally arose as he began feeling well enough to eat. Amelia would take him food, helping him eat if he needed it. One early evening, as he finished eating and was handing his bowl back to Amelia, Eleanor walked over and stood just outside the shelter.

"May I talk to you?" she asked in Dwarfish. Amelia turned in surprise, a questioning look on her face. "I just want to talk to him," Eleanor said in English. Amelia turned back to Duncan, who nodded slowly. She shrugged and moved back to the fire. Eleanor took her place, kneeling at Duncan's side. She looked at him, noticing the rake-thin body, the short, brittle dark brown hair and the deep purple under his questioning brown eyes.

"Thank you," she said.

Surprise filled Duncan's face. "I might not have wished to rape you, child, but I fully intended to steal anything of value you might have had on you. I do not deserve your thanks, or the efforts your friends have put into preserving my life. I am not a good man."

"You understand the difference between right and wrong, though?" Eleanor asked.

Duncan nodded.

Eleanor smiled. "Then you can choose to be a good man, if you want."

Duncan gave her a condescending look. "If only things were that simple, child."

Eleanor shrugged. "Things are that simple, Duncan. Every time you are faced with a decision, just think, 'What is the right thing to do?' Not the easy thing, not the fun thing, not the comfortable thing, but what is the right thing. You have done it once, Duncan, so just keep doing it."

He nodded thoughtfully. "I shall do my best, child."

"That is all any of us can do – and my name is Eleanor."

Duncan thrust a hand out. "I am Duncan, I am pleased to make your acquaintance."

Duncan grinned as Eleanor shook his hand. His grin was infectious and she smiled back.

"I will leave you to rest. Perhaps we can talk again later?" Eleanor said as he released her hand and she stood.

"Any time, Eleanor," he said softly.

Turning from him she found Conlan standing in front of her. His expression was so intimidating that Eleanor instinctively took a step back, the shelter's supporting beam jamming into her back. He stared at her and she stared back. *What does he want?* Her happiness drained from her. Freddie and Will were off checking their traps and collecting firewood, while Amelia was stood a short distance away watching them.

"I don't want you talking to him," Conlan snapped. Eleanor felt her anger rocket, and with all the self-control she had at her disposal she slammed it back down. She would keep control, at all costs she would keep control.

"He's dangerous, I'd have thought you would have realised that," he tried to reason through gritted teeth. Eleanor stared at him incredulously. Was he worried about what she was going to tell the man? Did he not trust her to keep her mouth shut? Her confusion must have shown on her face, because he sighed in frustration.

"Eleanor, he attacked you," he said, as if explaining a very basic point to a particularly stupid child.

"If he's such a danger, why did you rescue him?" she asked.

Conlan looked uncomfortable. "He begged for my help…"

Eleanor stared at him. "You're telling me you took pity on him? I don't believe you. You've been furious with me for weeks. Your strong emotions radiate from you, did you know that? I can feel them, I can feel your anger crash against me. You brought me here to help Mydren and instead I killed hundreds. You taught me how to fight and I used that knowledge with a stunning lack of restraint. You rescued him to preserve your honour and you don't want me speaking to him because you're worried I'm going to tell him something I shouldn't. You don't trust me."

Eleanor took several deep breaths, conscious that her rant had increased both her anger and, by extension, her energy levels. She closed her eyes for a moment, pushed the excess energy back into the earth and felt her anger drain away as she did so. When she opened them again, Conlan was staring at her, livid.

"You can be a total idiot on occasion – if I didn't trust you talking to people, I wouldn't have bothered teaching you to speak Dwarfish in the first place! I taught you how to fight so you could do exactly what you did, defend yourself! Is it so hard to believe that I'm capable of showing mercy? He told me he tried to stop them raping you. I believed him, but he's still dangerous; I'd feel better if you kept your distance."

"I killed four of his friends, I'm fairly sure I could protect myself again, if the need arose," Eleanor snapped. Frustration filled Conlan's face; he took another step towards her, reaching out to grab her arms, and instead walked into a solid obstacle. It was like watching him walk into a plate glass window. He staggered back, stunned and shaking his head slightly. Turning, he looked at Amelia, who in turn gave him a flat, uncompromising stare in return.

"What do they think I'm going to do to you?" he muttered. He turned back, seemingly about to say something when Freddie barrelled into him, knocking him to the ground, getting in several vicious punches to Conlan's head and chest before he got over his surprise enough to fight back. Conlan punched Freddie in the side, pushed him off and struggled back to his feet. "This is getting out of hand," he said quietly as Freddie glowered at him. Eleanor closed her eyes and tried to force her anger under control. She felt Freddie hand on her shoulder.

"Are you OK?" he asked. Still struggling to control her anger, Eleanor nodded, letting Freddie's comforting presence calm her down and ignoring the guilt she felt for using him.

"Freddie, I was just trying to talk to her," Conlan protested.

Will came running up behind Eleanor. "What did I miss?" he asked, as if he was asking about an episode of his favourite soap. *Maybe we are his favourite soap*, Eleanor thought, amused. The tension in her body immediately evaporated as she giggled. She felt the stiffness drain from Freddie's body in response.

"You missed Conlan walking straight into Amelia's energy shield," she said, unable to keep the grin off her face.

"And why was there a shield there in the first place?" Will asked, his tone even, but Eleanor saw the concern in his eyes. Sighing, she shrugged. Will gave Conlan a questioning look.

"I was trying to get her to stay away from him," he said, nodding in Duncan's direction. "He's dangerous."

Duncan frowned. He might not have understood the words, but Conlan had made the meaning very clear.

"Conlan, the man has a partially healed hole in his side. Exactly what sort of a threat do you think he poses?" Will asked.

"He's still dangerous. I was just worried about her," Conlan persisted stubbornly, not looking at Eleanor. Eleanor stared at him in utter disbelief.

"You're worried about me?! I'm miserable because I can't talk to you. You're my friend and I miss you, and I think I might have cracked where the sword is and I want to tell you about it, but I'm too nervous about upsetting you to even try. If you do actually care enough to worry about me, think a little more about the impact *you* are having on me and a little less about protecting me from external threats I can handle just fine on my own. *You* are the only person in Mydren I can't defend myself against."

His face empty, Conlan held her gaze for a moment and then took several steps back before turning and walking away. They watched in silence as he disappeared through the undergrowth. Eleanor went to follow him. Freddie grabbed her arm.

"Leave him."

Eleanor shook herself free. "No, this needs sorting, I can't live like this any longer."

He grasped her arm again, a determined look came into his eyes. "Then I'm coming with you."

Eleanor shook her head, gently pulling her arm free. "Thanks for the offer, Freddie, but I don't think he's going to talk to me if there's an audience." She turned and walked after Conlan before Freddie could object further. She heard him take several more steps after her and was relieved when she heard

Will.

"No, Freddie, let her go."

She found Conlan sitting on the bank overlooking the stream.

"Are you just going to stand there, Eleanor, or are you going to say something?" The low Dwarfish tongue carried a sharp edge.

"I do not know what to say," she said, watching his shoulders stiffen with annoyance, or perhaps it was anger – it was difficult to tell without being able to see his face. He continued to stare at the water tumbling past him.

"You not knowing what to say, well there is a first. You had plenty to say a moment ago!"

He paused and took a deep breath, before turning to look at her. "Eleanor, please, come and sit down. Let me explain a few things to you."

Apprehension twisted her stomach. Her longing to be close to him, fighting the instinct that told her to run from the anger flowing from him.

"What are you thinking?" he asked, watching the expressions shift on her face.

Eleanor shrugged and told him the truth. "I am trying to decide if the pleasure I get from being able to sit close to you outweighs the risk I am taking by putting myself within striking distance." Surprise and then shame blanked his face; walking over, she sat down next to him. "You are worth the risk," she informed him solemnly.

He turned his head back to look at the water, its brisk gurgling in tune with the sound of the breeze moving amongst the trees. When he finally spoke, his voice was flat and emotionless.

"I wanted to stop you apologising, before, because you did not need to, not because I did not accept it. I wanted to tell you that, but you were really upset, and now I understand why. You assume you are to blame for far too much."

"If I am not to blame, why are you so angry with me?" she asked. "And do not tell me that you are not angry, because I can feel it, even now."

He sighed. "I am not angry with you, I am angry with myself."

"Why are you angry with yourself?"

It took him a long time to answer. "I really do care about you, Eleanor, maybe not in the way you want, but I still want to protect you and support you. More importantly, I do not want to hurt you, but that is all I seem to do."

Eleanor shrugged. "I hurt you just as much as you hurt me."

Silence.

"Do you regret telling me how you feel?" he asked, his voice quiet and careful.

"Are you still trying to knock a tree down with your fist?" Eleanor asked.

"No."

"Are you planning to try to at a later date?"

Conlan shook his head, amused. "No."

"Then I do not regret telling you, although I do regret losing my mind."

"It was a little extreme, even for you," Conlan agreed.

"Recently, when I get angry, I involuntarily pull energy from the earth. Remember when Freddie used to go slightly psychotic when he had a little too much energy? Well it would appear to affect me the same way, in that it makes me stronger, quicker and very aggressive. Perhaps it affects all of us the same way; in fact, I think Amelia experienced it when I nearly killed you and Will," Eleanor sighed. "It is like having an alcohol problem you cannot control. I think it might have been triggered by causing the earthquake. Now I am aware of it I have more chance of controlling it, but when I attacked those men and you, I had no idea." As they stared at the water she considered the situation. She could not force him to love her, and he seemed to be angry with himself because he was hurting her, even though it was hardly his fault.

"Stop hating yourself," she ordered. "Let us just go back to the way things were, yes?"

He smiled. "I can try... I miss you, too."

Eleanor had a moment of euphoria, and on impulse she threw her arms around his neck. His body tensed in surprise, but he stiffly put his arm around her. *Better than nothing, I can live with this.* She could feel every knotted muscle in his body screaming his discomfort at having her so close, but he did not push her away and instead just waited patiently until she let him go, even managing a small smile as she did so.

"So, tell me about the sword," he said, his voice a little rough.

Eleanor sat back down. "One-track mind..." she grumbled.

"I am sick of sitting around doing nothing." There was such anger in his tone, such frustration, that again Eleanor got the impression there was more going on than he was telling her, only this time she was not going to let it drop. So she just looked at him, his face almost glowing in the last rays of the sinking sun, and waited.

"What?" he asked.

Eleanor gave him as hard a look as she could manage. "Sitting around doing nothing is not your only problem right now…"

Conlan raised an eyebrow. "When did you become so perceptive?"

Eleanor sighed. "I can actually read you pretty well, it is just that normally I do not bother asking you what is winding you up because I am usually too afraid it is me. However, recent events have convinced me that while I can see and in some cases feel your emotions, I often have no idea what is causing them. So I have decided to ask, instead of jumping to incorrect conclusions."

Conlan's body tensed again. "And if I do not want to tell you?" The hard edge had crept back into his voice. Eleanor gave him a serene smile.

"You do not have to tell me anything that you do not wish to; however, if you do not tell me, I will make my own assumptions and you will have to learn to live with the…" she paused. "What's the Dwarfish word for 'rants'?" she asked in English.

Conlan smirked. "No word exists. Mydren women don't 'rant', and if they did, the men in their lives wouldn't respond too kindly to it."

"Oh. Nevertheless, I would like to know what your problem is. Maybe I can help." Eleanor gave him a concerned look to complement the questioning growl she added to the Dwarfish.

Dropping his head, he reverted back to Dwarfish so he could layer his response with frustration. "I do not like being weak. Being surrounded by four of the most powerful people in Mydren is making me feel redundant. I do not feel involved and I will not until we get the connection working. I am so close and yet still useless. I arrived in time to watch you destroy Duncan's friends, I did not even get the chance to help you with that fight. I was…"

"… disappointed," she finished for him. Surprised, Conlan nodded in answer. "Conlan, I thought you were disappointed with me, for killing," she said softly.

Conlan chuckled. "Eleanor, if someone attacks you, please feel free to do them damage; after all, that is the whole point of knowing how." Eleanor felt her cheeks start to warm in embarrassment. *I've seriously misjudged him. Will's right – as far as Conlan is concerned, I'm deeply obtuse.* Not noticing her embarrassment, Conlan continued.

"I was proud of you, by the way; you made your enemy scream and run. I never got the chance to tell you."

Eleanor felt her love for him drop on her like a felled tree. It was the most wonderful, painful, joyful, hateful experience; it span around her head, making her feel dizzy and lightheaded. She wanted to kiss him, stroke his face, give some physical outlet to the surge of emotion within her but she resisted the temptation and sat firmly on her hands, addressing his comments instead in an attempt to distract herself.

"Conlan, you are not weak. We might be the four most powerful people in Mydren, but we are following *you*. We *will* get the connection working for you, I promise. And when we do, you will be the most powerful person this world has seen in over seven hundred years. Being a normal human being around us for a while before that happens will help you to keep some perspective, help you to remember that not everybody has power or strength and yet it does not make them any less important as people."

Conlan looked at her with his deep, penetrating gaze for so long that Eleanor began to feel uncomfortable.

"What?"

He shook his head. "Nothing, just some of the things you say surprise me."

He turned his head to stare back at the water, the sun setting behind the tree line. He appeared to be thinking, and not wanting to intrude, Eleanor sat with him in companionable silence. When he spoke again she jumped.

"I broke my promise." The growling undertone he gave the Dwarfish represented a grovelling apology.

"Yes, you did," she agreed. "I understand, Conlan; I know you were trying to protect me from Jarrick."

More silence.

"I do not deserve you."

His comment was a mere breath and so quiet that Eleanor was not sure if she had heard it or not, but her shattered heart responded to it regardless and she felt her love for him swirl around her insides again. Stubbornly refusing to admit that he did not love her back, she let the feelings fill her with warmth and smiled at him, knowing all her emotions were showing in her face and not caring. He knew. For once she was not going to hide it. In the sun's dying light he gazed at her, a small frown set between his eyes. He moved slowly and took her face in his hands, his touch sending electric sparks shooting through her body and making her feel delirious. He leant forward and kissed her forehead, and her mind dissolved into blissful rapture.

Releasing her, he returned his gaze to the sunset. Still totally stunned and operating on autopilot, Eleanor turned back to look in the same direction in the knowledge that there could have been juggling bears in front of her and she would not notice. She was so caught up in her spinning thoughts that it took her a while to realise that not only had Conlan failed to flinch, object or tense when she had leant against him, but he had actually put his arm around her and pulled her closer towards him. Her mind exploded in ecstasy again.

The velvet dark-blue of twilight, the first stars beginning to appear, the sound of the water as it travelled past, his breathing – slow and relaxed – the feel of his strong arm around her shoulders, the side of her body pressed against his. *A perfect piece of time.* The joy of it chipped away at some of the guilt and horror of the last few weeks, and every one of his breaths was a precious gift that helped to distort one of the faces of the dead in her mind. Gradually she began to let go of some of the guilt. She had made a mistake, and one she was sorry for – she could not ask the dead for forgiveness, but Conlan forgave her, and maybe that would be enough.

They sat in comfortable silence. It was getting late, but Eleanor knew she could sit there for all eternity, if he wanted to. She felt an energy string brush against her.

Are you OK? He didn't hurt you, did he?

No, Freddie, I'm fine. We had a chat, nothing explosive.

We saved dinner for you.

Eleanor could feel his relief, his concern.

We'll head back now, she said, pulling her energy free. Conlan drew his arm back and turned to look at her. Eleanor shivered, cold and uncomfortable. *Please don't let me go.* For one brief moment Conlan had held her and she had felt complete, less... broken.

"Who was that?" Conlan asked.

Grateful that her expression could not be seen well in the twilight, she did her best to lie diplomatically.

"Freddie, he is worried about us being out in the dark and wants us to come back."

"Liar," Conlan muttered. "Freddie was worried I had murdered you and was digging your grave at this very moment."

"Don't be an arse, Conlan!" Eleanor snapped, switching back to English, as she was unable to add the required insult in Dwarfish. "Freddie isn't stupid," she continued. "He knows you'd have had me dig my own grave before you murdered me."

Conlan was silent for a moment and then he burst out laughing. "I've missed you."

Eleanor gave him a sly smile. "Come on, let's go back. I'll tell you about the sword over dinner."

Will and Amelia were having an animated discussion about the uses for their Talismans when Eleanor and Conlan walked back into camp. Will's amused argument was that his was better than Amelia's, because at least he could use his to drink from. Freddie was agreeing with Will and Amelia was stubbornly insisting it was a stupid argument. Eleanor joined in with the mild teasing and then told them about the information she had gleaned from the book, reciting the short poem back to them several times and listening to them dissect it as she and Conlan ate their dinner. By the time she had finished eating they had only got as far as deciding that 'south freedom's hands' referred to the nomads who lived in the southern savannah. Conlan had explained that hundreds of years ago these proud nomads, the People of the Horse, had ruled the southern savannah, but he had no idea if they even existed any more. The southern savannah had become a no man's land. He had shown them the map in the back of Gregor's book, drawing a line across the bottom quarter of the continent, from the desert below Drent in the east all the way across, through to the volcanic Fire Mountains that made up the bottom of Mydren's central backbone to the coast in the west. Everything below the line was dangerous territory. At first, those fleeing the fighting in Mydren had gone there, and then those hiding from the Lords had found sanctuary. Eventually, wanted criminals had gone there, knowing that justice would not follow them.

"How long will it take us to get there?" Amelia asked. She still had Gregor's book on her lap and was tracing the route with a finger.

"A month," Conlan said, a frown on his face as he glanced at the shelter. Conlan wanted to leave immediately – Eleanor could feel it – but what were they going to do about Duncan? Will saw the look and interjected.

"Saving his life has consequences, Conlan – we can't just abandon him. Duncan's not well enough to look after himself and we can't travel with him, so we're going to have to wait."

"How long?" Conlan asked.

Will shrugged. "A month, maybe less."

Conlan's frown deepened. "That's too long; we will reach the southern savannah in the middle of the rainy season and we'll have to deal with storms and floods. We'd be taking a big risk."

"I don't think we have a choice," Will said, glancing at Duncan. There was a heavy silence, broken by Freddie.

"So, we know where we're going, but what about the rest of it? The poem makes it sound like we are going to have to give them something to get into the nomads' land, a 'gift beyond measure' – what does that mean?" Flashes of her dream pulsed through Eleanor's head and she answered Freddie's question before she realised what she was saying.

"When you give your heart to someone, you give them a gift beyond measure."

There was an uncomfortable silence while Will, Amelia and Freddie looked at Conlan, but his attention was solely on Eleanor, watching the painful emotions that she knew were marching across her face. She winced as she felt rips forming in her haphazardly stuck-together heart.

"So we have to give them a heart. Does that mean literally?" Amelia asked with a shudder. Glad that somebody had the common sense to talk over the atmosphere she could cut with a knife, Eleanor shook her head.

"I don't think its literal, Amelia. The people who wrote the book wouldn't want us to have to die to get the Talismans – kind of defeats the purpose."

"OK, so we have no idea what that means, but how about the last bit, 'think to the future, a deal to be made'?" Freddie asked, purposely missing the third line of the poem. They were all surprised when Conlan answered.

"I think this is about making them our allies. If the People of the Horse still exist, I think we're meant to get them to fight with us," he said.

"I agree, whoever wrote the book wanted to help us. I kind of messed up the green fish guys," Eleanor said.

"Kluthta," Will interrupted. Eleanor looked at him blankly.

Will smiled. "The green fish guys. They call themselves the Kluthta."

"Oh, OK," Eleanor continued. "I messed up with the Kluthta, so we should make every effort to get the People of the Horse onside."

"Will, you never did tell us the full story with the Kluthta," Freddie said, looking at Will expectantly.

Will shrugged. "Not that much to tell, really. The one who copied my memories was a priestess. They're a xenophobic race, so even if we hadn't fought them, we'd still have found it very difficult to make them our allies. Plus they are primarily water creatures, so land battles would have been out for them and the Lords of Mydren don't have a navy. They communicate telepathically and have very strong mental powers, many magnitudes stronger than mine, but they were unable to match with your brain waves. Perhaps in the future we could make contact again – trading with them could be beneficial."

"Not that helpful then," Freddie said, shrugging. Eleanor noticed the strange look on Amelia's face and wondered whether she thought Will was hiding something. *Should I ask him?* Amelia remained silent; if she did not feel the urge to push, it might be better to leave it for the moment. Eleanor made a mental note to ask Will about it the next time they were alone.

Thoughtful silence descended.

"It's late, I'm tired," Eleanor said eventually. Getting up she stretched and wandered over to the shelter where Duncan was already snoring. Wrapping her blanket around her she curled into a ball and for the first time in a very long time was immersed in deep, restful sleep.

Time seemed to slow to the point where Eleanor was convinced it was actually moving backwards. They filled their time as best they could. Freddie cleaned and sharpened every weapon he could get his hands on, and he even restored Duncan's blade to its former glory. Conlan became absorbed in the book Eleanor had bought him. Will and Amelia just seemed to be absorbed in each other. Now Duncan could be left on his own they would disappear for entire days, coming back rather wet and blissfully happy.

As the time inched past, Eleanor caught herself flashing glances at Duncan, wishing he would hurry up and get better, as she wanted to be off. She knew the others were unconsciously doing the same thing, although Conlan was quite consciously glaring at the man. It did not take long for Duncan to notice.

"Why is everybody suddenly giving me funny looks?" he asked when Eleanor brought him breakfast. The rain had eased off a little, and Will and Amelia had disappeared early, saying they would be back late, so Eleanor was providing meal services. She smiled apologetically but gave him the truth.

"We need to leave here as soon as possible, and we cannot do that until you are well."

"I am fine, I can cope on my own," he said, struggling to sit and wincing at the pain the movement caused. He looked sheepishly at Eleanor's raised eyebrow. "Well, almost..." he admitted. He looked at Eleanor for a moment and then took her hand. "You have done more than enough for me, far more than I deserve in fact, so if you need to go, you should go."

"The effort Will has expended keeping you alive would be wasted if we left you now, so we are going to wait," Eleanor said, smiling. Duncan smiled gratefully back and nodded his head slightly. Eleanor left him to eat in peace. Seeing the menacing glare Conlan was giving Duncan from where he was sat by the fire, she went and sat down next to him. He did not take his eyes off the injured man, who thankfully was eating his breakfast obliviously.

"He's said he's sorry. Actually, he's said it quite a few times now and I've forgiven him."

"I should have just finished him... I wanted to, I made a mistake," Conlan muttered, not looking at her. Eleanor cringed; she knew this callous disregard for life was not really Conlan. *Why is he behaving this way – is he that desperate to leave?*

"Conlan, saving someone's life is never a mistake. Duncan could be a good man, if he tried, and maybe he will after this. It's far better we change him than kill him," Eleanor said.

"You are far too forgiving."

Eleanor shrugged. "You, of all people, should be grateful for that."

Conlan glanced at her, with another mystery expression. "What if we haven't changed him?" he countered, his dark gaze returning to Duncan.

"And who are we to judge?" Eleanor asked, worried about where the conversation was leading. "I executed Jarrick. I judged him and found him unfit to continue breathing, so I took his life. I had no right to make that decision, nobody does – even kings shouldn't have the sole power of life and death over their subjects."

"The man who wrote the book you gave me is of the same opinion," Conlan said thoughtfully.

"Forgive him, Conlan, give Duncan another chance. He made a choice on the side of right, so let him know that it means something to someone else. Maybe then other people's lives will mean more to him," Eleanor said quietly.

She had not really expected her words to make an impact, as Conlan had been glaring at the man for weeks now, so she was shocked when he nodded, stood up and walked over to the shelter and sat down next to Duncan. Anxiety clawing at her insides, but not being able to hear what he was saying, Eleanor watched intently. At first Duncan looked terrified, pulling himself painfully away from Conlan until his back was pressed against the shelter wall, but as Conlan spoke quietly to him, he relaxed slightly. His face serious, Duncan responded. Eleanor wondered what Conlan was saying to the poor man. The conversation moved back and forth. Eleanor could not see Conlan's face but his body was relaxed, and slowly Duncan relaxed too, he even smiled occasionally. Transfixed by the sight before her, Eleanor did not notice Freddie sat next to her until he spoke.

"Is Duncan going to need rescuing?"

Glancing at him, Eleanor shook her head. "No, strangely, I think it's OK." She smiled, enjoying the burst of happiness Conlan's actions had unexpectedly exploded within her.

Much to Conlan's relief, Will finally agreed that Duncan, who could now stand and walk about if he was slow and careful, was fit enough to be left to fend for himself. Will had advised him to stay in the shelter for a while longer, until he felt rested enough to venture further afield. They had left him with food, water, blankets and a mountainous pile of firewood. As they had said their goodbyes, Freddie had returned Duncan's sword to him with some reluctance, as it was a beautiful weapon now that it had been polished and sharpened. Duncan had stared at it for a long time, gently pulling the blade from its lacquered wooden scabbard to admire it. Then with a snap he pushed the blade back and handed it to Will.

"This sword used to belong to my grandfather," he said. "He was an honourable man. I was never worthy of it and it became tarnished and damaged in my possession. The tarnish and damage are gone and you have done the same for my soul. I no longer need a sword, but you do, so have this with my grateful thanks." Will smiled at the man and took the sword from him. Duncan nodded and then slowly approached Eleanor where she stood next to Horse. "I have something for you, too," he said quietly. Confused, Eleanor stared. Duncan looked at her, his face solemn. "I know you practice magic, Eleanor. Your secret is safe with me, I promise. I know you think you caused the earthquake in Nethrus. You have accepted my apologies, but you have never asked for what I know you want; you have never asked for forgiveness, so I offer it to you now. The people of Nethrus? If you had anything to do with that, I am sure it was an accident. I experienced that earthquake and watched friends die, but I forgive you – on behalf of all the dead and wounded of Nethrus, I forgive you. If my forgiveness gives you one moment of peace, one moment of happiness, then I give your friends the gift of your smile." It was such a profoundly sweet and innocent notion that Eleanor was stunned. She knew that Duncan could not really absolve her of her crimes against the people of Nethrus, but hearing someone say she was forgiven was a deeply cathartic experience. Layers of grief, pain, self-loathing and guilt, already loosened by Conlan's forgiveness, fell away and she had a feeling of being so light she could fly. She knew that tears were running down her face, but she was also smiling, her heart filling with gratitude for this man. Duncan watched her with a wide, honest, pleased-with-himself grin on his face.

"Thank you, Duncan," Eleanor said between sobs and still smiling at him, her heart healing a little with every tear. Happiness flowing within, Eleanor unthinkingly pushed energy strings deep into the earth, wanting to share her joy. Her energy surged through the soil, denied so long this simple pleasure. The earth enveloped her, supported her and pulled her deeper. She eased her energy and delight into the world around her and let earth's energy flood through her soul.

It was Amelia's short intake of breath that brought Eleanor back to reality.

"Wow," Freddie breathed.

Pulling her energy back, wiping her tears Eleanor gasped as she looking around her. The clearing was alive with plant life; a thick, bright-green carpet of grass had grown up on what they had trampled down to mud during their stay. A profusion of multi-coloured flowers were visible in the grass – vibrant, velvety petals delicate in the cold wind and totally out of place in the grey autumn. The trees that enclosed the clearing had grown fresh leaves, and buds on their branches had begun to blossom, as if it was suddenly spring again. It was beautiful and it was impossible.

"Oops," Eleanor whispered, looking at Duncan's astonished face. He was so surprised that he totally ignored Conlan when he came to stand next to him.

"You are a goddess, I attacked a goddess," Duncan said, sounding utterly horrified.

"No, she is not a goddess, but it is a common misconception," Conlan told him, sounding amused. Noticing Conlan, Duncan glanced at him and then immediately turned back to stare open-mouthed at Eleanor.

"Then what is she? She did this... How did she do this? When you said she caused the earthquake in Nethrus, I did not think you meant literally... such power in such a tiny, delicate... What *is* she?" Duncan looked totally bewildered, frightened even. Putting his arm round Duncan's shoulder, Conlan led the man away, talking to him in quiet tones that Eleanor could not hear; every so often, Duncan would turn to look at her, eyes wide.

"I guess Duncan helped," Will said.

Eleanor nodded and smiled; it felt as if it was the first time she had done so in months.

Will smiled. "Then I'm glad he lived."

Eleanor held Will's gaze. "Thank you."

Will shrugged. "It was mostly luck."

"No, it was copious amounts of time, patience and skill. Duncan is grateful and so am I," Eleanor said, not satisfied until Will grudgingly accepted her praise. Freddie moved to her side, wrapping his arms around her.

"I'm glad you're feeling better," he whispered, using his low voice as an excuse to lean in to her, his lips grazing her cheek. It made her feel uncomfortable, but she resisted the urge to shove him back. She had no right to treat him that way, especially as she had encouraged this behaviour by relying on him. Since Conlan had rejected her there had been several times when he had been close, too close, looking at her in a way that felt more than friendly. *I used him, and that's going to have consequences.* Leaving Freddie as a problem she would have to deal with later, Eleanor forced her body to relax into his arms and smiled at him. His black eyes gazed lovingly back and Eleanor felt a small stone of dread drop to the bottom of her stomach.

Conlan had finished talking to Duncan and they were walking back towards them. Eleanor could see the amusement in his eyes. The stunned look on Duncan's face said everything; despite the dangers and despite his need for secrecy, Conlan had told the poor confused man the truth. Eleanor wondered why. Duncan approached Eleanor, and to her horror he dropped to his knees at her feet.

"I want to say I am sorry," Duncan said quietly, his head bowed. Eleanor looked down at him.

"You have said sorry several times, Duncan. I forgive you, so I do not need to hear it again, please get up."

"But when I apologised before, I did not know who you were," Duncan said miserably.

"Duncan, it should make no difference. I could be the lowest nobody or a goddess, but either way, what you had planned to do was wrong. You apologised and you seem to have changed your ways, so I accept that. I have no idea what Conlan just told you, but I do not need any different treatment. Now please get up before you make me angry." She stepped forward, intent on dragging the man back to his feet, if necessary. Duncan gazed at her in awe as she helped him up.

"I know that you have a dangerous mission ahead of you, so if you ever have need of my help in the future you need only ask."

Eleanor smiled at him. "You seem to know an awful lot," she said, giving Conlan a questioning glance. He shrugged and smiled. *So much for keeping secrets.* "Be careful what you offer, Duncan," Eleanor warned. "You may find that I hold you to it!"

Duncan laughed. "I very much hope so, my lady."

18

MERL

They finally managed to leave. Will grumbled that he had not finished his picture of Eleanor's flowers, and his drawings were never as good if he had to do them from memory. Duncan waved them off, and as they moved through the now blossoming trees, out of the wood, Eleanor's curiosity started poking her and she moved a little faster so that she was walking next to Conlan.

"What did you say to Duncan?"

Conlan turned and smiled at her. "I told him the truth," he replied. Eleanor frowned; this was not like him at all.

"OK, well I'm assuming you mean some of the truth, not all of it, so what exactly did you tell him?"

"I told him you were an Avatar, that the others were also Avatars and that you were here to help Mydren and that there were big changes coming," Conlan said, shrugging. Eleanor's frown deepened.

"That's some really dangerous information to be giving him; he could blab that to a Protector. That could have some unpleasant consequences for us and him."

"Blab?" Conlan asked.

"To 'blab', meaning to talk too much, to tell secrets you shouldn't," Eleanor said in flat monotone, well aware that Conlan was trying to distract her from her line of argument. He nodded and turned back to look where he was going, as if the conversation was over. Eleanor huffed. "You didn't answer my question."

Still looking ahead, Conlan smiled. "I did answer your question, but what I didn't address was your unspoken criticism of my actions." Annoyed by his calm, amused attitude she glared at him.

"Should I make it a spoken criticism?"

Conlan chuckled. "If you like."

Irritation making her shoulders tense, Eleanor nearly tripped over because she was staring at Conlan and not looking where she was going. He caught her by the elbow as she stumbled and pulled her back to her feet.

"Thank you," she muttered, embarrassed.

"You should look where you're going," Conlan commented. Irritation jumped into anger, and with a hand on his arm, Eleanor dragged Conlan to a stop.

"You're in such a good mood right now, it's scary!" she snapped. "Why did you tell Duncan about us? Are you trying to get him killed?" The humour vanished from Conlan's eyes. He stared at her, as if trying to work out what he should say. The fact that he had to think about his response did not fill Eleanor with confidence that she was going to like the answer. When he eventually replied, his voice was even.

"Against my better judgement I actually quite liked Duncan, and I wanted him to know the truth. I wanted him to tell people about us. The Lords of Mydren know we exist, and because of the earthquake their Enforcers will have told them we're a threat; we're getting closer and closer to having to fight them in open battle. If we have to do that before we've figured out how the connection works, I would prefer it if we had a sizeable army on our side! If Duncan tells people about us, tells people we're not to be feared, then maybe some of the populous will fight with us."

"That's a risky position to put the man in," Will said, worry hardening his tone. Eleanor turned; they were all staring at Conlan.

"Yeah! We should have had a discussion about this before you told him – this is something we should have voted on," Freddie said, giving Conlan an irritated look. Conlan looked back at them, unconcerned.

"I hadn't intended to tell him anything. I wanted to, but you're right, it's a risk. However, Eleanor's little... what's that word you used for gardens, Will?"

"Horticulture?" Will guessed.

Conlan nodded. "Eleanor's little horticultural explosion made it necessary for me to say something, so I improvised." He saw the look on Eleanor's face and his expression softened. "I'm not blaming you, Eleanor," he said quietly. "Sooner or later the people of Mydren were going to have to know who we are, so this just pushed up the timescale slightly. I warned Duncan about the dangers he was facing, but he wants to help; besides, I think the man is more than capable of taking care of himself."

Eleanor nodded. She was afraid – for Duncan and for them – and she unconsciously pulled back into Horse's warm, downy neck for support.

Horse gently wrapped her head over Eleanor's shoulder, laying it across her chest. Eleanor raised a hand absently scratching behind her ears. The comfort the animal gave her provided the courage to bring her gaze back to Conlan's. He had a small smile on his face, but such pain in his eyes that the bright green orbs seemed duller; Eleanor knew what he was thinking about, even before the wave of loss and sorrow washed over her.

"You miss Rand," she whispered.

"Very much," he agreed, his voice gritty and strained. She extracted herself from Horse and took his hand, giving it a squeeze.

"I miss him too," she said. "So does Horse – she had some very romantic intensions where Rand was concerned." She had been saving this piece of information for an occasion like this, and as Eleanor had hoped, surprise and then amusement took some of the pain out of Conlan's eyes and his smile widened, became more genuine. Horse was looking at him with her adoring brown eyes; he stepped forward, running a gentle hand down her nose, and then chuckling softly to himself, he turned and set off again through the trees and they followed after him.

For the first few days their journey was slow and arduous, as Conlan took them cross-country so that Nethrus did not come into sight at any point. Eleanor was relieved she would not have to witness the destruction again, but she was even more relieved when they made it back onto the track and started heading south. With Rand gone, they were not able to set the quick pace they were used to. Will's horse, now carrying him and Amelia, tired after only a few hours. Amelia's horse, not used to carrying Conlan's weight, would also slow at the slightest opportunity.

When they stopped yet again, Eleanor saw Horse turn her head to stare at her. Eleanor smiled, rubbing the animal's neck. Horse continued to stare at her. Surprised, Eleanor pushed an energy string into the animal's head and was nearly knocked off her back with the strength of the thoughts Horse sent her. Images of Eleanor and Amelia on Horse's back. Eleanor sent the animal feelings of concern, as she was just a small horse and she did not want to hurt her. The image she received back was as close to screaming 'hypocrite' as Horse could get. *I keep telling people I don't need protecting, so maybe Horse doesn't either.*

"Will?" Eleanor said, his blond head turning questioningly in her direction. "Horse thinks that she can carry Amelia as well as me, and she thinks she can do it at a far quicker pace than yours and Freddie's horses."

Will frowned. "Eleanor, Horse is a little small to be carrying two."

Eleanor nodded. "Yes, but she wants to help. Maybe we could give her the benefit of the doubt for a few hours?"

Will shrugged. "OK, but I want you to keep up regular checks, make sure she's handling the extra weight."

Amelia slid off the back of Will's horse, and Eleanor slipped her foot out of her stirrup so that Amelia could use it to mount. The tall woman pulled herself up behind Eleanor, wriggling to get herself comfortable on top of the bags and blankets strapped to the back of the saddle. Even sat on the raised piles of luggage, Amelia's feet nearly reached the ground. Worried, Eleanor pushed into Horse's head, wanting to know if she was OK. Horse sent her an image back of the overflowing cartful of produce her previous owner had made her pull, indicating that what she carried now was featherlight in comparison.

They looked ludicrous, but Horse had been right, she was able to carry Amelia and Eleanor at a far quicker pace and they began to make better time. Moving south, the weather began to get warmer. It was still grey and wet, but now it was humid during the day and cold at night. The landscape began to change, with rolling hills giving way to a flat, eerily quiet, mostly empty nothing that seemed to go on forever. The lush, green grass disappeared, replaced by tall, golden grasses that Horse did not enjoy eating. The soil became cracked, dry and bleached, and rain stood in huge puddles because the soil was not able to absorb it quickly enough. Vegetation was sparse, although the frequent precipitation made what little there was a bright, fresh green; flowers bloomed for a few hours and propagated, before they shrivelled in the damp heat. Prickly bushes that ripped and tore at anything that moved too close became common, ugly black tangles that broke up the endless landscape. The trees changed too, becoming shorter and more gnarled, twisted in the heat, their leaves stiff and leathery. Unlike the desert, Eleanor felt as if nothing here ever moved, as if it was stuck in time.

Food, or the lack thereof, was starting to be a worry again. They did see the occasional hare, its fur the same pale, sandy cream as the soil and rocks, but there did not seem to be enough of them. Eleanor had suggested they try one of the large chameleon-type lizards they came across on a regular basis and had been met with four slightly disgusted looks. Freddie commented that she had only suggested it because she knew she would not have to eat it. Slowly but surely, disgust had given way to resignation when they realised there was very little else to eat. As it turned out the lizards tasted quite good, they were easy to catch and had enough meat on one to feed four. Eleanor had stuck to eating the sweet, juicy pear-type fruits off the prickly bushes. They were difficult to harvest, leaving Eleanor covered in small scratches, but a couple were a meal in themselves, and supplemented with some of the nuts, beans and dried berries Will had packed for her and the flat, gritty bread cakes Amelia made from flour and water, it was enough. Horse liked the fruit too, and Eleanor discovered eating them had the side effect of giving both of them a natural repellent to the little biting gnats that swarmed above the warm, shallow standing water left by the frequent but brief thunderstorms. The track disappeared as they travelled further south, leaving them riding across hard, baked earth until it rained and the top layer of soil became slippery mud. They had not seen a soul in weeks, not that Eleanor was particularly unhappy about this, as from what she had been told and experienced, she was not sure she wanted to meet any of the criminal lowlifes that inhabited this surreal, flat place. Freddie had asked Conlan what his plan was and he had given him an amused smile – no plan, just keep walking until they found who they were looking for. On this occasion, knowing nothing about the 'People of the Horse', Freddie had shrugged his acceptance of the 'non-plan'.

"Eleanor, I think that bird is following us," Amelia said. She sounded concerned, her eyes fixed on a small dot circling high above them. Eleanor lifted her gaze to the sky, for once cloudless, and followed the bird's progress as it moved effortlessly through the air. The sky was an odd colour here, like the soft blue had a yellowy tinge to it, making it blend with the horizon – no end, no beginning, just a seamless circle of land and sky. It sometimes made Eleanor feel like she was stuck in the snow globe she had loved as a child, only it was rain that fell here, not snow.

"Eleanor!" Amelia's voice was sharp and impatient. "I said, do you see it?"

"Yes, it's just a bird, Amelia, it's not the first we've seen."

"Eleanor, it's a really big bird and it's following us. You don't think that's a little odd?" Amelia asked.

"My entire life is a little odd, Amelia, and so is yours. It's a bird. I don't care, but if you think it might be edible, Will is going to be interested." Amelia fell into wounded silence behind her.

Eleanor sighed. "Sorry, Amelia, that was mean."

"Yes, it was. Who rattled your cage anyway? You've been in a bad mood for a while," Amelia observed.

Eleanor looked ahead, seeing how far away Freddie was; too close, she decided, so she brushed an energy string against Amelia.

It's Freddie, isn't it? she asked the second Eleanor entered her head.

Yes.

What's he done?

He's been sweet, kind, thoughtful and loving, Eleanor replied miserably.

But he thinks it's going to go further and it's not, is it?

I don't know what he thinks, but sometimes he looks at me and I'm certain there is more to it than just friendship. What do I do?

Stop beating around the bush, Amelia advised. *Talk to him, tell him he's got no chance. Crush his hope once and for all. Eleanor, if I thought for one minute that Freddie was right for you I'd be saying go for it, but he's not. I can talk to Freddie, if you like, or get Will to do it, but it would be better if you do it yourself.*

No, I'll talk to him when we stop tonight… Thank you, I'm sorry I snapped at you. We'll keep an eye on that bird. If it's still there this afternoon we'll decide what to do about it, OK?

OK, Amelia agreed.

The bird was still there as the sun reached its apex and began its steady decline into evening. It was a hot day, the lack of rain making the heat dry for a change, but no less unpleasant. Eleanor was sweaty and getting a crick in her neck and eye strain from watching the bird do slow, lazy circles around them. The only variation to its behaviour was to drop its height. Amelia was right, it was a really big bird and it was following them.

"Is it a vulture? Does it think we're going to die?" Eleanor asked quietly.

"No, I don't think so. I'm not an authority on birds, but my mother was obsessed with them, so I picked up a few things. I think it's an eagle, or the Mydren version of an eagle," Amelia said.

"Really? What's it doing out here?" Eleanor asked, remembering the majestic mountain birds as they had soared over her head, looking for prey.

Amelia shook her head. "I have no idea. What are we going to do about it?"

"I think you need to talk to it," Eleanor answered.

"Pardon?"

"It's just a thought, but I can talk to the animals of the earth and Will could talk to the Kluthta, so maybe you can talk to birds, creatures of the air," Eleanor said, wondering if Amelia was going to laugh at her. There was silence. Eleanor glanced back to find grey eyes full of surprise staring back.

"Kind of makes sense," Amelia agreed. "But what about Freddie? I don't know any fire animals."

Eleanor giggled. "Me neither, unless they have phoenixes here, but then I've always thought fire was a bit like an animal anyway, because it eats, needs oxygen and multiplies."

"So how do I talk to a bird?" Amelia asked.

"I don't know... but I talk to Horse and other animals in pictures a lot of the time, and they talk back to me in the same way. Horse understands quite a few words, but she called me a hypocrite the other day and she had no word for that, just pictures," Eleanor said.

Amelia giggled. "Horse called you a hypocrite?"

Eleanor nodded. "Yes, I was being overprotective of her."

"Smart Horse."

"She is, very smart, but Rand was smarter; Rand I could have a conversation with," Eleanor said quietly, feeling her grief sting.

"He was a very special horse, Conlan's struggling without him," Amelia said. Eleanor's gaze drifted to Conlan's back, making sure he was out of earshot before she responded.

"I can feel his grief, can feel a lot of his emotions, and I think it's something to do with his shield getting thinner. Can't you feel it?" Eleanor asked. It was something that she had been wondering about for a while – why could she feel Conlan's emotions so acutely when nobody else seemed to notice?

"No, but I do feel Will's emotions sometimes, if they're strong, even if we're not talking in each other's heads, and I know he's felt mine. Maybe you feel Conlan's emotions because you love him, you're more open to it... I don't know, but if his shield is getting thinner that's a good thing, right?" Amelia asked.

Eleanor sighed. "A very good thing, except I don't know what caused it. Was it the hell Jarrick put him through? Or Rand dying? I don't want him to suffer again."

"I guess not, you'll just have to keep watching. I have huge amounts of faith in you, and I know you'll get there in the end," Amelia said.

Eleanor smiled. "Thanks... So are you going to talk to our feathered friend?"

Amelia giggled. "You're right. Our lives are odd!"

Eleanor focused on the bird as Amelia closed her eyes and took slow, deep breaths. At first nothing happened. Amelia's grip around her waist tightened, and she gasped and yelped loudly in Eleanor's ear, making her, and by extension Horse, jump.

"Oh no, Eleanor, I think I pushed too hard," Amelia moaned.

Watching the bird, Eleanor saw it falter, flap its wings weakly and then fold them entirely. The bird began to drop. Fast.

"Amelia, hold tight!" Eleanor yelled, thudding her heels into Horse's side and making her trot and then canter, forcing her to gallop, steering them to the left towards where the bird was plummeting.

"Amelia," Eleanor called breathlessly over her shoulder. "You need to create a shield and catch the bird... Can you do that?"

"Go faster," Amelia replied.

Eleanor entered Horse's head, urging the poor overloaded animal to greater speed. Doing her best to obey, Horse surged forward. Eleanor felt the wind rush through her hair and Horse's muscles as she powered along. This was something she was going to have to do again, when Horse was not carrying Amelia and luggage; it was exhilarating.

"Eleanor, stop!" Amelia ordered.

Eleanor pulled hard on Horse's reins, and the animal came to a skidding, sliding stop, front legs locked in front of her acting as breaks. The deceleration was so sharp that Eleanor flew forward, up and over Horse's head, but fortunately her feet came out of her stirrups as she did so. Still holding on to the reins, they pulled her over, feet flying over her head as she flipped and crashed to the ground. She landed on her back, the wind knocked out of her and bright spots dancing behind her eyes. Her vision slowly cleared and she found Horse's bemused upside down head loomed over her.

Eleanor had just taken her first lungful of oxygen when Will's face joined Horse.

"Are you OK? What was that about?" he asked, quirking an amused smile at her. Only having found the ability to breathe in the last second, Eleanor was totally incapable of speech. Will crouched at her side. "Do you want to sit up?" he asked. Eleanor shook her head – what she wanted to do was breathe. Horse dropped her head, rubbing a wet, bristly nose into her face. The poor animal was breathing hard after her mad dash, her light caramel-coloured hair dark with sweat. *Had Amelia caught the bird?*

"Is she OK? She hit the ground at some speed."

Amelia. Where was she? Eleanor could hear her but could not see her.

"I think she's winded, what's that?" Will said, looking over Eleanor's head at something behind her.

"It's a type of eagle, it's been following us," Amelia said.

"Is it dead?" Will asked.

"No, I entered its mind and stunned it. I caught it with a shield," Amelia said.

"Really? You caught it? That's brilliant," Will said softly, his voice full of pride. Eleanor heard the sound of hooves approaching.

"Will," she gasped. "Help me up." Firm hands helped her to sit; the world swam in and out of focus for a second, before settling back down. Amelia was stood at Horse's side, a huge bird in her arms. Its head lolled over her arm, eyes closed and its body still, which Eleanor decided was a good thing, because it had a set of the biggest talons she had ever seen on a bird. The claws were its most impressive feature, but it also had a large, sharp, curved beak and beautiful amber-brown feathers that looked ruffled and untidy after its headlong dive.

"What happened?" Conlan asked as he pulled to a stop next to Horse, Freddie stopping behind him.

"I knocked a bird out of the sky, and we chased after it so I could catch it. Horse stopped a little suddenly and Eleanor didn't. Will says she's winded," Amelia answered, looking down sympathetically at Eleanor.

"Why did you knock a bird out of the sky?" Freddie asked, walking over to take a closer look at the eagle.

"It was an accident, I was trying to talk to it," Amelia said.

"Let me guess, Eleanor's idea?" Freddie said, eyeing the bird's talons warily.

Amelia giggled. "Of course. The bird's been following us for most of the day, we wanted to know why, so Eleanor figured if she could talk to animals of the earth and Will could talk to the Kluthta, maybe I could talk to the bird. It just requires a more delicate touch than I gave it... Poor bird," Amelia said, jumping as it twitched in her arms. Freddie stepped quickly back as Amelia's eyes glazed over slightly and she tried again to talk to the slowly recovering creature.

"Why would a bird be following us?" Freddie asked, staring in apprehension as the talons flexed slowly.

"What's a bird that belongs in the mountains doing flying around here? Something doesn't feel right," Will said quietly as he stood, using a hand to shade his eyes, looking around him.

"Oh dear, we have a problem," Amelia said. "The bird is a pet, there are two men following us and... Ooww!" That was as far as she got. She staggered slightly, her eyes wide with fear, pain and shock. Will rushed forward and caught her as she swayed, holding her up, which was not an easy task with the bird in her arms. As Will struggled to keep her upright, his hands found something and he looked over her shoulder and down her back.

"Conlan, she's been hit with something, we're being attacked," Will hollered, horrified. He pulled whatever it was free, dropping it to the ground.

"Ooww!" Freddie gasped, raising a hand to his neck where a small, black dart was protruding. Pulling it out, he staggered sideways, toppling over into a clumsy heap, eyes rolling before they closed. Not knowing where the darts were coming from, Conlan's eyes flashed across their almost empty surroundings, his sword already drawn. Will gasped and staggered, a dart sticking out of his shoulder, and tried to ease Amelia gently to the ground, dropping her the last few inches. He pulled the dart from his flesh as he keeled over at Amelia's side and lay still. Eleanor watched in numb terror. *Are they dead?* She turned to look at Conlan as he came to crouch at her side.

"We need to find cover," he whispered, not looking at her, still trying to work out where their enemies were hiding. *Cover, where?* Eleanor shook her head, looking at where Freddie, Will and Amelia lay motionless.

"We can't leave them unprotected."

She was not going to admit they were dead until it was absolutely necessary. Conlan gasped and Eleanor's heart squeezed as she turned back to him. His eyes were wide, looking at the little dart sticking out of his chest. He winced as he pulled it free. Grabbing Eleanor's arm he dragged her away, heading unsteadily for the scant cover of a couple of prickly bushes twenty feet away. Too frightened now to resist, Eleanor followed. They had almost reached the bushes when Eleanor saw the second dart hit Conlan in the back of the neck. He gasped again, shuddering and collapsed to his knees, dragging Eleanor down with him. He pushed her into the dirt, covering her and using his body to shield her. With her face in the dirt and Conlan's weight pressing down on her, Eleanor could see very little. *Not good if I need to fight.*

"Don't move, Eleanor," Conlan whispered, his words slurred and halting. "Maybe they'll miss you." She felt his rapid, panting gasps begin to slow, until they resembled the gentle unhurried breath of sleep. Eleanor nearly wept when she realised that they were not actually going to stop.

For several slow minutes she did as he had asked. *Of course they're not dead.* If whoever had attacked them had wanted them dead they would just have used normal bows and arrows, not gone to all the effort of making drugged blow darts. So they wanted them alive and they had missed her completely, why? If she was conscious, she could fight. She struggled to get out from under Conlan's inert body; he was heavier than he looked. She eventually managed to pull herself free and went to take the sword from his hand, noticing the dart in his neck as she did so. Carefully, Eleanor pulled it out. It left a small puncture wound that bled, but not too badly. More worrying than the blood were the purple and red tendrils that radiated out under his skin from the hole the dart had left. They went around Conlan's neck, up into his hairline and down his back under his clothes. Whatever was on the dart was fast-acting and his body was desperately trying to fight it. She looked at the dart; it was maybe an inch long, made of a thin piece of fire-hardened wood, with a spike from a prickly bush as its tip. Tiny bits of feather had been added at the opposite end to the tip, which would give the dart some stability in flight. It would not have much of a range, especially as it required human breath to propel it; their attackers must be close.

Taking Conlan's sword, remaining in a crouch next to him, she scanned the few places of available cover and waited. They would come to her now, she was sure of it. She did not have to wait long, as she saw two figures stand up from behind a clump of prickly bushes about fifty feet to her right. Despite their height they appeared young; their movements were still the slightly uncoordinated confusion of youth, as if their bodies were a size too big for them. They wore plain, dusty clothes, baggy trousers and shirts with leather jerkins over the top, and the taller man carried a leather bag strapped across his chest. Their skin was dark, like Freddie's, but where Freddie had a beautiful golden hue to his complexion, theirs was almost black, like polished ebony. Eleanor wondered if she should blast them to bits, shuddering at the thought. *If they are same people who set the trap at the waterfall, we need to know who they are; besides, what if they have poisoned the others?* These men might be the only ones who could help them.

"You missed one, Yatt," the shorter of the two men commented as they moved closer, staring at Eleanor with curiosity. His Dwarfish sounded odd. Eleanor recognised the words, but the growl and snarl were all wrong. *An accent?*

"She is just a child. You know what *oppimun* does to an adult, what do you think it is going to do to her?" Yatt asked, looking at his accomplice.

"He said they all had to be unconscious before he got here, so dart her already," the short man said irritably. He seemed to be moving to check on Amelia, but as he crouched down, Eleanor realised he was reaching for the bird in Amelia's arms. Yatt turned to look at Eleanor, seemingly unconcerned that she was tensed, ready to fight and holding a lethal weapon in her hand. His thin, muscular body flexed slightly, and Eleanor could see lines of dots that decorated his face under his eyes and over his cheek bones.

"I am sorry, little girl," he whispered, raising a long, thin pipe to his lips. He was too far away for Eleanor to reach with her sword, and she knew if she moved there would be a dart in her before she got two feet. Should she throw her weapon? It went against all of Conlan's teaching, but then he had not exactly prepared her for this situation. She was going to have to wing it.

"Hey, Yatt! Osser is still alive!" The short man sounded overjoyed. Yatt dropped his pipe from his lips, but he did not take his eyes off Eleanor.

"Really? The speed he dropped? Why did the bird brain fall out of the sky in the first place?" he asked. His short friend was carefully lifting and examining the bird.

"I have no idea. I cannot see any damage on him. It was a great distraction though, they never saw us creeping up; we were able to get really close."

It was a short exchange, but it gave Eleanor a little time to think, her mind desperately trying to formulate a plan. This man, Yatt, had refrained from darting her because he was worried about the effect it would have on her. Maybe she could play to his compassion. Drawing her body in further and making herself look even smaller and weaker, she stared at him with wide, innocent, frightened eyes.

"Are you going to kill me?" she asked, making her voice a terrified, childlike squeak. The sword was shaking in her hand, which had not been planned, but Eleanor hoped it might help her case. Concern and sympathy filled Yatt's black eyes, followed quickly by guilt.

"I have not killed anything with these darts in a long time," he replied.

"Is it going to hurt?" Eleanor asked. If she knew the drug's effects, perhaps she could help the others to recover quicker, any and all information she could get at this point was a good idea. The guilty look on Yatt's face deepened.

"*Oppimun*'s effects vary depending on the victim's size and age, how many darts have pierced the flesh, where they hit and how long the darts have been in the skin. The results are unpleasant, but not fatal," he said.

"I am frightened," Eleanor whispered, staring beseechingly up at the man. Yatt hesitated, glancing down at his blowpipe.

"Hurry up and dart her, he will be here any minute and he is not someone we should mess with!" the short man snapped in Yatt's direction. The bird, Osser, was fully conscious and the short man was watching it preen its disorganised feathers.

"Shut up, Millice!" Yatt shot back, not looking at him. Yatt stared at Eleanor for a long moment and then put his hand in the inside pocket of his leather jerkin, taking something out. "This will help with the effects, I suggest taking half yourself and giving the other half to that man," he instructed, nodding at Conlan's still body. "He took two darts, and judging by the spread on his neck the second one was under his skin for a while. He will be very ill and I have no idea how the *oppimun* will affect you." He took a couple of careful steps forward, watching Eleanor warily, placed a small glass bottle on the ground and then stepped back. Eleanor shuffled forward, watching the blowpipe, and picked it up. The bottle was a little too big to fit in the palm of her hand, and inside was a dark green translucent liquid.

"Yatt, he is coming, I can see him, dart the girl!" Millice said, fear running through his voice. Eleanor wondered if she could keep Yatt talking long enough to catch a glimpse of their mystery accomplice.

"Put it somewhere safe, how about that man's jacket pocket?" Yatt suggested, nodding at Conlan again. Eleanor nodded and turned. Conlan was lying on the pocket nearest to her, so she leaned across his back to put the bottle in the pocket on the other side, realising her mistake as she pushed it deep inside. She felt the sharp stab of the dart hitting the back of her neck. Her responses already slowing, it took her an age to take her hand from Conlan's pocket. She pulled out the dart, staring at it in shock. A slow, steady burning was moving out from the impact and her mind was beginning to whirl. She felt, rather than saw, Yatt behind her. Her body felt weak, beyond her control and she slumped forward, dropping face down across Conlan's back. A gentle hand rested on her head, a comforting gesture.

"I am sorry, child," Yatt whispered. There was the sound of thundering hooves and the hand was gone. Her mind twisted and writhed, strange thoughts moving through it. The dragon appeared a few times, but now he was breathing fire and burning her neck. She struggled for consciousness and fought the drug. She needed to know who the man was; they needed to know more about this new enemy. Her breath panting in her lungs, she tried to lift her head, to look up at the man as she heard him dismount, but it was too hard.

"I take it there were no problems?" came a new deeper voice, the refined Dwarfish sounding odd after listening to Yatt and Millice.

"No, all unconscious as requested," Yatt replied. Through barely open eyes, Eleanor saw a pair of boots step into her vision at Conlan's side.

"Hello, Conlan, Daratus sends his regards."

That name, Daratus, it meant something; she should remember that, it was important. Lots of things were important. One of the boots pulled back, delivering a sharp, viscous kick to Conlan's ribs. His body jerked, causing the sword to drop from Eleanor's numb fingers, but there was no indication that the injury had been felt. *He's going to feel it when he wakes up.* Angry that she could not make her body move to protect him, darkness washed over her and the burning chased her down into fiery depths.

She was being burnt alive, her flesh melting and dripping from her bones, blood boiling. Flames were licking every inch of her skin, crisping it and pulling it tight so it spilt; thick fluids leaked out, heating, scalding and causing more pain. She screamed her torment and flailed her limbs, desperate to put the fire out. Murmuring voices filled her ears. *Why don't they help?* She screamed again, tried to speak, tried to beg for help. "Please..." was all she could manage. The murmuring became louder, more coherent.

"We need to suck the poison out." It was Dwarfish, refined Dwarfish – a stranger's voice.

"I have to put the poison in my mouth?" Will's voice echoed, strained and fearful.

"She is too small for this... it could kill her. I will do the same for Conlan, he has taken too much. I will take what I can from him." It was the stranger's voice again, but it was not a stranger, there was something familiar about it. Eleanor felt her body lifted. She was face down, an arm supporting her across the chest and her head dropping forward. Firm hands yanked on her jacket, ripping at her shirt and brushing her hair out of the way, the chill breeze soothing her burning flesh. There was something soft and firm on the back of her neck, where the deepest agony was located – suction, a strange sensation. The pain pushed her too far and her consciousness slipped for a moment. When reality returned, the suction had disappeared and there were spitting noises, then she felt the touch on her neck again. The fire continued to burn through her. She whimpered. Surely she should be dead by now? There could be nothing left for the fire to burn. The odd sensation on her neck disappeared again.

"I do not think this is working, all I can taste is her blood," Will said.

"You are right," the voice agreed. "It has had too long in their bodies."

Something flashed through Eleanor's mind – a bottle with green liquid in it. Something that was important... *Too important.* She heard an agonised groan and realised it had not come from her, it had come from somewhere else. A weak, sobbing cry filled her head, stabbing down to her heart, and she knew. Conlan was in pain. She had to help him. The bottle flashed in her head again. The liquid was green, like Conlan's jacket, in the pocket, a bottle to help him. She forced herself to focus and tried to move, which was impossible with any degree of control. She tried to open her eyes, but all she saw was blurry darkness. She tried to speak.

"Will." No response. She concentrated, drawing air into her lungs. "WILL!" The arms holding her jumped and tightened around her.

"I'm here, Eleanor, I'm trying to help but I don't know what to do."

Eleanor heard his anguish and felt his body tense as Conlan cried out again.

"In Conlan's jacket... pocket... bottle... cure..." she gasped. Will froze for a second, then he laid Eleanor gently on the ground. Her body writhing in the fire that burned it, she tried to concentrate, tried to stay conscious; her eyes open now, still seeing nothing.

"What are you doing?" the stranger asked curiously.

"Getting something," Will said. Eleanor felt hands on her body again, pulling her up, Will cradling her like a baby. "This green stuff?" he asked. She forced her head to nod.

"Give it... to him..." she rasped, her voice disappearing into a gasping cry as another pillar of fire engulfed her tormented body.

"I'll save him some, I promise. Open your mouth," Will ordered. Eleanor stubbornly shook her head. Conlan was far bigger than she was, he would need more.

"Eleanor, please, Conlan's not the only one suffering. If this is the antidote, you need it too," Will said, trying to force her mouth open with one hand while holding her up and holding the bottle. Eleanor shook her head again, sucking her lips into her mouth, keeping them tightly closed.

Will muttered under his breath but Eleanor felt her body placed back on the ground. She heard a gagging cough and hoped that some of the liquid had gone down Conlan's throat.

"What is that?" the stranger asked.

"A cure," came Will's distracted reply.

"Where did that come from?" The stranger sounded surprised.

"I have no idea," Will said. Eleanor felt her body lifted from the ground and Will brushing away the damp hair that was clinging to her face. "OK, he's had some, the rest is yours," he said, his irritation unable to hide his affection. Eleanor smiled, closed her eyes and opened her mouth. A splashed of liquid ran down her throat and she understood why Conlan had gagged – it tasted foul, like drinking stagnant water. She forced herself to swallow it before she started coughing. As the bitter, acidic liquid hit her stomach she felt it spasm, but slowly the fire dropped from a volcanic roar to a slow, steady heat, which after the previous pain was almost bearable. Relieved, she let the cool darkness claim her again.

It was the violent urge to throw up that dragged Eleanor up through darkness and into the bright daylight. Too bright, she closed her eyes tight again and moaned as the sunshine stabbed at her. It was hot; the heat beating down, but she felt cold.

"Eleanor? Are you OK?"

Freddie. She carefully tried to open her eyes again. Everything was still blurry. A camp had been made in the sparse shade of one of the gnarled trees that dotted the landscape. Their blankets had been rigged up to offer shelter from the sun. Freddie's face gazed down full of loving concern, and her already sickened stomach did another flip. *I need to talk to him...*Turning her head, she could see Will and Amelia sat a few feet away, looking at her.

Their faces were rather more blurry and greyer than Freddie's. Conlan lay asleep at Amelia's side, while a strange man sat on his other side. Something akin to panic squeezed Eleanor's already delicate stomach, but she had no clue why, as there did not seem to be any obvious threats. *What happened? Who's that? Amelia caught a bird... I have to remember something, it's important... lots of things are important. We got hit by darts... then what? There was a dragon, fire, green? A word... Douglas? There was a bird... and... and...* Eleanor stopped. Her mind had failed her. She was meant to remember something, something important, but it was gone, totally messed up. There was a memory, but it was so unclear it was useless, like corrupted data on a computer. All she was left with was the vague impression that something was wrong.

"Is she awake?" Will asked.

"Yes, I think so," Freddie confirmed. Eleanor struggled and he helped her to sit. Her stomach lurched and she felt another strong desire to vomit. Not wanting to throw up all over Freddie, Eleanor pushed herself onto all fours and then stood. Freddie tried to stop her.

"Eleanor, what are you doing?" he asked alarmed, standing with her and supporting her swaying body. She pulled his hands off her, took a dozen tottering steps out of their shelter, fell back onto all fours and threw up the world. Or at least that was what it felt like. The spasms squeezing her stomach made her retch until there was nothing left to throw up, and then dry heaves ripped at her insides. She felt a comforting hand rubbing her back and noticed with vague interest, through watering eyes, that her vomit was green. Eventually the spasms subsided. Even resting on all fours she was swaying, bright flashes sparked through her vision and a headache began cranking itself up to tear her brain apart. A piece of wet cloth was handed to her. Grateful, Eleanor wiped her face, knowing gloop was dribbling off her chin. When she had cleaned her face, she sat up gingerly and wiped the splashes of green vomit off her hands. The smell was so bad that she had to fight the reflex to throw up again. She dropped the cloth, and a mug of water was put in front of her.

"Take small sips," Will advised, his hand still gently rubbing her back. She turned to look at him and gasped. He did not look any better than she felt. There were deep purple bags under his glazed eyes and his skin was mostly grey but with a distinctly yellow tinge to it.

"You look like crap," Eleanor whispered in a rough sore voice.

Will smiled. "You too."

After several mugs of water, Eleanor felt able to stand again and Will helped her back to the others. All she wanted was to sleep. Freddie watched her return.

"Are you alright?"

Glancing at him, Eleanor shook her head. She felt unconnected, adrift, her mind had failed her and her body was telling her there was danger where none existed. On autopilot she moved to where Conlan slept between Amelia and the unknown man. The stranger looked up at her. He was an older man, his hair mostly grey, with a little of the original brown still present. His body looked strong, fit and muscled, toned sinews standing out on his bare forearms. Speckled green-brown eyes regarded her with interest from under bushy eyebrows, and a friendly smile emanated from his suntanned, weather-beaten face.

"Hello, Eleanor, I am Merl."

Eleanor smiled back. He reminded her of a grandfather she had barely known. *I can remember a man who died when I was seven, in another life, but I can't remember what happened a few hours ago! What's wrong with me?*

"Hello," she replied. "What are you doing here?"

"Merl came to our rescue," Will said from behind her. "He stopped the men who attacked us. Gregor sent him."

Eleanor's eye's widened in surprise. "Gregor, Conlan's grandfather?"

Merl nodded, his friendly smile reassuring. "I have worked for Gregor Baydon for many years and I have known Conlan since he was a small child." He reached a large, gnarled hand to ruffle Conlan's hair affectionately before returning his sharp, bright eyes to Eleanor. "Gregor has been worried about Conlan since he heard about the earthquake in Nethrus. I have been tracking you for a while. It looks like I found you just in time."

"Just in time?" Eleanor echoed.

"Do you want to sit next to Conlan?" Merl asked, a concerned frown on his face as Eleanor swayed in front of him. She nodded, smiling again as he shuffled aside, making room. Eleanor dropped down next to Conlan. His skin had the same grey pallor as Will and Amelia's, but instead of the yellow tinge, his had a soft green look to it. *Green again, that's important.* He was sleeping peacefully. Lifting his left arm, Eleanor curled up underneath it at his side. If she could hear his heartbeat, could hear him breathe, she would know if he needed her, and she needed the solid comfort of knowing he was there. She reached an arm protectively across Conlan's chest, rested her head against him and closed her eyes. His presence insulated her from the confusion and fear. She listened to his heart beat in time with hers, calming her – the steady, regular tempo lulling her to sleep.

She woke with a start, eyes snapping open to golden, early evening light. Her thoughts were still full of dragons breathing fire, green swirls spinning through her mind and a danger called Douglas. Conlan's breathing had changed, and his heart rate was quicker. She lifted her head and turned to look at his face. He smiled at her, eyes glassy.

"You look awful," he commented, the effort making him cough weakly.

Eleanor smiled back. "You look green," she replied.

"I think that's because I really need to throw up," he moaned. Eleanor understood that feeling and pulled herself up off him, offering him help to sit. As he moved he winced, a hand moving to his right side and rubbing his ribs. "Oooww," he breathed.

"What?" she asked, concerned. Conlan looked at her, confused, his fingers gingerly moving up and down his side.

"I have a bruise, where did I get that?"

Eleanor felt a flash of guilt, a vague feeling that she had not been able to protect Conlan, she shrugged. "I don't remember, my memory is like Swiss cheese at the moment."

Conlan rubbed his side. "'Swiss' cheese?"

"Cheese that's full of holes, I think the stuff in that dart affected my brain," Eleanor explained, trying to hide just how frightened she was by this concept, as her mind was all she had. Conlan groaned and moved his hand from his side to his stomach.

"Maybe talking about cheese wasn't the best idea. I really need to throw up."

With effort Eleanor helped Conlan up and away from the camp towards a group of prickly bushes, where he dropped to his knees and threw up green gloop with stunning effect. Trying not to look, Eleanor rubbed a comforting hand up and down his back. Will appeared at his other side, helping Eleanor to support him and then giving Conlan a damp cloth to clean himself with and water once he had finished. She watched the care with which Will supported Conlan, unconcerned about the mess he was making and interested only in helping him feel better. She felt gentle, warm affection radiating out from her heart.

"Eleanor, you're going a little green again, you don't have to stay. I can look after him."

The noxious odour of green vomit came to her on the light breeze and her stomach squeezed uncomfortably. Conlan began to retch again and Eleanor beat a hasty retreat back to the camp, watching from a safe distance.

"You two are the only ones who have been sick, what was in that bottle? Where did it come from?"

Eleanor jumped at the voice; Merl was stood behind her, watching Conlan with a worried look on his face.

"What bottle?" Eleanor asked.

Merl's worried look deepened. "You do not remember?"

"I think whatever was on the dart has messed with my memory, as the last thing I remember was Amelia catching a bird and then we were attacked," Eleanor said, shaking her head.

"You and Conlan were in a bad state when I found you. Will and I tried to suck the poison out, but it had spread too deep. Then you told us about the bottle of green liquid in Conlan's pocket, a cure you said. It worked, as you both stopped writhing, but it seems to have made you both quite ill," Merl explained, watching Eleanor's face carefully.

"I do not remember," Eleanor whispered. "But I do remember green being important."

"Do you remember anything else?" Merl prompted, his voice filled with gentle concern. Eleanor thought about it, trying to drag the disjoined corrupted data in her head into a coherent memory. Her mind resisted.

"I have a vague recollection of a dragon, someone called Douglas and that green is important. I think I failed to protect Conlan, but I do not know what I was meant to be protecting him from," Eleanor said.

Merl smiled sympathetically. "I think your head is rather messed up – there cannot have been dragons, as they do not exist, and Conlan, apart from a little sickness, is fine, so you could not have failed to protect him."

Eleanor shrugged, not feeling up to telling Merl why his logic was wrong. "Where are Amelia and Freddie?" she asked, glancing around her.

"The other two Avatars went to find us something to eat," he said. The thought of food made Eleanor's stomach coil in a very unpleasant fashion, a response compounded when Merl's words reached through her headache.

"Who told you we were Avatars?" she asked, her eyes narrowing in suspicion. Merl smiled reassuringly, but before he got the chance to reply, Conlan's voice, astonished disbelief ringing through it, called his name.

"Merl?"

"Hello, Conlan," Merl said, turning to face him with a wide, happy grin spreading across his face. With Will's help, Conlan was walking towards the man, giving him a surprised, pleased smile in return. He shook Merl's hand and the older man pulled him into a strong embrace and patted him on the back like a long-lost son. Confused, Eleanor pushed an energy string out to Will.

Who is this? Eleanor asked.

Merl claims he was sent by Gregor. I came round to find him trying to help you and Conlan; whatever was in those darts had more of an effect on the two of you than it did on us. Merl claims he killed two of the men who attacked us and chased a third man off. I've seen the bodies of the men he killed, the bird was dead, too; one of the men had a blowpipe and some of the darts on him. What happened, where did that bottle of green liquid come from?

Eleanor shook her head. *I really don't know, my memories are messed up. Something feels wrong, but that could just be my sense of equilibrium. I guess we should be grateful Merl showed up when he did. We knew the enemy was out to get us, and we still fell into their trap... again.*

"Is she alright? Her eyes look strange," Merl said, looking closely at Eleanor.

"She is talking to Will in his head," Conlan said. Eleanor felt Will's surprise that Conlan would divulge this information.

"Conlan, is it wise to give Merl information about us?" Will asked in English. "Don't you think his arrival is a little odd? He claims he saved us from our attackers, but it all seems a bit too much like a coincidence."

"Will, I've known Merl since I was two and I trust him. My grandfather has trusted him for nearly forty years. Can we give him the benefit of the doubt until he's had the chance to explain?" Conlan asked, sounding mildly irritated.

You don't think Merl can be trusted? Eleanor asked.

Actually, Freddie thinks Merl can't be trusted; I just think we should be careful.

"Is there a problem?" Merl asked as he eyes flicked between Will and Conlan as they spoke.

Conlan smiled at him. "No, could we sit please? I would like to ask you some questions."

Merl smiled amiably back at him. "Of course, you must feel awful and I am making you stand in this heat. I have questions for you, too." They walked back to where they had set up camp. The sun was beginning to set, so Will set about lighting a fire. Eleanor half-sat, half-crouched next to Conlan and Merl and listened to them talk.

"What are you doing here?" Conlan asked the older man.

Merl smiled. "Your grandfather sent me. He heard about the earthquake and knew it must be you, or rather her," he said, nodding in Eleanor's direction. "I have been tracking you for a while and I caught up with you as those three men were tying your unconscious bodies to your horses. There was a fight, I managed to kill two of them, but the third one got away. Will helped me to bury the ones I killed and their bird too, it attacked me." He pulled aside his shirt to reveal several long, recently scabbed over bloody claw marks which ran down his chest. "Ruined my favourite shirt," he grumbled.

"What did the man look like, the one who got away?" Eleanor asked.

"He had black skin, black eyes and black curly hair. He was tall, muscular, good with a sword," Merl told her, looking a little surprised she had spoken.

"The other two men, the ones you killed, did they look the same?" Eleanor asked, feeling something try to stir in her head. Merl nodded.

I can show you my memories of burying them later, if you want, Will offered.

Eleanor nodded. *Thanks.* Giving him a quick smile, she pulled her energy free.

"So how are you? Other than being a little green…" Merl asked with a chuckle.

"I am fine. But why did Gregor send you?" Conlan asked.

"He thought you could do with the help. He knew that if Nethrus was gone, you must have had an altercation with Jarrick, and after what you told him when you visited he was worried you may have been hurt, or worse. Is Jarrick dead?" Merl asked, his eyes moving up and down Conlan's body as if looking for injuries.

"Yes," Conlan replied flatly, giving Eleanor a glance she did not understand.

Merl sighed. "I remember him as a child – he was so sweet, he used to follow you around, copy everything you did. How did that turn to such bitter hatred?"

"I let him believe he was not loved," Conlan said quietly, giving Eleanor another look, but this one she did understand, as his expression was one of pure guilt. Eleanor gasped as she felt the emotional equivalent of his look wash over her; she had not known how badly he was feeling over what he had done to Jarrick.

"Why did you do that?" Merl asked. "I never took you for the callous type."

Conlan hung his head and sighed. "I thought I was protecting him, I thought if I kept him at a distance our father would ignore him. Apparently he hurt Jarrick anyway, only I left him to deal with it by himself. I made a mistake, one that cost Jarrick his life."

Horrified, Eleanor shook her head. "No, Conlan, that was my fault," she said in English.

He raised his head and gazed at her with one of his deep, unfathomable stares. "Whose emotions were you acting on?" he asked softly, the look in his eyes telling her he already knew the answer.

"Yours," she whispered honestly.

"Daratus has a lot to answer for," Merl said, employing a deep snarl to indicate he would like to make him pay for his crimes, politely ignoring the conversation Eleanor and Conlan were having. Eleanor's mind stuttered to a halt. *Daratus... not Douglas... Daratus, Conlan's father is called Daratus...* Terror pushed Eleanor's system towards panic, and her heartbeat raced, forcing out her breath in short gasps.

"Eleanor? Are you OK?" Conlan asked in English, moving forward and placing a hand on her shoulder.

"Is she alright? She does not look well," Merl commented.

"She is terrified," Conlan said as he held her gaze. She stared back blankly, not understanding where the fear was coming from, and so having no idea how to stop it.

"She just looks ill to me. How can you tell she is terrified?" Merl enquired, moving a little closer so he could study Eleanor's face.

"I can feel it," Conlan said softly.

"You can feel her emotions?" Merl asked incredulously.

Still not taking his eyes off Eleanor's face, Conlan nodded. Slowly his words reached through the terror's grip. *He can feel my emotions, too?*

"Eleanor," Conlan said. "Can you tell me why you're afraid?"

"Daratus... I think he sent the men, which means he knows where we are," Eleanor said, still speaking English and making a couple of mental leaps she had no evidence for, just a strong hunch. Merl was watching intently; Eleanor found the scrutiny a little creepy.

"Are you sure about that?" Will asked from behind her. Eleanor turned her head to find he had started the fire and was putting water on to heat.

"No, there's nothing sure where these memories are concerned... I'm sorry, I really can't remember..." she tailed off. Eleanor tried not to cry, but it was too late, the tears were falling. She wiped her eyes on her sleeve. Looking up she saw Freddie and Amelia step into the firelight; Amelia was carrying the dead body of a large lizard.

Freddie marched towards Eleanor and crouched at her side. He glared at Conlan.

"Take your hands off her," he snapped. Guilt flashing across his face,

Conlan took his hand from Eleanor's shoulder.

"It's not his fault, Freddie," Eleanor tried to explain. Freddie put his arms around her and Eleanor closed her eyes, resting her head against Freddie's chest, a wordless comfort.

"What happened?" Freddie asked over her head.

"Eleanor thinks Daratus knows where we are," Will told him.

"What was that about? Is she OK?" Merl asked.

"Eleanor thinks Daratus sent the men who attacked us," Conlan said.

"Does this mean she remembers?" Merl asked.

Eleanor shook her head, looking at Merl. "It is not a memory, just a strong feeling."

"So what do we do?" Will asked in English, including Freddie in his question.

"It's not really enough to go on, at least not until we find out more. We should keep going," Conlan said.

"OK, but could we at least take it in turns to sit guard at night?" Freddie asked, sounding irritated. "I'll start tonight."

"Are you sure? That dart didn't do you any more favours than it did the rest of us," Will said.

"I could ask Merl..." Conlan started.

"No!" Freddie snapped, giving Merl a distrustful look. "I'd feel better if it was just us," he added, making his tone softer as he caught the flash of annoyance in Conlan's face. Merl had noticed Freddie's look and raised an eyebrow at Conlan in question.

"We are just setting up some precautions," Conlan said.

Still suffering from the effects of the drug, they ate very little for dinner and went to bed early. Eleanor lay with her eyes closed, pretending to sleep but instead listening to Merl and Conlan talk. Conlan asked questions about his grandfather and Merl asked about their travels and activities. Eleanor realised as the conversation progressed that Conlan was giving very little information away. Each question he asked tested the extent of the knowledge Merl already had, and Conlan gave no information beyond this level. Merl knew they were looking for the Talismans, but he did not know what the Talismans were or where they had been before Nethrus. Eventually Merl asked what they were doing in a dangerous place like the southern savannah.

'We need to speak to the People of the Horse' was Conlan's terse reply. Merl asked if he could tag along for a while, in case they needed his help. Conlan agreed, but Eleanor heard the hesitation in his voice – he had listened to Will and Freddie, and he was being cautious. Explaining that he was still feeling unwell, Conlan called a halt to the conversation as Merl's questions became more insistent.

Eleanor listened to the night; out here the darkness was more alive than the day. She heard the whining barks of some sort of fox as it hunted the small weasels and shrews that inhabited the flat world around her. She had never seen any of these animals, but when she pushed her energy out she felt them. She was tired, but her mind did not seem to want to sleep. It occurred to her why as the silence beat against her – she could not hear Freddie snoring. Would it help if she went and slept closer to Conlan, so she could hear him breathe? She tried to stifle a yawn and failed miserably. Opening her eyes, she could see Merl sat a few feet from Conlan, staring into the fire. He raised his eyes and focused on something behind Eleanor's head, a questioning look on his face. Turning, she saw Freddie sat behind her, his back against a small, thin tree, his glittering black eyes returning Merl's stare. Merl pulled himself up and walked over to Freddie's side, crouching next to him.

"I am not the threat you think I am," he whispered in a pleasant tone. Not understanding the Dwarfish, Freddie just glared at him. The older man shrugged, moved a little distance away and curled up. He closed his eyes to sleep.

Freddie, Merl was just telling you he's not a threat, Eleanor said as Freddie pulled her offered energy towards him.

He can say it all he likes, but it doesn't mean it's true.

No, I suppose not, but if Conlan and Gregor trust him, maybe we should trust their judgement.

Silence.

Freddie, I need to talk to you about something. I was going to say something earlier but then we were attacked and...

You still love him. Freddie's voice was hard, cold.

Eleanor cringed. *Yes, I do, I think I always will. I've seen the way you look at me sometimes; you want more from me than I'm able to give. Can't we just be friends?*

More silence, but Eleanor could feel the sharp bursts of Freddie's pain slipping through his defences. Wrapping her blanket around her, Eleanor stood and shuffled heavy-eyed to Freddie's side.

Want some company?

He did not look at her, but gave a small nod of his head. Eleanor sat next to him, yawning again.

You need to sleep, you're still ill from that dart. Come on, lie down, Freddie said quietly, patting his thigh.

Freddie... Eleanor started, feeling uncomfortable.

Just friends, Eleanor.

She nodded and sank to the ground, guilt pulsing through her as she wrapped her blanket around her and rested her head on Freddie's leg. He stroked her hair tenderly as she drifted off to sleep.

The first rays of the morning sun were splashing liquid silver across the barren land when Eleanor woke to Freddie stretching his stiff back slightly, massaging the knots.

"Sorry, didn't mean to wake you," he said, offering her a tired smile as she sat up. They watched as across the fire Conlan stirred, wincing as he sat up and absently rubbed his side. He noticed their scrutiny, his expression another one Eleanor did not understand. She smiled at him but he did not return it; rather, he held her gaze for a moment longer, a frown knotting his forehead, before he stood and moved off to collect firewood.

"What did I do now?" Eleanor murmured, watching his back as he walked away. Freddie shrugged.

As they travelled they rotated the watch every night. Freddie had stubbornly resisted Conlan's suggestions that Merl be included in this nightly vigil. The argument had eventually come down to a vote. Will had agreed with Freddie, saying it was a sensible precaution. Eleanor had voted against Freddie, as she rather liked Merl. Amelia had pointed out she had nothing against Merl, but she agreed that she was not ready to trust him to watch over them as they slept. The result of the vote had put Conlan in a foul mood for days. Eleanor did not understand Freddie's reaction, as Merl had done nothing at all to arouse suspicion, he was funny, friendly and chatty, telling them stories about the things Conlan had got up to as a child. Eleanor enjoyed listening to his tales and asking whispered questions about Conlan she knew he would not have answered himself. Journeying further into the savannah they saw no one, so it was a big surprise to Eleanor when she was prodded awake, early one morning, with the sharp tip of a sword in her shoulder.

19

❦

THE SWORD

It had been Will's turn to watch over them, and as Eleanor's eyes flew open, her first thought was that Conlan was in trouble. She sat bolt upright, tense, looking for the danger and found it all around them. Twenty tall, muscular men stood in a rough circle along the perimeter of their camp, so confident in their numbers that not every sword was drawn. They all had ebony-black skin, short black hair and black eyes; they blended effortlessly into the early morning light. *Why are they just stood watching us?* Eleanor thought distractedly, watching as Freddie got the same rough wakeup call she had received. Will and Amelia were already awake. Will was sat very still, the sharp edge of a small blade pressed into his throat, while Amelia sat stiffly next to him, her gaze riveted on the man crouched behind them with his knife at Will's neck. The man did not acknowledge Amelia's presence; in fact, he looked bored. To her left Eleanor saw that Conlan and Merl were also awake, their expressions tight and guarded.

"Will, you were meant to be on watch," Eleanor said in English, giving him an accusing glance and receiving a withering one in return.

"They came out of nowhere, like ghosts," he replied, wincing as the blade at his neck bit deeper and drew a thin line of blood just visible in the shadows.

"Shut up," ordered the man holding the weapon, his Dwarfish sounding odd and yet familiar. Eleanor's mind tried to start a thought but it came to a stop as it hit the jumbled mess of corrupted memories. Angry at her uncooperative brain and at Will for letting the enemy get that close, Eleanor glared at the man.

"Why do you people always start with 'Shut Up!'?" she asked, underlying the Dwarfish with a heavy layer of irritation. "We just met you; it would be far more polite if you introduced yourselves first! Is there some book on taking us prisoner I do not know about, which states you must first tell us to shut up? I am just wondering, because I would have thought you could have come up with something a little more original!" The man stared back at Eleanor with open-mouthed surprise, while several of the other men sniggered. A peeved look settled onto his face.

"How about, 'Shut up or this man is going to lose a lot of blood'?" he drawled.

Without thinking, Eleanor answered the question. "Well, it is an improvement I suppose, but you still included the words 'Shut Up', so it's not really good enough." Eleanor saw the disbelief in his face change to anger. *I'm risking Will's life.* It was a dangerous game she was playing, but for some reason she wanted to trust this man. She did not feel threatened or even afraid, but then again she was not the one with a knife at her throat. The blade had not moved any further on Will's neck, so Eleanor decided to push her luck and trust her instinct about the man holding it. "My name is Eleanor, what is yours?"

"Nials," the man said, the surprise now in his voice. Eleanor wondered if he was surprised at her or himself for actually replying.

Eleanor smiled. "I am pleased to meet you, Nials. The man you are threatening is my friend, Will. He is actually quite harmless." Will flashed her an amused look. Eleanor ignored it and continued to focus on Nials. "You can take your knife from his throat," she continued. "You outnumber us, so what threat could we be?"

"I have orders to follow," Nials said.

"I am not a great believer of orders myself, unless I am issuing them, of course," Eleanor said conversationally, wanting to keep the man talking; information was good and could save their lives. "What are your orders?" she added with another smile.

"We have to keep you here until Urerla arrives." Again he sounded surprised, but this time Eleanor was fairly sure it was because he had answered her question.

Eleanor nodded. "I was wondering, would it hurt if you just asked us to stay put until Urerla gets here? I do not think threatening us is necessary, or do your orders state that you have to make us bleed? We have done nothing to threaten you, and frankly I am getting a little irritated with the general attitude of strike first, ask questions later. We are trying to help the people of Mydren and we just keep getting hit, stabbed and poisoned, I am starting to feel deeply unappreciated!" To Eleanor's surprise, Nials removed his knife from Will's throat and stood in a fluid, graceful movement.

"Thank you," Eleanor said.

Nials stared at her for a moment. "You might not want to thank me just yet," he replied with soft menace. "Perhaps I removed my knife from his throat so I could slit yours." Eleanor waited for the fear to rise, but none came. She smiled at him.

"Perhaps you did, but if you wanted me dead it would be far quicker to get him to do it," she reasoned, jerking her head back to indicate the man stood behind her, his sword drawn.

"Or maybe I would like the pleasure of taking your life myself," he said. Eleanor rose slowly to her feet; nobody tried to stop her. Walking towards Nials, she stopped well within striking distance and clasped her hands behind her back, giving him as much of an open target as she could. An energy string pushed rudely into her head.

What are you doing? Freddie demanded, his anger crashing against her. Eleanor ignored him, keeping her attention on Nials.

"Who is Urerla?" she asked.

"You are not afraid of me, are you?" Nials asked, sizing her up. Now she was closer, Eleanor noticed the small, raised, delicate pattern of scars that made a dotted line under his black eyes. She had seen scars like that before. The faces of the men Merl had killed jumped into her head. Will had got a pretty good look at them and Nials had the same black skin and the same ritual scaring under the eyes, although the pattern on one of the dead men had been far more complicated.

"No, I am not afraid of you. I actually want to trust you. Who is Urerla?" Eleanor asked again.

Are you mad? He could kill you!

Nials gave her a long appraising look. Eleanor concentrated on returning it with a calm, steady look of her own, recognising the hiss and spit of the fire behind her that told her Freddie was drawing energy.

Freddie, stop it, I'm fine. We're just talking. Do you really think Amelia would allow this man to hurt me? The heated crackling of the fire died down again.

You take far too many risks, Freddie muttered.

No, you're being overprotective, Eleanor replied, trying to stay calm. *I'm getting information, this is important.*

Well, let someone else do it, I don't want you putting yourself in harm's way, Freddie snapped.

"Urerla is the one who will decide what to do with you," Nials replied. Still caught up in her argument with Freddie, it took Eleanor a second to translate what Nials had just said.

"Why must something be done with us?" Eleanor asked.

"You are trespassing on our land, and we do not take kindly to that," Nials replied.

"You are the People of the Horse, we…"

She was interrupted by the sound of thundering hooves, and following Nials's gaze she turned to look. Three dark-coloured horses were approaching, their riders sitting tall. The horse in the middle was bigger than Rand had been, flanked at either side by slightly smaller animals that hung back a few paces from the lead horse. They moved at considerable speed. The figure astride the larger, lead animal had a slim, feminine grace and rode with practiced skill, but as she was riding out of the rising sun, Eleanor was unable to determine any further details. *Is this Urerla?* The woman pulled the charging beast to a halt, swinging her leg over the saddle and landing gracefully, almost before the animal had stopped. Those following her seemed to be bodyguards and came to a halt but remained mounted, eyes missing nothing of the situation in front of them or the surrounding environment.

The woman was clothed in the same light, rough material as Nials and the other men – slightly baggy trousers, a shirt tight over large breasts and a sandy-coloured cape, the hood thrown back to reveal her long black hair falling in tight curls around her shoulders. From her curved hips hung a thick belt, made of heavy gold links, charms and gemstones attached to it which jingled merrily as she moved. Her full, dark velvet lips were pressed into a disapproving sneer. Her black skin also bore the marks of ritual scaring, but her pattern was complicated, with several lines of dots under her eyes and down across her cheek bones. *Like the dead man.* Eleanor was impressed; she was a uniquely beautiful woman. Carrying herself with a calm, confident grace she sashayed towards them, her belt tinkling in the silence.

"Nials, you sent for me? Who are these people?" she asked, strong authority in her quiet throaty voice. Her eyes moved across the faces in front of her she did not recognise.

"I do not know," Nials replied. "We were waiting for you to question them." The woman nodded and stepped towards Freddie, openly scrutinising him with intelligent, iridescent black eyes. Freddie stared back at her as she appraised him; his eyes travelled slowly down her tall, strong, curved body and back up again, and an appreciative grin spread across his face.

Who's she? he asked in open admiration.

I think this is the person we were waiting for – this is Urerla, Eleanor replied as the woman turned and looked at each of them in turn. Freddie pulled his energy string back and continued to stare. Eleanor smiled as the woman's gaze passed over her; there was no return smile. The black eyes flicked back to Freddie.

"Who are you?" she asked.

Freddie knew he was being addressed, but having no clue what was being said he just smiled at her.

"He is the Avatar of Fire. He does not speak Dwarfish," Eleanor said. The woman glanced at her, a quizzical eyebrow raised.

"We can translate for you, if you wish," Will said, standing and stepping forward and causing Nials to move his hand to the dagger at his side. Urerla looked at Will. She did not seem surprised at the mention of Avatars.

"Who are you?" she asked.

Will smiled. "Will, Avatar of Water, it is a pleasure to meet you, Urerla."

"Another Avatar? What are you doing here? Who is in charge of your group?" she asked.

"I am in charge," Conlan said, standing. The guard behind him rested his blade against Conlan's neck, but he ignored it as he continued. "We have come to talk to you; we want the Avatar of Fire's sword."

Urerla turned to regard Conlan. "The sword is not for the taking. Which Avatar are you?" she asked, her cold gaze lingering over him.

"I am not an Avatar, my name is Conlan Baydon," he replied. For a long, strained moment Urerla stared at Conlan, then at Freddie and then back to Conlan again. She seemed to be working out what she should do next.

"My mother will need to decide what to do with them, we must take them back," she commanded. Nials snapped to attention. Eleanor felt there should have been a salute, but he just nodded his agreement to her order. Without another word Urerla mounted her horse in one easy motion, pulled the huge animal round and galloped off back the way she had come, her bodyguards whipping round their own mounts and following her. As they left, Nials started issuing orders.

Their captors watched them break camp. Once their horses were saddled and packed, Nials sent men round to disarm and restrain them. One of the men grabbed roughly at Eleanor, patting her down and looking for concealed weapons. He removed Remic's knife from her belt, turned her around and pulled her wrists behind her back. She felt thin ropes tying her hands in place. She did not resist, allowing them to help her onto Horse's back. When they realised that there were not enough horses to go round, Nials pulled Amelia onto his horse. Sitting her in front of him, they set off in the same direction Urerla had taken, the men leading their horses forward at a steady, mile-eating trot.

Eleanor was soon uncomfortable, as the ropes bit into her flesh, rubbing the skin and her arms began to throb from being forced to hold the same position. To make matters worse, the brilliant rays of the rising sun had given way to dark, heavy grey clouds, which made it feel like early evening, not early afternoon. It was still hot, unpleasantly so, and especially as Eleanor was unable to remove her jacket. The air thickened with the oppressive heat of an imminent thunderstorm. Eleanor and Horse jumped when the first flash of lightning ripped across the sky, searing its brief, jagged existence onto Eleanor's retinas, the rumbling thunder that accompanied it heralding the rain that fell in a steady, pounding downpour. Soaked through to the skin in minutes, Eleanor tried unsuccessfully to wipe back the hair clinging in annoyingly cold, wet tentacles to her face. The drop in temperature made her feel a little more comfortable, but the continuous forceful drubbing of the massive water drops began to give her a headache. She hunched her shoulders and endured it, wondering if they were going to get hit by lightning. As they travelled, her mind churned. She went through the memories Will had shown her several times, making comparisons; several worrying insights occurred to her. From the colour of their skin, their clothes and the ritual scaring on their faces, Eleanor made the logical assumption that both dead men had been 'People of the Horse', and from Merl's description the man who had got away was one, too. The complicated ritual scaring on Urerla's face was too similar to that of one of the dead men to be coincidence. *Were they related?* If this was the case, then none of their current captors could be trusted. *Gregor's book, I have to protect it, I need to find a way to keep it with me.* She wondered if she should try to keep the Talismans with them, but she decided it would be better if they did not draw attention to them – as long as nobody read the book, they were unlikely to be recognised. Eleanor wondered if Daratus had made a deal with the People of the Horse – were the whole tribe in on it? It would help if she knew what the man who had escaped had looked like. She tried looking into the minds of their horses, but discovered that the animals had been more interested in resting or eating, even Horse had taken a nap when she had seen Eleanor and Conlan hit the ground. She had thought it an odd time to rest, but she had not objected when the opportunity was presented.

They travelled for hours in silence. Eleanor used the time to come up with a plan to keep the book with her. It distracted her from the situation in which she found herself. She did not like the heavy rain and lack of light, interspersed with blinding flashes of lightning and thunder that made the air tremble. As the afternoon became early evening, Eleanor saw orange light flickering in the distance. As they got closer she could make out a large wall, which looked like a mud-built fortress, blending into the grey, wet world around it. The walls were perhaps thirty foot high, with large metal baskets spaced evenly along it, and in each basket blazed a cheery fire. Eleanor could make out dark shadows shifting behind them and felt eyes staring down at her.

As the massive battlements loomed over them, Eleanor saw a doorway further down the exterior which housed enormous, weather-worn wooden gates. As they approached there was yelling from the top of the wall, and with a whining creak that filled the gloom, making Eleanor shudder with apprehension, the wooden door swung open ponderously. Walking through the gates, a heady sense of power flowed through her, washing away her fear. She felt strong, confident and relaxed; whatever came next, she could face it. Up ahead, Eleanor watched Conlan straighten his shoulders and, despite his restraints, sit up straighter, looking more alert, relaxed and ready. He turned his head towards her and gave her the smile that made her insides go runny. She smiled back, knowing it was his strength and confidence she was feeling.

The inside of the fortress was not the military encampment that Eleanor had expected. There was a main 'street' of single-storied, flat-roofed mud buildings, each building leading into the next with no space between them. The occasional figure moved quickly through the rain, shoulders hunched, and Eleanor knew that eyes still watched them from the walls. Other than that, the place looked deserted. As they entered, the wooden gates were pushed back into place with a resounding crash that made Eleanor and Horse jump. The men pulled them forward, deeper into the wet, dark, quiet village. Their horses were stopped at a nondescript building that looked like all the others, the only difference as far as Eleanor could see being that the building before her did not seem to have windows, only a strong door with a dead bolt on the outside to lock it. Care was taken in removing them from their horses, the bolt was drawn back with a metallic shriek and they were ushered inside. Preparations had been made for them. The main room of the building made Eleanor think it must be a storeroom, apart from a pile of blankets against one wall, a couple of lit lanterns and a rough rug, which had been thrown over the dirt floor, the room was empty. A door at the back of the room stood open to another smaller room, and Eleanor could see a toilet bucket and assumed it had been set up as a makeshift bathroom. Nials moved among them, cutting through the ropes at their wrists. Eleanor heaved a grateful sigh of relief, feeling the muscles in her shoulders spasm at the sudden movement. She could see the cut on Will's neck. It was starting to heal but still looked a mess, so she could use it to put a plan into action.

"Nials, we need some of our bags," Eleanor said, her voice loud in the silence, all eyes turning towards her.

Nials shook his head. "No, you have what you need here; we will bring you food and drink."

"We need our medical supplies, Will has medicine that will help heal his neck," Eleanor replied, moving towards the still open door, intent on forcing the issue. Nials glance at Will, then back to Eleanor, moving to block the doorway as he did so.

"We will send our healers," he said.

Eleanor snorted in derision. "Have they treated Avatars?" she asked, fixing Nials with a hard stare. Nials glanced back at Will again. He seemed undecided. Eleanor gave him a little time, not taking her eyes off him.

Eventually he sighed. "Very well, which bags do you need?"

"I will show you," Eleanor said, moving out of the door and towards their horses as fast as she could before he thought to stop her. The two men holding their mounts' bridles gave each other surprised looks as she marched towards them. She went to Will's horse and pulled his medical bag down, releasing the strap and slinging it over her shoulder, and then she moved to Horse and took her satchel as well.

"What is in the bags?" Nials asked from the door of the building. Eleanor returned, opening Will's medical bag. The contents were obvious, although Will's sketch pad and pencils were tucked down the side. She then opened her satchel, lifting a couple of the bottles out and showing them to Nials.

"What else is in there?" Nials asked suspiciously, reaching to open the mouth of the bag wider.

"Just personal things, some books, money, nothing special. Would you like me to get it all out?" Eleanor asked, doing her best to sound bored. He had not reacted to the mention of 'books'.

Nials smiled. "No, I trust you," he said.

Eleanor smiled back. "Thank you." She had only deceived him a little bit and it was not going to do him any damage.

Nials and the other men left, bolting the door behind them. For a moment there was silence as everyone stared at her, confused expressions all round.

"You know that our physiology is no different to theirs, don't you?" Will asked in English.

Eleanor nodded. "Yes, Will, but they don't know that. I just wanted to make sure that Gregor's book stayed with me."

Will looked at her, another long appraising look, and she could see he was thinking. "Well I guess I'd better clean up my neck," he said, moving to sit on the rug. Eleanor carried the bags over, and she and Amelia dropped in front of him.

"What do we need?" Eleanor asked. Will looked into the bags.

"That bottle with the red liquid in it would be a good start, and there's some material you can use to apply it under the bandage strips."

Carefully following Will's instructions, Eleanor and Amelia cleaned the cut.

Amelia had wanted to stitch it, but Will had convinced them that applying a bandage would be enough. They had just finished when the shriek of the bolt being forced back snapped all their eyes to the door. It opened with a creak and several men entered carrying a large, hot metal pot of food, along with some bowls and spoons, a loaf of bread and a jug with some mugs. They placed the food and drink on the floor without a word, turned and left, the door closing with a bang and the bolt grinding into place.

"It would not take much for us to escape," Merl said thoughtfully. "I do not understand why you let them capture us in the first place."

Conlan sat down on the rug, serving food into the bowls and passing it round. Merl frowned at him.

"Conlan, you should not be serving us, we should be serving you!"

Conlan smiled at him and then concentrated on his task; he did not look at Merl as he spoke.

"We are not escaping, because I want them as allies, not enemies."

"Allies against what?" Merl asked.

"Did my grandfather not tell you? If he sent you out here I would have thought he would have explained what he was sending you into, or at least given you the option to decline. After all, you are risking your life right now."

Merl's frown deepened. Taking the food Conlan offered, he sat down on the rug next to him.

"He told me you were doing something vitally important. He said you might be in danger, that you might need help after the earthquake in Nethrus. I was to find you and do anything you asked. What is the Avatar of Fire's sword you asked for?"

Conlan ignored the question for a moment. "Eleanor, this food has meat in it, would you like some bread?" he asked in English. Eleanor nodded. Conlan tore off half the loaf and gave it to her. Will rooted around in his medical bag and produced a small piece of material, the corners pulled up and tied into a bag, and passed it too her. She opened it carefully to find a mix of nuts and dried berries.

Eleanor smiled. "Thank you."

Will shrugged and smiled back. "They were for emergencies – I think this qualifies."

Merl watched them, trying to understand what was going on.

"She is not eating?"

"She does not eat meat," Conlan answered, passing a bowl of food to

Freddie, who took it gratefully and plonked himself down next to Eleanor.

"Why not?" Merl asked, his tone implying it was the most ridiculous thing he had ever heard.

"I am the Avatar of Earth, Merl, and the animal that gave its life for the meal you are eating was my brother or sister. Could you eat one of your siblings?" Eleanor snapped, irritated.

Merl paled and shook his head.

"You asked about the Avatar of Fire's sword..." Conlan continued, as if Eleanor's outburst had never happened. Merl nodded, a look of polite interest on his face; Conlan gave him a warm smile.

Starting from pretty much the beginning, with Alaric and the first Avatars, Conlan gave Merl the abridged version of what they were doing and why they were doing it. He had just got to the part about the Talismans and how many they had and where they had been, when Eleanor felt an energy string brush against her.

Why is he telling Merl all this? Will asked. Eleanor was surprised by the emotionless look he had on his face compared to the worry in his voice.

Merl is risking his life being with us, he deserves to know why.

He must really think Merl can be trusted.

Eleanor thought about it for a moment. *Or he doesn't think it matters.*

Will gave her an odd look as he pulled his energy string back.

"You are looking for Talismans, which were hidden by Alaric's servants centuries ago, so that you can recreate the power of the Five, overthrow the Lords of Mydren and declare yourself king?" Merl was asking in wide-eyed disbelief, food forgotten in his hand.

"Yes," Conlan confirmed.

"What do these Talismans look like?" Merl asked.

Conlan looked at Eleanor. "Do you have Gregor's book?" he asked in Dwarfish. Slightly taken aback, Eleanor stared at him for a moment, before answering in English.

"Are you sure Merl can be trusted?"

"Yes, I think he can be trusted, but even if he can't I don't see the problem with him knowing what we're doing. If he's with us, who's he going to tell?"

Conlan said.

"OK, but we need to be careful, Conlan. The people who attacked us, they were 'People of the Horse', I'm sure of it. It might just be a few people within the tribe working with Daratus, or it might be that the whole tribe has a deal with the Lords of Mydren. Whatever the case, Merl needs to know that the book is to be protected."

"You realise that Merl could be working with Daratus," Freddie interjected, hard eyes on Conlan.

"Yes, the thought did occur to me," Conlan said mildly.

"Then is showing him the book a good idea?" Freddie asked.

"He's risking his life to be here, Freddie. I trust him, and even if I didn't, as I said, I don't really see how reading the book is going to do any damage if Merl is with us," Conlan said.

Freddie huffed. "You're in charge."

"Thank you for noticing," Conlan said, a sardonic smile on his face. Freddie gave him a mildly insolent smirk in return.

"Is there a problem?" Merl asked. Conlan shook his head as Eleanor pulled her bag towards her, rummaging until she found Gregor's book carefully protected in its piece of cloth. She handed it to Conlan and he sat next to Merl, opening different pages and showing him pictures of the different Talismans.

Eleanor sat next to Freddie, who automatically put an arm round her and then seemed to remember himself and withdrew it. Eleanor grasped his hand as it slipped over her shoulder, pulling it back around her and pushing a string out to him.

Freddie, am I hurting you?

Confusion filled his face. *No, Eleanor, why would you think that?*

Letting you hold me. I feel so guilty for doing it. Doesn't it hurt being this close and knowing it won't go any further? Eleanor asked, dropping her eyes, her shame making it impossible to look at him.

Eleanor, if Conlan allowed you to hug him, would you care what his motivations were? Eleanor's mind immediately provided her with the memory of Conlan's arm around her, holding her close as night fell around them. She had shut her mind down and simply enjoyed the moment.

No. If Conlan wanted me to hug him, I'd try not to question it. I'd just never want it to end.

Exactly, Freddie said softly. Eleanor felt a surge of affection and wrapped her arms around his waist, hugging him close to her. He hugged her back fiercely, resting his chin on her head. Eleanor felt another string brush against her.

Are you listening to what Merl is telling Conlan? Will asked. Eleanor turned slightly, giving the two men her attention.

"… are sure you have seen the crown before?" Conlan was asking.

"I am certain, yes, although this picture does not do it justice; it is a beautiful piece of craftsmanship," Merl replied.

"Where? Where did you see it?" Conlan asked, the excitement in his voice hard to miss.

"In a glass cabinet in the main reception room in the Central Tower," Merl said. There was silence.

Do you think he's telling the truth? Will asked, once he had translated what Merl had said for Amelia and Freddie.

I've no idea, Eleanor answered.

"How do you know what is in the reception room of the Central Tower?" Conlan asked, suspicion creeping into his voice.

If Merl noticed, he ignored it. His response calm and measured. "I went there a few times, with Gregor, on some of his attempts to reclaim custody of you and Jarrick."

There was another lengthy silence.

"Reclaim custody?" Conlan asked, softly.

"Did Gregor not tell you?" Merl asked. "Did you think he just let you go? Gregor spent years and a small fortune trying to get you back. He spoke to any Lord who would listen, tried threats, bribes, even blackmail, but nothing worked. At the time, your father was held in very high regard and he looked set to make it all the way to the Central Tower. You turned sixteen, became an adult and Daratus lost control of you. In my opinion the man was an idiot for thinking he could control you in the first place, you have your mother's stubborn streak. You started speaking out against him and ridiculed his decisions, showing him up as the weak, foolish man he is. He tried to discipline you, but having you flogged did not shut you up, so he took what he thought was the only step left to him and disowned you. Another mistake, if he had been smart he would have had you quietly killed. Gregor thought you would return home then, come back to him, he was hurt when you stayed away. He persuaded Lord Harris, you remember him? He persuaded him to officially acknowledge you as his heir, despite Daratus disowning you. Gregor wanted to leave his estate to you when he died. He has never stopped loving you and never stopped fighting for you."

More silence.

"I did not return because I did not want my father using it as an excuse to declare Gregor a traitor," Conlan said quietly. Eleanor shuddered as his pain washed over her. Freddie pulled her closer.

"Your grandfather is a powerful man, Conlan, more powerful in many ways than your father. Daratus would never have risked taking him on, but you were not to know that," Merl said sympathetically.

Silence again.

"How am I supposed to get the crown out of the Central Tower?" Conlan wondered out loud, with just a hint of despair in his words.

"I might be able to help you with that," Merl said, giving Conlan a mischievous smile.

"Really, how?" Conlan asked, desperate hope in his voice warring with the suspicion in his eyes. His hope appeared to be winning.

"Well, I might be able to convince someone to sneak the crown out... for a price," he said.

"That would be great, Merl. Would we need to go back to the Central Tower?" Conlan asked, clearly trying to control his excitement.

"No, I could send a message to the person I am thinking of and we could meet them halfway. Katadep would be a good place – there is a Protector stronghold there and my friend could find a reason to visit," Merl said thoughtfully.

What is Merl saying? Freddie asked.

Will translated again.

That sounds a little too good to be true, Freddie said carefully.

Eleanor nodded, seeing Freddie's concerned in Will and Amelia's faces. *But what if Merl can provide us with the crown?* she asked.

And what if Merl is working for the enemy? This could be a trap, Freddie answered.

Freddie, seriously, Merl loves Conlan, treats him like a son. You've seen it, do you really think he could be working for Daratus? Besides, if the crown is where Merl says it is, we've got very little chance of getting it ourselves. It might be worth springing a trap, just to get our hands on it.

You want to purposely walk into a Protector trap? Amelia asked, a little horrified.

We're Avatars, Amelia, we'd be more than a match for whoever they sent, and springing the trap would bring our enemies into the light, make them easier to fight, Eleanor reasoned.

Avatars have been killed before and Amelia has come close to losing her life – we are not invincible, Eleanor, Will said quietly.

Eleanor nodded. *We were taken by surprise when Amelia was hurt, and maybe the other Avatars got careless, made mistakes.*

What? Like knowingly walking into a trap? Freddie asked. Eleanor shot him an irritated look, but he stared back passively. He was serious, Eleanor realised, he was really worried.

I trust Conlan, he knows what he's doing, Eleanor said stubbornly.

Will nodded slowly. *I trust him too and Merl is growing on me. I say we give him the benefit of the doubt, but we need to be more aware of our own limitations.*

They dropped into silence again, listening to Merl and Conlan's conversation.

"How would you send a message?" Conlan was asking.

"Your grandfather is part of a large network of spies, so get me to a reasonably sized town and I can send the request," Merl said. Conlan nodded, looking thoughtful.

"Your Avatars are very quiet," Merl commented.

"They will be talking in each other's heads," Conlan said, giving them a brief glance.

"You are in charge – should you not know what they are saying?" Merl asked, his soft voice full of concerned confusion.

"I am sure they will tell me if they are discussing anything important," Conlan said.

Merl nodded. "It must be very difficult for you, not knowing what they are thinking or saying, especially when they hold all the power."

Conlan stared at him for a moment, but said nothing, moving to hand out blankets in silence instead.

Eleanor lay underneath hers, unable to sleep. At Merl's request, Conlan had handed Gregor's book over to him to read and they had held sporadic conversations about Avatars, Talismans and Conlan's shield as Merl had asked questions. Freddie turned over in his sleep, throwing his arm over Eleanor's waist and pulling her towards him, sighing softly as he rested his head against her back, his snoring starting up again. Conlan said goodnight to Merl, and Eleanor heard him lying down next to her, the rug underneath them not being big enough for him to get any distance. As he placed his blanket over him, Eleanor felt it cover her outstretched arm. She was just about to withdraw it, not wanting to invade his private space, when under the blanket she felt his hand close over hers. Surprised, she opened her eyes. He lay on his side, facing her. A small smile lit up his face and spoke of victory. They were so close, the sword and the crown were within their reach. His look gave Eleanor a warm glow. He stared at her for a moment and then closed his eyes to sleep. Her hand remained comfortably enveloped in his.

It was long before dawn when they were woken by the bolt on the door to their gaol being pulled back; the sound was so loud and grating that Eleanor sat up with a start, waking Conlan and Freddie as she did. Will opened his eyes but did not move, as Amelia was still asleep in his arms. The door was pulled open. It was dark outside and chilly air blew in, but it appeared to have stopped raining. Nials entered, staring at them with tired disinterest.

"Urerla wishes to speak with you, Conlan Baydon," he said quietly.

"In the middle of the night?" Conlan asked in a thick, sleep-clogged voice, underlying the Dwarfish with suspicion. Nials raised an eyebrow, looked at him coldly but said nothing. Rolling his eyes in annoyance, Conlan got to his feet and without looking back followed Nials. The door closed and bolted behind them.

"What was that about?" Freddie asked.

"Urerla has asked to see him," Eleanor said, noticing Will and Freddie giving each other a strange look.

"What?" she asked.

"Just a little odd, that's all," Will said, looking back at the door.

"Maybe the woman doesn't sleep much," Eleanor suggested. Freddie and Will gave each other another look she did not understand. Irritated, she glanced from one to the other.

"What?" she asked again.

Freddie gave her a wicked smile. "Think about it, Eleanor, why do you *think* a woman might be asking a man to join her in the middle of the night?" Embarrassed at her stupidity, Eleanor felt her cheeks turn crimson as Freddie's words fitted the pieces of the puzzle together.

"She wants to have sex with him?" she asked, wanting to be very sure that she had the right idea before she said anything else.

"Perhaps," Will said, giving Freddie an irritated glance.

Freddie sniggered softly. "Oh come on Will, you saw the look Urerla gave him, she was practically undressing him on the spot," he said, his grin getting wider. Eleanor felt her stomach twist and was angry at her body's response. She had no claim over Conlan. He could do as he pleased, but the thought of him in the arms of the stunningly beautiful Urerla made her physically sick. She was going to have to work hard to hide this feeling, she realised. It was unfair; if Urerla could make him happy, who was she to deny him or make him feel bad?

"As I recall, she gave you much the same look," Will retorted quietly. The smile on Freddie's face grew wistful, his eyes glazing slightly as he remembered.

"She is really beautiful," he said softly.

Will rolled his eyes and then closed them, pulling Amelia closer as he tried to get back to sleep.

Eleanor smiled at Freddie's expression. "You really liked her." Her voice snapped him back to reality and a guilty expression flashed across his face.

"She's very beautiful, but she has nothing on you," he said in a very serious tone.

Eleanor giggled. "Freddie, she has a lot on me! Height, curves, big breasts... manageable hair..."

Freddie reached a hand out and ran his fingers gently over her head and through her dark hair to her shoulders. "You have beautiful hair, but what makes you special is in here," he said, laying a hand over her heart for a moment. "And in here," he continued, gently tapping the side of her head with two fingers. Embarrassed again, Eleanor dropped her eyes.

"I guess I should be grateful that something detracts from my physical shortcomings," she muttered.

"Short being the operative word," Freddie said, smiling at her. Seeing his attempt to keep the conversation light, and to distract her from her embarrassment, Eleanor smiled back, slapping him playfully. Freddie groaned, grabbing his arm in mock agony and collapsing back down to the rug. Eleanor giggled again and lay down next to him, pulling her blanket over her.

"Freddie?" Eleanor whispered, her eyes fixed firmly on the cracks in the ceiling.

"Yes?"

"Do you think Conlan really would sleep with Urerla?" she asked.

There was a long pause.

"Honestly, Eleanor, I've no idea," Freddie said. She closed her eyes as thoughts of Conlan and Urerla together ran through her mind.

"And you just let him go?!"

It was a furious voice, yelling in Dwarfish, that woke Eleanor with a start. Her eyes shot open. Merl was standing inches from Will, glaring at him and jabbing his finger angrily into his chest. Will was staring back calmly.

"What would you have had me do?" he asked mildly.

"Stop him, protect him," Merl snapped.

"He is quite capable of taking care of himself," Will said, the hard growl he put through his reply implying that Merl was being an idiot.

"If he was, do you think his grandfather would have sent me to protect him? That boy has a truly astounding ability to get himself into trouble, he always has had. You are his Avatars, you should be defending him," Merl said, ignoring Will's unspoken insult. Will continued to hold Merl's angry glare with a cold, calm one of his own, but he said nothing more. Freddie gave Eleanor a questioning look.

"Merl thinks we should have stopped Conlan leaving, tried to protect him," she told him.

"Where did he go?" Amelia asked, watching Merl and Will with apprehension.

"Urerla asked to see him," Freddie said.

Having nothing to fight against, Merl backed off, moving to sit back on the rug. Pulling Gregor's book back into his lap he started to read again in hostile silence. Will sat back down next to Amelia, pulling her into his arms.

"Do you think we need to rescue Conlan?" Eleanor asked, looking at the worry in Will's eyes.

He shook his head. "No, we're trying to make them allies, remember? I'm sure he'll be fine – I can't figure out why Merl was getting so upset about it."

"He's just worried about Conlan," Eleanor said, fully understanding Merl's feelings. Will nodded, but he did not look convinced. Before they could discuss it further, the nerve-grating shriek of the bolt being pulled back and echoed through the room. Her attention flicked to the door as it was flung open, dawn's weak light flooding in. Conlan was shoved inside with enough force to send him sprawling. The door was slammed shut again, so quickly that Eleanor did not notice who had pushed him. His hands were tied behind his back, so he landed gracelessly, his head bouncing painfully off the floor. Will moved to help him, but Merl beat him to it, flashing an angry scowl. They watched as the older man untied the restraints. Conlan sat for a moment rubbing feeling back into his wrists; he had obviously been tied up for a while, perhaps since he had left their cell.

"What happened?" Merl asked.

"Long story," Conlan said, raising his head to look at Merl. As he did so, Eleanor noticed the bright red mark on his face in the very noticeable shape of a hand.

"Who slapped you?" she asked in English.

Conlan looked at her, rubbing his face.

"Urerla."

Eleanor smiled, she could not help it. If the woman was slapping him, Freddie and Will's suspicions seemed unlikely. "I thought we were trying to make them our friends, why did she hit you?"

Conlan shrugged.

"So, is she going to give us the sword?" Will asked, also sticking to English while sitting back down next to Amelia.

"She doesn't have it," Conlan replied.

"Then who does?" Freddie asked him.

"A rival tribe."

"Rival tribe?" Freddie spluttered. "We got the wrong 'People of the Horse'?"

Conlan nodded. "Many centuries ago the 'People of the Horse' fractured into eight separate tribes. In the beginning these tribes fought almost to the point of mutual annihilation for control of the others, but realising they were going to destroy themselves if they didn't stop the fighting, they found another way to deal with the problem. Every year they hold a 'meeting', where all eight tribes get together. Alliances are strengthened, marriages are arranged and trade deals are made, but the main purpose of the 'meeting' is to decide who will hold the 'Heart' for the coming year," he said, getting up and moving to sit next to them on the rug, Merl following.

"What 'Heart'? There are hearts mentioned in the poem from the book, but why is holding it important?" Freddie said, asking the questions spinning round Eleanor's head before she got the chance.

"The 'Heart' is what they call the sword, although to be more precise it's what they call the large heart-shaped diamond that's the sword's pommel, and it's important because the tribe holding the sword has ultimate control of all the tribes for that year," Conlan said.

"How do they work out who gets the sword?" Amelia asked.

"I wasn't able to get all the details on that," Conlan admitted. "But they have some kind of competition, a test of strength, courage and stamina between man and horse."

"They're not going to give up the sword easily, are they?" Eleanor said quietly.

Conlan shook his head, frowning. "No, I don't think they are."

"Is Urerla going to release us so we can find the tribe that *does* have the sword?" Will asked.

"Urerla doesn't have that kind of authority. That would be her mother's decision. Her mother is the leader of this tribe. I assume we'll be meeting her soon," Conlan said.

"So did you tell Urerla why we needed the sword? Did you explain that we'd like them to be allies?" Eleanor asked.

Conlan smiled. "Yes, but I think getting them to be our allies could be a little difficult."

"Why?" Freddie asked, beating Eleanor to it again.

"Because the 'People of the Horse' make alliances through marriage; they don't seem to recognise there might be other ways," Conlan replied.

Several thoughts lined themselves up in Eleanor's head, giving her an amusing insight, and she giggled. "That's why she slapped you – she offered you an alliance of marriage and you turned her down!"

Conlan dropped his head, looking embarrassed. "Something like that," he muttered.

"Was that wise?" Eleanor mused. "She's a beautiful woman, she could make a good queen and you would gain another army." Conlan raised his head, green eyes locking onto hers.

"You think I should marry Urerla?" he asked, disbelief in his voice. Eleanor shrugged and smiled at him. It took effort, but her voice was calm when she answered him.

"Conlan, you're going to be a king, and your choice of wife will therefore be very important. I don't think you should discount Urerla out of hand." There was a brief silence as Conlan stared at her.

"I don't want to marry her."

"Kings do as their kingdoms require," Eleanor said. "They marry to increase their lands, to strengthen their support, to turn enemies into allies or to strengthen their own position through having children. So she's worth considering." Conlan flicked his eyes to Will, Eleanor could not read the look that passed between them.

"She's right Conlan, that's the way kings and queens have done it for centuries in our world. If we manage to survive all this, who you end up marrying is going to be of great importance," Will told him. Conlan stared in hurt consternation, moving his gaze back to Eleanor.

"I'm not going to marry Urerla. Think of another way to get them onside," he said flatly.

Eleanor shrugged again. "I think you might have to," she said. "The poem spoke about a 'gift beyond measure' and 'a heart for a heart', plus finding yourself a queen would be thinking of the future."

"Eleanor, I'm going to say this once more and then we won't discuss this again. I'm *not* going to marry Urerla," Conlan said stiffly from behind teeth clamped tightly over his obvious anger. "And frankly, I'd have thought you'd be the last person suggesting that I should," he added. Eleanor smiled, knowing there was a large amount of hurt in it that she could not hide.

"Why?" she asked softly. "Because I love you? Do you not understand what that means? It means that you are more important to me than anything else in existence. I want you to be happy and I want you to find a queen who will support and protect you, be your companion, someone you can trust."

"That's what I have the four of you for," Conlan said, not taking his eyes from Eleanor's as she slowly shook her head.

"You need to have offspring, Conlan, and we can't help you with that. An heir will consolidate your throne, stop civil war breaking out when you die and bring stability to your rule. You're going to need a wife," she insisted.

There was silence. Conlan stared at her with another one of his enigmatic looks. Eleanor felt as if the others were holding their breath and waiting for something. It was Merl who broke the silence.

"What is the matter?"

Conlan turned to look at the older man, irritation marching across his face. "Nothing," he said coldly.

Merl looked from Eleanor back to Conlan, his eyes full of sympathetic concern.

"So what happened? Where have you been?" he asked. Conlan turned and repeated to Merl what he had learnt, leaving out the bit about Eleanor thinking he should marry Urerla.

Eleanor tuned him out, trying to calm down her churning mind. She had meant what she said – she wanted him to find a queen, be happy and have children – but that did not mean the thought of him happy with someone else did not hurt. However, she was not going to make him hesitate in his choice because he was worried about upsetting her. She knew she had shown him some of her pain, but he was not going to see it again. The others left her in peace, talking amongst themselves and wondering what the 'competition for the sword' might entail. It took a lot of effort, but Eleanor took all her hurt and shoved it deep inside, down to the bottom of a deep pit she kept for such thoughts – those she could not deal with. The bolt being pulled back brought Eleanor's musings back to the present. The door opened and Eleanor was blinded by the strong sunlight that illuminated their gloomy gaol. Several men entered, removed the remnants of the previous night's meal and deposited fresh food. They also replaced the lanterns, two of which had run out of oil during the night. Nials stepped forward.

"Urerla wishes to speak with the Avatar of Fire," he said in a carefully neutral voice, staring at Freddie who squirmed uncomfortably, a look of apprehension on his face.

"What did he say?"

"Urerla wants to see you," Eleanor told him. Freddie looked at her, eyebrows raised in surprise.

"If she can't have Conlan, maybe she'd settle for you instead?" Will said quietly with a smirk.

"It would be nice if someone did," Freddie muttered, giving Conlan a reproachful glance.

"The Avatar of Fire is going to need an interpreter," Eleanor said to Nials. The man nodded and smiled at her.

"Urerla is aware of this and has asked for you to accompany him."

"How am I going to speak to Urerla?" Freddie asked of nobody in particular.

"Eleanor is going with you as an interpreter," Will told him. Freddie stared at him in open-mouthed horror.

The others' laughter followed Eleanor and Freddie as they left the building and stepped out into the hot, bright sun, the door closing behind them. Eleanor squinted, as the light was disorientating. Firm hands took her wrists and tied them behind her back again. Her shoulders protested, but she did not resist. Freddie was likewise restrained. Eleanor felt an energy string brush against her. She pulled it in, feeling Freddie's hot, agitated presence fill her head. He said nothing, as he did not seem to know what to say; he just sent her his feelings of discomfort and fear. Eleanor smiled, sending him

understanding and her confidence that they would be fine. She felt him calm
slightly, but he did not withdraw his energy. They followed Nials in silence
through the village. Now the rain had stopped there were more people
walking around. Black eyes regarded them with a mixture of curiosity and
distrust. Eleanor noticed nearly everyone they saw carried evidence of ritual
scaring, and even the children who ran past them had the raised dots under
their eyes; she wondered if it was painful having them done. At the far end
of the village was a large enclosure with horses milling around inside. To the
left of this paddock was another mud-built, single-storey building. It was far
bigger than any of the other buildings they had passed and it looked as if it
had been added to over time in a very haphazard way. Huge wooden double
doors that reminded Eleanor of the gate they had entered the encampment
through stood open to reveal a dark, gaping hole. Eleanor could see nothing
within. On each side of the door stood a guard, black eyes endlessly
sweeping the environment in front of them, alert to danger. Nials walked
towards the doors.

"Urerla has asked to see these two," Nials said as he approached. The
guards looked Freddie up and down, before doing the same to Eleanor.

"I assume they have been stripped of weapons," one of the guards asked.

Freddie, are you still carrying any weapons?

No, they found them all. Why?

I just don't think it would be advisable to enter this building armed, Eleanor replied,
eyeing the guards warily.

"They have been searched, they carry no weapons," Nials confirmed. The
guard nodded and Nials continued forward into the building. Freddie and
Eleanor followed. Once through the door, Eleanor stood still for a moment,
allowing her eyes to become accustomed to the dark. Nials noticed her stop.

"Are you alright?"

Eleanor nodded and continued forward again.

Are you OK?

Yes, Freddie, it was just the change in light, it's dark in here.

Yeah! And creepy, Freddie agreed.

At the far end of the room, against the back wall, Eleanor could see a huge
cage; it stood the full height of the room and would easily have housed ten
men. Her eyes still adjusting to the dark, Eleanor walked a little closer,
curious about what was inside. Freddie followed her.

Up there, on that perch, he noted. *It looks like that bird Amelia caught.*

Eleanor followed his gaze to the top-right corner of the cage and saw what he was talking about. The bird was identical, and even the speckled golden-brown feathers appeared to match perfectly with the image she had in her head of the eagle Amelia had caught. Without warning, the corrupt file in her head suddenly swam into sharp focus and she remembered, the shock strong enough for the images to crash through her defences and into Freddie's mind, too.

"Osser," she murmured.

Well that explains where the green bottle came from, Freddie said, his voice a little shaky as Eleanor's memories faded. Eleanor realised that Nials was stood at her side; he had a strange scrutinising look on his face, an eyebrow raised in suspicion. Eleanor wondered what she had done.

"This bird is called Putt. She is normally livelier, but her son, Osser, is currently missing. She is lonely," he said, looking at Eleanor as if waiting for her to say something. The implications of his look charged through her head. *He thinks I had something to do with Osser's disappearance. I'm an idiot.* Having no idea what she should be saying, and worried about saying the wrong thing, Eleanor turned back to look at the bird, which stared at her with malevolent yellow eyes, reminding her of the dragon.

"Poor bird," she said softly in Dwarfish, layering the words with sympathy. Nials regarded her for a little while longer, giving her the chance to speak. When it became clear she was going to say nothing more he gave her one last glare, turned away from the cage and walked on, expecting them to follow. Nials led them through a door at the back of the entrance hall, walking into and down a long tiled corridor. They passed several doors, but Nials took them through the one at the far end, which led out into glorious sunshine. Once again, Eleanor was momentarily blinded. When her eyesight returned she found herself in a beautiful garden. Not quite as impressive as Conlan's mother's, but it was close and a lot bigger. There was a riot of brightly colourful flowers and the smell a familiar intoxicating scent that brought back strong memories of Conlan's smiling face. Several large trees housed in enormous earthenware pots offered dappled shade in various places, benches beneath them. Tiled paths wove through the plants, leading to larger squares of tiles with tables and chairs set out.

"Wow," Freddie breathed, looking around him. Nials smiled – no interpretation was needed. Like Jarrick's courtyard, the garden was boxed in on all sides with buildings which all had doors and windows opened to the stunning view before them. At one end of the garden was a tall water fountain, a large pond underneath it to catch the water. Urerla was sat on the lip of the pond, her hand making lazy circles in the water beneath her. She had changed her clothes and now wore a simple, loose-fitting, sleeveless white dress that seemed to be made of many layers of delicate, see-through material. She still had the heavy gold belt at her waist, and it jingled as she stood to greet them.

"The Avatar of Fire," Nials said a little stiffly, his face strangely emotionless. Urerla smiled, and the already stunning woman became instantly angelically beautiful. Freddie stared at her, wide-eyed and open mouthed.

Freddie, close your mouth, you look like an idiot, Eleanor said, amused when he jumped and snapped his jaw shut.

"Thank you, Nials, you may leave them with me," Urerla said, her eyes focused solely on Freddie, who had recovered enough to grin inanely back at her. Nials left the garden, Eleanor thought he closed the door with a little more force than he had needed to. Urerla took her eyes from Freddie for a moment to glance at Eleanor.

"And who are you, child?" she asked with a condescending little smile. Eleanor smiled back at her. If they could make allies with these people without having to marry Conlan off, all the better. Being friendly might help this cause.

"My name is Eleanor and he is Freddie," she replied nodding at her friend, who was still grinning, transfixed by Urerla.

"Is he really the Avatar of Fire?" she asked. Eleanor nodded. Urerla's eyes narrowed in suspicion.

"Can he prove it?" she asked.

Irritated on Freddie's behalf, Eleanor nodded. "Yes he can. Do you have fish in this fountain?" Urerla shook her head. Eleanor smiled grimly and turned to Freddie. "Freddie, Urerla wants you to prove you're the Avatar of Fire, could you please heat the water in this fountain?" Eleanor asked. Freddie broke eye contact with Urerla to look at Eleanor with a bemused expression and shrugged. Urerla jumped back as the water in the pond under the fountain began to boil gently; moving forward again, she held her hand over the water, feeling its heat.

That's enough, Freddie. Nice control by the way, where did you get the energy from?

You sound like you're praising a dog. The fire baskets on the walls of this place burn day and night.

Eleanor giggled. *Not a dog, more like a monkey.*

Freddie smirked at her. Urerla had turned back to look at Freddie, a strange look in her eyes that Eleanor did not understand, but she felt the tension in Freddie's body.

"Would you both like to come and sit with me for a while?" Urerla asked.

"She wants you to sit with her," Eleanor told Freddie, whose eyes were firmly riveted back on the beautiful woman in front of him. He nodded emphatically. Eleanor nodded too, not that Urerla seemed to notice. She led them through the maze of tiled paths that meandered through the garden, Freddie watching her hips sway as she walked, the gentle sound of her tinkling belt filling the air. She led them to a small bench under a weeping willow, whose branches offered a screen to prying eyes, giving them some privacy. The comfortable-looking sofa underneath was only designed for two, and Urerla guided Freddie to one end; her light, delicate fingers brushed against his chest, pushing him to sit. She sat down next to him, very close, their thighs touching. Eleanor huffed and with difficulty sat on the floor at Freddie's feet. They both ignored her.

"I need to tell you some things," Urerla said. Eleanor translated. Freddie nodded.

"I am getting older, and my mother has been insisting for a while that I find a husband. Unfortunately the choice is less than encouraging, as I want someone special," Urerla said, leaning into Freddie, her fingers running gentle circles around his chest as she looked into his eyes. Eleanor translated her words.

"Was Conlan not special enough for her?" Freddie asked with a sneer. Urerla heard his tone and looked questioningly at Eleanor, who faithfully repeated what Freddie had said. A pained expression passed quickly across Urerla's face before the angelic smile returned.

"I approached Conlan first because his was a higher status than your own, not because I found him more attractive. I thought it would be easier to convince my mother if my choice was high-born. But you are an Avatar and I was unprepared for just how impressive that would be," Urerla said in soft, silky tones. Eleanor rolled her eyes and translated in flat monotone.

Please tell me you don't believe this, Freddie.

Not a word.

"You want him to marry you? Why not just ask him?" Eleanor snapped bluntly at Urerla. The woman turned to glare at Eleanor with unconcealed dislike.

"You are very annoying, child. You are here to translate, nothing more," she said, her voice cold.

What did she say?

She said I'm annoying.

Wow, Eleanor, that's impressive – she's known you all of five minutes…

"I would very much like to be your wife," Urerla said, leaning closer still and running her hand slowly up the inside of Freddie's thigh as Eleanor translated.

She has a very persuasive argument, Freddie mused.

Freddie, if you are actually planning on having sex with this woman, I'd appreciate not having to translate the throws of passion.

Jealous much!

No, I'm just nauseated.

"Erm, Eleanor, could you ask her not to go any higher? Also, could you *politely* decline her offer?" Freddie said as he tried to pull himself up on the sofa and away from Urerla's questing hand, a task made difficult with his hands tied behind his back. At his words, Urerla looked expectantly at her. Thoroughly irritated with the whole situation, Eleanor glared back.

"Freddie does not wish to marry you, sorry. Also, he would appreciate it if you removed your hand, as you are making him uncomfortable," Eleanor said. Urerla glared at her, her lip curled in disgust, giving an ugly aspect to the beautiful face.

"You are entirely too bold for a child. Perhaps you need to be taught some respect," she said in a cold voice.

"Get in line…" Eleanor muttered in English, holding the woman's suspicious, irritated look. Urerla turned back to Freddie and smiled, then laying her body against his she kissed him savagely. Her many layers of dress covered both of them so Eleanor could not see, but judging from the wide-eyed surprise on Freddie's face, Urerla's hand had reached its target. Despite being forced into it, Freddie was kissing her back, Eleanor noticed with mild disgust. She rose to her knees and, standing with difficulty, walked away down to the far end of the garden, towards the exit, wondering how far Freddie would let Urerla go and if he would be given the chance to stop it. She could still feel his presence in her head, and if she concentrated really hard she could vaguely sense his feelings, which were currently amused pleasure. Eleanor had not really considered where she was going, she just did not feel like being witness to Urerla's desperate attempts to bag a husband. She reached the door they had entered the garden through and, with difficulty, trying to aim by watching over her shoulder, she managed to get her hand round the handle. Unfortunately as her fingers closed over the smooth metal, someone opened the door from the other side and pulled her backwards. With a 'woomph' of air from her lungs, Eleanor landed painfully at the feet of Nials.

"Eleanor? What are you doing here?" he asked, helping her to stand.

"What Freddie and Urerla are doing no longer requires my services as a translator, so I was leaving," Eleanor said without thinking. Nials gasped. Eleanor looked at his face and saw the raw fury fill his eyes before he turned from her, searching the garden for them. He heard Urerla giggle in delight from under the willow tree's branches. His body tensed, and with fists clenched he marched towards them.

Freddie, Nials has just found out what you're doing. He doesn't look very happy about it and he's heading your way.

Eleanor felt her mind fill with Freddie's panic.

Eleanor, help! Urerla doesn't understand me and she won't get off.

Eleanor ran towards where she had left Freddie and saw Nials draw the tree's hanging branches apart with such force that for an instant the air around him was filled with long, thin, falling leaves.

"Urerla!" he yelled, fury making his voice higher than normal.

Eleanor felt an echo of Freddie's pain as Nials hit him. Running faster, she arrived in time to see the second blow hit the side of his face. Nials had dragged Freddie from the sofa, pinning him to the ground a knee on his chest, gripping the collar of his shirt he was punching him repeatedly in the face, each blow making his head bounce off the stone beneath him. Urerla watched in horrified despair, tears running down her face, saying nothing and making no move to help Freddie.

"Nials, stop it, please. He cannot fight back," Eleanor said.

"Good," Nials snarled, hitting Freddie again. "That will make it quicker."

"Make what quicker?" Eleanor asked in confusion.

"His death," Nials replied coldly as he stood and began kicking at Freddie's prone body, his foot making bruising contact. Freddie grunted in pain and pulled his legs towards his chest in an attempt to protect his vital organs. In desperation Eleanor moved between them. Nials stopped and glowered at her.

"I have no wish to hurt you, Eleanor," he panted. "But I will if you do not get out of the way."

Eleanor nodded grimly. "I have no wish to hurt you either, but I will if you do not leave him alone. This was not Freddie's fault. This is totally down to her!" Eleanor said, giving Urerla a bitter, angry glare.

"How dare you!" Nials spat out, taking a menacing step forward.

Listen to me – fix Urerla and Nials up, get them together. They've been sneaking lustful glances at each other since we first met them...

What? Freddie, I don't understand...

Eleanor waited for a response, but when none was forthcoming she looked down. Freddie did not look conscious and she felt his energy string slip from her mind. Panicked, Eleanor turned to Nials.

"Untie me, I have to check him. I need to know he is OK."

"I want him dead, how dare he touch Urerla," Nials said, staring coldly at Freddie's inert form.

Exasperated, Eleanor glared at him. "Freddie has his hands tied behind his back, so how can he have touched anything? Urerla has been doing all the touching!"

"Why would she do that?" Nials demanded.

"Because she has been told she needs a husband, and like a lot of women she has overlooked the obvious to aim for the unobtainable," Eleanor said, seeing Urerla raise angry eyes to hers.

"Why should I not want someone special as my husband?" she asked, sounding very whiny.

Eleanor shrugged. "No reason. It just depends on what you class as special. You might think you want Freddie because he is an Avatar, because he is different and exciting, but he snores, he has no manners, his sense of humour is deeply twisted and he is probably incapable of fathering children."

Urerla stared at her. "He felt very capable to me," she murmured. Eleanor shook her head, trying to dislodge the rather unpleasant image Urerla had just put into it. Nials raised an eyebrow and glanced from Freddie to Urerla and back again. Freddie's energy string brushed weakly against her.

What are you saying? Freddie asked, sounding a little groggy, even in her head. Eleanor gave him a quick translation, relieved he was conscious again.

I have manners! he said indignantly.

No you don't, Eleanor retorted.

"So if I do not want Freddie, who do I want?" Urerla asked petulantly.

Eleanor smiled at her. "Well, how about Nials? He seems to be a good man and he came charging over here to defend your honour, however misguided. You could marry him."

Urerla dropped her head and sighed. "I have known Nials since we were children. He knows all my nasty secrets, knows what I am really like. He does not want me."

"Yes I do," Nials said softly, a slow grin spreading across his face.

Good call, Freddie! Nials just told Urerla he wants her, Eleanor said, impressed.

The way they were looking at each other it was sort of obvious. I think this whole thing with Conlan and I was Urerla's attempt to make Nials jealous. I guess it worked.

Urerla looked up at Nials, a stunning smile lighting up her eyes. "Why did you not say something?" she asked in confusion.

"I thought my feelings would not be returned, I was afraid of being rejected," Nials said, looking a little uncomfortable.

What are they saying now?

Nials says he didn't say anything because he was afraid of being rejected, Eleanor translated.

I can understand that, Freddie said.

Me too, Eleanor agreed. *Personally, I think he's very brave, Urerla strikes me as being a bit of a pain in the arse.*

Yeah, but she's a great kisser.

Eleanor glanced down at Freddie still lying at her feet; he gave her a smirk as he pushed his body to sit, wincing in pain as it pulled some of his new bruises. They watched as Urerla stood and walked hesitantly towards Nials. She stopped in front of him, trembling slightly, all the confidence she had shown with Freddie gone. Stepping towards her, Nials took her face in both hands and kissed her soundly. She wrapped her arms around him, and as he gazed down, Urerla smiled at him.

"I love you, I always have," she whispered. Nials hugged her tight to him, a look of disbelieving joy on his face.

Why can't love always be that easy? Freddie asked, and Eleanor felt a strong wave of his unhappiness. She dropped to her knees in front of him so she could look him in the eyes.

"I'm sorry, Freddie," she whispered.

He gazed at her, then leant forward and kissed her. Hot, soft lips pushed into hers. For a moment Eleanor was too stunned to respond. Freddie took this as a sign to continue and pushed harder against her, his tongue running along her lips and parting them, entering her mouth, urgent, forceful. It was the metallic, copper taste that brought Eleanor back to herself. Freddie's mouth tasted of blood. She gasped, pulling away out of his reach.

He grinned at her. "Sorry," he said, but he sounded anything but. "You were just so close and I wanted so much to know what it felt like."

"And has your curiosity been satisfied?" Eleanor asked tartly.

"If I said 'no', would you let me try again?" Freddie asked with a sly grin.

Eleanor glared at him and Freddie's confidence slipped.

"Please don't be mad at me, Eleanor."

"Promise me you'll never kiss me like that again without my permission," she said coldly, angry that he thought he could just push himself on her and it would not matter.

"I promise, I'm sorry." This time he actually sounded sorry. Feeling bad for hurting him again, Eleanor smiled, knowing she was sending him mixed messages but not caring.

"So who is the better kisser, me or Urerla?" she asked, giving him the chance to joke it off.

"A gentleman never kisses and tells," he said pompously. "See, I do have manners," he added with another wicked grin. Before he could say anything further, Nials appeared at his side. Stooping, he helped Freddie to his feet and then helped Eleanor up.

"Please tell him I am sorry," Nials said. Eleanor translated and Freddie smiled his acceptance of the apology.

"Thank you," Urerla said. "Thank you for pointing out what I could not see."

Eleanor smiled at the woman, who suddenly looked so much calmer and happier. "It was Freddie who noticed Nials was in love with you."

Urerla arched an eyebrow. "A truly remarkable man," she said softly, coming to stand in front of Freddie. He smiled at her and she kissed him gently on the forehead.

Freddie sighed. "Let me guess, another woman who just wants to be friends?" he mumbled.

Eleanor nodded. "It's your own fault for being such a wonderful friend."

Freddie rolled his eyes at her.

"I came here to tell you that Laurice wishes to see you," Nials said, his arm unconsciously wrapping round Urerla's waist pulling her closer. She melted into his body, sighing softly.

"Who is Laurice?" Eleanor asked.

"My mother, she leads our tribe and will decide what to do with you," Urerla replied.

"What is she likely to decide?" Eleanor asked as fear made a sudden grab at her. Nials and Urerla looked at each other with concern. Eleanor swallowed hard.

"She might decide to help you and direct you towards the tribe that holds the 'Heart', or she might just decide to have you escorted to the edge of our borders, or she could decide to have you executed," Urerla said. Eleanor blanched; execution was something she did not want to face.

"Urerla, you might want to talk to her before she makes her decision. We want to be your friends, your allies. Conlan *is* going to be King of Mydren, and an alliance with him would be beneficial to you, but if you try to execute us we will defend ourselves. We have allowed you to restrain us, allowed you to lock us up, but that was our choice. If you try to kill us we will destroy you," Eleanor said, seriously worried that these people might try something very ill-advised if she did not warn them. Nials snorted. The look he gave her was one of patronising amusement.

"We outnumber you four hundred to one, you would have no chance," he scoffed. Eleanor gave him a small smile.

"Actually, I could destroy every living soul within a hundred miles of here all by myself and there are four of us with that sort of power," she said. Turning her head and drawing a small amount of energy from the earth, she aimed it at a large palm tree in a big pot in the centre of the garden.

A loud cracking, splitting gunshot noise echoed around the courtyard and the tree and pot exploded. Disintegrated pulp expelled forcefully in all directions. From twenty feet away the air displaced by the explosion caused a shockwave and small pieces of tree and earth to patter against them.

"You are not a child," Urerla whispered, fear in her voice. She cringed against Nials' chest as he looked at the remains of the tree and back to Eleanor in horrified amazement. Not wanting Urerla to be frightened, just wanting her to understand, Eleanor smiled gently at her.

"No, I am not a child – I am the Avatar of Earth. I do not want to hurt you. We want to be your friends. Please tell your mother, please try to convince her that helping us would be a good thing."

The sound of the tree exploding brought running feet to the garden. Several men, including the guards they had seen on the door earlier, rushed into the garden from different directions with panicked faces and weapons drawn. They converged on Freddie and Eleanor. Rough hands grabbed their arms and sword points poked into flesh.

"I was assured they had been searched, that they had no weapons on them!" one of the guards snapped in a strange voice which was far too high for a man and sounded a lot like he had swallowed a squeaky dog toy. Still looking a little shocked, Nials nodded.

"They are not carrying weapons, Harnlyn, they *are* weapons," he said flatly.

"Then how do I disarm them?" Harnlyn asked with an expression of fearful distrust. Nials shrugged.

"You cannot and you might as well untie them and release them, as they are only tolerating their bonds because they wish to be our allies."

Harnlyn stared at Nials and Urerla, then back to Freddie and Eleanor. "If they are such a threat, would it not be safer to kill them?" With a shudder, Eleanor realised it was a serious question. Nials looked a little horrified.

"You see that tree?" he asked, pointing to the mess in the middle of the garden. Harnlyn nodded. "She did that," Nials continued, nodding at Eleanor. "From over here. She did not touch it, she just looked at it; it took no effort. What do you think would happen if she turned that power on you?"

Eleanor dropped her head in shame as images of Perry's body exploding flashed through her mind.

Harnlyn's panicked gaze oscillated between Nials and Eleanor. "Do they all have this power? Or is it just the child? Is there no way we can kill them?"

"We do not need to kill them, as they wish to be our friends. Just let them go," Urerla said pointedly.

Harnlyn controlled his mounting panic enough to flash Urerla a very patronising look. "How gullible you are – they say they can be trusted and you believe them!"

Nials and Harnlyn began to argue over what action should be taken; Eleanor tuned them out, hoping that Nials would win, otherwise she was going to have to kill again.

Are you OK? You look upset… What are they saying? Freddie asked.

Nials is telling this guy, Harnlyn, what I'm capable of doing. They've no idea, Eleanor replied, sending Freddie her feelings of self-loathing for the monster she knew she was. To her surprise Freddie sent her a memory, the memory of torching the three men who had hurt Amelia. As it played in her head, Freddie sent her all his feelings that went with it. His pain and grief over what had happened to Amelia and his strong desire to make someone pay for it burned brightly. There had been delight at finding the men and letting his power loose on them – how dare they hurt someone he loved?! Yet, as the men had staggered around the camp in burning, tortured agony, Freddie had felt guilt crash down on him. He had no idea why the men had attacked them. Did they have families? Had he mindlessly killed a young child's father? His previous existence had been about saving people from suffering the kind of death he had just unthinkingly inflicted. Then he had felt Eleanor pull her hand from his, the look of disgust on her face as she walked away from him. Watching the memory, Eleanor found herself playing back her own memory. Had she been disgusted? Yes, she had. Freddie's feelings of guilt and misery had intensified when he realised that even Eleanor did not believe his actions were justified.

You're not the only monster here, Freddie whispered as the memory came to an end.

I'm sorry I made you feel so bad; I had no right to judge.

Despite the men standing around them and the swords digging uncomfortably into their torsos, Freddie took a step towards her so that his body could touch hers.

"Do not move!" Harnlyn squeaked loudly in Freddie's surprised, uncomprehending face. "Nials and Urerla have vouched for you, but if you do anything I do not like, you will regret it!"

"He does not understand you," Eleanor said quietly.

Harnlyn glared at her warily. "Why not, is he stupid?" he sneered.

Eleanor bristled. "No, he just does not speak Dwarfish." *This man is an idiot.*

"Harnlyn, my mother asked to see them some time ago. She does not like to be kept waiting," Urerla said softly.

"I would be failing in my duty if I took these... abominations in front of my lady, Laurice," Harnlyn snapped.

"They are not abominations, they are Avatars," Urerla said, smiling at Eleanor.

"Same thing!" Harnlyn squeaked.

"Who told you we were abominations?" Eleanor asked, watching a guilty look cross Harnlyn's face.

Harish, I know that word. Did he just call us abominations? Freddie asked in surprise.

Yes he did, which is a little odd, don't you think?

Very, where did he hear it from?

I'm not sure, I asked him and he just looked guilty.

Could Harnlyn be working with Daratus? 'Abomination' was a Protector insult. It was a worrying development.

"I like them, Harnlyn, and I think my mother will, too," Urerla said, looking irritated by the withering look Harnlyn flashed at her.

"Take them to the audience chamber," Harnlyn snapped, not looking overly happy about his decision. Eleanor was dragged forward and towards a door on the other side of the garden. Freddie was dragged similarly behind her.

Should we be putting up a fight? Freddie asked.

No, not yet, we're going to see Laurice. Let's find out what she has to say before we burn our bridges totally.

Eleanor tried to pay attention to where they were being taken, but the building was like a rabbit warren and was even harder to navigate than the Dwarves' mountain. The hands gripping her arms were digging in painfully and it was distracting. Furthermore, the man holding her was doing so at a height that was comfortable for him, which meant Eleanor was forced to walk on tiptoe or risk getting pulled off her feet. After quite a few twists and turns, they entered a large, light, airy room. Still only a single storey high, Eleanor looked up to see that the ceiling was missing; she could see the cloudy sky through it. However, the room did not look like it ever got wet. *A retractable roof? Clever.* The small frame of remaining ceiling had been decorated to match the walls and floor with different sized squares of bright, bold colours. Red, green, blue, yellow; it should have looked gaudy, but for some reason it actually looked very sophisticated and regal. In the middle of the room was the only furniture – a simple wooden chair on a raised wooden platform – and in front of it Eleanor could see Will, Amelia, Conlan and Merl standing calmly within a circle of armed, mean-looking guards. Men and women stood around in small groups, talking in low voices, and every so often their black eyes would stray to the middle of the room as the result of either interest or suspicion. Eleanor and Freddie were dragged over to their friends. The circle of guards parted and they were shoved forward. Eleanor struggled to keep her feet. Falling forward, a body stepped in front of her, stopping her headlong dive for the floor as she fell against it. Standing up again, she raised her eyes to find Merl looking at her, a friendly smile on his face.

"Thank you," she said, returning his smile.

He nodded. "You are most welcome."

"Did you have fun with Urerla?" Will asked Freddie, a mischievous smirk on his face. Eleanor turned and saw Freddie's face flush with embarrassment.

"Did she do that to you, too?" he asked Conlan, ignoring Will.

Conlan chuckled. "She tried."

"What did he say?" Merl asked, watching the conversation. Conlan translated for him, which prompted Merl to ask what Urerla had tried to do. As quickly as she could, Eleanor told Merl, Conlan and Will what had happened to her and Freddie, also explaining about Osser and the memory that had returned. She had just got to the bit where Nials had dragged her backwards through the door, when Harnlyn marched towards them from the back of the room. The guards parted as he approached and he grabbed

Eleanor by the collar.

"You will not speak," he ordered in a harsh tone that was ruined by his high-pitched, squeaky voice.

Eleanor giggled. "You want to bet?" she countered, using a low growl through some of the Dwarfish to add a hint of a just how absurd she found the man.

"We are trying to make them our allies, remember?" The snarl Conlan gave to the word 'remember' made it a harsh rebuke.

"This man is an idiot," Eleanor said, turning her head to look at Conlan and trying to convey with her eyes that he could be working with Daratus, the subtext to her comment implying he was far worse than an idiot. Conlan's eyes became fractionally wider and he lifted his gaze to scrutinise Harnlyn's livid, speechless fury. Eleanor heard sniggers and whispers from their immediate vicinity; she was not the only one who thought Harnlyn was a moron. *Daratus should choose his accomplices better, unless Harnlyn had been chosen for the very fact that he was an idiot who would get caught, thus moving suspicion away from another, more devious enemy.* Eleanor was so involved in her churning thoughts that she did not notice Conlan had moved to stand next to her until he spoke.

"I regret not teaching my Avatar more respect. She will apologise," he said quietly.

Harnlyn finally found his voice. "She insulted me and I will not let that pass. She will be punished," he spluttered, but despite the words and the implications, his ridiculous voice still made Eleanor want to laugh.

Conlan sighed. "I cannot allow you to do that."

"Then you insult me, too!" Harnlyn's indignant squeak was made even more laughable after Conlan's beautiful, deep voice.

"That was not my intention," Conlan said softly, a thin layer of civility over a deep layer of menace.

What's going on? Freddie suddenly piped up in Eleanor's head, making her jump. Harnlyn eyed her suspiciously.

Long story. Basically, I just insulted Harnlyn and he wants to punish me, Eleanor replied, doing her best to retain her calm.

Harnlyn shook her again. "An insult of this nature demands ten cuts," he insisted, his voice moving to an even higher pitch as a result of his anger and obvious anxious stress.

Conlan's not going to agree, is he? Freddie said as his concern hit her.

I've got no idea... I don't know if the current situation is going to give him the option to stop it.

Not wanting to ruin Conlan's chances of an alliance just to protect her, Eleanor forced herself to cower, shake slightly and beg.

"Please, please do not hurt me. I am sorry – really, really sorry."

Running the memories of Conlan rejecting her through her head again, she felt tears building and lifted her watery eyes to Harnlyn, giving him a moment to see her terror before she spoke again.

"I was wrong to insult you. I was just frightened and stupid and said the first thing that came into my head. Why would you want to hurt someone as insignificant and small as me? Surely you have better things to do than punish a rude child?" she sniffled as the tears fell, wondering if she had taken it too far. Would Harnlyn see through her rather crass manipulation?

"She hardly seems worth it," said one of the guards behind them.

"Yeah, let her go, Harnlyn, she is just a child and you have frightened her enough," agreed another. Harnlyn looked at the faces around him and then back to Eleanor, dull hatred in his eyes. He let go of her collar. She staggered back and was caught by one of the guards behind her, who then pushed her back to her feet.

Did you just beg for mercy? Freddie asked.

Eleanor sighed. *Yes I did, was it convincing?*

Definitely – and I didn't understand a word of it.

Wonderful, she said flatly.

Harnlyn continued to stare malignantly at Eleanor before storming off out of the room. Conlan gave Eleanor a hard, disapproving look.

"He may be idiot enough to believe your act, but I'm not. This isn't over, Eleanor, we'll be discussing it further," he murmured in English.

"He called us abominations, Conlan, a Protector insult. He's not just an idiot, he's not to be trusted," Eleanor said. Conlan nodded, but he did not speak further. They lapsed into silence, waiting. Freddie even stopped talking in her head, although he did not remove his energy string.

The cloud cover above them had begun to dissipate and the afternoon light faded into evening before Laurice finally made her entrance. Eleanor's shoulders and arms were beginning to throb unpleasantly from being tied behind her back most of the day; it made her feel crabby and miserable. Blood had soaked the cuffs of her shirt and jacket from her failed attempts to loosen the ropes and relieve the strain. She regretted taking her leather cuff off, as at least one of her wrists would have been protected. Nobody else was complaining though, and Eleanor knew that Freddie was in a more damaged state than she was. A door at the back of the room was slammed open, and through some unseen signal the idle chatter that had filled the room ceased immediately.

Finally! I was beginning to think the stupid woman would never get here, Freddie said loudly in her head, making Eleanor jump. Next to her, Conlan saw the movement, or perhaps felt her surprise, and turned to look at her. Eleanor shrugged and Conlan gave her an irritated, disapproving glare before looking back at the woman who was walking towards them. Urerla was a stunning woman, but in comparison to her mother she was an imperfect copy. Laurice was tall, lithe and muscular, her black skin somehow luminous. She wore tight trousers and a rough shirt over long, toned legs and a large bust. There was a heavy gold link belt around her curvaceous hips; it was similar to Urerla's, but her belt held considerably more charms and precious stones, meaning it made more of a noise as she walked. Eleanor realised this was what had caused the silence to spread through the room – they had heard her coming. Laurice's perfectly proportioned body moved with a delicate grace that belied its strength, and her hips swayed in the same way Urerla's did.

Is that how women are meant to walk? Eleanor asked, noticing that Freddie, Conlan, Will and Merl all had their attention on Laurice, their eyes following her every movement.

Freddie laughed. *That's how some women are meant to walk, but if you or Amelia started walking around like that we'd never get anything done!*

Why not? Eleanor asked, slightly nonplussed.

Because it would be far too distracting. It's bad enough when you wear those tight short-sleeved shirts Callie gave you!

What's wrong with my shirts?

Eleanor, they show every curve of your perfect little body, just like a second skin, and it's very hard to concentrate on anything other than you when you're wearing one.

Is that ALL men think about? Eleanor asked irritably.

Freddie laughed again. *Pretty much, but we'd think about it a lot less if women stopped putting temptation in front of us.*

My mother was right! Eleanor muttered darkly.

Freddie's laughter was still ringing in her head as Laurice reached her chair and sat down. She crossed her legs gracefully and stared down at them. There were small laughter lines at the corners of her eyes and mouth that gave her the appearance of age, but she certainly did not look old enough to be Urerla's mother. She also had the raised dots of ritual scaring under her eyes; hers too were more elaborate than the ones Eleanor had seen in the general population. *Maybe it's so the royal family can be identified? Does that mean Yatt was a member of the royal family?* Laurice's black eyes showed the same intelligence as Urerla's, but they also held something else – a knowing, the impression of life experience; this was not a woman who would be easily fooled.

"Which one of you is Conlan Baydon?" she asked in a voice that sounded like a chiming bell, her eyes scanning across their faces.

"I am," Conlan said, stepping forward as far as their circle of guards would allow.

"I have heard some strange things about you and your Avatars. I am interested in hearing the truth," Laurice said, the underlying Dwarfish stating he had better tell the truth, or she was going to make him suffer.

"As I am interested in speaking it," Conlan assured her.

"Is it true that one of your Avatars destroyed my favourite tree in my private garden?" she asked mildly. Conlan's eyes immediately flicked to Eleanor.

Shrugging sheepishly, she nodded.

"Apparently it is," he said, giving Eleanor a disgusted look before turning back to Laurice as she spoke again.

"Is it true that this same Avatar was rude to Nials, my most trusted horseman, when she first met him?"

"Yes, she was rude, but in fairness she was trying to protect her friend by getting Nials to remove a knife from his throat," Conlan answered. Laurice raised an eyebrow at Conlan's defence of Eleanor's actions, but she did not comment; instead, she moved on to her next accusation.

"And is it true that this same Avatar also insulted Harnlyn, the captain of my house guard?" Laurice asked, her tone still deceptively mild.

"Yes, this is true, although the Avatar has apologised to Harnlyn and will be apologising for the loss of your tree," Conlan said. His voice was calm and steady, but Eleanor could see his fists clenched tightly at his sides. He was furious.

"You do not seem to have much control over your creations," Laurice observed. Conlan did not respond, just held Laurice's look until she spoke again. "It would seem your Avatar requires a lesson in respect," she said, standing. "Nials, bring Conlan Baydon and the wayward Avatar to my chambers and we will deal with this now. Lock the others back up."

Eleanor glanced at Conlan, she could feel his apprehension. Nials came from the back of the room, a stern look on his face, the circle of guards parted and he took Eleanor's arm, pulling her forward. Conlan followed.

What's going on? Freddie asked.

I think I'm in trouble. The tree I exploded was Laurice's favourite; she's going to punish me, Eleanor said. Even in her head, her voice sounded frightened and small.

Conlan won't let them hurt you, Freddie assured her.

Right now I think he'd be cheering them on. I think he's rather angry with me.

What should I do? Freddie asked. Eleanor felt his concern again.

I don't think there is anything you can do right now, but would you please leave my head? If they're going to do something unpleasant, I'd rather you didn't have to suffer it with me.

Are you sure? I don't mind, and maybe I could help.

Eleanor shuddered at the thought of losing control and screaming or crying with Freddie in her head. It would be a horrid thing to do to him.

No, really, I'll be better off on my own.

OK, but only if you're sure, Freddie replied, sounding hurt.

With her attention on what Freddie had been saying, Eleanor had not noticed the twists and turns they were taking, and she was surprised when Nials opened a large ornate wooden door onto what looked like someone's office. In front of them, across the room, stood a massive wooden desk, paper, books and writing instruments scattered messily across it, the chair behind it facing a large open window that looked out over the garden Eleanor had been in earlier. She could see people cleaning up the mess she had made of the tree. In the middle of the room, within the boarder of a rich, colourful rug, were two overstuffed sofas that looked as if they were rarely used. They faced each other, a low table in between. Along the back wall of the room were bookcases, filled to overflowing with books, papers and charts. There did not seem to be any order to it. In the corner of the room was an 'A' frame of polished wood, on which sat the most beautiful saddle Eleanor had ever seen. It was made of a snake-like leather, it had an almost metallic green colour to it and the stirrups and edges were adorned with small red gems that sparkled even in the fading evening light. Hanging on the wall, next to the saddle, was a painting so large that the bottom of the frame was inches from the floor, while the top actually touched the ceiling. The painting was the remarkably life-like image of a horse – a beautiful horse – its pure black coat shining over its defined, strong, muscled body, elegant grace with an air of noble, equine intelligence. It stood to attention, one front hoof lifted as if he was ready to spring out of the painting. Impressed, Eleanor walked towards the image and studied it slowly so that she would always remember it.

"That is Meran, my husband's horse," Laurice said. Eleanor jumped at her voice and turned to see the woman enter the room and close the door behind her.

"I am sorry I destroyed your favourite tree and insulted your people," Eleanor said quickly before Laurice could speak and say something irreversible like 'chop off her head!' "I speak and act without thinking," Eleanor continued. "But I really do not want that to reflect badly on Conlan, as it is not his fault I have no self-discipline." Expecting violence or at the very least someone to yell at her, Eleanor was surprised when Laurice laughed, a wonderful, full, rich sound of pure amusement.

"Child, do I look like someone who cares very much about trees or the fragile pride of men?" she asked, smiling at her. Confused, Eleanor looked the woman up and down and immediately noted the strength and confidence in her face and body and the intelligence in her eyes.

"No, you do not strike me as someone who cares about those things, so why are we here?" she asked bluntly.

"Eleanor, that was rude," Conlan chastised quietly, looking just as confused as she was.

Laurice gave him a scornful look. "Do not stifle her spirit; you will have need of it if you truly wish to be king. She has a disconcerting ability to see to the heart of people, which is a useful thing to know if you wish to rule. She certainly recognised Harnlyn for the fool he is," she said, turning to Nials. "Untie them, please, I do not believe them to be a threat. And can we have some light in here?"

Nials nodded and took a knife from his belt. Stepping behind Conlan he cut through his restraints, doing the same for Eleanor. She gasped at the sharp pain that ran through her shoulders as her arms moved from her previously locked position. Moving away from them, he began lighting the lanterns that were placed around the room.

Laurice scrutinised Eleanor for a long time before she spoke.

"To answer your question, child, you are here because I wish to thank you for helping my daughter see sense – you have made her very happy – and also to find out what you can tell me about Yatt, Millice and a bird called Osser. Nials was out looking for them when he stumbled across your group. He heard you mention Osser to your friend while you were looking at Putt. I would appreciate the truth," Laurice said in the same mild tone.

Eleanor looked questioningly at Conlan.

"Tell her," he said quietly. Eleanor nodded, turning back to Laurice.

"It is a rather long story," she said.

Laurice's eyes flashed with hope. "You have seen them then?"

Eleanor nodded. "Yes, I saw them but they are dead. I am sorry," she said, layering the Dwarfish with her grief and sympathy. Eleanor watched the hope in the woman's eyes die and be replaced by a deep pain. Laurice moved to one of the sofas and dropped gracelessly down to it. Feeling bad for her, Eleanor moved to crouch at her side so she could look into Laurice's blank face. Her black eyes burned with grief.

"I am sorry, they meant a lot to you?" she asked.

Laurice looked at her, agony in her eyes.

"Yatt was my son," she whispered. Seeing her distress and wanting to help, Eleanor reacted without thinking. Standing, she put her arms around the woman and hugged her close. Laurice stiffened, and realising her mistake, Eleanor released her.

"Sorry," she said.

Laurice quirked her a small smile. "There is no need for apologies. Come, sit. You had better tell me what happened."

Eleanor told Laurice the whole story, placing heavy emphasis on how Yatt had given them the antidote to the darts and had tried to help them, despite the situation. While Eleanor knew some of the story was new to Conlan, his expression remained a passive blank canvas throughout.

"He was irresponsible and reckless, but he had a good heart," Laurice said sadly. "This third man, could your friend Merl identify him, if he saw him?" she asked Conlan. Eleanor saw the threat in the woman's eyes.

"Perhaps, but you would have to ask him. Merl acted in our defence. Whatever your son's reasons, he attacked us," Conlan replied.

"I do not place blame on Merl," Laurice said softly, holding Conlan's gaze for several moments before looking over at Nials who was stood silently by the door. Eleanor could not read the look that passed between them, but Nials stuck his head out of the door, as if he was checking what was in the corridor. He then walked to the window and stared into the twilight gloom before shutting it tight and closing the heavy curtains across it. He turned back to Laurice and nodded. The woman looked at them for a moment, as if trying to make a decision.

"The news you bring me puts me in a difficult position. To help you understand, I feel I must explain, which means I must impart some very sensitive information. Can I trust you?" she asked. Conlan and Eleanor nodded in unison.

"Very well," Laurice said. "I am bringing you into a secret known only to Urerla, Nials and myself. Someone is trying to take my position from me. My husband died three moons ago. It appeared at the time to be an accident, but seeing as the only witness was his horse, we are unlikely to ever know the truth. There have been subtle attacks on my position since then, designed to undermine the respect my people have for me. Rumours and discontent at my decisions have abounded, and they never seem to come from the same person. It is proving to be impossible to track down the original source. Yatt took his father's death very hard. He never believed it was an accident, so he began investigating on his own. His suspicions fell on Harnlyn, and I am beginning to think he was right."

Eleanor nodded. "I think Harnlyn is working with or for a Lord of Mydren called Daratus, but I do not think he is your main traitor."

Conlan and Laurice looked at her questioningly. Eleanor smiled. "Harnlyn is a moron. Do you really feel he is capable of making your husband's death look like an accident or stirring up your people against you without being caught? I think Harnlyn is a decoy, perhaps even an unwitting one; someone with a far superior intellect is playing this game."

"What do you suggest?" Conlan asked. Eleanor closed her eyes and thought about it. They needed to flush out the real traitor, needed something important enough that he or she would handle it themselves.

"What is she doing?" she heard Laurice whisper to Conlan.

"Thinking," he replied, and Eleanor heard the hint of pride in his voice.

She smiled as several possibilities came to her.

"I need to ask some questions," she said, opening her eyes again. Laurice nodded.

"You brought Conlan and I here under the pretence of punishing me, so how were you planning on explaining that you did not, in fact, carry out the punishment?" Eleanor asked. There was silence. Eleanor looked from Laurice's pained expression to Nials' guilty look.

"Oh, you *are* going to carry out the punishment?" she whispered, frightened. *That changes things,* Eleanor thought as her mind began amending her plans, despite her fear.

"It would raise too much suspicion not to," Nials said, a strong current of apology running through the Dwarfish.

"What punishment were you planning on giving?" Conlan asked in a hard, cold voice. Nials hung his head, not able to look Conlan in the eye as he answered.

"Harnlyn was correct – ten cuts would be the expected punishment."

"I have no idea what that means," Eleanor whispered, knowing her terror was showing in her face and that it was strong enough for Conlan to be feeling it, too.

"It means as it suggests. Ten cuts down your side with a sword," Laurice said. Conlan rose to his feet.

"No, I will not allow it! Her body is too fragile to withstand such punishment. You will kill her."

"I will be careful," Nials said, still not able to look Conlan in the eye. Conlan stormed towards him, grabbing him by the throat and slamming him into the wall.

"I said 'NO'!" he snarled.

Nials struggled in Conlan's grip, not sure if he should be fighting back or not, his eyes flicking to Laurice in desperation. Worried that Conlan might actually damage the man, Eleanor leapt off the sofa and ran to his side. Placing a hand on his arm, she shook her head.

"Don't hurt him," she said in English. Not looking happy about it, Conlan nodded and let go of Nials' throat, leaving him coughing and spluttering as he returned to the sofa. Eleanor sat back down and stared for a moment at Laurice.

"This 'ten cuts', is this the only punishment available? Would there be any circumstances under which you may offer leniency?" Eleanor asked, pleased that she had managed to keep the fear out of her voice. Laurice considered this suggestion.

"Perhaps, if you were able to offer something considerable in return, I could reduce the punishment down to ten strokes instead," she said. "But I do not see how that helps, as you have nothing to offer."

"Ten strokes?" Conlan asked in a flat voice.

"Ten strokes with a horse whip," Nials said in a rough voice, rubbing his throat. "Not a serious punishment; we sometimes use it to discipline older children."

Eleanor looked at Nials in horror. *This is the best they can do?* She did not like it, but she had an idea and this was going to play right into it.

"If that is your best offer, I will take it," she said grimly.

"Eleanor, no," Conlan said, pain in his eyes. "You do not have to do this, we can fight our way out of here and find the tribe with the sword ourselves."

"It is alright, Conlan, I can do this," Eleanor assured him. "I have an idea; they will not get my blood for free."

"What do you have in mind, little Avatar?" Laurice asked, giving her an appraising look.

"You will give me ten strokes, telling everybody you reduced my punishment because I promised to read the mind of your husband's horse so I could tell you what happened to him," Eleanor said.

Laurice gasped. "Can you do that?"

Eleanor nodded. "I cannot guarantee that the horse saw anything, but your traitor does not know that. They will, however, need some time to think and react, but not too much time. You want them to be off-balanced, still in shock. So once you have punished me, explain that I needed time to recover and then lock us back up until tomorrow afternoon. Your traitor will be left with only three options to protect their identity: kill the horse, kill me or kill us both. You now know your traitor's next targets and a time frame for the attack. Do you think you can be ready?"

Laurice stared at her. "You are quite remarkable," she said softly, her growling undertone speaking of admiration and respect. "You said we would not get your blood for free. What do you want in return?"

Eleanor smiled. "I want you to swear your allegiance to Conlan. I want you to make your most solemn oath that you will fight at his side when he calls for you and that you will try your best to convince the other tribes to join him. I also want your help finding the tribe that holds the 'Heart' and to get it off them."

Laurice and Nials glanced at each other guiltily.

"You *are* the tribe that currently holds the 'Heart'," Conlan deduced. Laurice nodded.

"It would be unwise to advertise to strangers that we hold the 'Heart', so none of our tribe would admit to us having it. It is a security precaution."

"If you hold the 'Heart', does that mean you can make decisions for the other tribes? Can you swear allegiance to Conlan on behalf of all eight of them?" Eleanor asked. Laurice and Nials looked at each other again.

"Yes," Laurice confirmed.

"Then I wish to change my request. In return for my help in finding your traitor I want you to swear all eight tribes' allegiance to Conlan and agree to stand with him in battle when it comes. Oh, and I want you to give us the sword," Eleanor said, her voice calm and controlled. Laurice, Nials and Conlan stared at her.

"We will indeed be paying dearly for your blood," Laurice said softly. "I agree to your terms. I will swear allegiance to Conlan Baydon on behalf of the eight tribes and the sword will be yours before you leave."

There was an uncomfortable silence. Swallowing down her fear, Eleanor walked towards Nials. "You have a punishment to carry out," she said softly, irritated by her trembling voice.

"Eleanor, you don't have to do this," Conlan blurted out, the English carrying a distressed growl.

She smiled at him. "Please don't stop me. I need you to trust me, believe in me." She turned back to Nials, looking at him expectantly.

"Come with me," he said quietly, opening the door. Conlan was suddenly at her side.

"I am going with her," he said to Nials, who shrugged.

Eleanor shook her head.

"No, stay here... please." The soft snarl she put through the 'please' making it a begging request. Conlan held her pleading gaze.

"You should not have to face this alone, let me help you."

Eleanor sighed and shook her head again. "I know you care about me, so how do you think you are going to react?" Reluctantly, Conlan nodded and watched as she left the room.

Nials took her on another confusing route through the building's many dark corridors, lit by the occasional lantern hung on the wall. Trying not to think about what was coming, Eleanor concentrated on what they were gaining – the sword and a huge army for Conlan. *This is worth it*, she told herself over and over again. Nials led her into a dark room that smelt of horse sweat and saddle leather, a stable block she realised. As he moved around her, lighting lanterns, she saw more. There were several stalls along the walls – they all looked empty – and a large open square of space in the middle of the room.

"This is a quiet place. If you are able to refrain from crying out, we should not attract an audience," Nials said in a cold, empty voice. Too frightened to speak, knowing it would make her cry, Eleanor nodded.

"Take your jacket off and get down on your knees," Nials ordered in the same cold tone, pointing to the middle of the room. Eleanor dropped her jacket to the floor and walked slowly forward, her body trembling and legs barely able to hold her up. *They do this to their children! You can handle this!* she yelled at herself in her head. It did very little to dispel her terror. She dropped down to her knees and sat back on her heels. Nials crouched at her side and gently tugged at her shirt where it was tucked into the back of her trousers, pulling it free and up her back and over her head, leaving her arms still in the sleeves to allow her some modesty. She crossed her arms over her chest, holding the shirt to her, and leant forward slightly, feeling the chilly air create goosebumps on her skin.

"Do not let your body fall forward, Eleanor, keep straight," Nials said, his gentle fingers tracing the line of her spine over the vertebrae that pushed against the skin of her curved back. "If I strike the bones of your spine it will be very painful and I may cause permanent damage," he continued. "Do you understand?"

Again Eleanor nodded. Nials rested a light, comforting hand on her head for a moment before standing and moving across the room to pick up something. As he turned back towards her, Eleanor nearly passed out. Her heart pounded and beads of sweat sprang to her suddenly ice-cold skin. Fear squeezed her chest, and short, panting breaths were all she could manage. Her body trembled so hard that it was difficult to stay upright. Her mind spinning almost uncontrollably. She had expected to be hit with something like a riding crop – short and stubby; it would be painful, but it would mostly leave bruises. What Nials had in his hand was more like a bullwhip. Eleanor closed her eyes, wondering if it would help if she could not see it happening. It did not help. She heard the snapping swish of the lash's wicked tongue as it reached out greedily for her vulnerable flesh.

The first blow landed across her shoulders, a line of fire. Her body tensed and she gasped, shoving her hand into her mouth and biting down so hard that blood flowed over her lips and down her throat, but she made no further sound, forcing her body to keep upright and still. She had barely registered the first blow when the second one landed, the third and fourth agonies arriving in quick succession. Nials placed the lash over her shoulders and down her back, finding fresh unmarked skin with each stroke. Eleanor bit harder into her hand and tears filled her eyes. Desperate to pull away from the pain, she searched for a memory that might distract her. Conlan's face appeared, and leaning forward he kissed her forehead. The remembered bliss distracted her as the fifth and sixth blows fell, her body shuddering. The pain was beginning to make her mind falter.

Then suddenly it was over. Her body tensed in anticipation of the next pain, but none came. She could feel the deep, angry throb of the lines, warm blood running down her back from split, torn skin. The pain pounded over her in crashing, numbing waves, but it was manageable. Nials was at her side, his hand once again on her head.

"You did well, little one," he said softly, and Eleanor heard the distress in his voice. Gentle, careful hands helped Eleanor pull her shirt back over her head, and the material immediately stuck to the blood. Supporting her, Nials helped her to stand, the movement sending pain coursing through her back, spiking her brain and threatening to remove her consciousness as if someone was pulling a rug out from under her. She whimpered, swaying, her legs shaking.

"Take slow, deep breaths, you will feel better," Nials advised, still holding her firmly. Eleanor nodded and closed her eyes, expanding her lungs and letting the breath out in a slow, regular cycle. Nials was right; eventually she began to feel better.

"Do you feel ready to go back?" he asked. Still not able to speak, Eleanor nodded. Conlan would be worried, and she did not want to give him any further reason to be upset, as he was going to feel bad enough as it was. Nials led her back to Laurice's rooms; again, she paid little attention to the route, concentrating instead on getting her body used to the current level of pain surging through it with each step. If she could get more used to it, she could hide it better. She experimented moving her shoulders and gasped, staggering, using the wall for support to stop herself falling to the ground. Nials stopped and looked back at her, his black eyes full of sympathy and concern. He said nothing but waited until she had got herself together, before setting off again.

Conlan was up and across the room before Nials had finished opening the door. He stopped in front of her, agony in his eyes. He did not seem to know what to do or say. Behind him, still sat on the sofa, Laurice observed in guilty silence.

"I'm OK," Eleanor whispered in English.

"You don't look OK," Conlan commented in a rough voice.

"I'll live," she said, trying to make her voice stronger, giving him a smile and trying her hardest to convince him she was fine. "Plus now we have matching stripes," she added, hoping her meaning was clear. *You survived this, I can too.* He frowned at her for a moment and gave her one of his deep gazes before he spoke quietly.

"I know how much it hurts, Eleanor, you don't have to be brave."

Eleanor sighed. "Yes I do. I don't want this hurting you too, so I'm going to do my best to hide it. You can make it up to me when you rip out the traitor's still-beating heart and make him eat it."

Conlan tilted his head, giving her an expression she had never seen before; he looked proud of her, impressed. It was actually a very sweet expression that made her heart jump in her chest.

"I never realised you could be so bloodthirsty," he teased, smiling at her. She shrugged, immediately regretting the movement as pain twisted her stomach. She saw her pain reflected in Conlan's face and forced it back down inside.

Nials led them back through the dark, chilly night to the building where they were being held. As the door's bolt was pulled back, Conlan ran a hand over Eleanor's head, a soft comfort. She smiled gratefully at him and they stepped inside. The door slammed shut. Four pairs of eyes turned towards them as they entered. *I must look awful*, Eleanor realised as she took in the horrified expressions on her friends' faces.

"Will, Eleanor needs medical attention," Conlan said quietly. Concerned, his eyes flicking between Eleanor's face and Conlan's, Will retrieved his medical bag. Freddie jumped to his feet.

"Eleanor? Are you OK, what happened?" he asked softly. She had no idea what she should be saying, as her mind was putting too much effort into dealing with her pain; she just wanted to sleep. Not understanding her silence and wanting to offer comfort, Freddie wrapped his arms around her, pulling her into a hug. As he made contact with her back and shoulders, Eleanor cried out, pain clawing at her and tears spilling down her face. Surprised, Freddie pulled back and withdrew his arms, realising they were covered in blood as he did so. In total shock, he stared at the dark-red stickiness before staring back at Eleanor.

"They punished you," he whispered in horror. Unable to stop the tears now, Eleanor nodded. "Will, she's bleeding," Freddie said, unable to drag his eyes from the blood. Will moved to Eleanor's side, raising an eyebrow at Freddie's blood-stained hands and arms. He moved behind her and she heard him gasp.

"Freddie, she needs to lie down," he said with forced calm. Taking her hand, Freddie led her to the rug.

"Eleanor, lie down," he said softly.

"She needs to lie on her front," Will ordered, stating the obvious in a flat, empty tone while rummaging through his supplies for what he needed. Eleanor dropped to her knees. The jolt making her whimper again, and behind her she heard another gasp.

"What happened?" Amelia asked of no one in particular, horror raising the pitch of her voice and making it wobble.

"They punished her for exploding a tree," Freddie told her in an empty voice, helping Eleanor to drop forward. She moved her arms under her head. It hurt. Resting a tear-streaked cheek on her arm, she sighed as Freddie gently stroked her hair.

"You let them do this to her?" Merl asked. He sounded traumatised. Conlan gave no response. Eleanor felt an energy string brush against her and Will's furious presence filled her head.

He let them do this?

Eleanor sighed. *No, Will, I let them do this. I could have stopped them if I'd wanted. I made the choice to submit.*

Why? You're a mess.

This was worth it, I promise.

He had no right to ask it of you. Eleanor cringed as Will's anger and hurt battered against her – on top of her own pain it was too much and she started crying again.

I'm sorry you're upset, Will. Please don't be angry with me, I don't think I can take it just now. She briefly felt Will's guilt, before shuddering as his loving affection for her flooded through her body as a warm glow, wrapping round her carefully and separating her from the pain. He gingerly pulled up her shirt and began cleaning her back with an antiseptic that should have had her screaming in agony, but with Will supporting her mind, numbing the sensations, all she felt was a mild stinging.

I'm not angry with you, Will said. *I'm angry with Conlan for putting you in this position. I don't like seeing you in pain.*

I told you, Will, this was my choice – and it was worth it.

So you said, but tell me, is any of this 'benefit' your pain has brought going to directly benefit you? Shocked by the anger she could still hear in his voice, Eleanor was silent. When she did not respond, Will continued. *I didn't think so. You made a deal, agreed to suffer to help Conlan and he let you. Do you understand why I'm angry?*

Eleanor felt her own anger rising. Will was being an idiot; he knew how important this was. *It was my plan, Will, my idea. I'm quite proud of it actually, and anything that benefits Conlan benefits us too, you know that. I don't understand. Conlan made a deal and agreed to suffer in order to help Amelia. And you let him… you talked him into it. How is this different?*

Will rubbed a little too hard over one of the thick, bloody welts that went across her lower back and round her side. Even with him keeping the pain at bay, Eleanor felt it and cried out.

Sorry, Will said.

Actually, Will, I'm really impressed – you're talking to me, keeping the pain away and treating my injuries all at the same time.

Who says men can't multi-task? And you're changing the subject.

Eleanor sighed. *I don't want to talk about it anymore, what's done is done. We can't change it.*

How much are you going to give for a man who offers you nothing in return? Will asked in serious concern. *Where does it stop?*

It stops when my heart stops beating, and possibly not even then, Eleanor said with a calm, steely resolve. *And don't you think you're being a little hypocritical, especially given what you were prepared to do for Amelia?*

Eleanor, Amelia loves me in return, we have a relationship. She gives me so much; what do you get from Conlan?

A lot more than you think, Eleanor snapped.

Will snorted. *I hope so, because from where the rest of us are stood he's an uncaring, unfeeling, merciless bastard.*

No, Will, please don't think that.

Will huffed in exasperation, pulling his energy string free. Hot pain poured through her again. She winced but forced down her whimpering cry. Will tenderly pulled her shirt down over her back again. Freddie lay down next to her, his arm a pillow for her head so she could move slowly into a more comfortable position.

"Will, her hand needs attention, too," Freddie said in a pain-filled, brittle voice. Confused, Eleanor looked down and saw the half-moon bite mark she had left across the first knuckle and the side of her right hand, the ripped skin oozing blood in a steady pulse with her heartbeat; she had not even noticed it. Will knelt at her side and lifted her hand up slightly, not wanting to move her shoulders.

"You bit yourself?" he asked, his voice calm and clinical, despite the tension Eleanor could see in his body.

"I was trying not to scream like a baby and make an utter fool of myself," Eleanor muttered.

Will frowned but said nothing more. He cleaned her hand, wrapping a bandage tightly around it. "It really should be stitched. It's a deep wound, but your teeth haven't left a neat enough edge, so you're going to have to be careful, OK?" he ordered, giving her a stern look.

Eleanor nodded. She felt so tired. Freddie's arm was comfortable, and her eyes closed. Freddie covered them with a blanket. She tensed as the material fell across her, but it did not hurt as much as expected, as her back felt strangely numb. She wondered what Will had treated her with and why he had not used the same stuff the last time he had given her stitches. Maybe it was something Kona had told him about.

"Is she going to be OK?" Conlan asked, his voice as emotionless as Eleanor imagined his face to be.

"No. She's in pain, she's scarred for life and she's so totally besotted with you that she thinks this was a good idea!" Will snarled at him.

"Will..." Conlan started.

"Shut up," Will barked. "I don't want to hear it."

Eleanor wanted to explain, wanted to tell Will to leave him alone, but she was drained and her body would not follow her commands. The peaceful inky black was sucking her down, like water down a plug hole.

She was in the middle of a strange dream about being in the thick of battle, standing over Conlan's fallen body. Defending him. Her sword swung desperately around her at the enemy, a dark, faceless hoard. In her dream Eleanor felt something brush against her fingers and she looked down. Conlan was conscious and stopping her fighting because he was holding her sword hand, the blade immobile in front of her. She woke with a start, pain making her wince. It was quiet. Freddie's soft snores and the slow deep-sleep breathing of the others were the only sounds. *It must be late or really early.* Opening her eyes she found Conlan lying on his side next to her, pained green eyes staring back. Hidden under their blankets she could feel his fingers gently brushing up and down hers, stopping where the bandage started. It was a small, comforting movement, loving almost. Her need for him flowed through her. Ignoring Will's advice, she grasped Conlan's hand and held it tight. The delicate scab that had formed split open and blood began soaking her bandage, but she did not care. She wanted him to know that it was alright, that she was alright. She smiled at him and he slowly smiled back. She reluctantly released his hand, not wanting him to feel the blood; it would only upset him. He moved his hand forward slightly, resting it on her forearm and gently rubbing her skin with his thumb. Eleanor relaxed, sighing in pleasure and closing her eyes. *This is what Will and the others don't see, this is why they don't understand*, she thought, before she allowed the darkness to pull her back down into a deep, restful and dreamless sleep

The bolt thrown back in the lock woke Eleanor with a start. Her body tensed and pain shot through her. She whimpered, struggling to get up. Everybody else was awake. Conlan was watching her from against the wall. He did not look like he had slept. The others seemed to be ignoring him, although Merl shot him an angry glance as Freddie helped her to sit upright.

Eleanor smiled. "You let me sleep?"

Freddie nodded. "You looked like you needed it, looked so peaceful, so relaxed, we didn't want to wake you." Eleanor felt the ghost of Conlan's touch on her arm and sighed. The door was opened and warm sunshine washed over her, reminding her there was a world outside. The light was too bright, so she closed her eyes but did not turn her face away, feeling the joy of it wash through her. She knew the person who had opened the door may well be the traitor come to kill her, but for a few seconds it did not matter. A figure in the doorway blocked the light.

"My lady Laurice asks for you to make good on your promise, Avatar," a high squeaky voice spoke in an attempt at a harsh, nasty tone.

"Hello, Harnlyn," Eleanor said quietly, smiling at him. It must be afternoon already, as the traitor had made no move on her, unless this *was* the move, but Eleanor really could not see Harnlyn as a devious mastermind. She staggered painfully to her feet and walked towards him. Freddie stood, joining her.

"What are you doing?" Eleanor asked, glancing at him.

"Coming with you," Freddie said.

Eleanor's heart squeezed, horrific scenarios running through her overactive mind – the traitor attacking, Nials and his men fighting back, Freddie caught unknowing in the middle. She shook her head.

"No, stay here, you can't help me with what I need to do," she said, pushing him back with a hand on his chest. It was like pushing a brick wall.

"I'm coming with you," he said again. There was focused determination in Freddie's face. Harnlyn shoved him back so he could reach Eleanor, pulling her arms behind her back to tie them. She was unprepared for the rough movement, and the pain ripped up her back. She cried out, tears immediately flowing, and staggered, feeling weak and dizzy. Only Harnlyn's bruising grip on her arms kept her upright.

"No sharp comment, child?" he gloated.

"It would be a waste of my breath, you are too stupid to understand my better insults," Eleanor snarled, unable to stop herself and knowing it was a bad idea to bait him, but she did not want him thinking he had beaten her. Harnlyn let out a high, frustrated yell, which sounded like a woman in pain. With considerable force he flung her into the wall. Pain exploded claymores in her head. Through dazed, half-open eyes she watched Freddie launch himself at Harnlyn, pounding his fists into the man's surprised face. Will pulled Freddie off his bleeding, struggling victim and dragged him back, his arm firmly across his chest. Thankfully, Will had reacted before the two guards who had followed Harnlyn through the door had recovered from their shock enough to take matters into their own hands. A body crouched in front of Eleanor, blocking her view, hands roughly propping her up, dragging her back against the wall behind. Pain roared through her and made her body twitch involuntarily. She sobbed weakly.

"Sorry, Eleanor, are you OK?" Merl asked. Eleanor could see Conlan beyond Merl's shoulder, his body rigid, forcing himself not to intervene.

"What is going on here?" The deep voice echoed around the room, carrying the assumption of absolute authority. Surprised, Merl turned to face it and Eleanor got a view of this new stranger. It was another tall man with ebony skin, but not someone she had seen before. This man seemed older; his short cropped black hair had flecks of grey through it. He carried his strong, thick body with the confidence of one who knows his every order will be obeyed. He glanced disgustedly down at Harnlyn, before stepping over him towards Eleanor.

"Move," he ordered Merl in a voice of velvet-clad steel. Still staring in surprise, Merl stood up and moved out of the way. The older man crouched in front of Eleanor, his strong, unflinching gaze holding hers.

"I am Berick," he said, the growl he put through the Dwarfish implying a meeting of equals.

Eleanor assessed him. Cunning intelligence looked back from deep black eyes. He had the same elaborate ritual scaring under his eyes as Laurice, Urerla and Yatt. *A member of Laurice's family?* Without thinking, Eleanor raised a hand to his face and gently ran her fingers over Berick's scars. *Like reading Braille.* She smiled at him, he smiled back and she knew, without a doubt, that this man was the traitor. A strange calm followed this realisation. She would react quicker if she was relaxed.

"I am Eleanor," she said, annoyed at how fragile she sounded. He took her hand as she withdrew it from his face and gave it a gentle, friendly pat.

"I know who you are, Eleanor, Avatar of Earth. A woman of remarkable talents. My sister Laurice has told me what you are going to do, and I thought I would come and take you to meet Meran. Harnlyn cannot be trusted to behave in an acceptable fashion," Berick said, giving Harnlyn a contemptuous glance. Harnlyn looked back reproachfully, rubbing his jaw as he got to his feet. Firm hands took Eleanor's arms, helping her to stand, but the room spun; her overtaxed body headed towards shutdown. As she staggered, she was caught and lifted off the ground, held carefully against a strong body, arms trying to minimise the contact with her back, her head falling onto a shoulder. Merl, she realised. She looked over Merl's shoulder and caught Conlan's eye. She saw understanding. He flicked his gaze to Berick and Eleanor gave him a tiny nod.

"She is too weak to stand, I will carry her," Merl said to Berick, who nodded once, before turning to leave. Merl, Harnlyn and the guards followed him. Looking behind them as they walked away, Eleanor saw the door slammed shut and bolted. She missed the others already; she had not wanted them with her, they were safer where they were, but she felt their absence as a tearing pain. She fought down the guilt she felt for putting Merl in danger, it would be better for Conlan to lose Merl and one Avatar than two Avatars. She admitted to herself that if it came to it, she would rather Merl died than Freddie. Working hard to stop her body tensing, she looked around as far as her peripheral vision would allow without having to move her head, trying to spot Nials, wondering when he would strike and hoping he would not wait until she was dead before he did. Eleanor closed her eyes and let her mind drift. There was nothing she could do now – her plan would either succeed or fail. A strong unexpected burst of pain suddenly filled her stomach; not her pain, she realised, it was Conlan's physical pain. Concern for him flashed through her mind, but it faded almost as soon as she had felt it, as if Conlan had pushed her away, leaving her confused.

The sun's glorious warmth disappeared as they entered a building. Eleanor opened her eyes, allowing them time to adjust. She did not think she would be able to put up much of a fight if it became necessary, but being able to see would be an advantage. *At least then I can look death in the eye.*

"Eleanor? Do you want to stand?" Merl asked gently. She nodded against his shoulder and he placed her down, keeping a firm hold of her arm until he was sure she was not going to drop again. Once on her feet she looked around her and realised with a jolt of fear that they were in the stables Nials had taken her to the previous evening. She could see her jacket still lying on the floor where she had abandoned it. Many more lanterns had been lit, the soft orange light trying to compete with the brilliant sunlight that poured in through the open double doors at the far end of the room.

There was the shuffling of hooves, and Eleanor turned to see a man leading a horse forward from one of the stalls. The other stalls still looked empty. The horse moved slowly, tottering painfully forward like an old man with chronic arthritis. Eleanor gasped, her own pain forgotten, as she stared at the miserable creature before her. She knew this was Meran, but her logic found it incredibly difficult to match the horse before her with the one she had seen in the picture in Laurice's room. The once strong, muscled body was wasted, gaunt and hollowed out, flesh slipping loosely over sharp bones. Eleanor could see every rib, and his joints creaked as he moved. The black coat, which had shone in the painting, was dull and lifeless and missing in some places. Open sores stood angry red. The head dropped forward almost to the floor, listless eyes staring at nothing. Horrified, Eleanor pushed into the animal's head and immediately understood. The horse was grieving, blaming himself for his beloved master's death. Meran raised his head stiffly and looked Eleanor in the eye. Pushing deeper she found a keen intelligence, a brave and devoted heart and a strong sense of duty. Meran knew he had failed to protect his master and had given up caring about life as his guilt ate away at his soul. As Eleanor pushed carefully through the animal's mind, all sorts of interesting facts and information came to her. Meran struggled to pull his pain-scattered thoughts together, but he seemed to want to show her something important. Without her needing to ask, the tormented animal sent Eleanor the memory of his master's death. They were attacked by several men riding out of the sun. Meran had fought back, lashing out with his hooves, as his master had hacked and stabbed with his sword, but someone had managed to reach his bridle and had yanked it roughly down and round. Meran had bitten the arm, tasting blood, but it was too late, as his head twisted too far and he lost balance, falling heavily on his side, landing on his master and trapping his leg, making it impossible for him to avoid the blow to the head with a rock that killed him, his skull splitting. Meran had been pulled up, and it was then that he saw a figure riding towards them from the distance. *Berick.* Eleanor recognised the man as he approached.

"Good, no weapon damage, you did well," Berick said to a figure stood out of Meran's view. Shocked to his core, Meran could not take his eyes off his fallen master and the blood spreading from his crushed head.

"If we lodge his foot into the stirrup and drag him a short distance, it will look as if he fell out of the saddle for some reason and was dragged to his death," came the reply. The voice was hard and cold, but oddly familiar.

"Very well. Thank you again for your assistance. I assume there will be no loose ends?" Berick asked, looking pointedly at the three dead and two still-standing attackers, who seemed oblivious to the arrangements being made for their deaths.

"No loose ends," the cold voice agreed. "But you will keep up your end of the bargain; you will help me incapacitate Conlan Baydon and his group?"

"As we arranged, as long as you promise that whoever I send to you will not become a loose end. Why are you so sure they are coming?" Berick asked.

"I have it on very good authority that they will be here at some point," the voice said knowingly. Berick nodded, clearly wanting to know more.

The memory began to break up under the force of Meran's grief, and Eleanor knew she was going to get no more. Meran shuddered and she sent him the mental equivalent of a comforting hug. She tried to tell the animal that it had not been his fault, that the person Meran should be blaming was Berick. Eleanor felt something stir in the horse's beaten-down mind; it was anger, an understanding of its own memories through Eleanor's explanation that Berick had killed his master. Rage shot through Meran as he looked around him, taking in the world for the first time in a while. Worried that the horse would do something rash, Eleanor sent him a feeling that all was in order, that he would get his revenge, but he must wait and bide his time. Meran agreed, but Eleanor could see that his whole body was alert, an echo of the once proud animal in his eyes. She left her energy string in Meran's head, monitoring his mood, in case he changed his mind about attacking Berick, but the bigger part of her concentration was occupied analysing Berick's and the strangers' conversation. Laurice had said her husband had died three moons ago, approximately three months; her understanding of time was a little hazy here, but she felt fairly certain that she had only just destroyed Nethrus three months ago. Their attacker had been waiting for them and knew they were coming, even before she had announced herself to the Lords of Mydren with the earthquake. How had Daratus known? *What if Gregor was not as powerful as Merl had said?* Eleanor wondered, with a sinking dread, whether Gregor was still alive. Next time she found a jewellery shop with Remic's symbol, she would ask them to find out.

Eleanor's worried thoughts were interrupted when she saw four figures moving towards them through the open double doors, the sunlight making them nothing more than dark shapes until they got closer, but the swaying walk and tinkling of their belts identified Laurice and Urerla long before

Eleanor could actually see their faces. Nials stood at Urerla's side and another man she did not recognise stood at Laurice's side. All four had swords strapped to their waists.

"Berick, I'm surprised to see you here. I was told you were too busy to attend today," Laurice said. There was no trace of suspicion in her voice, which worried Eleanor, because if the woman could not conceive her brother as a traitor, convincing her was going to be difficult.

"Orno was not just your husband, Laurice, he was like a brother. I too wish to know what happened to him," Berick replied with a serious frown. Meran heard Berick talk, realised who he was and took an impatient step forward, pawing the ground with his hoof. Eleanor sent him soothing, calming feelings – his time would come, she assured him.

Laurice looked at Meran in surprise and ran an affectionate hand down his neck. "This is the most life I have seen him display in many moons. I wonder if he knows what is going on?" she whispered.

"Step forward, Avatar of Earth," Nials said, looking at her. Wondering when Nials intended to make his move, Eleanor nodded and walked into the middle of the room, trying not to stare at the fine spray of blood she could see on the floor. Her blood.

"Having spoken with Conlan Baydon, I am told you can read Meran's thoughts and memories simply by touching him," Laurice said. Eleanor nodded. "Then please, ask Meran how my husband died," she said, anguish in her voice. Eleanor stepped forward. She did not need to be touching the horse to talk to him, and Conlan knew that; was there a plan here? She took Laurice's place next to Meran, gently running her hand down the animal's neck. He turned to look at her. Through their link Meran sent her another thought, a desire to end it; when he had destroyed Berick he wanted his life to finish. Eleanor's heart twisted and she sent the horse a strong sense of a life still to live, of things still to do, that losing a loved one was not the end. The horse scoffed at her – what did she know? Eleanor sent Meran her memories of Rand, everything, all her love for him, and showed Meran how much Conlan had loved his horse. She then sent the memory of Rand's death, knowing that tears were running down her face. Meran watched the thoughts in his head and felt Conlan's grief. He identified with it. Eleanor tried to give Meran the impression that Conlan was also tormented by grief, yet he still kept going, still met each day with resilience, because Rand would not have wanted the master he loved to curl up in a ball and die, just as Eleanor was certain that Orno would not have wanted the horse he loved to end his life prematurely.

"Well?" asked Nials, his sharp question snapping Eleanor out of her conversation with Meran. She turned to face Laurice.

"Meran says Berick killed your husband," she said loudly and clearly. Laurice did not look surprised. She looked at her brother with burning hatred.

"Why?" was all she asked. Berick sneered at her.

"This is the first time the Nardar Tribe have held the Heart in over sixty years, and what are you doing with it? Nothing! Every year the Lords of Mydren get closer and closer to our lands, and what are you doing to stop them? I have made a deal. I get rid of you, take control of the Heart and the eight tribes, we swear allegiance to the Lords of Mydren and they leave us alone, our land is protected."

Eleanor saw anger flow through Laurice as she moved out of Meran's shadow so she could focus on Berick.

"Do you really think the Lords of Mydren will honour that promise?" Laurice asked, with utter contempt running through the Dwarfish.

"I suspect he knows they will *not* honour their promise," Eleanor said with slow calm. "But he does not care. He is going to get control – power – for the first time in his life. Meran told me that tribal power is passed down the female line, and a man can only take the role if no other option is available. He has been so close to true power his whole life, but never touched it."

"You would have destroyed your people, if you had succeeded?" Laurice enquired, her tone measured and only her eyes showing her fury.

Berick smiled at her. "But I have succeeded," he said. "Kill them!"

Eleanor saw movement and heard the metallic swish of swords pulled from scabbards as thirty men moved out of the stalls they had been hiding in and advanced upon them. Drawing energy from the earth she blasted at the nearest man. The air a few feet in front of her exploded in dazzling colour, bright green and golden brown, the colour moving across a circular barrier that surrounded them all. *Amelia's shield, Amelia is protecting us.* Eleanor's heart leapt in her chest; she was not alone, they were here. She resisted the urge to look around her. She would not give their position away – she would make their enemy think this was all her doing.

"I have erected an impenetrable barrier between us," she said to Berick. "Exactly how many loyal men do you have? Not enough, I am thinking, or subterfuge would not have been necessary in the first place."

Berick stared at her with malignant hatred, a slow grin spreading across his face. He drew breath to speak, but before he got the chance, the men stood around the edge of the shield began dropping to the floor one by one, screaming and writhing in agony for a few seconds and then laying still. Their movements looked familiar, similar to what Conlan had suffered when she had loosed Will's energy on him, but this was much faster, much more powerful. This was killing. *So that's what it looks like when Will releases drawn energy.* Berick watched in horror as his men dropped dead in front of him. The men looked at each other in terror, some tried to hide back in the stalls and several others began hammering their swords on Amelia's shield.

Harnlyn ran for the open door, bursting into flames before he had gone five feet. He toppled over, burning so quickly he did not even have time to scream. Eleanor raised her eyes from his smoking corpse and saw Will, Freddie, Amelia and Conlan stood in a line several feet beyond him, silhouetted by the light from the open door which framed them in sunlight. *My guardian angels.* She turned back to Berick, glaring at him, but he was looking at something over her head. He nodded, once. Eleanor whipped round again in time to see the guard at Laurice's side slam the hilt of his sword into Nials' face. The horseman's eyes rolled in his head. Blood flowing heavily from his nose and mouth, he fell over on his back, unconscious. Urerla stared in horror and dropped to her knees at Nials' side. The traitorous guard wasted not a moment and slammed her in the head, too. She collapsed over Nials, blood trickling from her hairline. Laurice was not as easy to dispatch, and as the guard bore down on her she drew her sword. Eleanor glanced back at Merl, who looked at her in horror. The guard and Laurice were too close for Eleanor to blast at him, so she ran towards Nials as the two circled. She heard the metallic clash of the first thrusts and parries as the two engaged; Laurice could hold her own. Eleanor checked Nials and Urerla's pulses and found that both were strong. However, Nials was choking on his own blood, so Eleanor pulled Urerla off him and turned the unconscious man over to make sure he could breathe by putting him into the recovery position. She then took his sword from him and turned to help Laurice.

Laurice was putting up a worthy fight, but the guard was stronger, had her off balance and was pounding at her with powerful overhead blows she was just about managing to deflect. As Eleanor watched the woman's defence crumble, the guard knocked her sword out of her hand, stepped forward and bashed her in the side of head. Laurice dropped to the ground. The guard stepped behind her, pulling her up by her hair and pressing his blade into her neck.

"It would seem I have the advantage again, Avatar," Berick said smugly. He was focused on Eleanor and did not seem to have noticed the others yet.

"You cannot win this, Berick, you must know that. The minute you kill Laurice, you lose all leverage. I will destroy you, and Urerla will take control of the Nardar Tribe. Your only option is to release Laurice and beg for her mercy," Eleanor told him. Berick seemed to consider this suggestion, the smug smile not leaving his face.

"Drop your defences," Berick ordered.

Eleanor sighed. Why did everything always have to be so difficult? "Berick, are you in a rush to die?" she enquired. Berick said nothing but nodded at the guard, who moved slightly. Laurice cried out in pain and blood began to dribble down her neck. He turned his gaze back to Eleanor, his meaning clear: your move.

Eleanor shrugged. "It will not save you, but I will drop my shield," she said loudly, hoping Amelia would take the hint. Berick stepped cautiously forward, his hand in front of him and smiling as he failed to encounter any resistance. Eleanor felt an energy string brush against her and felt Will's presence fill her mind.

You have no idea how good it is to see you, she told him.

We'd never willingly let you fight on your own, Eleanor. Nials came to see us after you left and asked us to step in. What are we going to do about Berick?

I promised Meran he could kill Berick.

"Drop your weapon, Avatar," Berick ordered.

You promised the horse revenge? Will asked. Concentrating more on her conversation with Will than Berick, Eleanor chucked Nials' sword to the side.

Yes, she said, feeling a little angry. *You didn't feel his grief, Will. He's punishing himself for failing to protect his master, so revenge was the least I could do. Can you kill the man holding Laurice?*

Unfortunately he's too close to Laurice – we don't have that kind of control. Anything we do at this point will be risking her life, too.

"If I cannot win, little Avatar, I will make sure that Laurice does not win either," Berick snarled. Eleanor felt Meran's mind as the horse realised that the man he wanted to kill was within striking distance; she told him to wait, the time was coming. The horse snorted impatiently.

"Is a lack of absolute power really so bad, Berick?" Eleanor asked. Not that she cared, but she needed time to think, and keeping Berick talking might provide it.

"Says an abomination of pure power," he sneered, launching himself into a rambling justification of his actions.

Will, I have an idea.

What do you have in mind, Eleanor?

Well, if you release drawn energy, people jitter to death in seconds, but when I took energy from you and released it at Conlan it was weaker. He didn't die, but it was unpleasant...

You want to pull my energy and release it at Laurice and the guard, reduce its impact?

Yes.

Freddie can do it, he has the best control.

OK, I'll tell Meran what we're going to do – that way, once Laurice and the guard are out of the picture, he can attack Berick.

OK, give me a second to tell the others.

While Will explained their plan, Eleanor told Meran what was going to happen, informing him that once Laurice and the man threatening her had dropped to the ground, Berick was all his for the taking. Eleanor felt his savage joy as she withdrew her energy string. Berick was still yelling and spitting a lifetime of impotent fury at her. Eleanor ignored him, glancing at Merl. The older man was staring back, obviously wondering what she was going to do next.

OK, they're ready, Will said. Eleanor watched as Will closed his eyes and Freddie's eyes almost immediately glazed over. Through her link to Will, Eleanor felt his energy fade as he dropped in a boneless heap to the ground. Eleanor turned to look at Laurice and smiled apologetically. Sensing that something was coming, the woman closed her black eyes and Freddie let Will's energy go. Laurice and the guard collapsed back, writhing on the floor and crying in pain, before lying still. Eleanor looked back to Berick, whose vociferation had come to a stuttering halt as he looked in horror at his sister's body. For several seconds nobody moved, then with an ear-splitting shriek Meran rushed forward, kicking his front legs out at Berick and hitting him with crippling blows to the stomach and chest. Berick fell back, and a spray of blood expelled from his mouth as he did so. He lay choking, blood running from the corners of his mouth and his face full of terror. Meran stepped over him slowly, lifting his front hoof over the sobbing man's head. Berick pulled his arms up in defence, but all it did was delay the inevitable as Meran stomped repeatedly down on the cowering man. Eleanor winced as she heard the bones in Berick's arms snap, the man releasing a gurgling scream of agony that was cut short by Meran's precisely delivered hoof to the side of his head. No longer able to watch, Eleanor turned her head away and closed her eyes, cringing at the wet splitting sounds.

Silence.

Eleanor opened her eyes. Meran had moved away from Berick's lifeless, bloody body. The horse stood, head bowed and shaking violently. Freddie and Amelia checked that Laurice, Urerla and Nials were OK, while Will lay on the ground, eyes dazed but open.

Will, are you OK?

I'm just tired.

Eleanor pulled her energy string free as he struggled to sit. Turning back, Eleanor saw Merl. The man still seemed to be in shock and stood like a statue, staring at what was left of Berick. Movement in her peripheral vision caught Eleanor's eye. The guard who had threatened Laurice was on his feet, moving swiftly towards her. A dagger glittered sharply in his hand. Surprised,

Eleanor stared, momentarily paralysed.

"Eleanor!"

The loud voice made her jump and then there were strong arms around her, pulling her away from the knife, a body moving to shield her, a grunt of pain, a heavy weight crushing her to the ground and pain strong enough to strip reality from her.

"Eleanor?"

Wincing, Eleanor opened her eyes and the fog cleared a little. She was lying on the ground and a hand stroked her head.

"What happened?" she asked, pushing her body to sit, Freddie helping her.

"Merl just saved your life," Freddie said as she sat. Merl was lying on the ground next to her while Will assessed a deep gash across his ribs. Reaching forward, Eleanor placed a careful hand on Merl's shoulder. He turned his eyes towards her. He had risked his life to save hers.

"Thank you," Eleanor whispered, smiling gratefully. "Are you alright?"

"I will be fine once this butcher has finished poking and prodding," Merl said, glaring at Will, who ignored him.

"Where's the guard?" Eleanor asked. Freddie pointed to the stable wall where the guard lay sprawled in an unmoving heap, watched over by Amelia. Conlan stood a few feet away, watching her with an expression she did not understand. He was standing awkwardly, like he was uncomfortable in his own skin. She smiled at him and he smiled back, although it failed to reach his eyes. Eleanor frowned as his smile dropped. She watched as he walked stiffly past her to Meran and began gently stroking the trembling horse's neck.

"What have you done to yourself?" he asked softly in Dwarfish. Meran lifted his head and locked his eyes on Conlan. A soft nose nuzzled into his face and then the broken animal dropped his head onto Conlan's shoulder, taking a deep shuddering breath, eyes closing. Conlan wrapped an arm around Meran's neck and with his other hand absently scratched behind his ears, just as he had done for Rand.

Urerla had come round, and once Will had assured her that Nials was going to be fine, she had pulled herself together enough to get help to carry Nials and Laurice to their beds so the healers could attend them. Laurice came round as she was being carried away. She insisted on issuing orders, smiling at Eleanor as she gave them their freedom back and made sure the traitorous guard was locked up for further interrogation.

It took a few days for Laurice, Nials, Urerla and Merl to recover. In the meantime, Eleanor and the others were allowed to go where they pleased; curious, appraising looks followed them. The full story of what happened appeared to have spread through the entire tribe, and small children kept coming up to Eleanor, begging her to blow things up. They had been given their own suite of rooms, overlooking the private garden, and Eleanor was enjoying sleeping in a bed again. She had even been able to have a bath. Despite the relaxed atmosphere, good food and comfortable bed, Eleanor's nerves were on edge. At first she thought it was worry for Merl, as the knife wound had been deep, but Will had stitched up the gash, promising Eleanor that Merl would be fine. She believed him. It was not Merl that was making her uncomfortable, and as she thought about it she realised it was Conlan's mood that was affecting her own and everyone else's. They were all trying too hard to pretend everything was great, yet it did not feel right at all. Conlan had said barely five words to her in three days. He left their rooms before she woke and came back after she had gone to bed; he had almost moved into the stables with Meran. She did not begrudge him this contact, as she knew how much he missed Rand and how much his attention would be helping Meran, but Eleanor still felt like he was avoiding her. With this thought in mind she wandered down to the stables to enjoy the relative peace and the cool air the early hour afforded her.

Horse saw her approaching and came trotting over with an excited nicker. Eleanor climbed onto the fence so she could sit and stroke her friend's nose. Looking out over the other horses, Meran was nowhere in sight. Having given Horse a long hello, she dropped down from the fence and headed towards the dark of the stables. Eleanor stood in the doorway, allowing her eyes to adjust to the gloom. Several stalls were filled with dozing animals. Moving down the building, Eleanor glanced into each stall. She heard Conlan's voice before she saw them. He was murmuring softly to Meran in Dwarfish.

"Is that good? I am glad you like it… You deserve it, you are so special, do not give up; you are strong enough to survive. You want some more? Here."

Eleanor smiled at the affection in his voice. In the last stall Conlan was stood with his back to her, feeding Meran treats. Eleanor was amazed at the difference three days had made. Meran was still thin and fragile, but he did not look like he was on the verge of dying. His movements were more fluid and graceful, as if some of his body's pain had gone. The look in his eyes was brighter and more alert, and he was interested in what was going on around him. He saw Eleanor and snorted a greeting. Conlan turned around, holding Eleanor's gaze for the first time in days. Silence stretched.

Meran, impatient for the tasty morsels he could see in front of him, nudged his head into Conlan's stomach. The expression on Conlan's face twisted into a rictus of pain. Gasping, he took a few steps back from Meran, face paling. The horse flashed Eleanor a concerned look and they both turned to look at Conlan as he stood, head bowed and arm wrapped protectively around his belly.

"What happened?" Eleanor asked, taking a step towards him.

"Nothing," he said, stepping out of her reach. "I'm fine, please leave me alone." His voice was hard and cold, but Eleanor could hear the misery underneath it – could feel it, even – as he refused to look at her. Worried, Eleanor took another quick three steps towards him. He retreated until his back hit the stable wall and he could go no further.

"You're in pain, why?"

Holding her gaze with a miserable one of his own, Conlan stared at her and shook his head.

"I'm fine," he insisted again.

Eleanor pushed gently into his stomach; he closed his eyes, jaw muscles clamping down on a groan, his body shuddering. Eleanor pulled his jacket apart, dragging his shirt up so she could inspect his abdomen. She got a flash of fist-shaped mottled purple, green and yellow bruises, before Conlan dropped the food he was carrying for Meran and drew his arms across himself, pulling his jacket closed and blocking her view.

"Please, I'm fine, leave me alone."

Hurt that he would not tell her the truth, Eleanor took a step away and tears slipped down her cheeks.

"Don't cry, Eleanor, I'm fine, truly."

"You won't tell me what happened – and that hurts," she sobbed, waiting for an explanation. In miserable silence he stared back. With a kick of frustration she realised he was not going to tell her and felt her mind trying to fill in the blanks. Who would want to hurt him? Had Freddie hurt him as revenge for her? Had Will let him do it? Did they not understand that all they were doing was hurting her again?

"Freddie," she whispered, seeing the confirmation in Conlan's eyes. Rage shot through her with such force that she started to shake. "I'm going to do that glorified fire-lighter some serious damage."

Conlan's hand caught her arm and he looked at her beseechingly. "Please, Eleanor, no. Freddie had every right to make me suffer. I should never have let you do it." Murderous rage created a pounding, throbbing cloud in her head. Her energy levels spiking, Eleanor shook his hand free and ran from the stables, heading towards their rooms. She knew Conlan was following, but she could run far faster.

She slammed the door open to Freddie's bedroom with such a bang that it jerked him from sleep. He sat up drowsily as she stormed towards him. Not wanting to kill Freddie, she had forced her energy levels back down on her run from the stables, but she was still fuming.

"Hi, Eleanor, I..." he started, his voice disappearing as he registered the look on her face. "Oh," he murmured.

"How could you?" she screamed. "How *dare* you hurt Conlan! You've wanted to do this for ages, haven't you? Inflict pain, make him suffer because I chose him over you. Why didn't you believe Conlan when he told you it had been my idea, that I talked him into it? Do you really think so little of me?"

Eleanor paused as the full impact of the pained, guilty look on Freddie's face reached her.

"You didn't ask him for an explanation, did you?" she continued. "You just attacked him." Her voice was a horrified whisper and her relentless mind presented her with another question that made her stomach hurt. "Did you even give him the chance to defend himself?"

Freddie did not seem to know how to respond, but the expression on his face said all Eleanor needed to know as she fought desperately to keep control of her rising energy levels.

"You hateful, spiteful, selfish loser!" Eleanor screamed, watching tears spring into Freddie's eyes.

"Enough!" Will insisted from behind her, moving to Freddie's side.

"I told you this would happen, I told you," Amelia said in quiet accusation from Eleanor's side, disgust on her face. The words tearing at her, Eleanor stared at Will.

"You helped Freddie?" Eleanor asked, her whole world turning slowly upside down. This was Will – he cared for and loved Conlan, surely he would not want to hurt him. Freddie she could understand, she could imagine him losing control, but Will? He was calm, level-headed... The expression on Will's face nearly pushed Eleanor over the edge, and her attempts to keep her energy levels down became a serious fight.

"Conlan understands violence, Eleanor; in fact, it's pretty much all he understands. What he allowed them to do to you was not acceptable, so we made that clear in a way he understands."

"Will, he trusts you. He didn't do anything wrong. How could you do that to him? If you tell him his actions are wrong he'll believe you. How can you let him think that he deserves to be punished for believing in me?"

"He let them hurt you; he could have come up with a better plan," Will said calmly.

"So you violently assaulted him to get your point across? You took a battered, emotionally fragile man who looks to you, his friends, to set an example – and you brutalised him? What does that teach him? How does that do anything other than compound his belief that you solve problems with your fists? How could you betray him like that?! I expected better from you, Will."

Disgusted, Eleanor turned to leave and found Conlan stood in the doorway. His expression was emotionally shutdown – closed, empty, blank – but the devastation and uncertainty in his eyes brought a lump to Eleanor's throat. She flinched as his emotional pain battered against her.

"I'm sorry they did that to you, they were wrong," she whispered.

"You promised not to tell her," Freddie accused in a thick, emotional voice.

Conlan dropped his head. Eleanor felt his shame wash over her, and instant white-hot rage made her energy level rocket. Deep inside her something snapped. She span round, pulled energy from the earth and started releasing it.

As she blasted away, Eleanor yelled. "Freddie, *you* might be a total moron, but I'm not!" One of the bedside tables shattered into matchsticks. "Conlan told me nothing. I figured it out. It wasn't hard." The end of Freddie's bed exploded, tipping it at a precarious angle, feathers filling the air. "I only know two men stupid enough to do something like that." The bedside table on the other side of the bed joined its mate as a scattering of wood. "I love him, Freddie, in a way you couldn't even understand." A portion of wall next to Freddie's head exploded out. "You don't love me! You can't, because if you did, you'd know that anything you did to hurt Conlan would hurt me too!" She screamed this last, exploding the ceiling down on Freddie's head. He and Will cowered under the falling masonry.

Dirt, dust and debris filled the air. Eleanor could see sky through the hole. Her blasting session had tired her and she stopped for a moment panting, letting the dust settle. Her rage slowly receding, a cold numbness took its place. A hand rested lightly on her shoulder. Turning, she found pained green eyes. Eleanor whimpered as he inadvertently assaulted her with his tormented emotions.

"Please, Eleanor, stop," Conlan whispered. She nodded, her energy levels dropping as her rage faded. Tears started, and not caring if he wanted to be touched or not, she wrapped her arms around Conlan and sobbed into his chest. He picked her up, carrying her as Merl had done, her head on his shoulder and putting as little pressure on her back as possible. It must have been uncomfortable for him, but he gave no indication of pain. Eleanor wrapped her arms round his neck and closed her eyes. She did not know where he was taking her, but she did not care; he was holding her, and that was all she wanted. He took her outside and then Eleanor felt them move into shade before smelling the strong scent of horses. She opened her eyes as he sat down, leaning back comfortably on the pile of clean straw at the back of Meran's stall, Eleanor lying against him. She wriggled slightly so she was not resting against his stomach and laid the side of her face on his chest, listening to him breathe. He kept his arms wrapped around her, his cheek resting on her head. Eleanor heard movement outside the stall and smiled as Horse stuck her head round, looking at her questioningly. Horse walked into the stall, dropped to her knees next to Conlan and lay with her head on his leg, staring at him adoringly. Meran turned to look at Horse lying next to Conlan and Eleanor, and with a snort he got painfully down to his knees before laying his head against Eleanor's leg.

Time ceased to have any meaning. Eleanor dozed, not really sleeping, not really awake, her mind blank and contented. She recognised that, for the first time, there was serenity. Conlan's strong arms around her, listening to him breathe, feeling warm, comfortable and totally safe, she was finally able to let go and stop her mind's perpetual churning. Horse and Meran lay next to them in quiet companionship, and Eleanor felt loved, felt the world begin to turn itself right side up again. Conlan did not speak but ran slow circles up and down her arm with light fingers, occasionally stroking her hair back from her face. Eleanor slipped into a level of bliss she had never felt before, a gentle joy. Conlan sighed, pulling her closer, and she knew he could feel how happy she was. As the day moved on outside, Eleanor ignored it, not wanting to disturb the perfect peace she had found. She did not move and hardly dared to breathe. She just wanted him to hold her forever.

She heard footsteps outside the stall. *Reality*, she thought with irritation as she felt Conlan's body tense.

"Hello, Laurice, I am glad to see you are feeling better," he said, his tone light and friendly.

"Laurice," Eleanor said, not opening her eyes. "I am sorry about the mess I made of Freddie's bedroom."

"I always wanted an 'open' roof in that room," Laurice said, unconcerned. Conlan chuckled and fireworks of pleasure went off in Eleanor's head, as not only could she hear the laughter she loved, but she could also feel it as it vibrated through his chest.

"You are very understanding," Conlan said, running gratitude and grateful thanks through the words. "Was there something we can help you with?"

"I was told I might find you here, but I was not told it would be unwise to interrupt. My apologies," Laurice said, and Eleanor could hear the amusement in the woman's voice. She expected Conlan to pull away from her, to deny Laurice's implications, but instead she felt his arms tighten slightly round her body.

"We are just sharing some quiet time. Eleanor was upset. Please speak," he said.

"I was planning on holding a celebration this evening to announce my daughter's marriage, and I was wondering if you, Merl and your Avatars would honour us with your presence," Laurice said.

"I cannot speak for the others, but I would be delighted to attend, thank you," Conlan replied, and he sounded genuinely pleased with the invite.

Eleanor smiled, still not opening her eyes or moving. "Thank you for the invite, Laurice, I would love to come. What time should we be there? Actually, what time is it now?"

Laurice laughed. "It is currently just before midday. We normally eat about sunset. I will send Nials to your quarters to fetch you and I will ask Urerla to locate the rest of your group and invite them. Should she be telling them where they can find you, if they ask?" she asked slyly. Again, Eleanor expected Conlan to pull away and ask Laurice not to tell the others anything, but again he surprised her by chuckling, sending Eleanor into raptures.

"You can tell them, if they ask," he said.

Eleanor heard Laurice walk away and smiled.

"We got invited to a party. That is so lovely of them."

Conlan did not respond and Eleanor sighed softly, allowing herself to relax again and letting the sound of his breathing bring back the warm fuzzy feeling of tranquillity and sanctuary. There was no thought, no stress, just delightful warmth and a calm refuge.

It was many hours later when Eleanor heard footsteps again. She felt Conlan's body tense, but his voice was gentle.

"Hello, Amelia."

"Hi," she replied tentatively.

From what Eleanor had heard she had tried to help Conlan, tried to point out the obvious. With that single thought, Eleanor felt all the misery and anger that her proximity to Conlan had faded into the background come back into sharp focus.

"Eleanor, are you ready to talk yet?" Conlan asked. There was no expectation in his voice. If she said no, she knew he would accept it, but she was going to have to face it sooner or later, and she did feel better, more whole and more able to deal with her hurt. She opened her eyes and sat up. Amelia was stood in the entrance to the stall. The expression on her face made Eleanor think of olive branches and sacrificial lambs. She wondered if Will and Freddie were in her head.

"Are they OK?" Eleanor asked, her guilt punching at her. "Did I hurt them?"

Amelia shrugged. "Freddie's got some bruises and Will has a lump on his forehead from the roof falling on him, but given the circumstances they were lucky."

"You should have put a shield over them," Eleanor said, her guilt taking another swipe.

A deep, serious looked moved into Amelia's grey eyes, and when she spoke, her voice was a cold whisper. "Merl had barely carried you out of the door when they jumped Conlan. They didn't wait for an explanation, didn't even ask for one. I tried to stop them, but they ignored me. I should've flattened them, but I was frightened of hurting Conlan further. They deserved what you did. I wouldn't have been able to control my energy that well."

Eleanor shook her head. "No, this is all my fault. I should have shot Freddie down far sooner and should have put more effort into explaining to Will. I knew he was angry."

Conlan sighed. "This wasn't your fault, Eleanor."

She knew arguing the point was a waste of time, but that did not change the fact that she was going to make it up to him.

"Will and Freddie are really sorry," Amelia ventured. Eleanor turned to glare at her for several heartbeats, before smoothing her expression into something a little friendlier. *Amelia is the olive branch here; it's not her fault they sent her.*

"They should be," Eleanor replied, managing to add a threatening Dwarfish growl to the English, making Conlan chuckle.

"Are you going to come back? We're going to the party soon and you need to change. I can help you, if you like," Amelia offered with a smile. Eleanor looked at her, bemused. Looking down at her clothes, they seemed perfectly adequate.

"Change?" she asked, and Amelia laughed.

"Eleanor, you have straw in your hair, you're covered in dust, have blood on the back of your shirt and you smell like Horse; it's a party! You need to have a bath and put on some clean clothes. I know you have a dress or two in the stuff Callie gave you."

Eleanor frowned. "Dress?"

This time both Amelia and Conlan laughed.

Eleanor huffed. "I don't like dresses," she said, knowing she sounded a little petulant, but the nightmare white dress was dancing through her head.

"I liked the white dress," Conlan said softly, as if he was reading her mind. It was disconcerting.

Eleanor stared at him incredulously. "It was hideous, I felt naked in it!" she muttered, dropping her head and feeling her cheeks turn crimson in embarrassment. Conlan placed a hand on her face and she shuddered at the pleasure that flooded her body. He firmly brought her eyes to his.

"You looked beautiful," he murmured.

Shocked beyond rational thought, Eleanor stared at him. He had just told her she was beautiful. He smiled at her and her heart tried to bounce itself out of her chest.

"Eleanor? Are you OK?" he asked, a small frown appearing between his eyes. Still unable to give a sensible, coherent response, Eleanor continued to stare at him. She was grateful when Amelia came to her rescue.

"She's fine, Conlan; you just surprised her, she really hated that dress. I'll take her for a bath," she said, stepping forward. With firm hands on Eleanor's arms, she got her to stand and led her from the stable.

Amelia was helping her to undress in the bathroom, steaming hot water waiting for her. Finally, Eleanor found her voice again.

"Amelia?" she whispered.

"Yes, sweetie?"

"Why did Will do it?" she asked, failing to keep the hurt out of her voice.

Amelia sighed and helped Eleanor into the large metal bath tub. "It takes a huge amount to get Will furious, but once he *is*, all common sense goes out of the window – you should know that. He's feeling unbelievably guilty and has no idea what to say to you or Conlan; neither of them does. They've been freaking out. Poor Conlan, he's been doing his best to hide his pain and stay out of your way. He's been hiding his misery because he knows you can feel it." Tears began running down Eleanor's face again; Amelia noticed and shook her head. "Please don't, or you're going to have red eyes for the party."

"I'm sure red eyes would make me look even more stupid than the dress," Eleanor muttered.

"You won't look stupid. Don't you want to look your best for Conlan?" Amelia asked. Eleanor stared. The thought had never occurred to her.

"Amelia, he sees me all day, every day. He's seen me soaking wet, covered in mud, covered in blood, covered in sand, half-asleep, throwing up, sweaty and tear-stained. I really don't think one night of me in a dress is going to make much of an impression against that opposition."

Amelia smiled at her knowingly. "He remembered the white dress."

Eleanor raised an eyebrow. "Yes, Amelia, he remembered the white dress that made me look like I was wearing nothing. I'd lay odds that Will and Freddie remember that dress rather well, too."

Amelia giggled. "Fair point," she agreed as she concentrated on washing the straw and dust out of Eleanor's hair.

Amelia had been right. There were two dresses in the bottom of the bag Callie had given her. She had no idea what they looked like – she knew that one was brown and the other was vivid green, but that was it. So she was surprised when Amelia led her back to her bedroom, still damp and wrapped in a towel, and showed her the two dresses lying out on the bed. They had both been freshly washed and pressed and they were beautiful. The brown one was warm and soft and made from an earthy brown, velvet material, which would hang heavily around her. Long sleeves and a square neckline, the top tapering to a tight waist and a full skirt completed the look. When Eleanor moved her hand across it a golden ripple followed her hand's movement, giving the impression of flickering gold streaks. The bright green one seemed to be made of silk, and the material made the colour shift hue in the light. It was a much more delicate material and it would brush her skin as she walked, like the white dress had done. It was also a full-length dress, but with short sleeves and a heart-shaped neckline. The bust and waist were fitted, with a small fishtail of material at the back.

"Which one do you want to wear?" Amelia asked, smiling at the blank look Eleanor gave her. "Would you like a suggestion?" she offered. Eleanor furiously nodded her head and Amelia laughed. "OK, well the brown one would go beautifully with your eyes, but the green one would be more comfortable in this heat and would match Conlan's eyes better."

"Why does that matter?" Eleanor asked in confusion.

"It doesn't, it was just something that occurred to me," Amelia shrugged. Eleanor was not convinced that was the whole truth, but she let it drop. Amelia left her in peace to dry off and dress, returning to brush and pin Eleanor's hair, which she pulled back off her face before handing her a pair of delicate brown leather ballet shoes she had never seen before. Eleanor looked at her questioningly.

Amelia smiled. "I borrowed them," she said by way of explanation. "You didn't think I was going to go to all this trouble and then let you wear your boots, did you?"

Eleanor shrugged, accepting that Amelia obviously knew far more about dressing up than she did. Once Eleanor was ready, Amelia organised herself and put on the outfit she had brought to Eleanor's room, a stunning, pale grey, loose-fitting, strappy dress that flowed like water over her slender body.

"You look beautiful," Eleanor said appreciatively.

Amelia smiled. "Ditto, sweetie." Her face was suddenly serious. "Eleanor? Have you given any thought to how you are going to react when you see Will and Freddie?"

"Yes, I've given it some thought," she said, her voice solid ice.

"And?" Amelia prompted. Eleanor saw the glazed look in Amelia's eyes and knew who would be inside her head eavesdropping.

"And they're going to apologise," she said softly. "Come in, Will!" she added. The door opened and Will entered. He looked strange. It took Eleanor several moments to realise that he was scrubbed, clean-shaven and wearing clean, pressed clothes that did not look like he had been living in them for weeks; she was not used to it. He wore a bright white shirt over dark brown trousers that she had never seen before. *Amelia has been very busy borrowing clothes.* Eleanor noticed the cartoonish-sized purple lump on his forehead, partially hidden by the soft blond hair he had brushed over it, and guilt punched her hard. She did her best to keep it off her face, though, as she was still angry with him. He was watching her, deep-blue eyes showing apprehension.

"I'm sorry."

Eleanor stared at him. "It's not me you need to be apologising to, Will."

Will nodded, dropping his gaze.

"Shall we go and join the others?" Amelia asked, ignoring the brittle atmosphere as she took Will's hand. They walked down the corridor to the living room they shared. Freddie was stood outside, also wearing new clothes, his outfit matching Will's. He looked nervous, his expression twisted by the slight swelling to his eye and several bruises standing out dark purple and red on his golden brown skin.

"What are you stood out here for?" Eleanor asked.

Freddie dropped his head. "Conlan's inside; I didn't want to face him on my own," he whispered.

"Coward!" Eleanor hissed at him, pushing past, opening the door and marching into the room. Conlan was stood by the window and turned to face her.

He smiled. Everything stopped.

He was washed and clean-shaven and had even brushed his hair into some sort of order. Like the others he was wearing borrowed clothes: black, tight-fitting trousers, black polished leather boots up to his knees, a white silk shirt with a soft collar and a jacket that dropped to midway down his thigh and seemed to be the exact same colour green as Eleanor's dress. *Amelia was right, the colour makes it look like his eyes are glowing.*

Eleanor smiled as her heart stuttered back to a semi-normal beat again. "You look very handsome," she managed. "Did Amelia steal several people's wardrobes to clothe you all?"

Conlan chuckled. "Apparently she went to a lot of trouble to get this jacket to match your dress. I'm unsure why it was important, but she assures me it is."

Eleanor shrugged, ignoring the twinge of pain across her back. "I have no idea either, but if it makes her happy…" Behind her, Amelia sighed loudly. Eleanor looked around the room and frowned. "Where's Merl?"

"He has chosen not to attend, as he is still a little sore. Laurice has people watching over him, he appears to be quite enjoying being waited on hand and foot," Conlan said. Eleanor nodded, amused. There was a cough from behind her and Eleanor turned. Will and Freddie were watching Conlan.

"We need to apologise," Will said softly. There was an uncomfortable silence

"I lost my temper," Will said slowly. "You didn't do anything wrong and we had no right to pass judgement. Please forgive me."

Eleanor decided he sounded genuine. Before Conlan could respond, Freddie spoke.

"I'm so sorry. I needed to take it out on someone and you were convenient; it was wrong, please forgive me, too." Eleanor looked at Conlan and saw the affection in his eyes.

"I forgive you," Conlan said, a grin spreading across his face as they raised their heads and smiled at him.

Eleanor hardened her glare. "Promise him you will never lay a hand on him in anger again," she ordered.

"I promise, Conlan, I'll never intentionally hurt you again," Will said, and Eleanor heard the guilty apology in his voice.

Freddie was silent for a few moments, but finally he took a deep breath. "I promise, Conlan, I'll never strike at you in anger again. I'm sorry," he whispered.

Conlan stood silently, emotions flashing rapidly across his face and shame filling his eyes. "And I make you the same promise," he said quietly, looking each of them in the eye and holding Eleanor's gaze. "All of you."

Will gave him a wide grin while Freddie nodded, although he still looked uncomfortable.

"Eleanor, do *you* forgive me?" he asked in a small, pained voice. Eleanor thought about it. Did she forgive him? She wanted to, and she knew it would cause problems if she was unable to, but she still felt hurt and betrayed.

"Freddie, you took the most important person in my life and you damaged him. I know why you did it, I understand and yes, I forgive you, but I trusted you. You destroyed that trust and I'm finding that very, very hard to deal with," Eleanor said, staring at his bowed head. Freddie nodded, eyes firmly down, and Eleanor saw tears drop off the end of his nose. Her heart squeezed for him. Stepping towards him she wrapped an arm around his waist and looked into his eyes. Reaching up, she wiped the tears from his bruised face. A tiny smile tried to lift the corner of his mouth. Resting her head against his chest she hugged him tight.

"Don't ever do that again, Freddie," she whispered.

"I'm sorry," he whispered back, carefully hugging her in return.

"Eleanor…" Will started.

A shot of anger ripped through her. "I've something I want to show you," she interrupted, and with no warning at all she slammed an energy string into him with such force that Will staggered backwards. Closing her eyes, Eleanor sent him her memories and feelings. She started with the deal she had made with Laurice and Conlan's objections – his distress, threatening Nials. Moving on, Eleanor showed Will every quiet word of encouragement and support, every tender, comforting touch Conlan had ever given her and the strange way he remembered everything she said. She then brought forward all the occasions he had made her feel better, had made the effort to make sure she was OK, and all the times he had made her feel better, without even knowing he had done anything. As she played these memories back, rapid snapshots playing against the background of her emotions, she realised that almost every one had been a private moment. Conlan had approached her only when there was nobody else paying attention. She showed Will the comforting reassurance Conlan gave her, the brief touches, the gentle stroking of her head and holding her hand under the blankets. Then she replayed some of the day they had spent in the stables, sending Will all her feelings of serenity, her joy at having the churning in her mind stop, her delight at discovering that he could do this for her. For a moment she dwelled on this, wanting Will to understand what it meant to her, before yanking her string back roughly.

"Now do you understand?" Eleanor snapped.

Astonished, Will moved his eyes to Conlan and gave him a stunned smile. Conlan gave him a lopsided grin in return.

"What did she show you?" he asked, apprehensive eyes flicking to Eleanor.

"She showed me just how wrong I was," Will whispered in Dwarfish, a grovelling growl of subservient apology running through the sentence.

Conlan chucked. "She is good at that."

Will nodded ruefully.

There was a knock on the door and Amelia opened it. Nials stood dressed in a fine silk version of the everyday clothes he normally wore. He smiled.

"Are you ready to leave?"

Conlan nodded. Amelia took Will's hand and pulled him after her. He still had an awestruck look on his face, and every so often he would glance back at Conlan, as if he could not quite believe he was looking at the person he thought he knew. Eleanor was surprised when Conlan took her hand.

"What did you show him?" he asked.

"You."

Conlan looked uncomfortable for a moment, before shrugging it off. As they walked towards the door, Eleanor turned back. Freddie still stood in the middle of the room. His face was empty and he had a look in his eyes Eleanor did not understand. She stretched her free hand back to him. Smiling, he walked quickly forward and wrapped his hand tightly round hers.

Nials led them back to the main audience chamber. Eleanor could hear the sounds of voices talking and laughing long before they reached their destination. It sounded like a lot of people. She was quietly glad for Conlan and Freddie's hands in hers, as they embodied confidence. Social gatherings had never really been Eleanor's thing. She liked the idea of parties, wanted to join in and have fun, but large groups of people made her nervous. *If I can't handle a party, how am I going to deal with a battle?* Feeling her anxiety, Conlan gave her hand a squeeze. Chastising herself for being utterly pathetic, Eleanor sought calm. Nials opened the main doors to the audience chamber, and the noise level jumped. Will and Amelia blocked her view, so Eleanor could not see much, for which she felt grateful. As they entered, silence fell so quickly it was like someone had pressed the mute button. Wondering what was happening, Eleanor jumped when Nials's voice rang out.

"My Lady Laurice, precious Urerla, Honoured Ladies of the Seven Tribes, Noble Horsemen, faithful friends, dependable allies and beloved family, I have the pleasure of presenting Conlan Baydon and his Avatars."

A moment of silence followed Nials's words.

"'Conlan Baydon and his Avatars'; he makes us sound like a Vegas lounge act," Eleanor muttered without thinking. Next to her Freddie slapped his hand over his mouth and looked pained as he fought to control his giggles, every naked flame in the room jumping. In front of her Eleanor could see Will and Amelia go rigid; she knew they were also trying desperately hard not to laugh.

Oops…

Conlan noticed the reaction of the others and looked down at her, an eyebrow raised in question. She smiled back innocently. Before he could say anything the assembled gathering broke out into riotous applause. To the huge swell of clapping hands, Nials led them forwards. Everything looked very different from the last time Eleanor had seen the audience chamber; the clapping was making her nervous again, so she concentrated on the room. The central raised platform with its wooden chair was gone and had been replaced by six wide tables that ran the length of the room, benches on each side, white cloths and flower arrangements covering the tables, cutlery and glasses arranged in each place, sparkling in the delicate, dreamy glow of lanterns and candles. At the far end of the room, towards where they were heading, a table had been placed horizontally across the others. This table only had settings on the side that faced the rest of the room, and instead of benches there were large, comfy-looking chairs with high arms and tall backs. Looking up, Eleanor could see the remnant pale orange and red splashes of the setting sun through the open roof, and a cooling breeze brushed her face. Everybody was stood clapping, cheering and smiling; it made her uncomfortable. Conlan, however, seemed relaxed and happy, a friendly smile on his face. *Growing up with a Lord of Mydren as a father, he must be used to it.* As they reached the end of the room, Laurice stepped forward. She was wearing her gold belt with a stunning red dress, similar to the one Urerla had been wearing in the garden, with lots of floaty layers of gossamer material. As she looked around at the many women present, Eleanor noticed this style of dress seemed to be the fashion; most women were wearing one in myriad different colours, styles and lengths.

Laurice clasped the hands of each of them to her in greeting, a radiant smile on her face. She directed them to their places personally. Eleanor was horrified to find they had been placed on the top table, with Conlan sitting next to Laurice. The only other occupants at the top table were Urerla, Nials and the leaders of the other seven tribes, whom Laurice introduced as they walked to their seats. Each woman had a different delicate pattern of ritual scarring across their faces, and all gave an air of strength and intelligence, appraising Eleanor with keen interest as they met her. She wondered what Laurice had told them.

As she sat in her place, Eleanor felt like every eye in the room was boring into them, analysing and scrutinising. Relieved to discover that she was to sit next to Conlan, with Freddie on her other side, Eleanor relaxed slightly, as at least she would have someone to talk to – a distraction from the watching black eyes. They took their seats as Laurice took hers, followed by the shuffling and movement of three hundred people climbing into their places at the tables in front of them. After this flurry of activity had passed, an expectant silence descended and Laurice stood, smiling at the people gathered before her. When she spoke, her clear, chiming voice carried to the far corners of the room.

"Beloved friends, thank you for joining me on this night of new beginnings. We have gathered here to celebrate the love my daughter and heir, Urerla, shares with my horseman Nials as they declare their desire to marry, to which I give my wholehearted blessing. We also gather to celebrate our new alliance with Conlan Baydon. I owe my position, my life and the lives of my daughter and her future husband to Conlan and his Avatars. In recognition of this, and on behalf of the Eight Tribes of the Horse, I swear my allegiance to him and offer such help and assistance that he may need in his battle to destroy the Lords of Mydren and claim the right to rule. My brother moved against me because he believed I was failing to act against the ever-growing threat the Lords of Mydren present to us and our way of life. I have not acted before because I never felt there was an option of defiance available. This is no longer the case; we have been offered the chance to show that we are a force to be reckoned with. I believe that Conlan Baydon will succeed, and I look forward to the day I see him crowned King of Mydren."

Laurice paused, smiling at Conlan who nodded his head in graceful acceptance. Eleanor looked down the table; none of the other tribe leaders seemed shocked or upset by Laurice's proclamation, so Eleanor assumed any disagreements that might have arisen had been argued out by Laurice beforehand. Laurice turned back to her people and continued speaking.

"As a symbol of our allegiance to Conlan Baydon, we are parting with our most treasured possession, the 'Heart', which has rested with our people for hundreds of years and was forged in our volcano's molten heat. However, it was never truly ours and I now pass it back to its rightful owner. Freddie, Avatar of Fire, please stand."

Eleanor looked at Freddie's confused face; he knew she had said his name.

"Freddie, stand up," Eleanor hissed urgently. Freddie flicked his eyes to Eleanor, before getting slowly to his feet. A guard moved from against the back wall and gave a sword, sheathed in an elaborately carved silver scabbard, to Freddie. Inch-long rubies glittered from it as Freddie turned it over in his hands, a look of excited awe on his face.

"Tell her thank you," Freddie said to Conlan, smiling as he ran tender fingers down the sword and then taking his seat again, not able to take his eyes off the weapon. Eleanor heard several gasps from the crowd at Freddie speaking English, but looking out at the sea of faces, as Conlan translated Freddie's gratitude in a far more elegant style than Freddie himself, Eleanor decided it was surprise and interest she had heard. Nobody seemed afraid, just curious and friendly. *Four down, one to go; all we have to do now is retrieve the crown, get rid of Conlan's shield and get the connection working. All this time... why does it feel like we're no closer?* Eleanor was so caught up in her thoughts that she jumped when Laurice addressed her.

"Eleanor, Avatar of Earth, please stand."

"Me?" Eleanor asked. *What have I done now?*

"Unless you know of any other Avatars of Earth I could be addressing?" Laurice asked, amused. There was polite laughter from the guests. Her heart hammering in her chest, Eleanor got up, stared at her feet and felt her stomach flip. Conlan reached for her hand and held it tightly. Eleanor smiled and raised her head. She looked at Laurice, trying to avoid glancing at the audience.

"Eleanor, Avatar of Earth, I owe you special thanks, as you helped my daughter find love, a gift beyond measure, and, with no thought for your own safety, stood in my defence and paid a heavy price. In recognition of this selfless courage I would like to offer you a gift of your choosing, anything you wish that is within my power to provide. What can I give you, little warrior?"

Eleanor stared at Laurice open-mouthed. She knew what she wanted, knew there was only one thing she could ask for. Glancing down at Conlan's hand holding tightly to hers made her feel a little braver and Eleanor steeled herself.

"Please may I have Meran?" she asked, looking Laurice in the eye.

A deathly hush fell over the room as if three hundred people were holding their breath. Laurice looked shocked. It was Nials who answered her from further down the table.

"Eleanor, you ask too much. Meran is a member of our family."

"Peace, Nials," Laurice said quietly. "The Avatar asks in innocence. I would know why she makes the request; she has a horse who loves her."

A strong hot blush blossoming on her cheeks, Eleanor dropped her head again and allowed herself another glance at her hand in Conlan's before raising her eyes to Laurice's, a face full of guilt. Laurice saw the look and understood.

"You did not ask in innocence, did you? You are well aware of the implications of your request," she said. Her voice was mild, but it still carried the length of the room. Eleanor heard more gasps and her heartbeat went into overdrive. Wondering if she was going to get punished again, she nodded.

"Meran told me about his 'status'," she confirmed, rushing into her explanation, her voice trembling slightly but wanting to get her point across before Laurice decided to stop her. "I have a horse I love and who loves me, but Conlan does not. He needs a horse fit for a king, he needs a strong, brave, dependable friend, he needs Meran and Meran needs him." Laurice regarded her in silence, so Eleanor kept going. "The People of the Horse bind their allegiances in marriage, but this is not possible in this case; however, Meran is a member of your family, and while the bond between horse and master is not a 'marriage', it can still be strong enough to act as a bind to your alliance." Then dropping her tone to a growl of desperate begging, the verbal equivalent of prostrating herself at Laurice's feet, Eleanor spoke again. "Please let us take Meran, he wants to come with us. If he stays here the grief will kill him."

Eleanor felt Conlan's grip tighten as Laurice stared at her thoughtfully. Her friends' eyes glazed over as Will gave a translation in Freddie and Amelia's heads as to what was going on. Time stretched and Laurice turned and held a whispered conversation with Urerla. Eleanor could feel every eye in the room glowering at her for what she had suggested. Eventually Laurice turned back to face her, holding her gaze with a strong, steady eye. Eleanor forced herself not to drop her head.

"Eleanor, Avatar of Earth. I offered you a gift and you risked my displeasure by making a request on behalf of another. Had I not offered you this gift, would you have asked me for Meran anyway?" Laurice asked. She did not sound angry, but Eleanor knew sometimes this was a greater indication of it.

"Yes, I would have asked for Meran, and for the reasons I have stated. Meran is a fine horse and a friend. He needs a new purpose. Conlan's horse Rand, another fine animal, died tragically not long ago, so they need each other," Eleanor said.

"A heart for a heart," Laurice murmured. Eleanor realised it was the third reference she had made to the sword's poem in the book.

"A silver sword in south freedom's hands; A gift beyond measure to enter their lands; A heart for a heart, a price to be paid; Think to the future a deal to be made," Eleanor quoted. Laurice stared at her in open-mouthed shock as the other seven tribe leaders began whispering furiously behind her back.

"These words of secret prophesy have been passed down from the mother to the daughter of the ruling families for generations beyond memory. We are told that when these words came to pass we would need to fight to change the world for the better. How do you know them?" Laurice asked. Eleanor could feel the crowd leaning closer, fascinated and excited at being let into this secret.

"We were given instructions on how to find the Talismans that we need, and the poem I have just recited was how we found you," she said.

Laurice smiled, as if everything had suddenly become clear. "My husband's horse is yours, along with my grateful thanks. I would ask, however, that you wait a few weeks before departing, in order to allow Meran some time to build up his strength. He is rather fragile at the moment."

Laurice flicked her eyes to Conlan, and Eleanor saw his head nodding out of the corner of her eye, but she was not taking her eyes off the woman in case she changed her mind.

"Wonderful, then let us eat!" Laurice said, her chiming voice filling the room. Eleanor dropped heavily into her seat as her legs gave way. Laurice's command appeared to be the signal for life to return to the room; the excited buzz of conversation rose and fell as doors in the back of the room opened and waiters and waitresses entered to serve the hundreds of guests. A plate was placed in front of her and Eleanor realised that her food was different from all those around her – it was one of her favourite vegetable dishes, a mashed pale-pink, carrot-like root that had a sweet sugary taste and was covered in slightly bitter, melted cheese. She looked at the array of eating utensils in front of her and tried to work out which one she should be eating with. There seemed to be no logic to how they were laid out, as they were arranged in a strange overlapping circle around the plate. She glanced at Freddie, but he looked just as bemused as she was. Her hand still in Conlan's, Eleanor gave it a light tug; he politely broke off his conversation with Laurice and turned to her.

"Yes?" he asked softly in Dwarfish.

"I do not know which…" she waved her free hand over the place setting, not knowing the Dwarfish word for 'cutlery', "… to eat with," she whispered. Amused, Conlan nodded and gave her a lesson in table etiquette, quietly telling her the names for each implement as well as their collective terms and explaining the order. There was a sort of logic to it, as they used their utensils in a spiral progression. Throughout his lesson, Laurice would occasionally offer additional information as to why certain things were done, telling Eleanor stories about poisoned leaders and the spiral of movement representing the spiral of life from birth to death. Freddie had entered her head so that Eleanor could translate for him, as he found the tradition and ritual to formal eating fascinating. As they ate and more courses were brought out, Eleanor realised there was an implement for each course, which meant there were going to be twenty-five in all, a sacred number, Laurice had told her. Considering the amount of food presented at each serving, Eleanor began pacing herself, and she suggested that Freddie do the same. He scoffed at her. Conlan, she noticed, took no more than two or three mouthfuls from each dish, but then Eleanor had not wanted to let go of his hand, so he was reduced to eating with one utensil. He did not seem to mind and actually seemed relaxed, happy and comfortable, which helped Eleanor shake off some of her fear. In addition, Freddie cracking dreadful jokes in her head as he attempted to get to grips with his dinner made her giggle, helping to calm her nerves further. Eleanor was impressed with Laurice's chefs; they managed to come up with twenty different dishes just for her, each one unique and wonderfully tasty. The last five courses were puddings and sweets. Eleanor watched Conlan finish his first full plate of food when a light spongy cake covered in thick, white, sweet, mint-flavoured custard was put in front of him. Loving the look of boyish delight with which he ate, she offered him her portion as well. He grinned at her, not needing to be offered twice, and swapped his empty plate for hers. He was slightly more restrained on the four further courses, but Eleanor smiled at the wistful looks he gave the uneaten sweet treats and cookies he had left as the plates were removed.

After the meal, hot bitter tea was passed round. Eleanor wondered if this was meant to help sober up those who had been drinking too much with their mountains of food. Eleanor had stuck to a cool, spicy, syrupy drink diluted in water; it tasted a little like ginger. She had never been a big fan of alcohol, disliking the loss of control that came with it, her mind requiring a permanently firm grip to function. Will, Amelia and Conlan managed to make a couple of glasses of the heavy, blood-red wine they had been served last the whole meal. Freddie had consumed several more glasses, but far from inebriated, he was just happy. Eleanor hoped it lasted.

Once the tea course was over, people began getting up from the tables and milling around the great room talking as an army of servants cleared away the mess and then the tables and benches, leaving only the top table and a large room. At the far end, a small stage area was erected and a band began setting up, tuning strange-looking instruments. The noise was shrill but strangely tuneful. Eleanor felt her heart drop into her stomach, which, on top of the huge meal she had just eaten, made her feel rather sick. *Music... Does that mean there's going to be dancing? Am I going to have to dance? In front of people?* Conlan felt her sudden terror and gave her hand a squeeze.

"Are you OK?" he whispered in English. She looked at him, loathing her fear.

"Am I going to have to dance?" she whispered back hoarsely. She saw the amusement sparkle in his eyes, but he made a huge effort to keep it out of his voice.

"Not if you don't want to," he replied solemnly. She nodded, somewhat mollified, and watched as the band finished setting up their instruments.

Nials and Urerla, as the happy couple, were the first to take to the floor. The music was a bright, lively tune in the tempo of a waltz. Both Nials and Urerla were good dancers and moved around the floor as if they were one graceful being, the subtle sound of Urerla's belt a backdrop to the band's music. Urerla clearly loved every minute of the attention and Nials loved Urerla's ecstatic smile, his eyes barely leaving hers as they moved together in a flowing, sensual dance. There was thunderous applause as the dance came to an end. As other people began to take to the floor, Laurice asked Conlan to dance. He smiled and rose from his chair. Leaning over slightly, he took Freddie's hand, placing it around Eleanor's.

"Freddie will keep you company until I get back, OK?" he said in English. Eleanor nodded and noticed the strange look on Freddie's face. It was quite a while before Conlan returned, as once Laurice had danced with him, all the other tribal leaders wanted to as well. Then Urerla had insisted on having a dance, Nials smiling indulgently as Conlan whirled her round through the other guests. Eleanor watched him travel lightly across the floor; he seemed to know exactly what he was doing and was thoroughly enjoying himself. Eleanor smiled, his happiness making her feel floaty and content. The dances moved on to more set pieces, with all the guests moving together in complicated steps, which seemed to be as natural to them as breathing. Conlan, laughing and joking with his various dance partners, did not seem to give the dancing a second thought. Will and Amelia were also dancing. Eleanor was surprised to see that Will also seemed to know what he was doing, just as he had known which knives and forks to use. They watched the dancers with interest and giggled at the less elegant attempts made by some of the more drunken guests. Freddie kept up a running commentary of silliness, and Eleanor added her own observations.

Eventually Conlan returned. Taking his seat and looking a little flushed, he leaned across to Eleanor and whispered in her ear.

"Dance with me, please. I want to make every man in the room jealous."

Eleanor smiled, a tight, warm feeling flooding through her, and whispered back.

"Flattery will get you nowhere. Besides, if you want to make every man jealous you need to pry Amelia out of Will's arms, not dance with me."

His cheek brushing hers, he whispered again. "If you don't say yes, I'm going to get down on my knees and beg... very, very loudly."

Eleanor felt a deep heated blush rise to her face at the thought. "How much have you had to drink?"

"More than I'm used to," Conlan admitted with a mischievous chuckle. Eleanor realised he was serious. She weighed up the embarrassment of her dancing against the embarrassment of having Conlan beg at her feet and decided that dancing would be a better idea. She nodded slowly.

"OK, but I have no clue what the dance steps are, and you're going to regret it when I break your toes." Conlan laughed, took her hand and helped her from her chair, leading her to the dance floor. Eleanor walked with her eyes firmly down, hoping nobody would see her. Conlan placed a light grip on her waist and took her hand.

"Eleanor, take your eyes off your feet and look at me."

Taking a deep breath and trying to calm her racing heart, Eleanor raised her head.

"Allow me to lead you and let yourself follow. Don't over-think it. I know these are difficult concepts for you, but try, OK?" Conlan instructed, grinning. Eleanor nodded, her anxiety making her a little sick. She concentrated on Conlan, the way his body moved, the hints he gave her with a flick of the eyes or a tensed muscle, about where he was going to move next. Time disappeared and she had no idea how long they danced. She was aware that the music style and tempo had changed several times, as Conlan changed his steps to match. Now Eleanor was a little more comfortable, his movements were quicker, more the beautiful fluid motion she had seen when he danced with Urerla. He looked down at her with a happy smile on his face, his eyes holding hers, spinning and twirling her. *I'm dreaming – this is all some strange fantasy my mind has cooked up.* The glow of candlelight, the full moon she could see shining down through the open roof, stars scattered across a cloudless sky, the blur of smiling, happy faces as she twirled past and Will's amused encouragement as Amelia tried to teach a giggling Freddie how to dance – they all worked to convince Eleanor that this could not be real.

Eleanor woke late the next morning, still tired and feeling like she had only just gone to bed. Her stomach felt swollen and stretched, too full. She needed to take a walk, and preferably a long one. Shambling out of bed, yawning and trying to get her eyes to open, she pulled her clothes on and smiled as her eye caught the green dress draped over a chair. It was physical proof that last night had not been a dream; she smiled again and ran her hands over the silky material. Walking down the corridor and heading for the outside world, Eleanor heard Merl's voice through the partially open door of the living room; she stopped and listened.

"She did what?" Merl sounded confused.

"Asked for Meran," Conlan replied.

"One of the most powerful people in Mydren offered her a gift of her choosing and she asked for a half-dead nag?!" Merl spluttered, disbelief making his voice louder.

"Meran was once a fine horse," Conlan said. "With the proper care he can be that again. Unfortunately it means that we must stay here for another two weeks while he has a chance to recover." There was a pause.

"Maybe we can use this time to our advantage," Merl said thoughtfully. "We could leave the others here, and you and I could travel to Termont. It is the nearest town where I can send a message to my friend, but it is a little off course. If we go now, when we leave in two weeks' time we can take the quicker, more direct route to Katadep."

"That is not a bad idea," Conlan said, and Eleanor felt her overfull stomach lurch. He was going to disappear off with Merl, just the two of them, with no protection. Was he mad? She debated marching in on them and demanding an explanation. She jumped as an energy string brushed against her.

Didn't you say your mother told you it was wrong to eavesdrop? Freddie asked, walking up behind her.

Merl is trying to convince Conlan to go with him to a town called Termont while we wait for Meran to get stronger. It will be just the two of them, in order to send a message, Eleanor told him, unable to keep the slight edge of panic out of her thoughts.

I'm sure he'll be OK. Let's face it, the Lords of Mydren want all of us, so nothing would be gained from apprehending just Conlan, Freddie reasoned.

You're being remarkably calm and practical about this, Eleanor noted.

That's because if Conlan does agree to go with Merl, I'll be going with him, Freddie told her.

Great, so then I get to worry about both of you, Eleanor muttered.

I'll protect him, Eleanor, I promise. I failed you once, but it won't happen again.

Eleanor felt tears prickle her eyes and hugged him, touched by his thoughtfulness.

I do love you, Freddie, you know that, right?

Yes I know, Freddie said, gently kissing the top of her head.

The door to the living room was pulled open and Freddie jumped, whipping his hands behind his back. It was a totally pointless gesture, as Eleanor still had her arms wrapped tightly around his waist. She wondered why he had done it. She turned her head and Conlan gazed at her, a small smile tugging at the corner of his mouth.

"Spying in doorways are you now?" he asked, amusement running through the dwarfish.

Eleanor blushed. "I just heard you talking as I was walking past…"

Conlan held her gaze as her cheeks turned an even deeper shade of red.

Is Conlan angry with me? Freddie asked.

No.

He's not jealous?

No, he's not jealous, why would he be jealous? Eleanor asked, slightly bemused.

It's different now… Freddie started, but then he stopped, unsure of himself.

Eleanor was so perplexed that she ignored Conlan and stared into Freddie's face. *Nothing's different, Freddie. I don't understand.*

He… cares for you, Eleanor. And Eleanor heard pain in his voice.

Freddie, he's always cared for me, just as he cares for you, Will and Amelia; he's just getting more comfortable with the concept. He's getting better at showing his feelings. Nothing has really changed, and anyway, I don't understand why he would be jealous.

Freddie shrugged and looked uncomfortable, as if there was something he wanted to say but did not think he should.

"Are they talking in each other's heads again?" Merl asked, coming to stand at Conlan's side. Trying to hide her embarrassment at being caught eavesdropping, Eleanor nodded.

"We were discussing your trip to Termont. Freddie wants to go with you."

"It is your decision, Conlan, he can join us if you want him to," Merl said. Conlan stared at them for a moment as Freddie gently returned his hand to Eleanor's waist.

"Pack your things and check your horse, Freddie, we're leaving at first light tomorrow," Conlan said. Freddie nodded and smiled. Conlan nodded, an odd look on his face, and he moved past them down the corridor with Merl trailing behind.

Freddie took Eleanor's hand and they wandered down to the stables. Horse and Meran were pleased to see them, and Eleanor spent some time petting and stroking the animals while Freddie checked out his horse, making sure all his kit was ready for the next day. Eleanor had never really paid much attention to Freddie's horse, or Will's and Amelia's for that matter. She looked at the very average chestnut-coloured animal in front of her.

"Freddie, what's your horse called?" she asked from her perch on the corral fence. She held Horse's head in her hands and scratched the animal's face absently, her four-legged friend dozing in blissful contentment. She knew there were people around them, children staring; she tried to pretend it was just her and Freddie.

"I call him John, but I've no idea what he thinks he's called. He doesn't answer to his name," Freddie said, not looking at her, his attention on 'John's' raised hoof as he checked it for splits or damage. Eleanor pushed an energy string into the animal's head and giggled.

Freddie looked at her over 'John's' back, gently placing his leg back down. "What?"

"Freddie, your horse doesn't want to be called John, because that's the name you call him when you're angry and frustrated with him. He wants you to call him 'Pal', because that's what you call him when you pet him and give him treats," Eleanor said. Freddie stared at her and then moved to the horse's head and took it in his hands.

"I'll call you Pal, if you like," he told it as the horse nuzzled his head affectionately into Freddie's chest.

"Why did you call your horse John?" Eleanor asked, thinking it was an odd name for a horse – not that she had any room to comment, considering her horse was called Horse.

"It's my brother's name," he said quietly as he checked Pal's other hooves.

"Do you still miss him?" Eleanor asked, feeling guilty that she had not given her family and friends a second thought in months.

Freddie sighed. "We were very close, best friends... I miss that."

"You have best friends, Freddie," Eleanor said, not understanding the bitter melancholy in his voice. Freddie looked at her.

"No, all I have is you. I don't think I'd be in a hurry to call Will, Amelia or Conlan best friends. Will and Amelia think I'm an idiot and Conlan is too caught up in himself to notice me."

Upset by his obvious unhappiness, Eleanor thought his words through. Will and Amelia did not think Freddie was an idiot. Will found his juvenile humour and lack of manners grating on occasion and Amelia did not like being the butt of some of his ruder jokes, but they both loved him, she was sure of it. Eleanor suspected that Conlan, on the other hand, found Freddie rather funny, just as she did. He certainly seemed to have had more patience for his jokes and behaviour recently. Perhaps it was time he got to know Freddie better, maybe then he would appreciate him a little more. Conlan could do with more of Freddie's silliness in his life, to stop him taking himself so seriously.

"Will and Amelia don't think you're an idiot, they just don't always appreciate your type of humour. They do love you," Eleanor assured him. "Freddie, can I ask a favour of you?"

"Always," came Freddie's immediate response.

Eleanor smiled. "While you're on this trip with Conlan, please make an effort to get to know him. Pull him out of himself, don't let him wallow in silence and don't let him spend the whole time talking to Merl in Dwarfish. Force him to talk to you, tell him about being a fireman. He'll be interested, I promise. Tell him that story about the woman in her nightdress with the cat, he'll find it really funny. If he gets difficult, tell him I asked you to talk to him."

"What if I irritate him?" Freddie asked.

"I irritate him – a lot – and we're still friends. Two people don't have to agree on everything and do everything the same way to be friends, Freddie. So long as you tolerate and try to understand each other's differences you'll get along great. You never know, he might surprise you."

Freddie raised an eyebrow and looked very doubtful, but he nodded his agreement to her request.

Dawn the next morning was cold and overcast. Dark, heavy rain clouds on the horizon hid the rising sun, making it feel earlier than it was. Merl was already packed and mounted, impatient to leave as Conlan and Freddie loaded up their things. Will and Amelia stood wrapped around each other in the chill, looking half-asleep. Nials had come to see them off and had given them some last minute supplies and instructions. Eleanor had not been able to get a quiet moment to talk to Conlan and she did not think hugging him and begging him to be careful would be something he would want her to do in public; however, not being able to say goodbye properly was making her miserable. Freddie saw her and walked over.

"Cheer up, I'll look after him and we'll be back in twelve days," he said, giving her a lopsided grin. At least she could hug him. She wrapped her arms around his waist, and as she did so she pushed an energy string out to Conlan and gently caressed his shield. Freddie pulled away, smiling at her; she gave him a smile back, which turned his smile into a wide grin as he mounted his horse. Conlan did not look at her, as his view was fixed firmly on the road ahead, but his eyes did hold a slightly glazed look and he had a small smile on his face.

Eleanor stood and watched them disappear into the distance while spreading her energy string out over Conlan's shield, wrapping round it and supporting it. She had no idea if he recognised it, but she only pulled her string back when she felt it start to stretch so thin it was breaking apart. As it did so, Eleanor realised that the itch that had started in her brand was now a burning pain, indicating that Freddie was travelling out of mental contact with them. Will came and stood next to her, rubbing his brand, too; it was similar to Amelia's, but his five wavy lines were horizontal across his wrist, not vertical, looking like waves on the sea. He put an arm around her shoulders, his voice soothing when he spoke.

"You've been stood here hours, Eleanor. It's starting to rain, come inside."

She nodded, allowing him to lead her back to their rooms, the weight of separation making her feet drag.

Trying not to dwell on the huge hole that Conlan and Freddie's absence had left inside her, Eleanor concentrated on getting Meran well. She was determined to have the animal restored to his former glory by the time Conlan returned. Thankfully, Meran seemed just as interested in achieving the same objective. With Horse's help she took him through his paces and started to strengthen his muscles, and with the help of Laurice's bemused chefs, she fed him lots of oil, fat and protein-rich food, cooked specially for him. Will and Amelia had given up trying to persuade her to sleep in her bed. Will had worried that one of the animals could move in the night and step on her or roll over and flatten her, but Eleanor had laughed herself silly at the notion and he had backed off, accepting that she was happier in the stables. What she had not told Will and Amelia was that sleeping with Meran and Horse's warm bodies near her was the only way she could stop the dark, evil thoughts that preyed on her in her sleep. Horrific nightmares of Daratus murdering Merl, Freddie and Conlan stalked her dreams. It was fear she was able to keep a grip on during the day, but it surged forth to swallow her whole in the chilly black nights. The smell of horse and the warm, dozing bodies pressed into hers reminded her of the day she had spent with Conlan, bringing a measure of the peace she had found and giving her a few hours of undisturbed rest; enough to keep her going.

The change in Meran was nothing short of miraculous. Eleanor had explained to him that he would be coming with them when they left and that he would be starting a new life with a new master to love him. The animal's anticipation and excitement were visible in his expressions and movements. His wasted body seemed to fill out before Eleanor's astonished eyes, new muscle tone showing through; his coat grew back to its old black shining lustre, and with Will's assistance his sores healed. He was a huge horse, Eleanor realised, as she brushed his coat and plaited his mane and tail. He was taller at the shoulder than Rand had been, but where Rand had been sturdy, solid and mature, Meran was lighter. Just as strong as Rand, Meran's strength was coiled inside him, making him high-spirited and playful like a teenager. On Eleanor's careful diet his energy levels began to climb, so to wear him out a little she took him for runs into the surrounding savannah – no saddle, no bridle, just her and Meran, Horse trying her best to keep up behind them. The wind in her hair, the pounding of hooves and the gentle undulation of muscle as Meran galloped at full speed for the distant horizon, made Eleanor want to whoop and cheer at the exhilarating, life-affirming experience. Nials had been horrified when he found out. There was a reason, he said, that they had ceased their nomadic lifestyle and lived in a fortress – just because she had not met any of the roving bands of thugs that called the southern savannah home, it did not mean they were not out there. Eleanor had told Nials what had happened to the last roving gang who had tried to jump her. To her surprise Will had backed her up, telling Nials not to worry, as she was very capable of looking after herself. Nials had given Eleanor a dubious look but accepted Will's reassurance. However, Will had insisted that she take her sword with her on her rides.

She brushed Meran's coat to a glossy shine, applying a little oil in places where the hair had not grown back fully and loving the warm, silky feel as she ran her hand over his body. The horse was jumpy and excited, mostly because Eleanor was jumpy and excited. They were due back later in the day and she wanted Meran looking his best. She had washed him, dried him, brushed him, combed and brushed his mane and tail, and she had even oiled his hooves. Horse watched, amused, but Meran seemed to love the attention. Eleanor had warned him not to get used to it, as she did not get many baths while they travelled, so it was unlikely he would. Once Meran was ready, she moved on to Rand's red saddle. Nials had helped her make the adjustments so it fitted Meran's narrow back, but she still needed to clean and polish it. Amelia came to visit, trying to get her to come inside to have something to eat. Eleanor had ignored the request, showing her how much work she still had to do. Sighing, Amelia had sat down next to her, grabbing a leather stirrup strap and a cloth so she could rub saddle oil into the cracks. They had finished the saddle and moved on to the bridle when their brands began to itch. Eleanor caught Amelia's eye and they grinned at each other. The pain in their brands moved up to an uncomfortable burning and Amelia helped Eleanor saddle Meran, which was proving to be tricky, as the animal was practically jumping up and down like a dog in his excitement. Taking light hold of his reins, Eleanor led him out of the stables and down towards the main gates. Meran had his head held high and his steps were very pronounced and elegant; he looked stunning and the red saddle looked amazing against the black of Meran's back, its silver studs sparkling in the afternoon sun. Will was already waiting for them, rubbing absently at his brand. He smiled appreciatively at Meran.

"Eleanor, he looks like a different horse, you did a great job," he said as they got closer.

Eleanor smiled. "I had help, lots of it... He's not fully mended yet, but he's eighty per cent there and certainly healthy enough to join us when we're ready to leave."

The gate was pulled open. In the distance Eleanor could see three figures and her heart leapt. It was only as they got closer that Eleanor realised she could hear laughter – uncontrolled, 'rolling on the floor' belly laughter – and with shocked surprised she recognised it as Conlan's. They walked under the gate, he and Freddie in fits of hysterics about something. Conlan was laughing so hard he was holding on to the front saddle to steady himself. Merl followed behind, a look of amused confusion on his face. Will and Amelia were staring wide-eyed at Conlan, as if he was some strange alien they had never seen before. He sat in his saddle, trying to get himself under control as Freddie leapt off his horse and pulled Eleanor into a tight hug, the pain in her brand disappearing as he did so. He kissed the top of her head and then pulled back, his nose wrinkled in mock disgust.

"Eleanor, you stink. Have you been living in the stables?" he joked.

"Yes she has," Will said, still not able to take his eyes off Conlan. Freddie frowned. Not wanting to ruin his good humour, Eleanor gave him a wide smile.

"So which story did you tell him to illicit that reaction?" she asked, nodding towards Conlan, who was still shaking with sporadic bursts of laughter. Freddie sniggered, looking unbelievably pleased with himself when he saw the expressions of surprise on Will and Amelia's faces.

"I told him about that guy who got stuck in his garden railings."

Eleanor giggled. "The one who claimed he had slipped?" she asked, remembering the story.

Freddie nodded, holding her gaze. "Thank you, I had a great time."

"Meran?" Conlan asked incredulously. He had managed to stop laughing and dismount, greeting Will and Amelia with a brief hug, which did nothing to remove the looks of surprise from their faces. He regarded the horse, a delighted grin growing as he walked towards Eleanor. At his comment, Freddie seemed to notice the huge animal standing behind her for the first time.

"Eleanor, he looks amazing," Freddie said, slowly moving around the horse. Eleanor watched Conlan approach. Not wanting to embarrass him by throwing herself into his arms, she pushed an energy string out to him instead, bringing him to a juddering halt in front of her. A shiver passed through his body and his eyes glazed slightly. She smiled at him and handed him Meran's reins.

"He's been waiting for you," she said. Conlan took the reins, brushing more of her hand than was strictly necessary. Not looking at the horse, he stared at Eleanor. Freddie came back from behind Meran and unconsciously wrapped an arm around Eleanor's waist. Conlan dragged his attention from Eleanor to the horse in front of him, running a careful hand over his back and studying the changes.

"Freddie, want to join me? I'm thinking of taking this fine beast out for a run," Conlan said as he swung himself gracefully into the saddle. Meran began to step from side to side in eager anticipation of his first run with his new master. Conlan reached forward and scratched behind his ears.

"Sure, but no lizard slippers, OK?" Freddie said, grinning as Conlan laughed again.

"Lizard slippers?" Eleanor asked, confused.

"Don't ask!" Freddie and Conlan said together, dissolving into more laughter.

"Are we going somewhere? We only just got back," Merl grumbled, watching Freddie pull his packs off his horse, abandon them and then remount.

"Freddie and I are going to have a run, you stay here," Conlan ordered without looking at him. He stared at the open gate and the empty horizon with anticipation. Meran leapt forward, going from a restless stand to full gallop in a matter of seconds. Freddie turned Pal around. "Cheat!" he called at Conlan's back, digging his heels into his horse's side and urging him to catch up.

Will and Amelia watched them go in stunned silence. Slowly, Will turned his head to look at Eleanor.

"What has Freddie done with Conlan?" he asked in English, with a totally straight face.

Eleanor smiled. "That's who he always was," she said, knowing all her love for him was in her voice.

The sun was setting when Conlan and Freddie arrived back. Eleanor was still in the stables. Horse had decided, since Meran was now Conlan's responsibility, that Eleanor should be spending time pampering her and had demanded a bathing, brushing and oiling. Merl had been in to sort out his horse and Will's, as Conlan had borrowed it. Eleanor had asked him how the trip had gone and the older man had smiled, telling her he had not laughed so much in years. Eleanor had nearly finished Horse's grooming session when she heard the sound of friendly chatting and hooves as Conlan and Freddie led their horses into the stables.

"... not fair, you have a fresh horse that Eleanor's been pampering for nearly two weeks, while Pal has been carrying me around for days. Of course you're going to win!" Freddie was saying.

"That's true, poor Pal having to carry you around, no wonder he didn't have the strength to keep up for more than half a mile," Conlan said teasingly. There was a pause and Conlan chuckled as the entered the stables. He noticed Eleanor, a pleased smile spreading across his face. Handing Meran's reins to Freddie he strode forward and pulled her into a tight hug.

"Thank you for restoring Meran, he's wonderful," He stopped and pulled back slightly while smiling indulgently. "Freddie's right, you stink. I think you need a bath."

"He's an amazing horse and he's so quick to learn – want to see something really cool?" Eleanor asked. Conlan nodded and then helped her to remove Meran's saddle and bridle and store the equipment. Running a gentle hand down Meran's nose, Eleanor smiled.

"Let's go for a ride," she said softly, taking a firm handhold of his black silky mane. Meran lifted his front leg so she could use it as a step to mount. Eleanor began giving him the simple one-word instructions she had taught him.

Lifting both his front legs off the ground, Meran twirled with ballet-like grace towards the stable's exit, moving out into the corral and Horse following behind to watch. Eleanor put Meran through his paces; showing off for his new master, the excited horse gave it his all, his hooves snapping up as he walked. Eleanor got him to side-step, move backwards, do the pirouette turns again and rear up, kicking his front legs in the air, all to the verbal commands she had taught him. She then got him to trot in a wide circle. Once he had found a regular rhythm, Eleanor brought her feet up underneath her, using her arms to balance while making very sure that she did not look at how far away the ground was. She stood up. Moving lightly on the balls of her feet in time to Meran's movement, she let the horse carry her for a few circuits. Still using verbal commands, she directed Meran towards the yellow mountain of straw in the corner of the corral. He stopped in front of it and at Eleanor's command he bucked, his rear flying high in the air, propelling her off his back, up over his head and into the straw. Scrambling out, Eleanor saw Freddie and Conlan rushing to help her.

"I'm fine," she assured them, giggling as they pulled her up. Conlan absently picked straw out of her hair.

"Can you teach Pal how to do that?" Freddie asked, a wide grin on his face.

She shrugged. "Maybe some of it. Pal is a lovely horse but he's not nearly as bright as Meran," Eleanor said, cringing at Freddie's look. "I'm not saying Pal is stupid, Freddie, because Horse couldn't do half this stuff either. What I'm saying is Meran is remarkable." Hearing his name, Meran trotted over and stretched a foreleg out, bending the other against his body and bowing to Conlan, his head almost touching the floor. Conlan raised an eyebrow at Eleanor. She rolled her eyes.

"That wasn't me, Conlan, that's all him. Meran has a few interesting habits of his own."

"Remarkable," Conlan said softly, echoing Eleanor as he reached out to stroke Meran's nose with affectionate wonder.

20

THE CROWN

They left for Katadep two days later. Half the fortress had come to see them off; Laurice, Urerla and Nials gave them all hugs and handshakes, having already stocked them up with provisions. Eleanor was torn between wanting to get back on the road, wanting to find the crown, wanting to make the next small move towards making Conlan a king and wanting to hide under the blankets in her bed. For no reason she could put her finger on she had a profound sense of dread about this journey, even before she had taken a single step.

Katadep was just over halfway between Laurice's fortress and the Central Tower. They would reach it by skirting the edge of the central mountain range for several months and then turning west. They were taking a slightly roundabout route, but it meant they would avoid large pockets of civilisation for as long as possible. That way, they would be able to forage and camp, saving what little money they had left between them for the nights they would have to stay in the city. Conlan had never been to Katadep but Merl had, telling them it was a more impressive city than Baydon and that it housed the largest Protector stronghold outside of the Lords of Mydrens' towers. Merl had a permanently excited look on his face, and his animated chat was light and friendly, which helped to dispel some of Eleanor's anxiety. As they travelled they went back to taking watch each night, Merl taking his turn; there had been no objections.

They soon settled back into their comfortable travelling routine and Eleanor relaxed slightly. Conlan seemed content, and he and Freddie spent quite a bit of time together with the result that Conlan laughed a lot more. Eleanor also noticed he was more tactile, occasionally even giving her and Amelia quick hugs. Eleanor never pushed him on this, not wanting to be rejected again, but when Freddie occasionally wrapped his arms around her she would drape an energy string around Conlan's shield, hoping he would understand that she would like to hug him, too.

As they got closer to Katadep they discussed plans, Merl explaining that his friend, Arran, would be at the Protectors' stronghold on the south side of Katadep awaiting Merl's contact. Conlan had asked what Arran wanted for the risk he was taking, and Merl had laughed: 'an awful lot of money' had been the reply. Conlan had looked confused, wondering how they were going to pay him when they had barely enough money for a few nights in an inn. Merl had smiled; apparently there was no need to worry about it, as Gregor would be taking care of any and all financial requests from Arran. Eleanor again felt her worry for the old man's safety – they were going to have to check he was OK.

Freddie had voiced his concerns that they could be walking into a trap. Conlan had listened as Freddie had explained his concerns. What if the Protectors had some secret weapon? 'Even superman had kryptonite,' he had said. Will had pointed out that Avatars had been destroyed before and the book had been very hazy about how this had been done. Conlan had told them that he trusted Merl's judgement; however, Freddie and Will's concerns had not gone unheeded.

As they got closer and closer to Katadep, Conlan's smiles disappeared and he retreated into a dark mood which seemed to get worse with every step they took. Eleanor could feel his fear. Only Freddie seemed able to get more out of him than snapped monosyllabic remarks. By the time the huge stone battlements of Katadep's outside wall were in sight, even Merl was silent and apprehensive. They entered the main gates of the city as they were closing for the night, the four Protectors on duty giving them a slow look up and down but waving them inside, the sun setting behind them cast long, eerie shadows. The further north they had travelled, the colder it became, as winter was still in its final throws through most of Mydren and Katadep was cold, wet and grey. Remnants of the snow that had fallen was still piled high in side streets and unused doorways, the once dazzling white reduced to grey, slippery sludge. Eleanor sighed, thinking of the beautiful mountains of home and the high lake covered with ice. A pang of homesickness, intensified by the fear that was steadily growing inside her, shook her body. Horse felt it and shuddered with her. The city was quiet, which was not surprising for a cold, dark wintery evening, but Eleanor did not like the silence. Their horses' hooves echoed loudly down the near-empty streets. Everyone seemed tense and hyper-alert, jumping at every noise – a yelling voice in the distance, a dog barking from behind a wall, two cats fighting in an alley. The horses were so spooked by the nerves of their riders that Eleanor had to enter their minds in an attempt to calm them down, as she was scared one of them was going to bolt. The only exception to this rule was Meran, who held his head high and like Conlan searched the streets and alleyways they passed for threats; he had lost one master, and it was not going to happen again. They eventually found the inn Merl had recommended. They had definitely stayed in better. The lovely inn in Drent sprang to Eleanor's mind, and by comparison this place was a dump; however, it was affordable and slightly warmer than sleeping on the streets. Merl obtained three rooms. Eleanor opened the door to the one she and Freddie would be sharing and sighed at the damp brown walls, peeling paint and the battered furniture; a musty, stale sweat smell hung heavy in the air.

"Not up to your standards?" Merl asked with an amused smile, unlocking a door on the other side of the corridor.

"I suspect my horse has stayed in better," Eleanor replied. Merl's laughter followed him into his room. The sound caused goosebumps to erupt all over her body, and for a moment she froze as nameless dread overtook her and she shook. Her paralysis was broken by the others coming down the corridor, carrying the bags they had taken from their horses. Eleanor walked into her room, still shaking slightly. She sat on the bed, which creaked ominously. Freddie came in, dumped their bags and closed the door. Looking round the room, disgust registered on his face.

"It might be more comfortable sleeping in the stables," he commented. When Eleanor did not answer, he looked at her. She was unable to hide her fear. He moved quickly, dropping onto the bed next to her. The frame groaned louder. Putting an arm around her, he pulled her close.

"It's nearly over, Eleanor. Merl and Conlan are going to send a message to Arran tomorrow morning, and then we find out where the meeting is going to take place."

Eleanor shuddered again, tears filling her eyes, her fear tearing round her insides like a hurricane.

"But what happens then?" she whispered.

Freddie shrugged. "We go to meet Arran. Either he gives us the crown or the Protectors spring their trap and we fight."

"This doesn't feel right, any of it. Conlan should've listened to you."

Freddie gave her a small smile. "Conlan *did* listen. We've discussed it and we have some ideas for plans if it's a trap."

"Why didn't he discuss this with all of us?" Eleanor asked, irritated at not being included.

"He wanted to think about it for a while – it's why he's been so quiet and moody recently. He's been working out contingency plans. He's going to discuss it with us all once he and Merl have sent the message to Arran."

"I can feel his fear, Freddie, what else have you been discussing?" Eleanor asked.

Freddie sighed. "I think we're far too confident in our abilities. The Lords have been in power a long time, so I'm sure they have a few secrets of their own. We're assuming they know nothing about fighting Avatars; however, we have a book of instructions, so maybe they do, too. Conlan and I have been trying to think of ways they could kill us, so we can be better prepared if it is a trap." Eleanor felt her fear surge through her again, her thoughts spinning.

"Freddie, if this is a trap, would telling someone who can help us be a good contingency plan?"

"Probably. Who did you have in mind?"

There was a knock at the door as Eleanor finished explaining about Remic's knife and the dwarves' spies. Freddie got up to open it and let Will and Amelia into the room. They had brought food, as there was not enough money left for them to eat the inn's questionable cuisine, but given the state of the bedroom, Eleanor was actually grateful for this small mercy. As they sat and ate the meagre provisions, Freddie repeated what he and Eleanor had been discussing, asking Will and Amelia for their input as they did their best to make plans, despite the large amounts of unknown factors.

Eleanor lay in the darkness, Freddie's arms wrapped tightly around her, and listened to the rats move through the walls and occasionally across the floor. Freddie could not sleep either, which was unusual for him. He did not want to talk but just lay still, holding Eleanor in a death-like grip, his breath flowing warm air across the back of her neck. Her mind endlessly analysed the information they had available to them and churned through plans and possibilities. Eleanor waited for morning.

"Where do you think you are going?" Conlan snarled at her. He and Merl had found her and Freddie walking down the corridor, heading for the exit. He grabbed her arm and marched her back to their room, Freddie and Merl trailing behind.

"We wanted to get a message to Remic, ask him to check that Gregor was OK and to make sure someone who could help us knew where we were," Eleanor said, pulling her arm free and glaring at Conlan.

"You should not be taking decisions like that without speaking to Conlan first," Merl chastised.

Eleanor flashed him an irritated glance. "If Conlan had been in his room, I would have asked. This is too important to wait."

"Remic is miles away, how is he going to check on Gregor?" Conlan asked softly, his anger gone and concern in his eyes as Eleanor returned her gaze to his.

"The Dwarves have a spy network. I need to present the knife Remic gave me at the right shop and they will help us."

Conlan looked surprised. "I wondered why you were so attached to that knife..."

"This is a Protector-run city, Conlan, it is not safe for her to go wandering around," Merl said, frowning.

"Give me the knife, tell me which shop and I will go," Conlan said, holding out his hand.

Eleanor shook her head. "No, I do not think you would be accepted, they would be expecting me."

"The knife, Eleanor," Conlan ordered. His voice was quiet, but the irritation was clear. Eleanor stubbornly shook her head.

"Eleanor, your master, your creator, has given you an order. Do you not understand that it must be obeyed?" Merl asked softly. *My master?* Eleanor looked at Conlan. His eyes held hers with one of his mystery looks, but he did not deny Merl's assessment of the situation.

Eleanor glared at Merl. "I am not some mindless slave he can order about! He is my friend, my love, my hope for the future, but he is *not* my master," she spat, and turned abruptly from Merl's open-mouthed shock and back to Conlan.

"I need to be the one who hands over the knife," she insisted. "I am trying to help, so stop barking orders at me and let me get on with it."

Conlan held her gaze in silence, body still, face expressionless while Eleanor counted time with her pounding heartbeats.

"Conlan, you want to be king and you cannot control even her. Why are you bothering to argue the point? Just take it from her!" Merl huffed. "We are wasting time."

Conlan glanced at Merl and then back to Eleanor. She realised he was quite capable of taking Remic's knife from her – time to remind them of the power she had at her disposal.

"You wish to disarm me?" Eleanor asked in disgust. "And who is going to do that, Merl? You?" She pulled a tiny amount of energy from the earth, and with a splitting pop she exploded the chair Merl was leaning against, depositing the man in a graceless heap on the floor. Floundering amid the splinters of wood and stuffing, Merl huffed and cursed himself back to his feet. Conlan's face was a mask of fury as he strode across the room, towering over her but very purposely keeping his clenched fists at his sides. Freddie took a step towards Conlan, while Merl put an arm across his chest and shook his head. Freddie glowered at him but stopped, his body stiff with the effort and indecision on his face as he tried to work out if he could take on both Conlan and Merl.

"We are in the middle of Protector City and you are using magic?" Conlan snarled. "Apologise to Merl!"

Dropping her gaze from his blazing green eyes, Eleanor nodded.

"I am sorry, Merl."

Merl said nothing and Conlan was motionless. She raised her eyes. He was looking at her thoughtfully. Will and Amelia entered the room behind them.

"Is everything OK, Eleanor?" Will asked in Dwarfish. His tone was mild, but his underlying growl carried suspicion.

"Your master was simply about to dispense some much-needed discipline," Merl snapped.

"My master?" Will asked, amused.

Merl looked at Conlan with a disapproving frown. "Do none of them understand your position?"

Conlan sighed and took a step back from Eleanor. "They are not my servants, Merl, they are my friends… my family. Eleanor, go, take Freddie. Make sure you walk just behind him, though, as men do not walk behind women in Mydren. Stay out of trouble and come back here as quickly as you can."

Eleanor rolled her eyes but nodded. Giving him a small smile she grabbed Freddie's arm, pulling him out of the door after her, before Merl tried to change Conlan's mind.

It took them some time to find the right shop. The city was far bigger than any they had been to before, and it sprawled over many miles. Down the street from their inn was a four-storey building with a flag flying over it. The sign over the door said 'Weaver's Guild'. It was an impressive building, standing higher than all those around it and high enough that they were able to see the flag from quite a distance, which gave them a reference point to use to get back. Eleanor walked as quickly as she could without looking suspicious towards the main shopping area she had glimpsed on the way into the city. Freddie walked a few steps in front of her as she gave him directions in his head. The jewellery shop with the mountain and diamond symbol over the door was halfway down the wide shopping boulevard. It had a large ornate doorway and a front window that glittered with beautifully crafted baubles designed to entice rich ladies. The shop had only just opened for the day as they entered. The sales assistant, a red-haired woman with pale, freckle-covered skin, looked them up and down before deciding they were not serious customers. She was wearing a full-length, plain-brown fitted dress with long sleeves and a buttoned up collar; her face and hands were the only flesh that could be seen. It seemed to be the standard outfit for all the women Eleanor had seen since arriving in Katadep. She had yet to see a woman in trousers.

"Can I help you?" the assistant asked coldly. Not sure if she should trust just anybody with her request for help, Eleanor smiled. It did not hurt to be friendly.

"We would like to see the shop owner, please."

"I do not think that will be possible," the woman replied, her voice dropping a few more degrees in temperature.

"Remic sent us," Eleanor said, the redheads' eyebrows nearly disappearing into her hairline in surprise.

"Come with me," she said, turning on her heel and heading towards the back of the shop. Eleanor jogged to keep up with her long legs and Freddie followed dutifully behind. The woman led them through a beaded curtain into a staffroom. There were tables, chairs, a messy noticeboard, drinks-making facilities, a fire blazing in the fireplace and pegs on the wall with an array of clothing hung on them. On the left-hand wall was a door marked 'Private'. The woman knocked politely.

"Come in," said a fragile male voice from behind it. The door opened. Eleanor and Freddie walked into a cramped office, a desk, chair and cabinet practically filling it. Behind the desk was a shrivelled old man in an embroidered padded velvet jacket. He regarded the woman with milky-grey eyes as he absentmindedly scratched his bald, liver-spotted head.

"I am sorry to disturb you, Father, but she claims Remic sent them," the woman said, her tone one of disbelief. At the mention of Remic's name, the old man's bushy, grey eyebrows shot up in the same expression of surprise his daughter had inherited. His eyes flicked in Eleanor's direction; he noticed her fully for the first time and scrutinised her, knowing eyes holding her gaze.

"Eleanor?" the old man said softly. Next to her the red-haired woman gasped. Relieved she would not have to explain who she was, Eleanor nodded and smiled. Walking forward, she lay Remic's knife on the old man's desk. The old man smiled back.

"It is a pleasure to meet you. My name is Judder and this is my daughter, Leda," he said, nodding towards the woman, who bobbed a curtsy. "We were told about you. Remic holds you in the highest regard, Avatar of Earth, and I am honoured that you would grace us with your presence. Now then, how may we be of assistance?"

Aware that she had very little time, Eleanor quickly introduced Freddie and then launched into a rapid summary of what was going on, telling the old man about Merl's friend, the crown and about the possibility of it being a trap, then telling him about her fears for Gregor. Leda went back to tend the shop and the old man listened as Eleanor tried to bring him up to speed,

Freddie standing quiet and watchful behind her. Even talking quickly, it took far longer than she had expected. When she had finished, she patiently answered the old man's thoughtful questions.

"If you are captured you will be taken to the dungeons in the Protectors' stronghold," Judder said, frowning. "We would be unable to rescue you from there, so you must get to the main gate. Once there we can help you, because if you do get caught, we will know and we will be waiting. Get to the gate."

Eleanor nodded, wondering how difficult that would end up being.

"And Gregor?" Eleanor asked.

Judder nodded. "That is a far easier request; however, it will take a day for the messages to get there and back, so you must return, if you are able." Eleanor nodded and thanked the old man. Judder had offered all the help he could, she had let someone know what was going on and she had done her best to make a contingency plan. It was time to go back.

For the people of Mydren it was lunchtime, and the streets thronged. Moving in and out through the crowds, Eleanor and Freddie headed back towards the flag she could see flying over the Weavers' Guild building while Eleanor told Freddie what Judder had said. Back at the inn Freddie quietly opened their bedroom door and they slipped inside. Will was sat in a chair by the sorry excuse for a fire that guttered in the grate, Amelia was sat on his lap, leaning against his chest, and they both had relaxed, spacey expressions on their faces. Eleanor knew they were talking to each other.

"How did it go?" Will asked as Eleanor sat down in the other chair opposite him. The bits of the chair she had exploded earlier were gone, burnt on the fire, she imagined. She gave them a rundown of her meeting with Judder.

"Did Conlan get back yet?" Eleanor asked.

"He came back briefly, but when he realised you weren't back he disappeared off again with Merl. That was about an hour ago," Amelia said.

The sun was setting when Conlan and Merl returned. Eleanor had begun to fret and was relieved when she heard his light tread on the floorboards outside the door. Without knocking, Conlan opened the door and walked into the room, his eyes landing on Eleanor still sat in the chair, Freddie sat at her feet. Merl followed behind, giving her an irritated look.

"Did you find the spies?" Conlan asked. Eleanor nodded, giving him a small smile as she pushed an energy string over his shield. He gave her a tired smile in return, dropping to sit on the bed, eyes widening as it groaned beneath his weight.

"So, are we getting the crown tonight?" Will asked.

Conlan nodded. "We sent the message to Arran. He has asked us to meet him in the park in the centre of Katadep a few hours from now. Merl and I have just been there to check it out; it's a huge area with trees and plants – lots of hiding places and perfect for an ambush, if you're worried the people you're ambushing might make a lot of noise."

"So if this is a trap, what's the plan?" Will asked.

"We fight back," Conlan said glibly.

"That's not a plan, Conlan, that's a knee-jerk reaction," Will observed mildly.

"I'm fairly certain these Protectors have never met anything quite like the four of you; however, you'll be pleased to hear that Freddie and I have come up with some plans," Conlan said seriously.

Eleanor and Freddie stood at the bedroom window watching Merl, Conlan, Will and Amelia walk down the street. None of them looked back. The moment they were out of sight, she and Freddie rushed around and gathered their stuff together because if they were captured, they did not want their belongings falling into enemy hands. Once everything was packed, Eleanor and Freddie rode through the dark, quiet streets of Katadep, pulling the others' horses behind them to Judder's house. Eleanor was surprised by their luck when they did not meet any Protector patrols. Judder looked a little bemused to see them on his doorstep, but he happily promised to take care of their horses and equipment until they got back. Eleanor kissed Horse goodbye, hoping it would not be the last time she saw her friend. With Freddie following close behind, they ran towards the park.

Somewhere in the darkness a bird screeched and Eleanor shivered. Freddie tightened his grip on her hand. She closed her eyes, trusting him implicitly to lead her. Conlan had not exaggerated, the park was huge. As they walked as quietly as possible through the undergrowth, Eleanor pushed multiple energy strings into the earth, her mind brushing the 'awareness' of the trees, plants and animals around her, looking for clues. She felt branches whipped back, uncomfortably close to breaking point; focusing all her energy strings in that area, Eleanor concentrated and visualised eight men moving towards a small clearing. Eight men were not an attack force, so maybe Arran was just being cautious, too. *Conlan.* Eleanor felt his energy and could not resist caressing it as she passed, before brushing a string against Will. He pulled her in. Amelia was already there, just as Freddie was in her head. Effortlessly, they bound their energy together.

Did you get everything to Judder? Will asked.

Yes. We're heading in your direction now, but so are eight other men. They're going to get there first, Eleanor said.

Eight men? That's not much of an ambush, Freddie said quietly.

Maybe Arran is just unsure about us, Amelia suggested before Eleanor got the chance.

They fell silent but kept their energy strings linked. Eleanor found it comforting and wondered if the others did, too.

As Eleanor and Freddie moved closer to the rendezvous point, she spent a few moments investigating the area, working out where all the men were positioned; three of them were stood out of sight in a rough triangle around the clearing in which their friends were stood. Using a passing shrew's eyes, Eleanor determined they were only armed with swords. The remaining five men were stood together, hidden in the darkness, and oddly they appeared to be unarmed. Eleanor gave the others this information.

This feels wrong, Eleanor whispered, letting some of her worry and fear slip through her mind's defences.

Yeah! I'm beginning to think this was a bad idea, Freddie murmured.

Well there really aren't enough for an ambush, so let's hope Amelia is right, Will said.

Still creeping forward, Eleanor and Freddie made it to the edge of the clearing, lying flat on their stomachs, the cold damp of the earth immediately seeping through Eleanor's clothes and body. Will and Merl were staking torches into the ground and lighting them so they could see when Arran arrived. Conlan stood next to Amelia, his eyes flicking around the surrounding darkness. Eleanor pushed an energy string out to him again and saw the smile that passed briefly over his face.

"Hello, Merl, it has been a long time."

The voice was quiet but it carried across the clearing. Will immediately moved back to Conlan's side. Eleanor had problems locating where the voice was coming from, but as Merl walked forward to greet his friend she understood why. The voice belong to one of the five men she had seen standing in the shadows. *No wonder I couldn't make them out in the dark.*

A long black robe covered him and a hood was drawn over his head, his face hidden.

Will gasped.

"Hello, Arran," Merl said.

Conlan froze, shock on his face. "Merl, this is an Enforcer," he said, his shock turning to fear. Will had stepped in front of Amelia, his face grim.

"Indeed he is," Merl replied, a nasty smile twisting his lips.

"I understood there would be four Avatars," Arran said, his voice emotionless.

"Two of them are hiding out in the bushes somewhere, some idiotic rescue plan if this turned out to be a trap," Merl said, the Dwarfish made an animal-like snarl by his irritation. Eleanor watched Conlan's body go rigid as he stared at Merl. In her head, Amelia gasped as Will translated Merl's words.

"This is not really satisfactory, Merl. You were given one job to do – get the Five here – and you have failed. Lord Daratus will not be pleased," Arran said, his voice still calm. The words were some sort of signal, and before he had finished speaking, both Will and Amelia collapsed to the ground, writhing, arms wrapped around their abdomens, sobbing cries filling the cold night air. Through their link, Eleanor and Freddie felt an echo of the paralysing pain.

Will, what's happening? Eleanor cried, panicked.

I don't know, but it hurts, like when Conlan tried to pull my energy but worse, so much worse... The thought faded as Will's consciousness began to fade; Amelia was already lying still next to him, her eyes closed. Frightened of being pulled down into black oblivion with them, Eleanor broke the link, dragging her and Freddie's energy strings free. They looked at each other in horror as Will's body stopped writhing. He lay still, eyes closed, but the rise and fall of his chest with each breath continued.

What do we do now? Eleanor asked.

Follow the plan, Freddie replied.

Horrified, Conlan knelt at Will and Amelia's sides, checking their vitals, searching Amelia's neck for a pulse. Relief in his eyes when he found one, he turned to glare at Merl.

"What have you done?" he demanded.

"You are so arrogant!" Merl snapped at him. "The Lords of Mydren have ruled for hundreds of years, do you think they would have forgotten how to deal with abominations?"

"I trusted you, Gregor trusted you..." Conlan said, unable to keep the hurt from his face.

"You and Gregor are fools playing with fire. You have created weapons of unimaginable power, and as I have witnessed time and again, you have absolutely no control over them!" Merl yelled at him.

"As much as this little chat is fascinating, we have two Avatars still to find, preferably before Lord Daratus learns of your incompetence," Arran said mildly. Merl winced at the word 'incompetence' and glared at Arran.

"My father does not tolerate failures, Merl," Conlan commented.

Merl marched towards him, throwing his first punch before he had finished moving. It was a clumsy attack driven by fury. Conlan ducked it and punched Merl back. The older man staggered onto his back foot, already off balance. Conlan maintained the advantage. Arran did not look interested in getting involved, so Conlan ignored him and focused on Merl. They traded punch for punch for several moments, but while each one of Conlan's landed punishing blows, Merl's did not. Conlan dealt Merl a vicious blow to the chin. The older man collapsed, staring up with dazed, hate-filled eyes. Looking bored, Arran flicked his hand. Conlan was flung off his feet and propelled through the air to impact against the trunk of one of the larger trees at the edge of the clearing with a sickening thud. He dropped to the ground, barely conscious. Eleanor gasped, pain twisting her gut. She made a move to get up but Freddie dragged her back down.

We can't help them if we get caught, he reasoned. *That's an Enforcer, and a powerful one if he could disable Will and Amelia; we need to think this through.*

There were five of them… five Enforcers? Eleanor wondered. *I have to help him, Freddie.*

He's still alive. If they wanted him dead, Merl would have killed him months ago, Remember the plan, Eleanor, we can't show ourselves. Again Freddie was the voice of calm, cold reason. Eleanor froze as Merl struggled to his feet. Wiping the blood dripping down his chin with the back of his hand, he walked purposely towards Conlan, who was on all fours, attempting to stand. Glazed, pain-filled eyes tracked Merl warily.

"I shall enjoy watching Daratus tear you apart," Merl snarled at him, delivering a solid kick to Conlan's ribs, the force of the blow enough to lift Conlan off the ground and propel him into the tree trunk again.

"Have you any idea what you cost me?" Merl continued, with another hefty kick. Conlan curled in on himself, trying to make as small a target as possible. Merl continued yelling and kicking. Eleanor shuddered with each blow.

"I loved her, loved her! Do you hear me?"

Kick!

"She was my world."

Kick!

"She was carrying my child and you killed her, your own mother!"

Conlan's head snapped up, a look of stark despair on his face.

"Merl... I..." he choked.

That was as far as he got. Merl kicked him in the head before he was able to say anymore. Conlan fell back, his body twitching then going limp.

Eleanor shoved her hand into her mouth to muffle her gasping sob, her teeth automatically fitting the scars.

"This is not helping us find the other Avatars," Arran observed. Merl looked back at Arran with flat, vicious eyes, a sneer curling his lips.

"Eleanor!" Merl yelled. "I know you can hear me. Give yourselves up or Conlan will suffer. Our orders were to bring him in alive, but there was no requisite that he be undamaged."

Eleanor pushed her hand further into her mouth, tears filling her eyes. Freddie kept a firm grip on her arm. For a moment there was silence. When there was no answer, Merl grabbed the back of Conlan's collar and the waist of his trousers and dragged him back into the light. Eleanor desperately wanted to blast him, but Conlan was too close. Merl resumed his savage kicking. Every blow sent needles of sympathetic pain through Eleanor's body.

"How much of this do you want him to take, Eleanor?" Merl asked, looking at the darkness around him, panting slightly from the exertion. Arran did not seem inclined to stop Merl's abuse and Eleanor could take it no longer. *Reason be damned. Plan be damned.* Fighting off Freddie's attempts to restrain her, Eleanor walked into the open, pulling free the sword at her waist. Using her energy to seek out the Enforcers she tried to blow them up, but they had a shield around them. It was far weaker than Amelia's, she would get through it eventually, but she did not have the time. Leaving the Enforcers for a moment, Eleanor concentrated on the three Protectors, killing them instead and hating the fact that incapacitating them was not an option. Then she brought her focus to Merl.

"Leave him alone," she snarled, her body poised for battle. Merl threw his head back and laughed at her, the hard, nasty sound echoing around the clearing. Eleanor watched, eyes bright with anticipation, as Merl stepped away from Conlan. He stepped towards her, just far enough away that she could blast him. She began drawing energy from the earth, but then a strange sensation hit her. It felt like someone had ripped open her stomach, forced their hands deep inside, grasped her vital organs and were now trying to yank them out. Pain shot up her spine, exploding through her head. Black spots swarmed across her vision. She dropped to her knees, her sword falling from nerveless fingers as she gasped for breath. Through half-open eyes she saw Freddie run towards her. Merl saw him and quickly retreated to Arran's side.

Freddie wasted no time and Eleanor watched as the torch flames shot higher and Freddie released his energy at Merl and Arran, only to watch in frustration as it dissipated against a shield in front of them, brilliant flashes of red and orange lighting up the clearing. Eleanor's pain-fogged mind recoiled back as the trees and shrubbery around them began to blaze. *Why's he setting things on fire?* Then she understood – the bigger the blaze, the more energy he could draw from it. Freddie was trying to get through the shield. Eleanor forced her addled brain to concentrate and work out what was going on. Freddie fought on at her side and fire flared around them.

Freddie, over there... the other Enforcers... Eleanor instructed, pointing in the general direction she had last seen the four figures.

Freddie turned his attention from Arran's shield, and the trees and bushes on the far side of the clearing exploded into a raging inferno. Eleanor felt the pain coursing through her body recede slightly. Freddie cried out and staggered in an attempt to stay upright, fighting off sudden obvious pain and continue his attack.

How are they doing this? Eleanor wondered.

Abruptly the agony was gone, leaving her shaking and weak. Freddie groaned and toppled over, clutching at his stomach.

Freddie, how can I help you?

There was no response, but Eleanor felt the dark shadow of his pain, his desperation to stay conscious, to keep protecting her. She stroked his hair as his eyes rolled in his head.

Eleanor, RUN! Get away! he managed before the pain intensified and he uttered a few last sobs before lying silent, his energy string slipping away from her.

She reached for his neck, checking for a pulse. It was there. Free of the debilitating agony for a moment, Eleanor crawled forwards.

Conlan's breath was shallow, his face pale and a number of bruises were blossoming. The steady trickle of blood from the corner of his mouth was enough to make her worry about the internal injuries Merl might have caused. She stroked his face, knowing she could not leave him, would not run. She would die with him, if that was their fate. With no warning the agony overtook her senses once more. She pitched forward into the dirt. This was the most intense pain she had experienced, and in a flash of clarity Eleanor understood why. The Enforcers were pulling her energy out, just as Conlan had tried to do to her all those months ago; the pain was familiar, as Will had said, only much stronger. Once Freddie had been drained of energy, all five of them must have moved on to her. Now she understood what was happening, Eleanor searched out their strings. There were only four. *Four Enforcers pulling energy.* Not sure how to counter the effect, she tried to pull the energy back, gripping onto their strings and pulling with all her strength, eyes screwed tight in concentration. The pain dropped slightly. It was having some impact, and as Eleanor became more comfortable with what she was doing she opened her eyes. Four black-robed figures stood around her, Arran stood in front of her with Merl at his side, smug and confident. Arran's hood had fallen back to reveal his features. He was younger than she had expected, in his late teens perhaps. His face still held some of the softness of a child, with the sharper angles of the chin and cheek bones that would make him a handsome man beginning to show through. There was something very familiar about him. His short hair was shocking white, making the hazel-coloured orbs of his eyes seem disproportionally large in his face. Eleanor shuddered at the cold cruelty in his expression, his eyes showing suffering well beyond his years. Investigating the four energy strings, Eleanor realised that one was weaker than the others and was not pulling as hard. Holding the tension in the other three strings, Eleanor concentrated on the weaker string and put all her remaining strength into ripping the energy from this one Enforcer. To her left, one of the black-robed figures swayed on his feet, staggered back and collapsed, all resistance to her pulling on his energy disappearing as he did so. Eleanor knew she was killing the man and shuddered as freezing, black despair seeped into her heart. Undeterred, she pulled out the remainder of the energy he had, feeling his shield flicker and fade, his heartbeat stuttering and stopping. She shifted her concentration and used the energy she had stolen to strengthen her grip on the other three strings. Two of them faltered at the shock of seeing their comrade fall. *Maybe I can still win this...* The thought gave her hope and she selected another energy string to focus her efforts on. As she concentrated, she realised the closer to their shields her energy string was pulled, the more pain roared through her body. If they managed to pull her energy through their shields, the pain was the horrific. Using as much of her remaining energy as she dared, Eleanor felt another of the Enforcers start to fail and sway on his feet.

Arran raised a thin, white eyebrow at her. Merl stepped forward, grabbing a handful of her hair tight to the roots, intent on dragging her to her knees. Seeing an opportunity, Eleanor surreptitiously slipped her hand into Conlan's boot, her fingers tightening around the handle of his knife. As Merl pulled her upright, Eleanor let out a scream of fury, and wrenching the knife free, plunging it to the hilt into the inside of Merl's thigh. Merl roared in pain. Eleanor gave the knife a violent twist. She knew she had succeeded when the gush of warm blood ran down her hand and arm. As she yanked the weapon free she felt the blood splatter warm across her face; she had hit a main artery. He would die.

Moving her attention to attacking Merl had left her open to the ongoing attack on her energy, and the haze of pain intensified as her energy was shredded through the remaining Enforcers' shields. As she struggled to take back control of the situation, Eleanor watched Merl stagger, then fall, landing heavily on his back. He gasped and groaned, his hands clasping his leg. Raising his head, he glared at her with murderous fury.

"*Drallup!*" he hissed, cold, hard and vicious. Eleanor realised she had heard this voice before. This was the voice Berick had been talking to in Meran's memories. Merl had killed Laurice's husband and Yatt, Millice and Osser just so he could get close to Conlan and gain his trust. Merl's head dropped back and he lay still. *Another death on my hands.* Eleanor turned away to find Arran's hazel eyes scrutinising her. So very familiar. The pain became excruciating as the Enforcers got over their initial shock. No one moved to help Merl. Now she understood what was happening, Eleanor moved her remaining effort into fighting back and pulling at their energy, but she was weak and could not keep up the fight much longer. *Need to finish this before I pass out.*

"Arran, she killed Karnos – are you going to help us?" one of the other hooded Enforcers asked, his voice strained and panicked and his eyes flicking to the body of his dead comrade. Arran sighed, as if this request for assistance was beneath him. Crouching down he reached out a hand and touched Eleanor's forehead. An immense jolt of pain shot through her. She jittered and then collapsed. It was like a version of Will's energy release, but without the potency. Not understanding, Eleanor's mind swirled under the increased assault from the three remaining Enforcers.

"You are using water energy," Eleanor gasped out, looking at Arran as she curled into a ball of agony at Conlan's side.

"I can access energy from all four elements as needed," Arran said. Still straining against her attackers and struggling to hold on to the energy she had, Eleanor tried to keep Arran talking, hoping to get some answers. If she lived to fight him again she was going to need all the information she could get.

"Can all Enforcers do that?" she asked haltingly, her words slow and laborious.

"You are full of questions," Arran observed conversationally, as if an Avatar writhing at his feet was a normal occurrence. He stared at her for a moment before answering in a slight bragging tone.

"While Enforcers are rare, I am the rarest. Most become comfortable with one element as children and soon become unable to use any other. I was identified by Lord Daratus very early in my life. I was trained to use all the elements equally, so I have access to them all, but not at quite the same level you and your friends enjoy."

"If you had this ability, why did you not use it when you attacked us at the waterfall?" Eleanor gasped, forcing the words out.

"What waterfall?" Arran asked.

Arran doesn't know about the waterfall. Does this mean that Lord Daratus is not responsible for that attack? Or did he just not tell Arran?

Eleanor could feel herself losing the battle as the darkness crept in at the edges of her vision. She tried pushing a string into the earth, wondering if she still had the strength to draw more energy, but her string was dragged away, energy being pulled along it at an alarming rate. *Arran's joined the fight.* He was strong, very strong, but as he pulled her energy, Eleanor felt no increase in pain. *Will didn't feel pain when I pulled his energy, but he did when Conlan pulled it. Conlan has a shield, so why is Arran different? Does he not have a shield?* As a last-ditch attempt to defend herself, Eleanor pushed an energy string at Arran. Conlan felt it when she had touched his shield, so maybe the young Enforcer would, too. Maybe it would distract him. If there was no shield, perhaps she could reason with him directly. Despite her assumptions, Eleanor was surprised when her energy barrelled into his, her consciousness entering his mind, a million thoughts crashing against her at once. There were too many for her to register them all, but her mind automatically absorbed and stored them. *What happened to his shield? Where are his mind's defences? I'm right, the pain is coming from having my energy pulled by Enforcers with shields.*

"Get out of my mind!" Arran ordered, delivering a precise, practiced blow to the side of her head, his cold hazel eyes chasing her into the nothing.

"Conlan."

The greeting was empty and emotionless. Eleanor fought the pain and exhaustion, forcing her eyes to open again. With blurry vision she saw Conlan, his hands tied behind him. He had been pulled up to his knees. A Protector held him up by gripping his throat and holding a fistful of his hair. She was lying on the floor of an empty room, big enough that Conlan's name echoed around it once spoken. It was cold. There was a fireplace but it was shrouded in darkness. Three flickering lanterns left the whole room wrapped in shadows that seemed to move with intent. Eleanor saw the scene reflected as an indistinct tableau in the windows, made black mirrors by the darkness outside.

"Father," Conlan replied, a matching emotionless tone.

So this is a Lord of Mydren...

The man standing in front of Conlan was tall with a solid body hidden under flowing dark blue robes that contrasted with the sharp pale-blue steel of his eyes. Eleanor could see Jarrick in them. His short hair was the same shade of brown as Conlan's, the temples shot through with grey. The face was cold, hard and smooth like a sculpture, and it was impossible to guess at his age, because emotion had left no tell-tale lines upon it. His body was perfectly still. *Maybe that was why Jarrick loved statues; they subconsciously reminded him of a father he could never reach.* Eleanor could see two other Protectors standing behind Lord Daratus. They stood at relaxed attention, confident that their services would not be required.

Eleanor jumped when Conlan's father lashed out and punched his son hard in the face. It was so hard that his head snapped to the side, wrenching him from the Protector's grip and depositing him on the floor. The Protector stooped and hauled him upright, holding on to Conlan's shoulders this time.

There was silence.

Lord Daratus was still, almost as if he had never moved. Conlan shook himself, spat blood and slowly raised his head. His father stared down at him.

"I disowned you. You are no longer my son, and for the short span of your life that remains you will not address me as such." There was no anger, no irritation, just an emotionless tone. Conlan shrugged, implying he did not care one way of the other, but Eleanor could feel the waves of fear and misery that were pouring from him. Hurting for him, Eleanor forced herself to her feet. While she was struggling with this monumental task, Daratus preached, waving something in Conlan's face.

"Is this what you want?" he asked. "This pointless piece of silver? This useless relic of a bygone age?" Conlan did not respond. His father hit him again. The Protector made sure he stayed upright this time. Eleanor realised that what Daratus was waving around was the crown. *How supremely confident he must be to have brought it within Conlan's reach.*

"What kind of a king wears a silver crown? It is so cheap, so pathetic," Daratus continued, heavy emotionless words battering down. "You are an idiot. We defeated the abominations in the past. Did you think we would forget how?"

Once she was standing, Eleanor tried to work out what she should do. She held no illusions that they could escape – there may only be three Protectors present with their Lord, but it might as well have been a hundred. Will and Amelia lay together where they had been dropped, eyes closed and faces pale. Freddie lay a little distance away; he was conscious but his eyes were vacant. They had no energy to run. The Protectors had not even considered them enough of a threat to bother tying them up. None of the Enforcers were lurking in the immediate vicinity. *Guess they don't consider us a threat at the moment either.* Inspecting her energy levels, Eleanor realised she was currently about as dangerous as a day-old kitten. While she could push an energy string out if she wanted to, there was no strength left in her to pull the energy she needed from the earth. However, the Lord and the three Protectors all had their attention on Conlan. No one had noticed she was standing, so she currently had the advantage of surprise. *But what do I do with it?* Conlan grunted as his father hit him a third time, the movement so quick that he was perfectly still again before Eleanor realised what he had done. There were very few options. Escape for them all seemed unlikely, and a solo escape would be non-productive. All she could really do was help Conlan. Maybe she could stop his father hitting him. Eleanor ran at the Protector that was holding on to Conlan. Her charging weight was enough to knock him over and drag them all down. They crashed to the floor, sliding a short distance on its polished wooden surface. Before they had stopped moving, Eleanor pulled the surprised Protector's dagger from his belt, positioning the blade under his chin and pushing just enough so that he gasped and froze.

"I could kill you," Eleanor whispered in Dwarfish into the terrified man's ear. "Remember that I chose not to." She removed the blade, slamming the trembling man in the temple with the dagger's hilt. She moved around him as he crumpled to the floor. Coming up behind Conlan she sliced through the rope at his wrists. Her strength failing her, she knelt next to him, panting heavily, her head spinning, as he pulled the bindings away.

"I was under the impression that the abominations had been left helpless," the Lord said, his gaze moving from Eleanor to the unconscious Protector she had left on the floor.

"That is what we were told, Lord Daratus," agreed the taller one of the two Protectors standing behind him looking at Eleanor warily.

"Go! Fetch Arran!" Daratus ordered. The Protector nodded and looked relieved to be getting out of the way as he ran for the door. Conlan had managed to get himself standing, pulling Eleanor to her feet as he did so. His father watched passively.

"You have made loyal little playmates for yourself. Does it know what it will suffer because of you?" the emotionless voice intoned, hatred making his eyes burn. Conlan was silent, so Eleanor answered for him.

"Drollup!"

The growling subtext she added implied that she considered him her inferior. She had no idea what *drollup* meant, but she had heard it used twice as an insult, and as it was the only Dwarfish insult she knew, she was going to use it.

Daratus raised an eyebrow at her. "You taught the abomination to speak?"

"Getting her to speak wasn't the problem, but getting her to shut up..." Conlan said quietly in English. Daratus glared at them, suspicion narrowing his eyes before deciding to ignore the comment.

"Then I shall tell it about the torture I will inflict." An eerie half-smile touched his lips but failed to reach his eyes. He gazed at Eleanor for a moment. "I will rip and tear its flesh, crush and break its bones. Before it dies in agony, I will shatter any remaining sanity – and Conlan will watch it all, so it can cry to him for help that will never come." His voice was the same cold, emotionless monotone, as if he was reading a shopping list, but for some reason this made what he was saying even more terrifying. Eleanor felt fear claw at her soul and she cowered, her back pushing into Conlan. He was trembling. She turned to look up into his face. Fury made him menacing.

He snatched the dagger from Eleanor's hand and flung it at his father. The movement had been quick, but the knife seemed to be moving in slow motion, tumbling end over end through the air. It slowed down and stopped its journey inches from Daratus's chest. He watched dispassionately as it fell at his feet, and then he turned to the door, where a hooded Enforcer stood. Eleanor felt another shiver of fear travel through her; it was like his black robes were pulling light towards him, as if he were a walking black hole.

"Arran, while your timing is impeccable, would you mind explaining to me why this abomination is still standing?" Daratus asked as the Enforcer gave him a slight bow, pushing his hood back. Merciless hazel eyes focused on her, and the familiarity struck her again before the feeling of having her energy pulled blurred her vision and took what little strength remained in her body. Eleanor collapsed, vaguely aware that Conlan had caught her and lowered her to the floor. She whimpered as Arran tugged at her tiny spark of energy, then he pushed into her head. Frightened, Eleanor tried to push him out, but he flooded her mind with agony. She experienced pain upon pain, an agony that made everything else she had so far experienced seem like the imitation of pain in comparison. While her mind twisted and writhed in torment, her body thrashed in unison. As distractions went, it was effective. She was unable to form a coherent thought, let alone kick the intruder out. He looted her head as she struggled, unable to stop herself screaming. Then the agony was gone, leaving her fighting for consciousness. Her muscles twitched spasmodically and her right arm was trapped painfully underneath her. She had no strength to move or even open her eyes. She felt violated, weak and pathetic; she had been unable to protect her thoughts and feelings from being known by the black-robed figure in front of her. She wanted to cry but lacked even the strength for that. Arran spoke, his voice as empty and emotionless as his master's.

"The Avatar of Earth is constantly connected to its energy source, so it recovers quickly. The Avatar of Air should also have this faster recovery time. I left it originally with barely enough energy to continue breathing. It should not have been capable of putting up a fight, my Lord."

"So why is it attacking my guards?" Daratus asked.

"Love, my Lord." The Enforcer spoke the word with distaste. "Its mind is complicated but its love for him..." a finger pointed accusingly at Conlan, "... is very clear. It is pushing itself beyond its limits to protect him."

Daratus laughed humourlessly and Eleanor shivered as ice-cold terror washed over her.

"Do you love it in return?" he asked. Conlan said nothing. As her consciousness started to fade, Eleanor heard the running feet of more Protectors. Rough hands pulled her up, her head rolling forward wrenching her neck. The pain helped her fight off the impending darkness. A cold, firm hand grabbed her chin.

"This one is resilient, strong. I shall enjoy breaking it," Daratus said.

Eleanor heard the sounds of a struggle, of fists hitting flesh. *Conlan.* She wanted to reassure him she was not afraid. She pushed an energy string out to him, feeling for his shield; she ran the string out over its surface, pretending she was caressing his face, wishing she could talk in his head. She knew he could feel it. The struggling stopped, but the sounds of violence continued.

"Stop!" Daratus ordered. "I want him conscious to witness the demise of his creations." Eleanor's faltering mind gave a start, trying to understand what she had just felt. At Daratus's words she had felt Conlan's shield fade slightly.

"You were always a disappointment, but you have also caused me a lot of trouble, Conlan; your actions have reduced my standing with the Central Tower. I intend to take that out on your abominations. Every blow, every pain I deliver will be your fault. I want you to remember that point as their dying screams fill your head. This futile stupidity is over, and I will take their lives in slow, agonising torture – because they believed in you."

Daratus's voice was finally carrying some emotion – a deep, seething hate. Eleanor felt Conlan's shield fade further, and an avalanche of information poured into her head as the final piece of the puzzle fell into place. Alaric had crawled into the earth, beaten and battle-weary. *He gave up.* Eleanor remembered her brief struggle to live after she had been shot, as it had become too hard. *I gave up.* Conlan had told her about having to wait for 'defences' to drop. He had not spoken in her head until after she had given up. The shield was a natural defence. Maybe it existed to stop people's emotions leaking out or to stop their energy being pulled from them, or perhaps it acted as their mind's defence from intrusion. In the end, the purpose it served was irrelevant; to get rid of it, she had to get Conlan to give up, to let go of his will to live. His father's words were having some effect, but could she continue? Would she get the chance? *Can I hurt him so much that he would want to die?*

To get the connection working, she was going to have to destroy him.

"Lock them up, I am already late for dinner. I will deal with them tomorrow," Daratus ordered. "Lock them up together. I want Conlan to look into their eyes as he contemplates what I shall unleash on them."

Eleanor felt Conlan's shield fade again, confirmation, if it were needed, of what she had to do. As they were dragged to the cells she concentrated on pushing her love for Conlan, her compassion and her mercy, deep inside her. Then she focused on all the dark, hateful things she had absorbed, feeling anger rise and the slow, small increase in her energy as it did so. She nurtured it, letting all the hurtful, bitter and unpleasant things Conlan had said to her run through her mind. She remembered what it had felt like when he rejected her, how helpless she had felt when he had stuck his sword into her chin and her misery and anger when he had hit her. She took all the dark, bitter emotions, all the pain he had inflicted on her, and focused on it, allowing it to grow into a seething mass of rage.

Her body was dropped onto a cold stone floor and she heard a cell door slam with finality. Eleanor took her fear and added it to the seething mass. *It's getting easier to keep myself conscious*, she thought as she forced herself to open her eyes. *Maybe I'm getting used to the lower energy levels.* The cell was an eight foot by eight foot bare, empty space lit by several lanterns. It made little impression. *I've met the dragon, so it was only a matter of time before the dungeons turned up*, she thought grimly as she tried to force her tired mind to concentrate on what she had to do. The move had woken Will; he was struggling to pull himself up so he could reach a still unconscious Amelia. Freddie had a haunted expression on his face, but he managed to smile at her weakly as she glanced at him. Conlan was sitting against the cell wall, his head in his hands. She felt something dark and hateful strain inside of her at the sight of him. He was the reason they were in this situation. Rage giving her strength, Eleanor pulled herself to her feet. Surprised, Conlan staggered painfully upright and stepped towards her. Moving with more speed then she thought she had, she marched towards him and shoved him roughly backwards using both hands.

"I trusted you, believed in you and now I'm going to pay for that with my life. You started this, brought us here and let us believe that we could make a difference. Why?" she snarled. Conlan stared at her, speechless. She shoved him again, his back hitting the cell wall. His legs collapsed out from underneath him and he slid down in front of her, his eyes still searching hers for some explanation. Eleanor felt his shield fade further – it was working. She forced herself to continue.

"We're going to die, Conlan. Your father is going to take great delight in tearing us apart. Will you enjoy that, too? Is that what this has been about? Do you enjoy watching people suffer? You've certainly gone out of your way to make sure I've suffered."

Conlan stared at her with uncomprehending distress. She buried her feelings deeper and narrowed her eyes. Sneering, she continued. "What possible motivation did you have? It was never some noble cause; you're far too selfish for that. This was about you, wasn't it? It's always been about you! Your father disowned you, took away all your fancy things and your power, so you created a mission for yourself and made yourself feel important again, but it's no fun without people to lord it over, is it? So you created us, a captive audience you could torture to your heart's content." She slapped him hard in the face, her hand making contact with a sharp crack against the bruises Daratus had left. The already bloody lip started seeping again. His eyes came back to hers filled with raw, naked pain. Will was at her side. One look at the misery in his expression and she nearly faltered.

"Eleanor, don't…" he whispered. She glared at him for a moment while pushing an energy string into his head.

Trust me, she pleaded. *You promised.*

She pulled her string back; she could not afford to get into a debate with Will about what she was doing.

Her voice took on a cold, remorseless tone. "I know you didn't want to tell him how we felt, Will, but I'm not going quietly to my death. You might be able to suffer in silence for him, but I'm not!" Eleanor could see the indecision on Will's face – he had promised that he would trust her, no questions, no discussion, when she asked for it, but Eleanor suspected he had not thought he would have to watch her tear his best friend to pieces to honour the promise. His expression changed and he looked at her thoughtfully. He nodded once and then moved away, a pained look on his face, letting Eleanor finish what she had started. She saw the hope of rescue die in Conlan's eyes and pounced on it.

"Did you think Will would stop me? Will feels exactly the same way! Your actions are not just going to destroy him, they're going to destroy Amelia as well. He's going to watch the woman he loves tortured to death in front of him. Have you *any* idea what that will feel like? No, of course you don't. You have no idea what love is, do you?" she hissed.

"I'm sorry…" Conlan whispered, devastation filling his face.

Eleanor slapped him again, this time hard enough to make her hand throb. He put up no resistance as his head jerked to the side. She would not give him the chance to speak further, knowing that if he interrupted her monologue she would crack, and she was only going to get one chance. The moment he guessed she was not one hundred per cent for real, it would stop having its effect. Eleanor could feel the shield fading rapidly but it was not enough, she had to keep going. She slapped him again, with all the strength she could muster, the sharp sound echoing round the cell. The tormented despair in his eyes as he brought them back to hers emptied her mind of thought. She glared at him, thinking fast.

"Now you decide to say you're sorry?! I didn't think you even had that word in your vocabulary! Don't you dare speak, nothing you utter is worth listening to," she screamed. He stared at her, tears welling up. Eleanor felt her resolve start to crumble and wanted to reach for him, to beg his forgiveness, but his shield was so thin now. Her gaze drilling into him, she imagined she was burning a hole right through his heart with her hate and fury, steeling herself for what she knew she must do. She dug her nails into her hands and the pain pushed the exhaustion back a little. When she spoke again her voice was cold, bitter thunder.

"We're going to die. Slow, bloody, agonising deaths. We gave you everything, is it enough? Are you going to grieve for us as you watch our bodies broken and torn? This is just another game to you, isn't it? You've betrayed us to our deaths, just like you did your mother!"

Please let that be enough!

Conlan recoiled from her words like he had been bitten by a snake. She struggled to keep the bitter hatred in her look as he stared at her, totally wrecked, tears trickling slowly down his face. His shield was so thin. She could feel all his pain. All his shame. All his guilt. He truly believed what she was saying, believed she hated him. The shield was going to disappear, she knew it. She just had to get him to let go of life.

"Conlan, this is the end. I'm going to take your life," she lied, her words razor-sharp. "I know Will would like the satisfaction of watching you die, and if you're not around to witness it, perhaps your father will make our deaths easier."

"End it," he whispered.

Eleanor forced herself to snarl at him. "Not nearly good enough. Beg for your death, as no doubt we will end up begging for ours." Eleanor watched his pride drain from him; defenceless, stricken, he stared at her and nodded slowly, his face blank, his eyes deep pits of agony, fear and self-loathing.

"Please, Eleanor," his voice catching at her name. "If it will help you in any way, I'm begging you, take my life." He closed his eyes, waiting for the killing blow, tears running. Eleanor wondered where he thought she had got the energy from to blast at him. He took a slow, deep, shuddering breath.

He thinks it's his last, Eleanor realised, her heart shattering as she felt his shield finally collapse in on itself, disappearing completely. She dropped to her knees and gently placed her hand against the angry, red imprint she had left on his face. She tenderly rubbed her thumb across his cheek, pulling away the tears. He opened his eyes to stare dully at her.

"I'm sorry, Eleanor," he whispered again, his distress crashing over her and swamping her mind. Without warning, her consciousness was swept up into the chaotic maelstrom in his head. Conlan's mind felt like a tornado was moving through it – thoughts, feelings, fears, spun around her in dizzying confusion and battered against her, threatening to tear away her sanity at any moment.

It was a mistake! His horror-filled thought stabbed through her mind and heart over and over, reverberating through her as he used it to rip at his soul. There was no antechamber, no quiet place they could talk. If she wanted to understand, she was going to have to talk directly to his mind.

I guess the shield was his mind's only defence, like Arran. Avatars are different, our defences are on the inside.

Eleanor concentrated on the images spinning and flashing in front of her, trying to block out the thoughts Conlan was using to beat himself up with. It was too much, he was going into overload. She needed to focus and inhabit one memory so she could pull herself together. In desperation she yelled into the chaos.

Your mother… show me your mother.

The image of a beautiful green-eyed woman swam into view and solidified, the memory expanding and pulling Eleanor in until she felt a part of it, seeing it all through Conlan's eyes. Around her was the garden she had visited, Conlan's mother's garden; it was better kept, but still the riot of glorious colour she remembered, the wonderful heady smell of flowers in bloom filled her consciousness. It was a warm summer's day, and she saw his mother's smiling face as she held him in her arms. He reached a hand to stroke the smooth, petal-soft skin of her face, a tiny hand – he could have been no more than one or two. He was warm, comfortable and blissfully happy, the smell of the flowers and the drone of the occasional insect were lulling him to sleep.

"My beloved," his mother whispered to him, her voice musical, the growling language a kitten's purr on her tongue. "My special boy, one day you will be a great leader and I will be so proud. I love you, with all my heart, but I know that I do not deserve you." She leant over him, kissing his forehead, and Eleanor felt the child's unconditional love.

The scene changed, another took its place – a well-worn track of thoughts, Eleanor realised. Conlan had played these memories back to himself many times. Underneath the thoughts that were embedded within the scene, Eleanor became aware of the thoughts that had been added over time. She felt his vow to his mother as he got older that he would make her proud, would atone for her death in any way he could.

The next scene showed winter. Conlan was older and standing tall. He would be four or five maybe. He watched his mother walking through the dead flowers as his breath made clouds in the still, frosty air. His mother held her hand out over a frost-bitten plant and Conlan gasped in awe as the flower regenerated before his eyes, growing strong, vibrant and beautiful once more.

"It is a secret, beloved, not to be told," she whispered, serious green eyes holding his. The child nodded, feeling pride at being trusted with a secret.

Magic… Conlan's mother was a natural, connected to the earth.

The image changed again. A room, Gregor's library, a child's hand held over dying flowers in a vase. Concentration. If his mother could do it, perhaps he could learn, too. Was that leaf a lighter shade of green? Wonder. Then a feeling of being watched. The child turned his head. A servant, not one he liked, stood in the doorway staring at him with calculating eyes. The only feeling at the time had been fear; but over the years Conlan had added layers of self-loathing and regret to this memory. This was where it had happened. This was where he had unknowingly betrayed his mother.

Gregor's study faded and a new memory solidified. This time there was a lot more detail. This memory had been obsessed over and played so many times that it stood out sharply in contrast to the slightly faded quality of the other memories. Around her was the hallway of a great house, Gregor's, Eleanor assumed. Heavy wooden front doors shuddered under repeated blows, the crashing noise and angry yelling muffled from the other side of the door.

"Open for the representatives of the Lords of Mydren!"

His mother stood, beautiful even in her terror, at the foot of a large sweeping staircase that disappeared into darkness. Conlan knew that Merl and his grandfather were away on business, knew the servants would not get involved, so he had run to protect her, placing his small frame between her and the danger. The doors gave way with a creaking crash and men wielding swords, Protectors, swarmed in. One of the men marched up to them, grabbing Conlan's arm roughly.

"Conlan, son of Lord Daratus and Helena Baydon, you are accused of practicing magic. You will come with us!" he snapped.

No! The child thought stubbornly, fear pulsing in his veins. With all his might he kicked the man, who let go of his arm, yelping in surprise. He may have only been a child, but Conlan had been trained in the best places to apply his strength. He punched and kicked with all the force of his fear, but the man was stronger and slammed a meaty fist into the side of Conlan's face, lifting him off his feet. He landed, stunned, the force knocking the wind from him. His mother ran forward, holding a tiny, delicate hand out, as if this would fend them off.

"It is not Conlan you want, it is me," she insisted. Her admission of guilt hung in the air and a slow smile spread across the Protector's face.

Eleanor gasped. *They knew already. They just needed her to admit it.*

Heavy, brutal hands grabbed at her. Conlan tried to stop them and they knocked him roughly back down, trampling him in their rush to get to his mother. The Protector Conlan had attacked walked towards him, rubbing at the bruises the child's small fists had inflicted. He grabbed Conlan by the neck and lifted him up so they were face to face, blowing rancid, alcohol-coated breath at him. The Protector drew his knife and waved its glittering sharpness in front of the child's terrified eyes as he kicked with desperate futility at the air and tore, with ineffectual fingers, at the bear-like hand squeezing his throat.

"Something to remember me by, boy," the Protector sneered, cutting deeply into Conlan's face and dragging the blade down.

The child jerked, letting loose an agonised, breathless scream. Shame crashed over him on hearing his mother's sobbing distress in the background, hating himself for not being able to take the pain like a man, for not being able to protect her, for putting her in the position of having to protect him in the first place. He was flung back to the floor and watched numbly from barely open eyes as his mother was manacled and gagged. A well-aimed punch to the head rendered her senseless; a hammer-blow to the boy's heart, smashing it to pieces, the fragments tearing through his soul. They dragged her through the broken remains of the door, the last sight he had of her blurred by his tears. Silence and cold, shadowy darkness, watching his blood pooling on the carpet with disinterest.

Eleanor dragged herself away and pulled out from behind the child's eyes. The scene dissolved, colours running, draining away, leaving only darkness. The boy, still lying on the floor sobbing softly, was enclosed in a circle of light from somewhere unseen above. This was no longer a memory.

Conlan, Eleanor whispered. The boy whimpered, pulling himself into a tighter ball. Desperate to comfort the grieving child and wanting nothing more than to put her arms around him and tell him it would all be OK, Eleanor moved forward. As she reached for him, the strength of her need to help him surged through her and she discovered she had arms, a body. She knelt next to him and ran a loving hand over his head. He lifted himself up, wiping tears with the back of his hand, smearing blood from the knife wound.

What are you doing here? The words were spoken by the boy, but the anger underneath them belonged to the man.

I want to help you, Eleanor replied simply.

You cannot, she is dead and it is my fault. As he spoke the words the blood ran more freely down his face and the bruises became more pronounced. Horrified, Eleanor shook her head.

Conlan, what happened to your mother was not your fault. Play your memory back again, slowly, and look at the faces of the Protectors when your mother says that she is the one they want. They knew, Conlan, they knew. They just needed her to admit it, and like cowards they threatened her child so that she would confess. They brought manacles with them that would never have fitted a small boy. Why? Because they knew they would not be leaving with you.

The darkness shifted around them and once again the memory played out, the focus and clarity shifting from Conlan's mother to the men around her. Eleanor watched from the shadows. The memory came to an end. The child pulled himself up from the floor and stood up, eyes wide, comprehension dawning.

I never noticed.

Eleanor opened her arms and the boy ran into them, hugging her tightly, his body trembling as the darkness became brilliant shining light.

It was not your fault, she whispered over and over again.

Eleanor felt herself leave Conlan's mind, but she was unsure if she had elected to leave or had been pushed out. She opened her eyes; his were still filled with fear and pain. Whatever had just happened in his head did not appear to have reached his conscious mind.

"Your shield's gone, Conlan," Eleanor murmured.

His confusion tore at her, and the unrelenting hideousness of what she had just done to the man she loved ripped through her. She had made him beg for her to kill him. *What kind of a monster am I?* She moved her hand from him so quickly that he flinched. *What have I done?* Unable to stand her own guilt and his pain any longer, she curled herself into a ball, shaking, broken sobs tearing through her until the exhaustion swept her away from the nightmare of her own creation.

Eleanor felt her energy twitching, pulling her from the blackness. It was attempting to pull energy from the earth to replace what she had lost. She tried to concentrate, to speed the process up, but she lacked the strength and the effort was pushing her back towards unconsciousness. There were whispered voices, too low to make out the words. Her head was resting on something comfortable and warm, while her back lay on cold stone. A warm hand gently brushed her hair off her face. *Freddie.* She opened her eyes. She was on the far side of the cell to Conlan and Will. They were sat next to each other, talking in soft voices. Amelia slept at Will's side, her head resting on his outstretched legs in the same way as she was lying on Freddie's. Seeing Conlan slammed remorse painfully into her, but she pushed it back. *Not now, I can't give in to this now, we need to get out of here.* She pulled herself up.

Freddie smiled at her. "Are you OK?" he whispered.

Eleanor shook her head. "I don't deserve to be. Why are we over here?"

Freddie's smile faded. "Will suggested it might be an idea to get you out of Conlan's range for a while." Eleanor felt guilt grind into her, twisting her stomach and making her head throb; she looked into Freddie's eyes. Something had changed – there was distance, a new and uneasy wariness.

"I had to do it, Freddie."

He nodded slowly. "I know you did, but I never thought you could be that cruel, that brutal. That had to come from somewhere." Shame burning in the pit of her stomach, Eleanor dropped her head. There was darkness inside of her that she had never really acknowledged before, and she had let that loose on Conlan. *I never even wondered if he would be strong enough to take it.*

On shaking legs she stood up and walked hesitantly to the other side of the cell, dropping to sit on the floor in front of Conlan. He and Will stopped talking and both turned their heads to look at her. Will gave her a long appraising look. Conlan stared at her, green eyes cold as stone.

"I'm sorry," she said. "I had to do it, had to say those things. I didn't mean a single word of it."

"You were very convincing."

Four words, but they carried so much anger, so much bitter menace, that for the first time in a very long time Eleanor felt fear as she looked into Conlan's eyes. Trying not to tremble, she nodded.

"I had to be, it wouldn't have worked if you had suspected anything." Tears falling, her eyes dropping, she did the only thing she could think to do. "Please, Conlan, I'm sorry. Please, I had to do it." There was silence. She raised her head slightly to view his face. It was a mistake. The look he gave her froze the blood in her veins and made her energy twitch with fear and shame.

"How am I supposed to trust this plea for forgiveness? You seem very good at manipulating me," Conlan said, his words poisoned-filled barbs. Eleanor stared at him. She had no answer. She had betrayed his trust.

"I can show you the truth, if you really want to know," Will said.

Conlan turned to look at him. "How?"

"You don't have a shield anymore, so I can show you the inside of her head, show you all her motivations, every thought, every fear, every hope and dream. I can show you her soul," Will said solemnly. Eleanor's heart rate doubled, her breath painful as she panted her terror; he would find out, he would learn the dirty, evil secret she carried. It would destroy everything. She moaned as Conlan nodded his agreement.

"Will, no… please, no," she whispered, flinching away from him.

Will glared at her.

"I won't let you, I'll keep you out," Eleanor said, a measure of strength returning to her voice with her sudden anger. Will laughed, a vicious sound that sent a shiver up her spine.

"If I want to get into your head, you won't stop me. If this is what Conlan needs, he can have it. I suggest you submit."

Before Eleanor could answer, Will's energy slammed into her head, physically knocking her over. Her mind filled with pain, a more intense version of the pain Arran had inflicted on her. Wave after wave of agony, like being dropped into a vat of acid, every nerve ending screaming. It made her body and mind shudder, writhe and jerk. A harsh breathless sobbing escaped her gritted teeth. How was he doing this? She knew Will's energy levels were as low as hers, so the only conclusion was that it was part of his 'mind-meld' abilities that were not affected by his lack energy. She had no hope of being able to push Will out, but as the pain stopped, allowing some coherent thought, she realised he had not tried to push past her defences.

"She's putting up strong resistance. This could take a while," Will said, staring at her coldly.

I'm not putting up any resistance. Her thoughts cut off as the pain came again, this time with a greater intensity. It was too much for her exhausted body and her movements became sluggish.

"No, Will, enough!" Conlan said, anguish in his voice. The pain left and she lay still, eyes closed, fighting the need to pass out.

Will huffed in frustration. "Do you want to know or not?"

"Not like this, I can't do this," Conlan whispered.

Eleanor felt a gentle hand on her face searching her neck for a pulse.

"Eleanor? Can you hear me?"

She once again forced her eyes to open, to find Freddie leaning over her. He smiled but Eleanor could still see the fear in his eyes. *He's afraid of me.* Tears rose in response to the hurt this thought caused. She had done as Conlan wanted, so why did nobody understand? Freddie helped her to sit up, allowing her to rest against him, supporting her. Conlan stared at her, his eyes still hard. Eleanor could not bring herself to look at Will.

"What you did was horrific," Conlan whispered. Sighing, he dropped his gaze. "But I can't hate you for it. You knew exactly what to say, you knew about my mother. How?"

Eleanor tensed in anticipation of a surge of emotional torment from him, but none came. He looked confused, as if he too had expected pain that had failed to materialise.

"It wasn't your fault," Eleanor whispered. Conlan gave her a sharp, suspicious look. In a stronger voice she answered his question, wondering what he was thinking. "I knew about your mother because Jarrick and Merl mentioned her. The rest of it... I know you. I took the solid core of your being, your strength, your courage, your desire to do the right thing, your responsibility to the people of Mydren, the care you have for us, and I turned it into something sick and twisted." Her voice dropped back to a whisper and she hung her head. "I'm not proud of myself, Conlan."

"Was there no other way?"

Eleanor could not look at him as she answered. "The only other way was to cause you such physical injury that you would believe yourself to be dying."

"That would have been kinder," Conlan muttered.

Eleanor nodded. "Yes it would, but there'd have been no guarantee you'd have survived, and even if you had, you'd have been in no fit state to get out of here." Eleanor could feel him staring at her, but she could not raise her head. When he spoke, he sounded resigned.

"I suppose I deserve it for breaking your heart."

Eleanor gasped in shock. *Is that what he thinks? That I considered it payback?* She shook her head, her eyes meeting his. "No, Conlan, don't think that. You didn't deserve what I just did to you. I wasn't acting out of revenge. I don't want to hurt you. I'm sorry... please." The tears were falling again, but she brushed them away, angry at herself for being pathetic. *No time to fall apart now.* Again she tried to push the guilt back, but it was side-stepping her attempts and hitting her with iron fists whenever it got within range.

"A lot of people have tried to break me. My father would be amused to know that all it took was a tiny girl with a few well-chosen words," he whispered bitterly. Eleanor felt the extent of the damage she had caused as his hurt tore through her. There was no time. The more urgent problem of escape was what mattered.

Taking a deep breath, Eleanor accepted what the pain in his eyes and the hurt that was crashing over her were saying.

"You can't forgive me, I understand that, but since this isn't going to get resolved right now, please can we focus on the matter in hand."

Anger and indignation flashed across his face. "What matter is that?"

"The life and death one, you know, the one where we get out of here in one piece and live to fight another day," Eleanor said, Conlan's look telling her he no longer considered himself to be in one piece.

"How are you going to do that?" Will snapped. "None of us has the energy to spare. Those hooded bastards have been back twice since you passed out, just to make sure we're kept barely conscious. So tell me, little miss genius, what's your plan?"

Eleanor finally forced herself to look at Will's glaring expression. It made her shake. What Will had done made her fearful and uneasy, but he was right.

"I don't have a plan," she admitted.

"Then we're going to die anyway, only you decided to torture Conlan first,"

Will sneered. Eleanor felt the tears running faster, but she made no attempt to brush them away, she was too stunned. She had assumed that Will, at least, would understand.

"Leave her alone, Will," Conlan said, sounding as tired as he looked. "She's doing the best she can; she got rid of my shield. Besides, she's not the only one to consider torturing me an acceptable price for a necessary action."

Will ignored the pointed look Conlan gave him.

"Don't tell me you forgive her!" Will said in angry disbelief. Conlan seemed to consider this for a moment.

"I forgave you," he noted softly, smiling at Will.

Eleanor felt a small seed of hope burst into unexpected life. "I'm so sorry I hurt you, and if we get out of this alive I promise I'll make it up to you, but please will you help us figure out a way to escape?"

Conlan sighed, the distrust and anger fading from his eyes. "I forgive you, Eleanor." Her heart stopped. He smiled, her heart jump-started painfully and the world stopped instead. "You did what I asked," he continued. "I have no right to complain about the methods. I'm just hurt that you found it so easy to do that to me." He rubbed his red cheek ruefully, but the smile remained. Eleanor winced at his words.

"For the record, that was the hardest thing I have *ever* had to do," she whispered. An energy string brushed against her. She grasped it but nearly flung it out of her head as she felt Will's wary presence.

I'm sorry, Eleanor. You were never in any danger from me. I just wanted him to see you in pain. I needed to cut through his hurt, the despair and rage you created in him. I needed to remind him just what you mean to him. I would never have let him anywhere near your mind.

You were faking? Eleanor asked incredulously.

He forgave you, didn't he? We don't have time for him to sit around and brood about this. Now stop feeling sorry for yourself! Will snapped, pulling himself from her head.

"Eleanor? Are you OK?" Conlan asked, and Eleanor realised that she had been staring at the floor for a long time. She was not OK. This was way out of her league and she had no idea how they were going to get out of the cell, let alone the stronghold, and the knowledge of what was coming was paralysing her. Taking her silence as a sign that something was wrong, Conlan moved forward and placed his hand on her face. He lifted her eyes to his.

"What Will did to you, does it still hurt?" he asked, giving Will an angry sideways glance.

"No, and Conlan, please don't look at Will like that. You have no idea how lucky you are to have a friend who cares about you as much as he does. I understand why he did what he did and I forgive him, you have no right to be angry with him," Eleanor said, her voice cold and calm, her emotions under firm control. Conlan looked back at Will. Eleanor could not read the look that passed between them, but Will smiled.

"So what's wrong?" Conlan asked, turning back to her. Eleanor pulled her head from his hands and pushing back into Freddie's solid warmth she stared at the floor, very aware of just how hard her body was shaking.

"What's wrong?" she repeated. "Have you looked around recently? I'm frightened, Conlan. Terrified. We have no idea how we're going to get out of here, and I really don't want your father to rip me to pieces. My fear is freezing my brain. You're my family, my world, everything I love. We have precious few hours of life left and what have I been doing? I've destroyed you, made Freddie afraid of me and pushed Will into attacking me. I suppose I should be grateful Amelia is still asleep!" she choked down a sob as she finished her rant. Knowing her despair was slipping from her control, she kept her eyes firmly on the floor.

Conlan reached for her face again, forcing her eyes to his and staring at her for a long moment before he spoke. "Eleanor, you've figured out the book and how Avatar energy works. You've passed a *maldra scelpa*, rescued me on several occasions, removed my shield, helped me find an army and provided me with the most intelligent horse I've ever met. You've got us further than I ever thought possible, so don't quit on us now."

She stared at him. Calm green eyes filled with faith and hope stared back. It hurt. *Go down fighting? It's not as if we have anything more to lose!* She nodded and took a deep breath, pushing her feelings back down, but her voice still quivered when she spoke.

"What have I missed? You said the Enforcers had been back?"

Conlan sat beside her as Will answered, his voice flat. "They come back, pull whatever energy we've been able to recoup, and then they leave again."

"Hurts like hell," Freddie grumbled.

"I think that's because they're pulling our energy through their shields," Eleanor said slowly. "If you can find their energy strings you can pull the energy back, but possibly not with the low energy levels we have at the moment."

"Can't you just hide some energy somewhere?" Conlan asked.

Will smiled. "Sorry, we don't come with spare batteries."

Conlan looked confused. "What's a battery?"

"Something that stores energy in our world," Will answered.

Batteries?

Eleanor yelped in delight, waking Amelia up with a start. Moving forward as fast as her aching body would allow, she knelt in front of Will and kissed him hard. Rocking back, she smiled, amused by his surprised look. A slow smile met hers.

"Will, you're a total genius!" she enthused.

Will looked doubtful. "I am?"

She nodded and sat back down, running through the plan in her head and looking for problems. Will watched her for a moment, then noticed Conlan, Freddie and Amelia all staring at him.

"What?" he muttered almost to himself. "*She* kissed *me*!"

Feeling happier and lighter, Eleanor allowed her mind to churn through angles and possibilities. "How often do the Enforcers visit?"

"Every few hours," Will informed her.

Eleanor nodded, factoring in the time scale. "When are they next due?"

"Now," Conlan said, glancing at the cell door with apprehension.

"I have a plan," Eleanor said, unable to take the smile off her face.

"That's great, but could you calm down a little and explain it?" Conlan asked.

Eleanor nodded. "Right... plan, yes... I do actually have a battery," she stuttered, the excitement making her a little agitated.

"Still not making sense to the idiots, so maybe Will the genius could explain," Amelia said with a smirk.

Will shrugged. "No clue what she's on about."

"Calm down and explain yourself," Conlan said. She could hear the irritation creeping into his voice.

She took a slow, deep breath and tried to keep her voice level as she explained. "That's what the Talismans are, or at least what the gems in them are – they're batteries, sort of. They store energy, our energy. I've played with it a little, but I didn't really give it much thought because I never envisaged a situation where I'd need stored energy."

"So we *do* come with spare batteries," Will said, smiling at his own joke.

"Just a shame we don't have them on us anymore."

"Well that's just it. Obviously the sword, wand and chalice are with Judder." She then reached inside her shirt for the chain and pulled it out, dangling the diamond in front of them. "I forgot about this, though."

"How much energy is in there?" Will asked, watching it swing to and fro.

"A lot. I spent a long time filling it, wondering if it would reach a limit, but it didn't." Still smiling, Eleanor put the diamond safely back under her shirt.

"So what's your plan?" Amelia asked, a look of hope in her eyes that Eleanor found she desperately wanted to keep there.

"We let the Enforcers come back and empty our energy down again, then we have two hours. I'll share the energy out between us, enough so that you can pull your own. We blast our way out of here and make for the main gate. Hopefully Judder will have stood by his word and be there to help us," she said, a happy smile on her face.

"You don't need to give me that much energy, Eleanor, this city has extensive aquifers; besides, your energy always makes me feel like I'm being buried alive," Will said, shuddering slightly.

"Well it's that or torturous death... your choice," Eleanor countered.

Will smiled cheerfully. "Buried alive... "

The cell door slammed open.

Eleanor jumped and twisted towards the four Enforcers as they entered. Arran stepped forward, his large hazel eyes staring at her malevolently. The energy-draining sensation ripped through her but there was no pain, which meant only Arran was pulling her energy.

Conlan lunged forwards, and in one fluid motion Arran pulled his attention from Eleanor and gestured with his hand, slamming Conlan into the cell wall where he struggled briefly like an insect pinned to a card, before going limp and dropping to the floor. Arran whipped back and calmly continued pulling Eleanor's energy, almost before she had realised he had stopped.

"Find their strings and take the energy back!" Freddie ordered. Forcing himself to his feet and giving Conlan a worried frown, he strained against the efforts of the Enforcers.

Stunned by the sudden violence, Freddie's words jerked Eleanor into action. She tried to pull the energy back, and for a moment she held Arran in check, smiling grimly at the surprise on his face. Arran took a step towards Freddie, and Eleanor knew exactly what he was going to do.

"Why are you doing this?" Eleanor asked through gritted teeth, desperate to distract him. Arran stopped and stared at her silently, looking a little surprised. Despite his lack of response, Eleanor kept talking. "We are trying to free Mydren, we want to free magic. We are trying to change this world for the better so in the future no child born with magic talent will be dragged from its parents and tortured into serving a Lord's whims. We are trying to help people like you, Arran."

He narrowed his eyes, focusing further. Another tugging sensation joined Arran's, and pain filled her world. It felt like the core of her being was being ripped out. An Enforcer with a shield was assisting Arran. *If he moves into my head now, he'll see our plan.* Fear of discovery stopped her fight and she collapsed, registering Arran's satisfaction through half-closed eyes. She thrashed weakly against cold stone, dimly aware that Amelia was sobbing.

The pain left. Eleanor lay panting before the Enforcers. Arran glared at her and waved his hand once more. Freddie was buffeted off his feet and flung into the cell wall as Conlan had been, dropping like a sack of wet flour. He tried to rise, but Arran flicked his hand down and Freddie was slammed forcibly into the unyielding stone floor, a whimpering cry escaping him with the sharp exhalation of air from his lungs and the audible crack of ribs.

"Resist me again and he will suffer further," Arran said, pointing a long white finger at Conlan, his merciless expression firmly back in place. Yet Eleanor had seen a flash of something in his eyes. The Enforcers turned and left the cell in a flapping of black robes, like crows over road kill.

Silence.

Conlan stirred and groaned as he forced himself up. Moving to her side, he made sure she was breathing before moving to Freddie. Eleanor could hear panting and pained breaths from across the cell.

"Freddie?" Conlan whispered.

Eleanor tried to move, to get up, to help Freddie... the world retreated into black.

"Eleanor, Eleanor..." The soft growl penetrated the dark. "Will, I think she's coming round." A gentle hand brushed her face and then gave it a light slap, the sensation bringing reality into sharp focus.

"Hey!" she muttered, raising her hands in weak defence.

"Eleanor, come on, open your eyes," Will ordered. "We had a plan, remember? We can't get the energy out of your diamond – we tried – so you have to do it. Wake up." The light slap again. "Wake up, Eleanor, you're being pathetic."

Irritated, Eleanor opened her eyes. Conlan was cradling her and Will was leaning over her, grinning.

"Freddie?" she asked, trying unsuccessfully to get Will's features into focus.

"I'll live, Eleanor," came the whispered reply. "Assuming we get out of here."

With Conlan and Will's help, Eleanor sat upright and took a few deep breaths while waiting for everything to stop spinning. Freddie was sat against the wall next to her, one arm wrapped around his ribs. His breath was laboured, his expression glazed and blood flecked his lips. Shocked by the pain she could see in his eyes, Eleanor moved slowly to kneel in front of him. Reaching forward she took his face in her hands.

"Don't you dare die on me, Freddie," she said, and leaning forward she kissed his forehead. Freddie smiled at her, slowly shaking his head.

"No dying, got it," he murmured.

"Eleanor, the plan? Now, please, you've been out for a while and time is slipping by," Conlan said, sounding rather exasperated. She turned and held his gaze, which garnered another one of his unfathomable looks. She nodded, reached for the diamond and wrapped her hand around it, feeling the comforting vibrations of the energy stored within. Eyes closed, she pushed a string into its lattice and pulled the energy free.

It was like releasing the cork off a champagne bottle after spending ten minutes shaking it up. The energy exploded through her – too much, too fast to control. Panicking, she made futile attempts to remove the string. Her levels passed normal and began climbing, her body shook and the surging power began to get painful. She had to release it, had to get rid of it, but they could not afford to waste the energy. She opened her eyes to find Conlan's concerned face in front of hers. *Mustn't release the energy.* Not really thinking about what she was doing, she acted on instinct and grabbed Conlan's wrist. The moment their skin touched, the excess energy flowed from her into him, like a burst dam, their energies linking effortlessly. He gasped, pain creasing his features and body slumping forwards. Eleanor kept a tight grip on his wrist and struggled to regain control. Eventually the flow slowed enough to make control possible. Eleanor withdrew her energy string from the diamond and took short, panting breaths.

Raising his head, Conlan swore softly in Dwarfish, his body shaking as he looked at her bewildered. She smiled and reached a hand to stroke his head as she let go of his wrist. Slowly sitting up he rubbed it and looked down in surprise. There was a raised imprint, like the rest of them carried, but the symbol burnt into the inside of his wrist was a five-pointed star within a circle. Closing her eyes for a moment to catch her breath, Eleanor found she could almost see her energy glowing within him. Luminous green and brown flowing streams wrapped around his own glowing white energy. Conlan was holding a lot of energy, but he seemed to be showing no ill effects.

"What was that?" he asked, still rubbing his wrist.

"I think that was the connection. You don't take energy, Conlan, *we* are not yours to control; *you* belong to *us*. We give you energy. You currently hold so much that I can see it glowing, I can feel it. Please try not to release it at us. Can you feel it?" Eleanor asked slowly and gently, not wanting to scare him into accidentally exploding them.

Conlan closed his eyes, and a grin, like a child opening a much longed for birthday present, spread across his bruised face. "It feels warm and sort of earthy."

Eleanor smiled. "OK, hold that thought, keep your eyes closed and just concentrate on what it feels like. I'm going to help the others and then we'll see if you can use it, OK?"

Working as quickly as possible, Eleanor carefully rationed out what was left of the energy in the diamond. The change in her friends was instantaneous; colour returned to their faces and their movements became more fluid and stronger. Freddie claimed his pain had reduced and Amelia was not the only one with hope in her eyes. Conlan had not moved from where Eleanor had left him kneeling on the floor, his eyes closed and a small, dreamy smile on his face. Not wanting to startle him, she kept her voice low as she spoke.

"Conlan, keep your eyes closed for the moment, OK? Tell me about the energy."

Conlan nodded. "I can feel it inside me. It's part of my own energy, but separate. It feels like you, like your personality is stamped on it."

"OK, Will is going to send you some of his energy," Eleanor said, looking at Will. The only visible evidence of this transfer was Conlan's widening smile.

"Wow," he breathed.

"You can feel that, too?" Eleanor asked.

"It's so different from yours – wet, cold... calming," Conlan whispered.

"That would definitely be Will. Can you differentiate between the different types of energy?" Eleanor asked as she watched his face for signs of pain that would indicate he was holding too much.

"Yes, as easily as I can tell the difference when I look at the two of you, the colours are obvious," he said.

"Colours?" Freddie asked.

Conlan smiled, eyes still firmly closed. "Like the colours when you release your energy at Amelia's shield. Eleanor's energy is green and brown, Will's is purple and blue. It's beautiful."

"OK, next step. Freddie is going to send you some of his energy," Eleanor said, nodding at Freddie, who grinned at her in turn.

"Hot," Conlan muttered, then he chuckled. "Impatient; definitely Freddie, red and orange."

"My turn," Amelia said quietly.

"Oh, Amelia… so beautiful," Conlan murmured. "Your colour is silver-grey. Your energy feels so light, but it's so strong."

Amelia looked surprised at Conlan's comment. "Sure you're reading that right?"

Conlan nodded. "Strong, so very strong, as strong as Eleanor's."

Will smiled and hugged Amelia to him. Amelia smiled faintly, looking a little stunned.

"Conlan, can you feel your hold on our energy?" Eleanor asked.

Conlan shook his head. "No, I'm not holding it, it's just there."

He's not holding the energy back; maybe that's just us. Perhaps we have to hold our energy in and he has to push the energy out. Still speaking in a slow, calm and quiet voice, Eleanor made another request of him. "When you feel ready, Conlan, I want you to open your eyes. *Please* try not to release the energy you're holding, as the damage you could cause would be quite spectacular. You have enough of our energy to level this building."

"You're not exactly filling me with confidence, Eleanor."

"Sorry, but you need to be aware of the potential you're carrying."

Slowly, looking like he expected something horrific to happen at any second, Conlan opened his eyes. Eleanor and Amelia gasped.

"What?" he asked, his gaze travelling over them anxiously.

"Your eyes are glowing," Will said, when he realised Eleanor was too awestruck to respond.

"They are? Is that normal?"

Will shrugged and they all turned to look at Eleanor. She stared at the bright-green orbs. They had always glowed with his life, his intelligence, but this was something completely different. It was like they were backlit. They were so brilliant emerald green that she felt she could sit and stare into them forever. *I wonder if he can see in the dark now,* she pondered, the thought coming out of nowhere. With effort she snapped herself out of her mind's desire to lose itself in Conlan's stunning eyes.

"I have no idea if it's normal and frankly no time to think about it now. So long as you're not in pain, I'm going to class all of this as a success and move on," Eleanor said briskly.

"I'm not in pain, it just feels a little strange. It's like whispered voices you can't quite hear," Conlan said, smiling.

"That would be destiny talking, sweetie," Amelia said quietly, running a gentle hand over Conlan's head. Eleanor smiled. Destiny was not just talking, destiny was yelling.

"You have energy and you're connected to us; the brand on your wrist proves that. Now you need to release some of our energy in a meaningful fashion," Eleanor said, consolidating her thoughts on the matter as she spoke. "This is where I come a little unstuck, as I have no idea how to test this. As I said, if you let go of all the energy we gave you, you're going to bring this building down on our heads. I was sort of hoping that your control would be different from ours, because if it isn't there seems little point in having a 'centre'. I was hoping that you would be able to release our energy in well-aimed, controlled bursts, basically the opposite of what happens when we release ours."

"Your energy releases always seemed very controlled to me," Conlan said. "You blasted that chair right out from under Merl. What happened to Merl, by the way?"

"He's dead," Eleanor said flatly.

"I did him a great wrong…" Conlan stopped, frowning, as if what he was saying did not make sense to him.

"It wasn't your fault," Eleanor whispered again. Conlan looked at her, his eyes glazing over again as memories ran through his head.

"Oh," he murmured as tears once again filled his eyes.

Conlan crumpled. His body trembled violently. Eleanor pulled him into her arms. She expected him to push her away, but he wrapped his arms around her, buried his face in her neck and sobbed. Not being able to feel his relief as Eleanor could, not understanding, just wanting to help, Amelia reached for his hand. On his other side Freddie put a hand on Eleanor's shoulder as a sign of quiet support. Will reached an arm around Amelia.

For one brief moment they were all physically connected, and with the speed of a star exploding, their consciousness was thrown to all corners of the globe, as if they had been pushed into space on the top of a rocket and they were now looking back down at the planet they had left. Mydren spread out in all its natural glory before them. Eleanor could feel the control all the elements exerted on their environment, could see how easy it would be to manipulate. The experience was similar to when the four of them had balanced their energies together, but on a much larger scale. She could feel the wonder of the others and could feel Conlan's palpable awe.

What is this? Conlan's question echoed through their heads. Eleanor felt them all try to answer it at once, but it sounded as nothing more than white noise. When there appeared to be no response, Conlan panicked. Was he here alone? How did he get back to his body? As his concentration wavered they began to fall, plummeting back towards Mydren at a stomach churning speed. Conlan was clearly in control, even if this was not evident to him. Their returning consciousness hit hard enough to affect their physical bodies and wrenched them apart.

Still reeling from their 'crash landing', Eleanor was unprepared when she was dumped out of the connection and back into the raging chaos of Conlan's tormented mind. It was like being stuck on a merry-go-round that just got faster and faster, images flashing past, confusing, scary. If she did not concentrate she would lose herself. She could feel the others trapped as she was, but with even less idea of what was going on. A calm refuge was needed so they could marshal their resources and detach themselves. An image jumped out at her from the maelstrom and stopped all thought. As she focused on it she moved into a memory. It was her, or at least it was someone the same size as her, because all similarity between herself and the creature in Conlan's memory ended there. The figure stood, soaking wet, looking into the distance with an apprehensive look on her face. *Before we found the chalice*, Eleanor remembered. *We were swimming. I was thinking about the dragon.* Conlan was thinking about something else entirely, and Eleanor knew that if she could have blushed she would have done. He was absorbed by her casual grace, the way her wet clothes showed her curves, her beautiful face, hair falling artfully across it in wet streams. In his eyes she glowed with an inner light that he felt drawn to, like an addiction, a voracious desire he simply added ever more fuel to, but never satisfied. His need for her was almost painful. Eleanor asked the question without thinking, *How do you really feel about me, Conlan?* realising too late that the others had joined her in this corner of Conlan's mind.

Image after image snapped before them, his thoughts, feelings, desires and fantasies coming with them. Eleanor stood in the white dress, looking so small and vulnerable but so unbelievably beautiful. His memory of her righteous rage as she had moved with determined power and control, fighting Duncan and his friends, shone in glorious splendour. Her eyes glistened as they held his, soft, chocolate-brown, flecks of amber moving through them depending on her mood. When she was angry with him they looked almost gold, and when she allowed her love for him to show through they were a deep, rich-brown he wanted to disappear into forever. Hundreds of images. Recurring feelings of pride, gratitude, adoration, wonder, amusement and devotion. She felt his overwhelming desire to protect her, but over and above all of it Eleanor felt his love. A huge feeling. She filled his every waking moment and he felt her absence as a physical ache. His love was different. She had felt Freddie's love for her and Will's love for Amelia, but this was something beyond that. While all the Avatars loved dearly and with all their hearts, they held some of themselves back. Eleanor knew what Will held back from Amelia, frightened she would run from the dark side of his soul. She did not know what Freddie held back, but she could guess. Conlan did not love like that, though. He would hold nothing back if he ever admitted he loved her. For Conlan it was all or nothing. He did not know how to limit what he showed. With a shock, Eleanor realised that she had known he loved her, her heart had known. Her physical being had recognised his love in the way he touched her and cared for her, and she had unknowingly responded to it. This was why her love for him had never faltered, because her heart had overridden her logical mind.

Thinking of her calmed Conlan's mind. She reached out to Will. Too embarrassed to discuss what she knew they had all just seen, she skipped straight to business.

How do we get free?

I don't know, Will answered, sounding incredibly tired. *Maybe Conlan has to expel us?*

Eleanor felt Amelia's presence come closer.

Maybe if we all speak together? she suggested.

Eleanor felt joint agreement as Freddie found them.

OK, she agreed. *What do we say?*

If we just have to get his attention, we could just yell his name, Freddie offered.

Right, said Will. *After three: one, two, three.*

All four of them, their energy strings entwined, yelled 'Conlan!' as loudly as they could in his head. Conlan's shocked reflex action brutally shoved them out.

Stunned, Eleanor opened her eyes. Their bodies had been forced back. Conlan now sat alone in the middle of them, as if surrounded by a toddler's discarded toys.

"You were in my head, all of you. Where were we?" he asked, his voice shaking.

"I think that was the true power of the connection," Will said, sitting up. "I think we might need to practice a lot more!"

"Understatement of the century," Freddie muttered, wrapping his arms around his ribs protectively.

"What did you see in my head?" Conlan asked quietly.

"You lied to me," Eleanor said seriously, knowing he would know exactly what she meant.

"Maybe I had my reasons."

"Maybe you did, but please don't," Eleanor said, wanting him to say more, wanting him to admit out loud that he loved her.

The silence stretched out.

Will coughed. "Er, remember that life and death situation? Well we're still in it; could you perhaps leave this for later?"

"This is important, Will," Eleanor said without looking at him.

"Eleanor, I'm not stupid, none of us are. We're all very aware of the significance of what's going on right now between the two of you, but we need to get out of here, and sooner rather than later. I think its a few hours before dawn, so most people will be asleep. We stand a much better chance of escape," Will said, looking apologetic.

"What if we die trying to escape?" Eleanor whispered sadly. "I want to hear him say it, just once."

Conlan stared at her. Then taking a firm, careful hold of her face he leaned in, pushing his lips into hers. He kissed her with passion and desire, but it was under tight control; he was cautious and tender, as if he was afraid of breaking her. She stared into his eyes, unable to close hers; she never wanted him out of her sight again. She pushed a little harder against him, seeing his surprise as she opened her lips and ran her tongue along the soft line of his mouth, tasting blood. Thankful that Freddie had shown her how, she pushed her tongue gently into Conlan's mouth, caressing and tasting, the world no longer of any interest. For a moment he responded, a quiet moan escaping him, before the reality of the situation, of the three people staring at them, forced him to pull away. He spoke in a whisper.

"I love you, Eleanor."

Eleanor felt his love as it flowed over her, and for several seconds it eradicated everything from the universe but him, his glowing green eyes holding hers. Tears made rivulets through the streaks of dirt and blood on her face.

Conlan frowned. "That wasn't meant to make you cry."

Eleanor smiled, the tears still falling. "I've waited a very long time to hear you say it. I'd given up hope that you would. I'm stuck in a cell, waiting to die and I feel like someone has beaten me black and blue with a bat, but right now I'm the happiest I've ever been." Heedless of their injuries, Eleanor threw her arms around his neck and he pulled her against him. *If I hold him tight enough, do we merge into one being?* She slowly moved a string out over his now glowing, pulsating energy ball and felt him shiver involuntarily at the touch. He moved his head back to hold her gaze with a soft, slightly spaced-out expression; she smiled and ran her hand tenderly down his face, her thumb rubbing against his scar, ignoring the stubble, the cuts and bruises, and seeing only the bravest heart and the strongest soul she had ever met.

Will coughed again and Conlan jumped, looking at him over Eleanor's shoulder.

"I know this is a bad time… " Will said, letting the unspoken assessment of their situation hang in the air. Conlan nodded and reluctantly let go of his death-like grip. Eleanor sighed, her body felt uncomfortable when he was not holding her. Freddie was grinning at her and trying hard to be happy. Amelia had a knowing smile on her face.

"Come on, I'm sick of this place, let's go," Eleanor said, getting to her feet. Will helped Conlan to stand. Eleanor watched him, his head bowed as he took a few deep breaths and his muscles shifting beneath his clothes, as if he was trying to fit back into his body. Things had changed, and she could see it. As Conlan straightened his shoulders and pulled himself to his full height, he unconsciously wrapped his defences around him, but it was not distance or silence that protected him now. It was love. Eleanor could feel it and knew the others could, too. His love pulled them close and protected them. Raising his head, Conlan noticed Eleanor's scrutiny and smiled. She shuddered as every hair on her body stood to rigid attention. Here was a king. She fought the irrational urge to kneel and acknowledge this fact. The pain, anger and guilt that had always seemed part of him were gone, and strength and compassion now shone from his glowing green eyes. Eleanor heard Amelia's sharp intake of breath as she saw the same thing. Conlan noticed their response.

"What?" he enquired, but the suspicion that normally accompanied this question was also gone. He sounded amused.

Amelia opened her mouth and then closed it again, her eyes wide. Conlan's smile grew and he pulled Amelia close, kissing the top of her head.

Initially Conlan had wanted to go after his father. Will and Freddie had talked him out of it, though, pointing out that they had no idea where he was and that none of them was in a very healthy state. As such, they needed to fall back, regroup and get to grips with how Conlan's control worked, before they got into any serious battles. Conlan had tried to release the energy he was holding, but with no result. Will had entered his head to help him figure it out, but he had not been successful. Being only able to talk to Conlan's raw mind had not helped. Frustrated and knowing they were running out of time, Conlan had called a halt and asked Amelia to push the cell door out of its frame. They had stepped cautiously over the splintered door, hanging half off its hinges, and into the dark corridor beyond. Freddie led them through the black. Conlan had been disappointed to discover that glowing eyes did not give him the ability to see in the dark, although Eleanor had pointed out that it did look eerily cool seeing them floating next to her. If ever he wanted to scare someone to death, that was the way to go.

At the end of the long corridor they reached a spiral stone staircase, and as they climbed it became lighter, the soft orange glow of lanterns making it possible to see. They could hear boisterous voices coming from above. Creeping up the last few stairs on their stomachs, Will and Conlan scouted out the room and then slithered back down.

"There are three Protectors playing cards near the top of the stairs," Conlan whispered. They nodded, as they could all hear the animated conversation that was accompanying the game. "There is another Protector," Conlan continued. "He's sat in a chair near the far wall and Arran is sat by the door. It seems to be the only exit. The door is bolted from the inside, so we just need to get to it and we can get out."

"We need to get rid of Arran and the Protectors," Will breathed. Conlan nodded.

"I could incinerate them, if you like," Freddie offered.

Conlan frowned. "I was thinking something a little less lethal and less likely to draw attention."

Will shook his head. "We can go hand to hand, but I think they'd outclass us right now. Anyway, Arran can create a shield and then raise the alarm."

"Leave Arran to me, I can deal with him," Eleanor whispered.

"Oh, you sound so masterful," Freddie muttered with heavy sarcasm.

"Not helping, Freddie," Eleanor snapped, unable to maintain her irritation when his cheeky grin stole across his face.

"Eleanor, if you want Arran, he's all yours," offered Conlan. "We'll move into the middle of the room, using Amelia's shield to conceal us, and once we're in position Amelia can push the shield out and knock the Protectors off balance. Will and I will then jump them. Freddie, stay out of the way, you're not up to it," he ordered, ignoring Freddie's peeved look. Moving as quietly as they could manage, they emerged into the room, Amelia altering her shield to hide them. The room was small and windowless, and bare stone walls and un-sanded, dirty floorboards completed the decor. The three Protectors sat round a rickety table covered in the small coins they were using to bet on their card game. The other Protector was sat to the side reading and with his back ramrod straight in a wooden chair, his eyes closed as if in meditation - Arran. Eleanor felt her heart skip a beat as her breath came in fast, fearful pants. Conlan took her hand and the fear dropped slightly. They moved slowly towards the middle of the room, and they were almost in position when a floorboard beneath them let out a loud groan. They froze. Eleanor's heart pounded so hard in her chest that she was sure the whole room must be able to hear it. Arran's eyes shot open and his gaze tracked from side to side. The Protectors noticed his movement and nudged each other, sniggering.

"You," Arran ordered, pointing to the Protector nearest to him without looking at him. "Stand in front of this door."

"I had a good hand," the man grumbled. With a sigh of irritation the Protector put down his cards and shambled to the door, stretching stiff, tired muscles as he moved. His shoulder brushed the edge of Amelia's shield but he did not seem to notice. He stood with his back to the door, looking bored.

"You," Arran ordered again, pointing at the Protector who was sat reading. "Go and check they are still in their cell."

"Think they might have disappeared into thin air?" the Protector asked with glib disrespect as he lay his book down. Arran glared at him but the Protector merely shrugged and grabbed a lantern from the wall, his unintelligible mutterings of annoyance following him down the stairs.

Conlan lay a hand on Amelia's shoulder, and letting go of Eleanor's hand he held up three fingers, then two, then one. Amelia pushed out her shield.

Eleanor did not see what happened to the Protectors. There were thuds, yells and the sounds of violence, but her attention was focused entirely on Arran. The moment the attack had started, Eleanor had yanked at his energy, pulling it from him forcibly. His face had shown surprise when she first appeared, the expression changing to shock as he realised what she was doing. Looking into his face as fear and confusion flowed across it, a whole raft of strange thoughts and coincidences tumbled through Eleanor's head. A sudden flash of insight was so startling that she felt her energy shudder, but her gut told her it was right. So what was she going to do about it?

Arran had no hope of fighting her – and he knew it. It had taken four of them to defeat her last time, and then it was only because they had caught her by surprise. As she pulled his energy, she carefully drained it back into the earth; she did not want to go psychotic, she needed a level head. As his energy levels dropped, Arran fell to his knees in front of her. His eyes were empty. When Eleanor was confident that he posed very little threat, she stopped pulling. He stared up, swaying slightly and trying to keep upright. She heard the sound of the other Protector returning from the cells below as his feet pounded up the stairs, his panting breath, a heavy thump and then silence. Eleanor did not bother to look; she held Arran's hazel eyes with a penetrating gaze of her own.

"Are you going to stare at me until the sun rises and they find you, or are you going to kill me?" Arran asked. He did not seem overly interested in which option she would choose, he just sounded tired.

"I have no desire to kill you, Arran. I would like you to join us, we could do with your help," Eleanor said quietly.

Surprise moved back onto Arran's face. "I do not understand."

Eleanor smiled. "Really? Which part?"

Arran raised an eyebrow at her, the expression was so familiar. "I have spent the better part of the night torturing you and your friends. Why do you not want me dead?"

"Did you do any of that for your own ends?" Eleanor asked.

"I was following orders," he said flatly.

"Why do you follow orders, Arran?"

He looked startled by the question and his forehead creased into a heavy frown. "If I do not follow orders I am punished," he said quietly, the Dwarfish filled with humiliation.

"You do not have to live like that, not if you do not wish to. We can offer you friendship, understanding and protection. Come with us, please," Eleanor implored.

Arran stared at her and she stepped forward, placing a hand on his shock of white hair.

"Why do you dye your hair?"

Arran's eyes widened. "How do you know?"

Eleanor shrugged; she did not want to get into that conversation just yet. Without warning he grabbed at Eleanor's hand, and water's electrical energy sparked through her. It was not a powerful jolt, as he did not have the strength left to pull enough energy for that, but in her current weakened state it was sufficient to drop her to the floor in a heap, gasping for breath, eyes rolling and disorientated.

"NO!"

A yell of such fury and ferocity. Eleanor turned her head and forced her eyes to focus. Conlan moved swiftly towards her, flinging his arm out across his body as he approached. Out of the corner of her eye Eleanor saw Arran's body flung across the room by air's pushing force. The white-haired Enforcer thudded into the wall, the force of his body's impact knocking mortar loose. He dropped to the floor and moaned.

"Eleanor," Conlan whispered. Strong arms wrapped round her as she struggled to sit.

She smiled at him. "You released some energy," she observed, looking back at Arran's semi-conscious body.

"Instinct, but I think I might need more practice. Did I kill him?"

"No, I don't think so," Eleanor said, surprised by the look on Conlan's face. "Did you want to kill him?"

"He tried to kill you," Conlan pointed out, conflicting emotions warring across his face.

"No, he didn't, he didn't have enough strength to give me anything more than a nasty shock and he knew it – he's just not someone who gives up easily. He's your father's personal Enforcer, Conlan, and I want him to join us," Eleanor said. Feeling a little better she pulled herself unsteadily to her feet and walked over to where Arran lay panting, his glazed eyes trying to focus on her. He was not able to sit up, so she lay on her side next to him so she could look into his eyes. Slowly, Eleanor reached a hand out and stroked his face.

"Do not touch me, abomination," he hissed.

Eleanor sighed and withdrew her hand. "Is that you talking, Arran, or the nonsense you have been filled with?"

"I will not listen to you, abominations lie," he muttered, the effort making him cough weakly.

Eleanor smiled. "Yes, sometimes we do, but we try hard not to."

"Why are you still talking to me? Just kill me and get it over with," Arran said, and Eleanor realised with a sick feeling in her stomach that he really expected her to kill him.

"I am not going to kill you, Arran, and neither are any of my friends. I cannot force you to join us either, if you wish to stay here that is your choice, but if you ever get tired of being treated badly, come and find us," Eleanor said, smiling sadly. "It would upset me if I was ever forced to face you across a battlefield."

Arran still looked confused as he lost his grip on his consciousness, his eyes closing. Will knelt at his side, checking for a pulse.

"He's still alive, do we take him with us?" he asked, blue eyes moving to Eleanor.

She shook her head. "He must make the decision to join us of his own volition."

"If he does turn up, how do we know we can trust him?" Freddie asked.

Eleanor sighed, feeling only pity. "He doesn't have a shield, Freddie, it's been stripped from him. Will can read Arran's soul, if we need him to."

"There's more going on here than you're telling us," Amelia said, her eyes narrowing in suspicion.

Eleanor smiled. "Am I that transparent?" All four of them nodded. She looked back at Arran's still body, gently stroking his head. "Yes, I think there's more going on here, but let's see if Arran decides to join us, before I start telling you my theories."

They crept from the dungeon's antechamber and through the stronghold's corridors, getting lost several times before they found the main entrance. Despite their energy levels they were all struggling under a bone-crushing weariness. Eleanor was beginning to worry about how she was going to ride. Conlan had seen her occasional faltering steps and had offered to carry her. She had given him such a contemptuous glare that he had backed off, hands raised in surrender and a slightly hurt look on his face. The exhaustion was making her crabby, but she was not an invalid. Will was not carrying Amelia, and Freddie was still putting one foot in front of the other.

"Do we have to walk across the courtyard?" Freddie whispered. "It's kind of exposed."

They were hidden in the darkness of a doorway in the corner of the courtyard, the main gates so tantalisingly close that Eleanor was tempted to make a run for it. The courtyard was maybe forty yards across of empty space. The night was still, quiet and freezing cold, but Eleanor could see the sky starting to lighten above the courtyard's buildings. Could they wait until daylight and then sneak out? The gates were closed – this was not a great obstacle to her – but blowing them up would make a lot of noise. If they could wait until daybreak, maybe they would open the gates anyway, but if they waited someone would notice they had escaped. Eleanor was still thinking this through when she heard shouting and running feet.

"They have escaped, secure the gate."

"Someone call a healer!"

"Inform Lord Daratus."

Behind her, Conlan swore softly.

"There goes the element of surprise. I assume they're yelling about us. We might as well make a run for it," Amelia whispered.

"We could really do with putting more effort into the planning stage of our 'plans'," Freddie muttered.

Eleanor smiled as Conlan leaned into her, lips brushing her neck, the soft vibration of his voice felt more than heard. "Eleanor, can you take out the gate?"

She nodded. "But could we make sure there's nobody in front of it before I do? It's going to be a rather big explosion."

As she spoke, a troop of thirty hastily-dressed Protectors came stumbling out of a door into a vaguely formal arrangement in front of the gate. A door ten feet to their right slammed open and Eleanor was surprised to see Arran march out of it. Well, 'marching' was a generous term. He obviously wanted it to look like he was in firm control of himself, but his movements were stiff and pained. He was met in the middle of the courtyard by the other three Enforcers, who looked around warily. Eleanor felt air brush past her face as Amelia raised a shield to hide them.

"Managed to slip past the mighty Arran, did they?" the Enforcer's sarcastic tone carrying clearly in the frigid air. The other two sniggered.

"There is only one way in and out of this place, so they will have to come through us to get out," Arran said, ignoring the jibe.

"So if they got out, how come you are not dead?" the sarcastic Enforcer asked. Arran shrugged. Another door into the courtyard slammed open and another troop of Protectors, ready for a battle, filed into the courtyard, followed by Lord Daratus.

"ARRAN!"

Lord Daratus's voice filled the courtyard with cold authority. Eleanor saw Arran flinch and his head drop.

"Yes, my Lord?" he said in an empty, emotionless tone. Daratus strode across the courtyard until he was stood in front of the four Enforcers.

"You allowed them to escape?" he asked.

"No, my Lord, I did not allow them to, they were just stronger than me. Even your son showed magical talent, his eyes were glowing and he flung me into a wall without touching me," Arran said calmly. Lord Daratus lashed out, catching Arran in the face and knocking the young man onto his back.

"He is no longer my son, Arran," he said in the same emotionless, bored voice.

"No, my Lord," Arran agreed from the floor, a hand pressed against his face as blood dribbled from his nose. His tone was respectful, but Eleanor could see the hate in his eyes.

"He showed magical talent?" Daratus mused. "He tested with very minimal talent as a child and proved unworthy of training. This must be the power of the Five we were told about. Arran, if they were able to break out of their cell and overpower you, why are you not dead?" Daratus dropped his vicious pale-blue eyes to glare down. Eleanor was impressed when Arran stared back calmly.

"They did not want me dead," Arran said truthfully.

"Why not?" Daratus asked, and there was a nasty threat under the question.

"I do not know, my Lord."

"I am disappointed. This will not go unpunished, but you may redeem yourself a little if you are able to apprehend the Five before they leave the stronghold," Daratus said, turning on his heel and walking from the courtyard.

"All of a sudden I feel really sorry for that kid," Conlan whispered. Eleanor nodded as she watched Arran force his body to stand, fighting his pain. He hung his head, humiliated, as the sniggering turned to sneering laughter.

"So what now?" Will murmured, staring in dismay at the sixty armed Protectors between them and the gates.

Eleanor stepped back against Conlan, who automatically wrapped his arms around her, her back fitting perfectly into his chest and stomach. She laid her head against his arm and closed her eyes. In the silence, Eleanor felt the serenity that listening to Conlan's breathing brought her, and slowly she pushed her mind into concentrating on the problem in hand, looking for a solution. Information poured through her mind and she discounted nothing, allowing all possibilities equal consideration. Eventually, the thoughts consolidated. She opened her eyes, and her friends looked at her expectantly.

"I have a plan. It's a little complicated, so I'm going to explain it as I go along. Is that OK?" Eleanor whispered. They nodded at her.

"Amelia, I need you to create some fog – really damp, moist-laden fog – in the courtyard. Can you do that?" Eleanor asked.

Amelia shook her head. "I don't know how."

Will rolled his eyes. "Amelia, just pull a cloud down into the courtyard, one that's full of rain."

Eleanor stared at him and grinned. "I said you were a genius!"

Amelia closed her eyes, her face a mask of concentration, as she focused on the task while keeping the shield in place.

The light in the courtyard slowly darkened as a huge grey cloud moved overhead. At first the Protectors did not seem to notice, their focus on the shadows around the square. As the cloud moved down, there were gasps and mutters of suspicion and fear. Arran looked up for a moment, his eyes narrowed, and then he lowered his gaze. Eleanor gasped audibly. She knew he could not see her, but before the cloud's dark grey mist obscured him from view, Eleanor felt sure he had known she was there.

"Hold your positions," Arran yelled through the courtyard, his voice muffled by the thick, damp air.

"Mist, now what?" Amelia asked. She looked as grey as the cloud, and Will caught her as she staggered against him. "We have to hurry," Amelia whispered. "I can't hold the shield much longer."

"Conlan, can you help Amelia? I need Will a moment," Eleanor said. Conlan nodded and put a shoulder under Amelia's arm to support her; she dropped her head groggily against him. Will brushed her hair out of her face and turned to look at Eleanor, a questioning look on his face.

"I need you to electrocute the cloud," Eleanor said. Will stared at her and a smile spread across his tired face.

"How does that help?" Freddie asked.

"The water in the cloud will radiate my energy charge out, hitting them all at once. It may not be not enough to kill them, but it will certainly stun them. But I suspect that was Eleanor's plan all along," Will said, his grin getting wider as Eleanor nodded.

"Clever," Freddie said appreciatively.

"On occasion," Eleanor agreed.

Will stepped briefly around Amelia's shield, careful not to touch the tightly packed vapour, and released his energy. Eleanor saw it pass through the cloud as small flashes of purple light, like a mini electrical storm. They heard the yelps, groans and cries of surprised pain and then the thuds as bodies dropped to the ground. Eleanor hoped her plan did not result in more deaths on her conscience. Once the flashes had dissipated, silence fell.

"We have very little time before the cloud breaks up. We have to go... now. Run!" Amelia ordered, dropping her shield. Will pulled Amelia into his arms and Conlan supported Freddie. Using the walls of the courtyard as a guide, they ran into the cloud and aimed for the exit. The cloud made it difficult to see, which had sort of been Eleanor's point, but it meant they were almost on top of the gate before they saw it, the Protectors' unconscious bodies lying before it.

"Amelia, you need to push the Protectors out of the way," Eleanor whispered, panting and looking around fearfully. The cloud was beginning to break up and they were about to become easy targets.

"Amelia isn't capable at the moment," Will said quietly. Eleanor looked at her friend's limp body cradled against his chest.

"Conlan," Eleanor whispered. "Can you do it?"

He smiled and nodded. Leaving Freddie to stand on his own for a moment, he walked a little closer. He took a slow, deep breath and swept his hand from one side of the gate to the other. The Protectors' bodies slid and tumbled against each other as they moved with bruising speed into a pile in the far corner of the gate. Conlan turned round and gave Eleanor a grin. She smiled back. She would have to be careful, but he had created enough room for her to blow up a sizeable chunk of the gate without killing anybody. She waved her hand, indicating they should move out of the way.

"STOP!"

Loud, hard and angry, the voice shattering the silence made them all jump. They turned round to see Arran standing ten feet behind them. He looked dazed, but he was upright and walking towards them.

"I cannot let you leave."

"You may have noticed we were not asking for your permission," Conlan said in a calm, relaxed tone.

Arran glared at him. "Lord Daratus will not be pleased. I must make you stay or die trying."

"Are those your only choices?" Conlan asked, his voice still calm and very non-threatening.

"What do *you* want?" Eleanor asked. Arran stared at her, and from the look on his face she assumed nobody had ever asked him this question before. He did not seem to know how to answer, but before he got the chance Conlan flicked his hand and the young Enforcer was once again knocked off his feet, slamming into the wall near the far side of the gate.

"That was unnecessary," Eleanor chastised.

"Eleanor, the sun is rising, the cloud is dissipating and Amelia isn't able to create a shield right now. I know you like the boy, but we don't have time for this," Conlan said, irritated. Eleanor walked away from him and towards where Arran had fallen; she was surprised to discover him still conscious.

"You have a very high pain threshold," Eleanor said, crouching at his side and gently running a hand down his face again. He did not ask her to stop, did not flinch away; he just stared, his glazed eyes holding hers. His voice was an almost inaudible whisper when he spoke.

"Please, just kill me. I am sure it will be kinder than what *he* will do to me."

Eleanor smiled at him sadly, still stroking his face.

"I am sorry, Arran, but I cannot do that. You have a destiny." She leaned forward and kissed his forehead. "When you are ready, come and find us," she repeated. His eyelids were dropping – he was fighting it, but his consciousness was fading. Sighing, Eleanor got back to her feet. Conlan stood behind her with a look on his face she did not understand.

"He has a destiny?" he asked, confused.

"What? Did you think you were the only one?" Eleanor snapped at him. Hurt flashed through his eyes. It stabbed at her but she ignored it and pushed past him towards the gate, drawing earth's energy as she walked. She had barely come to a stop when she released her explosive force at the gate. An almightily splitting crunch rent the air, the gate fragmented and bits of wood blasted in all directions. Being careful of the jagged edges she had left, Eleanor stepped through the hole and out into the street. She had taken fewer than ten steps when five men surrounded her. From behind them came a red-headed woman, and Eleanor smiled in recognition.

"Avatar of Earth, my father sent us, please come," Leda said.

"Who is this?" Will asked warily, the Dwarfish heavy with suspicion.

"A friend, we need to move quickly," Eleanor said.

They moved as fast as they could through the quiet streets. Will was struggling to carry Amelia and move at any speed, but he refused to let anyone else help him. Leda led them to a small building that looked like a warehouse. Inside were their horses, packed and ready to go.

"We will take you to the city gate. The Protectors there are in my father's 'debt' so they will allow you to pass, but we must hurry before reinforcements arrive from the stronghold," Leda said.

Eleanor hugged the startled woman. "Thank you, Leda, and thank your father."

Leda smiled and handed her two thick white envelopes. "It's the information you asked for and a letter from Remic. It has been an honour to be of service to you, Avatar of Earth."

They mounted, Amelia waking enough to get on her horse but still looking tired and pale. Moving as fast as they dared through the cold, icy streets, Leda guided them to the city's gate, her red hair streaming behind her. True to her word, the Protectors opened up for them; they did not even have to slow down. Leda and her men pulled their horses to the side. Eleanor gave Leda a wave as they shot past, heading for the open countryside and freedom.

21

THE BEGINNING

They had run with the assumption that every Protector in Mydren would be chasing them, but after several days it became apparent that this was not the case. Conlan and Will circled back frequently, but there were no Protectors in sight. Nevertheless, Conlan pushed them hard. For the first two days and nights they ate up the miles, moving as fast as the track and horses would allow, adrenaline keeping them conscious and in their saddles. After forty-eight hours, even Horse and Meran were flagging and desperate for rest. Conlan pulled them off the track and led them out into the wild beauty of Mydren. The lack of sleep was making it difficult to think. Eleanor wanted to talk to Conlan, but there was never a moment. She caught him looking at her occasionally and smiled. There would be time to talk later, when they were safe, but for the moment she had to concentrate on staying awake and on her horse.

Eleanor sat slumped in her saddle, the freezing morning rain drumming down on her. She was soaked, ice-cold and exhausted, and her bent posture was giving her backache. She rode in a daze as the countryside slid past. She had a vague idea they were heading south. Not that it mattered, as any direction away from Katadep would have been fine with her. The days and nights were merging into one long uncomfortable nightmare. She had watched another sunrise from her saddle and she knew she was going to have to rest soon or she was going to collapse. Horse's tried, trudging plod kept lulling her to sleep and she would wake with a start as she felt her body slipping from the saddle. Freddie was slumped in his saddle. Amelia rode at his side, helping to steady him. He had not complained or fallen behind, but his exhaustion and pain were plain in his face. He was not going to be able to keep going much longer either. As the unseen sun marked time across the grey sky, Eleanor watched Freddie deteriorate, until he collapsed against Pal's neck, reins dropping from his hands. Will and Conlan had left to do another check, to make sure there were still no Protectors following them. Eleanor felt herself start to slip from her saddle and Amelia moved her horse up to her side. She lay a hand gently on her head.

"Eleanor?"

Eleanor shuddered and pulled herself upright, the world spinning.

"Let me hold you for a while, Eleanor, let me help you" Amelia said softly. Stubbornly shaking her head, Eleanor tried to sit more upright, to give the impression of a strength she no longer possessed.

"Help Freddie," she said, her voice a thin whisper. It sounded alien to her.

"I can help you both, if you'll let me," Amelia said, an edge to her voice. She raised her eyes to Amelia's and steel grey regarded her, seeing straight through her facade. Slowly, Eleanor nodded and Amelia smiled, the soft mothering look returning. Carefully, as if she was indeed holding a sick child, Amelia helped Eleanor across to her horse and wrapped a blanket around her. Sighing, Eleanor relaxed. Amelia urged her horse forward again so she could walk at Freddie's side, a hand through the waist of his trousers to stop him from falling. Eleanor entered their horses' minds, carefully explaining what was happening and that they could not move at anything faster than a walk without risking Freddie falling off, but that was fine by them, as they were just as tired as she was. Eleanor closed her eyes, the gentle movement and comfortable warmth soothing her into a pleasant doze.

Eleanor heard the pounding of hooves behind her. She hoped it was Conlan and Will, but she would gladly have welcomed screaming hoards of Protectors, if they would let her stop and sleep. A horse was brought to an abrupt halt beside them, but Eleanor could not bring herself to open her eyes.

"Eleanor is not your burden to carry, Amelia," Conlan said irritably.

"Eleanor is *not* a burden, Conlan. She is a tired, battered friend in need of my help, as is Freddie," Amelia told him, the hard edge back in her voice.

"If they needed help they should have said something," Conlan persisted.

"No, they shouldn't have to say anything; you should have seen what I did and offered. Have you any idea what they've just suffered for you?" Amelia snapped back.

Silence.

"Maybe we should stop for a while and get some rest?" Will ventured. There was more silence.

"OK," Conlan agreed softly. "Give Eleanor to me."

"I can handle Eleanor, Conlan, but if you want to move faster than a walk, Freddie is going to need your help," Amelia said, the edge still in her voice.

"You've been through the same torture that they have, Amelia," Conlan said, choking on the words. "I'll help Freddie, but let Will hold Eleanor, you need a break."

"You told me I was strong, Conlan," Amelia said. "Don't change your mind just as I was starting to believe you."

There was another heavy silence.

"Freddie?" Conlan said quietly. "Freddie... I know you're tired right now, but we're going to find somewhere to rest. I'm going to get on your horse behind you, to help you stay in the saddle, OK?"

There was no answer. Soon they were off again and Eleanor once more relaxed into the comfortable fog. The sounds and even the movement around her seemed distant. Only Amelia's warm body was real. Behind closed eyelids, Eleanor knew the daylight was fading. She heard the muted whisper of wind through trees, and memories of her first night in Mydren came back to her. She felt the world close in slightly as they moved across the boundary of the forest Conlan had brought them to. She could imagine the trees standing around them in blank regiment as the sun sank into night – ominous to some, but she felt only comfort and sanctuary.

Amelia pulled her horse to a stop. Eleanor heard Conlan and Will try to ease Freddie gently from the saddle. His soft groan reached Eleanor clearly in the chilly air.

"Sorry," Will said.

"I'm just glad I'm off my horse," Freddie murmured.

Drifting now, her eyes closed and her body limp, Eleanor felt herself lifted from Amelia's arms. *Conlan*. He held her close, his stubbly cheek gently brushing her face as he whispered.

"Maybe now you'll let me carry you for a while."

Eleanor could hear the love in his voice. She wanted to say something, but she had no idea what, and exhaustion dragged her into darkness before her tired mind could think of a response.

Five seconds later she was awoken by gentle shaking. She was warm and comfortable, and she knew that strong arms were holding her close.

"Go away," she mumbled, not opening her eyes. "I'm asleep."

"We have to keep going, Eleanor. Come on, get up, and wake Freddie while you're at it."

Surprised, Eleanor opened her eyes. It was day, just, the light still grey. Conlan was stooped over her. The arms wrapped around her were Freddie's. Confusion knotted her brow. Why was Freddie holding her? Why did Conlan not want to hold her? Lifting her head she could see Will and Amelia asleep behind her.

"I think we need more rest, Conlan," Eleanor said, still not moving.

"You can have all the sleep you want in a few days' time when we have some distance between us and Katadep." Glowing green eyes held hers, expectant, waiting for her to complain, which made her want do the opposite. She wondered if Conlan knew this. She nodded and Conlan smiled slightly, before moving to wake Will and Amelia.

"Freddie?" Eleanor said, rubbing the arm wrapped around her waist.

"Just a few more minutes..." he murmured, and despite his injuries he tightened his grip around her.

Their day-and-night headlong dash became a monotonous, endless trek. Travelling from sunrise to sunset, they barely had enough strength to eat before dropping into oblivious sleep. Eleanor's eyes often closed before her body hit the cold, damp earth, not caring if she had a blanket or not and just wanting sleep's release. Without fail they were woken what felt like moments later, to have the waking nightmare continue. Eleanor was a little hurt each morning when she woke to find Freddie's arms around her. Conlan seemed different around her, careful, like he did not want to get too close. He hugged her when she asked for it, eventually giving in to her requests and holding her while she slept, but as soon as he knew she was awake in the morning, he was up and off. She made several attempts to kiss him and he gently rebuffed her, looking pointedly at the others asleep around them. She was hurt and confused; she knew he loved her, so why was he reluctant to touch her? Why was he keeping her at arm's length?

After eight days of travel, Conlan felt they were far enough away that they could stop for a few days' rest and make some plans. The light had begun to fade and the temperature was dropping, and a steady, freezing drizzle had soaked her through again. Another wood, more trees, cold, damp earth. Eleanor did not care. She dismounted and took Horse's saddle and bridle off, dropping them to the ground with her bags and folded herself down on top of them, something in her bag digging into her chest. It hurt, but not enough for her to bother moving. The darkness was calling and she rushed to embrace it.

When she woke, there was a warming fire blazing in front of her. Her blanket was draped over her and Conlan's jacket was folded under her head. She lifted herself slightly. Will and Amelia were next to her, Will's arms wrapped protectively around Amelia's body even in exhausted sleep. Freddie was sat across from her. He saw her stir and smiled.

"How long have I been asleep?" she asked drowsily. Her throat was dry and her mouth felt like something had died in it – her tongue, perhaps. There was a water skin lying next to her head. Grateful for someone's thoughtfulness, Eleanor grabbed it and took long, slow swigs until she felt better.

"Three days," Freddie said, watching her drink.

"Where's Conlan?" she asked, looking round as she put the stopper back and lay the water skin down where Will and Amelia would see it when they woke up.

"Collecting firewood."

Eleanor slowly sat up. Pulling Conlan's jacket on, she smiled. She could smell him on it and sighing she hugged it. It was like having him wrap his arms around her, and a warm glow pushed out from her stomach and through her tired and battered body, somehow making everything seem better.

"Cold?" Freddie asked.

She shook her head. "Just makes me feel safe."

Freddie gave her a long look, an odd expression on his face; it made her guts twist in apprehension. She felt an energy string brush against her and she pulled it in.

Did I do something wrong, Freddie? You seem… unhappy.

Not unhappy, thoughtful. I thought I knew what love was, but if you had done to me what you did to Conlan, I wouldn't have been able to look you in the face again, let alone forgive you. I love you, Eleanor, but not like he does.

I'm sorry, Freddie, Eleanor whispered, feeling awful for him.

No, Eleanor, don't feel bad, he insisted. *It's OK, I'm glad you're happy. I'm just not looking forward to being the odd one out. I liked having you around. I didn't feel quite so lonely, but if I'm honest you scare me quite a bit, and you deserve better than that.*

Eleanor felt tears welling up in her eyes. *I scare you? I wouldn't hurt you, Freddie…*

Yes you would, if it was necessary; you have a ruthless, brutal streak in you. That's not a criticism, Eleanor. You have no idea how glad I am you're on our side, but it does frighten me and that's my weakness… Conlan doesn't have that fear. Wincing, Freddie slowly and painfully stood, moved to her side and wrapped his arms around her. There was no obvious hesitation or fear in the move, which made her feel a little better. Resting her head against his chest she sighed, wiping her tears away.

You're still my friend, Freddie; you're not suddenly going to go invisible.

Freddie laughed. *I'm going to hold you to that.*

Eleanor smiled as he pulled his energy string back. She was still exhausted and the warm fire was making her drowsy. "I think I need to sleep some more."

"OK," Freddie said, releasing his hold. Instinctively she wrapped her arms around him. Freddie gasped at the pain.

"Sorry, please don't let go," she whispered, relaxing as Freddie hugged her close to him and let her sleep against him. She drifted again, the warm fire, Freddie's firm hold and Conlan's jacket all combining to make her feel safe, relaxed and loved.

"Is she OK?" Conlan's soft growl made her smile; she did not feel able to open her eyes and felt a strange surge of pleasure over the fact that she did not have to. She had spent so long overriding her body's urgent and increasingly desperate pleas for rest that it felt wonderful to finally be able to give in to it.

"She's fine, just tired still."

Eleanor felt Freddie's reassurance rumble through his chest as he unconsciously pulled her closer.

"You can sleep too, if you want to. I'll keep an eye on everyone," Conlan offered.

"Thanks."

There was genuine gratitude in Freddie's tone and a friendly camaraderie that Eleanor had never heard before. Freddie seemed to have finally got over his distrust of Conlan. Moving with care, Freddie wriggled himself so he could lay down, panting a little at the pain. Eleanor let her limp body fall with him, laying at his side, head on his arm, his gentle snoring relaxing her back to sleep.

Something brought her from deep sleep to wide awake almost instantaneously. Sitting bolt upright, she stared wide-eyed and frightened. A fire blazed in front of her, her blanket covered her, it was dark and cold.

"What's the matter, sweetie?"

Gasping and feeling foolish for her fear, Eleanor turned towards the voice. Amelia smiled at her. Will, his arms wrapped tightly around Amelia and his back leaning against a tree trunk, watched her carefully. Conlan and Freddie were nowhere in sight. Her mouth and throat felt like she had been asleep for days again.

"I think I just had a bad dream," Eleanor said, her voice dry and rough. Amelia moved to crouch at Eleanor's side, handing her a water skin and stroking her hair as her friend drank greedily. She was still wearing Conlan's jacket.

"I think that's to be expected after what we've been through recently," Will said quietly, giving her a strange look she did not understand.

"What?" she asked.

The hint of a smile tugged at the corners of his mouth. "Nothing, it's just you've been talking in your sleep a lot since we left Katadep."

Eleanor felt the blood drain from her face.

"Oh, what have I said?" she whispered, not sure she wanted to know.

"Mostly you've been mentioning Arran," Amelia said, not looking at her.

Eleanor felt embarrassment heat her cheeks. "In what context?" she stuttered, panic straining her voice.

"Not really a context, you've just been calling out for him, telling him to come and find us," Will said.

"Well I want him to," Eleanor said.

"Why? What's so special about that kid?" Will asked, a genuinely confused look on his face.

Eleanor smiled. "Quite a lot, actually." Will looked at her expectantly. She had not intended to tell them unless Arran turned up, but if she was talking about it in her sleep, then maybe she should tell them before she inadvertently blabbed it out. "He practices magic, like we do, but he has the ability to draw energy from all the elements. Apparently this is rare, as most natural magicians learn to rely on one element in childhood and are then unable to access the others later in life, and of course he has no shield."

"How did he lose it?" Amelia asked, looking distressed; Eleanor knew she was remembering what it had taken for Conlan to lose his shield.

"From what I was able to piece together from my brief visit in his head, Daratus tortured him as a child, to the point where he gave up," Eleanor said softly, unable to keep the pain she felt for him out of her voice.

"As a child?" Amelia said, horrified.

Eleanor nodded sadly. "He was taken from his mother the moment he was born and tested for magical talent. He then spent the next ten years locked up in a cell, being forced to practice and expand his abilities."

"Do a lot of Enforcers have their shields stripped from them?" Amelia asked.

Eleanor shook her head. "From what I picked from Arran's mind, only those with a prodigious talent have their shields stripped – it makes them easier to control."

Amelia stared at her in pained silence.

"How did Daratus know he was going to be born with magical talent?" Will asked.

"An educated guess, I assume. After all, his mother had high magical ability and one of her other children had displayed some magical talent," Eleanor said, watching the thoughts and expressions race across Will's face.

"Who was his mother?" Will asked.

"Helena Baydon. Arran and Conlan are half-brothers," Eleanor said quietly.

Amelia sat down on the ground with a bump, staring at Eleanor with open-mouthed shock. Having already worked out some sort of idea, Will handled his shock a little better, but they both looked at her for several long minutes before Will broke the silence.

"Do you have proof?"

"No, but I'm right. The only person who knows the truth is Daratus. Arran and Conlan have no idea, and even Merl didn't know," Eleanor said.

"Merl? Merl was Arran's father," Will said as the pieces fitted together for him. Eleanor nodded.

"Are you going to tell Conlan?" Amelia asked.

"I hadn't intended to, not unless Arran turns up. I was just really hoping that he would come and find us," Eleanor said. There was another lengthy and stunned silence as Will and Amelia attempted to come to terms with the information Eleanor had given them.

"You liked him," Amelia said quietly.

"Eleanor likes everybody," Freddie said as he and Conlan stepped into the firelight, carefully dropping the ingredients they had found for dinner in front of them. The glowing green eyes were still a surprise each time she saw them. And still beautiful. He was wearing Will's spare jacket, and the dark brown looked good on him.

"Who were you talking about?" Conlan asked softly, not looking at her.

"Arran," Eleanor answered, wondering what he had heard. She decided it could not have been anything she did not want him knowing yet, or Freddie would have said something. Conlan nodded, as if her answer was expected, but he said nothing else. They needed to talk, away from the others. Her nerves squeezing at her stomach, Eleanor stood up, and picking up a lantern she walked over to him, making her steps purposeful and confident. She stood in front of him, a hand held out.

"We need to talk."

Conlan's blank expression turned to apprehension and he slowly shook his head. Eleanor smiled at him.

"That wasn't a request, Conlan, that was an order. Get up." Her voice was quiet, but there was no mistaking the steel of resolve beneath it. Reluctantly Conlan got to his feet, took Eleanor's hand and allowed her to pull him away from the fire. Eleanor walked through the dark wood in silence, looking for a suitable place to stop but mostly trying to calm her nerves. Conlan's hand in hers was a pleasurable torment and she was tempted to move inside his head to see if he felt the same way. *His head is always going to be a temptation.*

She found what she was looking for in the roots of a fallen tree – a small cave-like shelter that would be easy to heat with a small fire. She collected some wood and kindling and used the lantern's flame to light it. Conlan stood watching in silence. Eleanor could feel his uncertainty. Once the fire had caught, she piled up some bigger pieces of wood beside it and sat in the mouth of the small natural shelter wondering if she should speak first or allow him to.

"I don't think I can do this," he said, the words laced with so much pain that for a moment Eleanor could only stare at him. *What can't he do? Love me?*

"I don't understand," Eleanor whispered, feeling her world start to wobble.

"I've learnt to share you with Freddie. It's been really hard, but I know you love us both and I just want you to be happy. Freddie is a good man, he loves you and I trust him, but I barely know Arran. I'm not sure I'd trust him if he did show up here. I don't think I can share you with him, too," Conlan said, his face wrapped in shadows. Eleanor could not see his expressions and she did not understand his words. *He thinks he's sharing me with Freddie?* Too stunned and confused to speak, Eleanor stared at him as Conlan kept talking, as if he had to get everything off his chest before she stopped him. "You love Arran, I heard it in your voice. You've been calling for him in your sleep. In Mydren having several wives is acceptable, but a woman having several husbands is not. Will has told me that in your world attitudes to love and relationships are different and that marriage is not necessarily part of a relationship, but this is so painful for me... I want you all to myself and it hurts that I can't have that. I'm really hoping Arran stays away."

Eleanor felt his misery wash over her. *How did I manage to give him the idea he was sharing me?* Struggling to find the right words, Eleanor stared at the shadow standing across the fire from her.

"I want to love Arran, just as I love Will, Amelia and Freddie. They're my family. I'm hoping that Arran is going to choose to be a part of that, but there's only one thing that's going to make me happy, and that's you. I love Freddie, but Conlan I'm *in love* with you. There's a really big difference. I know it took a lot for you to admit you loved me. I know you're afraid, that the things you love get taken away from you, but you are all I want. All I've ever wanted."

"I don't understand," Conlan whispered.

"I can't make it any clearer, Conlan. I want you and only you. I think I fell in love with you as I was dying. I've been feeling guilty for months about not missing my old life, my old home, my family and friends, but you made everything here so vivid. I felt more alive than I ever thought possible. This life became my solid reality because you fill it. My old life was just the dream I had while I waited for you. You're my anchor to this world, to life, and I love you." She was surprised at just how true the words were.

"After everything I've done to you? Why?"

Eleanor sighed. "Well it's certainly not your easy-going nature."

Conlan chuckled and Eleanor felt her heart do summersaults. He walked over and sat down next to her. She stared into the fire's depths for a moment, gathering her thoughts.

"I've seen inside your head, Conlan. I saw flashes of your childhood. I know what happened with your mother, although I don't understand how you decided it was your fault. You survived where so many others would have crumbled, and somehow you survived with your soul intact and I love you for that. I've felt your love, for me and the others. I know how much you care, even if you won't admit it. I ripped you to pieces and you forgave me, still loved me. You're wonderful; you deserve to be loved, so please, Conlan, let me love you," she begged.

There was silence; she turned to him. The fire's dancing light revealed the awestruck look on his face, his soft, glowing, green eyes shining with his love of her. A second later she felt this love surge through her, the emotion so powerful it was like a heavy storm wave crashing down. Her body shuddered as the warmth spread. She reached a shaking hand towards him. Slowly running her fingers down his face, he shivered but did not pull away. Eleanor moved closer, taking his head in her hands and drawing his stunned face to hers, not taking her eyes from his. She leant in and brushed his warm soft lips with her own. Pulling back slightly, she whispered, "I love *you*. I want *you.*"

Conlan smiled – the look she adored – and she gently brushed her lips against his again, running her fingers through his hair. Placing her hands on his chest, Eleanor pushed him back onto the ground, crossing her arms over him so she could support herself, and she looked into his face. She felt his heart beating under her hand. Leaning forward she pushed her lips into his, harder this time, still unable to take her eyes off him. Under her hand his heart rate increased. He kissed her back, slowly and gently, moved his tongue between her lips, tentatively exploring. The taste of him, the warmth of him and the loving look in his eyes filled her mind, and for a while all life and creation revolved around them. He ran his hand from her shoulder down to her waist and she sighed in pleasure. Then he carefully but firmly pushed her away. Panting, he stared at the roots and earth of their makeshift shelter's roof. Eleanor sat up, worried.

"I don't want you to stop", she whispered. "I want you and I want to give you something I will give to no other man, no matter how many hugs and kisses I give Freddie or anybody else. I'm giving myself to you and only you."

Conlan shook his head, deeply concerned. "I can't do it, I could really hurt you."

Her confusion deepening, Eleanor stared at him. He saw her look and tried to explain. "I mean you're tiny, Eleanor, delicate... I... " In frustration he took her hand, spread the fingers out and pushed his own hand against hers, palm to palm. Her hand looked like a child's in comparison.

He looked at her, his eyes full of loving concern. "You don't see yourself this way. Your personality always makes you seem larger than life, but you barely reach up to my chest. To me you're a tiny, beautiful, perfect, delicate, fragile being that I desperately want to protect. Please don't let me hurt you anymore."

"So what was your plan? Love me at arm's length for the rest of your life?"

"I never really believed this would happen," he admitted a little sheepishly.

"Surprising, considering the amount of fantasies you've had about it," Eleanor murmured.

"Eleanor, I... " Conlan started, blushing deep red.

Eleanor glared at him. "Shut up, Conlan. I want this. I want you, and I want to make you mine, wholly and completely mine."

"I am yours," he whispered, pulling her back down on top of him and pushing his lips against hers. He kissed her so hard and with such passion that she forgot to breathe, forgot how to think, forgot who she was. She knew only him, and the world revolved around them at a dizzying speed.

She felt a moment of apprehension as he rolled her onto her back, his weight pushing her into the ground, before a burning longing wiped all thoughts from her mind. He kissed her with more confidence, supporting her head with one hand while moving the other slowly down her side and thigh and then back again, up to her face. With the pad of his thumb he gently rubbed the scar he had left under her eye. Pulling away slightly, he frowned.

"Are you sure about this?" he asked, his voice husky.

"I have never been surer about anything in my life."

He leaned into her neck, kissing her and chucking softly. She could feel the vibrations through her chest and his breath warmed her skin. *I love you.* She gently wove her fingers into his hair, pulling his head tighter into her neck. His breath came in short bursts as he ran his hand tenderly back down her side, moving back up and then under her shirt. The burst of molten lava that flooded her veins and the electric current that surged through her as his hand touched her bare skin made Eleanor shudder, the burning longing becoming an acute need, more important to her than oxygen. As he slowly moved his hand back to her face he felt the thin scar under her chin where he had stabbed her. *The time Freddie nearly killed you.* He pulled back once more, a little breathless, the frown back on his face.

"Do you have any scars on your body I'm not responsible for?" he asked. She could see the shame in his eyes again. Eleanor grinned wickedly.

"Oh yes, but you'll need to give me a thorough inspection to find them." Love burnt the shame away, and an amused smile spread across his face as he pulled her close again.

"I'll go slowly," he whispered. "If it hurts, I want you to stop me." *Not in a million years.* It was her last coherent thought before she gave herself over completely to the glorious sensations he was stirring within her.

The flickering firelight illuminated his face; he looked calm, contented… peaceful. Eleanor lay across his chest, her chin resting on her hands so she could look at him. *I've never seen him this relaxed before; I've never seen him peaceful and conscious at the same time either.* He was staring up at the dirt of their shelter's roof, his eyes distant. The air was chilly as it nudged the fine sheen of sweat down her back, and her skin felt so sensitive that it was almost uncomfortable. She was happy, completely happy, and she knew that no matter what happened now she would always have this feeling held protectively in her heart, reassuring her that she was loved. If there had been pain, she had been totally unaware of it; she smiled smugly. As usual, Conlan's fear for her was unfounded. As he had entered her, she had unthinkingly entered his head, driven by the overpowering need to be as close to him as possible. It had not been the maelstrom she had encountered the last time. On the surface it was calm and blissfully happy. His head was full of love, wonder and mindless, comfortable joy, and Eleanor had felt his longing to simply stay in the moment they were currently occupying, to lose himself forever in the warmth of her soft, yielding body.

She lay her head against his chest, listening to the steady beat of his heart and knowing all she had to do to speed it up was run her fingers lightly down his side. Neither of them had been able to sleep, but she had not wanted to talk either – she had just wanted to feel him hold her close and listen to his heartbeat, listen to him breathe. She drew all the love and desire she felt for him into one pulsating mass, and pushing into his head she let it flow through him. He gasped, a soft groan escaping him and his body trembling. His love, need and desire for her surged through his mind in response. He pulled her close and she felt his bliss.

"You're in my head," he whispered a little awed.

"I should have asked," she apologised, withdrawing her energy.

"Eleanor, I'm yours. Heart, mind, body and soul, everything I am is yours. You don't need to ask," he said softly. She smiled, turned her head and ran a light trail of kisses across his chest, amused and pleased by his body's immediate response. He rolled her carefully onto her back again, looking up as he did.

"Wow," he breathed. Confused, Eleanor followed his gaze. What had been damp, muddy, bare winter earth was soft grass and flowers. Trees had burst into bloom and the grass had grown into a thick mattress under their discarded clothes. It was hard to see the full extent of the transformation in the flickering light of the fire, but given her current level of bliss Eleanor suspected that it would rival what she had inadvertently created in front of Duncan.

Eleanor giggled. "I guess you made me a little too happy."

He smiled down at her. "There's no such thing," he whispered, kissing her. Then using gentle, caressing lips he began exploring her body. She closed her eyes, moaning softly. She was totally unprepared for the energy string that crashed into her with such force that her head snapped back, bouncing on the grass. She gasped in agony.

"Freddie," she whispered as his frantic presence filled her head.

Eleanor, we need you back now! Freddie cried, sending her the image of heavily armed Protectors surrounding them, a hooded, black-robed figure watching.

"Eleanor, Eleanor, what's the matter?" Conlan hollered in the background.

We're coming, Freddie. Hold on, we're coming.

Eleanor sat up as Freddie left her head. "We have to go, they need us," she said, reaching for her clothes.

"This had better be a matter of life or death," Conlan muttered, fumbling for his own clothes. "Or Freddie's a dead man!"

Eleanor was too panicked to explain just how serious the situation was. She was dressed and running back to the camp as fast as her legs and the moon's shadowy half-light would allow, before Conlan was even half-clothed. He had called after her and begged her to wait, but she had ignored him. Images of bloody massacres flew round her head. She made no attempt to be subtle, they would hear her coming, but she was beyond caring. She charged back into the camp, the sight before her bringing her up short. Amelia was kneeling on the ground next to their camp fire, her eyes closed, biting her bottom lip as she concentrated. She was cradling Will's head in her lap. He was sprawled unconscious before her, a sword still gripped in his hand. There was blood running down the side of his pale face. Freddie was kneeling next to Amelia, a reassuring hand on her shoulder and whispering to her. The Protectors stood around them. One had a sword drawn and was using it to poke cautiously at the air in front of him, looking surprised when he met resistance. The Enforcer was stood to one side, his face deep in shadow.

The six Protectors started moving towards her as Conlan came running up to stand at her side. He took in the scene as she had, and cursed in Dwarfish. Unsure of the level of threat they were facing, Eleanor waited. The Protectors reached them, and the one with the sword re-sheathed his weapon. Eleanor felt Conlan's confusion. *What are they doing?* As they had made no overt threat towards them, Eleanor refrained from simply blasting at them. With less than five steps between them, the Protectors stopped. The one at the front moved forward.

"We have come to offer you our assistance," he said, kneeling before them. As he did so, the other Protectors around him fell down to their knees. Surprise wiped Eleanor's mind for a moment.

"You have this effect on way too many men, Eleanor," Conlan said in English, amused.

She smirked at him. "Worried about the competition?"

He pulled her close, her back resting against him. "Not anymore," he whispered.

They stared at the Protectors for a moment, before Conlan addressed them.

"If you are here to help us, why is my brother bleeding?" he asked, a nasty edge to the Dwarfish. Eleanor smiled. The word he had used, 'brother', was an old one, one that appeared in Gregor's book, but Conlan had said it was not used much anymore. The word meant brother in its truest meaning, as in a person who shared his blood, and Will was this and much more.

The Protector who had knelt first raised his head, and Eleanor had a strong sense of déjà vu. "He attacked us, my Lord. We were simply defending ourselves. Please accept our apologies," he said. Eleanor felt the whole of Conlan's body tense at the word 'Lord'.

"You think I am a Lord?" he asked quietly.

The Protector grinned. "We choose to follow you, as we want to help you bring down the Lords of Mydren. How would you like us to address you?"

Eleanor's churning mind gave her the reason why this Protector looked so familiar.

"This is the Protector you didn't kill," she said, attaching a Dwarfish bark of astonishment to the English almost without thinking about it.

Conlan looked confused. "Pardon?"

"That night, after Bremen," Eleanor clarified. "This is the Protector I asked you not to kill." Conlan stared at the man in surprise.

"What's he doing here?"

Eleanor shrugged.

"Please get up off your knees. You may address me as Conlan," he said to the patiently waiting Protector. "How did you find us?"

The Protector stood and pointed to the black-robed figure standing silent as a statue behind them.

"Arran found you. The Avatar of Earth appeared in his dreams, and she told him where you were located."

Eleanor felt Conlan's embrace tighten further.

"Is there something you want to tell me?" he whispered in English.

Eleanor looked over her shoulder at his awestruck face. "I'm as surprised as you are, Conlan. I didn't know I was doing it, but Arran uses the energy of Earth just as I do. We're both connected, just in the same way the dragon and I were connected. It's possible I unknowingly guided him here in my sleep."

Arran walked towards them and removed his hood as he did so. His hair was no longer white but a soft brown; it suited him. His face held the emotionless, blank expression Eleanor had come to associate with anyone who spent too much time with Daratus. His eyes, however, showed all his uncertainty and fear. Eleanor smiled at him, and stepping out of Conlan's arms she moved round the Protectors and stood in front of him.

"I am here as you asked," he said simply.

"I am so very glad you are," Eleanor said, her smile beaming wider. A smile, not very sure of itself, and obviously not used to being there, spread across the young man's face. Eleanor opened her arms wide, offering him a hug. Arran took a hesitant step forward and pulled Eleanor against him. She held him until she felt his body relax a little.

"Welcome home, Arran. We are delighted you have come to join us," Eleanor whispered.

"I brought you a gift," he said, pulling back. The smile on his face seemed a little more confident. "Well actually I brought Conlan a gift," he said, nodding at Conlan who had not moved. He gave Arran a friendly smile as the Enforcer walked towards him, fishing something out of the bag strapped over his shoulder as he did so. He held out the crown and Conlan took it, staring down at the thick band of silvery metal in his hands.

"Thank you, Arran," he said softly. "You took a huge risk bringing this to me and coming to join us. I am grateful."

"Just promise me that Daratus is going to pay," Arran said. Eleanor could not see his face, but she heard the bitter hatred in his voice.

Conlan nodded. "Yes, Arran, I can promise you that," he murmured. His voice was still soft, but the Dwarfish implied a shared desire to see Daratus punished.

"So, are you ready to become a king now?" Eleanor asked Conlan in English.

"It doesn't seem such a ridiculous notion anymore," Conlan said thoughtfully. "However, the forces we have aren't nearly enough."

"No," Eleanor agreed, a smile spreading across her face. "But they're a good beginning…"

Acknowledgments

No author gets this far without guidance, support and proof readers, and I am no exception. I would particularly like to thank the following:

My husband, John, without whom this book would not exist, his steady, calm, unfailing devotion gave me the courage to allow the world to meet Eleanor. Bossy Boots is very grateful my love!

Unending thanks to my dear friends and proof-readers, Chantal Robinson, Ailsa Cane, Shelley Bryon, Kate Yates, Conchi Diaz, Jon Smith and Laura Williams. Thank you for all the effort you put into reading my drafts and for the great advice and constructive criticism that came from everyone. Especially Ailsa, who managed to put a red pen through half the book and make it a hundred times better. I really appreciate it, couldn't have done it without you guys, love you lots, coffees on me.

Thanks to my cousin, Richard Burgess, vet extraordinaire, for patiently answering all my bizarre questions on equine murder and not trying to have me committed.

Thanks to the band, Within Temptation who created the inspirational music this book was written too. Their album 'Silent Force', has, from continuous playing, become the soundtrack of this book for me. I encourage you to enjoy their music.

www.within-temptation.com

If you enjoyed this book, please come and find out more at:

www.Mydren.com

About the Author

Sara Burgess lives in Manchester with her long-suffering husband, her beloved bear-dog Sweep and three cats: Frodo, Gandalf and Gimli. She has lived in Florida, Spain and France and has at different times in her life been a video shop assistant, bank clerk, school teacher, supermarket till worker, hotel receptionist, bookshop assistant, archaeologist, software trainer and she currently works as an Intranet Evangelist to pay for her first love: writing. In her infrequent spare time she enjoys the movies, opera, bike-riding, reading and hanging out at DaVinci's with the 'crew'.

Printed in Great Britain
by Amazon.co.uk, Ltd.,
Marston Gate.